THE DEAD RIDER.

FROM A DRAWING BY E. R. HUGHES. (Mas., Nov. i., v. i.)

THE NOVELLINO

OF

MASUCCIO

NOW FIRST TRANSLATED INTO ENGLISH

BY

W. G. WATERS.

WITH ELEVEN FULL PAGE ILLUSTRATIONS

BY HUGHES.

LONDON:

PUBLISHED FOR THE TRADE.

Contents

PAGE.

Contents

PAGE.

PAGE.

PAGE.

Introduction

THE middle period of the fifteenth century is one which every writer on Italian history or literature will approach with interest or even delight. It is probably at the present time being worked more zealously and more studiously than any other; wherefore it would be out of place to set down here any vague generalities concerning it. Pope Paul IV., speaking a century later,* compared the ruin and confusion of his own age with the states system which produced rulers like Francesco Sforza, Cosimo dei Medici, Francesco Foscari, Nicolas V., and Alfonso the Magnanimous, and likened the Italy of the time to a well-tuned musical instrument and the states of the aforenamed rulers to the strings thereof, cursing the while the memory of Alfonso of Aragon† and Ludovico of Milan, wretched lost souls who had disturbed this harmony and compassed the ruin he was fated to behold. These good times of the Pope's retrospect may be roughly identified with the period of Masuccio's literary activity, and the people who then lived and moved in town and country, as the originals of the interesting series of literary pictures which he has left us in his work.

The "Novellino" is a collection of fifty stories, each one told by the writer separately, without any striving after continuity. Masuccio does not trouble himself, like certain others of the Novellieri, to construct a setting for his work, and to feign that the tales are told in turn by the various members of a gentle company brought together by hazard. He tells us that all his novels are true,‡ and

* "Relatione di M. Bernardo Navagero alla Serma. Repca. di Venetia," 1558.

† Alfonso II., grandson of the Magnanimous, and mentioned by Masuccio as Duke of Calabria. He fled before Charles VIII. in 1495, and abdicated without striking a blow.

‡ "E invoco l'altissimo Dio per testimonio che tutte sono verissime istorie, le piu nelli nostri moderni tempi travenute." —Parlamento.

that in many cases he is only setting down what he has learnt by the evidence of his senses.* Each novel begins with a dedication to some personage of note, and ends with divers comments by the author. These comments in a measure fill the place of the chorus in Greek drama, and exhibit more completely than the narrative itself Masuccio's own view of the episode therein chronicled. Now and again the terms employed in the novel might leave an impression that evil-doers were being let off too easily, were it not for the scathing denunciation of offence and offender as well, written in the "Masuccio" at the end.† The book begins with a Prologue dedicated to Ippolita, Duchess of Calabria, a patroness of learning and learned herself, and of extraordinary virtue, if the words of Francesco Tuppo in his short dedication to the early editions of the work are to be taken seriously.‡ After a few flowery tropes Masuccio strikes the note which is dominant throughout the entire work, to wit, the profligacy of the ministers of religion, and in the first ten novels he assuredly lays on the scourge with a will. His treatment of this, and indeed of all other subjects, is bluntly realistic, and his constant excursions into real history and his allusions to actual personages show how vastly his essay in story-telling differs from the pure fiction and fictitious history of Boccaccio and Ser Giovanni, and from the fairy tales of Straparola.

Under Alfonso the Magnanimous the literary renown of Naples rose to a point never attained before or since. In his zeal for the cultivation of learning this remarkable man rivalled the activity of Cosimo dei Medici. Like Cosimo he favoured the foundation of an academy of letters, and the learned men he entertained, first and last, at his court, certainly equalled in numbers those who frequented Florence at the same time. Laurentius Valla, Beccadelli, and Pontano all enjoyed his favour, and Filelfo during his turbulent and wandering life spent some time at Naples. Alfonso maintained a long correspondence

* "Siccome per verissimo ho sentito e con piu esperienze toccato con mano."—Novel XXV.

† Novel III. may be taken as an instance.

‡ "Quale guardando la inaudita pudicitia tua."

with Leonardo Aretino, and Poggio was employed by him to make a translation of the "Cyropædia" of Xenophon. It may be assumed that Masuccio enjoyed the friendship of Beccadelli and of Pontano, seeing that he dedicates to each of them a novel; others he inscribes to the men of affairs about the court, such as Antonello de Petrucciis and Francesco Scales; others to the high nobles of the kingdom, and others to the various members of the royal house of Aragon.

Between Alfonso and his natural son, who succeeded him as Ferdinand I., the difference was vast indeed. It is almost impossible to believe that such a father could have produced such a son. Pontano, who was in Ferdinand's employ both as secretary and ambassador, when writing after the king's death* tells of horrors which might rank with the most hideous barbarities of Ezzelino or Bernabo Visconti. He was cruel and treacherous as a tiger, brutal in speech, lustful, and avaricious. He would spend lavishly to make some display of gaudy and ostentatious pomp, but he would never fail to replace, by the judicial murder of some rich official and the confiscation of his estates, the treasure thus expended. In duplicity, cruelty, and irreligion, he was no unfit match for the contemporary occupants of St. Peter's chair, but it will be vain to search for any such presentment of him in the pages of the "Novellino." Masuccio, a noble by birth, a courtier by profession,† and secretary to Ferdinand's trusted friend and counsellor, Roberto di Sanseverino, could ill afford, whatever he might know and believe, to set down in his book a true picture of the king.

The best that can be said of Ferdinand's rule is that, within the bounds of his own kingdom, the peace was fairly kept. Stained as he was with every vice, he was a

* "De Immanitate," vol. i., p. 318, Ven., 1518: "Ferdinandus rex Neapolitanorum præclaros etiam viros conclusos carcere etiam bene atque abunde pascebat eandem ex iis voluptatem capiens quam pueri e conclusis in cavea aviculis: qua de re sæpe numero sibi ipse inter intimos suos diu multumque gratulatus subblanditusque in risum tandem ac cachinnos profundebatur."

† The "Masuccio" to Novel XLIV., which is filled with fulsome praise of the Duke of Calabria, as bad a man as his father, may be taken as an instance of the writer's servility.

far-sighted and capable ruler, and, after the suppression of the rebellion of the Angevin nobles, who had been incited to revolt by the refusal of Calixtus IV. to grant him investiture of Naples, he managed for many years to keep his own kingdom quiet, though he did not fail to stir up strife amongst the neighbouring states at every opportunity. No one of his lieutenants did such splendid work in the subjugation of the Angevin revolt as Roberto di Sanseverino, and as a reward for his services he was made Prince of Salerno and Lord High Admiral of the kingdom. Masuccio became his secretary, and, under the favour of such an exalted personage, his social and literary advancement must have been comparatively easy.

The period covered by Masuccio's maturity is the fortunate one of Ferdinand's reign, the time of comparative quiet between the Angevin war and the Revolt of the Barons in 1485, in which fell so many illustrious heads, and which prepared the way for the final ruin of the Aragonese dynasty. Porzio in his history of this movement has set forth fully the causes which led to it, and demonstrates how well justified the barons were in the action they took, and how it was that, at the mere sound of the trumpets of the army of Charles VIII., ten years later, the Aragonese monarchy fell like a house of cards. Of Masuccio personally there is very little information to be gathered. There is no record of his birth or of his death. He was probably born about 1420,* and that he was still living in 1474 is certain, for in the Parlamento, or epilogue, to his book he mentions the death of Roberto di Sanseverino, an event which took place in that year. Seeing that he was Sanseverino's secretary, and that the great majority of his novels are dedicated to prominent Neapolitans, it may be assumed that his life was chiefly spent in Naples and the neighbourhood. Dunlop has set down,† and Roscoe has copied a statement that he passed the greater part of his life in the service of the Dukes of Milan, but for this

* In the Pinto MS., quoted by Settembrini, it is stated that Masuccio's name appears as a witness to a legal document in 1441. He must therefore have been twenty-one years of age at that date.

† "History of Fiction," ii. 172.

there is no warrant, beyond that given in a few inconclusive words at the beginning of Novel XI. After 1474 Masuccio fades entirely from view. The references he makes to himself in the "Novellino" are few and unimportant; more suggestive is one which occurs in a work by Pontano, an epitaph written to his memory, and a composition scarcely worthy of that writer's high reputation as a Latin scholar.

"TUMULUS MASUTII SALERNITANI FABULARUM EGREGII SCRIPTORIS.*

"Hic quoque fabellas lusit tinxitque lepore,
Condiit ornatis et sua dicta jocis.
Nobilis ingenio, natu quoque nobilis, idem
Et doctis placuit principibusque viris.
Masutius nomen, patria est generosa Salernum,
Hæc simul et vitam præbuit et rapuit."

In the story of Messer Goro and Pope Pius II., Luigi Pulci refers to Masuccio, and furthermore dedicates his story to the Duchess of Calabria in terms which suggest that he had been encouraged by reading the many pleasant tales of Masuccio to make this essay in fiction, and to beg the illustrious lady to accept the same, as she had already accepted the dedication of the "Novellino."† In the appendix to Toppo's "Biblioteca Napoletana," written by Leonardo Nicodemi, there is a passage which claims for Masuccio the honours of a poet, but no fragment of his verses has come down to posterity.‡

Masuccio was born of the Guardati, a noble family of Salerno. In his admirable introduction to the edition of the "Novellino" published in 1874, Signor Luigi Settembrini has been able to supply certain fresh facts concerning

* Aldine edition, 1518, p. 72.

† "Raccolta dei Classici Italiani," Milano, 1804, vol. ii., p 142. "Masuccio, grande onore della citta di Salerno, molto imitatore del nostro M. Giovanni Boccacio, illustrissima Madonna Ippolita, mi ha dato ardire a scrivere alla Vostra Eccellenza, leggendo a questi di nel suo Novellino molte piacevoli cose, le quali poi che io intesi essere da V. S. graziosamente accettate e lette, ho fatto come i navigante i quali sogliono addirizzar le loro navi dove le loro mercatanzie intendono aver ricapito."

‡ In the "Masuccio" to Novel XXX. he gives a hint that he might, if occasion should demand, become a rhymester, "con un fiume di proprii e convenienti adiettivi quasi in rima posti."

the family aforesaid, taken from some private genealogical records to which he had been given access. These tell of a certain Luise, or Luigi Guardato, the descendant of a long line of fighting barons, who was secretary to Raimondo Orsini, the prince upon whom Alfonso the Magnanimous had conferred the lordship of Salerno. This Luigi was numbered amongst the oldest nobility of the Seggio del Campo, presumably the aristocratic quarter of the city, and by his marriage with Margherita Mariconda became the father of the writer of the "Novellino." It is further recorded that Masuccio himself married Cristina Pando, and had by her four children. The MS. then goes on to deal with the branch of the Guardati which settled at Sorrento, descendants of which in 1874 were still living.

Masuccio's place in the political and social world may best be realized from the dedications of his novels. From the terms of these it would appear that he must have been intimate with many of the most prominent of the public men of his time, and amongst these may be numbered seven or eight of the leaders in the Barons' revolt of 1485.* It has been noted already that he was secretary to Roberto di Sanseverino, and from the fact that he dedicated to Antonello, Roberto's successor, one of his novels, and wrote a cordial and flattering exordium to the same, it may be inferred that he was on intimate footing with the son of his patron. Under these circumstances it is almost certain that, had Masuccio been living when the revolt of the Barons broke out in 1485, some mention of his name would have occurred in the quasi-judicial proceedings taken against the leaders of the conspiracy. From the appendix to Porzio (ed. 1859), it may be gathered that he was not—even if alive—the secretary to Antonello de Sanseverino, for the names of all the secretaries of the implicated barons are given in the records relating to their trials, and Masuccio's is not amongst them. The fact that a member of his mother's family, Andrea Mariconda, was Vice-Protonotario, and one of the judges who dealt with the accused conspirators, might account for the ab-

* Novel IV. is dedicated to Antonello de Petrucciis; XIII. to the Conti di Lauria; XVIII. to Antonello de Sanseverino; XXX. to the Prince of Bisignano; XL. to the Conte di Tursi; and XLVIII. to the Duca di Melfi.

sence of his name, but the balance of probability seems to favour the view that he died before the outbreak of the revolt, and was spared the spectacle of the ruin and death of his friends.

No further facts of any importance are forthcoming concerning the personality of Masuccio, but, without wandering into the mazes of constructive criticism, it may be permitted to cite from the "Novellino" itself certain passages which warrant a tentative estimate of his character and leanings. Masuccio seems to have rated himself as one with a message to deliver; his work was perhaps the earliest example of the *Tendenz-Roman;* his phraseology gives one the impression that he wrote with his feelings at a white heat, and when a man delivers his soul in this wise he will generally contrive to let it appear what manner of man he himself may have been. Pulci speaks of Masuccio as "molto imitatore del nostro M. Giovanni Boccaccio," and there is perhaps some analogy between his position in the Aragonese court and that which Boccaccio had occupied in the Angevin. In the Prologue and in the several dedications there are divers over-laboured touches which suggest that he was trying hard to play the courtier, and to consecrate his life to the delectation of the Duchess Ippolita and her ladies; but, judging by the earnest spirit he displays otherwhere, it is hard to believe that he set about his work only with the object of telling witty stories of amorous intrigue and sombre ones of tragic adventure.

In the very Prologue to the work he announces his primary theme, by proclaiming himself the scourger of priestly vices. There is evidence enough and to spare to be gathered from other sources that a censor of this sort was badly needed, but there is also evidence just as strong concerning other evils and abuses which Masuccio lets pass unrebuked. It must be remembered, however, that in all ages the flagellators of existing offences as well as the teachers of new and purer rules of life have chosen their special fields of labour, and Masuccio apparently did not deem himself strong enough to attack the forces of evil on all sides. The cruelty, the avarice, the treachery, and the lust of the rulers of the land, and the misery of the people subject to the caprice of one of the most infamous of tyrants, did not greatly stir Masuccio's indignation or pity. These were public evils and public wrongs. They existed in every land and in almost equal degree, and with the facile acquiescence of an Italian in things constituted and with the traditional *pazienza* he was content to bear them, grievous as they were, rather than take arms against them. If they touched him, they touched everyone else as well, and the course of past events had proved over and over again that the struggles for redress and reform which had been begun against the forces of constituted authority, were by no means foreordained to success, and that the outcome of such attempts as had been specially fortunate had rarely been worth the trouble and danger of the enterprise. It may have been a train of reasoning like this which led Masuccio to suffer the ills springing from bad government to go unscathed by his satire, but prudence may very likely have intervened and counselled him that to criticise the acts of a king like Ferdinand would be to place his neck in the hangman's noose.

It is when Masuccia begins to deal with the offences which spring from the corruption of this or that particular class or caste or sex; of those foul blows which are dealt us by the hands we are especially led to trust; and of the foes which lurk within a man's own household, that he seems to find his true vocation. If the words which a man speaks or writes are ever to be taken as evidence of the mind that is in him, then assuredly Masuccio may be credited with ardent hatred of the offences he denounces. Putting aside occasional lapses into licentiousness of expression as accidents inseparable from the age in which he wrote, it is almost impossible to doubt his sincerity as a would-be reformer of manners. It is true he makes now and then reservations and exceptions which appear to us strange and inconsistent. Once he excuses and even commends a cardinal with respect to dealings which he would certainly have censured had he been writing of a friar.* Again, after the manner of Boccaccio, he wishes for the friend to whom the novel in question is dedicated,

* Novel XV.

fortunes as happy as those of the youth whose successful intrigue with a married woman he has just chronicled;† but in estimating these seeming incongruities some heed must be taken of the change which, since his day, has come over the ordinary conception of sexual love. Masuccio lived in the lingering shadows of the middle ages, and was on this account the heir of a tradition by which certain forms of adultery attained a place, if not amongst the domestic virtues, at least amongst the venial sins. The air was as yet heavy with the miasma bred from the dismal swamp of cramped and artificial life led by womankind in those dreary centuries. The courts of love of France and Provence declared more than once that love between husband and wife was impossible, and the drift of existence within the narrow limits of a feudal castle went far to confirm this proclamation. Love, however, of one sort or another was inevitable, so it found its expression in the faithful unfaith covenanted between *dame* and *serviteur*, in relations the type of which is made familiar to us in the Arthurian romances and in the early Celtic love stories. These relations were shaped by the personal preferences of the lovers themselves, and had but slight regard of the moral obligations repudiated by their adoption. In these early love gestes the youth rarely addresses the maid; he is attracted rather by the mature woman with character and passions developed by the independence she has enjoyed since she was brought out of her seclusion and commanded to marry a man whom she had seen twice or thrice before—a mate chosen, not to please her fancy, but by reason of the fiefs and towns under his control. The loves of such women with the men whose *métier* it was to solace their weariness and woe, occupy a large portion of the ballad and romance literature of the middle ages. Tristram and Yseult, Paolo and Francesca, are but the most noteworthy examples, the finest flowers of this unwholesome passion-nourished thicket of exotic bloom, worked up into pathetic stories and set before us instinct with life and beauty, from having passed through the hands of the great artists who have dealt with them.

† Novel XII.

With the lapse of time the custom aforesaid became so universal that toleration of the same was inevitable, and after a cycle of toleration came something like approval, or, at any rate, very lenient censure. It is worthy of remark that this new bond of vice very soon put on the guise of virtue, by demanding the absolute fidelity of one offender to the other. If only this faith were duly kept, every other crime consequent on the intrigue would be passed over with indulgence. In the version of Tristram and Yseult given by the Minnesinger, Gottfried von Strassburg, both of the lovers are commended to sympathy and compassion, the inextinguishable fidelity of one to the other, the rejection of all else the world had to offer for the sake of love, being regarded as the supreme exhibition of virtue. To take another, and more familiar instance, Dante, with all his austerity, deals out but mild condemnation to the ill-starred lovers, seeing that he places them in the least terrible circle of the Inferno for the punishment of their offences, and in our own day the severe respectability of Tennyson has allowed us to nourish no slight sympathy for the loves of Lancelot and Guinevere.

The prevalence of this legend of infected passion and impure fidelity, and its survival down to Masuccio's time, must be held largely accountable for the fact that he, who writes himself down over and over again as the scourger of female depravity, should constantly mete out very light censure to offences which seem, judged by modern standards, wellnigh as flagrant as those which he visits with his fiercest denunciation.* To take as an example Novel XXIV., it may be remarked that he begins the story by relating how, as a matter of everyday occurrence, a gallant youth fell in love with a fair dame, the wife of one of the chief gentlemen of the city. He writes about the youth in the kindliest spirit, praising him warmly as he describes in what seemly fashion he essayed

* The influence of mediæval sentiment may also be traced in Novel XLI., where Messer Ciarlo consents to serve his friend in furtherance of his amour by taking a part somewhat similar to that played by the companion in the "Aubade" of Gerault de Berneil, who sings to warn his friend that the dawn is breaking and that it is time to leave his ladylove (Taylor's "Lays and Songs of the Minnesingers and Troubadours," p. 247).

to win the lady's favour, and demanding from the reader subsequently the deepest sympathy on account of the failure of his enterprise. And in dealing with the lady he does not condemn her for her infidelity to her husband, but because she preferred the embraces of a Moorish muleteer to those of the proper gentleman who had elected to make her his partner in adultery. The speech and action of the lover too, when he takes up the story, serve to demonstrate how strongly the spirit aforesaid had infected current sentiment. He, having caught the lady *flagrante delicto*, does not confine himself to chiding her on his own account, but goes on to rate her soundly for the betrayal of her husband, whom he praises as a gentleman adorned with every excellence. All this is in full harmony with mediæval feeling as to the relation of the sexes. The woman who favours her lover, and him alone, is scarcely regarded by Masuccio as unchaste or worthy of blame, and in the first part of the book he has little or no censure for those who commit themselves with monks and friars, but reserves all his condemnation for the male offenders. The women against whom he writes as the vilest of created beings are those who, not content with a husband and a lover to boot, abandon themselves to some unclean intrigue with a Moor, or a dwarf, or a muleteer.

Masuccio seems to have set out his work with the view of making it serve two principal ends; one to provide a number of diverting stories for the Duchess Ippolita, and the other to shame into better behaviour womankind and all persons wearing the religious habit. Boccaccio and Sacchetti, before his time, and all the Novellieri of the Cinquecento who followed, concern themselves with the same class of subject, but none of them proclaims him so emphatically a *censor morum* or shows such deadly earnestness of purpose. He entered upon a path already well trodden, and a vast host of imitators followed upon his heels; wherefore the mass of literature of the same character as the "Novellino" is a huge one. Masuccio's work would, without doubt, have gone down to the oblivion which has fallen upon Sermini and Sabadino and a host of others, had he not been gifted with the sense of artistic construction which enabled him to set out his pictures with a few firm and rapid strokes.* There is no attempt at polish or elaboration; the secret of his immediate success, and of the recognition still given to him by the historians of fiction, comes from his unerring faculty in hitting at once upon the central point of whatever subject he may have in hand, and his rare judgment in selection and subordination, never failing to let the point aforesaid stand out as the main instrument for enforcing the moral, or illustrating the argument under consideration.

Masuccio's canvas is a limited one. A few of his stories are in the vein of genuine buffo, a few more are tragedies pure and simple, but the majority of the residue will be found to treat of one or other of his two particular themes, the castigation of profligate clerics and unchaste women. He devotes one part of the work to each of these specially; but in the other parts he never lets a friar or a woman escape the lash if he finds a chance of laying it on. The most scathing passages, and those which give the most evident signs of sincerity, are those which occur here and there in the "Masuccio" at the end of the stories. These in places almost smoke with the fire of his rage, and, intermixed with his rough-hewn and occasionally incoherent phrases, are to be found passages of real dramatic power. As an instance may be quoted the conclusion to Novel XXIII., in which, after screaming himself hoarse over the crimes of women, he finishes with these words: "Would that it had been God's pleasure and Nature's to have suffered us to be brought forth from the oak-trees, or indeed to have been engendered from water and mire like the frogs in the humid rains of summer, rather than to have taken our origin from so base, so corrupt, and so vilely fashioned a sex as womankind;" or the frightful indictment at the end of Novel VI. which he prefers against women who put on the habit of religious houses—an in-

* One of his happiest efforts is in the Prologue to Part III., which deals with the profligacy of women. He seems to have realized that it would need some special effort on his part to make the stories immediately following acceptable to the Duchess Ippolita; so by the aid of Mercury he exhibits her as the presiding genius of the shrine of chastity, and lets her excellencies shine out all the brighter from comparison with the turpitude of the residue of her sex.

dictment which is, as he declares, supported by the clearest evidence of his senses;* or the introduction to Novel II., where he prays God soon to make an end of purgatory, so that these friars, being unable to live any longer on the offerings made to them therefor, may be forced to go and work with the mattock.

There are two streams of tendency which sway with peculiar force the common life of the Southern Italians, to wit, the physical side of the sexual passion and the sentiment of religion, and Masuccio may have been impelled unconsciously by the working of these to turn the course of his censure especially against wanton women and lewd friars. While the sun shines, while there is food enough for to-day's meal, and while to-morrow's may be won by an hour's work, while Beppino and Ninetta are conscious of the prick of passion in their veins, they think of little else but love-making, and Beppino is not content merely to sigh after his inamorata or to worship her beauties from a distance. Far from it. Sexual love around the shores of Parthenope was then, as it is now, of that elemental and primitive character of which we find some echo in Lucretius when he writes of that overmastering force which sways the material universe as potently as the bodies of men and women. In Latin countries, as compared with Teutonic, woman is more especially regarded as the instrument of pleasure, and the Neapolitan is subject to a superadded influence of similar nature by reason of the stream of Oriental life which at different periods overflowed his frontiers. Therefore, whenever Beppino may have found that his pretty plaything, which he dreamt of keeping entirely for his own diversion, had befooled and perhaps robbed him, he would roar as loud as Polyphemus over his

* "Taccio anco quanto dir si potrebbe circa lo sposare con li frati, dove io medesimo non una ma piu volte sono intervenuto e visto e toccata con mani."—Novel VI. There is a confirmation of his accusation in a passage in Kemnisius, Ex Concil. Trident., Part III., "de celibatu Sacerdotum": "Memorabile quod Ulricus epistola refert, Gregorium, quum ex piscina quadam allata plus quam sex mille infantum capita vidisset, ingemuisse, et decretum de celibatu tantam cædis causam confessus condigno illud pœnitentiæ fructu purgasse."

wounded pride, and Masuccio's screed against the whole sex may very well be taken as the concentrated expression of this widely-spread sense of injury and resentment—Beppino, and his interpreter as well, being too oriental in feeling to realize that they themselves should be ruled by the standard they would apply to womankind. From the same source a subsidiary explanation of Masuccio's hatred to the priesthood is forthcoming. As soon as the heavens are clouded, when the world wags ill, when love is under an eclipse, and when the fires of passion begin to burn low, when the lovers find in the place of their spent passion no subject with which their fancy may engage itself, man, and woman also, will turn towards what they are pleased to call their religious duties. Beppino, with many thefts, and perhaps a homicide or two upon his soul, and Ninetta, with a long string of petty sins, and infidelities out of number, will both repair to the priest for the mending of their evil case by the promise of a safe entry to Paradise upon terms not too hard. Now, if they should find—as they assuredly would in many cases—that these men, the physicians of their souls, had become what Masuccio calls "rapacissimi lupi," what more natural than that they should cry out that they were being cheated of their dues, that it was both useless and unseemly to go for religious consolation to men no whit better than themselves. Thus the priestly offence would become something more than a peccadillo, and an outcry would arise against profligate and avaricious clerics, to be caught up and accentuated by Masuccio and other censors.

To illustrate still further the intensity of Masuccio's hatred for women, his twenty-first novel may be compared with the first story of Il Pecorone. The two tales deal with the same theme exactly,* and are substantially the same in detail, the only noteworthy difference being that Masuccio brings into the narrative a certain friend of the hero, a man described as impervious to all the wiles of the sex, and lets him discourse at great length on the falsehood of women and the folly of all those

* This tale is given by Painter in the "Palace of Pleasure," No. XLVII., a translation of Ser Giovanni's version.

who trust them. Ser Giovanni in his version of the tale is content to let the frailty of the lady in question be revealed simply by the action of the story, assuredly the more artistic method of treatment, but the temptation to preach a sermon on his favourite theme was evidently too strong for Masuccio to resist.*

For Masuccio's hatred against the religious orders another and a more cogent reason than the one already alluded to is not far to seek. The character of the Popes, and of the major part of the high ecclesiastics who ruled Christendom during the last half of the fifteenth century, was bound to be reflected in the morals of the inferior clergy. The contrast between the ideal life, laid down for all Christians alike by the cardinal maxims of the Founder, and the actual career of fraud, and lust, and cruelty, and bloodshed which was followed with few exceptions by the princes of the Church, appeared no doubt less glaring to the contemporary observer than it is to us, but there are abundant instances in the religious history of the time which may be cited to show that this flagrant corruption and the spectacle of sin sitting in high places provoked the wrath of all the men of pure and holy lives still surviving amongst the corruption of the times. Revivals or revolts against the nefarious practices of the priesthood were almost continuous after the notable movement begun by Arnold of Brescia in 1139, and the laudatory terms in which Masuccio speaks of men like San Bernardino, San Vincenzo, Giovanni Capistrano, and Roberto di Lecce—all of them men of holy lives and revivalist leaders—show how fully he appreciated the evils they attacked and how completely his sympathy was with them in their work.† It is not enough for him to accuse the great mass of the vowed professors of religion of every crime under the sun. Over and beyond this he warns his friends

* Settembrini, in a note ("Il Novellino," p. 54), advances a somewhat whimsical reason for his ill-humour towards women, declaring that it arose from the contemplation of the numerous evils which came upon the kingdom through the profligacy of Joanna II.

† In the "Parlamento" he reiterates his praise and appreciation of all priests and monks who lead honest and godly lives.

that they may not hold converse with anyone wearing the religious garb without loss of character and the good opinion of all worthy men. Even the illustrious Pontano*—one of the last to be suspected of clerical leanings—is rated soundly in that he is too much given to the society of these enemies of the human race,† and by way of pointing his lesson Masuccio goes on to tell a story which sets forth the impiety and blasphemy of the friars in a fashion which would be hard to excuse were not the sincerity of the writer and his zeal for reformation so transparent.‡

At the end of the first part he gives notice that he has said his last word about the priests, admitting at the same time that he has hardly touched the fringe of the question.‖ Here and there it is true he finds a good word for the religious orders, speaking generally, and in well-guarded terms,§ but every individual ecclesiastic, except the revivalist leaders above-mentioned, who appears in the "Novellino," is more or less corrupt and depraved. In Novel XVII. there is a prior who is a companion of thieves and a receiver of stolen goods; in Novel XVIII. a friar of St. Antony swindles a farmer's wife in rascally fashion; in Novel XXIX. another acts the part of Hende

* Novel III.

† Pontano wrote the following words to be inscribed on his own tomb: "Labor, dolor, ægritudo, luctus, servire superbis dominis, jugum ferre superstitionis, quos habet caros sepelire, condimenta vitæ sunt." They scarcely exhibit him as the favourer of clerical dominion.

‡ He writes: "Aprasi adunque la terra, e una con li lor fautori la moltinudine di tanti poltroni vivi tranghiottisca, non solo per castigamento de' presenti ma per timore ed eterno esempio di tutti i futuri scellerati loro pari."—Novel III.

‖ "Essendomi al tutto disposto di tal perversa e malvagia generatione piu avanti non trattare, quantunque a bastanza non abbia scritto."—Novel X.

§ "Questo ben dirò io, e per fermo confesso, quanto de' fatti loro in le passate dieci novelle e in altre parti ho ragionato, non lo avere con intentione fatto di lacerar quelli che a compimento le loro approvate e santissime regole osservano: li quali avvengadioché rari siano, o con difficultà giudicar si possano, pur quelli tali sono indubitatamente e lume e sostenimento de la nostra fede e cristiana religione."—Novel X.

Nicholas in Chaucer's "Miller's Tale;" and another in Novel XXX. plays the pander to the Prince of Salerno. In fine, it may be noted as an instance worth remark that in Novel XXXIII., which is recognized as the first modern rendering of the story of "Romeo and Juliet," there is presented, instead of the pious and dignified Friar Lawrence, a base fellow who must needs be bribed for the service he does the lovers in joining them secretly in wedlock, and again when he provides the drowsy potion for the ill-starred Giannozza.

In dealing with a work of fiction so important as the "Novellino," it is almost inevitable that a comparison with the "Decamerone" should suggest itself. It has been noted already how Luigi Pulci spoke of Masuccio as a imitator of Boccaccio; there is likewise a passage in the "Novellino" itself which hints that its writer was fired to follow so illustrious a leader;* but however sincere and earnest his desire may have been, his attempt was not a successful one.† In temper and in parts as well, the two men differed so widely that any such essay was bound to fail. Boccaccio was a scholar, and a fastidious one, while Masuccio, if he knew the rules of grammar, certainly did not always regard them. Boccaccio sat serene apart from the rough humours of the people; they diverted him, and it was his pleasure to use them for the delectation of his readers. He did not, like Masuccio, take vice in hand primarily to correct it. He would laugh at it—often indulgently—and at virtue as well, were the laugh necessary to round off his work to perfection. His scorn of formal religion after the spirit of it had been crushed out by ecclesiasticism may have been as sincere as Masuccio's fulminations against the vices of the clergy; but he does not limit himself to the castigation

* Prologue to Part III.

† Agostino Doni, in his "Libreria" (Venice, 1558), writes, p. 80: "Quanti ci sono che s'inviluppono in qualche laberinto d'altri, chi accusa Dante, chi defende il Petrarcha, altri armeggian con 'l Ariosto, e altri concorrono con il Boccaccio a novellare, lascio stare hora dei roba le novelle d'altri, o che gli toglie le dittione intere per non far satira. Benedetto sia il Salernitano che al manco non ha robato pure una parola del Boccaccio, anzi ha fatto un libro il quale e tutto suo."

of vice and hypocrisy. He makes a travesty of real piety, and excuses or even praises what the sincere professors of religion in all times would have condemned, and never once lapses into such enthusiasm as Masuccio displays in speaking of San Bernardino and the pure and earnest men who followed him. His regard for treatment is careful enough to satisfy the exacting standard of contemporary teaching. How much more highly he rated it in comparison with subject than did Masuccio is evidenced by the setting forth of the two books. The "Novellino" is given to the world as a mere bundle of stories, a succession of rough-hewn powerful studies brought out without forethought or design from the workshop. It wants even the conventional knitting together furnished by Ser Giovanni and Il Lasca to their collections, and constituted as it is, must stand or fall on its own merits, whereas, in the case of the "Decameron," were the tales themselves robbed of three-fourths of their interest, the work as a whole, would still attract and fascinate on account of the extraordinary beauty and delicacy of the setting, which must ever be ranked amongst the acknowledged masterpieces of literary craftsmanship. It is hard to realize any contrast more telling and dramatic than that exhibited between the dainty personalities of the immortal ten, taking their gentle pleasure in their fair retreat, and the pavid crowd stricken with the horror of the pestilence and cowering in the streets and alleys of the city below—between the brilliant masquerade of life in all its humours and all its phases set forth to the listeners by each story-teller in turn, and the grim and almost tangible presence of Death lurking just outside the garden doors.

In the "Novellino" all that Masuccio does in the way of setting and introduction, is to write a Prologue and classify his stories somewhat roughly into five groups, each group being preceded by a short prologue of its own.

The first group deals with the offences of priests and friars, the second with the mishaps which befall those who are over-jealous, and with divers amusing tricks played by cunning knaves, the third with the profligacy of women, the fourth with various love-stories and adventures, and the fifth with noble deeds wrought by illustrious personages. Masuccio writes with all the fire of a southern Italian. Whatever he has to say he says, careless as to what terms he shall use for the expression of his meaning. With such a temperament, and such a method of treatment, it will be readily understood by all those who remember the character of the subjects he commonly elaborates that he must often be coarse in diction. He is undoubtedly often coarse in form, but there are few traces in his rugged sentences of that corrupt purpose which shows itself too often amidst the delicate periods of Boccaccio's prose. His manner of speech is not widely different from that used by the Neapolitan of to-day, and he uses it with a touch of pride and satisfaction, writing himself down as the *materno poeta* in the very first phrase of his book. While Pontano and Poggio and other humanists and story-tellers were writing in Latin, it was his object to show whether, with his handling, the Neapolitan idiom might not give as good results as the Tuscan was giving to Pulci and the Ferrarese to Boiardo. His Italian, though involved and inelegant,* is not dialect, as Roscoe affirms in his notice in the "Italian Novelists;" it is, however, sufficiently tinged with popular idiom to show that he had gathered his experience by mixing with men of every class, and that his view of life was a large and comprehensive one. Though he lived about the court, and wrote at times in sycophantic terms, he showed himself quite at home in describing the life of the common people, both in town and country. The pages of the "Novellino" are full of racy characteristic types of Salernitans and Neapolitans. There are the peasants, working as hard then as they work to-day in the Campania Felice and in the mountain vineyards, and the traders and craftsmen of the towns, with their humorous tricks and coarse practical jokes put one upon another, the details of common

* Signor Settembrini in his footnotes to the latest edition is frequently compelled to admit that certain passages, though they show the author's meaning, are obscure, while others baffle comprehension entirely.

life, the doings of the persons concerned, being all sketched with the firm and easy touch of experience.

If full credit be given to the claims advanced by Francesco Tuppo in his introduction to the early editions of the work, it would appear that, had it not been for the forethought of a certain John Marco and of Tuppo himself, the "Novellino" as a complete work would never have seen the light. From the fact that Masuccio wrote a Prologue to the whole book, and a Parlamento or Epilogue, and prologues to the several parts, it is evident that he left his work complete in manuscript; but the terms of Tuppo's introduction raise a doubt whether he was alive when the edition of 1476 was printed.* In Novel XXII. he speaks of his present old age,† and Novel XLVI. must have been written after 1470, as in it he alludes to the capture of Arzilla by the Portuguese in that year. It is certain that he lived to the end of 1474, but the fact that Tuppo addresses the first edition to the Duchess Ippolita, as Masuccio had dedicated the MS. to her,‡ certainly lends colour to the view that the writer was no longer on earth to discharge this task which fell to Tuppo's care. Again, had he been alive, when his writings were torn up by the officer of justice, presumably at the request of some one or other of the victims of his lash, he would scarcely have let his work appear without some mention of this attack upon him and his mission.‖

Leaving Masuccio's personality in the shadows which bar all further investigation, a short consideration may be given to the history of the book itself. The first edition was printed at Naples in 1476 by Reisinger of Strasburg, who had brought thither the art of printing five years before. Of this edition only one copy is known

* A passage in the "Masuccio" of Novel XXX. shows that the tales were circulated and read—presumably in MS.—as they were written.

† "E con la presente senectu cognosco de' fatti loro."

‡ "Quello como per Masuccio fo ad tua serenita intitulato, cusi stampato a te illustrissima mia Idea pia Ipolita duchessa de Calabria sera per me indirizato."—Introduction Ed. 1483.

‖ Tuppo's words seem to imply that divers copies of the book in MS. were in circulation before 1476.

to exist, the one in the Bibliotheque Nationale in Paris. The second edition appeared at Milan in 1483, and the third at Venice in the following year. The fourth, of 1492, also of Venice, has for frontispiece a very fine woodcut representing Masuccio offering his book to the Duchess for acceptance, and at Venice also the five succeeding editions—the last in 1541—were printed. The tenth, "l'editione della gatta,"* was brought out without date or place, and, as it was the first to appear after the institution of the Index, was greatly mutilated. The eleventh appeared in Lucca in 1765—"in toscana favella ridotto"—and in 1874 Signor Luigi Settembrini brought out at Naples the edition which the present translator has followed. Signor Settembrini—to quote his own words—thus set to work: "Io mi propongo di restituirlo all' antica lezione per quanto m'e possibile." This task he has performed most thoroughly, and he has not shrunk from bringing back certain passages to the orthodox obscurity or even incomprehensibility of the earlier editions, rather than suffer them to remain in the unauthorized lucidity which the anonymous Tuscan editor of 1765 had shed over them by his emendations. There is no evidence that a complete translation of the book into a foreign language has ever been made. Painter gives Novel XVII. in a form which suggests that it must have been taken from an altered French version; Roscoe includes six, greatly changed from the originals, in his "Italian Novelists;" and a translation of nineteen into French has recently been published. In conclusion, I must acknowledge my heavy obligation to the learned introduction which Signor Settembrini has prefixed to his work, a contribution not merely to the elucidation of this particular book, but of the whole literature of Southern Italy.

* It has a cat and kittens on the title page.

Dedication by Francesco Tuppo*

MOST illustrious Ippolita of Aragon and of Visconti, who by thy own virtues art more goddess than mortal, what though in this inept beginning o' mine the lyre of Orpheus would in sooth be the more fitting instrument wherewith to attempt not only to enumerate but to call to mind thy noble and queenly converse, thy great courage, and thy unheard-of munificence—thou who art the one and only rock of beauty from which flows the spring of chastity. Nevertheless when I, who am entirely devoted to thy most illustrious ladyship, consider those happy years of youth which have been thy portion with us by virtue of thy state as the future queen of this our Ausonian kingdom, since thou hast become in lawful matrimony the spouse of my earthly lord and master, Alfonso of Aragon, Duke of Calabria, the first-born of the invincible and mighty lord, Don Fernando, the peaceful and fortunate King of Sicily, Hungary, and Jerusalem: when I consider thy chastity, the like of which has never before been heard of, that regal and mysterious secret in which thou sharest as an only daughter, and how thou art equal to the Sibilla Cumana in resource, and in humanity superior to all the Roman, Greek, and Trojan ladies who ever lived: when I consider all these things in my mind, I am fain to become an image of stone more quickly even than those who look at Medusa's face. And of a surety our Parthenopeans may well bless great Jove for having in these our days endowed with the gift of thy most excellent virtues this land of ours, which, on account of thy holy prayers, can never be blasted either by human or divine wrath.

Finding myself on this account entirely bound over to your sublimity (as my rustic pen declares,) I will never cease so long as my lowly spirit is master of this

*This dedication is omitted in all editions after that of Venice, 1484.

worn and weary body of mine to praise and extol your virtues to the skies, and like a devoted slave to show myself ready to do whatever I can for your most illustrious ladyship. Wherefore [this book] having come into my hands by the means of Johan Marco the Parmesan,* that most excellent copyist of all the letters ever [written] in the world, a servant of the king, and a very dear friend of my own, it seemed to me that such a book ought not to be kept back from fame. Now, although the original [writings] were torn in pieces by the very hand of the magistrate,† and burnt by those who learned therein certain news concerning their own households, nevertheless my craft was great enough to preserve a copy of the same; and, seeing that it had been already dedicated to your serenity by Masuccio, I now in like manner address it, thus printed, to you, my most illustrious goddess, the pious Ippolita, Duchess of Calabria. Farewell.

Of your illustrious ladyship the faithful servant,

FRANCESCO TUPPO OF NAPLES.‡

* There is a mention of Johan Marco, Cinico, in the poems of the Count of Policastro, one of the sons of Antonello de Petruciis, who was executed after the conspiracy of the barons. See D'Aloe in his appendix to Porizo's "Congiura dei Baroni."

† Auditore, minister of grace and justice.

‡ Francesco Tuppo was a doctor of laws and a clerk in the royal service. He was the author of a version of Æsop's Fables, rendered into the Italian, which was printed in 1486.

Prologue

THE NOVELLINO OF THE NOBLE MAKER IN THE MOTHER TONGUE, MASUCCIO GUARDATO OF SALERNO, DEDICATED TO THE MOST ILLUSTRIOUS IPPOLITA OF ARAGON, OF THE HOUSE OF VISCONTI AND DUCHESS OF CALABRIA.* HERE BEGINS IN AUSPICIOUS WISE THE PROLOGUE:

SINCE I clearly understand and hold as an indisputable fact, most illustrious and exalted lady, that it would ill become me to compose a book to the music of my mean and harsh-toned lyre, that it would become me even less were I to call the same after my own name, I see that, in so doing, I might be more justly rebuked for my temerity than commended either in great or small degree for my gifts of eloquence. Nevertheless, having from my most tender youth busied myself in the exercise of my wit, coarse and unpolished though it be, having written down with my rude and sluggish hand certain novels, the truth of which is approved by real and authentic events which have come to pass in former times, and in these our days, and having sent these same to divers worshipful persons—as in sooth the titles of the stories themselves will clearly demonstrate—the desire has often come upon me to gather together all such of these as may be scattered abroad in divers places,

* Ippolita Maria, the daughter of Francesco Sforza by his marriage with Bianca, the natural daughter and only issue of Filippo Maria Visconti, the last Duke of Milan of that family. She married in 1465, Alfonso, Duke of Calabria, the eldest son of King Ferdinand I. and grandson of Alfonso the Magnanimous. She had by him two sons and one daughter: Ferdinand, who succeeded to the throne of Naples on his father's abdication, Don Pietro, and Donna Isabella, Duchess of Milan, wife of the Gian Galeazzo Sforza who was dethroned and slain by Ludovico Moro. She was a woman of intelligence and a patron of learning. Constantine Lascaris was her tutor in Greek, and dedicated to her the Greek Grammar published at Milan in 1476, the first Greek book printed in Italy. She died at Naples in 1484 and was buried in the Church of the Annunziata.

and, by the collection thereof, to form the present little book, calling the same—on account of its trifling worth—The Novellino, and dedicating and sending it to you, who are the mainstay and light of this our Italian land.

This I do in order that you, with the fluency of your accomplished tongue and the excellence of your rare wit, may castigate and polish the many rusty places you may find abounding therein; then, after you shall have cut off and taken away any superfluities you may discover, you may—*licet indigne*—give it a place in that excellent and glorious library of yours.* And although there were at work divers causes which almost drew me back from this scheme of mine, and dissuaded me from entering upon this work, still, when I happened not long ago to call to mind a certain instance, greatly in the mouths of the vulgar, which actually occurred in our city of Salerno not many years since, I felt comforted thereby and spurred on to carry out my proposed work. What this instance aforesaid was, I intend to let you know before I write further.

I must tell you, therefore, that in the days of Queen Margaret,† of happy and illustrious memory, there lived in this our city a certain Genoese merchant, a man of great wealth, engaged in traffic on a vast scale, renowned by name in all parts of Italy, and called Messer Guardo Salusgio. His family, moreover, was one of the most honourable of the city. Now it chanced one day that this same merchant was walking backwards and forwards in front of his bank, which was situated in a street called La Drapperia, a quarter in which were to be found many other banks, and jewellers', and tailors' shops as well. During his walk it came to pass that he espied lying just

* The Aragonese kings collected a fine library in Naples. It was sacked by the French under Charles VIII. in 1495.

† Daughter of Charles of Durazzo, who was beheaded in 1348. She married her cousin, Charles III. (Durazzo), by whom Joanna I. was deposed and murdered. She was the mother of Ladislas, King of Naples, d. 1414, and of Joanna II., d. 1435. She was a woman of great ability and courage, and it was on this account that Ladislas, who was an infant when his father died, was able to retain the throne. She died in 1412, and lies buried in the Cathedral of Salerno, where a gorgeous tomb, the work of Baboccio da Piperno, was erected to her memory.

at the feet of a poor tailor who was there plying his trade, a Venetian ducat; whereupon he, being quite familiar with the impression and device thereof, although the coin itself was all muddy and bruised, knew straightway what it really was, and without any hesitation stooped down and said, smiling the while, "By my faith, here is a ducat." The wretched tailor before him, who was patching and mending a doublet in order that he might earn for himself a little bread, when he saw what had come to pass, was so much overcome with poisonous envy, by his extreme poverty, and by rage and vexation as well, that he turned his face to Heaven, clenching his fists in the tempest of his fury, and uttering curses against both the justice and the power of God, ending with these words, "It is well said that gold runs after gold, and that the ill fortune of the miserable never changes. Here am I, a wretched wight, who have laboured hard all through this day without earning as much as five tornesi* by my toil, and I forsooth find round about me nought but sharp stones, which pierce and ruin my shoes. This man, who is master of a mighty store of treasure, has now picked up a golden ducat at my very feet, a thing which he needs just as much as the dead need incense." While he was thus lamenting, the wise and prudent merchant betook himself into the shop of the silversmith who lived opposite, and charged the latter to restore the ducat to its original beauty by the means of fire and of the tools he used for such work. Then, with a pleasant smile upon his face, he turned towards the poor tailor and addressed him in these words: "My good man, you were very wrong to murmur against God in such fashion because He acted with a wise purpose in thus letting me find this ducat, forasmuch as, if it had chanced to fall into your hands, you would very soon have parted with it. Nay, even if you had kept it, you would have put it away all alone by itself amongst your poor rags, and would not have placed it where it should be; whereas, now that it has come into my possession, it will fare in just the opposite wise for I will take care that it be put amongst its fellows in a fine and numerous com-

* Tornese, an old French coin worth the third part of a French crown.

pany of coins." And after he had thus spoken, he returned to his bank and threw the coin which he had picked up on the top of many thousands of florins which were already there.

For the reason then that I have composed—according to the illustration of the fable above written—a little book of my own out of certain novels which were scattered about, some here and some there, I have long wished, because of all these reasons which I have mentioned aforetime, to send the same to you, most worshipful silversmith and super-excellent adept in works of this sort, albeit you will find them, like the ducat, very muddy and sadly beaten out of shape. Thus you may correct and beautify my book with those tools of yours which are always ready at hand, and when it shall have become fair and seemly, it may peradventure be deemed worthy of a very humble place amongst your sumptuous and most elegant volumes.

And this same book of mine in its new place will only lend a fresh and a greater adornment to the whole; for, as the philosopher hath it, when things of an opposite nature are brought into close conjunction, their inequalities become the more manifest therefor. And over and beyond this, I make my prayer to you that, at some future time when leisure may be granted to you from your other duties, you will not look upon it as an irksome task to read these novels of mine, because I am well assured that you will find therein many merry conceits and delightful jests, which will prove to you an unceasing source of pleasure and recreation. And if, peradventure, there should be amongst those who listen to them some canting bigot,* some follower of those false ministers of religion—concerning whose wicked lives and nefarious vices I mean to record some pretty stories in the first ten of my novels—some fellow who would willingly rend me with his ravening teeth, I beg you that you will on no account turn aside from the path you have undertaken to tread because men of this sort may declare that I am a blasphemer, and that I have uttered evil slanders against the servants of God with my

* "Santesso." The edition of 1483 gives "sanctesso," and that of 1484 "sanctese."

envenomed tongue. In a strife like this, indeed, I ask nothing more but that Truth herself should, in the time of my need, take up arms in my defence, and bear witness on my behalf that I am not moved to act in this wise on account of any desire of mine to speak ill of others, or of any personal or particular hatred which I bear towards men of this sort.

But, on the contrary, so as not to hide the truth in any way, I have been seized with the wish to bring to the notice of some powerful prince or other, and likewise to the notice of divers other particular friends of mine, certain instances, some of which have happened in our own day, and some in times not very long past. By the consideration of these the persons above-named may furnish themselves with full information concerning the many and varied methods, and the wicked devices, by means of which foolish, or rather, not very wise, laymen have, in past times, been tricked and befooled by these false professors of religion. My purpose in doing this is to make sure that those now living may become more wary of such folk, and that the generations of the future may be prepared so as not to suffer themselves to be led into entanglements by this vile and corrupt crew, working under the cover of simulated righteousness. And furthermore I, recognizing the fact that amongst the ministers of religion there are some good men,* perceive that I am of necessity constrained to follow their example, and to imitate their doings in certain matters. I feel this chiefly because the greater number of monks and friars, as soon as they get a cowl over their heads, seem to fancy that full licence has been granted to them to put the worst slanders upon all laymen, both in public and in private as well, adding that all such men are surely damned, and many other bestialities for which they ought to be stoned.

Now if perchance they should be minded to contend in opposition to me by making the assertion that, when they preach, they rebuke and scourge the sins of the wicked, I can easily answer them thereanent by remarking that, when I write, I do not set down words against the virtues

* Orig., *cognoscendo io li religiosi assai bone persone.* The sense seems to require "*tra*" before "*li religiosi.*"

of the good. And in this wise, without any trickery or favour given to one above another, we shall all transgress and all be chastised by the same stripes. Therefore, seeing that I am disposed to follow their example and to write with all truth concerning the many villanies and the corrupt lives of every one of them, no one at all ought to feel any displeasure thereanent. Nevertheless, with regard to those whose ears are choked with holy water* in such wise that they cannot bring themselves to listen to aught spoken amiss concerning those vowed to religion, it seems to me that the best and only remedy for their infirmity will be to let them go their way in God's name, without ever reading or hearing tell of these novels of mine. And, keeping up their commerce with the friars, they will get to know more thoroughly every day that passes how profitable such conversation is both to their bodies and to their souls. And as such men as these are abundantly furnished with all sorts of charity, they will continually impart the same virtue to their associates. And you, most worshipful and beauteous lady, reading my volume with your wonted friendliness, may perchance find therein some flowerets intermixed with the many thorns; which thing will cause you now and then to remember the least of all your servants, your most humble Masuccio, who, without ceasing, recommends himself to you, and prays the gods for the increase of your happy and prosperous estate. Farewell.

* Orig., *ammassate de santa pasta*. "Pasto is by metaphor much used for court holy water, fond entertaining hopes to feed fools withal."—FLORIO.

MASUCCIO.

THE brief and inept exordium addressed to your most famous serenity being now finished, I will let follow straightway the novels, or rather the stories, which I have already promised; and in the first ten of these, as I have before stated, will be set forth divers hateful deeds of some of these professors of religion. Amongst these will be found certain tales which will not only rouse the astonishment of those who listen thereto, but their inward grief as well; some there are which will not be passed in review without merry laughter and rejoicing. Amongst the rest, the first novel is dedicated to the invincible and most puissant king our lord and master; and, when this shall have come to an end, I intend to deal with divers other themes, some diverting, some moral, and some pitiful and worthy of your tears, going on in the order which follows.

Novel the First

ARGUMENT

MAESTRO DIEGO IS CARRIED BACK DEAD TO HIS CONVENT BY MESSER RODERICO. ANOTHER MONK, THINKING HIM TO BE ALIVE, STRIKES HIM WITH A STONE, AND THEN FEARS HE MAY HAVE SLAIN HIM THEREBY, WHEREFORE HE TAKES TO FLIGHT, MOUNTED UPON A MARE. BY A STRANGE CHANCE HE MEETS, RIDING ON A STALLION, WITH LANCE IN REST, THE DEAD MAN, WHO FOLLOWS HIM ALL THROUGH THE CITY. THE LIVING MONK, HAVING BEEN ARRESTED, CONFESSES HE IS GUILTY OF THE HOMICIDE, AND IS DEALT WITH AS A MALEFACTOR, BUT THE CAVALIER MAKES KNOWN THE TRUTH, AND THE FRIAR IS DELIVERED FROM THE DOOM HE MERITED NOT.

TO THE MIGHTY KING, DON FERDINAND OF ARAGON*

EXORDIUM

MOST mighty and glorious king, both in the present day, and in times past as well, the number of skilful poets, of eloquent speakers, of most excellent writers, who have laboured and still labour in elegant prose and in noble verse, in Latin and in the mother tongue, to celebrate the plentiful honour and the endless renown of your most serene Majesty, has been so great,

* Ferdinand I. was the natural son of Alfonso the Magnanimous. He was born in 1431, and succeeded to the kingdom on his father's death in 1458. He married (1st) Isabella of Chiaromonte, by whom he had the following children: Alfonso, Duke of Calabria, who succeeded him; Federico d'Altamura; Giovanni, who became Cardinal; Francesco, Duke of Saint Angelo; Beatrice, who married Mathias, King of Hungary; and Leonora, Duchess of Ferrara; (2nd) Joanna, the sister of Ferdinand, King of Aragon, by whom he had a daughter, Joanna, who married his nephew, King Ferdinand II. He died in 1494.

that I am persuaded my rude and homely style must appear to you not otherwise than as the black spot in the centre of the pure white ermine.* Nevertheless, since your Highness has deigned with your accustomed courtesy to assure me that it would give you great pleasure were I to set down in writing some record which may preserve the memory of that remarkable adventure which happened in the kingdom of Castile to a certain cavalier and a minor friar, I desire, with what speed I may, to obey these your wishes and I would sooner fail in respect to what I write, than by my silence seem to fail in any way in dutiful obedience towards you. For this reason, and not on account of any rash humour of mine, I have determined to enter the difficult labyrinth, and boldly presume that this unworthy script of mine may be read, peradventure, by so puissant a king. Wherefore I beg you, with all the humility which the occasion demands, that it may please you kindly to accept the same, hoping that when your other occupations may give you leisure, you will not find it tedious to peruse it in the company of your stalwart and active children and foster-children. And, in addition to the fact that the story in itself is noteworthy, you will find therein divers pleasantries and feats worthy of all praise wrought by certain friars, the record of which will, I doubt not, only serve to increase and augment your reverence and devotion to men of this sort. Therefore your most faithful Masuccio, casting himself at your feet and seeking your good grace, implores that he may not be reckoned by you amongst the number of those whose names are no longer held in remembrance. Farewell.

* Ferdinand was the founder of the Neapolitan Order of the Ermellino.

THE NARRATIVE

I WILL tell you then, most righteous king, that in the times when our lord and king, Don Fernando of Aragon,* of happy and illustrious memory, your most worthy grandfather, and the ruler of the kingdom of Castile, bore tranquil and protecting sway, there lived, attached to a religious house in Salamanca, an ancient and very noble city of the above-named kingdom, a certain friar minor named Maestro Diego da Revalo, who, being no less well versed in the learning of the Thomists than of the Scotists, had been deemed worthy to be chosen and appointed one of those who, in consideration of a generous salary, should expound this teaching in the excellent schools of the famous university of this city. In this calling he made the wondrous fame of his learning widely known throughout all the kingdom; and, besides this, he would now and again preach certain short sermons more noted for their useful and sensible tone than for any great show of devotion. And being still a youth, and of a very comely presence, and graceful as well; being subject, moreover, to the heats of amorous passion, it happened that one day, while he was preaching, his eye fell upon a young lady in his congregation who was endowed with the most marvellous beauty. This lady, who was called by name Donna Caterina, was the wife of one of the chief gentlemen of the city, to wit, Messer Roderico d'Angiaja; and the friar, as soon as ever he beheld her, was mightily pleased with the sight of her. Therefore Master Cupid, by means of the fair seeming of her beauty, dealt a stroke of love to his heart already inflamed. After he had come down from the pulpit he betook himself to his cell; and there, having cast aside all his theological reasonings and sophistical arguments, he gave himself up entirely to thinking of the fair young woman who had so potently captivated him. And when he came to know the high

* Ferdinand the Just, King of Aragon and Regent of Castile. He married Eleanora of Castile, and was the father of Alfonso the Magnanimous. He died in 1416.

estate of the lady, and whose wife she was, and to realize what a crazy task he was taking in hand, he set to work to persuade himself to abstain from attempting such an enterprise as this. Nevertheless, he would now and again say to himself, "Love, when he wills to bring his forces into play, has no regard for equality of blood; for, were this necessary, the great ones of the earth would not for ever come plundering our coasts. Therefore Love, in justice, should allow us to love those above our station, as he has allowed our superiors to stoop to those below them. No one is smitten by the strokes which Love deals while taking thought of the same; they come ever unexpectedly; wherefore, if I have been surprised unarmed by this sovereign Love—against whose attacks men strive in vain, seeing that they can in no wise resist them—I am deservedly overcome. And having thus become his subject, happen what may I will throw myself into this fierce battle, and if I only gain therein death and the riddance of all earthly pain, at least my soul will with boldness and confidence take its flight, because I shall have dared to spread my snares in such exalted ground." And having thus spoken, without going back to the first negative arguments he had used, he took up paper, and, with many deep sighs and scalding tears, wrote to the lady of his love a fitting and elegant letter, praising in the first instance her beauty, more divine than mortal; then setting forth how completely he was overcome by the same in such degree that he was now waiting either for her favour or for death; and concluding by saying he knew well enough that, by reason of her high estate, he himself was in no way worthy to be allowed an audience with her, still he besought her, of her compassion, that she would deign to grant him time and opportunity whereby he might be able to have parley with her in private, or at least to accept him as her humble servant in the same wise as he had chosen her as the one supreme queen of his soul. Then, having brought his letter to an end with divers other flowery speeches, and having closed and several times kissed the same, he gave it to his clerk, with directions as to whither he should convey it. Now this clerk, being well trained to service of this sort, hid the letter in a secret receptacle on his left side, such as men of this kind are wont to have about them, and went his way to the place whither he had been ordered to go. When he had duly come there, he entered the house, where he found the gracious lady with many of her women-folk about her, and, having given her becoming salutation, he spake thus to her: "My master recommends himself to you, and begs you that you will let him have a little delicate flour wherewith to make wafers for the host, concerning which thing he has written more at length in this letter." The lady, who by nature was very discreet, no sooner saw the letter than it seemed to her certain what sort of message it would bear to her; and, having taken the same and learnt by reading it what was the drift thereof, she was by no means affronted to learn that the writer was enamoured of her, although she was very honest and chaste in her life.

In truth, she reckoned that she herself was fair beyond all other women; and, as she read, her heart rejoiced greatly when she perceived what high praises were lavished on her beauty, following the example of that woman who, together with original sin, acquired that innate passion of vanity which has now infected all the residue of the female sex; for women hold the universal belief that all their fame and their honour and their glory lies in nothing else than in being loved and courted amorously and praised for their beauty, willing rather to be accounted fair and faulty than to be accredited with the highest virtues and an ugly face. Nevertheless, she holding with good reason all friars in strong dislike, made up her mind that she would in no wise grant Maestro Diego one jot of what he asked, nay rather, that she would give him his answer in terms of scant courtesy. Furthermore she resolved that, on this occasion, she would say naught of the matter to her husband; wherefore, abiding in this purpose of hers, she turned to the clerk, and, without showing that aught had occurred to disquiet her in the least, she said to him: "Go tell your master that the one who owns my flour wants it all for his own purposes; therefore let him take thought to seek some elsewhere. Tell him, likewise, that there is needed no other reply to his letter; but if he should still desire one, let him give me due notice, and then, as soon as my husband shall have come back to the house, he will straightway set to work to do for him the favour which this proposal of his deserves."

This unsympathetic answer was duly conveyed to Maestro Diego, but it in no wise lessened his ardour; indeed, his love and his desire seemed rather to burn with a fiercer flame therefor. He let relax not a whit his pursuit of the enterprise he had undertaken; and, because it happened that the house of the lady was quite near to the convent, he began once more to cast his amorous glances upon her with such constant importunity, that she could not gaze out of a window, or go to church, or to any other place without doors, and not find the provoking monk continually hovering around. Wherefore it happened that this matter became known to all the neighbours who dwelt near by, and was furthermore brought to the notice of a great part of the city. For this reason, the lady at last told herself that the affair was one which she ought no longer to keep from her husband's ears; fearing, at the same time, that, if it should come to his knowledge through the information of anyone else, over and above the danger thereof, she might be held on the score of the same to be something less than an honest woman. So finding all her thoughts to be in full agreement over this matter, she laid it before her husband point by point, one night when they were together. The husband, who was a gentleman of worship and high-spirited as well, found his anger so fiercely kindled by what he heard, that he with difficulty held himself back from going in that self-same hour to carry fire and sword against the convent and all the friars therein. But after he had calmed his rage somewhat, and spoken many words of praise anent the prudence and honesty of his wife, he bade her give a promise to Maestro Diego, and to let him come to the house on the following evening in such fashion as might seem to her to be most fitting and convenient, so that at the same time he might bring to pass the satisfying of his own honour, and the deliverance of his dear and well-loved wife from any danger of contamination. The rest of the plot he bade her leave to his own care.

Albeit that it was difficult for the lady to imagine to what issue the affair would come, nevertheless, in order to comply with the wishes of her husband, she answered that she would do as he directed, and as the clerk was for ever coming back to her, seeking by some new craft to sap the stubborn rock of her chastity, she said to him one day: "Commend me well to your master, and tell him that the great love he bears towards me, together with the scalding tears which, according to his letters written to me, he sheds for me without ceasing, have at last found a resting-place in my heart, in such wise that I now seem to belong more to him than to myself. Now, as our good fortune has willed it, Messer Roderico is gone this day into the country, where he will stay the night, lying at an inn. Wherefore, when the clock shall have struck three, let him come to me privily, and at that hour I will grant him an interview according to his wishes. But I earnestly beg him that he will say naught concerning this affair to any friend or companion of his, however intimate he may be." The novice, marvellously delighted, went his way and delivered this gracious message to his master, who forthwith became the happiest man the world had ever held, notwithstanding that the brief time which must elapse ere the given moment would come seemed to him a thousand years.

And when the hour drew nigh, and after he had well perfumed himself, so that he might in no wise suggest the friar, Fra Diego, deeming that he would require all his strength to gain the prize in the course he proposed to run, made a good meal of the choicest and most delicate meats that could be gotten. Having put on his accustomed habit, he betook himself to the lady's door; and, finding this open, he entered straightway. Whereupon a waiting girl appeared and conducted him, as if he had been a blind man, through the darkness into the hall, where he deemed that he would be joyfully received by the lady herself; but in lieu of this he found awaiting him the master of the house and a certain trusty varlet of his. These two, having taken a firm grip of him with their hands, strangled him without making any disturbance over the deed.

After he had made a dead man of Maestro Diego, the gentleman began to rue somewhat that he should have sullied his puissant hands by killing a minor friar; and, realizing that mere regret would never mend the matter, he considered it best, both for the sake of his own honour and through fear of the anger of the king, that he should rid the house of this dead body; so he forthwith devised in his mind a plan to convey it back to the convent. Wherefore he hoisted the body on his servant's back, and made the man bear it into the friars' garden. Then, having easily found entrance into the premises, they conveyed it into that part of the house which the friars were accustomed to use as a privy, where by chance they found amongst the tumble-down seats only a single one which was in order; indeed, it is ever a thing to be remarked, that a greater part of the houses of the Conventuals* have more the semblance of robbers' caves than of habitations of the servants of God. On this one seat they set the dead friar, making it appear that he had come there for his needs; and, having left him, they returned home.

Now while Maestro Diego was being bestowed in this fashion, it happened that another one of the friars, a young and merry fellow, was seized about midnight with a sudden natural longing to betake himself to the same spot; so, having lighted a little lamp, he went in haste to the place where the dead body of Maestro Diego was

* The disputes in the Franciscan Order over the pontifical explanation of the monastic rule and the vow of poverty, which led to the secession of the Fraticelli and the formation of the "Beghards" and the Brethren of the Free Spirit in the latter part of the thirteenth century, came ultimately to an issue in the division of the order into two branches, the Conventuals and the Observantists; the former procuring license to live under a rule of mitigated severity, and the latter adopting the original rule of St. Francis in all its severity. The separate organization was finally established during the pontificate of Leo X., and in the early part of the sixteenth century the Capuchins, founded by Matteo di Basio, were established as an offshoot of the Observantists. In France the stricter Franciscans are known as Cordeliers.

seated. He saw at once who was there, and, believing him to be alive, he drew back somewhat without saying a word, for the reason that, on account of some envy and dislike of one another as friars, there was between these two a fierce and mortal hatred. The young brother waited in a corner until the man whom he deemed to be Maestro Diego should have finished what he had in his mind to do; and, after he had tarried some long time in thus deliberating over the matter, and without noticing any sign of moving on the part of Maestro Diego—feeling moreover that his necessity was growing urgent—he said to himself more than once, "God's faith, this fellow sits there, and refuses to make way for me, for no other reason than to show me, even in a matter of this sort, the enmity which he bears towards me through his ill will, but in this instance he will find his spite of no avail, forasmuch as I will endure as long as I can; then, if I find that he remains firm set in his obstinacy, though it is open to me to repair otherwhere, I will not do this, since it is against my will." Now Maestro Diego, like a vessel which had fixed her anchors in firm ground, made no sign of movement, great or small; whereupon the friar, finding himself able to hold out no longer, cried out in a rage, "Of a truth it cannot be God's pleasure that you should put such an affront as this upon me, and I, on my part, can endure it no longer." So taking up a large stone, and going close to Maestro Diego, he dealt him therewith such a blow on the chest that he fell over backwards without moving one or other of his limbs. The friar then perceived how shrewd a stroke he had given, and next marked that his foe lay quite still where he had fallen, wherefore he began to fear lest he might have killed him outright with the stone. He took a glance at the body, now believing one thing and now another, and at last went close thereto, and then, after he had viewed it by the light of his lantern, he knew for certain that it was the body of a dead man (as indeed it was ere this mishap), and believed that he himself had assuredly killed him in the manner above described. Whereupon, wailing over the catastrophe, and fearing lest, on account of the ill will known to subsist between them, he should be suspected of the fatal blow, and be mulcted of his life thereanent, there more than once came into his mind the resolution to hang himself by the neck; but, having given the matter better consideration, he determined to carry the body out of the convent and to fling it down in the street, in order to keep off from himself all suspicions which men in the future might have against him for the reason already mentioned. So, having it in his mind to carry out this design, he suddenly remembered the public and shameful court that Maestro Diego had persisted in paying to Donna Caterina; then he said to himself, "And where, forsooth, could I take this fellow with greater ease, and with less suspicion to myself, than to the door of Messer Roderico's house, seeing that it is hard by, and furthermore, men will certainly believe that this man, going after the wife, has been slain by the husband."

Speaking thus to himself, and without further canvassing the matter, he hoisted Maestro Diego on his shoulders, after no little trouble, and carried him up to the door aforesaid, out of which, only a few hours before, he had been dragged a corpse, and there left him. Then, without having been observed by anyone, he made his way back to the convent.

Now although the work of reparation he had just done seemed sufficient so to ensure his safety, nevertheless it occurred to him that it might be well for him to withdraw himself from the place for a time on some colourable pretence; wherefore, as soon as he had thus decided in his mind, he betook himself to the cell of the superior and spake in these words: "Father, the day before yesterday, for the reason that we were lacking in beasts of burden, I had perforce to leave behind me the greater part of our day's work at the house of a man much devoted to our order in the neighbourhood of Medina. Wherefore, with your blessing, I would fain go fetch our goods, taking with me the mare we have here in the convent, and by God's good will I will come back with the same to-morrow or the day after. When he heard these words, the superior not only gave the friar full leave to do as he proposed, but gave him likewise high commendation on account of his forethought. As soon as the friar got his answer he set his affairs in order, and, having prepared the mare for the journey, awaited the dawn to set forth on his way.

Messer Roderico, who all that night had slept little or not at all, through disquiet over the deed he had wrought, when at last the day was near at hand took occasion to send his servant into the purlieus of the convent, in order that by listening he might discover whether the friars had yet come upon the dead body of Maestro Diego, and what they might have to say about the matter. But as the servant went forth to discharge the errand which had been given him, he espied Maestro Diego himself seated before the door with the air of one who might be holding a disputation, a spectacle which gave him no little fright—such, in sooth, as a man may well feel on looking at a dead body—and, having run back into the house, he quickly called his master, and, bringing out his words with difficulty, pointed out to him how the dead body of the friar had been brought back thither. The gentleman was mightily amazed at this mischance, which in sooth gave him cause for still more doubt; nevertheless, being reassured by the justice of the enterprise in which he believed himself to be engaged, he prepared to await with good courage for the successful issue of the matter. Therefore, turning towards the dead man, he spake thus: "You, then, must needs be the plague of my house, seeing that neither dead nor alive can I hale you therefrom! Nevertheless, out of spite for the person who brought you hither, I will take care that you only return to the place whence you came on the back of a beast, seeing that in your lifetime a beast you were yourself." And having thus spoken, Messer Roderico gave order to his servant to fetch from the stable of a neighbour of his a stallion which was there kept for the use of the mares and the she-asses of the city.

Thereupon the servant made good despatch, and, having fetched the stallion equipped with saddle and bridle and all other necessary gear, the two together hoisted up the dead body aforesaid on the stallion's back, in such manner as Messer Roderico had already determined. Then, when they had bolstered him up in the saddle, and bound him fast therein, they furnished him with a lance, duly set in the rest, and put the reins in his hand as if they were minded to send him to the wars. Having got him thus in array, they led him to the place in front of the church of the friars, and there they tied the horse to the gate and straightway went back home.

By this time the young friar began to think that he would do well to set off on the journey he proposed to take; wherefore, having first opened the door of the convent and then mounted his mare, he sallied forth, but when he found Maestro Diego stationed there in the accoutrement before described, he was fain to believe that the dead man before him was threatening to kill him with the lance he carried. Of a sudden he was stricken with so terrible an access of fear, that he stood in no small danger of falling down dead on the spot; moreover, there came into his mind the dreadful suspicion that peradventure the spirit of the friar had once more entered the dead body, and that, by way of punishment, it had been ordained that Maestro Diego should follow him about whithersoever he might go, according to the beliefs of certain simple folk. And while he stood thus confounded and terror-stricken, not knowing which way he should turn, the stallion perceived by the odour he sniffed that a mare must be somewhere near about; and, getting himself in order for the work, and neighing the while, he strived to get anear her, thus throwing the poor friar into greater terror than ever. Nevertheless, recovering his wits somewhat, he made as if he would urge the mare along the road, but she, turning her dugs towards the stallion, began to play with her heels. The friar, who was not the best horseman in the world, was wellnigh upset hereby, and without waiting for a second bout, he clasped the mare's sides tightly with his legs, and struck his spurs into her flanks. Then, hanging with both his hands on to the pack-saddle and loosening the reins, he let the beast go whither fortune might take her. The mare, when she felt the spurs driven so firmly into her flanks, was incited thereby to start off, at the top of her speed and without guidance, along the first road which lay open before her, and the stallion, seeing that the prey he longed for had taken to flight, snapped in his violent passion the slender cord by which he was tethered, and rushed after her in fierce pursuit.

The poor friar, perceiving that his foe was on his traces, and turning to look over his shoulder, saw Maestro Diego there with his lance firmly clasped in hand, as if he were some fiery knight entering the tilt-yard; whereupon this last fear of his put to flight the first; and, as he thus fled, he began to cry out aloud, "Help! help!" Now, because of this shouting and of the clatter made by the uncontrolled horses, all the townsfolk betook themselves to the doors and the windows—it being by this time broad daylight—and each one looked on in amazement. Then rose up a great shout of laughter at so novel and strange a sight as the chase of one minor friar on horseback by another, this one looking no less like a dead man than that. The mare, uncontrolled as she was, ran now here, now there, through the streets, taking whatever road seemed to please her best, and behind her the stallion, hot and furious, kept up the pursuit. There is no need to tell how narrowly the friar more than once escaped being wounded by the lance. The huge crowd of people kept on following them with cries and whistlings and howlings, and on all sides were heard the shouts, "'Ware of yourselves! Stop him!" Some hurled stones, and others belaboured the stallion with sticks, each one of the crowd being keenly set on the task of separating them, not from any feeling of compassion for the fugitives, but rather from the desire to know what might be the names of these men, whom, on account of the rapidity of their flight, the bystanders were not able to recognize. And, thus harassed, they made their way by chance to one of the gates of the city, where they were brought to close quarters and captured together, the dead and the living monk as well; whereupon it was at once made known who they were, to the no little amazement of all those who were round about.

Then they led away both the friars on horseback to the convent, just as they were taken, and the superior and all the brethren as well were mightily grieved when they saw them brought in. The dead man they buried straightway, and prepared to give the living one a taste of the strappado; but he, as soon as he was tied up thereto, feeling in no way disposed to undergo the torment, made full confession that he had taken Maestro Diego's life for the reason written above, but he could give no clue as to who could have set the dead friar on the horse's back in such fashion. And because he made this confession, they spared him the torture of the strappado, but they condemned him to harsh imprisonment, and, furthermore, they sent their officer straightway to the bishop of the city to beg him to strip the friar in question of holy orders, resolving at the same time to deliver him over to the secular power, which might pass sentence upon him for homicide according to the commandment of the law.

It chanced that in these days King Fernando paid a visit to Salamanca, and during his stay there they related to him this story. Now, although he was a prince of marvellously proper carriage, and greatly grieved, moreover, at hearing of the death of one so noteworthy as Maestro Diego, nevertheless, overcome by the diverting humour of the episode, while hearing tell of the same in the company of his barons, he laughed so heartily thereat that he could scarce stand upright on his feet. And when the date was come when they must needs set about passing upon the friar the unjust sentence for the crime he had never committed, Messer Roderico, who was in sooth a gentleman of great integrity, and at the same time very well regarded by the king, stimulated by zeal for the truth and clearly convinced that his own silence would be the only reason for the infliction of such a wrong, at once made up his mind that he must die rather than keep hidden the truth concerning the deed. Wherefore, being in the presence of the king, where were also assembled divers barons and many other people, he spake thus: "My lord, the severe and unjust sentence pronounced against this innocent minor friar, together with the real circumstances of the case, induce me to give an explanation of the occurrence in question. And now, if your majesty will grant pardon to the man who dealt out to Maestro Diego the death he richly deserved, I will bring him here into this presence, and let him relate to you upon approved evidence and in full detail how the deed may have come about." The king who was both a very merciful man and one anxious to learn the truth, listened to this prayer for pardon in free and generous wise; and, as soon as he had received this assurance, Messer Roderico, in the presence of the king and of all the bystanders, gave a minute account from the beginning of the amorous passion of Maestro Diego for his wife, and of the letters and messages he had sent thereanent, and of all the other things devised and done by him in the matter up to the last hour of his life. The king, having already heard the statement of the young friar—a statement which seemed to him to be fully in harmony with the words which had just been spoken—and holding Messer Roderico to be a gentleman of worth and honour, without any further examination of him at once gave credit to the words he had just listened to. Then, all amazed as he was, he spent much time and trouble in turning over in his mind the nature of this strange and complicated affair, laughing heartily to himself the while. However, in order not to allow the undeserved sentence which had been passed upon the innocent friar to take effect, he made them bring him and the superior as well into his presence. Then, before his barons and nobles and all the other people who were there, he made it clear and manifest in what fashion the whole business had been brought to pass. For this reason he gave command that the friar, who had been condemned to suffer a cruel death, should forthwith be set at liberty, and the friar, when this had been done, and his name purged of all stain, took his way back to the convent rejoicing greatly. Messer Roderico, having been pardoned at the same time, was extolled with the highest praise in all the parts round about for that he had wrought such a deed. And thus the wonderful report in a very brief space of time was noised through all the kingdom of Castile by swift flying rumour, causing men to rejoice amain as they listened thereunto. The same report, having been carried from those parts into these our regions of Italy, had already been told, albeit briefly, to you, O most puissant king and lord; and now it is my grateful duty, by following your commands, to make it worthy of lasting remembrance, a merit it may be held to possess if one will closely examine the outward features thereof.

MASUCCIO

BOTH the quality and the method exhibited in the strange and novel and unforeseen chances of the story I have just told to you, most illustrious lady,* will, I doubt not, give you and all other listeners occasion to declare (after laughing thereanent as much as is meet) that our Maestro Diego got the return he richly deserved for the fervent passion which consumed him. And besides this, it seems certain to me that some will be found to maintain that, if he had chanced to be a spiritual brother or even one of the Observantists, he would never have come to such a pass of unbridled lasciviousness, and, by the consequence thereof, have met an end so gloomy and terrible. And although in other parts of this my little work I shall try to do full justice, by bringing before your notice these gross he-goats, and by answering for their deeds—by distinguishing between the life and works of Conventuals and Observantists;† nevertheless it occurs to me that it might be well now to touch somewhat briefly on this subject, by affirming that it would without doubt be much better for the whole of Christianity, if we had on earth no other religion besides that which Christ left behind him by the instrumentality of his glorious apostle, St. Peter. And because this has been partially corrupted in the lapse of time, even the ministers thereof, and also the brothers who are called Conventuals, show us clearly by their conduct how, and to what extent, we ought to guard ourselves against them, forasmuch as their outward seeming, and their garb, and their gait, and all the works of their hands, are but so many terrifying voices and clamours crying out: "Put not your trust in us." And for this reason, all those who are of the fine flower of intellect will judge the matter truly, and tell us how we ought not merely to hold blameless, but rather to praise highly, all those who refuse to go about with bent necks in mean garb and with a hypocritical face in order to deceive others. But supposing that to these men, who walk abroad

* Ippolita, Duchess of Calabria. † See Note, p. 19.

clad as gentle lambs while they are in sooth very wolves in soul, there should be granted the same opportunity which came to Maestro Diego, I do not for a moment doubt but that they would take good care to set about debauching our households as often as chance might permit. May God help those foolish laymen who are so meagrely endowed with wit that they know not how to recognize these crowds of sham friars and monks, who have borrowed their art from lying mountebanks, and go wandering abroad through divers kingdoms and countries preaching all new fashions of fraud—idling, thieving, and wantoning, and, when all other arts fail them, they feign to be saints* and to exhibit their power as miracle-workers. One comes with the waistcoat of San Vincenzo,† another adopts the rule of San Bernardino,‡ and another brings forward the ass-halter of Capestrano.§ In these, and in a thousand other diabolical ways, they

* Orig., "*se fingono santi.*" Masuccio is probably alluding to certain hangers on to the numerous religious revivals of the thirteenth and fourteenth centuries. One of the most noteworthy of these revivalist leaders was the Dominican monk, Fra Giovanni of Vicenza, who began to preach in Bologna in 1233. Amidst all the discord and bloodshed which then desolated Italy, he preached chiefly peace and the forgiveness of injuries. He then visited Padua, and most of the Lombard cities, and at last set to work to pacify and unite all these in one political bond. His head seems to have been turned by the marvellous success which met his efforts, for he began to burn religious opponents as heretics in Padua, whereupon the people rose against him. He was deposed from his leadership, and sank into obscurity.

† San Vincenzo (Ferrier) was born at Valentia in 1355, and joined the Dominicans as a preacher. Peter of Luna detected his abilities, and took him to Paris with him in 1391. When Peter became pope as Benedict XIII., he made Vincenzo his confessor, but the friar was soon disgusted with the sloth and corruption of Avignon, and in 1397 resumed his preaching. He travelled all over western Europe. At the Council of Constance he urged the deposition of the three popes, though one of them was his patron. He died in 1419, and was canonized in 1455.

‡ See Note to Novel XVI.

§ Fra Giovanni da Capestrano was a Franciscan Observant who opened a revivalist campaign at Brescia in 1451, and wrought many marvellous cures. See Muratori, "Istoria Bresciana," vol. xxi., p. 865.

encroach upon our possessions and honours. And although these doings of theirs re-echo in every place, and the report of them is blown about through the whole universe, nevertheless, in the following fable dedicated to that most serene prince your very worthy consort, I will farther tell you of a strange cheat which a certain Dominican friar, a child of the devil, put upon the person of an illustrious German lady under the guise of holiness. And from the end of this my story we shall be able to adduce the argument that, the straighter and loftier the trees these wretches attack, the more boldly and audaciously will they lay on with their felling axes, in order to bring the trunks down to earth. All this I will show to you clearly.

THE END OF THE FIRST NOVEL.

Novel the Second

ARGUMENT

A DOMINICAN FRIAR PERSUADES MADONNA BARBARA THAT SHE WILL FIND HERSELF WITH CHILD BY A CERTAIN RIGHTEOUS MAN, AND WILL IN DUE TIME BRING FORTH THE FIFTH EVANGELIST. BY MEANS OF HIS FRAUD, SHE BECOMES PREGNANT BY HIM; AND THEN HE, UNDER THE COVER OF A FRESH DECEIT, MAKES GOOD HIS FLIGHT. THIS DEED HAVING COME TO LIGHT, THE FATHER OF BARBARA MARRIES HER TO A MAN OF MEAN ESTATE.

TO THAT MOST SERENE PRINCE, ALFONSO OF ARAGON, THE MOST WORSHIPFUL DUKE OF CALABRIA *

EXORDIUM

DIVERS people there are, my most serene lord, who, being filled with the desire to put on a semblance of wisdom and integrity, and, with the idea of letting themselves be regarded by the herd of common people as good men and richly endowed with virtue, are wont to hold conversation with those who have taken upon themselves the religious habit, and to show themselves to the eyes of the multitude spitting out their paternosters and browsing at the feet of the saints. In what measure the men who employ such means as these are defiled by nefarious crimes and the most wicked vices, all those who may have come into close commerce with them will be able to vouchsafe, simply by giving true testimony of what they know. By false knaves of this sort I am blown upon,

* Son of King Ferdinand, who died in 1494, and husband of Ippolita Sforza, to whom Masuccio dedicated the Novellino. He renounced the sovereignty of Naples in 1495, and died the same year. He was born in 1448, and was known by the nickname of "Il Guercio," the squint-eyed.

bitten, and lacerated without ceasing, because, as they maintain, I have set my pen and my tongue to work in such fashion that I seem able neither to write nor speak at all except to bear witness against the friars. These men, in sooth, affirm that the greater part of the friars are duly obedient to the rules of their orders, and though here and there a wicked man may be found amongst the brethren, the vast quantity of good friars we see around us will in itself prove a stubborn fact to show that the number of them is practically infinite. And, as I have no desire to win the good word of these muttering hypocrites, I will hereby make answer to them in terms which will serve for ever, and tell them that the plain and open villainies worked by these malignant clerics, every day and in every place, with some fresh cunning, some new trick, confirm without ceasing the truth of my words. And from all such men as are lovers and fair judges of truth and honesty these assertions of mine will win a lasting reward of praise.

It occurs to me, therefore, my most gracious lord, to say with regard to this subject that it would be vastly more easy to find a given hundred soldiers, the half of whom should be good and worthy men, than to pick out of a whole chapter of friars a single one without some ugly stain upon him. But, supposing that the number of worthy friars may be ever so much greater than that of the worthless, the issue thereof would be no less an evil, in like manner as it often comes to pass in a perilous battle, during the course of which it may happen that a single mean coward will work mischief greater than is the good which arises from the feats of ten brave men. And in exactly similar wise would fare any ill-starred layman who might chance to give to such a treacherous crew any more faith than is necessary, seeing that aught of intercourse or familiarity with a single perfidious, secret-working, and ribald friar will bring upon us an amount of overwhelming shame and loss far greater than any honour and profit we might draw from the intimacy with a hundred just men.

Against all such as these—and to serve as their well-deserved and eternal punishment—it seems to me there is naught else to be said but to pray that God may soon make an end of Purgatory, so that these friars, being no longer able to live by the offerings made to them thereanent, may be forced to go and work with the mattock, thus returning to an estate from which the greater part of them have sprung. But in any case I desire in this most veracious story of mine—a story which I have addressed to you as my earthly master—to withdraw myself somewhat from the consideration of the general offences of the friars, and by descending to tell of one particular person, to show you in what wise a certain preaching friar, a man accounted of singular excellence amongst the Dominicans, contrived by the means of a strange cheat to capture in his subtle snares one of the most illustrious ladies to be found in all Germany.

THE NARRATIVE

THERE is in the mouths of men a story approved by a sufficient show of truth, which tells how, in years only a short time past, there lived in Germany a nobleman of high estate called by name the Duke of Lanzhueta,* a man wealthy in lands, and in precious stones, and in other possessions of this sort beyond any other baron of Germany. To this gentleman fortune had granted the gift of one only daughter, to whom he gave the name of Barbara, and she, as she was the single child of the house, was loved by her father with a deep and single love. In like manner, the extraordinary beauties of her person were celebrated and held in high esteem in all parts of the empire. Now this damsel, while she was yet of tender age, inspired peradventure by the Holy Spirit, or moved now and again thereto rather by some childish fancy than by any regular desire, promised by a solemn vow on her part that she would keep herself a virgin as long as her life should last, and thus, having dedicated her virginity to Christ and decked herself with all virtues and praiseworthy manners, so that she seemed to the eyes of the world as one overgone in devotion, she came to the marriageable age.

* Query, Landshut in Bavaria.

When it was made known to her that divers noble barons were proffering requests with no little importunity to her father to gain her hand in marriage, it seemed to her that of necessity she would be constrained to make known this inclination of hers; wherefore, in a manner entirely befitting the occasion, she informed her father, and her mother as well, of the same, but they both of them could only bring themselves to listen to news of this character with great harshness of demeanour and with much arguing thereanent. And, howbeit they used their wits as best they could, with many threats and with allurements also, to make her draw back from the course she was so obstinately set to follow, they knew well enough how firmly she was bent on treading the path upon which she had entered, and on this account, plunged in sorrow such as they had never before tasted, they determined to bring the matter to a peaceful issue, and to set down such an accident to the charge of nature.

As soon as Barbara had let appear what her inclination really was, and had caused to be set up in her chamber an oratory fashioned in very devout wise, she not only gave herself over to perpetual prayer, but vexed and mortified her delicate body with fastings and discipline after a manner which was a wonder to behold. The fame of so great sanctity soon spread itself abroad in the upper and the lower parts of Germany, and in these regions of Italy as well, and on account of this report in a very short time an innumerable multitude of religious persons, and of other people likewise, came together round about the city where dwelt the duke aforesaid. These people put forward all manner of excuses to account for their presence, and, in exactly the same way as the vultures and famishing wolves run after decaying carcasses, these human birds and beasts of prey did their best to win as booty both the fame and the fortune of so illustrious and extraordinary a lady.

Now amongst these there came a certain rascally friar, whose name I either do not know or do not wish to make public; indeed, for certain reasons of decency I intend to keep silence as to whether he was an Italian or a German. This man, forsooth, being a brother of the Dominican order, had gained much renown as a skilful preacher, and, using in most arrant wise the arts of a charlatan, he went rambling from place to place in Germany, which is, as you know, a rude and barbarous country, carrying with him the handle of the knife with which Saint Peter Martyr was slain, and other trifles, reputed relics of their San Vincenzo, and making it appear to the crowd of gulls he attracted that he wrought divers wonders with his unbounded and miraculous power.

It chanced that the fame of this man was brought to the notice of Madonna Barbara, a thing which he himself greatly desired to come to pass, having taken due foresight to attain this same end. Whereupon she, being mightily anxious to see him, sent word for him to come to her. The friar, not forgetting to put in practice all his wonted mummery, set out quickly to obey her summons, and, after the lady had given him reception, and honoured him as a saint, she made known to him the unchangeable resolution she had adopted, begging him at the same time that he would, of his kindness, give her counsel, and ending with a prayer for his aid towards the salvation of her soul. The friar, who was both young and robust in body, no sooner looked upon the beauty of the lady—which forsooth was more divine than human—than he fell straightway in love with her, and, for the reason that he felt himself now so sharply assailed by lustful desire, it wanted but little more to cause him to fall into a swoon at the very sight of her; nevertheless, having recollected his wits, he gave the most admirable commendation to the holy resolution she had formed, praising and blessing continually divine providence for having chosen to take so worthy a virgin out of this guileful world. Moreover, he argued before her parents that a character and disposition so perfect as was that of their daughter had not been created for their benefit alone, but for the profit of all womankind, present and future as well. Likewise he persuaded her, seeing that her intercourse with people of the world might be fraught with danger to his purpose, that she ought to set herself apart from the world in a society of ladies, who should be virgins likewise; putting herself under obedience to some religious order, in such wise as to cause to be formed another choir of virgins upon the earth, who would be ever at the service of Christ Jesus.

Now after he had held much converse with the damsel herself, and with the duke and his wife as well, and had made it appear to them all that the advice he gave was the best that could be given, holy in its character, built on the foundation of true reason, and such as would surely bring consolation to Madonna Barbara, the friar in a very short space of time persuaded them to let build a vast and magnificent monastery, which, according to his wish, was called after the blessed Catherine of Siena, and settled in such wise that the governance thereof might never fall into strangers' hands. In this house, together with Madonna Barbara, a great multitude of damsels of noble birth secluded themselves from the world, and there, under the ordinances and rules laid down by the aforesaid friar, they began to establish a very sanctified and perfect way of life—living in such wise, indeed, that no other than God, who alone knows the hidden secrets of all hearts, would have been able to find out that, by the working of the tainted soul of one wicked wretch, the great devil himself had already taken bodily possession of them. This fellow, in order to become privy to every inward thought of the young maidens, never ceased to exhort and persuade them that, in order to flee from the temptations of God's great adversary, there was to be found no course so meet and salutary as the constant resort to the holy practice of confession. Wherefore, fully carrying out this direction without suspecting aught of the great and hidden malignity which lay behind it, they set up a ravening wolf as the pastor of their gentle flock. He, being now well assured that he had baited his hook in the right way, perceived that the time had come to put in operation his lustful and nefarious design; so, having by cunning means got into his possession a certain little book belonging to Madonna Barbara, in which were written divers prayers of a very devout character, together with figures of the saints and of the Holy Ghost, he wrote therein, late on a certain evening, the following words in letters of gold, coming as it were out of the mouth of the Blessed Spirit: "Barbara, thou shalt find thyself with child by a righteous man, and shalt bring forth the fifth evangelist, who will give to us whatever may be wanting in the writings of the others; spotless thou shalt remain, and blessed shalt thou be in the sight of God." Having done this, he closed the book, and early the next morning he put it back in the place whence he had taken it the night before. Likewise he got ready many other slips of paper, dainty blue in colour, and inscribed in letters of gold with words of a similar nature. Having put these aside, he waited to make use of them in such a way as would best serve the purpose he had in view.

Barbara, having gone into her cell at the accustomed hour to recite the prayers she was wont to use, and having turned over the leaf whereupon was figured the Holy Ghost, perceived what manner of words had been there written afresh, and was utterly confounded at the sight which met her eyes. But after a little, having gathered together her wits somewhat, and having mastered the meaning of this awesome announcement, she felt herself assailed by no little wonder and confusion and anguish. She then set herself to read it over again, ever finding greater travail as she went on, and even became as one bewildered in her youthful, girlish, and as yet unsullied mind. Wherefore, wonder-stricken as she was, she tore herself away from the prayers she had just begun to say, and ran as quickly as she could to her spiritual father. And when she had drawn him somewhat aside, the maiden, conquered and overcome by girlish fears, showed to him the book with the gilded writing therein, weeping plentifully the while. Directly this met the eyes of the friar, he made a great show of being altogether stupified with amazement, and, having signed himself with the sign of the cross, he addressed Barbara in these words: "My daughter, in my belief this thing is naught else than a temptation of the devil, who, ill pleased at the sight of your state of perfect righteousness, is seeking to set before you some perilous snare, in order to cause you to fall into eternal perdition. Wherefore I now admonish you, on behalf of God Himself, and of the sacred obedience you owe to Him, that you never, at any time whatsoever, lend a believing ear to this or to aught else of a similar character. Nevertheless, I commend you highly for that you have laid this thing bare to me. But you must be careful always to act in like manner for the future. Of this I assure you, and I lay it upon you as a penance, to carry out my commands, for be well assured the snares which have been lately set to catch your soul will not be likely to become harmless* except you make use of the well-tried remedy of holy confession. But by the help of this you shall go forth strong and enduring, ready to do battle with the accursed enemy of God; so that in the end you will win for yourself a double palm of victory, seeing that your strength will make itself perfect in weakness."

Thus with these, and with many other words of a like sanctimonious character, he let her spirit quiet itself somewhat from the agitation which his carefully-devised trickery had produced, and having gone out of her presence, he called to him a certain young clerk, according to a plan which he had already formed, and made this fellow hide himself within side the oratory set up in the lady's chamber, giving him at the same time certain of the slips of paper of which mention has already been made, and directing him how and at what time he must send them forth to do their work. The gracious maiden, after she had gone into her chamber and set herself to prayer, beseeching God with all humility of heart that He would duly give her advertisement of any such event, was all of a sudden surprised at seeing one of these slips of paper fall into her lap. Having taken this in hand and read it, and remarked how richly adorned it was, and how it bore on its face words of a like purport in confirmation of the incarnation of a new evangelist, she fell at once into a violent fit of trembling. When she had risen from her knees and made ready to depart, she saw fall down a second missive, and then a third; indeed, before she left the place, there descended of these no less than ten. Then she went forth from the chamber, overcome with the direst fear, and called the friar, and, half dead with agitation, showed him the aforesaid pieces of paper. This wolf in

* Orig., *che si fatte insidie sopra dite non abbiano a dormire.*

holy garb, letting his visage give token of the amazement which, as he feigned, possessed him, then said: "My daughter, of a truth these be things to raise in our hearts the greatest possible wonder. Such things may not be passed over without taking the most serious counsel thereanent; forasmuch as it is quite as likely that they are being revealed to us by divine inspiration as by the opposing principle. Wherefore it seems to me that we ought neither to let ourselves run heedlessly after this belief, nor to keep ourselves obstinately fixed in our original opinion, but rather that we should apply ourselves to the blessed exercise of prayer; you on one part, and I on the other, will lift up our prayers to God and beg Him that, of His supreme and infinite goodness, He will deign to give us clear assurance whether this revelation be true or whether it be false, whether we ought to give heed to it or to flee therefrom. Moreover, on the morrow it is my intention to hold a celebration in your chamber, when, by the instrumentality of the wood of the true and holy cross, and of other relics fitted for the purpose, we will put to flight all the works of the devil, and will see what thing Almighty God will show to us."

To Madonna Barbara it seemed that all this advice given by the friar was most godly, and worthy to be carried out. Wherefore she made answer that it would please her mightily to follow all his counsels. And when the next morning had come, the friar got up in good time, and set in position all his artillery in order to pay his oblation to Satan. Then, having first given the signal to the young clerk that he should betake himself to the spot where he had before stationed himself, the friar entered the chamber of the lady, being received by her with tokens of deep reverence, and with a seeming of sanctity and devotion he began to celebrate mass. As long as the holy office went on, from the beginning thereof until the end, the young clerk did not cease from casting down the aforesaid slips of paper, of which his master had given him no small quantity to be used in this fashion. The young girl, when she saw them thus put forth without ceasing, and in such vast numbers (and each one bearing to her the same message), and perceived that neither her prayers, nor her vigils, nor all the other forms of discipline she had practised, had worked for aught else than to confirm her in her belief, was fully persuaded that such a revelation as this could only come forth from the Holy Spirit. Wherefore, exulting within herself on account of this mighty fortune which had befallen her, she began to think of herself as blessed indeed, and furthermore believed that it was ordained that things should fall out for her in such fashion as was described on the slips of paper. When the mass was finished, and when she had duly gathered up the papers which had fallen down so finely both upon herself and upon the friar—papers which bore every mark of having been prepared and written by the hand of some blessed angel, she stood as one altogether possessed with joy and gladness.

The friar, to whom it seemed that the time had fully come when he might go and pluck the last and the most luscious fruit of so fertile a garden, now said: "My daughter, I see indeed, by reason of these signs, so numerous and so clearly manifested, that this thing is the will of God, and that any endeavours on our part to gain further assurance thereanent would be held to be nothing else than a presumptuous desire to pry more curiously into those things which spring from the divine intelligence, which, as thou mayst clearly see, is openly showing its desire to produce a treasure so precious from that thrice happy womb of thine. Therefore, if we should still show ourselves to be unbelieving, I fear mightily the divine judgment would come upon us. At all events, so as to have no further hesitation as to the final confirmation of this matter, let us see whether in any part of the Holy Scriptures there may be found aught predicted of the same."

Then, having taken up the Bible forthwith, and turned over the leaves to a certain place in which he himself had put a mark, he came upon the passage in the Gospel of John where it is written, "And in the presence of his disciples Jesus wrought many other wonderful works which are not written in this book." When he had read this, he turned to the lady and spake thus: "We have no need of any farther witness. Behold and see how all our doubts are smoothed down! Of a truth, this one shall he be, concerning whom our evangelist makes mention—he who shall furnish us with all these things in which the others are lacking. Wherefore, if we should now go on questioning over and above what is necessary, it may be charged against us as presumption, and I, forsooth, will leave this burden to be borne by you alone, if you should still show yourself incredulous." The damsel, making answer to these last words of his, said: "Alas! my father, why should this saying, which in sooth is known to you alone, keep shut up in your inner consciousness all my welfare and all my hope? However, I shall always be ready to carry this thing into effect in such measure as may seem to you fitting and desirable."

The friar, seeing that the business was now brought to such a pass that it only remained for him to give the finishing stroke to his work, said: "My daughter, you speak indeed with wisdom, but there yet hangs in my mind one doubt unsatisfied. It is this: how shall we set to work to find the person in whom we can place sufficient trust, and who will be fitted for this business, bearing in mind that the whole world swarms with men altogether given over to fraud and treachery?" Madonna Barbara, who was treating the matter with the utmost purity of mind, then made answer: "My father, these writings of ours tell us concerning this thing that he who is to be the maker of this one must be righteous and holy even as you yourself are, so I do not see who can better bring to pass this thing with me than you, especially as you are my spiritual father." To this the friar replied: "In truth I do not know how this deed can be wrought by me, seeing that I, as well as you, have promised to keep my body in chastity as long as I live. Nevertheless, it seems that I assuredly would be no just man were I to consent to allow your holy and most delicate flesh to be sullied by the touch of other hands; and, over and beyond this, I myself am well fitted and furnished for the increasing of the Christian religion. At the same time, I will not now neglect to remind you that you must never let yourself be carried away so as to speak of this thing to anyone; for I doubt not at all that God would hold it for no trifling sin if it were to come to the knowledge of anybody else. And in this case, whereas now you are justly held to be the most highly blessed woman of this our age, you would be turned into a foe and a rebel against God."

The gracious maiden, giving him no other answer than the most solemn promises, affirmed that as long as she lived she would never make known this thing to anyone. "Now leave me," said the friar, "and this same evening, without farther delay, we will make a beginning of this work; but because unions of this sort ought to be entered into for the praise and glory of the most high God, we must needs occupy ourselves with continual prayer until the hour of our coming together, in order that we may enter these holy and divine mysteries with devout minds."

With this conclusion to his speech he betook himself to his own chamber, after he had been graciously dismissed by Madonna Barbara, and considering well in his mind how from his fruitful loins the holy evangelist would take being, he did not allow himself that day to defile his body with coarse food, such as he was wont often to consume in order to deceive others by a show of holiness, but took for the invigorating of his flesh the most delicate viands, the most exquisite sweetmeats, and the most sumptuous wines, all in temperate measure.

At last, when the hour was come which had been awaited by him with such keen desire, he entered with cautious tread the chamber of Madonna Barbara, who, still fasting and bathed in tears, had never once given over praying, and now, when she beheld the friar, rose upon her feet and gave him worshipful reception. Now he, albeit he was all on fire with lust to take his pleasure of the lady, and that every moment until he should find himself in her loving arms seemed to him a thousand hours, made up his mind nevertheless not to set about the amorous sport with aught of hasty lasciviousness, but to begin by seeing for himself whether the damsel was as fair to look upon naked and in candle-light as she was when clothed by day. Wherefore he bade her to strip herself naked, and she, although feeling the while smitten and overwhelmed with the deepest shame, obediently did all that he bade her do. When she had taken off all her clothes, and when he had divested himself of the greater part of his habit, he let kindle two great torches, and, having placed the lady betwixt these, and casting his eyes upon her flesh, delicate and smooth as ivory, which with its brightness outshone even the light of the enkindled flambeaux, he felt himself filled and overcome with so great concupiscence that he let himself fall almost as one dead into her arms. Then, when he had recovered himself and placed himself before her on his knees, he made her be seated as if she were his sovereign lady, and with joined hands and bent head he thus spake: "Thee I adore, O most blessed womb, in which, in times soon to come, there will be generated that which will be the light of universal Christianity." And having thus spoken, and kissed her in the middle of her lilywhite loveliness, he fastened with greedy desire upon her sweet and rosy lips, and, without letting her go for a moment, he threw himself upon the bed, which had already been prepared, holding her in his arms. In what fashion they occupied themselves all the night through it may be figured by each without much difficulty; but I know well, according to what the lady said when, in after times, she told of what happened, that they attained not only the number of the fifth evangelist, but to the seven gifts of the Holy Spirit.

Madonna Barbara, although she took the repast provided for her only in a spiritual sense, nevertheless, when she considered the same in her mind, came to the conclusion that this thing was the sweetest and most delicious pleasure that mortals could take or taste; so in the end it happened, the sport being so mightily pleasurable, that every night they found themselves fresh and eager to recommence the amorous struggle until such time as they should be fully assured that the evangelist had indeed been begotten. Passing their time in these delights, it fell out before long that Madonna Barbara became with child, and when this fact made itself apparent to both of them by manifest signs, one day the friar, being in fear of his life should the thing be known, said to her: "My daughter, thou seest that, forasmuch as it has thus pleased God, the end desired by us so greatly is now fulfilled, and that thou, being pregnant, wilt, by God's pleasure, be duly brought to bed, on this account I am minded to take counsel with the Holy Father himself, and to announce to him the divine miracle which is about to ensue, for the reason that he may despatch hither a certain two of his cardinals, whose place it will be to canonize your offspring at his birth, and by this cause he will be esteemed of greater excellence and far above all other saints."

Madonna Barbara, who, as it has been already said, was of pure and simple mind, readily gave credence to these words, and, assailed by a fresh passion of vainglory, felt no little pleasure that such a course as this should be taken on her account. The friar, seeing clearly that the vessel containing the new evangelist waxed greater in size every day that passed, got everything in order to quit the place; and, having taken from her divers other meals of pastry to stay his failing stomach, and bidden her farewell with little pleasure or contentment, he set forth on his journey, and in a short time found himself in Tuscany. What other feats he may have wrought after this, and what regions he may have traversed in order to beguile others by his tricks and craft, let him search out who is not already possessed with indignation. And it can, I trow, be held as a sure and certain fact that this precursor of Antichrist, into whatever land he may have come in the course of his wanderings, made all those who may have lent credence to his words to have a taste of the divinity of the angels in Paradise. Concerning Madonna Barbara, whom he left pregnant behind him, and who waited for a long time in vain the coming of the promised cardinals, I do not feel myself obliged to go seeking what fate may have been in store for her, nor what may have happened to her on the birth of her child. I only know right well that of this kind are the fruits and the leaves and the flowers which will assuredly come forth from the conversation and intimacy of these cheating friars.

I THEREFORE ask you what manner of human cleverness is there extant upon earth which shall be found sufficient for the warding off of the constant attacks such as we see delivered with all kind of deceit and treachery by these friars, whom I will never call holy men, but rather ministers of the chief of the devils? These same friars, having lately become aware of the fact that every man gifted with the flower of intellect must needs have full knowledge of the reprobate side of their corrupt lives, have, as a last remedy, schemed to pass themselves off as would-be saints. And in order that the devotees who favour them may be made to put faith in their manifest deceits, and so that the credulous may touch these frauds with their hands, I declare that these friars put forward certain creatures who have been plucked from the gallows and reduced to the last extremity of misery, and, having corrupted these with some small sum of money, they induce one to feign to be lame, another to be blind, and another to be oppressed by some incurable ailment or another. Wherefore, looking round and observing the dense and swarming crowd of ignorant people fascinated by their tricks, and not knowing what other thing to bring forward, they make a sign duly agreed upon before, for their gang of murderers to approach them, and these fellows, merely by touching the tassels of their robes and by the virtue of the relics which belonged (as the friars declare) to some departed saint of theirs, may be heard to proclaim with loud voices that a cure has been worked upon them simply by touching the holy preacher. Upon this they all cry out for mercy, bells are rung, long processes and authentic statements are drawn up, and by the means of such devilish working as this, the fame of such doings, spreading itself abroad and flying from one kingdom to another, forces even those men who can discern clearly enough the falsehood of the whole affair, to make believe that they take lies for the truth, forasmuch as were they to act otherwise they would be held and proclaimed to be heretics by the senseless multitudes and by the hypocrites. And over and above the experiences of these our days, which have been so clearly made manifest to us, we may well call to mind, as bearing on the truth of this matter, what has been taught to us in the preceding novel as to the manner of fruit we may expect to gather from their holiness. And albeit you must give in full measure your grief and pity to the noble lady aforesaid, on account of the suffering and betrayal put upon her by such a vile poltroon, nevertheless, the one which I now will let follow will not come to an end without giving you cause for much pleasure and merriment.

THE END OF THE SECOND NOVEL.

Novel the Third

ARGUMENT

Fra Nicolo da Narni being enamoured of Madonna Agata, procures fulfillment of his desire. The husband happening to come upon them, the wife declares that the friar, by the virtue of certain relics, has delivered her of a distemper which afflicted her. But, having found the friar's breeches at the head of the bed, the husband becomes disturbed in his mind, whereupon the wife assures him that the breeches formerly belonged to San Griffone.* This the husband believes, and in the end the friar causes them to be conveyed back to the convent in a solemn procession.

TO THE MOST ILLUSTRIOUS POET JOANNE PONTANO †

EXORDIUM

IF, most-noble-minded Pontanus, we ought to be as careful concerning the honour and profit of our true friends as concerning our own, I, although I, am only to be reckoned amongst the least of yours, am bound by every obligation to further your honour and well-being both by will and deed. Wherefore, knowing you to be adorned by so many peerless virtues that we may with justice call you the light of rhetoricians and the mirror

* The earlier editions give San Bernardino.

† Giovanni Gioviano Pontano, one of the most illustrious men of letters of the fifteenth century, was born in 1426, at Cerreto, near Spoletto. He studied at Perugia, and went in early manhood to Naples, where he attracted the notice of the celebrated Beccadelli (Panormita), the founder of the Neapoli-

of poets—knowing likewise of the other excellent parts you possess in such unbounded measure, I cannot on any account keep silent when I see all these excellencies sullied by a single spot which might easily be wiped away. By this spot I mean to indicate that constant practice you have of holding intimate converse with monks and friars of every sort—a practice which, in a man of your integrity, is a greater and a more reprehensible failing than the hatching of a plot with a bond of heretics. Of the truth of what I say you yourself may be the judge, seeing that none others than usurers, fornicators, and men of evil condition are ever to be seen associating with them, and these, forsooth, seek their company chiefly in order that, by thus foregathering with hypocrites, they may learn how better to deceive their fellows. Therefore, seeing that you yourself are not a wolf, it is not seemly that you should line your cloak with a wolf's skin.* I pray you get yourself out of so reprobate and damnable a path, and, above all, be firm, not only to withdraw yourself entirely from the society of such as these, but also to drive them from your house for good, even as if they were people smitten by some contagious plague. By following such a course as this you will shake off from yourself all possibility of future suspicion, and will give these creatures no opportunity of approaching you through the doorway of your friendship, and of contaminating, as is their wont, those who are about you. Now, in order that I may never behold you rushing down such a precipice as this, I will point out to you (with whatever authority my words may carry, and as a supplement to the arguments given above,) a farther example for your future action in the following

tan Academy. By Beccadelli he was introduced to the notice of Alfonso the Magnanimous, and from this time onward he was continually in the royal service, either as tutor, secretary, or ambassador. His literary fame rests on his Latin verse, of which he was a voluminous writer. On the death of Beccadelli he became the head of the learned society of the capital, and it was perhaps rather from him than from his predecessor and patron that the Academy of Naples received its formal constitution. When Charles VIII. entered Naples, Pontano greeted him with a congratulatory oration, an easy transfer of allegiance which Guicciardini censures severely. He died in 1503.

* Orig., *non conviensi della sua pelle foder arsi il tuo mantello.*

novel, which I have dedicated to you, and show you what recompense the friendship of a holy friar brought to a physician of Catania, who was addicted more than most men to the society of folk of this sort, and who, though he was of a very watchful and jealous nature, was deceived, and flouted likewise, by the subtle devices of his wife and of the friar.

THE NARRATIVE

CATANIA, as we all know well, is reckoned a noble and illustrious place amongst the other famous cities of the island of Sicily. There, in times not long past, resided a certain doctor of medicine, Maestro Rogero Campisciano by name, and this man, although he was full of years, took to wife a damsel called Agata, sprung from a very honourable family of the city before-named, who, according to the opinion current in the place, was the fairest and most graceful lady at that time living in the island. On this account her husband held her as dear as he held his own life.

Now because it very rarely or never happens that a man who is hotly in love escapes long from the plague of jealousy, this good doctor in a very short space of time became so jealous of his wife, without any other reason than the aforesaid, that he forbade her to hold converse with anyone, using just as great severity towards her friends and relations as towards strangers. And although he had very close relations with a community of friars minor in the city, being the keeper of their funds, the procurator of the order, and intimately acquainted with the whole course of their affairs, nevertheless, for the better safeguarding of his treasure, he commanded and laid a charge upon his wife that she should keep herself from all traffic with the friars, just as if they had been dissolute laymen. It chanced, however, in the course of time, that there arrived in Catania a minor friar called Fra Nicolo da Narni, who, though he put on the air of a hypocrite, and was wont to walk clattering along with a pair of wooden sandals like prison shackles, with a leather patch on the breast of his frock, with bent neck, and a gait fitted for the canting knave he was in sooth, was nevertheless a fresh-coloured, comely young fellow. And besides this, he had studied at Perugia,* and had gained considerable knowledge of the doctrine there taught; was a far-famed preacher, and already enrolled as a fellow of the confraternity of San Bernardino—a fact he never failed to make known to any one he might meet. He declared, moreover, that he had in his possession certain relics of this saint, by the virtue of which God had already shown, and still continued to show, many miracles. On account of this, and of the devout name enjoyed by his order, he drew to his preaching a marvellous great crowd of listeners, and in this wise it happened that, on a certain morning when he was preaching, he espied amongst the crowd of women in the church the aforesaid Madonna Agata, who seemed to him to be as a carbuncle stone in the midst of a mass of the whitest pearls, and, letting fall upon her many glances from the tail of his eye without in any way interrupting his sermon, he said to himself over and over again that the man who should be held worthy to enjoy the love of such a beautiful young woman might indeed reckon himself most fortunate. Agata, as was the wont of all those who came to hear the preaching, kept her eyes steadily fixed on the preacher in admiration, and, since he appeared to her to be a young man comely beyond ordinary, she breathed a wish to herself (without letting her thoughts run into any undisciplined excess of lust) that her husband were made more in the likeness of this handsome friar, and at the same time she began to think and to deliberate that she would like to go some day to make confession to Fra Nicolo. And thus, holding fast to this conceit of hers, as soon as she saw him come down from the pulpit she threw herself in his way, and besought him that he would vouchsafe to hear her. The friar, though he was inwardly overjoyed at her request, made answer to her, so as not to allow the corruption of

* Perhaps this mention of Perugia may be satirical on Masuccio's part, Pontano, to whom this novel is dedicated, having been educated there.

his mind to show itself on his countenance, that it was no part of his duty to hear confessions. Whereupon the lady replied: "But may not I, for the sake of Maestro Rogero, my good husband, ask to enjoy some privilege at your hands?" To this the friar answered: "Ah, then you are the wife of our procurator? For the respect I bear to him I will willingly listen to your confession." And when they had withdrawn themselves somewhat aside, and the friar had taken up his position in the place where they were accustomed to hear confessions, and the lady had gone down on her knees before him, she began to confess herself according to the accustomed rule. After she had laid bare a certain portion of her offences, telling the friar of the inordinate jealousy of her husband, she begged him of his kindness to let her know if there were any means within his power by which he could manage thoroughly to clear out of her husband's head all such delusions as these, believing perhaps that such ailments might be healed by herbs and plasters as her husband was wont to heal the sick folk under his charge. The friar set gladly to work to take into consideration a proposition such as this, for it seemed to him that now his good fortune was about to open for him the door which would give him the means of entering the path he so keenly desired to tread; wherefore, after he had given Madonna Agata consolation in somewhat flowery terms, he thus answered her: "My daughter, it is no marvel that your husband should be so jealous of you; indeed, were his mood otherwise, he would be held by me, and by every other man as well, to be something less than the prudent gentleman he is. Nor ought he to be charged with fault on this account, seeing that this circumstance arises solely from the working of Nature, who, having produced you adorned with so great and angelic loveliness, has rendered it impossible that anyone should ever be the possessor of you without suffering the sharpest pangs of jealousy."

The lady, smiling somewhat at these words, saw that the time had now come when it behoved her to return to the attendants who were awaiting her; so after certain other soft words had been spoken, she begged the friar to give her absolution. He therefore, having heaved a deep sigh, turned towards her with a pitiful countenance, and thus made answer: "My daughter, no one who is himself bound can give release to another, and for the reason that you in so short space of time have made me a slave, I can neither absolve you, nor loose myself, without aid from you." The courteous lady, who was by birth a Sicilian, quickly comprehended the real meaning of this ambiguous speech, remarking besides what a good-looking young fellow he was, and feeling no small gratification that he seemed to be so mightily taken by her beauty. Still she was somewhat surprised to find that friars took thought of such matters, because, on account of her youth and the careful guard kept over her by her husband, she had not only been kept from all dealing with religious persons of every sort, but had even been made to believe that the making of men into friars differed nought from the making of cocks into capons. However, she saw clearly enough that Fra Nicolo was more of a cock than a capon, and with a longing such as she had never before known, and with the firm resolve to give him her love at all hazard, she thus answered him: "My father, leave all your cares to me, forasmuch as I, coming here a free woman, must now return home the slave of you and of love." To this speech the friar replied, his heart filled with the greatest joy he had ever known: "Since then our desires run towards the same point, can you not devise some way by which we both of us, breaking forth at the same moment from this cruel prison, may taste the full joy our lusty youth permits?" To this she answered that she would willingly agree to this, supposing that a way could be found for its accomplishment, adding these words: "And now at this moment I am reminded of a plan whereby, in spite of the inordinate jealousy of my husband, we may be enabled to carry out our intention. For you must know that almost every month I am wont to be afflicted with a very grave distemper of the heart, so severe that it robs me of all power of sensation, nor up to this present time have I been able in the least degree to remedy the same by any device of the physicians. Indeed, certain women of experience in such matters have declared that my ailment proceeds from the womb, because I am young and fit to bear children, but by reason of the age of my husband I am not able to do this. Wherefore I have thought that on one of those days when my husband goes to ply his calling in the country, I might feign to be taken ill with one of my accustomed attacks. Then, having sent for you in haste, I might beg you to lend me certain relics of San Griffone, and you, on your part, must be prepared to come with them to me secretly; and afterwards, by the aid of a very trusty maid of mine, we can meet and take our pleasure together."

To this the friar, overjoyed, replied: "My daughter, may you be blessed by God for the excellent plan you have devised. It seems clear to me that we are in duty bound to carry it out, and I forsooth will bring with me a certain good friend of mine, who will not let your trusty waiting-woman complain that she is neglected while we are enjoying ourselves." Then, having spent some time over the conclusion of the business, they parted with many warm and amorous sighs. As soon as she had returned home, the lady made known to her maid the plan she had devised with the friar for their common gratification and pleasure, whereupon the maid, who was mightily pleased at the news, made answer that everything her mistress might command should straightway be prepared.

It chanced that fortune was very kind to them, forasmuch as the very next morning Maestro Rogero betook himself to visit his patients outside the city, according to the prescient surmise of his wife, who at once, in order to let no delay interfere with the course of the affair, began to call upon San Griffone to come to her aid, feigning to be afflicted with an attack of her customary distemper. Then straightway the maid addressed her, as if by way of counsel: "Why do you not send for those sacred relics of the saint which have such miraculous fame amongst men of all sorts?" Thereupon the lady, according to the plan they had arranged between themselves, making believe that she could speak only with great difficulty, turned towards the maid, and spake thus: "Nay, I beseech you to send and fetch them," and to her the woman, as if she were filled with pity, replied: "I will go myself for them." So, having set forth at the top of her speed, and

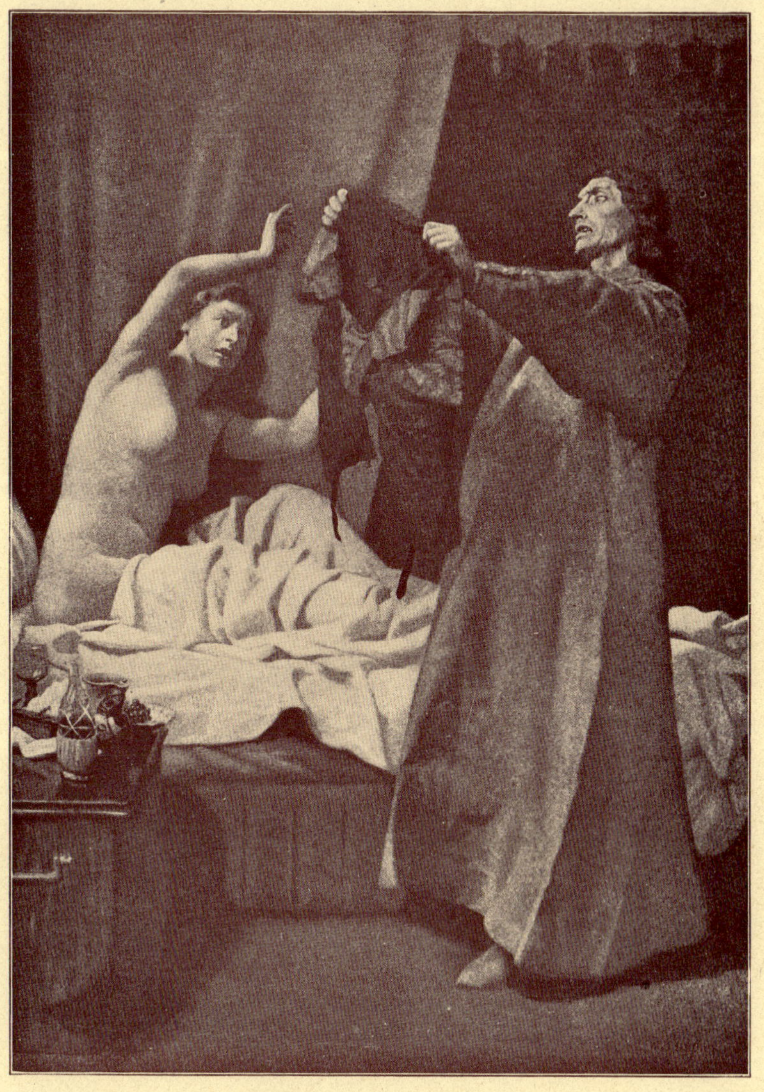

A RELIC OF SAN GRIFFONE.

FROM A DRAWING BY E. R. HUGHES. (Mas., Nov. iii., v. i.)

found the friar and given him the message which had been arranged, Fra Nicolo, together with a certain companion of his, a sprightly young fellow, and one well fitted for the business in hand, straightway set forth on his errand. When they were come into the chamber, and when Fra Nicolo, with a very devout look upon his face, had drawn anear the side of the bed upon which the lady was lying alone, she, who was tenderly awaiting him, received him with the greatest humility, and said: "O father, pray to God and to the glorious San Griffone on my behalf." To this the friar replied: "May the Creator make you worthy of what you ask; but you on your part must give evidence of devout behaviour, and if you are willing to accept His grace through the virtue of the holy relics I have with me, it is right and becoming that first we should resort with hearts full of contrition to the holy rite of confession, so that the soul, being brought back to health, the body may with ease be cleansed of its distemper." The lady answering, said: "Of a truth I have anticipated, and never wished for aught else than what you speak of, and this grace I beg most earnestly at your hands."

When they had thus spoken together, they gave courteous dismissal to all such persons as chanced to be in the chamber, so that there remained therein no one else except the maid and the companion who had come with the friar. Then, having securely locked themselves in, so that they might be in no danger of interruption, each lover began incontinently to raise the flame of desire with his lady. Fra Nicolo got upon the bed, and deeming that he might reckon on perfect security, took off his breeches in order that he might the better use his legs when freed from such impediment, and flung the garments aforesaid on the head of the bed. Then, having folded the lovely young woman in a close embrace, he began with her the sport so full of delight and so keenly desired by them both. The friar, who did not meet with such good luck every day of his life, gave full proof of his manhood, and once and twice reaped the full harvest of his desire; but, just as he was preparing for a third essay, he and Madonna Agata were made aware that Maestro Rogero on horseback was down below, he having come back sooner than they had anticipated from his journey. The friar in great haste flung himself off the bed, overcome with fear and vexation, and forgetting entirely the breeches which he had laid at the bed's head, while the waiting-woman, not at all pleased that the business she had begun with her swain must needs be abandoned, unfastened the door of the chamber, and, having called to the people who were waiting in the hall without, bade them come in at their pleasure, adding that, by the grace of God, her lady was now well-nigh entirely healed of her ailment, and praising God and San Griffone.

In this wise the matter stood when Maestro Rogero came into the chamber, and, as soon as he realized that something strange had happened, he was no less disturbed at finding that friars had begun to frequent his house than at the fresh indisposition of his beloved spouse; but she, observing at a glance that his humour was mightily changed, cried out: "Oh! husband, of a truth I should have been a dead woman by this time if our good father the preacher had not come to my aid with the relics of the most blessed San Griffone. These, as soon as he brought them near to my heart, took away all the pain and agony I suffered, just as a plentiful flood of water quenches a little fire." The credulous husband, when he heard how a remedy had at last been found for an ailment hitherto deemed incurable, fell a-thanking God and San Griffone with no small satisfaction, and at last, turning to the friar, gave him unbounded thanks for the great benefit he had wrought, and thus, after exchanging certain other speeches in devout and saintly discourse, the friar and his companion took their leave in the most seemly wise, and went their way back to the monastery.

Now, as they were walking along, Fra Nicolo began to feel somewhat cold about the breech, and then it came into his mind how he had left behind him at the head of the bed the garment he usually wore; whereupon, overcome beyond measure with grief and confusion, he turned to his companion and told him of the accident which had befallen him. His friend consoled him as best he could, and bade him cease from disquieting himself, forasmuch as the maid, who would be the first to find the breeches would assuredly hide them, and, laughing as he spoke, added these words: "My master, it is quite clear that you are not wont to put up with inconvenience of any sort, since it seems that you needs must, wherever you may be, straightway clap clothing upon those parts of yours. But perhaps you follow the example of the Dominican friars, who always take their dogs about with them unconfined by leash of any sort, and, although they often get fine sport, it is nevertheless a fact that hounds that are leashed are always keener and more holding in their grip when they come upon game." To this the friar replied: "What you say is true enough, but would to God that no scandal may arise on account of the fault I have committed; and, tell me, how did you fare with the prey I let fall into your clutches? For my own part, I know that in my hawking I managed to capture a brace of partridges, and, just as I was trying for a third, Messer Rogero came back." His friend answered: "I am no smith myself; but what do you say of a workman who managed to make two nails out of one heating of the furnace, and had got one finished complete, and the other only lacking the head thereto, when the girl, cursing the hour she was born, cried out, 'Here is the maestro at the door'? And thus the work which you had put in my way was left incomplete." Said the friar: "May God be willing to grant me leave to go back to the sport I was forced to give over, and then you, too, if you should still be in the mood therefor, may turn out your nails by the hundred." To this the friend replied: You will not find me wanting, but in sooth I believe the feathers of those two partridges you took are worth more than all the nails they make in Milan." At this speech the friar laughed heartily, and with many other witty words concerning their late adventure, they went on, joking between themselves.

As soon as the friars had left the chamber, Maestro Rogero, going close up to his wife's side and caressing her neck and her bosom, demanded to know from her whether the pain which had molested her had caused her great suffering. In the course of their conversation over this and over other matters, it chanced that Maestro Rogero, stretching out his hand to compose the pillows under his wife's head, caught hold of the laces of the breeches which the friar had left there.

When he had drawn them forth, and observed of a surety they were of the sort commonly worn by friars, he cried out with a face changed mightily: "What the devil can be the meaning of this? O Agata! for what reason are these friar's breeches here?" But the young wife, who was very wary and prudent (and love, moreover, had recently aroused yet more her intelligence), made answer without delaying her speech a moment: "And what can be the meaning of the long story I have just told you, my husband, if these be not the miraculous breeches which formerly belonged to the glorious San Griffone, and which our good father, the preaching friar, brought hither this morning as one of the most famous relics of the saint? Wherefore Almighty God, by the virtue of these, has already shown me great favour, and though I was fully assured of being entirely freed from my trouble, yet for greater security, and for piety's sake as well, I besought Fra Nicolo, when he was about to take it away, that he would leave it with me until the time of vespers, at which hour he or some others should send for it." The husband, when he heard this answer so ready and so well fitted for the occasion, either believed it in truth or made as if he believed it; but, having within him the nature of a jealous man, his brain was buffeted about without ceasing by the two contrary winds which this accident had stirred up; nevertheless, without giving any farther answer to the remarks of his wife, he held his peace. The wily young woman, being well assured that her husband was still somewhat disturbed in his mind, now began to scheme how she might by a new stratagem clear out entirely from his breast all the suspicious thoughts he there nursed; so turning towards her maid, she said: "Go now at once to the convent, and as soon as you shall have found the friar preacher, tell him to send and fetch the relics which he left with me, for by God's mercy I have had no occasion to use them more." The discreet waiting-woman, comprehending fully what the lady in truth wanted to say, went with all speed to the convent, and bade them quickly summon the friar preacher, who came straightway to the door, deeming peradventure that she had come to bring back the keepsake which he had left behind him. But he put on a smiling face as he spake to her, and asked her what news she bore. "No good news, in sooth," she answered, with a very ill grace, "thanks to your carelessness, and it would have been worse but for the prudence of my mistress." "Tell me what it is," cried the friar; and then the girl related to him, point by point, all that had happened, adding that it seemed to her there was no better way out of the affair than that they should send from the monastery to fetch the aforesaid relics with a certain parade of ceremony without further delay. Then the friar said, "Keep your mind at ease;" and, having taken leave of her and bidden her to hope that all things which had been ill done would straightway be repaired, he sought out the superior, and spake to him in these words: "Good father, I have just committed a most grievous sin, one for which in due time you can punish me as I deserve, but just now I beseech you to give me instant help, as the needs of the case demand, in order that this mischance may be set right without delay," and then Fra Nicolo set forth the whole story in as brief a fashion as possible. The superior, finding himself perturbed in no small measure over the affair, took the friar sharply to task for his imprudence, and thus addressed him: "See now what comes of working miracles! A clever fellow you are, in sooth! You fancied, indeed, that you could go safely to work; but, if you found you must needs take off your breeches, could you not think of some other way of hiding them, either in the sleeves or in the breast of your gown, or in some other secret place about your person? You, wonted as you are to be mixed up in such scandals as these, recked naught as to the great burden of conscience and obloquy of the world with which we of your order shall have to battle. Of a truth I know not what reason there is why I should not forthwith send you to prison as you richly deserve. Nevertheless, seeing that at the present moment it behoves us to endeavour to mend matters rather than to inflict punishment, and that the affair concerns especially the honour of the order, we will postpone your chastisement to some future time."

Then, having set ringing the bell of the chapter house, and let assemble all the friars, the superior told them how, in the house of Maestro Rogero the physician, God had that very day wrought a most evident miracle by the virtue of the breeches which formerly belonged to San Griffone. Having told them the story in the fewest possible words, he persuaded them that it behoved them to go forthwith to the house of the aforesaid physician, and bring back therefrom the holy relic with high solemnities and a procession, whereby they might give honour and glory to God, and cause the miracles of the saint to be held in yet higher esteem.

When the friars were duly mustered and ranged two by two, they took their way towards the house in question with the cross at the head of the procession. The superior, clad in a sumptuous cope, bore the tabernacle of the altar on his arm, and marching along in silence they came to the physician's house. When Maestro Rogero became aware of their presence he went out to meet the superior, and demanded of him the cause of this unwonted visit, whereupon the latter, with a joyous face, made answer to him in terms he had before arranged: "Well-beloved Maestro, the rules of our order require that we should carry in secret the relics of our saint to the house of anyone who may wish to have them, and in like manner if it should happen that the sick person, through any failing of his own, should receive no benefit from the ministration, that we should privily fetch them home again in order that the fame of miracles should not be diminished thereby. But in cases in which God, through the means of the above-named relics, may have willed to exhibit miracles past gainsaying, it is our duty to fetch the holy relic back to our church with all the ceremony and splendour we can afford, thus proclaiming abroad the miracle which has been wrought, and recording it in public form. And for the reason that your wife (as you must already know) has been freed from the dangerous disease which afflicted her through the working of our relic, we are now come in this solemn fashion to bear it back to our house." The physician, when he marked how the whole congregation of friars was come thither with so great a show of devotion, at once settled in his mind that these holy men would never have gathered themselves together to work any ill purpose; so, accepting as gospel truth the fictitious reasons of the superior, and driving away entirely all suspicious thoughts from his mind, he spake thus: "In sooth, you are all right welcome;" and, having taken the friar preacher by the hand, he led him into the chamber where Madonna Agata still was. She, who had in no wise gone to sleep over the business, had now the breeches all ready, and wrapped in a white and perfumed linen cloth. The superior, when they were displayed to him, kissed them with the deepest reverence, and made the physician and the lady do the same, and in the end all those who were assembled in the room kissed them likewise. Next, after they had placed the breeches in the tabernacle which they had brought with them for that purpose, and after a sign had been given to the company, they all began to sing in unison *Veni Creator Spiritus*, and in this order, traversing the city and accompanied by a huge crowd, they bore the relic back to their church and there placed it above the high altar, letting it remain several days in order that all those who had already heard of the miraculous occurrence might pay their devotions to it. Maestro Rogero, being very keenly set on increasing the reverence of the people round about towards the order aforesaid, let pass no opportunity of telling the story to whatsoever gatherings of men he chanced to encounter as he went about his practice, both within and without the city, setting forth the solemn miracle which God had wrought through the healing power of the breeches of San Griffone. And while he occupied himself in the discharge of this office, Fra Nicolo and his friend in no wise forgot to make a fresh trial of that rich hunting-ground which they had already explored, to the great delight both of the mistress and of the maid. Madonna Agata, independent of any sensual delight she might enjoy, came to the conclusion that this operation was in truth the only one of any service to cure her acute attacks; for the reason that it brought relief to the very seat of her distemper. Besides this, being the wife of a physician, she had often heard tell of that text of Avicenna in which he lays down the dictum, "that those remedies which are approximate and partial may give ease, but those which are continuous will work a cure." Wherefore, having tasted both the one sort and the other with much delight, she was duly conscious that, through the opportune ministrations of the holy friar, she had been entirely freed of the incurable mother-sickness which had plagued her so long.

MASUCCIO

HOWBEIT the novel I have narrated above abounds in pleasurable entertainment, and may well be re-read and re-heard, nevertheless I would rather, if there be any repetition of the same, that it should take place in the presence of those who are wont to follow me up without ceasing with their bows ready bent, taunting me with bitter words and reproving me for writing against these false world-deceivers, in order that (putting aside the deceit practised and the adultery committed by this ribald monk) they might in their whisperings and murmurings give full consideration to the fact that this open heretic, this notorious despiser of Christ's faith and work and doctrine, should not only have willed, but should have dared indeed to place within the chosen vase and veritable receptacle of the most sacred body of the Son of God, a pair of stinking breeches, lousy, and filled with a thousand different kinds of dirt. Moreover, let any man read of Christ's supreme agony, and he will not find that the traitorous Jews, although they slew Him with the greatest iniquity and insult, ever cast upon Him contempt equal to that which I have described. Let the earth, therefore, open wide her mouth and swallow alive this swarm of dastardly wretches, together with all those who support them, not only as a punishment for present offences, but as a warning and eternal example for all future ungodly men who may be like unto them. However, so as not to allow for a moment that these grumblers, styled my adversaries, have any power to restrain me from saying, according to the style in which I have begun, what I in sooth think concerning these soldiers of Lucifer, I will further demonstrate—little as they may like it—how a most subtle scheme was taken in hand by two accursed friars in order that they might gather together money, and by means of their greed get made prelates. You may learn clearly how this was done by the exhibition of their fraudulent miracles which they made.

THE END OF THE THIRD NOVEL.

Novel the Fourth

ARGUMENT

Fra Girolamo of Spoleto makes the people of Sorrento believe that the bone of a certain dead body which he has gotten is the arm of St. Luke. His accomplice contradicts this statement, whereupon Fra Girolamo prays to God that he will demonstrate the truth of his words by the working of a miracle. Then the accomplice feigns to fall down dead, and Fra Girolamo by prayer restores him to life. Having by the fame of this double miracle collected a great sum of money, Fra Girolamo becomes a prelate, and hereafter lives a lazy life with his comrade.

TO THE MAGNIFICENT MESSER ANTONELLO DE PETRUCIIS,* THE SOLE AND WELL-TRUSTED SECRETARY TO THE KING

EXORDIUM

DESIRING to make a beginning of my letter to you, I can but feel, my magnificent chief, that you—a very ocean of rhetorical style—must needs look upon my writing as nothing better than the vile bawling of a blind man of the common herd, even though the lyre

* Antonello de Petruciis was born of humble parentage at Teano. He was taken into the service of the state by Giovanni Olzina, the secretary of Alfonso the Magnanimous, and ultimately became secretary to Ferdinand I. Two of his sons perished in the conspiracy of the barons, and he himself was beheaded two years after in 1487. It is probable that the crime for which De Petruciis perished was his great wealth, since it was a maxim of Ferdinand to let his officials fatten themselves by extortion, and then after their judicial murder to seize upon their estates. In the edition of 1483, this novel is dedicated to Petruciis under the title of Messer Antonio d'Aversa.

of Orpheus and the eloquence of Mercury should be granted to me. This, then, is the only reason why I have deferred until this present time to write the following novel; and now, being well assured that it is highly diverting and good of its kind, I have resolved to send the same to you, all unadorned and unpolished as it is. And although it happens that this particular story can be of little profit to you yourself, seeing that you have knowledge enough and to spare concerning the ways of the world, nevertheless, should it happen to be read by certain others, they will, I doubt not, take therefrom some most useful counsel. Peradventure it may appear to these to be a sufficient argument why they should guard themselves carefully against the new and fraudulent sect known as the Saints—people who with all manner of guileful arts and subtle frauds make pretence of performing miracles, and prepare the way to steal away from others their honour, their wealth, and their peace of mind as well. Now, although I do not anticipate that any eloquence would be of virtue sufficient to sum up the whole volume of the wickedness of these men, nevertheless, merely by culling one small flower out of a wide plain, I may cause you to comprehend fully the details of a deceitful trick practised by a certain minor friar—a trick against which, according to my judgment, no human shrewdness would have been of any service.

THE NARRATIVE

AT that time when the French King James,* heretofore known as the Count de la Marc, became the husband of the last princess of the house of Durazzo, there came to Naples a certain minor friar who was called by name Fra Girolamo da Spoleto; and this

* Jacques, Comte de la Marche et de Castres. In 1415 he married Queen Joanna II., and shortly after the marriage he caused certain of her favourites to be put to death, and tried to keep the queen herself a prisoner. A riot broke out, and he fell into the queen's hands, and was thrown into prison. He escaped, fled to France, and became a Franciscan friar.

man, according to outward seeming, showed himself to be as holy as any of the saints, and was wont to spend the whole of his time as an itinerant preacher, not only in the city of Naples, but in the neighbouring towns as well. In all these places he acquired an amazing reputation and reverence.

Hence it happened that one day when he chanced to be at Aversa,* there was exhibited to him as a most wonderful spectacle the body of a certain knight well known to fame, which corpse many years before had passed into the keeping of a monastery of preaching friars. This dead body, either because it had been very well preserved, or peradventure on account of the temperate manner of life used by the knight while he was living, or for some other reason, was still in so sound and perfect a state, that not only was every bone thereof well settled in its right position, but the skin was in so little degree fallen to decay that, by touching the head, the lower parts of the body would move themselves. Sir Friar, as soon as he had well and carefully surveyed the sight before him, forthwith began to consider in his mind how he might contrive to get into his possession some member or other of the corpse aforesaid, in order that he might, by the aid of such member, to be styled by him a sacred relic, sweep into his purse hundreds and thousands of ducats. In the spending of these he deemed that he might not only live a life of lazy self-indulgence, but might even—as is the wont of such men—lay them out profitably enough to win for himself the rank of a prelate.

For, in sooth, if we take good inquisition of those round about us, we shall easily perceive how vast a number of friars have become prelates at the cost of luckless and witless laymen; this one rising to the post of inquisitor into heretical opinions, and that one becoming a collector of money for the furnishing of a crusade;† to say nothing of those others, who, by the instrumentality of papal

* Petruciis, to whom this novel is dedicated, was brought up at Aversa.

† Masuccio probably had in mind the attempt of Pius II. to promote a crusade for the recovery of Constantinople at the Council of Mantua in 1459.

bulls, whether these be genuine or false, grant full remission of sins, or through the power of money make promises to gain for anyone a safe abode in Paradise; thus, by hook or by crook, winning for themselves a bellyful of florins, in spite of the fact that such traffic is expressly forbidden by the most sacred rules of their religion.

But we will now return to our brother Girolamo. As soon as ever he had perfected his design, and had suborned the sacristan of the place, he contrived, although the latter was a Dominican, by the favour of the Prior of Santa Croce, to get possession of the arm, together with the right hand of the corpse aforesaid. Upon this member not only might one see the skin intact, and likewise some of the fine hairs growing thereupon, but the nails thereof were so smooth and firm that they might well have been taken for those of a living man. And so as not to let there be any delay in despatching the business Sir Friar forthwith swathed the holy relic in divers wrappings fashioned out of fine taffeta, and placed it, together with certain sweetly-smelling gums, in a casket, and then got his affairs in order to depart thence.

When he arrived in Naples he there fell in with a certain trusty comrade of his, and one no less skilled in the arts of cozening than himself, a friar known by the name of Brother Mariano da Saona, and these two made an agreement to betake themselves together into Calabria, a province inhabited by a very gross and stupid race of peasants, and one exactly fitted to serve them for the trial of their tools. The following is the course they decided to adopt: Fra Mariano, having disguised himself with great care in the habit of a friar of the order of Saint Dominic, went down to the port, and there searched about to find a ship in which he might make the voyage into Calabria, and Fra Girolamo likewise, accompanied by other three of his comrades, repaired to the seafaring parts of the town, laden with wallets for travel, and there, having by chance come upon a bark belonging to Amantea,* the captain of which was minded to put to sea at once, they all of them took passage in the same; the one party of friars, meantime, showing themselves to be in no wise well affected

* Orig., *Mantioti.* Amantea is a small seaport of Calabria.

towards the other, in the same fashion as one set of cheats, of the sort which haunts the country fairs, will bear itself towards another set, what time the two may foregather in some wayside inn. Then, when all things had been duly set in order, and when the sailors had dipped their oars into the water and stretched the sails to the breeze, they set forth on their voyage.

When they were come into the neighbourhood of Capri, on a sudden there rose up behind them a squall of wind so violent and so fraught with danger to them that all the sailors cried out forthwith that they could in no wise make head against the same. Wherefore, being almost shipwrecked, they came to a decision, albeit much against their inclination, to run the ship ashore on a little strip of beach near to Sorrento; and having with no little difficulty drawn the ship up to land at this spot, they all leaped on shore and took their way into the town, where they determined to tarry until the weather should have become more propitious for their voyage.

In this manner our good Fra Girolamo amongst the other travellers went with those who were of his company to the monastery of the Conventual Brothers, while Frate Mariano, who had become for the nonce a Dominican, took lodging for himself at the inn amongst the other laymen. When Fra Girolamo looked and saw how stormy the sea still was, and knew therefrom that some time must yet elapse before it could be calm, he made up his mind, worthy man, so as not to waste any more time, to show to the world then and there his first experiment with the virtues of that sham relic of his, bearing in mind more especially how he had in times past heard tell that this aforesaid city of Sorrento, over and above the fact that it was a place of great renown, was a very ancient city, more ancient, indeed, than any other in the kingdom. On this account, therefore, he came to the decision that the inhabitants thereof, being as yet infected with pristine dulness of intellect, would serve his purpose equally well as would the peasants of Calabria as subjects upon whom he might successfully try the experiment he had devised.

Wherefore he took care to let his good comrade, Fra Mariano, have privy information of what he was about to do, and then—the day following happening to be a Sunday—he begged the head of the convent to go to the archbishop, and to let him know that he, Fra Girolamo, had planned—with the sanction and blessing of the archbishop—to deliver a religious discourse on the following morning at the great church. And for this reason he begged the archbishop that he would cause intelligence of the same to be spread abroad, both within and without the city; forasmuch as he had determined in his mind that, as soon as he should behold assembled in the church a sufficient number of people, all showing themselves to be duly devout in their demeanour, he would, for the sake of the honour and glory of God, exhibit to their sight a certain holy relic, of a surety the most sacred they had ever beheld.

The archbishop, who was himself of the true Sorrentine type, straightway gave undoubting credit to Fra Girolamo's words, and at once sent forth his decree, not only into the city itself, but into all the country parts lying round about, that everyone should, for the reason aforesaid, betake himself to the place named in a reverent mind, in order that he might give ear to the preaching, and behold the sacred relic which was now to be shown to the people of Sorrento by a servant of God. In the end it came to pass that the news aforesaid was spread far and wide through all the country, so that on the appointed morning there was gathered together round the church such a vast multitude of people that within there was not space enough to contain the half thereof. When the hour was come for the preaching to begin, Fra Girolamo, accompanied by many other friars performing the ceremonies meet for such an occasion, went up into the pulpit and forthwith began to preach a long discourse concerning works of mercy and the holy duty of almsgiving. Then, when it seemed to him that the right moment had come, he, having first uncovered his head, began to speak in the following words:

"Most reverend monsignore, and all you other noble gentlemen and dames, and fathers and mothers of mine in Christ Jesus, I doubt not but that some report of my preaching in Naples will have come to your ears; for, in that place, by the help of God's mercy, and not through any merits or virtues of my own, I have, as often as I have preached, been listened to by an extraordinary number of people. Wherefore, having heard of the fair fame of this very noble city of yours, and of the humanity and piety dwelling in the hearts of its citizens—together with other accounts which have come to me concerning the beauty of your country—I have many times set my heart upon coming hither to lift up my voice and proclaim to you the word of God, and to take the while some joy and pleasure with you in this fair and gracious air of yours—an air which I, in good sooth, imagine is mightily well suited to my temperament. Seeing, however, that there has been issued to me a command from our Father the Vicar-general, that I should straightway betake myself into Calabria, there to assume the charge of various offices in certain of the towns to which I had been summoned, I found that it was necessary for me to turn upon my path somewhat, and to make my way towards that place whither I had already been commanded to go. Now, as I believe is well known to you, I myself, together with all the others who had embarked with me, arrived lately in your city, for the reason that the ship in which we took passage was driven into your gulf by the force of adverse winds and tempestuous seas, in spite of all the strivings and labours of the crew, all on board having narrowly escaped destruction.

"But I do not believe that this coming of mine into your city has been in any wise brought about by these contrary winds, but by the sacred working of the will of the Creator, who has thus graciously vouchsafed to satisfy in part my earnest wish. And in order, forsooth, that you also may be made participators in the aforesaid bounty, I am now minded to bring before your eyes a most marvellous relic, which thing cannot fail to serve for the increase of religion and piety amongst you. This relic is nothing else than the arm and the entire right hand of that most excellent and glorious writer of the words and deeds of Christ Jesus our Redeemer, Saint Luke the Evangelist, which precious thing the Patriarch of Constantinople gave to our Father Vicar. Whereupon this latter despatched me into Calabria therewith, for the reasons aforesaid, forasmuch as there has never been in this province up to the present time either the body or the limb of any saint whatever. On this account, my friends here gathered together, let each one of you in devout fashion uncover his head before looking at this precious treasure which our great God, more through the working of a miracle than through any act of mine, has granted you leave to behold. Now, first I will notify to you that I hold a bull from our lord the Pope, by the terms of which he grants the highest indulgence and complete remission of sins to every man who will give alms according to his ability in honour of the relic aforesaid, in order that, with whatever treasure can be thus gathered together, we may let construct a tabernacle of silver, set and adorned with precious stones, to serve as a fitting shrine for so excellent and precious a thing."

When the friar had made an end of this discourse, he drew forth from his sleeve a sealed bull, forged according to a cunning device of his own, and forthwith the whole of the people who were there present believed with unquestioning faith in the instrument he laid before them without ever having read a single letter of the same, and then each individual person drew near to make his offering, although it was no easy matter to do this on account of the crowd. Fra Girolamo, as soon as he had delivered in due course the fictitious story which he had concocted for the occasion, called to his associates and bade them bring to him the casket wherein had been placed the holy arm. Then, having let kindle a great quantity of lights round about, he went down on his knees, and, holding the sacred relic in his hand with a mighty show of reverence and with his eyes full of tears, he first of all kissed the border of the casket in which was shut up this false relic which he had prepared for the beguiling of others. Next he turned with great solemnity towards his companions, and then straightway began to sing a pious laud of Saint Luke, with full pontifical rites. At last, when he marked that all the people were standing, as it were, wonder-stricken, he opened the casket, and immediately there issued therefrom a most marvellous odour. Next he removed the wrappings of fine taffeta, and, having taken up the relic and uncovered the hand thereof and a small portion of the arm, he spake in this wise:

"This thing which I have here is the blessed and holy hand of that most faithful scribe of the Son of God; this is the blessed hand which not only wrote down so many excellent things concerning the glorious Virgin Mary, but likewise many times made a picture of her face and figure as she was in the flesh." And while he was thus earnestly set upon recounting the praises of the saint aforesaid, lo and behold! from a distant corner of the church, Fra Mariano da Saona, clad in the Dominican robes which he had lately put on, made all the people clear a way for him with the greatest persistence, and, shouting with a loud voice at Fra Girolamo, his confederate, began to declaim against him in the following wise: "Ah! vile rogue that thou art, coward and traitor both towards God and man, why art thou not overwhelmed with shame as thou utterest so monstrous a lie in affirming that this thing is in truth the arm of Saint Luke, forasmuch as I myself know for certain that at this moment his most holy body rests entire at Padua? In good sooth, this rotten bone you have here must have been dug up by you out of some grave, in order that you might deceive others therewith. Indeed, I am mightily astonished at the conduct of monsignore here and of these other reverend fathers in the church, men who might with reason condemn thee to be stoned, a punishment surely meet for thy offences."

The archbishop and all the people there assembled were not a little amazed when they listened to this strange saying, and, reproaching Fra Mariano with sharp words on account of his utterance, they commanded him to hold his peace forthwith; but he, in spite of this rebuke, ceased not to bellow forth his exclamations; nay, rather he showed himself all the more clamorous and persistent in persuading the crowd assembled that they should lend no belief to aught that Fra Girolamo might tell them. And now the affair had been brought into this tangle, it seemed to Fra Girolamo that the time had fully come when he should set himself to work the false miracle he had so carefully prepared. Wherefore, feigning to be somewhat disturbed in mind, he made a gesture with his hand to the people, signifying thereby that they should keep silence, forasmuch as they still continued to murmur; and when, after a short time had elapsed, he marked that everyone present was anxiously bent on hearing whatever he might have to say, he turned towards the high altar, where there stood an image of the Crucified, and, kneeling down before the same, he took up his speech, weeping plentifully the while:

"Jesus Christ my Lord, Redeemer of the human race, God as well as man, Thou who hast moulded me in Thine own image, and hast led me here through the merits of Thy most glorious body and by Thy human flesh without spot or blemish, and hast ransomed me by Thy most bitter passion, I now implore by the merits of those marvellous wounds which at one time Thou gavest to our seraphic Saint Francis, that it may be Thy pleasure to show forth a miracle about which there can be no gainsaying, here in the presence of this most devout concourse of people and of this valiant friar, who in sooth, acting the part of an enemy and of an antagonist to our religion, has come hither to put a slight upon my truthfulness. Deal with us in such a manner that, if I now say what is false, Thou shalt hurl all Thy wrath upon me straightway, and slay me at this very moment. But if, on the contrary, I speak nought but the truth in declaring that this is indeed the arm of Saint Luke, the most worthy recorder of Thy life and doings, then, O Lord! not for the sake of vengeance, but that the truth may be clearly made manifest, send down Thy judgment upon him in such a manner that, however much he may wish to do it, he shall be able, neither by word of mouth nor by gesture, to acknowledge his fault."

Scarcely had Fra Girolamo come to the end of this exorcism of his, when, all on a sudden, Fra Mariano—according to the plan already settled between the two—began to writhe all over, and to twist his hands and his feet, to howl aloud and to babble with his tongue in such wise that not a single comprehensible word issued from his lips. His eyes rolled from side to side, and his mouth was all awry, and, giving himself the semblance of being drawn together in all his limbs, he let himself fall backwards as one who had lost all control. As soon as the people who were there in the church perceived that a manifest and undoubted miracle had been wrought, they forthwith began to cry one and all for mercy in such wise that had it thundered aloud the sound thereof would scarcely have been heard by reason of the shouting.

Fra Girolamo, perceiving that the people had been enticed into the mood he desired, now began to cry out at the top of his voice, in order to inflame them yet further and to complete the trick he had set out, "Praised be God! Silence, O my people!" And when he had calmed the excitement of the congregation by these words, and had made certain of them take up Fra Mariano, who now seemed to be as one dead, and lay him down in front of the altar, he began to speak in this wise: "Oh! all ye of high estate, both ladies and gentlemen—all ye peasants likewise—I beseech you, by the virtue of the blessed passion of Christ, that you will all kneel down, and will devoutly recite a paternoster in honour of Saint Luke, by the merits of whom may God not only bring this poor man back to life, but may He likewise restore to him the lost use of his limbs, and his speech as well, in order that his soul may be spared the descent into eternal perdition."

No sooner had the friar uttered this command, than they all straightway fell into the posture of prayer, and, on the other part, Fra Girolamo, having come down from the pulpit and taken out a little knife, pared off a small shred of the nail from the miraculous hand, which thing he put in a beaker of holy water, and then, having opened wide the mouth of Fra Mariano, he poured down his throat the precious liquor, saying the while: "By the virtue of the Holy Spirit, I command you that you rise up forthwith and return to your former state of health." Now, Fra Mariano, who up to this present moment had only with great difficulty kept himself from laughing aloud, swallowed the beverage which was offered to him, and, perceiving the full drift of the affair, he suddenly raised himself upright on his feet, and opened his eyes like a man who had been stunned by a blow, and began to cry aloud, "Jesus! Jesus!" The assembled multitude, as soon as they perceived this fresh and undoubted miracle, likewise began to shout, one and all of them, "Jesus! Jesus!" like those who are terror-stricken and stupified with amazement. Some of them ran to ring the bells, and some to kiss and to touch the vestments of the preacher, bearing themselves in such a manner that it seemed as if each one of them was driven by some religious frenzy to believe that the last and universal judgment of all men was indeed at hand.

Fra Girolamo, who was now minded to make a quick despatch of the business which had brought him hither managed with no small difficulty to make his way once more up into the pulpit, whereupon he gave command that they should at once place the holy relic in front of the altar and, when this had been done, he made all his companions range themselves in order round about it, some holding lighted tapers in their hands, and some busying themselves to clear a space by the altar in such wise that every single person might be able, without hindrance, to offer prayers or oblations, according as he would, to the holy arm. And even after there had been collected from the crowd—the greatest that had ever been seen gathered together in that place—a vast sum of money, it chanced that certain women in the congregation were seized with an unbridled access of charitable frenzy, so violent that they tore off from their persons the pearls and the silver and the other precious jewels which they were wearing, and made an offering of the same to the holy evangelist.

And when they had in this manner kept the holy relic exposed to view for the whole of that day, it seemed at length to Fra Girolamo that the time had come for him to make the best of his way back to his home with the booty he had already gathered together. Wherefore, having made a signal to his companions in very cautious wise, they dexterously packed up everything belonging to them, together with the arm enclosed in the coffer. Then all the people assembled in the church took their way towards the convent. Fra Girolamo, who by this time was esteemed and reverenced almost as a saint by the archbishop and all the people, was by them honourably escorted back to this place, and, having had these notable miracles of his publicly authenticated, he himself, with Fra

Mariano and his other companions, and the great store of booty they had collected, went on board their ship the following morning, the weather being fine and propitious for their voyage.

Thus, sailing before a favourable wind, in a few days they came to Calabria, where they at once set to work with all kinds of fraudulent tricks, with so great success that, having filled their pockets full of money, and traversed all the regions of Italy, both those inland and those lying on the sea-board, they gathered together very great wealth by the virtue of the miraculous arm and by their many tricks of knavery, and at last returned to Spoleto. Having come there it seemed to them that they stood on safe ground; so Fra Girolamo, through the agency of a certain lord cardinal, bought for himself a bishopric—not by simony, indeed, but by a new form of collusion invented, and called by them "procuration,"* Then he, together with his colleague, Fra Mariano, passed a life of idleness, and indulged themselves in every pleasure as long as they lived.

MASUCCIO

THE last novel has in a measure shown us with what great cunning these fraudulent and most rapacious wolves strive and scheme to get possession of our goods, working for the most part in such fashion that no human precaution is of any value to defend us from their craft. And the practice of theirs which assuredly tends most strongly to kindle our anger and contempt is their continual preaching in condemnation of

* Masuccio probably means the delegation of ecclesiastical duties by the holders of benefices to others who agreed to discharge these duties for a small portion of the revenues. These were nearly always Mendicant Friars, and having got possession of the benefices, they were confirmed in the same, notably by Sixtus IV., who had himself been a Franciscan, by the bull of August 31st, 1474: *Amplissimæ gratiae et privilegia fratrum minorum conventualium or dinis S. Francisci, quæ propterea Mare Magnum nuncupantur.* On this account the real control of Church affairs fell almost entirely into their hands.

avarice, which thing they regard not only as a deadly sin, but also as an offence as unpardonable as heresy itself. But, we on the other hand, may see that avarice is not merely to be looked at as the universal and inborn passion of those who have put on the religious habit, forasmuch as we may behold them one and all following her closely, and embracing her even, as if she were some beloved friend or sister, or as if such doings had been expressly decreed and ordained as a precept of obedience by their rules.

Thus, if I made the statement towards the end of the foregoing novel that our Fra Girolamo bought a bishopric for himself, and that in these days simony has changed its name, no one need be at all astonished at this saying of mine, seeing that it must be plain to the intelligence of anyone that no man, however eminent his virtues may be, or however much of time and money he may have spent in studying in the Roman courts, can ever hope to rise to any grade whatever in the prelature save through the help and favour of the master of the mint. Nay, indeed, a man will find that he must needs purchase his prelature even as if he were purchasing by auction a horse at a fair, and he will find likewise that, over and above the bribes in the shape of gifts and stipulated sums of money handed over to those who favour his cause, he will also be obliged to pay liberally certain others to secure against molestation by them. Wherefore we should not wonder when we find men speaking of this thing, which is in sooth unlawful possession, as a due and deserved income. From this fact, therefore, we can set forth the argument that friars and priests and monks have invented a new language full of strange idioms, forasmuch as now, in speaking of the most heinous crimes, they add to, and trick out, the names of these with some well-known words out of the Holy Scriptures. And thus eating and drinking at the cost of the crucifix, and living a life of idleness at our charges, they make a mock both of God and man.*

* In Masuccio's time the Mendicant Orders had the privilege of performing all the sacraments, and likewise the very lucrative one of allowing sepulture in their habit, thus giving direct transit

Since these men are wont to describe as "the secret of their rule" the most abominable sins which can be wrought on earth to the dishonour of God and of nature, and practise these same offences without sparing or fear or shame, each one may easily figure to himself how they will act with regard to other crimes which are less revolting. I, who am minded to give farther intelligence concerning their doings public and private, am led on by the desire to let continue these novels in the same strain which I have already taken up. Therefore I will bring forward some other well-approved testimony against the monks, and in the novel which follows—the fifth—I will let you know how a ribald priest, besides singing the "Gaudeamus," and the "Per incarnati Verbi misterium," and the "Veni Sponsa Christi," and working other iniquities, was wont to call the sword which he carried about with him "Salvum me fac"; and likewise how, having transferred this name to another weapon, he cried out that he was bent on seating the Pope in Rome, and in driving out the Turk from Constantinople.

to Paradise. The Popes—Sixtus IV. especially—sided with them in their disputes with the parish priests, and under this patronage they became very aggressive and unscrupulous in their dealings with their opponents. In a report made by Giovanni Francesco Carafa, afterwards Paul IV., to Clement VII., there is a passage illustrating their methods: *Si viene ad homicidi non solo col veneno, ma apertamente col coltello e con la spada, per non dire con schiopetti.*

THE END OF THE FOURTH NOVEL.

Novel the Fifth

ARGUMENT

MASSIMILLA, BEING AMOROUSLY LOOKED UPON BY A PRIEST, AND BY A TAILOR AS WELL, PROMISES HER FAVOURS BOTH TO THE ONE AND THE OTHER. WHILE SHE IS TAKING HER PLEASURE IN HER HOUSE WITH THE TAILOR, THE PRIEST COMES FOR WHAT HAS BEEN PROMISED HIM, AND TRIES TO GAIN ENTRY BY FORCE. WHEREUPON THE TAILOR, BEING MIGHTILY ALARMED, SEEKS SHELTER IN THE GARRET. THE PRIEST COMES IN AND SAYS THAT HE HAS A WISH TO SEND THE POPE TO ROME. THE TAILOR, SEEING THAT A FESTIVAL IS AT HAND, DEEMS THAT IT OUGHT NOT TO BE UNGRACED BY MUSIC, SO HE BLOWS A NOTE ON THE PIPES, WHICH PUTS TO FLIGHT THE PRIEST. THEN THE TAILOR TAKES POSSESSION OF THE BOOTY LEFT BEHIND.

TO THE MAGNIFICENT MESSER ANGELO CARACCIOLO *

EXORDIUM

AMONGST people of the common sort there is a saying, times and often to be heard in the course of conversation, that one may find other ways of paying debts than with money; and if anyone has ever held this proverb in esteem, or has had cause to make use thereof, I, assuredly, shall be the one now to have recourse to it in my dealings with you. And as it happens that, from the beginning of our friendship to this present time, I find myself under so many and divers obligations to you that not only am I altogether unable to

* Besides this Novel Masuccio dedicates two others—No VII. and No. XX.—to various members of this noble family and likewise makes one of them a character in Novel XLIV.

enumerate them, but am unable even to call all of them to mind. And because to people of magnificent estate like yourself, things of small value, offered by those to whom you are bound by ties of true friendship, are wont to be more acceptable than sumptuous gifts, I have resolved to acquit myself of a small portion of the debt which I owe you by offering for your acceptance the novel which follows. I beg you, therefore, to receive it with all affection; and, if the uncouth idiom of my mother tongue* should be entirely, or even in part, displeasing to you, I beg you to pluck only the fruit of my uncultivated and unskilled handiwork, and leave the blossom thereof alone. Farewell.

THE NARRATIVE

IN the most authentic records, and those most worthy of being kept in remembrance, we may read concerning the high estate and the wealth which in times past existed in that delightful region lying on the sea-coast by Amalfi; and although, in dealing with these bygone days, we may speak in this, or even in a more boastful strain, nevertheless, when we look upon its present condition, we must see that not only is the wealth gotten through mercantile enterprise greatly diminished, and the sumptuous palaces fallen to ruin, but that the inhabitants thereof can to-day only get them a sustenance with great difficulty. Therefore, coming back to our story, I will tell you that not far from the city, (the name of which so delightful is the site thereof) in a certain sense describes it, there was situated a village in which, not a great time ago, lived a priest, Don Battimo by name, a man who, albeit he was country bred, was in no wise lacking in skill and understanding. He was young, and very robust in body, and on the whole was more given to the

* *Materno*. This is a favourite word with Masuccio, especially as applied to the language in which he wrote. In the Exordium of the First Novel it occurs, and in the *edizione della Gatta* was changed into *volgare*. He likewise calls himself *materno poeta* in the heading to the Proem.

service of the ladies round about that to the celebration of the holy office and the prescribed services of the hours. Wherefore, through the frequent following of sport of this kind, he brought it to pass that divers poor wights of the neighbourhood found their brows decked with ram's-horn crowns.

At last it came to pass that one day he let his eyes fall upon a certain young woman, a neighbour of his, whose name was Massimilla, the wife of a poor carpenter; but she, although on account of her great beauty she was wont to pique herself not a little whenever she might ensnare the fancy of a lover, when she became aware that the priest was in no small degree taken with her, never deigned to bestow upon him any greater favour than a single pleasant glance; perhaps because she had let her thoughts stray in another direction. The priest, a man by nature both eager and fickle, as soon as he realized that he pleased the young woman but little by making eyes at her, and that his prayers and flattering speeches had no effect upon her, began to follow her up with the greatest importunity with cries, and even with threatening words, in such a manner that she, more through weariness and fear for herself than through any longing she felt for him, at last gave him her promise that one day, when her husband might happen to be out of the way, he might have his will of her.

On this account the priest rested content to let affairs go on as she had promised; and while he, in good faith, kept back awhile his ardour, it happened that a young man belonging to another village near by, a tailor, Marco by name, fell in like manner very hotly in love with Massimilla. Now this young man, being gifted with very moderate skill at his craft, spent the greater part of his time in frequenting the feasts round about, and making very pleasing music upon a bagpipe which belonged to him, and, seeing that he was both in face and person a very seemly fellow—and, besides this, always furnished with a store of fresh quips—he was readily welcomed wherever he might go. Wherefore he found far greater reason for following business of this sort than for exercising his original trade. And because, as I have already said, he was enamoured beyond all bounds with the aforesaid young woman, spending his time in ogling her after the most courtly and gentle fashion he knew how to use, in order to cause her to regard him in the same wise, and because he was so mightily persistent in his amorous pursuit, it came to pass that one day he got from Massimilla a promise like to the one she had given with so much distaste to the importunate priest. On this account Maestro Marco was almost beside himself with delight, and looked forward to the departure of the luckless husband with no little pleasure and longing, a thing which both the priest and the wife herself awaited with just as great anxiety. As their good luck, which forsooth was bad luck for the poor husband, would have it, not many days passed before he had occasion to go as a sailor on board a caravel which was bound on a voyage to Palermo.

A very short time after his departure there happened to be held a festival in a certain place which lay quite near to his home, and Maestro Marco, having been bidden to the same to make music with his pipes, was delighted beyond all measure when he found there Massimilla, who had gone thither with some other peasants. Wherefore, having given each other many loving glances during the day, when the hour came for the ending of the revels Maestro Marco made his way to the young woman's side very cautiously, and with as few words as he could make serve his purpose, begged her that, of her kindness, she would keep the promise she had made to him some time agone. The young woman, to whom the mere promise had seemed an affair light enough, now in discreet and wary fashion prepared to fulfil the same, a matter which likewise offered little difficulty; so, after exchanging all sorts of soft speeches in the manner of rustic lovers, she said to the young man: "In a very short time from now I shall go my way hence, and shall pass along the road which cuts across from here. Therefore, do you keep good watch, and, as soon as I shall have gone away, follow me at once, so that we may contrive to come into some safe and well-chosen spot such as our business demands."

Now there belonged to Massimilla a little house with a garden attached thereto, situated upon the side of the

MARCO THE PIPER.

FROM A DRAWING BY E. R. HUGHES. (Mas., Nov. v., v. i.)

mountain above the hamlet, in which place her husband plied his calling instead of in a shop, working there at timber for ship-building. Now and then, indeed, in the time of summer, he would go with all his household and abide there altogether, and to this place the young woman deemed she might go with safety and take her pleasure with Maestro Marco, not only for the portion of the day which had yet to run, but likewise for a good part of the following night. Maestro Marco, highly delighted with this march of affairs, turned to a little boy of his who was with him, and, having given him the bag belonging to his pipes, bade him carry the same back to his house, while he stowed away the mouthpiece in his girdle. Then, when he had marked that Massimilla had left the festival, he followed quickly upon her track, as soon as he thought that he had given her time enough. And, having each traversed the country intervening in about the same time, they met once more at the cottage which had already been designated as the place of their foregathering, and, having entered therein and made fast the door, they duly settled themselves to the pleasant task they had in hand.

The priest, knowing nothing whatever of all this, and harbouring not the least suspicion of such a man as Marco, was only aware that the husband of Massimilla had taken ship to Palermo, and that she herself had been at the merry-making. Wherefore he, deeming that she would by this time have returned home, and foreseeing that he would find her at her wonted dwelling-place in the village, made up his mind to put his fortune to the touch; so, having set himself upon the road, accoutred with a huge cutlass which he styled his "Salvum me fac," he took his way with leisurely steps, as though he was walking for his pleasure, towards the dwelling of Massimilla. This he found to be fast shut from the outside; whereupon he at once settled in his mind that she would surely be in the place where she really was, forasmuch as she was accustomed often to go thither. He knew the spot well enough, and the sort of path which led thereto, and, although this seemed to him somewhat hard to tread on account of the fierce heat, he turned his steps towards the hillside, and, urged on by love, at last arrived at the cottage aforesaid, puffing and blowing not a little from shortness of breath.

Thus, at the very same moment when Maestro Marco was just beginning to kiss and fondle his lass, the priest, believing that she was within and alone, knocked at the door with no little delight in his heart. The young woman giving over her kissing for the nonce, cried out, "Who is without there?" And to this the priest made answer: "It is I—your own Don Battimo." "In sooth that might be good hearing at any other time," replied the young woman. Thereupon the priest answered: "And do you mean to say you know not what my will is, at such a time as this when, forsooth, there is neither your husband nor anyone else to stand in the way? Open to me, I pray you." Hearing these words she cried, "Ah! go away, and God go with you, my good man, for the reason that I am, at present, in no way ready to do what you propose." The priest, mightily upset at this answer, cried out, without taking further heed of his words: "By God's faith, if you do not open to me forthwith, I will beat your door down to the ground, and will then have my will of you, whether you like it or not; and afterwards I will go and proclaim your disgrace through all the country."

Massimilla, understanding clearly from the nature of the words spoken by the priest that he must surely be in one of his headstrong moods, and that he would as soon carry out his threat as utter it, turned to Maestro Marco, who was shaking with fear in every limb just like herself, through knowing what a reckless, giddy-pated fellow the priest was, and thus addressed him: "Dear heart of mine, you must understand clearly enough how great is the peril in which we both of us are placed on account of this unchained devil and accursed of God. Therefore I beg you, for the safeguarding of us both, to get yourself quickly up that little ladder into the pigeon loft. Then, when you shall have have mounted to the upper floor, and drawn up the ladder after you, you must stay there for a little time, being careful the while to make no sound of any sort. Meantime I hope that by one method or another I may get him to quit this place—and may bad luck go with him!—without suspecting aught as to how we have been occupying ourselves, and without taking away with him anything that is ours."

Now Maestro Marco, who, as far as courage was concerned, was much more like a sheep than a lion, straightway agreed to carry out exactly the hasty advice of the young woman, and at once set himself to follow all the directions she had given him, and as soon as he had gained the loft he put his eye to a crack that there was in the floor, and waited with no slight pangs to see what indeed might be the issue of the jest. Meantime the priest still kept on clamouring that the door should be opened to him; and as soon as the young woman saw that her lover was safely stowed away, she ran with a smiling face to undo the door, and, putting her hand upon him with a merry laugh, she let him see clearly that she had a mind to talk with him. The priest was inflamed with desire to possess her as fierce as that of the starving wolf for the timid kid, and without either good manners or restraint he began not only to cover her with kisses—as forsooth Maestro Marco had done a minute ago—but even to bite her in his amorous rage, neighing aloud as if he had been some fierce war horse. Feeling himself now fully ready for the fray, he declared that, come what might, he was determined to send the Pope to Rome. Hereupon Massimilla, who knew well enough that she was all the while observed by Maestro Marco, cried out, "What Pope may this be, and what merry words are these which you speak?" And though she put on an angry look, she made but a weak defence of herself. The priest, who every moment became more and more inflamed with desire, cut short his words and straightway determined to proceed to deeds; so, having dexterously turned her over upon a little couch and got himself valiantly in order for the first course, he placed his hand upon his sword and cried out, "Now the Pope is going into Rome." And this time, in sooth, His Holiness wore the pallium meet for such festivals, and presented himself more than once before the very altar and the tribune of Saint Peter. Maestro Marco, whose vexation had by this time in some degree driven away his fear, was, as it has already been noted, a very witty fellow; wherefore, finding himself now in perfect safety from any assault, and seeing what manner of game it was that was going on, albeit it was to him a very hateful spectacle, he took counsel with himself how he might play some new jest; so, having taken out from his girdle the pipe he carried there, he said to himself, "By my faith, this is not the sort of festival they hold when the Pope makes his entry into Rome—not a note of music of any sort do I hear." And then forthwith he put the pipe to his mouth and began to blow thereon a most wonderful entrance march, making all the while a huge clamour and stamping on the floor, which was made of planks. The priest, who had not yet come to the end of his sporting, as soon as he heard the music and the loud confused clatter which was going on over his head, was at once seized with the fear that the kinsfolk of the young woman and of her husband must be at hand, *cum gladiis et fustibus*, with the view of putting injury and shame upon him; so, mightily dismayed and using greater speed than he had ever yet put forth, he gave over the game which he had begun without being able to finish. Calling to mind the whereabouts of the door and finding the same open, he gave play to his legs the swiftest he knew how to employ, and made his way home without once stopping or turning his head to look behind him. Maestro Marco, as soon as he was assured that this fresh scheme of his had come to a happier issue than he had ever deemed it could attain, made his descent with a gladness of heart much greater than had been the fear with which he had gone up, and found the young woman almost choking with excessive laughter, so much so that she had not yet risen from the couch. Wherefore he at once resumed possession of the booty which awhile ago he had lost; and as the Pope had been duly honoured with music when he had made his entry into Rome, so Maestro Marco now brought the Turk into Constantinople with a mighty pleasant spell of dancing.

MASUCCIO

MAKING a quip of my own, I will say that there are grounds for the belief that Massimilla got far more pleasure from the retreat of the Turk out of Constantinople than from all the pomp of the Pope's entry into Rome. But for the reason that she by herself cannot give judgment I will leave it to be reckoned out in considering a similar spectacle of two nuns in a story which I intend to set before you at once—these ladies, having given reception both to clerics and to laymen without taking any trouble about the music, made it abundantly clear how, *in causa scientiæ*, they knew readily how to play their part in saving themselves.

THE END OF THE FIFTH NOVEL.

Novel the Sixth

ARGUMENT

On a certain night two nuns take their pleasure with a prior and with a priest. This thing coming to the knowledge of the bishop, he sets himself on the watch and seizes the prior at the gate of the monastery. The priest remains within, and the nun who is with him is made aware that the bishop is demanding entry. She, by means of a trick, induces the abbess to get out of her bed, and then conceals the priest therein. The bishop discovers him: the nun remains free of all blame; the abbess is disgraced, and together with the priest condemned to pay a fine of money.

TO THE MOST SERENE ROBERTO DI SANSEVERINO, PRINCE OF SALERNO AND ADMIRAL OF THE KINGDOM *

EXORDIUM

IN no one of my novels, most serene prince, have I as yet discoursed, either in great measure or small, concerning the amazing cunning and the subtle devices which are so often brought into play by a good number of the women under religious vows, when sudden emergency may make a call therefor. On this account it seems to me that it would serve a useful or even necessary purpose to give you some news concerning their manners and customs, seeing that I desire greatly to dedicate to you

* Roberto di Sanseverino was Masuccio's great friend and patron. San Severino, the town from which the family takes its name, is situated between Salerno and Avellino, and in the principal church there are tombs commemorating certain notable bearers of the name—Tommasso di San Severino, high constable

some fresh essay in story-telling from my pen; in order that, if you should at any past time have heard tell of divers good works wrought by such as these, you may now be confirmed in your belief as to their virtues by the account I shall give you of certain performances of theirs wrought in this present day, and furthermore that you may be brought to see clearly how these women, by means of the tricks they learn in the monasteries, manage to overcome the defects of nature in spite of the weakness of their sex, and occasionally by their cleverness confound the counsels of very prudent men. The following tale will bear full testimony to the truth of what I have said. Farewell.

THE NARRATIVE

IN that noble and ancient city, your own Marsico,* as perchance may be well known to you already, there is a most famous convent of ladies of the very highest worth and repute, in which, during the year which has just passed, there were no more than ten nuns, all of them in the flower of their youth and adorned with great beauty of per-

of the kingdom in 1553, and several of the princes of Salerno. This Roberto was the son of Giovanni, who bore the title of Count of Marsico. The last-named died early, leaving his young children to be brought up by his wife, who seems to have educated them in all the arts necessary to enable young noblemen to play their parts in those turbulent times. Roberto had come to man's estate in 1459, when the war broke out between Ferdinand I. and the Angevin faction, headed by the Prince of Taranto and the Duca di Sessa. He at once entered the service of the king, and distinguished himself so greatly in the successive campaigns, that when peace was restored after the defeat of the Angevin forces at Troia in 1462, Ferdinand created him Prince of Salerno, dispossessing Felice Orsini, who had joined the rebels. Masuccio was secretary to this prince, and seems to have been profoundly attached to him, judging from the terms he uses in alluding to his death in the "Parlamento" at the end of "Il Novellino." Prince Roberto died in 1474.

* A town in Calabria and a noted haunt of brigands. Sanseverino was Count of Marsico when the lordship of Salerno was conferred upon him.

son, and at their head an abbess, an old lady of very good and holy life. Now the abbess, though assuredly she had not let pass in vain her own days of youthful bloom, nevertheless was wont without ceasing to exhort the company of nuns under her care that they ought not, in the flight of time, to spend and to waste the early stage of their life, affirming, with numberless arguments, that there was no grief so sharp as that which arises from the consciousness of time spent in vain, and from making such discovery only when there is available little or no space left for repentance or amendment. And although, considering the excellent disposition of her charges in general, there was no cause for her to weary herself greatly over a matter of this sort, still amongst the other nuns there were two of high family and gifted with marvellous shrewdness of wit, one of whom—although she was never baptized by the name of Chiara—I will nevertheless, by a change of style, call Chiara. And hereby I shall only be giving her her desert, seeing that she knew very well, whenever occasion might demand, to make clear any business she might have in hand like a wise and discreet damsel. The other I will christen on my own account, and will call her Agnesa. These two nuns, either because they may have been fairer to look upon than any of the others, or perhaps because they were more observant of the precepts and ordinances of their superior, as soon as they perceived that the bishop of the city had, in a very severe and special letter, forbidden the intercourse of their own monastery with any person of whatever sort, made up their minds that they would in no wise submit to any such command, but on the contrary they would, with increased care and scheming, call up all their wits to the task of satisfying their wanton desires, and to employ various and strange expedients therefor.

On this account, letting such thoughts as these rule them, the natural effect followed in due course, so that in a short space of time certain plots of ground, having been well cultivated the while, brought forth abundant fruit in the shape of divers little monks. Thus there was established between these two an indissoluble friendship and perpetual alliance, and so carelessly did they set about wielding the razor, that they seemed rather to be flaying than shaving.* Seeing that they took small care to keep these doings of theirs hidden and secret, but let them come to the knowledge of divers people, the whole matter was made known to Messere the bishop, as to many others. Now it chanced one day that he betook himself to this reverend and holy house, peradventure in order to confirm and strengthen the dwellers therein in well-doing, and, as fate would have it, he too found himself hotly inflamed by the charm and the beauty of Sister Chiara; and, after having laid upon them many commands of his, and certain new provisions, he went back to his house a man differing vastly from what he was when he had set forth. As soon as he was come there he began to indite billets and to compose sonnets to let his Chiara know, in a few words, how he was altogether consuming away on account of the love he had for her. Chiara, when she had for several days held him in her lures in order to make his passion burn yet more fiercely, and when she had perceived that he had a countenance like the work of an unskilful artist, decineated peradventure after the similitude of one of the earliest of Adam's stock,† she made up her mind, once for all, to place his name in her tablets as one to be held in ridicule. Over and above these imperfections, he was miserly beyond all measure—a quality which did not at all commend itself to the grasping claws of Madonna Chiara.

The bishop having been made aware of this fact, and likewise that he had been gulled by his ladylove; and furthermore that, though she was as bright as a diamond to all the rest of the world, she was as thick as mud to him,‡ took it into his head to learn who might be the gallant upon whom this lady had directed her thoughts; and seeing that he was himself a lover to whom very few roads of this sort were strange ground, he very astutely made an inquiry into the matter, and discovered that the reverend Prior of San Jacobo was wont to take his pleasure with Sister Agnesa, while Chiara would hold high festival

* Orig., *che piuttosto scorticare che radere saria stato giudicato.*

† Orig., *da li primi di Adam.*

‡ Orig., *e che questa ear Chiara per altria ma torbida per lui*—a pun upon the lady's name.

with another priest called Don Tanni Salustio, a man of much wealth. Moreover, he ascertained that, for the sake of companionship, these two were accustomed to betake themselves together almost every night to the monastery to find pleasure and contentment with their paramours. Wherefore, having gotten particular knowledge of the affair, the bishop made up his mind that he would set to work with all possible means to get these two artificers into his hands, not only so that he might famously well pluck out of them the luxuriant plumes which they carried, but also that he might take vengeance for the insult which had been wrought to himself, a man who had proved to be more fortunate and adept in gaining his bishopric than in winning a way into the good graces of Madonna Chiara. And thus, while he made it his practice to go every night in person, taking with him a troop of ravenous clerical wolves, to the neighbourhood of the monastery to carry out as best he could his twofold plan, it happened that on a certain night, when the prior was taking his departure, he stumbled onto the lair of his enemies, and was by them taken in hold. Then, being brought before Caiaphas the high-priest, trembling the while with something else than cold, although he had not yet been questioned as to aught, the thought came into his mind that, by making a charge against his comrade, he might ward off from himself the anger of the bishop. Wherefore he straightway declared he had come thither to do naught that was blameworthy, but had simply gone into the monastery with Don Tanni Salustio, whom he had just left with Chiara in her cell.

The bishop, who was not a little gratified in that he had got his hand upon the prior, was at the same time no less eager to capture his companion as well; so, having bound the prior securely and sent him back to his house, he placed in order his artillery, so that he might be able to win an entrance undisturbed into the monastery, and next considered how he might, without risk, lay a firm grip upon Salustio, should such a thing be found possible.

Now Agnesa, who had been in a watchful and suspicious mood since the prior had left her, at once heard sounds outside which told her of his capture, and although she grieved for him from the bottom of her heart, nevertheless, as soon as she became aware how the bishop was seeking to gain admission to the monastery, she ran with all speed to the cell of Chiara and made known to her in as few words as possible what business was afoot. Chiara, albeit she heard the aforesaid news with the utmost disgust and confusion, being fully aware of how great evil might ensue thereanent, nevertheless, in no way lost heart over the business, but like a shrewd and courageous woman, and reinforced by a sudden counsel of resource, determined upon a way by which she might free herself from the quagmire so full of peril which lay manifest before her. So, having made stand up on his feet the priest, who as luck would have it had already discharged his crossbow more than once, and had made several fine marks on the target, and given him directions to hold himself in full readiness, she betook herself at the top of her speed to the chamber of the abbess, and calling upon her with a voice trembling with fear, she cried, "Madonna, run, run, for a snake or some other hurtful beast has broken in amongst your young chickens, and is eating them all." The abbess, being alike old, and one vowed to religion, and a woman, was monstrously avaricious, and, although it irked the old lady greatly to be thus disturbed, nevertheless, in order to defend her own possessions, she quickly threw herself out of bed, and betook herself with the gait of a wolf towards the farmyard where her fowls were kept.

Chiara, who was meantime standing keenly on the watch, when she perceived that her scheme had come to the issue she desired, without farther delay haled the priest forth from her cell, and, having taken him by the tail of his shirt—his clothes all bundled round his neck—she led him with nimble steps to the chamber of the abbess just as if he had been a beast going to the shambles. Then, when she had made him get into the abbess's own bed, she hurried swift as the wind back to her chamber.

Now almost at this very moment the bishop with his band of followers gained an entrance to the monastery, and, having gone into the dormitory, he came by chance across the abbess, who with a stick in her hand was coming back from the farmyard victorious, though she had found there no serpent. As soon as she saw the bishop with so disturbed a visage, she said to him, glancing towards him in turn the while, "Messere, what strange doings are these, that I find you here at such an hour?" The bishop, who by the savagery of his hideous face might well have struck terror into a bear, thereupon turned to the abbess, and related to her point by point everything that had occurred, saying in conclusion that he was firmly fixed in the determination to lay hands on Salustio, and on Chiara as well, by one means or another. The abbess, mortally grieved that an accident like this should have happened, and proclaiming her own innocence in the business as well as she was able, made answer that she was ready to satisfy his wishes in every way, and at the same time very well contented with all he had asked. The bishop, who was very much disturbed in mind at being thus forced to lose more time, forthwith led the way, with the abbess and his band of assistants following, to the cell of Chiara, and, having come there, they knocked at the door and called out to her that she should open to them forthwith.

Now Chiara in sooth had not slept at all that night; nevertheless, making believe to have risen from her couch all heavy with sleep, without arraying herself completely in her habit, and rubbing her eyes, she came to the door of her cell, and displayed herself in no wise troubled by what had happened, and said, smiling somewhat the while, "What is the meaning of all this array?" The bishop, now more fiercely inflamed than ever with love of her, and finding her more beautiful than ever when viewed under so searching a light, nevertheless, by way of giving her a strong shock of terror, cried out: "Ah! worthless wench that you are, we are come here to deal out to you the punishment meet for those guilty of sacrilege, and you begin to give us your japes and your jokes, just as if we did not know that Salustio has been lying with you this very night, and is, indeed, now inside there." The abbess, who was a prudent dame, was incited by the ill turn which seemed to have come to Chiara's fortunes; wherefore, before the latter could say a word in reply, she assaulted her with a torrent of injurious words, showing plainly that in her fury she was quite ready to lay hands on her. Chiara, knowing all the while that she had already settled her own bear in the other's lair, answered the abbess in the following terms, speaking somewhat disdainfully, "Madama, you have come running here in too great a rage against me, and have sought to throw stain upon my good name in a fashion contrary to all honour and duty; but I place my hopes in God and in the glorious apostle Saint Thomas, to whose service we are vowed, and entreat them so to bring it about that Messere shall not go forth from this place until he shall have gained clear and open knowledge of my innocence, and of another's guilt. Indeed, he who delivered Susanna from the false accusation of those villainous elders, will likewise deliver me from this infamy which is now cast upon me." And having thus spoken, with feigned tears and much show of anger, she went on to say, "Ravening wolves as you are, come into my cell according to your habit." The bishop, who was fully satisfied in his mind that the priest was indeed within, by a quick movement entered the room with all his followers, and searched every part thereof so narrowly that they left unvisited no corner in which even a hare could have hidden itself, but by no amount of searching could they find him whom they wanted to find. Wherefore the bishop, having left the cell full of wrath and anger, cried out: "In good faith, we will leave no spot unsearched till we find him." The abbess, so as they might make inquisition of the cells of all the nuns, cried out: "Sirs, in God's name search every place, and make a beginning in my own chamber." And in the same strain spake all the other nuns, who had run together to the spot on hearing the uproar which was being made.

Since the bishop seemed inclined to entertain this suggestion in the sense in which the abbess spoke, he straightway gave orders to two of his own followers to enter at once the chamber of the blameless abbess, directing them at the same time that they should only make a pretence of searching the chamber, as a place in no way to be suspected, in order that they might quickly be able to come to the other apartments. Whereupon they at once entered the room, and marking that the surface of the bed showed that someone was beneath, that at once decided within themselves that there must be a man therein; so, having drawn back the clothes, they found there the wretched Salustio half dead. As soon as they recognized who the man was, they fastened upon him like so many hounds of the chase, at the same time crying out "Ecce homo." As soon as the noise of this hurlyburly came to the ears of the bishop, he quickly made his way into the chamber with as many of his men as yet remained with him. Everyone will easily be able to judge for himself how completely overcome with amazement they all must have stood when they thus came upon the priest, clad only in his shirt, lying in the bed of the abbess, and more especially to figure the grief-stricken and betrayed abbess herself, who, standing as if she had been thunderstruck and stupified by this dire calamity, seemed to all those who looked upon her to be in sooth dead. She searched her memory, and was sure that no such man was in the bed when she had left it. Neither did she know whether this spectacle which she saw was to be reckoned as a dream, or as the truth, and it seemed to her that it was alike forbidden to her either to deny or to acknowledge this thing as real.

Madonna Chiara, as soon as she saw how the defence she had devised had been brought to serve as a remedy, and had come to the issue she desired, now dared, without taking much heed of what she said, to let burst forth over Messere the bishop, and over the poor beguiled abbess as well, a torrent of unseemly and monstrous words, saying, amongst other things, "By God's cross, I will send word to-morrow to my kinsfolk to bid them come and fetch me out of this public brothel, where priests are wont to come at night and to be found in the very bed of the woman whose bounden duty it is to hold up a good example to the others of the monastery. Hag of Satan would that fire might fall down from heaven, and by a miracle take her away from the face of the earth!" And uttering these words, and others of a like nature, she betook herself to her cell, and, angered amain, made fast the door thereof, leaving without the bishop and all the others overcome with amazement. The bishop, his rage now transformed into the deepest shame and grief, turned upon the wretched woe-begone priest, and made his followers quickly tie his hands and legs as if he had been a thief. Then, without saying another word by way of farewell to the grief-stricken and disgraced abbess, or to the other nuns, he went home to his house.

On the following morning, after he had considered the institution of a trial which should set to work to condemn both the prior and the priest to the flames, he made it appear to them, by the means of certain good friends, that he had abated somewhat the fury of his rage, and accordingly the fire, which, together with divers other dreadful torments, he was anxious to heap upon these sacrilegious sinners, became something vastly different through the working of the greedy humour of San Giovanni Bocco d'oro,* and thus his word proved to be of such great and singular virtue that not only were the peccant clerks freed from the death penalty which they so well deserved, but over and beyond the remission of their sins, there was granted to them plenary authority by means of which they were able to sail at will the seas which they had thitherto ploughed, and likewise over any other sea which might offer itself to their valour, without any penalty whatsoever, because, like true children of obedience, they made to Messere the bishop an offering of the tenth part which was due from them, in such wise that God ever multiplied their gains from good to better.

Behold, then, my most illustrious lord, in what manner the sagacious Chiara by her ready resource delivered herself out of the snare set for her by Messere the bishop, and, bringing under censure those who had threatened her with death by fire, came forth unharmed from her perilous situation.

* The sum of money given for a bribe, or bribery in general. See Busk's "Folk Lore of Rome," for an account of the saint.

MASUCCIO

IN order that I may not appear, in this my task of story-telling, to swerve backwards and forwards from one subject to another, I have passed over, and still intend to pass over, certain secret matters of some value, and even indispensable, which are to be learned concerning divers of our cloistered women; and amongst the aforesaid I would include all those who are under the heel of the friars. I will therefore keep silence about the various sects and the mortal feuds which take rise between the friars and the seculars, and likewise how those nuns who perchance entangle themselves with laymen are held and esteemed to be worse even than Jewesses; how they are without respite imprisoned, chased from one place to another, and persecuted as if they were heretics; while certain others, laden with favours and dignitites, are put in office, granted full leave to do whatsoever they list, and, lastly, enjoy the greatest prerogative of all. I keep silence, likewise, concerning all that might be said on the subject of the marriage of these women with friars, cases of which I myself have chanced to fall upon more than once, and have seen the evidence thereof, and have touched the same with my own hands. How they make sumptuous marriage feasts, inviting thereto from this convent and that their friends, who present themselves with equipages laden with all manner of rich goods. They sing the mass, and they forget not to hold high revel, and to pass all manner of scoffing quips, and to dance to the sound of hidden instruments. With the consent of the abbess and of their prelate they execute marriage contracts, duly written and sealed; and then, having supped off all manner of sumptuous meats, and performed every other ceremony pertaining to the rite of marriage, they go to bed one with another without showing any fear or shame, just as if their union had been contracted with the full sanction of their own fathers, and by the laws of marriage.

CHIARA'S INDICTMENT.

FROM A DRAWING BY E. R. HUGHES. (Mas., Nov. v:, v. i.)

Now, although in the novel which I have just told you I have written with knowledge and forethought a certain thing in incorrect fashion—inasmuch as I said that the well-cultivated gardens of the amorous nuns were wont to produce much fruit in the shape of divers little monks—I am now determined, let this contrary statement cost me what it may, that I will not be longer silent concerning a matter which ought assuredly to be regarded with the utmost severity and detestation. I declare, therefore, that these women, in order that they may not become pregnant, make use of innumerable devices of a nature such as decency forbids me to mention. And what shall I say of them, when, the ass having escaped from his head-stall and the prolific seed having engendered its natural fœtus, they employ, so as not to suffer their offspring to come to its full maturity, an immense variety of medicines, and, both above and below, make use of so many other detestable and poisonous beverages, that by this continual vexation the innocent souls of their children are slain and violently sent down into the pit of hell before ever they have had time to taste their mother's milk, or to behold the eternal light of the skies, or to be sprinkled with the waters of holy baptism? And if any man shall declare this thing which I have written here to be a lie, let him cast his eyes upon the fœtid sewers which run from the convents, and he will find there clear proof of the murders committed therein, and he may furthermore find a burying-ground full of the tender little bones of the victims hitherto slain, not smaller than that which Herod made when he slew the innocent children of the Jews.

I know not what more I can say about this matter, save only to declare that the patience of God endures too long, and that I, having neither the ability nor the knowledge to write fully concerning the thing which I have set before you, am minded to come to the telling of my next novel in the briefest fashion I can compass; of which same novel I not long ago gave certain intelligence to the magnificent Marino Caracciolo, a most noble Parthenopean. And although grief for my dear and worthy brother* darkened my wits in such manner that I myself knew not

* Francesco Guardati, brother of the writer was a priest.

at all what path I ought to follow in order to make a beginning of my writing; nevertheless, being now comforted by his prayers, and incited to my task by his many letters, I have persuaded myself at last to put pen to paper.

THE END OF THE SIXTH NOVEL.

Novel the Seventh

ARGUMENT

FRA PARTENOPEO IS SEIZED WITH LOVE OF MARCHESA, AND MAKES PRETENCE OF BEING AN ADHERENT TO THE KING IN ORDER TO WIN THE FAVOUR OF THE COURT. BY THE MEANS OF A TRICK HE GETS POSSESSION OF A KEY OF THE MONASTERY, AND A COMPANION OF HIS BRINGS MARCHESA TO HIM IN HIS CELL. HE GIVES HER MONEY, WHICH SHE ENTRUSTS TO ANOTHER LOVER OF HERS. THE MATTER IS NOISED ABROAD: THE FRIAR IS CAUGHT IN DISGRACEFUL CASE, AND CONDEMNED TO PERPETUAL IMPRISONMENT.

TO THE MAGNIFICENT AND HIGH-BORN MARINO CARACCIOLO.*

EXORDIUM

SO weighty, and so just and reasonable as well, are the causes through which I find myself drawn into circumstances of heavy and unwonted affliction—circumstances which make my life appear to be naught else than a continual weariness to me, that there should be no need for you to be in any way amazed, my illustrious Marino, by the fact that up to this present time I have kept silence with you, and have written to you no line. For you may clearly observe that the hostile assaults of my spiteful fortune have not in the end prevailed so as to hinder the great love which I bear you from finding a dwelling-place in my heart, but on the other part have stirred up my anguish-stricken mind and nerveless hand to write to you this present letter, and to give you a full

* Marino Caracciolo is the subject of Novel XLIV. He was a favourite of Alfonso, Duke of Calabria, and filled many high offices of state. He fell at Otranto in 1480, fighting against the Turks.

account of a certain event which has lately come to pass here. This I propose to do, not only to satisfy to some extent your just and reasonable wishes, but also to serve as a lasting warning for yourself, and for anyone else who in future times may happen to read it, illustrating in what fashion we should be on our guard, without ceasing, against the snares and ambushes of malignant hypocrites, and men whose religion is a counterfeit. Forasmuch as these, under the fraudulent seeming of their religious garb, resemble, not the savage wild beasts, who, driven by the barking of dogs and the uproar of the huntsmen, take refuge in their wonted haunts in the forest, but rather are like to tamed wolves, which, having become domesticated, will, when flouted and rebuked, seek the shelter of our inmost chambers, and there, protected by the cover of their natural and ill-advised presumption, encroach upon our honour and our very flesh and bones, as well as everything else we possess. Wherefore, in addition to many other experiences, this one I am about to relate shall serve you as another and a most certain proof.

THE NARRATIVE

THE clear-voiced rumour, which has already made itself heard throughout the universe, will carry a true report to those who come after, how, following upon the death of that exalted and glorious prince, King Don Alfonso of Aragon, King Don Fernando the Victorious, as the heir and only-begotten and dearly-loved son of the above-named monarch, occupied the throne of this our Sicilian realm as peaceful king and lord. In a very brief time from the date of his accession, he was duly invested with the kingdom by our most holy father the Pope,* and crowned and anointed as the most worthy sovereign thereof. When he had taken from all his barons

* Calixtus III. was Pope at King Alfonso's death in 1458, and died in the autumn of the same year. The Pope here referred to must be Pius II., as Calixtus claimed Naples as a fief of the Church, and incited the nobles to rebel in favour of the Angevins. Pius at once favoured Ferdinand's cause, and crowned him in 1459.

and from the people as well, the homage that was due to him, and had entered into complete and peaceful possession of his kingdom, it was the will of envious and wicked fate—fickle and ill content that such perfect peace and quiet should prevail—that the flame of a deadly and pestilential war* should be kindled throughout the whole realm before the second year of his tranquil rule had elapsed.

Now in the course of all these convulsions of the state and vicissitudes of fortune the magnificent and most illustrious city of Naples showed itself more constant in faith than any other city of Italy, harassed and oppressed as it was by the perpetual sight of its enemies delivering their assaults and pursuing their depredations even in the portions of the town which they had been unable to subdue. For these, and for many other reasons as well which I find it needless here to mention, the city aforesaid became as a place wellnigh depopulated. And, amongst the other fugitives, a large proportion of the members of the religious orders—of whom the number was exceedingly great—finding no longer in the city those fertile feeding grounds to which they were accustomed, and feeling the greatest distaste for discomfort of any kind, abandoned whatever rule of order they may have adopted, and betook themselves whithersoever it might appear they would enjoy the greatest facilities for playing the sluggard, albeit they had proclaimed themselves openly vowed to hunger and cold and travail for the sake of the love of Christ.

Some few of them, however, remained behind in the city, and amongst these was a certain holy friar, by birth a Neapolitan, a preacher of great force, and holding the first place as a father confessor. In sooth, he was in no less degree inclined to examine narrowly the various beauties of the ladies and inform himself as to their riches, than he was to spy out in them any vices or want of faith which might peradventure exist. And although I know and am well acquainted with the name of this man, and of the order to which he belonged—an order of which he falsely pretended to be an obedient member—I, nevertheless, for the sake of decency, will keep silence thereanent, and will simply speak of him in this place as Fra

* The war between Ferdinand and the Angevin leaders.

Partenopeo. This friar, unlike the others of his kind, showed no inclination to betake himself out of the city, but chose rather to remain within the walls, in order that he might be able without any restraint to have a more ample field for the prosecution of divers wicked practices of his which he had, up to that time, kept hidden and secret. In this manner, having changed himself from a shepherd into a wolf disguised under the gentle semblance of a lamb, he went about with bent neck, barefoot, and clothed in rags, so that to anyone who did not know what kind of man he really was, he would have appeared to be another Saint Ilarione.* Wherefore, after he had claimed for himself a marvellously great fame and sanctity through putting on this outward seeming, he beguiled not only many people of private estate, but even our lady the queen,† by the course he pursued. Now he would feign himself to be a headstrong partisan of the Aragonese, and now would bring into play various other deceptive tricks, working with such subtlety that in the course of time he made himself the master of all the secrets of state, however private they might have been.

It chanced that in the course of his wicked life—which, in sooth, was entirely pleasing to his own taste—he one day garnished his purse with several hundred florins, and taking with him as an associate another friar, Ungaro by name, and a rascal just as worthless as himself, the two passed by the Pendino de' Scigliati, where they saw a certain damsel, a Sicilian by birth, and endowed with a beauty which was a marvel to behold, who abode there, and was accustomed—albeit much against her will—to make public traffic of herself for the sake of gain. The reverend father, although he had just come back from a piratical emprise which had yielded him rich gain—gain which he had in friendly wise shared with his partner—as soon as he caught sight of and closely scanned these exquisite beauties which were exposed for sale so cheaply and for the smallest price, was seized with the desire forthwith to secure for himself this tempting bit of merchan-

* One of the earliest followers of Antony of the Thebaid. He lived forty-eight years in a morass near Gaza.

† Isabella di Chiaromonte, wife of Ferdinand I.

dize at one stroke, so fiercely was he inflamed with desire to possess the damsel. Wherefore, having drawn anigh her, he addressed her in these words, spoken in devout wise: "My daughter, will you endeavour to come to-morrow to our church for the health of your soul, and for your own satisfaction?" To him the damsel made answer that she would willingly betake herself whither he asked her to go.

Taken thus in the toils, and inflamed with desire, he went back to his house, and, having made manifest to his dear friend Ungaro how great was his passion, and informed him of all the schemes he proposed to carry out thereanent, he awaited with the greatest impatience the coming of the following morning in order that he might bring his work to its completion. And when the aforesaid time had come, and when he had gone up into the pulpit, he had scarcely made a beginning of his sermon when hi eyes fell upon the looked-for damsel as she entered the church, attired in such comely and modest fashion that the amorous flames in his captured heart—now, in sooth, newly bound by love's fetters—were kindled two thousandfold. As soon as his sermon had come to an end, there gathered around him quickly a crowd of people, both of men and of women, some to ask advice of him, and some to beg favours. But he, having firmly fixed his thoughts upon another matter, said to them: "My children, have you not heard the words of Christ in the gospel which was read to you this morning, telling you how there is more rejoicing and praise in the celestial choir over the conversion of one soul which has wandered astray, than there is over ninety-nine of those who are perfect and stand in no need of repentance? And now for this reason I am taken with the desire to see whether I cannot cause to enter one single spark of spiritual love into the frozen heart of this poor young girl here."

Having thus spoken he took the damsel by the hand, and led her to the seat where confessions were wont to be heard; and, after he had wrapped himself in his cloak, he began, with a great show of kindness, to put questions to her as to the cause which had led her to place herself at the service of whatever man might desire her, and to submit to be the slave of those who make a traffic in human flesh.* The damsel, albeit through the character of her life she was in no wise lacking in understanding, was unable to fathom the deep malignity of his hidden heart; so, weeping plentifully, she recounted to him in the briefest fashion she could use the complete history of the unfortunate thing which had come to pass with her. Thereupon, in answer to her, the friar spake: "My daughter, He who alone is privy to the secrets of all men shall be my witness as to how great is the bitterness of heart with which I have listened to the story of your ill-starred fate, and likewise how great an injury I rate it that I see you still abiding in this guilty condition. And on this account, whenever you may make provision to withdraw yourself entirely from the same, and to become worthy of a husband, I now make to you the offer of all my wealth, which you will find great enough in itself to suffice amply to furnish you with a fair and most convenient estate. Over and beyond this, I desire that, from this day forth, you should take into your entire possession both this body and this soul of mine, provided that I may behold you delivered from that gloomy prison in which, according to what you have yourself told me, you abide with such great distaste; giving you good assurance that, with your gracious and prudent seeming and with your loveliness—which, in sooth, is more divine than human—you have taken possession of me in such wise that, in the last few minutes, I seem to have become your property much more than my own; in short, I am yours entirely. Therefore I beseech you, my sweetest life, to let your pity move you, both on your own account and on mine as well, to consent to seek retirement in the house of a certain widow lady, who is devoted to our order, with whom you can continue to abide without any ill-fame or scandal whatsoever. When you are there it shall be my care to see that you enjoy all those things in which you take the greatest delight, until such time as the Creator shall be pleased to send to us some worthy and discreet youth to whom I may give you for his wife, which thing I, in my heart, desire most keenly."

* Orig., *e fattasi serva degli beccarini di carne umana.*

The damsel who up to this present moment had been very far indeed from gathering any inkling of this matter, which, in working upon the friar's gross lasciviousness, had made him burn thus ardently to disclose to her his passion, now, like a prudent girl, saw clearly that a certain report which she had heretofore judged to be a false one was indeed true, to wit, that this infernal crew of worthless poltroons held the better part of Christendom as their prey. Wherefore she, who knew well enough how to dispose of the wares she had to sell, as soon as she perceived how the friar was so keenly set on purchasing them for his use, forthwith made up her mind that, not only would she be careful not to give them away for nought, but that she would only sell them at the very highest price. So she answered him in these words: "My father, I thank you, forsooth, for your great goodness and charity, but I must tell you, so that you may know the truth of the matter, that I am on terms with my good man such as will in no wise suffer me to do always the thing I would; for the reason that he, being a sprightly youth and rich, as well as much loved and very popular in this our city, would, I doubt not, cast a thousand lives in jeopardy to keep me for himself, should he find that there was any danger of losing me; and then, after that, might spoil the look of my face by way of saving his honour.* Nevertheless, time has a way of setting things right, and on this account you will see that I, if I may be able to serve you in any way whatever, shall be no less eager to give myself to you than you have shown yourself eager to be mine."

The friar, perceiving that the affair would at least come to the issue of satisfying the greater part of his desire, and caring very little for aught besides, then made answer to the girl, whose name was Marchesa, in this fashion: "You speak very wisely, O my daughter, and may God bless you; but when shall we find occasion and commodity to be together, seeing that I am in no wise inclined to put faith in that bravo of yours?" To this the damsel replied, "There is no need at all to be fearful on the score of him; for, over and beyond the fact that he is by nature much

* Orig., *e doppo per suo onore guastarmi della persona.*

given to secrecy, and is in the way of gaining for himself no little profit thereby, it is beyond all belief, as you indeed have already said, that he should seek to give himself a blow on the foot with the mattock.* Wherefore, make yourself easy on this account, and leave the rest of the trouble to me." Then said the friar, "Since the view you take is one which also pleases me, there remains nothing more to be done for the carrying out of our design than that, at the hour to-night when I shall send a trusty companion of mine to you bearing with him a dress of our order, you should betake yourself in his company to me disguised in the habit of a friar, while I will devise means by which I may, acting with all due caution, give you reception in my cell."

The damsel was quite content with this proposal, and agreed to abide by the directions which the friar gave her. Then he, filled with desire, besought her that she would let him have a kiss by way of earnest; whereupon Marchesa, in order that she might thereby make burn still more violently the flame of his passion, put out to him, in as pleasing fashion as she could, her serpentine tongue, being prevented by the iron grating which was fixed to the seat of confession from bestowing upon him the full boon of her delicious mouth. With this touch of sweetness she stole away and went forthwith to her own house, where by chance she found the man who was her keeper, and him she at once began to address in the following words: "My good Griffone, I went this morning into the street, hoping that someone or other would take me for his pleasure; but now, if you will be wise and prudent, you will see that I have caught a bird by the beak, one well furnished with feathers, the plucking out of which will be fine sport for us for many months to come." Then, having made a beginning at the very first, she told to him the whole story, point by point, to the end thereof. Griffone, when he had listened to it, was mightily diverted with the same, and in sooth the time seemed to him to be as long as a thousand years until there should come in sight that

* Orig., *cercasi donarsi la zappa ne lo piede.*

Hungarian flyboat, sent to take in tow the Sicilian bark.*

Now to come to the other part of the story. Brother Wolf, who was all this while in a state of the greatest joy, and at the same time keenly set upon bringing into speedy execution the project he had framed, went quickly into the presence of the queen, so as to make sure of securing himself from any molestation on the part of the other friars, and began to address her in these words: "Sacred majesty, it is a thing clearly known to me that no man occupying a station like mine finds it seemly and convenient to wait upon the favour of any earthly power. Wherefore I, looking at myself only as a Christian man, find myself obliged perforce to conform to the will of our lord the Pope, as the Vicar of Christ upon earth, and the most holy Shepherd of our blessed mother the Church.† Nevertheless, though it seems to me that I am right in doing this, I am not only bound as a faithful partisan to our lord the king and to your majesty, but am also eager to undergo in your service the most cruel of martyrdoms, just as I should desire to suffer the same for the sake of our holy Catholic faith. It occurs to me, therefore, my sovereign lady—not thereby to speak evil of others, which thing may God forbid—that the greater part of our brothers are men such as might be rated by the world as of little or no account, for the reason that they are not endowed with the same righteous and prudent purposes as I myself harbour. In any case, therefore, some irretrievable cause of offence may very well arise, and on this account I, knowing well enough that I must needs guard myself very carefully against them, find that it behoves me to provide myself with some safeguard in the business I propose to undertake. Wherefore, if I should bring into my cell by night any faithful partisan of yours, and devoted to me as well, who might let it be known to me

* Orig., *mille anni gli parea che la fusta di Ungaria venesse a rimborcare la Siciliana barca.*

† Pius II. favoured Ferdinand, for the reason that he was unwilling to stir up a war which might tempt the Turks to invade Italy. Calixtus III., during the few months he lived after Ferdinand's accession, favoured the Angevin cause.

what men are thinking of or doing in the city, or perchance to instruct me by what secret and hidden means we may be able to put our hands upon moneys for the service of our lord the king, or to hold converse with me on a thousand other things which may come up for discussion, I would fain have such as these conducted into my presence, this one dressed in the habit of a friar, and that one and the other under various disguising garbs. Moreover, the gatekeepers at our convent are so exceedingly sharp, that in their curiosity to spy and to peer minutely into the smallest particulars attending the coming of anyone to our gates, they would bring it to pass that any such visitors as these I have spoken of would assuredly determine in their minds to return whence they came, rather than to trust themselves in the hands of those they know not. Now in what measure, from one hour to another, an accident such as this might work, either for the wrecking or the furtherance of the fortunes of our lord the king, your majesty may find it easy to determine. At any rate, it seems to me—and on this matter I make my prayer to you in the most urgent terms I can find—that in order that we may free ourselves from all actual and all possible dangers as well, you should without delay give your command to our prelate, and bid him furnish me, for my absolute use, a key of the monastery, to be employed by me in the service of your interests. I would likewise beg you to direct him to give due admonition to all those dwelling within the convent, that no one of them should, under any pretence whatever, give trouble or molestation to any person who may come to have speech with me, whether by night or by day; and furthermore that he should assign to me, for my sole use, a chamber apart from the others, in which I may at any hour give private audience to my visitors without letting them be put to any inconvenience thereanent."

The queen, who put the fullest and the most unquestioning faith in all that the good friar told her, was at once persuaded that his most adroit speech was based upon true and sincere motives, wherefore she first thanked him abundantly in return for the same, and then, having summoned into her presence a certain courtier who had her fullest confidence, she despatched him forthwith to the superior of the convent with the command that the aforesaid request of Fra Partenopeo should at once be complied with, without any exception whatever being made thereto.

When, therefore, everything which the friar demanded was thus fully carried out according to his wishes in a very brief time, and when, having got possession of the key, and without any delay furnished with all requisites a chamber fitted for any gallant, the night so keenly longed for came at last. Then Fra Partenopeo despatched his friend Fra Ungaro to bring thither Marchesa disguised in the habit of a friar; and he was not called upon to suffer any long delay, for he soon saw returning this trusty hunter of his, who, without the aid of hounds of any sort, was already bringing home the booty. He went at once to meet them, and, having taken the lady in his embrace, he covered her with the most passionate and burning kisses and led her within into the chamber, uttering the while a thousand sweet and loving words. When they had despatched the feast, which was fully worthy of the occasion, the friar gave leave to his friend Ungaro to depart, whereupon the two lovers went to bed to take their pleasure, and there to give tangible proof that friars still knew full well how to make others dance to the sound of the drumsticks, forasmuch as it may be remarked that before the matin bells began to ring the cock had nine times crowed.

Now Fra Ungaro was stationed all this time without the chamber, and hearing within so much sportive clatter like the beating of a paper-mill, and being himself vastly unlike a man of stone such as Medusa might have made, but, on the other hand, one full of lusty life, his own amorous fancies began to arise and to torment him somewhat. Finding himself assailed by these lecherous heats even more than was his wont, he was minded forthwith to have recourse to the same practice which the scullions use in the kitchen when, overcome by their greedy appetites, and fearful lest they should mar and befoul the meat meant for their masters, they eat dry bread savoured merely by the smell of the roast. Now in what fashion the business was brought about by the friar I ween anyone will be able to understand without farther explanation from me.

And when at last the morning was come, and the reverend father was minded to send the young woman back to her home well content with the result of her errand, he having given her certain of his more precious jewels, and opened his strong box filled to the brim with money, said to her, laughing the while: "Dear soul of mine, men of our condition are not wonted ever to touch money, wherefore do you now take as much thereof as may please you from this my store." After hearing these words she did not wait for many invitations, or show herself unwilling to do as the friar asked; but, having stretched forth her delicate hand, she straightway caught up therein as much of the coin as she could seize. Then, after she had once more put on all her attire and given the friar a close and amorous kiss, she took her way back to her own house under the conduct of Fra Ungaro, and, having come thither, she threw the money into the lap of Griffone, discoursing to him at the same time as to what point the affair had come already, and how she had set a bait for the friar in such wise that they must assuredly capture him, and in a very short time strip every bit of flesh from his bones.

Thereupon they together regaled themselves with a sumptuous feast, and, being keenly set upon laying their hands upon the residue of the friar's money, it came to pass that Marchesa let her feet travel full often in the road she had begun to tread. To her, and to the friar as well, sport of this kind gave much content, though for different reasons. Howbeit, the amorous passion of the friar grew stronger day by day, and the charges therefor and the gifts to the young woman showed no sign of waning. However, that strong box we have before mentioned as brimful was now emptied of its contents to such degree that a blind man might with ease have discerned the bottom thereof; whereupon Marchesa, for the reason that she was one well versed in traffic of this nature, soon found out how things were going with him, and then, with feigned pretexts of all sorts, began to refuse to continue her visits to the friar, for which reason he, who was entirely under the sway of his unbridled lust, perforce became aware, albeit very late, that the young woman was attracted to come to him for the sake of his goods, and not for his own sake. Therefore he began to sharpen his wits and to cast about as to how he should set to work to fill up once more that empty chest of his with a fresh store of money, and having, through the assistance of his friend Fra Ungaro, discovered in the church of their monastery a vast quantity of coin which had been hidden therein by a certain citizen who was now banished the state, he took possession of about five hundred florins of the same, and gave the residue thereof into the keeping of the court, betaking himself after this to the prosecution of his interrupted amours.

Then, having secured himself with the greatest care with regard to those about him, he would not only repair by night to the ill-famed house of Marchesa in the company of his friend Fra Ungaro, but they would even go thither often by day, demeaning themselves in such wise that the report of their iniquitous doings was spread abroad by the mouth of everyone, and was made a public scandal. When things had come to this pass, particular information of the same was given to the prelate of Fra Partenopeo's monastery by the mouth of a certain noble youth, who perchance may have been one of those beloved by Marchesa. The prelate, in order no longer to suffer the perfect religion he professed to be sullied by association with such a son of perdition, got information how, on a certain night, Fra Partenopeo was going unaccompanied by Fra Ungaro to take his pleasure with Marchesa; wherefore he betook himself secretly at the same hour to the house of the young woman, accompanied by a large number of the friars of his monastery and of other gentlemen, devoted friends of the order. And when they had got the culprit safe in hand, over and above the cruel scourging which they gave to Fra Partenopeo, whom they found stark naked in the bed with Marchesa, they condemned him to lie for the rest of his life in prison, where he finished his days in bitter misery.

MASUCCIO

IF the severe and altogether merited punishment dealt out to our brother Fra Partenopeo may have been in the past, or may prove in the future, to be the cause of making other men withdraw themselves from reprobate vices, and from working every day some fresh evil, it may not only be called laudable in itself, but may be held up to high commendation, and be kept in lasting memory by men of righteous lives. But forasmuch as the contrary may peradventure come to pass, it seems to me that we must not on any account suffer men in such case to live their lives in peace while thus steeped in wickedness. And since that we may in all truth set down a generation so froward as this as being endowed with a nature like to that of wolves—which beasts, when through some accident or other a certain member of the wolfish pack may chance to meet with a wound, and therefore be unable to follow with the others, will all turn upon him and mangle him in their rage as if he had been one of their foes—so in like manner these reverend signors bear themselves at those seasons when there may chance to fall upon any member of their order some grave and manifest scandal, some offence too glaring to be shielded from view by the fraudulent cover of their religious habit. Then no amount of cruel and continuous scourgings, or endless persecutions, or sentences of lifelong imprisonment, will suffice for his condemnation; and for their adoption of such a course as this there are two most manifest reasons. The one is to give warning and affright to the other friars, so that they may not by their heedless carriage let their doings of this sort get into the mouths of the crowd and become common scandal; the other is that they, as persecutors of ill-deeds, may obtain yet greater credit and trust from the laity. And to show you that such is the truth, I will tell you that, not many days agone, finding myself with certain members of this order, and talking with them concerning this very same matter, one of the number—and one moreover by no means the least in credit and repute, and a man on very familiar footing with me—addressed me in these words: "My good Masuccio, if on account of one ship which may have suffered shipwreck on the voyage from Alexandria all the other vessels should refuse to go to sea, not a single grain of pepper should we ever eat. Of a truth the gibbet is put up for the unlucky ones."

From discourse such as this one may take as evidence the fact that the most nefarious wickedness which these men commit appears to them to be nothing more than what is permitted by well-approved usage, so that they give themselves up to the practice thereof without feeling the least prick of shame or of conscience. Neither the fear of God, nor the risk of a shameful death, has any power to hold them back when once they begin to throw off the cowl. And therefore, to bring forward more cogent evidence than that given above, I will set forth clearly in the novel which follows certain words spoken, without any regard to decency whatever, by a famous preacher and reverend master in the Holy Scriptures, in answer to certain scholars, words as bad as any lewd soldier could have uttered.

THE END OF THE SEVENTH NOVEL

Novel the Eighth

ARGUMENT

A YOUNG LAWYER, HAVING NO TASTE FOR HIS STUDIES, SELLS HIS BOOKS AND LIVES JOVIALLY WITH THE MONEY HE RECEIVES THEREFOR. A PREACHING FRIAR PROMISES THAT HE WILL MAKE THE DEAD ARISE FROM THEIR GRAVES ON A CERTAIN DAY WHEN THE YOUNG LAWYER AND DIVERS COMPANIONS OF HIS HAPPEN TO BE PRESENT IN THE CHURCH, WHEREUPON THESE CONSIDER HOW THEY MAY ANNOY THE PREACHER WITH A WITTY PLEASANTRY, BUT HE TAKES HIS REVENGE UPON THEM AFTERWARDS BY A PROMPT AND APPROPRIATE REPLY.

TO THE NOBLE AND VIRTUOUS FRANCISCO SCALES, THE SECRETARY TO THE KING

EXORDIUM

I AM of opinion, my most courteous Scales, that at the opening of this our friendship it appertains to me as a duty to make a beginning of our written intercourse according to the custom which friends well agreed are wont to follow amongst themselves. On this account I, not wishing to appear in any way ungrateful for all the honours and choice fruits which have come to me through your most pleasant friendship, propose to approach you at this present season, not merely with such familiar correspondence as men are accustomed to hold one with another, but in the light of an exceptional friend. And, in addition to this, it has occurred to me that it would prove to you a seemly diversion, and one worthy of consideration, were I to tell you, out of the store I have, a certain tale. This same story, when you shall read it over at your leisure, may serve to remind you of the discreet conversation we have held one with another. And albeit it is never a matter of praise for a man to be on over-intimate terms with those vowed to religion, you shall, nevertheless, be brought to see clearly how much less blameworthy in certain men is the conversation which they show to the world every day in their outward seeming, than the things which abide in the core of their hearts. Farewell.

THE NARRATIVE

NAPLES, that noteworthy city, deservedly set down as the chief place of this our Sicilian kingdom, is, and will ever remain, most flourishing in arms and in letters, as exemplified in the excellences of its highborn citizens. There, not many years agone from this our time, lived a certain doctor of laws, of honourable descent, very rich, and of excellent manners and repute. This man, over and above the other goods granted to him by fortune, was blessed with one only son, who was called by name Jeronimo di Vitavolo. Now, seeing that the father had bestowed all his love upon this youth, and was greatly desirous to leave him, when he himself should pass to another world, endowed with divers virtues which—putting riches on one side—should abide with him as immutable possessions, he set himself with all diligence to lead the youth's steps into the paths of study. And when the father was brought to understand that his son's head was one by no means fitted for a career of this sort, and had, moreover, many times poured out his grief thereanent, both to himself in solitude, and to his near kindred as well, he sent word to his son Jeronimo, and bade him come to his bedside, he being withal full of years, and bound in a very short time to taste of death. Thereupon he appointed his son the inheritor of all his goods, and, having laid a charge upon the youth how that it was his bounden duty to give good heed to the study of the law, he bequeathed to him also all his books, which were of very great value. Thus, having put in order all his affairs, in a very short space of time he passed away from this perishable life, leaving behind him a highly honoured name, and was borne to the tomb with high and sumptuous ceremonies.

Jeronimo, who now occupied the place of master and head of the house, found himself in possession of many thousand florins in ready money. Wherefore the youth, seeing that he himself had endured no labour and weariness in gathering together the same, forthwith made up his mind not to place his affections in possessions of this sort, and at once began to array himself in sumptuous garments, to taste the pleasures of the town in the company of certain chosen companions of his, to indulge in amorous adventures, and in a thousand other ways to dissipate his substance abroad without restraint of any kind. Not only did he banish from his mind all thought and design of continuing his studies, but he even went so far as to harbour against the books, which his father had held in such high esteem and reverence and had bequeathed to him, the most fierce and savage hatred. So violent, indeed, was his resentment against them that he set them down as the worst foes he had in the world.

On a certain day it happened that the young man, either by accident or on account of some occasion of his own, betook himself into the library of his dead father, and there his eye fell upon a vast quantity of fair and well-arranged books such as are wont to be found in places of this sort. At the first sight of these he was somewhat stricken with fear, and with a certain apprehension that the spirit of his father might persue him; but, having recollected his courage somewhat, he turned with a look of hatred on his face towards the aforesaid books and began to address them in the following terms: "Books, books, so long as my father was alive you waged against me war unceasing, forasmuch as he spent all his time and trouble either in purchasing you, or in putting you in fair bindings; so that, whenever it might happen that there came upon me the need of a few florins or of certain other articles, which all youths find necessary, he would always refuse to let me have them, saying that it was his will and pleasure to dispense his money only in the purchase of such books as might please him. And over and beyond this, he purposed in his mind that I, altogether against my will, should spend my life in close companionship with you, and over this matter there arose between us many times angry and disordered words. Many times also you have put me in danger of being driven into perpetual exile from this my home. Therefore it cannot but be pleasing to God—since it is no fault of yours that I was not hunted forth from this place—that I should send you packing from this my house in such fashion that not a single one of you will ever behold my door again. And, in sooth, I wonder more especially that you have not before this disordered my wits, a feat you might well have accomplished with very little more trouble on your part, in your desire to do with me as you did with my father, according to my clear recollection. He, poor man, as if he had become bemused through conversing with you alone, was accustomed to demean himself in strange fashion, moving his hands and his head in such wise that over and over again I counted him to be one bereft of reason. Now, on account of all this, I bid you have a little patience, for the reason that I have made up my mind to sell you all forthwith, and thus in a single hour to avenge myself for all the outrages I have suffered on your behalf, and, over and beyond this, to set myself free from the possible danger of going mad."

After he had thus spoken, and had packed up divers volumes of the aforesaid books—one of his servants helping him in the work—he sent the parcel into the house of a certain lawyer, who was a friend of his, and then in a very few words came to an agreement with the lawyer as to the business, the issue of the affair being that, though he had simply thrown the books out of his house and had not sold them, he received, nevertheless, on account of the same, several hundred florins; and with these, added to those which still remained in his purse, he continued to pursue the course of pleasure he had begun.

And on this account, either because he was now very rich, or because of his wit and pleasant humour, it came to pass that he was always to be seen in the company of the most proper young men of the city. Wherefore, happening to repair one day with certain of his friends to the venerable church of San Lorenzo, he found there in the pulpit a very learned father preaching to the people, and giving notice that, on the following morning, he purposed to deliver a sermon on the subject of the Last Judgment, in the course of which he intended to make rise up again the dead kinsfolk of anyone who might chance to be there. On hearing this, it came into the mind of the aforesaid Jeronimo to frame in appropriate wise a witty saying which should bear on the matter in question.

When the morning was come, the young man, with his band of friends, and a certain doctor of laws whom they had taken into their company, made their way into the church, and, having withdrawn themselves apart in modest fashion, waited with pleasure for the moment when the preacher should make a beginning of his sermon. When at last the preacher went up into the pulpit, and with the utmost fervour began to discourse concerning the Last Judgment, standing with his head uncovered, and moving himself in exactly the same manner as a falcon uses when it is freed from the hood, he turned himself without ceasing towards a part of the church where there was sitting a certain widow lady with whom he was deeply enamoured, managing the while to continue his sermon without break or interruption of any sort. Now when he had come to that terrible phrase, "Venite mortui ad judicium," as soon as the words had passed his lips a couple of trumpeters, whom he had concealed in the pulpit, began to blow a harsh and frightful blast in such fashion that the whole congregation was altogether astonished and amazed—nay, they were even as people thunder-stricken and confounded. I will not stop here to mention certain good folk (who had come peradventure from Grosseto), who, as soon as they heard the sound, began to run about, now here, now there, amongst the tombs, expecting that, in good sooth, the dead would then and there arise from their graves.

Jeronimo, in the meantime, was standing apart with the companions who had come in with him, and laughing heartily at the brutishness of the stupid crowd of peasants. As soon as he perceived how there arose from them on every side weeping and lamentation and cries for mercy, without understanding in any way the cause of what they did, it seemed to him that the time had at length come when he might let forth that witty speech of his which he had duly fashioned in his mind; so, having drawn from his purse a counterfeit florin, he turned towards the doctor of laws, who was still in the company, and spake to him in this wise: "I am well assured that amongst those who will first rise from the dead will be my father, for the reason that no one could possibly match him in the scanty provision he made for me, and that he will certainly want to know from me the reason why I have not prosecuted my studies, and will now and again require at my hands those books of his, and will lay to my charge a thousand other complaints. Wherefore take this florin as your fee, and then as my advocate you can reply in my name this morning in such wise that we shall for certain win our cause." When he had brought this speech to an end, and when all those standing by had listened to this witty jest of his, they were all so struck with admiration at the grace and the finish of his words, that the doctor of laws, and all the others as well, began to laugh so loudly that it seemed as if they must split their sides. The preacher, who was high up in his pulpit, and some distance removed from the spot where the young men stood, turned himself round in the fashion which prudent steersmen use when they would know from which quarter the wind blows, and without any difficulty perceived what Jeronimo had done, and heard the loud laughter which the young men in his company sent up on account of the weeping and lamentation of the rest of the uncouth crowd in the church. At the same time he was in no wise sure that they suspected aught as to the trick he himself had just played; so, seeing that he was a very astute practitioner, a ready and excellent speaker, and over and beyond this a man entirely free from hypocrisy, he determined in his mind that he would get to know from them the cause of their laughter, and, if it should prove to be that which he suspected, to cap their jest with a ready and well-fitting answer of his own. Wherefore, as soon as the sermon had come to an end, he betook himself without a moment's delay to the place where

Jeronimo and his troop of friends were posted, and, having saluted them all with a friendly smile, he addressed them in these terms: "My good young gentlemen, if it be not an unseemly request to make, I beg you that you will let me know the reason why, when all the rest of the people in the church were weeping and lamenting, you were all laughing so merrily." Jeronimo, deeming that the priest was curious to know this thing on account of some silly conceit, as is the wonted behaviour of many of those holding similar rank, and knowing naught what the lining of his cloak was like, came forward and answered him in the following words, desiring at the same time to give him a smart hit by way of repartee: "My father, you have in sooth made us feel absolute faith in the fulfillment of your promises, wherefore we are here awaiting the resurrection from the dead of a very lovely young woman who died of the plague when our city was last visited by that pest. She, when the sickness was on her, was abandoned by her husband, a man void of all merciful feeling; wherefore she sent for me, who loved her more than I loved my own life, and I straightway did all I could on her behalf by the calling in of physicians, and by the employment of every remedy I could think of as fitted for the case, and such as would naturally be suggested by the great love I had for her. On account of what I had done in her behalf, and to show her gratitude for the benefits she had received at my hands, she gave herself entirely to me in the presence of several witnesses, promising that when she should be restored to health she would choose to belong to me, and not to her husband. The poor young woman, however, died on account of her sickness, and she lies buried in this your church. Now I am possessed with the thought that peradventure her husband may by this time feel a tardy repentance for his niggard cruelty, and that, when the report of this resurrection of the dead, which you proposed to bring about, should come to his ears, he would repair hither, accompanied by the whole of his kinsfolk, in order to lead back his wife to his house. Therefore I, bearing in mind these facts, on my part brought hither my advocate, and paid him a very high fee, in order that he might defend this most just cause of mine, and lay the same plainly before you with all boldness and confidence, knowing well that you are a veritable adept and most excellent arbiter in everything connected with the amorous passion. Wherefore, if it had come to pass that the marvel you promised had really happened, my advocate would have laid down publicly a most righteous exposition as to what ought to be done. But when in the end we saw how this feat you promised to do turned out to be nothing more than a vain fiction, coming to the same issue which your plausible speeches so often find, we laughed thereanent, and made sport in such fashion as you perceived."

The crafty friar, as soon as he heard this egregious and well-composed version of the story—albeit he no longer entertained the suspicion he had originally taken up—determined in his mind that the speech he had just listened to should not remain without a rejoinder which should be worthy of it, or even go beyond it, and at the same time he resolved to teach these young men what kind of fat his brain was made of.* Wherefore, having turned himself towards Jeronimo, he spake in these words: "You there, who are laymen, are accustomed to take your pleasure with your ladies as long as they remain young, but as soon as old age comes upon them, and they are found fit for no better task than to charm worms out of children or to nurse the mother sickness,† you hand them over to us in order that we may flay them. And when they come to us, confessing their sins, and telling us long stories of all the delights they enjoyed with you whilst they were in the flower of their youth, we get nothing else from listening to such discourses but a redoubled increase of our troubles, already too heavy for us to bear. And when it happens that some one or other of these may quit this life, they are quickly despatched to the care of the friars, and then we, wrapping up the decaying corpse greatly against our will, are bound to bury it. In this wise, therefore, you take your delight in women while their flesh is soft and delicate, and we are vexed and troubled through having to care for their decaying bones. Now, on account of such reasons

* Orig., *de che grasso il suo cervello fosse condito.*

† Orig., *medicare le matrone.*

as these, you may well understand in what fashion we poor friars are tormented by such as you, and how it is that, of all the things there are in the world, we can win by our industry naught but such rewards as I have just described to you. But we have one grievance which we find it hard work to bear with patience, and by this I mean the fact that we are not allowed to keep for ourselves in peace and quiet those women who have put on the monastic garb, whom we from the beginning of time have most justly claimed as our own. And would to God that you might find it enough to only lay hands on that one portion of womankind which does not already by the claims of reason belong to you, and that you would give over your incitements to them to rob us, as is their habit, and then to hand over their plunder to you. If indeed there be anyone who can give true testimony of this thing, I surely am he, forasmuch as, since I have been in this city of yours, to my own great concern I have come to know well in what fashion the matter is brought to pass. And our religion would assuredly be in a perilous state were it not that certain fellows of our kind, and not of the best complexion—to whom you with scant wit give far too much credit, albeit that they take upon themselves the style of Observantists—have assumed the task of reviling your honour and your estate as well, and for the love of our order inflict upon you vengeance for the aforesaid injuries. And you, unsatisfied still with the deeds above recited, now come and put into our hands dishes filled with dead and putrifying things, so as not to turn in any way from the path which you have begun to travel. Nevertheless, if it should chance that any one of you may desire to make a final trial as to whether or not I am a worthy judge of all varieties in amorous commerce, and a supreme arbiter of the humours thereof, let him bring to me a handsome girl alive and healthy, and, after I shall have set her apart for my own uses—as I hope reason will allow—and after the inquiry shall have been brought to its appointed end, I will deliver concerning the question in hand a decision so complete and so just, that it cannot fail to be pleasing in the highest degree to the girl herself; and, however much every one of the litigants may cry out for an appeal, no appeal of any sort will be permitted. May you all live in peace, and may God be with you!"

Jeronimo and all his companions were astonished and even confounded by the commendable and witty reply of the friar, and all agreed in declaring that this one, at least, could claim to be somewhat less base than the others of the lazy crowd of rascals of the same sort; but I myself, with the scanty wit I call my own, would persuade everybody to drive them all as far as possible away from the bounds of their dwelling-places without making any distinction whatever.

MASUCCIO

I DOUBT not but that there will be found many men of this our time, of the sort which takes great delight in reproving others, who will seize this opportunity of lecturing me, and will condemn me inasmuch as I declared that the preacher described in the foregoing novel ought to have had some measure of censure dealt out to him on account of his lascivious remarks. Although I could easily, by my own reasoning powers, make answer to such as these, still, in order to give greater weight to my statement, and as an example to posterity, I find I shall do well to bring forward as a defender of my position the irreproachable authority of our new Saint Paul. I speak of Fra Roberto da Lecce,* the herald of truth. He, forsooth, holds as a firm conviction, and one which he proves by the most valid arguments, that those priests who observe perfectly all the precepts of their several rules in such wise as they were settled and appointed by their holy founders, have, in these our days, grown very scarce on the earth. Then, coming at last to give particular information concerning his own minor friars, he declares

* He was a Franciscan of the Observantist Order. There is a notice in Graziani of his preaching in Perugia in 1448. He preached from a stone pulpit, which is still to be seen outside the cathedral, to a crowd of 15,000 people in the piazza below. On Good Friday he commemorated the Crucifixion by a sort of

that, amongst these, those friars who are eager to be known as Observantists are notoriously found wanting in those most weighty duties which were laid upon them by their seraphic Saint Francis, while they keep inviolably certain useless and superstitious practices. That is, they themselves wear sandals more coarse and ill-made than ever Saint Francis saw, so as to show themselves humble and poor and obedient in the sight of the ignorant multitude. They garb themselves in patched cloaks of various colours, with a leather strap for a buckle and a bit of wood for a button, and use all manner of other similar marks of hypocrisy, such as were never written down or thought of in their holy rules.

Nor, on the other hand, will I keep silence as to how these men—disobeying the necessary rules of humility—trespass on all that is necessary for the cultivation of the same, and become not only proud, puffed up, and full of ostentation, but also more covetous of fame and rewards than any other men who live—how every day that passes they rebel in their obedience towards their prelates. These last offenders are for the most part those who, having taken up the calling of preaching, ride about the country on mules, attended by servants on foot, and with asses laden with provender—men who might be more readily taken for herbalists or quacks than for the servants of God.

But what shall I say of those confessors who observe the precepts of religious piety so far as these forbid them to touch money which they know to be counterfeit, but at the same time heap up as much of good coin as they can lay hands on; in sooth it seems as if the insatiable voracity of such as these can never be satisfied. And thus, openly

theatrical show—a barber of the city, naked, bearing a cross on his shoulder, and a crown of thorns on his head, came out of the cathedral and went in procession through the city. His preaching led to a vast increase in the ranks of his order. In 1482 he was in Rome when the Orsini and Colonna feuds threatened to become a civil war, and on one occasion, when the piazza in front of the Pantheon was filled with fighting men, Fra Roberto came out of the church of Sta. Maria sopra Minerva, and merely by holding out the crucifix and praying for peace put an end to the conflict.

going astray from the two distinct precepts and solemn vows aforesaid, they maintain that they have been dispensed therefrom by the authority of the supreme Pontiffs; from the third vow, that of chastity, they daily grant unto themselves dispensation without papal authority of any kind whatever. Wretched indeed is the lot of those who allow their households to hold any intercourse with them. We may begin, therefore, by laying it down as certain that such of these as do not practise aught of superstition or hypocrisy should be honoured and held dear and commended as being the least wicked of the breed, and that all the others should be hunted out and banished by us into exile for life by a perpetual decree. But to leave off talking about them for the present, I will go on to speak in this next ninth novel of mine about a certain priest who, having been denied the privilege of taking carnal knowledge of a young woman, the wife of his gossip, brought all his wits into play in order to compass the object of their common desire.

THE END OF THE EIGHTH NOVEL.

Novel the Ninth

ARGUMENT

A CERTAIN PRIEST HAS AN INTRIGUE WITH THE WIFE OF HIS GOSSIP. THIS HAVING COME TO THE HUSBAND'S EARS, HE IN HIS JEALOUSY FORBIDS THE PRACTICE; WHEREUPON THE YOUNG WOMAN PRETENDS THAT SHE IS POSSESSED BY A SPIRIT. ON THIS ACCOUNT THEY SEND THE HUSBAND ON A PILGRIMAGE, AND THEN THE PRIEST GOES BACK TO TAKE HIS PLEASURE WITH THE WIFE WITHOUT BEING SUSPECTED BY ANYBODY.

TO THE NOBLY-BORN MESSER DRAGONETTO BONIFACIO. *

EXORDIUM

IN calling back to memory, my nobly-born and distinguished cavalier, how we two together have many times and often considered, while confabulating on various subjects, how very limited and scanty is the faith that one can and ought to give to anything concerned either with priests or with monks or with friars, I am now reminded that I might, for the further confirmation of these opinions, while telling you the story of a mighty humourous adventure, furnish to all well-advised listeners tidings concerning the unwonted craft which priests have lately learned to use in their goings and comings. These men forsooth, perceiving that the society and conversation of women are denied to them because of their religious vows, now scheme to become allied to young and beautiful women by the tie of spiritual brotherhood, thereby making no account of the violation of the most glorious sacrament of baptism—a rite which contains within itself

* In the later editions this novel is dedicated "Al magnifico Messer Cavalerino d'Arezzo."

so large a portion of the essence of our Christian faith. Therefore, with regard to such men as these, who go about betraying Christ, making a mock of San Giovanni,* and cheating and flouting their neighbours, it may be said that, neither living nor dead, can we manage to deliver ourselves out of their clutches. For these reasons may God by a lasting miracle give light to the minds of each one of us, so that we may be able clearly to spy out the hidden treachery of these wretches, even as thou, most sagacious Cavalier, hast most excellently done in thine own case.

THE NARRATIVE

PIETRA PULCINA is the name of a village situated in the Valle Beneventana, a place inhabited by a clownish race of people, fitted for the labour of the fields, or the tasks of the dairy and the cattle-shed, rather than for any other kind of traffic or profitable calling. Now in this place there lived, some time ago, a priest who was young, and a very good-looking fellow to boot; and, although all his learning consisted in being able to read a little, nevertheless, by the assistance of Madonna Santa Croce,† the special protector of the ignorant, he was appointed archpriest of the village aforesaid. Though it happened that he was, by a very long way, more fitted to be a feller of trees in the forest‡ than a shepherd of human souls, nevertheless he set himself to the discharge of his new calling in the best fashion he knew how to use, and, over and beyond the fact that in a very short space of time he became the spiritual brother of the greater part of all the men and women in the village aforesaid, it may be recorded that on all needful and prescribed occasions he gave to every one of his parishioners the spiritual sacra-

* St. John the Baptist.

† Probably an allusion to the "Santa Croce" spelling book, the earliest manual for children. This was still used in Italy a few years ago.

‡ Orig., *inversatore di bosco.*

ments. The end of it was, that this young man, after the manner of those who think it but a trifle to enjoy a bout of amorous sport whenever opportunity offers, cast his eye over a certain young woman of the place, the wife of a gossip of his, and one endowed with extraordinary beauty. Her name was Lisetta, and in a very short time the priest found himself hotly in love with her.

The aforesaid young woman was the wife of a peasant, also a youth, who was called by name Il Veneziano, and he, after having followed the calling of a mercenary foot-soldier in the wars not long past, at last came back to his own country, bringing with him the rewards which peace gives commonly to those who serve for gain; and then, subduing the earth with the mattock and the plough in the sweat of his brow, he passed his life honestly in the company of his fair wife. It chanced, however, that Lisetta very soon discovered how this gossip of hers was enamoured of her, and, recognizing him in his new office and dignity as the first man of the place, she ascribed to him the attributes of the highest station, and often, when communing with herself alone, felt no little pride thereanent. Indeed, she would willingly have given him all he asked for, had it not been that her husband, as one well versed in such affairs, became in a way jealous of her, insomuch that he never missed taking her with him to bear him company whenever he went, according to his wont, to his daily labour in the fields.

Now it happened one day that the young woman fell ill, and had perforce to remain at home in the house while her husband went forth to labour with his oxen. The archpriest, as soon as he got intelligence of this, straightway began to lay his plans for no other end than to make love to his gossip's wife, and, walking past the house where Lisetta dwelt, he called out, "Good day, gossip mine." She, having come to the window all filled with gladness at the sound of his voice, and having given him back a fitting salute, demanded of him whither he was bound at such an early hour. To her the priest, laughing the while, answered in this wise: "I in sooth am come hither this morning, now that your husband is gone afield and you for once left behind at home, to beg of you that you will give me the loan of his mare to go as far as the vineyard, for the reason that he himself is so much of a niggard that not only does he refuse to let any man mount her except himself, but scarcely allows another to set eyes upon her save when he may be present." Lisetta, who was very well advised, understood perfectly what sort of mare it was he was alluding to, and made answer to him, smilling as she spoke: "Good gossip, your thoughts have assuredly played you false to-day, forasmuch as you are come hither at a time when, however willing I might be to make you the loan you ask for, I am unable to do so, seeing that the mare has hurt her back in such a way that she may not, on any account, go out of the stable; indeed, this very morning, as soon as it was dawn, my husband wanted to have a ride for his pleasure, but on account of the failing I have just described to you he found that he could in no wise do what he willed."

The archpriest, who understood quite well what thing it was that Lisetta alluded to, then replied: "But this thing indeed is really a stroke of good luck for us, seeing that I cannot imagine that such a chance should have happened at a better time, I being especially well furnished at this present moment with a supply of fodder which I will presently put before the mare; nay, I will take such good care of her that another time you will, I am well assured, be all the more ready to lend her to me." "Alas!" cried the young woman, "you men are all alike, saucy fellows and boasters as you are. I, for my part, have never yet set eyes on a mare which, being ill, was in any way made well again by the boon of a grain of corn." "And why not?" said he; "but now pray to God that He may soon let her be fit for riding, so that there may ensue some actual deeds which shall bear yet stronger witness of the truth of what I say." "Now go your way, and God go with you," said Lisetta. "By the time five or six days shall have passed I hope the mare will again be fit for the saddle, and we will make a trial to see whether it is so." And after they had conversed together some time longer in a similar strain, the priest took his departure and went home.

After a short space of time had elapsed the mare was

found to be so far restored that she was able to sustain any burden, however heavy, which might be put upon her, and Il Veneziano made such use of her as pleased him. Then the young woman determined in her mind that she would carry out the promise which she had given to the priest, and on this account she remained at home one day alone for some trumped-up reason which she gave to her husband, instead of going to the fields with him. As soon as the archpriest knew what had happened, he betook himself, without losing a moment of time, to the door of the farm where the young woman dwelt, and entered therein without being observed by a single person. There he found the mare all in order, and, as soon as he had with a very few words arranged the stirrups to his liking, he mounted and rode so shrewd a bout, that before he had given over using his spurs he found that he had ridden a good two miles and a half, so that in a very short time he had fared a longer distance than he needed. And if the mare had not chanced to stumble and fall down in the course of the journey, on account of the great speed at which they went, he would with perfect ease have come to the end of the third mile, according to the purpose he had originally formed. And in order that his deeds might not be out of harmony with his words, he showed himself mighty generous of his provender at the end of every mile. Wherefore, with the greatest delectation to himself, he went on his course all through that day without having any notion, when evening at last began to fall, what number of miles he had covered since he set forth, and in this wise they continued the journey they had begun.

Now, when at last the hour had come when Il Veneziano would be returning from his fields, the archpriest went his way in right and proper fashion, having left the mare somewhat wearied, but not yet satiated with fodder, in the stable. But when it came to pass, somewhat later, that Lisetta's husband, either stirred thereto by the vice of jealousy or through having been made acquainted with what had passed, warned her, and forbade her, unless she might wish to meet her death at his hands forthwith, that for the future she should take good care to hold no intercourse whatever with the archpriest, the goodwife, calling to mind how vastly more abundant and generous were the favours provided by her good gossip than those of her husband, who forsooth was mightily niggard in this respect, was as one half dead with grief and vexation, and straightway let the archpriest know the turn affairs had taken—news which was to him fully as irksome as it was to her. Then, after many and varied expedients put in practice by them in order to find a secure means of foregathering, they hit at last upon a plan which was of a surety more diverting than dangerous.

By way of putting this project of theirs into execution without farther delay, our good Lisetta, when she was going out of church on a certain Sunday morning, made believe, in the presence of all the people there assembled, that she was possessed by some spirit or other, and straight way began to twist about her hands and her eyes and her mouth in the strangest fashion, howling and crying in such wise that all the people who were there fled from her presence as fast as they could. Now her husband, who indeed loved her more than he loved his own life, as soon as he saw what strange thing had come to pass, was stricken with wellnigh mortal grief, and, weeping bitterly the while, he led her back with him to his house. His grief having by this time in a measure chased away his jealousy, he let summon forthwith his gossip the archpriest, and, shedding abundant tears, he entreated him that he would quickly speak some conjuration against the possessing spirits, and consider what holy prayers he might use in order to compel them to go forth from his wife. The archpriest, coming forward with an air of the deepest gravity, and beginning his rite of exorcism with the accustomed forms, thereupon demanded to know of the spirit whom he might be. To this question the young woman, according to the pact between the two, made answer in these words: "I am the spirit of the father of this poor young woman, and am condemned to go wandering wretchedly about this world for the space of ten years."

Il Veneziano, when he heard these words, straightway believed it was his father-in-law who spoke, and addressing him, he said, with much weeping and tears: "Alas! I beseech you, for God's sake, that you will come forth from where you are, and that you will no longer torment your own daughter." Then the spirit in answer spake thus: "In a few days, indeed, I will go hence; but I tell you plainly that I will then take up my abode in your own body, where I shall remain all the residue of the time during which, as I told you, I am condemned to purge away my sins. This I will do because you yourself were glad when I died."

Poor Veneziano, as soon as he heard these terrible tidings, took no farther concern as to the trouble which at present molested his wife, being entirely occupied with the woes which threatened his own person in the future; wherefore he cried out, altogether overcome by his fears: "Ah, wretch that I am, is there indeed to be found no cure for my troubles? Cannot this doom, which has been pronounced against me, be revoked either by the way of almsgiving or by the offering of some other possessions of mine?" "Yes, indeed," replied the spirit; "that is, if you are inclined thereto." Then said Il Veneziano: "What do you mean by talking of my inclination? Surely I would sell everything I have, down to my jackass." To this the spirit made answer: "Your task then will be to go on a pilgrimage of forty days, and to visit forty churches, at every one of which you shall cause to be said a mass for the remission of my sins; and you shall furthermore leave due directions to the archpriest, your good gossip, against whom you have in very wicked wise taken up a jealous suspicion, that in the meantime he shall say the same number of masses in this place, and that he shall come hither every day and recite the canonical hours in the hearing of your wife, for the reason that his prayers are much more acceptable in the presence of God, he being so much more a righteous man, and one full of the gifts of the spirit. Therefore, from this time forth, I charge you that you show towards him the highest trust and devotion, forasmuch as by the virtue of his prayers I have good hope that you will not only receive the gift of grace, but that God will always in the future give rich increase to your flocks and your herds."

Il Veneziano, hearing that after all there was to be

found a remedy for the terrible misfortune which he, without the least doubt or suspicion, believed had been prepared for him, made answer without hesitation that he would at once let everything be duly carried out. Then addressing himself at once to his reverend gossip, he besought him that he would without fail let ensue all the above-named directions, promising at the same time to sell the finest pig he possessed for the forwarding thereof. Then, without further tarrying, he set forth on his journey.

The archpriest, who all this time had feigned to let fall tears from his eyes, while he was in truth laughing inwardly, took up forthwith the charge which had thus been laid upon him by his gossip, and, having resumed possession of the goodwife and of what few goods she had about her, it may be held for certain that, before the husband made his way back from the devout pilgrimage he had undertaken, it was necessary, in order to drive out from the afflicted body of the young woman the evil spirit aforesaid, to lay a whole hundred of blessed ones, which work these two accomplished with the greatest pleasure and delight to themselves. And thus at one and the same time the masses—which in sooth were never begun—were finished;* Il Veneziano returned, having accomplished his pilgrimage; Lisetta was freed from her trouble; and the spirit expelled by the archpriest. For the future Il Veneziano ever bore himself most complaisantly towards his reverend gossip, so that never again from this time forward was he in any way jealous of his pretty wife. And she, forsooth, in the season of her affliction, had laid bare, after the fashion which spirits are accustomed to use, all the secrets both as to men and as to women which had given her annoyance, telling such secrets after the similitude of certain others which the archpriest had more than once imparted to her during the practice of confession, thus following the infamous usage and damnable habit of this most wicked generation.

* Orig., *le non cominciate messe furono finite*—an Italian bull.

MASUCCIO

IN sooth the things which I have set before you in this last novel of mine are mightily diverting, and such as may not be passed over without much laughter. Amongst other matters there is the stumbling of the mare which prevented the worthy horseman from coming to the end of that third mile—a sort of journeying which may well seem hard of belief to all those who have not had experience of the same. But, the humour notwithstanding, we may and we must ever regard as things to be held in the deepest hatred that most malignant nature and that nefarious way of life of this village archpriest, and of the greater part of the whole body of the clergy. For they treat as a thing of no account the most holy sacrament of baptism, and make no more difficulty about breaking through and violating the same, or in laying bare the secrets confided to them in the sacred practice of confession, than they would feel over the most trifling mistake committed during the repetition of any of the offices of religion. And when they make confession one to another concerning any of these execrable vices aforesaid, or even of worse sins (if, indeed, worse can be committed), for which they richly merit the penalty of perpetual imprisonment, or even the painful and horrible death of burning by fire, they will impose upon each other such a trifling penance as a single paternoster, just as if the offence had been no worse than spitting in church. But if by chance there should fall into their clutches any layman charged with offences similar to the above-named, then, besides raising a terrible storm about his head, they would launch condemnation against him as a heretic, and would on no account consent to grant him absolution unless he should first hand over to them divers of the possessions of Madonna Santa Croce. That these words of mine are the truth I will show you in my tenth novel, which I will let follow forthwith (the last, moreover, which shall deal with the doings of this folk), how an old confessing priest —not in any village or rude country place, where his ignorance might in a way have been his excuse, but in the mighty city of Rome itself, and in the very centre of Saint Peter's—made, with the utmost wickedness and cunning, a market of the joys of Paradise to whatsoever persons might be willing to purchase the same, just as if they had been mere chattels belonging to himself. This thing was told to me as a true fact by a man whose word is worthy of all credit.

THE END OF THE NINTH NOVEL.

Novel the Tenth

ARGUMENT

FRA ANTONIO DE SAN MARCELLO IN THE COURSE OF HEARING CONFESSIONS SELLS THE GIFT OF PARADISE, AND ACCUMULATES VAST SUMS OF MONEY BY THIS PRACTICE. TWO MEN OF FERRARA CONTRIVE, BY PUTTING UPON HIM A MOST SUBTLE CHEAT, TO SELL HIM A FALSE JEWEL. WHEN HE COMES TO KNOW OF THE FRAUD, HE DIES WRETCHEDLY, ALMOST MADDENED BY THIS TROUBLE.

TO THE NOBLE AND HIGH-BORN MESSER FRANCESCO ARCELLA*

EXORDIUM

MY most righteous Arcella, if we mortals would only well and carefully consider the full extent of the sublimity and immensity of the mercy and the abundant grace of the most high God towards the generations of men, we should have it clearly made known to us how, from the very first moments of our procreation, He did not deem it enough merely to make us after His own image and similar to Himself; but, in addition to this, desired to confer upon us full domination over sea and land, hills and plains, and to make all generations of beasts, which reason not, to be our tractable subjects and useful for our being. And notwithstanding that our first parents, by their foolhardy greed, sought to bring upon themselves, and upon all those who should come after them, inevitable and eternal death, God, in order to demonstrate to us in all His deeds His abundant liberality and sublime love, deigned to send down to us His only Son, in His desire to redeem us from condemnation, and

* In the later editions this novel is dedicated to Messer Francesco Lavanguolo.

to let this Blessed One suffer a death of most bitter pain upon the wood of the cross, thus opening to us straightway the closed doors of Paradise. And over and beyond all this, so as to leave undone naught by which He might make clear to us all how true was the kindly affection He felt towards us in His benignant love, He left to comfort us here on earth, when He Himself willed to return to the Father whence He came, that most glorious bishop Saint Peter, his worthy successor, conferring upon him ample powers which should afterwards go down for ever to all the sacerdotal clergy as the workers of His will, whereby they might always be able to give us our share in the true city of Paradise, at whatever time we might call upon them for the same.

But one thing there is which must needs cause us the greatest astonishment when we regard it, to wit, the infinite patience which God the Creator of all shows in allowing still to live upon earth certain of these aforesaid agents of His holy mysteries, men who by this same authority sell the reward of Paradise in their office as confessors, as if it were a thing belonging to themselves, to others who look upon it as a chattel to be bought and sold. According to the means of the would-be buyer, and the sum of money he may be willing to spend, these men will pretend to give away or to withhold a higher or a lower place round about the throne of the most high God, never considering in their dealings the difference which there may be between one man and another—whether he may be a homicide, and of most wicked life, and given to every vice, or one of seemly carriage, and honoured by all, on account of his good and decent way of living. All they require is that their greedy avaricious hands should be abundantly salved with coin.* And were it not for the fact that I have made up my mind to molest these

* Baptista Mantuanus, who is cited by Bayle to illustrate the vices of Sixtus IV., writes in his poem, "De Calamitatibus Temporum":

"Venalia nobis
Templa, sacerdotes, altaria, sacra, coronæ
Ignes, terra, preces, cœlum est venale, Deusque."

Under Innocent VIII., his successor, the system of spiritual corruption was farther elaborated by the establishment at Rome wretches no more by the pricks of my pen, I would here bring before you so many instances well worthy of belief from times past, and, in addition to these, so many true witnesses as to their doings in these days, that you yourself, and many others besides, would wonder beyond measure how it is that divine justice does not straightway consent to let all such men be blasted by lightning, and sent down to the lowest centre of the abyss. Nevertheless, I will set before you one instance, showing you what manner of deed was wrought by a certain old priest in order to gather together money, and how he, after having sold Paradise to an enormous number of innocent Christian people, and thereby opened to them the gates thereof,* found these same gates, according to his deserts, shut in his face when the time came for him to depart from this life.

THE NARRATIVE

IN the days of Pope Eugenius IV.,† that most worthy prince of the Christian state, there lived in Rome a certain priest full of years, a good Catholic, reputed to be a man of pure and holy life, who was called by name Fra Antonio de San Marcello, and was a member of the Order of the Servites.‡ For many years past he had exercised his office amongst the other penitentiary priests

of a bank for the sale of pardons, and every sin had its price. In the chronicle of Infessura there is a story of the Vice-Chancellor, who, being asked why criminals were allowed to pay instead of suffering for their misdeeds, replied, "God wills not the death of a sinner, but rather that he should pay and live.

* It is somewhat remarkable that Masuccio should allow a corrupt sale of spiritual privileges to be valid for its purpose.

† Formerly Cardinal Condolmieri. He succeeded Martin V. in 1431. He was a Celestine monk, and a man of hard and stubborn character. His first act as pope was to attack and despoil the Colonnas, the kinsfolk of his predecessor. The Cardinal Prospero and Antonio, Prince of Salerno, were the chief victims. He summoned the Council of Basel for the reform of the clergy, and the Councils of Ferrara and Florence for the re-union of the Eastern and Western Churches. He died in 1447.

‡ The Servites were founded in 1233 by an association of Florentine citizens. They adopted the Augustinian rule, with

who served the confessionals at St. Peter's, and he always continued the practice of his calling without putting on a stern and wrathful face, as is the custom of some. He, on the other hand, by his kindly greetings and gentle manners, persuaded all the penitents to come to him to confess their sins; for, as surely as water will extinguish a burning fire, so holy almsgiving, done through the means of sincere confession, will purge away sin both as regards this world and the next as well. Indeed, if by chance there should have gone to him any penitent who had been guilty of all the misdoings and unpardonable crimes which lie within the possibilities of the sinful spirit of man, if only this sinner should have filled his hand full of anything beside wind, the friar straightway brought the penitent face to face with Saint John the Baptist.*

And thus, while the friar went on for many years heaping up this enormous gain, and being held and reputed by all those who knew him to be little short of a saint, it came to pass that the greater part of those coming from foreign lands, and of the Italians as well, would under no circumstances let themselves be shriven by any other than he, thus filling his pockets every day with various sums of money. Although he had by such practices as these heaped together many thousands of florins, and was often wont, with a hypocritical look upon his face, to make some pretence of adding to the buildings of his monastery, still, so rare and so insignificant were the sums he gave away, that, compared with the huge revenues he enjoyed, they stood for nothing more than the taking of a beakerful of water out of the Tiber.†

certain variations. They received the sanction of the Pope in 1255, and in 1487 Innocent VIII. put them on a level with the other mendicant orders.

* Orig., *pur che la mano d' altro che di vento gonfiata li avesse, di botto dirimpetto a San Giovanni Battista il collocava.* The first of these allusions is a parallel to the other Italian saying: *stare colle mani piene di mosche.* The reference to St. John the Baptist is probably a suggestion of bribery money, as in Florence coins were struck bearing the image of the saint, the patron of the city.

† Orig., *altro non era che un bicchiero d'acqua di Tevere aver tolto.*

Wherefore, after a certain time had elapsed, there arrived in Rome from Ferrara two youths, the one named Ludovico and the other Biasio, who, as is the practice of men of their sort, were accustomed to travel without ceasing through the world from one place to another, carrying with them false money and counterfeit jewels, and many other artful frauds, for the beguiling of all those people who might be to the leeward of them.* Before long these two received intelligence of the great riches cf Fra Antonio, and likewise how he was more avaricious than any other old priest in the place—how the only reason why he still went on taking his seat in that penitentiary of his arose from his intense passion of greed. And as for the seat itself, seeing that he continually made therein a trade and barter of places in Paradise, it might have been called more appropriately a publican's counter. Over and beyond this, it came to their knowledge how the good friar maintained a close intercourse and commerce with certain changers of money—men well versed in every language, and such as trouble themselves with the practice of no other calling than to change the money of their own country, sitting thus always in front of St. Peter's for the convenience of those strangers who nowadays come from the other side of the mountains. The two Ferrarese found out that not only did Fra Antonio seek the services of these men for the exchange of the various moneys he received into Italian coin, so that he might the better hoard them up, but that he also went to them for advice with regard to certain gems which, from time to time, came into his hands as offerings.

Wherefore, after they had got possession of minute information as to his ways and dealings, they took counsel together as to how they might best add Fra Antonio to the number of those whom they had cozened. For this reason Biasio, being well skilled in the language of Castile, pretended to be a Spanish money-changer, and, having hung a money-changer's tray about his neck, took up his station early one morning with his stock of coins amongst the others of his calling in front of St. Peter's. Then, whenever Fra Antonio might happen to pass either into or out of

* Orig., *che gionger si poteano sotto vento.*

the church, Biasio with a merry face would salute him by taking off his cap. For several days he continued to use this behaviour towards the priest, who, on his part, began to wish to know more of the man who greeted him so courteously; so one day he called to the fellow in good-humoured wise, and bade him tell straightway what was his name and from what country he came. Biasio, as soon as he perceived how things were going, was over-joyed thereanent, forasmuch as it seemed to him that the fish was at last beginning to scent the bait; wherefore in cunning fashion he thus made answer to Fra Antonio: "Messere, my name is Diego de Medina, and I hold myself at your pleasure. I am come hither forsooth, not so much to ply the trade of a money-changer, as to purchase any fine precious stones, either set or unset, which may fall into my hands, seeing that of such wares as these, I, by God's mercy, am a very skilful judge, through having lived for a good portion of my life in Scotland, where I managed to master a number of secrets connected with the jeweller's art. But in any case, my father, I am altogether at your disposition, and, if there should come into your hands any of the money of my country, I am prepared to assist you in the changing thereof for a very small profit. I will do this both on account of the respect I have for your cloth, and on account of the affection I have towards you in this acquaintance of ours, so recent and to me so very dear."

The friar, when he perceived how becoming was the speech of this man, and when he furthermore ascertained how great was his skill and knowledge as a lapidary, was in no small measure pleased with him; wherefore, reckoning that he had met with a great stroke of luck in finding such a friend, made answer to him in these words, his face beaming with joy the while: "Now see, my Diego, you must know that all good and true love is reciprocal. On this account, seeing that I am held here to be a man of particular authority, and one to whom, peradventure, more penitents come than to any other confessor of this church, I beg you, if such a request may not seem irksome to you, that, should any man of your nation, or, indeed, of any other, come before you, you will send him to me.

And anyone coming to me in such wise, I will hold to be specially recommended on account of the love I bear to you; and, besides this, I myself will do as much or even more on your behalf if ever you should require it." And in this manner, after they had mutually thanked one another, and had determined to treat one another exactly as if they were father and son, each one went about his own business.

Now Ludovico, in furtherance of the scheme devised between him and Biasio, had put on the disguise of a Provencal sailor who had fled from the galleys, and was now spending his time in going about St. Peter's, begging from this one and from that. Indeed, he knew so well how to play the part of a cozening knave, that, putting on one side the business he had chiefly in view, he picked up* from almost everyone he met a great quantity of alms, what though the sums themselves were but trifles. Meantime, as he went rambling about the church he did not fail to keep his eye fixed constantly on the pennant,† and when at a certain moment he perceived that Fra Antonio was unencumbered by any duty at the confessional, he humbly crept towards him with loitering steps, and besought him that of his goodness he would deign to listen for a few moments.

The good friar in sooth had a purse for every man's money, and although, judging by appearances, he deemed the fellow before him to be mightily poor, he nevertheless turned towards him, and, having made him kneel down at his feet, he signed over him the sign of the holy cross; whereupon Ludovico addressed him in the following words: "My father, although my sins are very great and heinous, I have not been moved to come to you so much to unburden myself of these, as to reveal to you a great secret which I would sooner commit to your keeping than to the keeping of any man in the world, for I clearly perceive that you are endowed with every virtue, and devoted to the service of God. I know not what spirit it may be within me which is urging me, either by my own good luck or by the fortune in store for you, to do this thing. I

* Orig., *arravogliava*—Neapolitan dialect.

† Orig., *con l'occhio sempre al pennello.*

only know that I feel myself compelled to make it known to you alone. But there is one favour I ask and implore of you, by the true God and by the holy sacrament of confession, and this is that it may please you to keep my secret close. Of the necessity of this request of mine, you, I am well assured, will be convinced forthwith when you shall have heard the nature thereof."

Fra Antonio, who comprehended clearly enough from the ring of the words that there was some gain to be made out of the fellow before him, immediately turned towards him, and, having made mental appraisement of his value, he thus addressed him in benignant wise: "My son, it was surely the good counsel of your soul which persuaded you to trust to my keeping this thing you mention. Still, I will not refrain from reminding you that you may lay bare before me this, and any other secret matter you may have, without any doubt or suspicion; for you must know that when you speak your confession will be made to God and not to me. And no form of death, let it be ever so shameful—to say nothing of the eternal damnation which would follow the same—would be held to be an adequate punishment in this world for the man who would be base enough to reveal the secrets told to him in holy confession."

Ludovico, who in sooth was a very cunning knave, here began to let fall plentiful tears, saying the while, "Messere, I believe all that you say, but still the fact remains that the matter in question must needs prove to be a mighty dangerous one as far as I am concerned, and that I am troubled with many doubts as to whether it can ever be brought to pass without letting fall dishonour upon me, or even putting me in danger of my life." On the other hand, the friar, whose greed was now keenly aroused, went on without pause to bring into play all his cunning, and persuaded Ludovico as best he could, with all sorts of cogent arguments, to stand in no doubt in a case of conscience. When Ludovico, with just as great cunning on his part, had kept back the secret from the friar for a considerable time, and when he saw at last how keen the old man's curiosity was to have knowledge of the same, he began to tell a story, in very timid fashion,as to how he had been detained by force on board a Catalonian galley for a long time, setting forth everything in due order, and ending by confessing how he had at the present time concealed on his person a carbuncle stone of immense value, which jewel he himself, while on board of the galley aforesaid, had stolen from the dead body of one of his comrades, a Greek, who had died of fever, and how he alone, of all the people on board the galley, knew that the Greek was wont to keep sewn up in the bosom of his coat this precious jewel, which he and a certain German had very cunningly stolen, together with certain other articles of great value, out of the treasury of St. Mark. Ludovico next went on to tell how by their evil fortune they had been made prisoners by this said galley, and how, the ship having been wrecked through missing sight of the lighthouse, he and divers others had made good their escape therefrom, and by the help of God had managed to find their way to Rome.

Now when Ludovico had brought to an end this well-planned discourse of his, he added, weeping as he spoke, "My father, I know well enough that if I carry about me this precious jewel on such a long journey as I needs must make to reach my home from this place, it may very easily come to pass that, by reason of this stone, I may some day be taken and hanged by the neck. Wherefore I would not mind parting with it for a sum much less than its just value. And because, as you yourself must see, that God has apparently sent His spirit upon me in such wise that I have been led straight to you, and because peradventure He may have ordained, on account of those many good works of yours of which I hear the fame, that so great a treasure as this carbuncle of mine should sooner belong to you than to any other man, I implore you, for all the reasons aforesaid, that you will do your best to let this business of mine come to an issue in such manner that no scandal of any kind may arise thereanent. I will let you see the jewel I have told you of, and, if it should chance to please you, you shall give me therefor just as much money as will suffice, when I shall have returned to my home, duly to bestow my three daughters in marriage; for I have this very day heard intelligence of them, letting me know that they are still alive, but reduced to a state of extreme misery and want. I ask you to give me so much and nothing more in exchange for my precious gem."

Fra Antonio, when he had heard the end of this skilfully concocted story, not only gave full credit thereto, but was so much delighted with the news that it seemed as if he would jump out of his skin for joy, and, after he had given his promise, with many flowery speeches, to keep secret whatever might be told to him, he asked Ludovico to let him see the gem in question. The fellow still pretended to be in a timid and reluctant mood, but, after the friar had gone on for some time urging his request, he drew out at last from his breast, feigning to be shaking with fear the while, a piece of crystal set in fine gold with a bit of ruby-coloured foil at the back thereof, the whole thing being arranged in such masterly wise that it seemed of a truth to be a carbuncle of the finest. From its size and from its beauty it was indeed a marvellous thing to the eye, and it was so well draped in cloth of taffetas, and so cunningly disposed, that every passer-by looking at it would have taken it for real, and no one but a lapidary would have detected the underlying fraud. Then Ludovico, taking the stone in one hand and carefully shading it with the other, cast a glance around him, and finally displayed his gem to the gaze of the greedy and rapacious wolf before him.

Fra Antonio, as soon as he had looked at it, was altogether confused and amazed at the sight thereof, for indeed it seemed to him as if it must be of even greater value than he had at first thought possible, and it straightway occurred to him that in this matter it would be well for him to seek the counsel of his Castilian friend; wherefore, turning to Ludovico, he said, "In truth the gem seems to be a very fine one; nevertheless, it may happen that your companion told you a falsehood. But, that there may be no doubt in the affair, I will, if it pleases you, show it privately to a friend of mine who has great skill as a lapidary and, if it should veritably prove to be what it is in outward seeming, I will give you not only what you ask for it, but as much as lies in my power to disburse."

To this speech Ludovico replied: "No, you must not do this thing, for it may happen that I shall be thereby condemned to suffer as a thief." Then the friar answered: "Of a truth you need have no doubts on this score, for I give you my promise that I will not leave the church, but only go as far as the great door, where there is, as I know well, a certain Castilian, an eminent lapidary, a very worthy person, and my son in the spirit to boot. To him I would wish to show the gem, using the greatest caution over the business, and when he shall have inspected it I will come back to you." To this Ludovico replied, by way of answer: "Alas! alas! it seems certain to me that you will be the death of me, and that this is my last day of life. Indeed, I would never grant your request were I not forced thereto. But, at the same time, if I grant it, I beg and warn you to take good care how you trust Spaniards, seeing that they are men to whom little faith is due." The friar replied: "Ah! leave the care of this to me, for, were he to prove the greatest villain the world holds, he would not get the better of me, forasmuch as he loves me as well as he does his own self."

Thus, leaving Ludovico in the church, Fra Antonio hurried away to the place where Diego was awaiting his coming with no small longing. As soon as the rogue saw him, he greeted him with his accustomed salute, which the friar duly returned, and then the latter, having taken Diego aside somewhat, displayed to him the precious gem, begging him at the same time that he would, for the sake of the love he had for him, tell him truly what might be the value thereof. As soon as Diego saw the stone he began to feign to be overcome with the greatest astonishment, and then, with a smile, he said: "Messere, is it possible that you want to make a gull of me, seeing that this is assuredly the Pope's own carbuncle?" The friar, overjoyed at these words, then said: "Do not trouble youself over the matter, but simply tell me what, according to your judgment, might be the value of it." Whereupon Diego, still laughing in his sleeve, replied: "What need is there for me to do this, since you know the gem better than I do. But I see how the thing stands: you are anxious to put my skill to the test; and, since it pleases you that it should be so, I am well content. So, without keeping you any longer waiting, I will tell you that no one in the world save the Pope or the Venetians could pay for this gem the price which it is really worth." The friar replied: "By the love that you have for me in your soul, I beg you to tell me what might be the value of it." "Alas!" said Diego, "although at this present time gems are of very small value,* I, poor as I am, would nevertheless rather be the owner of this carbuncle than of thirty thousand ducats." And after gazing upon the stone once more he kissed it, saying: "Blessed be the earth which produced thee!" Then, when he had restored the carbuncle to the friar, he went on: "But tell me, by your faith, does this gem indeed belong to the Pope?" "It does indeed," the friar answered; "but I must tell you that it is absolutely necessary this thing should be kept a secret, forasmuch as His Holiness does not wish that anyone should cast eyes upon it until it shall be set in his mitre, and I am now about to have it inlaid therein."

When he had thus spoken Fra Antonio took his leave, and, rejoicing in his heart at what he had heard, returned to Ludovio, and said to him: "My son, the gem is in sooth a very fine one; still it is not of such great value as you deem. Nevertheless, I will take it, and let it be set in a crucifix for our church. How much, therefore, have you determined in your mind to ask for it?" Ludovico answered: "Ah! do not talk in this fashion. I indeed know quite well what the thing is worth, and if I could carry it away with me without putting my life in peril thereby, I should assuredly become one of the richest men in the world. But I have determined rather to bestow it safely in some private place here, than to take it away with me and to sell it at a risk in other parts. To get me some aid in this my extreme need I therefore place myself entirely in your hands and beg you that you will act towards me in such wise as God and your conscience may inspire you, especially as you stand in need of the gem for the use of your church." The friar answered: "May you be blessed, my son! but, seeing that we poor priests have no other source of income than the alms which are bestowed upon us by devout persons, and seeing likewise that you yourself are a poor man, it will be necessary that we should

* Orig., *ancor che oggi le gioie sieno a terra.*

use some sort of discretion in our dealings one with another. And in order that you may have some experience as to how things are with me, I will tell you that I can now at this present time hand over to you two hundred ducats; and, if it should happen that at some future time you should come back to this place, I will not fail to make you a partaker in whatever grace God may have sent to me in the meantime."

Ludovico, when he listened to this speech, began to weep afresh, and cried: "Alas, alas! Messere, you call yourself a man of God, and yet you have the conscience to mention so small a sum. May it never be the will of God that I should fall into such an oversight as this!" Then said the friar in answer: "Now do not distress yourself, my good man, and weep in this fashion without reason, but tell me plainly what sum you want for your jewel." "What do I want for it?" cried Ludovico. "I trow that if I should let you have it for a thousand ducats I should be bestowing a greater benefaction upon your church than all those who have raised it up from the laying of the first stone." Fra Antonio, who on one side was moved by the vilest avarice, and on the other by greedy desire to be the possessor of this most magnificent gem, began to bear up to the wind, and Ludovico was fain to strike his sails somewhat;* so that at last, after a long bout of haggling, they both stopped half-way—that is, they agreed the price should be five hundred ducats.

Thereupon they took their way together towards San Marco, and Fra Antonio, as soon as he had come into his chamber, put the fine carbuncle safely away in a casket, and gave Ludovico in exchange for the same five hundred ducats in fine gold. Having received these and a benediction as well, Ludovico, with the friars' assistance, straightway sewed the money up in his coat, and this done, he departed, making his way swifter than the wind towards St. Peter's. When he arrived there he gave a signal to his companion, who was awaiting his coming, doubting

* Orig., *Frate Antonio che da un canto la pessima avaritia, e da l' altro la gulosita de la ricchissima gioia lo stimolava, de l'orza a montare incominciato, e Ludovico a calare in poppa.* Masuccio keeps up the nautical metaphor throughout this story.

somewhat the while. They met later on at a certain place which had already been settled between them; and now that they have set their sails to the wind, I beg you, good Fra Antonio, to find them if you can.

The friar, as soon as the bargain was completed, found himself mightily well content therewith, deeming that this purchase of his had made a very rich man of him. Furthermore, he was minded to sell the aforesaid jewel into the service of our Lord by the help of a certain lapidary, who was his dearest friend and also his gossip. Therefore, having sent for this man and bade him come straightway, he showed him this magnificent stone, using no little parade and ceremony the while, and thus addressed him: "What think you of this, my good gossip? have I not made a fine purchase, although I am naught but a friar?" As soon as the gossip saw the stone, he began to laugh, and when the friar perceived this he demanded, albeit he himself was still smiling, "What are you laughing at?" To him the lapidary answered, "I laugh in considering the multitudinous and multiform cheats which men versed in the world's ways contrive for the beguiling of those who are gifted with little forethought, and at the same time I declare that there are very few men who would not have known this stone to be a false one." "How!" cried the friar; "is not this stone a good one? What may its value be? Examine it well and narrowly, for the love of God." The gossip made answer to him: "I have already examined it, and I now tell you for certain that there is naught of value about it save the gold in which it is set, and that would not amount to more than ten ducats at most; and, in order that you may yourself be assured of this, I will make it clear to you forthwith." Then, having taken in hand a knife, he dexterously wrenched the stone out of the setting therewith, and took away the foil which was there, and straightway let Fra Antonio see that the stone was perfectly clear crystal, which appeared in the rays of the sun as something little better than a lighted candle.

When the friar fully realized the trick, it seemed to him as if the heavens were falling on his head, and that the solid earth were being rapt from beneath his feet. Then, in his savage fury and overwhelming grief, he raised his hands and began to lacerate his face with his nails, which were old and crooked. His gossip marvelled greatly at what he saw, and spake thus to him: "What ails you, my good gossip?" "Alas! my son," Fra Antonio replied, "I am a dead man, for I have paid for that thing there a price of five hundred golden ducats. But, for God's sake, give me your company as far as St, Peter's, where I trow we may find a certain Castilian money-changing thief who assured that the stone was genuine. Of a surety he must be in fraudulent league with the one who sold it to me." The gossip made a mock of this scheme; nevertheless, to give the friar satisfaction, they took to horse, and spent the whole of that day in searching for Mary all over Rome;* and in the end, when they failed to find her, the good friar made his way back to his home sad and grieving amain. Then he took to his bed, and, through lamentations and scourging himself, and beating his head against the wall, he brought himself into such a state of fever, that, without taking any heed to provide for the reception of the blessed sacrament, he passed away from this life in the course of a very few days.

In this wise, therefore, the great sums of money heaped up by him in making a barter of the celestial home, proved —most justly, be it said—in the end to be the cause which operated most powerfully in procuring his eternal exile therefrom. Indeed, at this last setting forth of his he was not able to carry away with him coin enough to satisfy the claims of Charon—that dread steersman—in order that he might make the passage from the river's brink to the city of Dis. From which voyage may God deliver me and every other faithful Christian man! Amen.

* Orig., *e tutto il di cercata Maria per Roma ne finalmente trovatala*, a saying equivalent to the English "To look for a needle in a haystack."

MASUCCIO

SO numerous are the hidden and secret tricks and the fraudulent wiles which these men who wear the garb of religion are wont every day to put upon ill-fated laymen, that there is no need to marvel if they themselves should now and again be cheated likewise in artful and ingenious fashion by certain others no less wary. Indeed, so little are they accustomed to be duped themselves, that they get into the way of presuming overmuch, and lose restraint over themselves in the matter of knowledge, holding it to be a question beyond dispute that no man could ever have the will or the power to put a cheat upon them. Wherefore, if it should happen at any time that one of them should fall into the snare which has been set for him by a layman, he will suffer so much bitter grief thereanent that he will be like to fall a victim to death, and be bereft of all hope—according to the instance set forth in the foregoing novel.

For the reason that I have fully determined to write no more of the doings of this perverse and wicked generation (although, indeed, I have not said half enough about them), and for the future to put the bar of silence upon my lips and to molest them no more, I find that I must needs leave unnoticed an enormous mass of their secret doings, such as could only by the rarest chance come to the knowledge of laymen. Nor will I enlarge, however much my pen may lead me on thereto, upon the deadly and cruel enmities and the depraved jealousies which exist, not only between one form of religion and another, but between the inmates of the self-same convent, or concerning those, just as great, which prevail in the courts of the great princes of the Church. And we can say nothing worse of them than to mark down how they seduce certain besotted laymen to take up their quarrels, so that about the tribunals and in the piazzas these latter contend publicly over the same, the one becoming a partisan of the Franciscans, and the other of the Dominicans, besides causing a thousand other beastlinesses concerning which I will be here silent. Wherefore, leaving them henceforth in full possession, without any hindrance whatsoever, of the many hundred years they have enjoyed, we will direct the course of our pleasant travel into other parts, and let him who may in the future desire to follow up the search as to their conversation and habits, continue the same for himself, and bear the burden of the pursuit. This one thing, however, I will declare and firmly maintain, that all those deeds of theirs which I have set forth in the past ten novels, and in other places, have in no wise been recorded with the intention of wounding those priests and friars who duly observe to the full the approved and holy rules laid upon them—men who, although it happens that they are few in number, and on this account difficult to be judged by us, are without doubt the light and the sustenance both of our faith and of the Christian religion. And if we come to consider the matter with care, there will be found no cause for marvelling that in such a vast multitude very many wicked and vicious men should exist; seeing that, although it chanced that the great and omnipotent God created in the first instance the whole of the angelic choir good and perfect, no small wickedness was afterwards found even amongst the most exalted ones thereof, so that they were hurled down from heaven by divine justice into the nethermost centre of the pit. And, also, what shall be said of Christ, our true and only Redeemer, who came to take upon Him our human flesh on account of the sins of our first parents? Was there not found amongst the small flock which He Himself had chosen that most wicked traitor, Judas, who sold Him for a price into the hands of the perfidious Jews? But in these instances neither the sin of the angels nor that of Judas prevailed in any way to stain the righteousness of those who remained faithful. By the aforesaid arguments we may in truth come to the conclusion that the monstrous vices of those priests who are wicked hypocrites can in no wise wound or offend the virtues and perfections of those who are righteous; nay, rather, the more egregious the exhibition made of the sins of the wicked, the brighter will be the glory with which the integrity of the just will shine. Forasmuch as a black crow, when placed beside a white dove, will only serve to enhance the purity of the dove's plumage, so in like manner the detestable doings and the manifest ill deeds wrought by these iniquitous wretches against the majesty of the eternal God will without ceasing exhibit the worth and beauty of the righteous life.

But because in these latter days it is no easy matter to distinguish the good from the bad, who, as I have already said, transform themselves from pastors into wolves wrapped round with the raiment of the gentle lamb, I will continue instant in my chiding of them until I make an end of my reproofs against them altogether, at the same time declaring that it would be more convenient and advantageous if we could contrive to live without these scandals, and that it would be well if their officers—who should naturally be the best judges of the coin they let circulate—were to mark them all with some strange and novel stamp, so that at a first glance it would be an easy matter for each one of us to recognize the counterfeits as branded traitors.* But seeing that such a matter would have to be proposed in their general chapters, I, having many other things to attend to, will leave the world as I found it. Wherefore, having brought this first part of my book to a happy end, we will, with the permission of the Creator and the good pleasure of my listeners, pass on to the second.

* Orig., *come signati giudei fossero.*

HERE ENDS THE FIRST PART.

PART THE SECOND

Prologue

HERE BEGINS AUSPICIOUSLY THE SECOND PART OF THE NOVELLINO, IN WHICH WILL BE FOUND TEN OTHER NOVELS SETTING FORTH, WITHOUT OFFENCE TO ANYONE, THE HISTORIES OF DIVERS FLOUTS AND SCATHES PUT UPON JEALOUS MEN, TOGETHER WITH MANY OTHER DELIGHTSOME ADVENTURES, IN SUCH ORDER AS WILL BE FOUND BELOW.

NOW indeed I have at last in my defenceless bark come out from amongst the dreadful waves and the raging winds which have vexed it during the narration of the nefarious and unbounded crimes told in the foregoing stories—not indeed without bodily hurt and much weariness of spirit—and have steered myself into the longed-for harbour of safety, there to relax my tired bones and worn-out limbs. Having repaired my rent sails and set in order all the other tackle and rigging of my ship, having taken heed that the season has put on a new aspect, and that the sea, now calmed down, will allow me under the fresh breath of the gentle zephyr to plough its depths in peace, having marked likewise that all the planets and the fair seeming of the skies show themselves friendly and favourable to my emprise, it seems that I ought straightway to direct the course of my bark into these joyous and delightful regions, giving my sails to the wind while this prosperous calm prevails. Then, having entered into these charming and gracious parts, I will gladden my hearers with pleasant and dainty discourse, and make myself an occasion for mirth and gratification to them. For their consideration—and before this benign star of mine shall have come to its appointed end and ceased to let shine the light under which I have begun this work—I will now set down ten other novels, which will form the second part of my Novellino. In these I purpose to tell divers other pleasurable jests, set forth in a strain which ought to give offence to no man. And my manner of procedure will be to intermingle the stories in such wise that the one to follow shall depend on the one just told. Wherefore in the beginning—and I do this not without good cause—I will deal in a due and fitting manner with the vicious infirmity of jealousy, and the poisonous results issuing therefrom, a subject which will be set forth after a droll fashion in the first novel, dedicated by me to the most illustrious lord, Don Federico of Aragon.

Novel the Eleventh

ARGUMENT

JOANNI TORNESE, BY REASON OF HIS JEALOUSY, CAUSES HIS WIFE TO DISGUISE HERSELF IN MAN'S ATTIRE WHENEVER SHE GOES ABROAD WITH HIM; BUT A CERTAIN CAVALIER, HER LOVER, ENJOYS HER IN THE PRESENCE OF A FRIEND OF THE HUSBAND, WHO IN A STATE OF FRENZY TAKES HIS WIFE HOME AFTERWARDS: THE DOINGS OF THE WIFE ARE NOISED ABROAD, AND JOANNI DIES OF VEXATION, WHEREUPON THE WIFE AGAIN MARRIES AND LEADS A MERRY LIFE.

TO THE MOST ILLUSTRIOUS PRINCE, DON FEDERICO D'ARAGONA, THE SECOND SON OF THE KING.*

EXORDIUM

MY most goodly prince, although jealousy has been described by many of our poets as a kind of amorous passion brought into being by the soft and gentle flames of love which has become somewhat excessive, nevertheless, on account of the untoward effects wh'ch arise therefrom, this distemper must be judged as an intolerable punishment, and one only to be borne with the greatest mental and bodily suffering. Wherefore, so harsh and so biting to the taste are the fruits which this poisonous plant produces, and so sharp and cruel is the bitterness thereof, that rarely or never is there to be found one fallen under the sway of it who, while deeming that he will steer clear of the furies of Charybdis, will escape destruction in the whirlpool of the barking Scylla. In

* He was the last king of the Aragonese dynasty who ruled in Naples. The second son of Ferdinand I., he succeeded his nephew Ferdinand II. in 1496. He was deposed in 1501, and died at Tours in 1504.

the novel which follows you will be instructed concerning a new form of jealousy, and a very strange sort of safeguard employed by a foolish and jealous fellow, who was bent not merely on preventing his wife from being regarded with amorous looks by gallants and lovers, but bent also on contriving so that she should not be espied by anyone in feminine dress: and likewise how it happened that, through his own handiwork, she was one day enjoyed as it were under his very eyes by a certain cavalier who was her lover.

THE NARRATIVE

TO come therefore to the matter I propose to deal with, I will tell you that in the times of my most illustrious lord, Duke Filippo Maria Visconti,* there lived in Milan a certain handsome and noble cavalier called by name Messer Ambrosio del Andriani. This same cavalier was young, rich, of very goodly person, and of excellent manners; and, being led by the generous bent of his rare intellect to become acquainted with the dignities and the famous deeds of the various princes of Christendom, he went searching after the same in many places both within and without the bounds of Italy. At last there was brought to him report of the magnificent state and the triumphal feasts which King Alfonso of immortal memory, your grandfather, was accustomed to maintain and to celebrate without intermission in the city of Naples, and on this account he determined to be a witness of these likewise, and thereby to satisfy his desires to the full. So, having put a thousand florins in his purse and furnished himself with horses and servants and raiment worthy of his condition, he took his way towards Naples.

When he had come there, and had well surveyed the many stately quarters of the city and the delightsome surroundings thereof, he came to the conclusion that the

* The last of the Visconti and grandfather of Ippolita of Aragon. He died in 1447. The terms used in speaking of him in this place have been held to imply that Masuccio was at one time in his service.

Naples in which he was now abiding was no less fair than the Naples he had prefigured in his mind. Thus for this reason, and for that which had originally led him thither, he determined in his mind to tarry there, enjoying himself and living merrily as long as the money he had brought with him should serve his needs. It happened that he foregathered with certain gentlemen of Capuana,* and, having been taken by these now to festivals, now into churches, and now to joustings, places where great crowds of ladies were gathered together, he said one day to his companions, after he had well considered the dames around him, that in his opinion the ladies of Naples were better furnished with graceful presence and with womanly worth than rich in superabundant beauty. Whilst he was discoursing in this strain, a certain youth, one of his most intimate companions, Tommaso Caracciolo by name, who chanced to be present, affirmed that what the cavalier had just said was no other than the truth, and added somewhat on his own account, speaking thus: "If it should ever be your fate to catch sight of a young woman living at Nola, the wife of a certain shoemaker named Joanni Tornese, I doubt not at all but that you, following the example of divers others I have already heard speak on the matter, would straightway confess that this young woman is the most beautiful you have ever seen in Italy. But to bring this thing to pass seems to me almost impossible, seeing that the husband keeps her shut up in such fashion that no one, however closely related to her, can ever get sight of her, on account of his unheard-of jealousy, and on account of certain suspicions which have been kindled in his mind from a report that the Lord Duke of Calabria, having been inflamed by the fame of her marvellous beauty, seeks to put her to the proof.

* That is, of the Seggio di Capuana, which was the aristocratic quarter of Naples. The Seggi of Naples and of the other southern cities were relics of the Greek foundation. They were, according to Giannone, "Istoria Civile del Regno di Napoli," particular districts, generally situated somewhere near the gates, in which certain influential families were wont to congregate for social intercourse and for political union. They were practically the same as the *Oratriai* of Athens. In Naples there were four, Capuana, Forcella, Montagna, and Nido—the last a corruption of Nilo.

And if another tale be true which a neighbour of his, who is also a servant of mine, told me for certain (but I know not in sooth whether I ought to lend any credence to the same), you will hear a very strange report concerning her, and this is that the husband, so as not to leave her at home alone in his absence, is in the habit of always taking her with him to whatever place he may visit disguised in man's attire; and thus, without incurring any suspicion, he goes on his way rejoicing, and enjoys the merriest time that is possible for a peasant in this our land. Wherefore, if it would meet your wishes, I would suggest that we might go and make an attempt to get sight of her beauty."

Thereupon, without any farther parley, they set forth in company and betook themselves to the shoemaker's shop. Having come there, Tommaso said: "Master cobbler, have you by chance some pairs of neatly-made shoes which you can show to Messer Ambrosio here?" Whereupon Joanni replied: "Assuredly I have, at your pleasure." And having let enter the cavalier, he made him sit down on a bench, and began to fit certain shoes on his feet. Tommaso, who sought to lengthen out the time of such business, turned to them and said: "Come now, I will go on and despatch some affairs of my own at a place near by, while you are engaged in finding a well-fitting pair of shoes." And excusing himself with these words he went his way, and the shoemaker began forthwith to try the shoes on Messer Ambrosio, keeping his head bent down low as it is necessary for a man to do when engaged on such a task.

Messer Ambrosio in the meantime held his head erect, turning his face around on all sides, for the reason that every thought of his was bent on catching a glimpse of the beautiful mistress of the house; and, as his good fortune would have it, he fixed his eyes upon a little latticed window, and saw at the same the woman herself, who was looking down upon him in the shop below. As he had good space of time wherein to get a clear and perfect sight of her, he looked well at her, and in the end, after he had feasted his eyes on the rich and priceless beauties which were exhibited in her face, it seemed to him that she was in sooth endowed with an excellence of beauty far greater than that which his friend Tommaso had led him to expect. Thus, on account of the length of time which Master Joanni took in settling him with a pair of well-fitting shoes, he found plentiful opportunity not only of scanning closely her face, but also of letting her know by various soft and amorous signs how hotly he was burning with love for her sake.

Now the young woman, who was of a very wary temper, was well assured that, on account of her husband's extreme watchfulness, she would never find an opportunity of satisfying the cavalier's wishes by any act of hers, and, although she was filled with delight at the thought that she herself had seemed pleasant in the sight of such a gracious gentleman, she determined not to exhibit to him any sign of her goodwill or to return him any gracious answer. And in this fashion the fitting on of the shoes at last came to an end; whereupon the cavalier, having paid to the shoemaker double price for his wares, thus addressed him, with a merry look on his face: "In good sooth, I have never in all my life worn shoes which, according to my taste, have fitted me so well as these; wherefore see that you have ready for me every day a fresh pair of the same fashion, for which I will not fail to pay you always the same price." The shoemaker, overjoyed at his good luck, held it to be indeed a most fortunate accident which had led so gallant and magnanimous a cavalier to come into his shop, and, deeming that he might draw great profit from such custom in the future, he said: "So be it, in God's name! and I, on my part, give you promise that each time you come to my shop you shall find yourself served better and better."

In the meantime Messer Ambrosio returned to his friend Tommaso, rejoicing mightily, and telling him in what generous wise his kind fortune had dealt with him at the outset of the adventure, affirming at the same time that the face of this woman was by far the most lovely he had ever seen, but that with regard to the rest of her person he could give no opinion, for the reason that he had been able to get no glimpse thereof. He summed up his speech by begging his friend to give him freely whatever prudent counsel he might have to offer concerning the affair in question. Tommaso, although he harboured but little hope that the business would come to the issue the other desired, began, like the exceptional friend he was, to try to be of some service to Messer Ambrosio, and to sharpen his wits as best he could, without in any way letting drop the discussion or leaving the spot. In their conversation they ran over all such ways and means as fervent lovers are wont to dream of in crises of this sort, and when at last they fixed upon a particular one which seemed to them propitious and fitted to their needs, they proposed to bide their opportunity until the conditions of time and place should prove to be such as would let them conveniently carry their scheme into effect.

Now, seeing that the cavalier followed without fail his purpose of going every day to buy a fresh pair of shoes at the wonted price, it happened that the shoemaker, in order to lure him on to further spending, began to address him in yet more servile fashion, and would now and again invite him in the morning to partake of a light collation in a private apartment he had at the back of his shop, the cavalier feeling no small gratification at these blandishments. The friendship thus begun between the two men continued, and when the day of Santa Catarina had come, a day upon which great crowds of people are wont to betake themselves to Formello, Messer Ambrosio began to walk up and down in front of the Castello,* his lodging being very near thereto, and to speculate as to whether he might catch sight of Joanni Tornese at the festival, with his fair wife arrayed in the fashion already noticed. He had not waited there long when he espied from a distance Joanni Tornese with a young scholar leaning on his arm coming towards him; whereupon he straightway understood that the thing upon which he had already reckoned had indeed come to pass.

Now, as Joanni was going along, it chanced that there met him on the way a very close friend and gossip of his, and as they walked on in company this latter demanded to know who might be the young man he had with him;

* The Castello Capuano, which was built by the Hohenstaufens, and was their principal residence. Opposite to it is the church of Santa Catarina a Formello.

whereupon Joanni answered him, as he had answered divers others before, that the youth was a brother-in-law of his, a student of medicine from Nola, who had come thither on a visit to his sister. Whilst they were talking in this strain they came to the spot where the cavalier was walking backwards and forwards, and after they had all saluted him by doffing their caps, and had been saluted by him in return, he fixed his eyes steadfastly on the face of the young scholar, and was soon well assured that the one he saw was she whom he had been awaiting with such keen desire. Then, with a joyful look on his face, he asked them whither they were bound, and they replied that they were on their way to Santa Catarina; whereupon Messer Ambrosio, having joined himself to their company, went along with them, and in the course of the way spake thus: "And I too on my part had purposed to go thither, and I was tarrying here by myself, awaiting the coming of my servants or of certain of my acquaintances who might bear me company; but, seeing that none of them have come, I will go with you." Then, having set out all together on their way, they arrived at last at the place where the festival was being celebrated, and found there assembled a vast crowd of people. On this account the cavalier had now and again a chance of pressing the hand of the young scholar to let her know clearly that he had recognized her, and when she, knowing perfectly well who he was, made answer to him in the same fashion, it seemed to him that his wishes were about to be fully accomplished, and he was satisfied beyond measure thereanent.

Early that same morning Messer Ambrosio had given full instructions to the host with whom he lodged as to everything that was necessary to be said and done for the carrying out of the project he had in hand, and had likewise despatched all his servants on various errands, so that not one of them would be seen until late in the day, Therefore he kept company with these people until the festival had come to an end, and then took his way back with them towards his lodging. When they had arrived in front of the house where he was staying, he took Joanni by the hand and began to speak to him in these words: "Good maestro, you have so often bidden me to your board, and have done me so much honour in your own house, that now it seems to me right and seemly that you, together with your companions, should stay here and take your breakfast with me this morning, although I am a stranger in these parts." Joanni, who, as we have heard before, was of a very jealous temper, and feared the very birds of the air for his wife's sake no less than men, felt very little in the humour to take her into an inn, albeit she had changed her woman's garb for that of a man. So more than once he refused the proffered invitation, and demurred to accept it; but at last, moved by the fear of giving offence to his friend, and urged on by the eager persuasions and promptings of his worthy gossip, he was induced to accede to Messer Ambrosio's request.

When all the company had gone together up to a small terrace where they found ready prepared a well-decked table, the cavalier called for the landlord forthwith, and demanded of him what had become of all his servants; whereupon the host answered and said that they were all gone to the market to buy oats and fodder. Hearing this, Messer Ambrosio feigned to be mightily disturbed, and said: "Though they should all be hanged by the neck we will carry out the affair we have in hand; wherefore do you have a care to give us something of the best for our repast." To this the host made answer in words which had been previously settled: "Messere, I have here prepared no delicate viands of the sort that would suit your taste." "How is that, you lazy rascal?" cried the cavalier. "In sooth I have a good mind to scoop out your eyes with this very hand. I have spent in your house more than two hundred florins, and now that I have brought hither with me these friends of mine, at whose hands I have received a thousand tokens of honour and kindness, you are not ashamed to tell me that you have nothing that is fit for us to eat." Whereupon the host, feigning to be frightened out of his wits, answered: "Do not be angry, messere, for were the king himself in the house you should be served straightway." But the cavaeier, turning towards him in a furious rage, said to him: "Be off with you, then, beast that you are, and see that you put to roast for me some of the best capons you have." The landlord forthwith departed to carry out these orders, and the cavalier still kept up the show of being in a raging mood; whereupon his guests exhorted him to have patience, forasmuch as in any case he might, without fail, regard them as his devoted servants. Messer Ambrosio thanked them kindly and said: "In sooth, I am well minded to hang up one or other of these varlets of mine, when they shall come back, for having left me, as you see, alone by myself all day; and this over and beyond the failure of his duty on the part of the landlord."

Now Joanni saw nothing of the snare which lay hidden beneath these words; so, in order to appease him and to show himself willing to do aught which would gratify him' he said: "Is there anything you want, for we too all hold ourselves as being bound to serve you?" To this Messer Ambrosio replied: "And I look upon you as my brothers; but it happens to-day that I am in want of a little sauce or relish which is called mustard; indeed, I am in such a humour this morning that I could not eat roast meat without some of the same therewith. One of my servants knows the place where they sell it at a fair price and good in quality—somewhere, I think, in the old market. Now, seeing that I have no one here to send for this mustard, how can I be otherwise than angry with my servants on account of this fault of theirs?" Joanni had already begun to be somewhat out of humour with himself with regard to the offer of service he had made, for he would assuredly have felt monstrously ill at ease at leaving his wife alone for so long a time. Wherefore, without making any other proposition, he kept his tongue between his teeth. Messer Ambrosio, seeing the course things were taking, turned towards Joanni and spake thus: "Ah, my good maestro, if the task will not be very irksome to you, I beg you that you will go fetch for me this sauce, and by the time you shall have come back our dinner will be ready."

Poor Joanni as he listened was mightily ill-pleased, but it seemed to him that he would be behaving in an unseemly fashion were he to refuse to do so slight a service. And again he searched his brains in vain for any plausible excuse he might advance why he should take his wife along with him. Wherefore, not being able to hit upon any safeguard other than the help of his gossip, he went up to him and in a whisper recommended the young scholar to his care; and then, having taken from the table a sauceboat, he flew as quickly as he could to fetch the sauce. The cavalier, as soon as he saw that he was gone, turned towards the gossip who had been left on guard, and cried out: "Alas! after all I have forgotten the best part of what I wanted to tell him." Said the gossip: "And what do you still want?" Then the cavalier answered: "I wanted some oranges, but in my rage I quite forgot to tell Joanni of my need." The other replied, deeming the request to be made in good faith: "I myself will go and fetch you some forthwith, for as it happens I have some of the finest oranges in the world at my shop, which were brought to me yesterday from Salerno."

Having thus spoken, he forthwith went on his errand; whereupon Messer Ambrosio, being left alone with the young woman, and thinking there was no time to be lost, took her by the hand, and said: "And now, master physician, I am minded to tell you privily concerning a certain ailment with which I am troubled." Then, having led her aside into a chamber and taken her up to the bed which was therein, after that weak demur and resistance which those whose desire is solely towards practice of this kind are accustomed to put forward, they made upon the swiftest wings of desire a flight of supremest rapture, and scarcely was this finished when the gossip came back with the oranges. Finding the chamber door locked, he marvelled greatly within himself thereat, and having put his eye to a chink which he discovered, he beheld the cavalier, after he had taken his pleasure with the young woman, holding her in his arms, and giving her many secret and tender kisses. This thing which he saw caused him no little trouble, and, having turned himself away with an indignant face, he was assailed with the thought that the cavalier, overcome by nefarious vice, had borne himself lasciviously towards the fair young scholar who had been left in his keeping.

Accordingly he went down to the entrance door, where he met Joanni; and the latter, not seeing his wife in company with the gossip, at once asked where his brother-in-law, the young scholar, might be, bearing himself the while like a man stunned and almost beside himself. To him the gossip answered in the following words: "Would to God that I had bitten out my tongue this morning, rather than have persuaded you to tarry in this place, forasmuch as I have now no longer any faith in that cavalier with whom you are on such intimate footing. At first, indeed, I reckoned him to be a man endowed with all the virtues, but I have lately discovered him to be as great a villain as ever lived." "Alas!" cried Joanni, "and what may have happened?" The other answered: "May God send him a bad year, forasmuch as this man, putting in practice the same guileful tricks by which he induced you to leave this place, also despatched me to fetch these oranges; and when, on my return, I found him locked in the bedchamber with your brother-in-law, I played the spy upon him through a chink of the door, and found that he was dealing with the young scholar as though with a fair and beautiful woman."

When poor Joanni heard this terrible news, he stood like a man who is neither dead nor alive, overwhelmed with confusion and quite beside himself. In this humour he went upstairs, where he found the cavalier seated at the table, and holding the young scholar in conversation as if nothing out of reason had happened. Then, turning towards him, and carried away by his grief and anger, he said, in a voice broken by sobs: "By my faith, sir, the Milanese courtesy* which you have shown towards me has indeed been great. But, seeing that you have been fain to eat the meat without waiting for the sauce, you shall now relish the sauce as best you may without ever again enjoying another taste of such a dish." Then Joanni, having dashed the sauceboat down on the table and seized his wife by the hand in a tempest of rage, cried: "Get up now, in the devil's name, and let us return home, seeing that we have paid our shot† without eating our

* Orig., *una gran cortesia Milanese.*

† Orig., *che senza mangiare noi avemo pagato lo scotto.*

meat, and I, to make things worse, have brought you the sauce." Then, threatening her with a downright blow, he went his way with her.

The gossip who did not fathom the depth of the inward grief of Joanni, followed him down the stairs and kept on reproaching him that he should have cast so great an ignominy upon so distinguished a man, and all for the sake of a boy. "What can it matter? Do you mean to say you think he will become with child? Well, if it is done, it is done, and what need was there to fall into so grave an error, and to lose such a friend on account of so small an offence." But Joanni, as he made his way with hasty steps, was thinking of naught else than how he might convey his wife back to his house, and for this reason, and because of the fierce anger which was raging within him, he did not trouble to give his gossip a word in reply. The good gossip, however, would not on this account give over his reproaches, but kept on urging him straightway to repair the fault which he had committed on such trifling ground of offence. At last his molestations became more than Joanni could bear, so, all trembling with rage, he spake to his gossip thus: "Alas! my gossip, it will not be any fault of yours if I do not this morning curse God and all those who dwell in the courts of Paradise. Cannot you see that this is my wife?" "But how can that be?" said the other. "Why should you take her about with you in this fashion?" Thereupon Joanni, with plentiful tears, told him the reason why he had acted in this wise.

The gossip, who was a shrewd fellow, first read Joanni a severe lesson for his folly, and then went on to counsel him thus: "My Joanni, you were indeed ill-advised; and, on account of the crazy scheme you fashioned, a heavy and a deserved punishment has fallen upon you. You wanted to jump out of the frying-pan and you have fallen into the fire.* Alas! my poor fellow! How is it that you were not warned how wicked and corrupt the world is grown in these our days, and that it is much more difficult to keep guard over pretty boys than over women, and especially over such an one as this, who is in truth a lure for these hawks incarnate? In good sooth I have wondered a thousand

* Orig., *cercasti saltare della patella per dare in su la brasa.*

times this morning that she was not snatched away from your arms. But now that the thing is done, and that you can blame no one thereanent except your own self, I will say that it befell you through your ill luck, and that in the future you had better make use of some other safeguard. If God has given you a woman for a wife it is not meet that you should seek to transform her into a man. I do not say that you should neglect to use whatever guard and precaution may be necessary with a young and beautiful woman, but of a surety you ought not to employ methods so unheard-of and so strange. In the end, forsooth, they will be found of little advantage; for when wives are fully minded to deceive their husbands, there never has been found in human ingenuity any precaution which has availed aught for the frustration of their intention. And be well assured that you are not the first, nor will you be the last, to receive buffets of this kind. Do but take an example from those men of eminent worth who have often fallen into snares like this. These prudently hide their mishaps whenever they can, so as not to add a lasting shame to the grief they feel already."

Thus, with exhortations and arguments such as these, and with divers others to boot, the good gossip went with Joanni as far as his house, pacifying him as best he could, and having left him there—for the reason that he saw no cause why he himself should be counted in the number of the duped ones—he made his way as quickly as he might back to the inn, where, having found the cavalier in the company of his good friend Tommaso, he joined himself to the party, and they all together made merry over the joke that had been played and over the dinner which had been ordered. Joanni, after long weeping and lamentation, died of grief; whereupon his wife, glad to be rid of him, married again, and tasted all the pleasures which belong to blooming youth without being transformed from her own and most comely seeming.

MASUCCIO.

THE jest which was put upon Joanni Tornese for having let go abroad his wife disguised as a man induces me to go on from the beginning I have made in similar strain, and to tell of another most artful trick played by one of our Salernitans upon a certain host who was as inordinately jealous of his wife—a story which will differ indeed somewhat from the one I have just told, inasmuch as in it the lover put on the disguise of woman's attire. This lover, for the reason that all other methods of putting into execution his longed-for project were denied to him, brought his marvellous craft into action in such fashion that the husband himself was induced to conduct him to the very bed in which he afterwards lay with the wife, over whom the closest watch was kept. For the reason, however, that this husband never in after times came to know aught of what had occurred, he was not bound to let his life come to an end therefor, as was the case with the wretched Joanni, who, as soon as he was aware of the shame which had been put upon him, died outright.

THE END OF THE ELEVENTH NOVEL.

Novel the Twelfth

ARGUMENT

A CERTAIN YOUTH, BEING ENAMOURED OF THE WIFE OF AN INNKEEPER, PUTS ON THE GARB OF A WIDOW WOMAN, AND ARRIVES ONE NIGHT WITH ALL HIS ATTENDANTS AT THE HOUSE OF THE INNKEEPER AFORESAID. THE HOST, INDUCED BY PLAUSIBLE ARGUMENTS, PUTS THE PRETENDED WIDOW TO BED WITH HIS WIFE, WHO, AFTER WITHSTANDING SOMEWHAT, TAKES PLEASURE WITH HER LOVER, AND THE HOST, UNWITTING OF WHAT HAS BEFALLEN, IS PAID TWOFOLD.

TO THE EXCELLENT SIGNOR FEDERICO DAVOLOS,* THE MOST WORSHIPFUL COUNT AND CHAMBERLAIN.

EXORDIUM

I AM persuaded, excellent and most virtuous signor, that if we take into account the chief philosophizing investigators of those higher intelligences which guide the vicissitudes of the heavens and the order of the planets, as well as the great inventors and adepts who, working both by argument and judgment, deal with every product of Nature—I say, if we take the aforesaid, each one by himself or all together, we shall find that they have never been endowed with such subtlety of intellect and lively ingenuity as Love, our great lord, has lent and will for ever lend to the better part of those who in their fervent passion follow the glorious course of his victorious banner. And in sooth those who consider well how amazing, and altogether beyond comprehension, are the wiles of wicked women when they are minded to play

* He was the husband of the lady to whom Novel XXI. is dedicated. He came from Spain to the service of Alfonso the Magnanimous, with whom he was a prime favourite.

THE WIFE OF THE AMALFITAN.

FROM A DRAWING BY E. R. HUGHES. (Mas., Nov. xii., v. i.)

their husbands false, will likewise find therein no small reason for wonderment. Wherefore we may assuredly give judgment and affirm that, in cases where the foresight of a crafty lover is conjoined with the evil nature of a wary woman, no human knowledge or circumspection will ever be found to supply a sufficient rampart against it. All this, my most prudent signor, you will be able to understand on your own part, and you may likewise give instruction, the truth of which no one can call in question, anent the same to all the rest of mankind now living on earth.

THE NARRATIVE

IN the years when this our city of Salerno was ruled by the sway of that glorious Pope, Martin V.,* the traffic of the place increased to a mighty volume, and merchandize in enormous quantities was brought thither without ceasing from every nation under the sun. On this account a vast number of outland handicraftsmen and others gathered together there and took up their abode, and amongst the rest came a certain worthy fellow from Amalfi, called by name Trifone, who was minded to follow the calling of an innkeeper in his new home. He brought with him his wife, a young woman endowed with no small beauty, and hired an inn in the street of our Seggio del Campo,† and likewise acquired another house in the quarter of the Porta Nova, situated in a very decent and secluded court—a spot near which no one

* Ottavio Colonna, elected pope at the Council of Constance in 1417, under the title of Martin V. His election is a landmark in the history of the papacy, inasmuch as it put an end to the Great Schism, John XXIII., Benedict XIII., and Gregory XII. being deposed in his favour. In one of her many disputes with Sforza, Joanna II. conferred Salerno upon Antonio Colonna, who held the city in the name of his uncle the Pope, by way of enlisting the papal influence on her side. Her successor, Alfonso of Aragon, took the city from the Colonnas and gave it to Raimondo Orsini.

† Salerno, like Naples, was divided into Seggi. The Seggio del Campo was Masuccio's own quarter of the city.

would pass unless he should have some colourable reason therefor.

After he had duly settled his wife and his family in the aforesaid house, it happened that a certain gentleman of our city of the most honourable lineage, whose name for many good reasons I have determined not to disclose in this place, fell deeply in love with this young woman, the wife of Trifone. Now this gentleman, who in sooth was tormented with the fiercest pricks that ever lover felt, could devise no method whereby he might find some place in which he might satisfy his desires; nor was he bold enough, seeing in what close custody the over-jealous husband kept his wife, to patch up a conspiracy with her in order to procure their foregathering. Wherefore he determined to employ in this affair the arts of a certain old woman who was well known to him, one of those pedlars who go wandering about the streets offering for sale such trifles and gewgaws as ladies love. One day, after he had made his wishes known to her, and given her all necessary instructions for the forwarding of the same—together with promises of liberal reward in case of success—she, who was both ready and anxious to serve him, went her way to set about the business. After having traversed divers of the quarters of the city she came at last to the one in which the young woman dwelt, and having come there, she addressed now this woman and now that, offering her wares for sale the while, until at last she approached the door where stood the innkeeper's wife; whereupon, without letting anyone hear what she said, she spake thus: "And you, my pretty lady, cannot I sell you any of my dainty wares? I know full well that if I were as young and handsome as you are I would not fail to buy some new thing every day, and thus, by letting art improve what Nature made, render myself beautiful beyond compare." "Alas!" cried the young woman, "you only wish to make a jest of me." Then replied the pedlar, "By the Lord, I speak no more than the truth when I declare that there is a rumour spread through all the parts hereabout that you are by far the most beautiful woman in the kingdom. And although I heard certain gentlewomen, in a house where I chanced to be of late, speak in envious and unreasonable wise in disparagement of your beauty (so that they might thereby commend their own) and declare that you were not of high birth, and divers other things of a like character—remarks such as women of this class are wont to utter, forasmuch as their eyes are ever ready to start out of their heads when they espy beauty in one of our condition, nevertheless there was present a young man of a noble house (I know not whether you may have acquaintance with him), who made answer to them in such terms as their speech deserved, and ended by declaring that, as far as beauty was concerned, not one of them was worthy to pull off your shoes."

The young woman, when she listened to these words, replied: "God help them then! and, if it be not unseemly to ask, it would please me mightily to know the names of these said gentlewomen, and also that of the noble youth who spoke in my defence." The old woman, who was all the time craftily spreading her nets, replied: "I will not just now let you know the names of these ladies, forasmuch as I am not minded to speak ill of anyone, but I feel I need not hold back from you the name of the young man." And then, without waiting farther speech from the other, she gave both his name and his family, and added: "But what words he spake to me over and beyond what I have told you, I do not mean to reveal to you unless you shall first swear to me that you will hold them secret."

The young woman, after the fashion of her sex, was altogether overborne with curiosity to know what these words might be, and gave her promise never to reveal them to anyone; whereupon the crone, using the deepest cunning the while, began to speak in this wise: "My daughter, I would in sooth be unwilling to counsel you in any matter which might perchance come to an issue fraught with dishonour to you, and, besides, this I would remark that it is not wise to give ear to everything men may say. He indeed told me that he loves you more than he loves himself; that he is enamoured of you in such fashion—so he swore—that he had, for love of you, lost both his sleep and his appetite as well, and was consumed like a burning taper. And although I have reminded you, and still remind you, that it behoves you to keep guard over your honour and your good name, than which there is no more precious possession in all the world, still I cannot keep silent my tongue and hold back from telling you that, as I view it, you could commit no more heinous sin than let such a youth as this die of his pain. Indeed, it seems still worse, when one considers how praiseworthy and amiable are his ways; how well-mannered he is, how liberal, and how honest. He was, in sooth, most anxious to give me a pretty little ring, in order that I might convey the same to you on his behalf; but I, being doubtful about your feelings towards him, told him I could not, at present, do such a thing. If you only knew what it is that he desires of you so ardently, I am assured you might easily find a way of granting it to him without letting your honour suffer at all thereby. He declares to me that he asks for naught else than that you should be willing to accept his love; that, as a reward for this devotion of his, you should show some disposition to give him a little love in return; and that, if at any time he should send you some small gift, you will deign to accept the same and to wear it for his sake. Now, my daughter, prayers like these do not seem to me to be very difficult to grant, and you, forsooth, ought to give ear to them sooner than any other young woman I know, so that you may not let your youth slip by without plucking some of the flowers thereof, remembering always that, for the sake of your honour, you are forbidden to taste its luscious fruits."

The young woman, when she listened to these tender words, tricked out with so many specious arguments by the cunning go-between, felt that she was, as it were, almost constrained by necessity to take the young man for her lover, albeit she was most honest by nature and in no wise disposed to overstep the bounds of her innate goodness. Wherefore, turning to the old woman, she spake to her thus: "Come now, Madonna, I will let you go back to the gentleman and tell him that for love of his worth and goodness I am willing to accept him as my one and only admirer, but let him be well assured that this is all he need ever expect to get from me. Tell him, likewise, to have good heed that he keep the matter a secret, and not fall into the error which besets most young men, who, as soon as they find themselves amongst their merry companions, go boasting, not only of the things they do, but also of the things they have never done and never seen. Tell him, too, that I would sooner die than that this matter should come to the knowledge of my husband, who is more jealous than any other man in the world."

When she heard this the crone was satisfied that in this first essay of hers she had worked to some good purpose, marking that the affair was certainly moving in the right direction; so she made answer to the young woman in this wise: "My daughter, your words are indeed most prudent; but I would wish you to know that this young man, amongst his other remarkable virtues, is gifted with a most secretive nature, and, as God may let me make a good end, I swear that when he laid bare this secret of his to me, he not only made me promise him with more than a hundred oaths that I would never let it become known to anyone, but also on his own part trembled like a reed, and the colour of his face took to itself a thousand varying hues with every moment that passed. Wherefore I beg you not to let any doubt as to his secrecy, keep you back from giving him your love, for of a surety the day will come when you will pique yourself on having the handsomest and the worthiest gallant in the world, and one, moreover, upon whose silence and secrecy you may fully rely. And although the favour which you here concede to him may seem a great one—and indeed you have given him all he asked—nevertheless I will not cease to call up in your mind the thought of the loss you will suffer if you should thus persist in letting waste your flowering youth in such wretched fashion. If, forsooth, ill fortune and the action of your parents have been the means of giving you so ugly and so baseborn a man for your husband, that is no reason why you should insist on being your own enemy; nay, it is rather a cause why you should cast about to find some means of giving yourself pleasure, seeing that there is no grief so bitter as the regret of old age over the neglected opportunities of youth." And then, putting on an air somewhat of mystery, she went on, saying: "Do you know what I will say to him as coming from you? I will tell him that it will be all his own fault if he does not find out for himself some way by which you and he may foregather."

To these words of the crone the young woman replied, putting on some show of indignation as she spoke: "By my faith, you will do well to have a care that you tell him no such words as these. It will suffice well enough if you tell him those which I directed you to bear to him and no more." Then said the old woman: "I beseech you that you will not be angry with me, nor wonder why it is that I am thus importunate; but I swear to you, by the sign of the cross* which I now make, that if I should not bear back to him some good news he will assuredly make an end of himself. However, I now recommend him to you as much as ever I can; and, in order that he may lend belief to the gracious answer you have given me to bear to him, I now beg you to take care to let yourself be seen by him to-morrow in the church of Saint Agostino, and when he shall rub his nose in this wise and say to you, 'I commend myself to you,' you shall reply to him as you brush your hair aside from your face, 'And I myself to you likewise.' In such fashion you shall pass the time until Fortune shall send you a better way of enjoyment." To this the young woman answered: "And I, too, on my part, will be generous to him and commend myself to him a thousand times. Tell him to come to-morrow morning, and tell him likewise that I cannot remain long in the church."

Therefore, when the crone had gone her way, the young woman stood some time letting fresh fancies engage her heart, in which, by reason of the impressive words she had just listened to, she seemed to feel a worm gnawing without ceasing. The old woman went straightway in search of the lover, and when she had found him she told him, point by point, everything that had happened, and what had been the result of her embassy. The youth, hugely delighted at the news she brought to him, was early astir the following morning, and went without delay to the appointed spot, where he at once espied the young woman, who had made herself even more lovely than she was as she stood, fresh from the hand of nature. And not only did

* *Orig., io ti giuro per questa croce.*

he get from her a greeting vastly more gracious than ladies are wont to give on such occasions, but he was also granted the promised answer to his covenanted signal; wherefore he found himself in such a state of joy and delight as he had never before known.

To pass briefly over the affair, the lady at last left the church, and the lover made his way home to ponder and to consider in what fashion it would be granted to him to pluck that supreme fruit of love which he so greatly desired, and having run over many and various expedients for the compassing of this end, he settled at last after much deliberation upon a certain one. By this he determined that, happen what might, he would make his way into her house in such a manner that she should perforce grant him that boon which he desired beyond anything else in the world, and indeed had already begun to taste in anticipation. Having laid bare his plan to certain gentlemen of Capuana,* who had come into the city to spend the holy season with the archbishop, who was their kinsman, they sent off late one evening a number of mules and horses great enough for the purpose they had in view to a certain spot outside the city. Then, when the lover, in the garb of a widow woman, and wearing a riding-hood and a bonnet, and two other youths similarly disguised in women's garb, had gone thither and duly mounted the pack-horses which had been prepared for them, they took their way, accompanied by the rest of the party on horseback, towards the city as soon as the night had fallen.

Now when they arrived at the Seggio del Campo they found that the host of the inn aforesaid, as soon as he heard the trampling of the horses, came out after the fashion of hosts and said to them: "Sirs, are you minded to take up your lodging here?" And to this one of the company replied: "In sooth we are. Have you good stalls for our beasts and beds for ourselves?" "Indeed, sir, I have," the host answered; "you have but to dismount and you will be served in the best fashion." The one who had spoken then drew the host aside and said to him: "See good host, the excellent character you bear has led us to seek your roof to-night; nevertheless, we find it fitting to

* Of the Seggio di Capuana in Naples.

demand of you that guarantee of security which the exigencies of our present affairs demand; for you must know that we have here with us the daughter of the Count of Sinopoli, who has recently been left a widow through the death of the late Messer Gorello Caracciolo, her husband. Now we are at present conducting her back, in her mourning, as you see, to her father's house, and we are unwilling for the sake of decency to allow her to sleep at an inn this night, should it be found possible to bestow her elsewhere. Wherefore, out of your courtesy, we beg you that you will do your best to find some worthy woman with whom she may take her lodgment this night, together with the two maids who attend upon her; and if you shall do this we will pay you for such accommodation double what it may be worth."

To him the host replied, saying: "My lord, I know no one in this quarter of the city who is of condition good enough to do this thing which you ask. Nevertheless, I will offer to do for you all that lies within my power. The truth is, that my own house, where my wife, who is a very young woman, resides, is not far distant from here; wherefore, if it be pleasing to you, the lady might well lodge with her. As to the payment for the same, that shall be left to your pleasure." Whereupon the gentleman, turning to the widow lady, said: "You see, Madonna Francesca, how it is. It seems to me that you will be vastly better lodged in the house of this worthy man in the company of his wife and of your maids than here with us in the inn." Then the lady, with a low voice, answered that she was quite content with what had been suggested, and the host, having left them in charge of a youth who would point out to them the way, ran forward quickly to the house. When he came there he summoned his wife, and gave her orders that she should, as quickly as she could, get the bedchamber in order, forasmuch as a certain countess, a widow still in her first youth, must needs find lodging with them for the night. The young woman, whose thoughts were far removed from all deceit and trickery, made answer to her husband in the sincerity of her heart: "My husband, you know what the house is like. Nevertheless, I will do all that is possible." Then said the husband: "See that the place be put in readiness for her forthwith, and prepare for her warm water with perfume thereto; for she will assuredly have great need of the same, seeing that she is covered with mud of the roads."

In the meantime the lady, escorted by two gentlemen of the company, had arrived at the door, and the two, having let her dismount from the saddle and taken her in their arms, led her into the bedchamber, the two attendant maids following after them. As soon as she had come into the room she made a sign that she was minded to undress herself, and straightway gave dismissal to those who had come in with her. The host, when he perceived what she did, felt that it became him not to remain; for which reason he, turning towards his wife, thus addressed her: "I commit the service due to this lady into your hands; wherefore look narrowly that everything be daintily prepared for her supper and for her night's rest. See, too, that you lock yourselves securely within the house. I meantime will go back to the inn to see to the wants of her followers and of the other guests who await me there." And having placed these commands upon her he went his way, and for their better safeguarding he locked them in the house from the outside, and having given the key of the door to one of the lady's attendants, he went back with them towards the inn.

Thus the young woman was at last left alone with her lover, and, holding him in very truth to be a woman like herself, she was mightily eager to be of some service in helping the so-called lady to disarray herself, and it seemed as if it were a thousand years before she could indeed discover whether or not the lady was comely to look upon. She took away with her own hands the gear which concealed the stranger's face, and then, after she had gazed upon the same attentively, and had remarked therein somewhat of the seeming of her lover, she drew back quickly, overcome with shame and timidity. Now he, when he perceived that she stood thus confounded, began to be fearful lest there might befall some danger of the sort which so often arises through the imprudence of young women; so he straightway determined that the season had now come when she might be made privy to the trick he had devised. So, catching her by the hand, he folded her in his arms, and began to speak to her in the following words; "O sweetest life of mine, I am in truth your faithful and constant lover, and I have come hither to you in this fashion because, what with the great jealousy of your husband on the one part, and your own exceeding honesty on the other, every way of accomplishing my wishes seemed blocked to me, save and except this one alone, which was disclosed and laid open to me by Love, our sovereign lord. For the reason that I have been led by him, as you see, into your sweet embraces, I implore you that, for the sake of the good name of both of us, and for our gratification as well, that you should, in discreet and cautious wise, allow me to have delight of the passionate ardours which now consume me, and turn towards your one and most devoted servant with all the concord and quietness which prudent women use, so that we together may pluck those sweet and most pleasant joys which are the fruit of our youth."

The young woman, what though she was sorely angered at what had been done, and more than once made trial to free herself from her lover's embrace, knew, nevertheless, that if she should cry out for help it would only serve to bring lasting disgrace upon her. Moreover, from the beginning she had been kindly affected towards the young man; so she straightway took counsel with herself, and made up her mind to give him what, peradventure, she would not have refused him had she been quite free to follow her own wishes, and turning towards him said: "As my husband's want of wit has proved to be the means of bringing you here, I do not mean to drive you away, and thereby run into disgrace which will last my life and then, since I have been, as it were, given into your hands, it seems to me that there is naught left for me to say, but to beg you, in the name of heaven and of that virtue to which your nobility binds you, that you will have good care of my honour if you satisfy your desires with me." The lover rejoiced greatly when he listened to these words, and kissed her passionately, telling her at the same time there was no need for her to doubt or fear at all, forasmuch as he would be ever ready to sell his own life, should such a thing be necessary, for the preservation of her honour and good fame.

Then, after he had subdued her spirit with this and with divers other gentle and flattering speeches, these two lovers, before they moved from the spot where they were, tasted the first fruit of their love; and then, when they had refreshed themselves with a delicate repast, and gone to bed together, they spent the whole night in delightful wise, being overcome with desire the one for the other. Moreover, they came to an understanding together, in order that they might in the future compass the satisfying of their desire in less hazardous wise, and, when the daylight broke in the east, the gentlemen who were escorting the newly-made countess having got in order their pack-horse train, and found their lady ready dressed for the road, set her on horse-back at once, and paid the good host a sum of money much greater than was his due. And, albeit they made as if they were journeying towards Calabria, they nevertheless went back that same night to their homes joking and making merry not a little. Lastly, the lover gave a very generous guerdon to the crone who had acted as go-between, and for a long time tasted much pleasure and delight in the company of the young woman. And to such a happy fate may Love lead you, my most worthy signor, whenever you may especially desire to partake of the same.*

MASUCCIO

THE trick which was put upon the Amalfitan innkeeper may in sooth be set down as very singular and very neat as well. The fellow, moreover, must have been beyond measure stupid to have shown such complaisance. And I doubt not that we shall find many ladies of the sort who are chary of their words, and are over-nice in finding fault† in order that they may be rated as prudent dames, who will declare that if they should ever hap-

* There is perhaps no other phrase in the "Novellino" which is so manifest a borrowing from Boccaccio as this.

† Orig., *le quali parlano raro e sputano tondo.*

pen to fall into such a case as was the young woman's I have just described, they would sooner kill themselves than consent to yield to the wishes of their lover. Wherefore I know not for the moment how to make answer to such as these, except to pray to God that He will not grant to them such great favour as to bring them into the condition of having that thing forced upon them which they most earnestly desire above aught else. But in sooth their wisdom and forecast are so great that they must rarely find themselves brought into such straits and perils as these; moreover, they are generally most studious to let follow whatever working the lover may desire, concerning which matter I will speak more at length in another place.

But what shall we say of the noteworthy craft and the masterly methods discovered by the old crone who acted as go-between by which the lover won his way into the good graces of his mistress? We might in sooth say much thereanent; but, because in this our time the art of the pander has come to be such a fine and subtle one that not only old people, but very young ones as well, are found who can ply the same most skilfully even in their sleep, I will hold my peace, and say no more about it. Wherefore, passing on to a fresh subject, I will tell a story of another noteworthy cheat put upon the person of a governor of our city, a native of the Marches, by a young Salernitan. This jest, forsooth, was so hugely fine and facetious that even now as I write thereanent I cannot in any way keep back my laughter; and that it is true many who are now alive in our city can bear me witness.

THE END OF THE TWELFTH NOVEL.

Novel the Thirteenth

ARGUMENT

PANDOLFO D'ASCARI IS MADE GOVERNOR OF SALERNO. HE TAKES A WIFE AND FAILS IN HIS DUTY TOWARDS HER. A CERTAIN YOUTH OF THE CITY BECOMES ENAMOURED OF HER, AND PLAYS A STRANGE JEST IN THE MATTER OF A SWORD OF HIS. ONE DAY THE GOVERNOR'S WATCH CAPTURES THIS YOUNG MAN AND TAKES HIM BEFORE THE COURT, WHEREUPON THE SWORD AFORESAID IS DISPLAYED TO VIEW, THE GOVERNOR'S WIFE BEING PRESENT. THE GOVERNOR IS MIGHTILY INCENSED AND BANISHES THE YOUNG MAN; BUT, THE STORY BEING NOISED ABROAD IN THE CITY, THE GOVERNOR DIES OF VEXATION, WHEREUPON THE YOUNG WIFE TAKES HER PLEASURE WITH HER LOVER.

TO THAT MOST EXCELLENT GENTLEMAN, BERNARDO SANSEVERINO, CONTE DI LAURIA*

EXORDIUM

IF, my most excellent and worthy sir, I have been somewhat remiss in writing to you up to this present time, it has been for no other reason than because I am of opinion that the matter with which I have heretofore busied myself, would not only have failed to give you any pleasure, but would even have called up in your mind something of irksomeness or distaste. Wherefore, in order to avoid any such unseemliness as the aforesaid, I have at last found out a fashion of writing which will, I doubt not, assure me that you will always in the future

* He was a younger son of Roberto di Sanseverino, and perished in the conspiracy of the barons. Masuccio has probably given him a wrong title as Porzio speaks of "Barnaba, Conte di Lauria" ("Congiura de Baroni," p. 50; Florence, 1884).

extend towards me that accustomed courtesy of yours in benevolent and pleasing wise. Therefore I will let you read in the following novel concerning the flout which a certain governor of our city, a man jealous beyond all bounds, had to endure—a jest which in the end brought upon him great loss and injury. In this, too, you will be able to judge clearly how dangerous and foolish an undertaking it is to go about equipped with arms which are of no service, and to try to battle with weakly muscles against that poisonous viper which is able to hold its own even in circumstances of the greatest peril. Assuredly likewise those, to whom both powder and flint are lacking, will find it a sorely difficult task to fight against the inexpugnable rocks. And although the lesson I teach may not in any way concern yourself, for the reason that, however great the quantity of artillery that might be needed for any enterprise, you would always find yourself most excellently furnished with the same, nevertheless it ought not to be in any way irksome to you, for that I now bring before you good and valid proof of this same fact: to learn how to provide for the future, and especially to secure yourself against the instability of fickle fortune, so that such mischance as happened to the governor aforesaid may never happen to you.

THE NARRATIVE

IT was formerly the custom of our princes of the house of Orsini* to send us here as a governor a creature of the sort which is, in sooth, vastly more familiar with the management and feeding of cattle than in the exercise of the functions of a magistrate. On this account they once sent us, amongst the rest, a certain man from the Marches, Pandolfo d'Ascari by name, one not only penurious, as is the disposition of all his countrymen, but miserly beyond all measure. Now this governor brought with him a great crowd of ill-disciplined underlings, very

* For the grant of Salerno to the Orsini, see note, p. 171, to Novel XII. After the rebellion of Felice Orsini the lordship of the place was given to Roberto di Sanseverino, Count of Marsico.

badly furnished with accoutrements, and divers men disguised after some new fashion in masks. Nevertheless, amongst those of more honour and repute, there was an old grey-headed man, his assessor, who, albeit he had a long tale of years behind him, would still have been found better stocked with knowledge as to how to manage or set a pattern on the weft in the loom than to say aught, little or great, concerning the laws.

Now the governor, having at last entered into the discharge of his office with no little pomp and bravery, issued to the guard which was wont to keep the watch a certain order by which he forbade any frequenting of the streets by night, or the carrying of arms; and, over and beyond this, he put forth many other new rules and regulations. And howbeit it happened that he and all those about him were, as it has already been remarked, very ill furnished with arms of the sort which are used in assaults upon men; still, by reason of something which in after time was made plain to the sight of all, it was discovered, by a most unlucky accident, that there was in the governor himself a similar lack in those other weapons and instruments which are more especially at the service of the ladies. E non ostante quello, come la sua disavventura volse, una certa infermita nel suo piccolo e genital membro gli sopravenne, per medicamento de la quale i medici in tal maniera il conciarono, che non ostante che bifurcato gli remanesse, gliene avanzo si poco che per nulla saria da essere stato giudicato. Now this man, when he was at last in a way cured of his ailment, notwithstanding the fact that he was now old and impotent, never ceased to follow out a certain project of his with the utmost assiduity and care—the project aforesaid being nothing else than the taking to himself a wife. At last he fell violently in love with a young Genoese damsel of very high birth and exceedingly fair to look upon, who, a few days before this, had come out from a certain religious house into which her father by reason of his poverty had sent her to become a nun.

Although the head of the order and all the chapter of the brotherhood put forth all their efforts to save themselves the loss of so valuable a booty, nevertheless, when they saw clearly that the damsel was altogether determined to lay down her life sooner than go back for any time into the convent, and were finally convinced that all their toil would be futile, they put aside their grief and trouble and began to rage violently against her, and ended by pronouncing against her the public sentence of excommunication, seeing they could in no other method work their vengenace upon her. On this account the lovesick governor, taking no heed of the fact that he was old and worn out, or that the girl had been a nun—which thing should have been of no small weight—but considering solely her youth and beauty, took her for his wife, all poor and penniless as she was. Then with great feastings and rejoicings he brought her home to his house, and gave her to wear the raiment suited to a person of high estate. Wherefore his imagination, as it ever befalls in the case of old men, swelled within him in such wise that he began to let forth boasts and threatenings as to the wonders he was going to work; nevertheless on the bridal night it happened that his powers were found wanting in such degree that, in lieu of the marvellous deeds he had bragged about, he was able to accomplish nothing better than kissings and bitings, on account of which what though he began to put forward a lot of fictitious arguments in his own defence, the young wife knew well enough, from this one trial, in what most wretched state of life she was fated to pass her flowering youth.

The governor, although it took him some time to learn that kisses alone are of little avail in business of this sort, but rather act upon ladies like a spoonful of lard thrown upon the fire, and that the mare's appetite will not grow less lusty merely because there is a lack of fodder, made up his mind at last to set about his task in no niggardly fashion, however ill-accoutred therefor he might find himself. But in sooth his powers had declined to a point which would suffice no more for the satisfying of the craving appetite of the lady, than would a meal of falcons stay the hungry stomach of ravening wolf. Now after she had spent her life for a certain time in this sad and bitter wise, it chanced that a certain doctor of laws of this our city fell violently in love with her. He was young, of a seemly person, of great worth, and of a very honourable family; and after he had by many and various experiments tried all the roads by which he might win an entry into her favour, and met with little success in his enterprise on account of the extraordinary caution exercised by the jealous husband, he made up his mind to commit his venture entirely to the good offices of fortune, and to rid himself of all trouble thereanent.

Wherefore, being of this mind, and having taken into his confidence a young man who was a citizen of the place, it came into his mind to play off a noteworthy joke upon the governor, and in his very presence to let the young wife know how well fitted he himself was to give her succour in the particular need which pressed so heavily upon her. The young man remarked how every day the catchpoles of the court would make their rounds about the city, seizing the arms of any one they might meet, and taking the bearers thereof straight off to the prison of the governor, who meantime was wont to continue all day in his chamber with his fair young wife. Mandato il popolano secretamente ad un maestro lignaiuolo, e fatta fare una forma virile oltra la natural misura grossa e ben formata, e quella fatta colorire e appropriare che quasi di vera carne parea, e a la coda fatto acconciare un manico di spada, e postala dentro un lungo fodero, a lato ce l'appicoe. And then with divers other companions of his he set himself to walk boldly up and down in the presence of the officers of the court, and they, as soon as they caught sight of him, straightway gathered round about him like hungry wolves, and, greedy for prey, called out to him, "Give us here those arms of yours, and come before the governor at once, and pay the fine enjoined by the proclamation." The young man, highly pleased at the turn things had taken, refused to give up his arms, but said that he was quite willing that they should take him into the governor's presence, where he would forthwith let them know what the reason was which led him to carry arms. So, having placed him in the midst of their band, they haled him along with much shouting and violence towards the palace; and, when the officers and their prisoner had entered the apartment, they found there the governor playing chess with his young wife, the grey-headed old judge bearing them company.

When he heard the uproar made by the entry of this crowd of people, the governor lifted up his eyes from the board and saw before him a young man carrying arms; whereupon, giving over his game of chess, in which in sooth he had not done much more than give his wife a kiss, he rose to his feet and turned to the young man, deeming the while that he might make a good profit out of this business, and thus addressed him: "Tell me what authority allows you to carry arms; and, failing this, what presumption of your own has thus stirred you up to break the law, seeing that no man of this city, however high his rank may be, ever takes it upon himself to go armed?" To this the young man, with a smile upon his face, made answer: "Messer, the arms I carry are in no way those which can do hurt or injury to any man, but are rather concerned with a vow made by a certain gentleman of my acquaintance." Now when the governor listened to these words he was seized with the belief that the young man was making a mock of him, and, boiling with rage, he caught hold of him by the breast with one hand, while with the other he grasped the hilt of the counterfeit sword, and strove with all his might to draw the same forth from its sheath. The young man on his part clung tightly to his weapon, and called out, "Messer, I beg you will not do me this wrong. I assure you this is no deadly weapon which I have here. Let me go about my business; for if you still detain me, I will avail myself of the censure of the Syndic."*

The governor thereupon became more inflamed with rage than ever, and fully made up his mind that he would

* Orig., *me ne aiutero dal Sindacato.* In the Italian cities there was a communal right by which the people were able to pass in review and even to censure the action of their rulers, whether they were under the head of the state, or under some baron like the Orsini, Lord of Salerno, at this time. This right the origin of which is hard to trace, was jealously guarded, and was not finally abolished till 1805. Any citizen who might feel himself aggrieved by anything done by the governor, might avail himself of the *Sindacato*, and go to the municipal magistrates, who at the end of the year would call upon the governor to give an account of his administration.

get possession of this weapon, what though he might have to steal it. Therefore, having called upon all his catch-poles to help him, he at last hauled it out of its scabbard, whereupon the lady herself, and all those who were present, were able to see what strange thing it was he held in his hand. Then everyone began to laugh louder than he had ever laughed in his life at the expense of the governor, upon whose face every little vein might have been counted, so grievously was he angered by what had happened. On this account he, inflamed with no little rage from the fact that he had found something differing vastly from what he had sought, was on a sudden struck by an idea that he could fathom the reason how this thing had come to pass, and for a while he stood all giddy and confused, bearing this strange ensign gripped tight in his hand, and feeling that he could neither with decency retain the same or put it away from him.

However, when he had got his wits back somewhat, and had come to the determination to let the youth smart under a severe punishment for having thus gone about bearing counterfeit arms, he turned to the old judge and said: "Master Judge, quid videtur vobis?" The lubber-headed old man made answer to him in his doggrel speech: "Messer, in good truth this man ought to be held worthy of being visited with grievous chastisement, but 'De jure longobardo,'* we can in no way reach him." The governor, who had, though very late, been brought to see that this assessor of his was a fool, now made up his mind that he would on his own account make full inquisition into all the circumstances which could have tended to bring to pass the matter now before him. Therefore, turning towards the young man, he thus addressed him: "By God's faith, you shall not go forth from this place until you shall have told me, albeit against your will, all

* In Italy the Gothic and Lombard legal systems introduced many new principles into Roman jurisprudence. The Lombard laws were issued by King Rotharis in 643. The Lombards at this time were Arians, so the Church had no co-legislation with the temporal rulers. For nearly five hundred years the Lombards ruled the south of Italy from Capua to Tarentum—a fact which will explain the survival of their jurisprudence instanced in the text.

that it is expedient to tell concerning this affair." The young man, seeing that now fortune, step by step, was working favourably for the success of his enterprise, spake in reply, without losing a moment of time, and said: "Messer, since you are determined to know what there is to tell about this thing, I will lay it before you with all respect to Madonna, whom I see here present. Non sono ancora molti di passati che al cotal dottore legista una fiera e pericolosa infermita del suo secreto membro gli sopravenne; al quale niuno argomento di medico non valendo, ed essendone quasi disperato, ebbe ricorso ultimamente a quello che tutti li fedeli cristiani deveno avere, e cosi fece voto a questi nostri miraculosi santi martiri Ciro e Joanni, ogni anno una volta appiccare una statua de cera a misura, ne piu ne meno de sua grossezza, dinanzi li loro devotissimi corpi, per li meriti de li quali e divenuto sano come fosse mai. E volendo el suo voto mandare ad effetto, ne trovando in questa citta maestro alcuno che'l voglia o sappia fare, gli e stato bisogno far scolpire la presente forma a la soa somigliante, e commettere e pregare a me che la porti in Napoli, e qui ad un singolare maestro mio amicissimo la faccia in cera formare: onde parendomi disonesto portarla discoverta, l'avea acconciata al modo di spada come voi vedete. Ecco dunque il gran male che io ho fatto, se di cio si merita punitione, sia col nome di Dio che io sono per riceverla apparecchiato." The lady in the meantime had found full opportunity to look at and examine the weapon in question, and, holding it as a fact that all this which her lover had referred to was indeed the truth, she gave over the laughing mood which had until now possessed her, and began to sigh very deeply, and, considering how vastly what she saw differed from something else she knew but too well, she cried out in a rage, "Messer, I beg you to throw away forthwith that wretched thing you have in your hand, and in God's name let this man go, so that we may let finish our game of chess."

Hereupon the governor flew in a great rage, but knowing well enough that he could not in the course of justice inflict any punishment on the young man, and that, the more he should bandy words with him, the more fresh cause of offence he would encounter, he cast down the harmless weapon upon the floor with a furious gesture, and then, turning towards the young man, said: "Down before me, you gallows thief. Of a truth you are of a villainous and execrable breed, and, as far as I myself am concerned, I deserve all this and worse because, having been informed that you were unwilling to come here, and knowing, moreover, that the Salernitans will deceive the devil himself, I ought never to have wanted to see what you had to bring forward as a proof; but by my faith you shall never trick me again, forasmuch as I will quit this town and betake myself otherwhere. Now get you gone from here, and may bad luck go with you, and see that this city be clear of you in the space of two hours; for if I catch you here after that time, I will have you seized as a rebel against the state."

The youth, when he saw that the whole affair was likely to come to an end in words, and that he had at the same time done excellent service to his friend, took little care as to what might follow; and, having picked up his weapon from the floor, and tendered his thanks to the court, went out from the chamber. Then, having gone round all the public places and the various quarters of the city, he made bitter complaint on the subject of his exile, and on every side he told over and over again the story of what had befallen him, causing the while the greatest laughter and merriment amongst those who listened to his words.

Now some time after this it chanced that the prince* aforesaid made a journey to Nola, and while he was there in the presence of all his courtiers and of a number of other people all carrying arms, someone told to him from beginning to end the story aforesaid concerning that governor he had sent from the Marches to rule Salerno, and how the affair had come about. After he had laughed mightily at hearing the story, he found himself so hugely diverted thereat, that he caused the same to be related to him over and over again in the presence of all the people standing around, and afterwards he gave full licence to the young doctor of laws to return to the city. Not only did the latter go back to Salerno, but he likewise, by

* Probably the Orsini prince who was then Lord of Salerno.

virtue of the favour aforesaid, always hereafter went about the city carrying arms, and divers of his companions did the same. Henceforth none of the catchpoles of the governor ever took upon themselves to seize their weapons, fearing always lest they should have put upon them another trick like the last. The governor, being well advised that he was now become a byword and laughing-stock in the place, felt as much regret that fate had ever led him to Salerno as he felt for having taken to himself a young damsel for a wife. Wherefore, on this account, or perhaps because he was stirred thereto by his excessive jealousy, he contrived to have granted to him the favour of changing his abode and going to Sarno, as soon as his time of office had expired. And after he had gone thither, either through his former illness, or by the fresh fatigues he underwent, or from some other cause, he fell sick, and in the course of a few days breathed his last. Therefore, his wife who grieved very little for his death, was left without children and with a good store of wealth; so she went back to her father's house forthwith. Moreover, she bore in mind the long and fervent love which the young doctor of laws had nourished for her, and she did not forget that bird of his which he kept in its cage. So, regarding herself as free, and a lady in her own right, she contrived in very discreet and cautious fashion that he should be introduced to her, and, being in no wise anxious to contract fresh nuptials, they both together repaired the loss of their time in the past, spending their days in the most blissful fashion as long as their lives endured.

MASUCCIO

I CAN call to mind that I have many times heard argued between wise and learned men the question with regard to vows of that sort which certain people are wont to make in this world during those times when adversity presses heavily upon them—vows which, through some failing or other, they are unable to carry out afterwards. In these discussions I have heard it maintained that these same vows may by the power and authority of the Pope be changed, both in respect to their form and their nature. Now for this same reason I am well assured that our doctor of laws, having had due instruction in this matter, and at the same time having been interdicted by the action taken in the case by the governor from letting fashion his own *ex voto* in wax and hanging up the same once every year before the shrine of the two sainted corpses aforesaid, was granted a dispensation which allowed him, in such a sacred cause, to substitute for the same an offering made after the manner of the flesh, in such fashion as men were wont to use in days past, not once a year, but many times a month, making their oblations in the holy temple of the valley of Jehoshaphat; peradventure so that they might be able to cite the same as more valid testimony in the day of judgment.

But now putting on one side jesting of every sort, I declare with all assurance that he who finds himself plagued with the two vicious infirmities above-named, to wit, avarice and jealousy, may indeed hold himself to be the most ill-starred of men, because, over and beyond the pricks which will without ceasing assault him within and never let his life be guided for one second by content, it often happens that he will meet disaster through the working of those troubles which he has always dreaded and shunned, seeing that all the subtle counsels and devices of thieves are laid so as to purloin cunningly from him who keeps the closest watch. And that I may expound the truth of the matter—over and beyond what I have said in the last three novels here set down—I will go on in a similar strain with my discourse, and will show in the next place a manifest example of this truth by means of what befell a certain old man of great wealth, avaricious and jealous beyond bounds. This same old wretch was at the same moment beggared of his honour, his goods, and his peace of mind, and, by reason of his jealousy, taken as if he had been a fish upon the well-baited hook.

THE END OF THE THIRTEENTH NOVEL.

Novel the Fourteenth

ARGUMENT

A CAVALIER OF MESSINA FALLS IN LOVE WITH A YOUNG NEAPOLITAN GIRL. HE LEARNS THAT HER FATHER IS VERY AVARICIOUS, WHEREFORE HE CONTRIVES TO BECOME ACQUAINTED WITH HIM, AND PUTS HIM IN THE WAY OF MAKING VAST GAIN IN TRAFFIC. AFTER A TIME HE PRETENDS THAT HE MUST NEEDS RETURN HOME, AND OFFERS TO LEAVE BEHIND HIM IN PAWN A SLAVE, THE SAID SLAVE BEING ONE WELL INSTRUCTED AS TO THE DEED HE HAD IN VIEW. THIS SLAVE, A WOMAN, BEGUILES THE YOUNG GIRL, AND THE TWO PLUNDER THE OLD FATHER AND TAKE TO FLIGHT IN COMPANY WITH THE LOVER. FINALLY THE CAVALIER MARRIES THE DAMSEL; THEY RETURN TO NAPLES, AND ARE HAPPY IN THEIR LOVE.

TO THE MOST EXCELLENT MESSER JACOBO SOLIMENA, PHYSICIAN OF SALERNO*

EXORDIUM

IN what degree that most envious and rapacious sin of avarice, with the detestable vices accompanying it, has spread itself over the entire universe, and in what fashion, when once it may have fixed its claws into a man, it seizes hold of and tears out of him every virtue he may possess, you, the new Æsculapius, will easily be able to judge by the aid of those rare abilities which you possess. And again, because I have not, as it seems to me, touched sufficiently hitherto upon the effects produced by jealousy, I am inclined, before passing on to other themes, to put on record my belief that this passion of jealousy is

* In "Tumulorum," Book II., Pontano refers to "Giacomo Solimene Medico."

not always to be regarded as the result of excessive love, but verily and indeed in most cases may be set down as springing from extreme meanness of spirit, seeing that the greater part of jealous people are either old, or ugly, or impotent, or such chicken-hearted wretches that, whenever by chance they may see a man of a better outward seeming than their own, they regard him as one who would be able to give better satisfaction to their wives than they themselves can compass. And because from my earliest years I have ever known you to be of the number of magnanimous and liberal-minded men, as well as an excellent physician for the cure of every form of infirmity which may beset us, it has seemed good to me, at the same time that I give you intelligence as to the novel which follows, to implore you that, out of your great knowledge and resource, you will proffer to your own Masuccio wholesome remedies, and such as are fitted for the cure of the one passion and the other, in order that he, having duly received instruction from you, may with no mean authority hand down to posterity the fruits of your marvellous knowledge.

THE NARRATIVE

MESSER TOMMASO MARICONDA,* my grandfather and a kinsman of your own, was, as no doubt you know well, a very notable and elegant cavalier, and one who in his time was held in no small repute and esteem in this our city. Now this gentleman, when he was aged and full of years, took vast delight, as is the habit of old men, in telling to his listeners great numbers of very remarkable stories, all of which he would set forth with the most distinguished eloquence, and with the most marvellous memory. And amongst others I well remember to have heard him tell, when I was a very young child, as a real and undoubted fact, how, after the death of King Charles III.,† there arose in our kingdom

* The Mariconda were a noble family both in Naples and Salerno.

† Charles III. of Durazzo, who deposed and murdered Joanna

grave and prolonged warfare provoked by the habitual tyranny of the house of Anjou. At this time there chanced to be in Naples a certain cavalier of the city of Messina, called by name Giuffredi Saccano, a man who was a vehement partisan of the house of Durazzo; and one day when, according to his habit, he was making a round of the city on horseback, he happened to espy at a window a very lovely young damsel, the daughter of an old man, a merchant, whose name at this moment I cannot rightly call to mind. Now, as he was beyond all measure delighted with her appearance, he found himself straightway inflamed with a violent passion for her, and, as the kindly fortune of both of them willed it, the young girl, whose name was Carmosina, perceived in her heart that she had found favour in the eyes of this gentleman. Although she had never before known what manner of thing love might be, and had scarcely ever set eyes on a man, the affair now came to a strange issue, and one almost unheard of before, inasmuch as one flame set those two hearts ablaze at one and the same moment. Indeed, they were both stricken therewith in such fashion that neither one nor the other could move from the spot. Nevertheless, after a certain time had passed, being drawn away by modesty and bashfulness, they parted one from another, though not without sorrow and regret on either side.

Whereupon Messer Giuffredi, being well assured how love had all on a sudden levelled two mortals to the earth with a single blow, and that nothing but the advent of some favourable opportunity was needed* to allow them to satisfy their sympathetic desires, gave himself up entirely, as is the habit of lovers, to the task of searching out who the maiden might be, and what was her parentage. At last he discovered who her father was, and learned besides that he was an old man inordinately jealous and avaricious, inasmuch as he was possessed by these vices even beyond the common measure of old age.

I., and was the father of Ladislas and Joanna II. The wars referred to were those waged by Margaret, his widow, on behalf of her son, against Louis of Anjou. Charles died in 1386.

* Orig., *e che altro che attitudine non gl' impediva.*

Furthermore he ascertained that the miser, in order to escape the prayers of suitors to bestow his only daughter in marriage, was accustomed to keep her always closely shut up in the house, treating her the while worse than the meanest servant.

Now the cavalier, having thoroughly informed himself concerning the things written above, began to feign to be enamoured, now with one and now with another of the young women who dwelt near to the damsel's abode, so that he might be able to advance some colourable reason for betaking himself into that quarter, and at least gladdening his eyes with the sight of the walls which contained her, if he might not see her in person. When this became known he was set down by many of his friends as nothing better than one who fills himself with wind,* and his cunning sagacity was made a mock of by all the fools of the place. But he, caring naught for all this, and following resolutely the purpose he had framed, contrived to contract a close and intimate friendship with the damsel's father, who was engaged in the traffic of merchandize purchasing very often from the old man divers wares at a monstrous price, for which things he had no need whatever; and over and beyond this, in order to inveigle the miser still more, he would not fail to bring other clients every day into the warehouse, so that the old man made fresh profits without ceasing.

Seeing that the old merchant drew very great advantage from his traffic with the cavalier and his friends, he let grow up between himself and the young man so close a friendship and intimacy that all those who knew him were mightily astonished thereat. However, after a time the cavalier, being seized with the desire to bring his scheme to the end he had designed, found opportunity one day to shut himself up with the old merchant in the warehouse, whereupon he began to address him in the following words: "For the reason that I stand in need of counsel and help in my affairs, I feel that I cannot do better than have recourse to you, whom, on account of your goodness, I love and reverence as my own father. Wherefore I will

* Orig., *non altro che per un pascivento giudicato.*

not hold back from laying bare all my secrets to you, and I will first let you know that, at a season now many years past, I left my father's house, and since that time I have been detained in this city on account of the love I bear to your king and of the circumstances of the war. And things have fared with me in such wise that, up to this present time, no chance has been offered to me of going back to my country. But now for several days past I have been urged by my father, who has sent many letters and messengers to me concerning this matter, that I should forthwith betake myself to see him once again before the season of his old age shall be sped. As I cannot refuse to hearken to these commands of his or to the voice of filial love, I have made up my mind to go to him straightway, and, after having tarried with him some short period, I intend at once to return hither, and to take up again my service under my lord the king. Now as I know of no one to whom I can more conveniently entrust my confidence on such an occasion than to you, I come to ask you whether you would be willing to take under your charge certain possessions of mine, and to keep the same for me till the time of my return. And above all this, the chief concern I feel is on account of a certain female slave of mine, one whom I am most unwilling and aggrieved to sell by reason of her worth and goodness. But, on the other hand, finding myself sorely beset by the lack of thirty ducats, and being kept back by my honour from requesting any friend of mine to make me a loan so trifling, I have determined, finding myself placed in this doubtful position, rather to take security of you alone in this business, and to give you the trouble to advance me the sum aforesaid, leaving in your hands the slave as a pledge for the same. If at any time before I shall return you may find an opportunity of selling her for the price of seventy ducats, which is the sum I gave for her, I will beg you to deal with her as if she were your own."

The old man, who in sooth was far more of a miser than of a sage, began to busy his brains in canvassing and considering what possible profit might come to him if he should consent to do the cavalier the service that was demanded, and, without detecting aught therein of the nature of fraud or debating the affair further with himself, made answer in these words: "See here, Messer Giuffredi, the love which I bear towards you is so great, that I assuredly could never bring myself to answer no to any request you might make of me, supposing that the thing demanded lay within my power to perform, and for this reason I am strongly disposed to accommodate you with whatever sum of money you may want for your purposes. And besides this, I will keep the slave on your behalf, in order that you may not suffer ill through having to sell her. Then, when you shall have come back here safe and sound—supposing always that the slave should have done what was needed of her—I will settle my account with you in such fashion that you will find you could not have been better treated even if you had been my own son."

The cavalier, rejoicing greatly at the answer he received from the old man, then replied to him saying, "In sooth I did not expect any other answer from you, and it seems to me that to render you thanks therefor would be superfluous, but may our Lord God grant that I may be able to lay before you clearly the product of this our friendship to our common profit and advantage." And after he had thus brought his discourse to an end he took leave of the old man, and having mounted his horse according to his wont, he made his way along the street in which was the lodging of his lady-love; and, as he passed along, by the working of the fate which ruled the lives of the one and the other, he espied by chance the form of the damsel partially revealed at the casement of her chamber—a boon granted perchance for the satisfaction of both of them. Then drawing herself back from the window like one bewildered, she cast down upon him a sweet and piteous glance; whereupon he, looking cautiously around him and observing no one in the neighburhood, and conscious that he had no time to spare for the making of long speeches, said to her, "My Carmosina, be comforted, forasmuch as I have at last found a means by which I shall be able to deliver you from your prison." And having thus spoken he went his way, God speeding him.

Meantime the young damsel, who had understood quite

clearly the purport of her lover's words, was in no small measure comforted therewith, and although it did not enter her head to hope that from such a speech could ensue any working which might make for her advantage, nevertheless, the bare hope roused in her breast thereby gave her heart, though she knew not wherefore. The cavalier, when he had returned to his house, called his slave into his presence and said, "My good Anna, the business which we discussed and arranged is already set in order, wherefore see that you prove wary and prudent in the affair which you will have to bring to pass." And although the slave was already well instructed in all the arts and methods she would be called upon to employ, nevertheless the cavalier caused her to rehearse several times afresh the concerted plan of their subtle stratagem.

When a few days had elapsed, and when he had set everything duly in order, the cavalier went once more to the old merchant and addressed him in the following words: "Alas! how irksome it is to me to withdraw myself for ever so limited a time from your friendship, which has been so precious and so profitable to me. Of this he who truly knows all our secrets will be a witness. Nevertheless, as it is convenient for my purpose that I should take my departure this very night, for the reason that all preparations for my passage are now complete, I have come hither to take my leave of you, and besides this to fetch the money which I begged you to advance me as a loan. Also I am come to bid you send for the chattel you wot of." The old man, who could have prayed God for nothing better, was overjoyed at this news, seeing that he had begun to feel some apprehension lest the cavalier might have repented him of his proposal. Whereupon, without further delay he counted out the thirty ducats, and, having done this, he sent to fetch the slave, who forthwith went to his house, taking with her certain small and delicate things which were the property of the cavalier.

Now when the evening was at last come, Messer Giuffredi, accompanied by the old merchant and certain others of his friends, betook himself to the seashore, and then, having embraced them all and bidden them farewell, he embarked on board a light galley which was about to set sail for Messina. But when the aforesaid ship had fared a short distance from the port of Naples, he made the shipmen place at his service a small boat (which matter in sooth he had already arranged with the captain), and in this he had himself conveyed to Procida.* Having come there, he found lodging in the house of a certain friend of his, and there he tarried until three days had passed. On the night of the third day, when the hour had come which he had appointed with the slave and with other associates of his, Sicilian fellows keen to act and well set towards any deed of dangerous adventure, he returned to Naples and made his way into the city in very cautious wise. Having come there, he took secret lodging, together with his associates, in a certain house hard by that of the old merchant—a dwelling which, through the ill times brought about by the wars, was at that period quite void of occupants, and there they all abode hidden and silent until the following day came.

In the meantime the cunning and quick-witted slave had gone to the merchant's house, and had there met with most friendly and joyful reception from Carmosina. The last named, knowing full well from whom the woman had come, in a brief space of time became on very intimate terms with her; whereupon the slave, spurred on by remembering how short was the time in which her purpose would have to be accomplished, laid bare to the damsel point by point the reasons for which she had come thither, using the while the most consummate arts and the most skilful discourse, and furthermore telling her exactly what her master had settled with her concerning the matter in question, and heartening the damsel little by little by the arguments she brought forward to carry out in daring fashion the enterprise to its issue, so as to secure for herself and her lover a lasting time of peace and happiness. The young girl, who for many reasons was even more strongly minded than the cavalier towards this end, did not suffer the slave to waste more time in adding one lengthy argument to another, but told her straightway that she was fully prepared to consent to every one of the proposals just made by her, and likewise to follow all the

* An island lying between Ischia and the mainland.

directions laid down by the cavalier, whom she herself loved as she loved her own life.

To these words the slave replied: "My daughter, if it should happen that you have a few little things of your own which you would like to carry away with you, I would counsel you to get the same in order at once, seeing that our plan will have to be put in execution this very night. You must know also that my master and his servant and certain other companions of his are now concealed in the house next door to us. This fact I have learnt from a signal which I have this day seen displayed from the house in question, and, as you well know, it would be an easy task to get into it from our paved courtyard." When the young girl heard how short was the time before her flight, she gave the slave a hundred kisses, and told her that she possessed nothing of her own, either great or small, which she could take away with her, but that she had made up her mind to abstract from the store of her avaricious old father a much greater sum of money than anyone could have reckoned sufficient for her dowry.

When they had brought the matter to this conclusion, and when the midnight hour had come, and the old man and everyone else in the house were fast asleep, Carmosina and the slave broke open a chest and took out therefrom jewels and money of a value exceeding one thousand five hundred ducats, and, having bestowed these safely away, they silently crossed over the courtyard and came to the spot where the cavalier was awaiting them. He, with the greatest joy, took the young girl in his arms and covered her lips with ardent kisses. Further pleasure they did not enjoy, seeing how precarious was their present abiding-place; wherefore the whole company set out on their way, and took the road which led to the seashore. Having cautiously issued from the city through a breach in the wall behind the slaughter-houses, they found their bark ready armed and fully equipped for a swift passage, and ready to cast off at a moment's notice. Whereupon they all went on board the same, and, having dipped their oars in the water, they found themselves at Ischia before many hours had elapsed. Then the cavalier and all those accompanying him presented themselves before the lord of that place, who chanced to be a particular friend of Messer Giuffredi, and one indeed who had been made privy to the whole affair. From this gentleman they all received most kindly and hospitable reception, and while they were abiding there the lovers, deeming that they were now upon safe ground, partook of the first and sweetest delights of their reciprocal love, and rejoiced the one as well as the other with no less joy over the circumstances of their flight.

In the meantime the old father, when the daylight came, first found that neither his daughter nor the slave whom he had taken in pledge were in the house, and then became aware that he had been robbed of his money and of his jewels to boot, and for the last-named loss he felt no less grief than for the first; indeed, how sore were his tears and lamentations each one may judge for himself. Moreover, no one need wonder to hear that he found his affliction so sharp and cruel that he was over and over again fain to hang himself by the neck therefor. And thus, overcome by his losses and the shame that had been put upon him, he spent his days in continual weeping shut up in his house.

Meantime the enamoured couple in Ischia lived their lives in the greatest delight, and by reason of their constant intercourse it came to pass that the fair damsel became with child. Which thing, when the cavalier came to know it, caused him the greatest delight, and he forthwith made a resolve to treat her with a worthy spirit of generosity, and at the same time to give full satisfaction to God, to the world, and to himself. Wherefore, having despatched a message through the intervention of the lord of Ischia to the father of Carmosina and to divers of his own kinsfolk, these aforesaid all came to Ischia, and, when they were all there assembled, and after certain contracts had been duly signed, the cavalier, by the favour of the king and with the universal approval and general rejoicing of the people of Naples, took Carmosina for his lawful wife. Thus, having exchanged the secret sport of Venus for the career of married folk, they went back to their Neapolitan home and passed their days in great happiness as long as they both lived. In this manner it may be seen how the jealous, miserly, and foolish old man atoned for the deed after all the damage had been done.

MASUCCIO

THE fortunate ending which I have let ensue to the story I have just completed will, I make little doubt, give cause to many of those who may read the same to hold up for approbation with unbounded praises the great foresight and sagacity of the young girl, who, marking how she was thus kept in this wretched plight and held to be meaner than the meanest hireling, contrived to procure for herself so seemly and valiant a lover; and, besides this, to obtain out of the hoard of her miserly old father a greater sum of money than would have been given to her as a dower, becoming in the end the wife of her lover with honour and happiness. Now the things above written, although in sooth they may be laid less to her charge than to that of Love, who awakened her slumbering wits and thereby taught her how to bring to an issue with the greatest courage those lessons which he himself had taught her, I for my part do not intend to praise, nor do I intend to advise any woman, however lavish may be the promises of her lover, to imitate Carmosina in this matter, and suffer herself to be carried away in such fashion. For, admitting that the issue of the affair was a fortunate one for our Carmosina, it must nevertheless be borne in mind that the tempers of men are not all of the same quality and inclination, and that the course of action which the cavalier followed, urged thereto by his innate goodness and uncommon virtue, may perchance be censured as faulty and poor-spirited by others, who are so minded that, if they should find themselves in a similar case, would plume themselves upon having done a valiant deed of prowess when they should have robbed their sweethearts of the flower of their virginity and afterwards left them in scorn to their disgrace. And even though each individual girl should feel well assured that in her own case the end must needs be a fortunate one, I still judge that she would be taking the wiser part who might follow a course opposite to that adopted by Carmosina, forasmuch as it is by far better never to put oneself in peril of meeting ruin at the hands of another, than to escape the danger though running near the precipice.*

And furthermore I am persuaded that it is a fact to be controverted by no one that the inordinate suspicion combined with the senile avarice of the old merchant were the real causes of the flout that was put upon him, and of the heavy loss which accompanied it. If afterwards there followed a reparation of the same in the creditable issue of the matter, it was assuredly not because the execrable vices of the old man did not exhibit their poisonous results, which results seem to me so monstrous and horrible that I am driven, out of sheer confusion, to cease to talk of them. And, for the reason that in the novel which I will next let follow it will behove me to treat of things greatly differing from, and even exactly opposite to this suspicious humour, I will for a season give over all discourse concerning this mean imperfection, and, still holding myself in the company of Madonna Avarice, I will exhibit to you the execrable conduct of a greedy, avaricious loon, by the means of which discourse you will be able to comprehend clearly how such a vice may become master of a man's understanding, and rob him of all virtue, honour, and content.

* Orig., *che presso il pericolo non periclitare.*

THE END OF THE FOURTEENTH NOVEL.

Novel the Fifteenth

ARGUMENT

A LORD CARDINAL IS ENAMOURED OF A CERTAIN LADY, AND BRIBES THE HUSBAND OF THE SAME WITH A SUM OF MONEY, IN ORDER THAT HE MAY LET HIS WIFE BE BROUGHT INTO THE CARDINAL'S APARTMENT. ON THE MORROW THE HUSBAND COMES TO TAKE HER BACK, BUT THE LADY BEING VASTLY CONTENTED WITH HER PRESENT LODGMENT, REFUSES TO ACCOMPANY HIM, THOUGH HE URGES HER THERETO WITH MUCH FRUITLESS DISCOURSE. IN THE END HE TAKES THE MONEY WHICH WAS PROMISED TO HIM, AND IN DESPAIR GOES INTO EXILE, WHILE HIS WIFE LIVED A PLEASANT LIFE WITH THE CARDINAL.

TO THE MOST WORSHIPFUL MESSER ANTONIO DA BOLOGNA PANORMITA*

EXORDIUM

ONLY because there comes over me a desire to write to you, most famous and illustrious poet, the light and glory of our Italian nation, my wit and my tongue, my hand and my pen, seem, as it were, to be so confusedly involved the one with the other that no one of them can or will return to its accustomed duties. Nevertheless, I am inspired with new confidence to catch up my weapons from the ground, and am heartened to address to you the novel which I send herewith, when I call to mind how I have seen you on divers occasions take no

* Antonio Beccadelli was born in 1394 at Palermo, and was afterwards named from his birthplace, Il Panormita. He was educated at Siena, where he had for a fellow-student Æneas Sylvius Piccolomini, and ultimately became one of the leading humanists of the time. He went first as professor of history to Milan, at the invitation of Filippo Maria Visconti, and later on became secretary to Alfonso the Magnanimous. He was also tutor to Prince Ferdinand, afterwards king, and died in 1471.

little pleasure in listening to the undisciplined variations and the coarse speech of the common people, and thrust aside, in favour of these, writings in the most elegant and meritorious style, as if no masterpiece of lofty rhetoric could ever excite or command the admiration of you, who are our new Apollo, or lead you to take pleasure therein. In the course of reading this novel you will be told of a very strange contract and a very unusual act of barter made between a certain Mantuan, who was in sooth a foolish blockhead, and one of our new Pharisees. This latter, deeming that he peradventure might one day win for himself the succession to the chair of the glorious Peter, and being in no wise disposed to allow the chief pastorate of the Church to fall into the hands of men of outland nations, desired rather that the same should remain fixed in those of his own descent, wherefore he did his best to beget children of his own. And as with a certain show of authority these cardinals have come to wear the crimson mantle and hat in remembrance of the red blood of Christ which was sprinkled upon the wood of the Cross, so in like manner they affirm that it is lawful for them to have children of their own on the strength of that other text in which God said, "Crescite et multiplicanimi." But for the reason that my falcon does not essay a flight high enough to assail the life and the carriage of such as these, will not stop to censure them in this place, but will at once go on to tell the story which I promised you.

Panormita was a voluminous writer of the smooth and polished Latin verse so fashionable in his day, but his name is chiefly remembered in connection with the authorship of the "Hermaphroditus," a poem obscene enough to incur even the censure of Poggio. There is a story told of him, to illustrate his enthusiasm for the classics, how he sold a farm in order to purchase a MS, of Livy. His books were condemned and forbidden by the church and the Minor Friars; Bernardino da Siena and Roberto de Lecce publicly burned the "Hermaphroditus," and the author's portrait as well. In spite of ecclesiastical censure Panormita enjoyed the patronage and friendship of the Emperor Sigismond, Alfonso of Naples, and Cosmo di Medici (he dedicated to the last named the "Hermaphroditus") and of many scholars—Guarino and Poggio amongst them—who were fascinated by his elegant style, while condemning the licentiousness of his subjects.

THE NARRATIVE

I BELIEVE that it is a thing well known throughout the universe, how that most blessed Pope Pius II. let summon and constitute a sacred and general council in the city of Mantua,* in order to set on foot an expedition to be undertaken by all the Christian powers against the Turk. Now the Pope having gone thither accompanied by his whole college of cardinals, awaited the gathering together of the princes and potentates of Christendom whom he had summoned thither in order that he might give his directions concerning all the needful preparations which he was persuading them to adopt for the carrying out of so noble an emprise. It chanced that there was amongst the others a certain lord cardinal, concerning whose name and dignity I will keep silence,† who, although he had not yet passed out of his flowering youth to the age which comes after, was nevertheless charged with the execution of the more weighty offices of the apostolic court. In addition to this, he had been endowed by nature with a most comely presence. I will not linger now to tell of the sumptuous apparel he used, or of his fine and richly-decked horses, or of the honourable troop of gentlemen who were in his train, or of the magnificence of his kingly manner of life. And what shall I say concerning his magnanimous spirit, which, being endowed with every liberal virtue, was vastly unlike that of all the others, and in time became most saintly and gracious through its abundance of every grace and gentleness; so that in the end he was accounted to be the most seemly and affable gentleman to be found in any of the chief places of Christendom?

* In 1459.

† Signor Settembrini puts forward a theory that this cardinal may have been Roderico Borgia, afterwards Alexander VI. He was raised to the purple by Calixtus III., his uncle, in 1456, as Cardinal of Valenza; and Summonte, "Storia Napoli," lib. v., p. 246, says, while treating of the Council of Mantua, "il Cardinal di Valenza restò con grandi entrate, e vicecancelliere della sede apostolica."

THE PRICE OF A WIFE.

FROM A DRAWING BY E. R. HUGHES. (Mas., Nov. xv., v. i.)

It happened that this same cardinal took up his abode in a palace belonging to a citizen of repute, round about which there dwelt a vast number of ladies marvellously beautiful in person, and amongst these there was one who, without doubt, outdid all the others of the city in beauty; and she, as fate would have it, was more than once observed by the lord cardinal aforesaid, who thereupon felt that he could take pleasure in her and in her alone. Like the mighty hunter that he was, he was powerfully attracted by this fair booty, and determined to leave nothing undone which might help him to come out of this enterprise a victor. And because the house where the young woman dwelt was very near to his own, and the windows opposite to each other, he found on this account abundant opportunity of gazing upon her, and of admiring her loveliness at his convenience.

Now because he received information after a time that this lady was more modest and virtuous than any of her neighbours, and because he found himself unable to induce her to look upon him even once with kindly eyes, while he used all kinds of gracious arts to commend himself to her favour, he began to feel that the hopes he had hitherto cherished were beginning to forsake him. Still, being fiercely urged on by the pricks of love, and knowing well that difficult undertakings are not to be brought to an issue without sore travail; remembering, likewise, that those objects which men attain with ease have but small savour and quickly pall, he at last fixed upon a certain scheme after he had well canvassed divers others. He determined to see whether he might not be able to entrap the husband of the lady aforesaid by his love of gold, knowing as he did that this man was very needy and very avaricious at the same time. Thus the husband, having been summoned, without any farther delay went to him forthwith, and was at once conducted into the presence of the lord cardinal in his chamber. After having welcomed him with many words of civil and familiar greeting, the cardinal made him sit down beside him, and then addressed him in these words: "Sir, as I well know you to be a man of prudent nature, it does not seem to me to be in any way necessary that I should use lengthy speeches and persuasive reasonings in making clear to you a certain matter which you may easily perceive to be one which must make for your lasting peace and contentment, and at the same time enable you to escape both from your present troubles and from those which await you in the future. Wherefore I must let you know that the charm of the great beauty of your most virtuous wife has seized upon me in such wise that I can find for myself no rest on account of the same. I know well enough that by no forethought or reasoning can I bring forward any plea which would permit me to require such a service at the hands of yourself, who are her husband; but when I considered how, for reasons of affection and of upright dealing as well, no other person would be able to set this affair in order so well as you, or to keep the same a secret from all ears, I made up my mind to have recourse to you, rather than to any other trusty agent, to act as a go-between on my behalf in the matter aforesaid, begging you that for the sake of giving me the satisfaction I so much desire, and for the gathering into your own pockets such advantageous profit, you will deign to grant me this boon which I long for so earnestly. And although the thing I speak of is of so great value and worth that I cannot be said to buy it, nevertheless you must understand that this service I ask of you will not have been given to me for nothing. but sold at a very high price, seeing that I desire no other thing than that your wife should forthwith take full possession of myself and you of all my wealth. Now if it seems good to you to do this thing, I beg you to tell me so without delay and not keep me waiting, in order that you may straightway perceive what will be the consequences of all the bounty and the rewards which I intend to bestow upon you."

The worthy man was, as I have before said, poor, and besides this avaricious beyond measure; wherefore, when he listened to the magnificent offers made to him by the cardinal, whom he knew well to be very rich and very liberal likewise, he at once considered that assuredly a very great profit must accrue to him from this business, and at the same time persuaded himself most confidently that with his craft he would be able to lay the plot in marvellously subtle and secret fashion. In sooth, the things afore-mentioned sufficed amply to confound his wits, to break through the respect he ought to have felt for the matrimonial tie, to lead him to hold cheaply the good opinion of the world, and to injure with such a disgraceful blow both himself and his eternal happiness. Therefore, without letting his thoughts busy themselves longer over the affair, he made answer to the cardinal in a few words: "Monsignor, I hold myself in readiness to do this service you require of me, for the reason that it is your part to command and mine to fulfill your every wish and pleasure."

When the husband had thanked the cardinal many times for his bounty, he took his leave with a joyous countenance, and, in order to let no long delay interpose before the business should be set in progress, be began on the following night to canvass the same in a very roundabout fashion with his wife, shielding himself as often as he needed behind the pretext of their pressing poverty, concluding his speech by affirming that a dishonest action, if it should be wrought in such cunning wise that no one might be cognisant thereof, may be held not to have been committed at all. The wife, who was a very discreet woman, not only took this discourse of his in excessive ill part, but likewise, being hotly inflamed with anger thereanent, she poured out upon him the vilest abuse, ending by declaring that, if at any future time he should allow himself to think of such a matter, and much less to speak of it, she would without further paltering make it known to her brothers.

The husband did not trouble himself greatly because his wife made so haughty a reply the first time he spoke to her of the affair; and, when he had allowed a few days to pass by, and when a moment fitted for his purpose seemed to have recurred during a conversation with his wife over divers pleasant things, he once more preferred to her in well-considered fashion the same request as he had made to her before. Whereupon she, showing herself more inflexible than ever, went forthwith to the house of her brothers, and with great displeasure told them the whole story of her husband's vile doings, and these, as soon as they heard what she had to tell, were greatly angered and caused their brother-in-law to come to them and let him know what things they had heard concerning him, threatening him sorely and casting foul words at him on account of the misdeeds he had planned against the honour of them all.

But he, who had already pondered over and prepared the answer he was minded to give, said, without aught of amazement, and even smiling somewhat, "Good brothers of mine, of a truth you might have made inquiry of me with more decorum, and then I might well have taken away all your suspicions, but since one is forced to endure all manner of things when dealing with a number of others joined in alliance, I will tell you the truth concerning the matter which your sister and my wife has related to you. Wherefore you must understand that I, having become suspicious that the cardinal, who has his lodgings over against ours, was seized with an amorous passion for her, and furthermore that he, by the help of certain of my household, had secretly woven a plot against me, made up my mind to try a final experiment in respect to her, holding her, young and fair as she is, to be an honest woman, what though I am somewhat uncertain as to the chastity of women in general. Then, if she should be found honest, as I have always found her, I resolved to praise her thereanent, and to withdraw myself from all suspicious mood both in the present and for the future as well. If, on the contrary, I should have discovered in her any falling away from virtuous carriage, I should have set myself, with your concurrence, to give her such usage as might be meet for her deserts. But now, for the reason that I have, by God's mercy, ascertained and proved her virtue, as you see for yourselves, I have let vanish from my mind all suspicion of any kind, old or new, and from this time forth I shall be careful to treat her with still greater consideration than heretofore."

The brothers, after they had lent ear to this excuse thus set forth in plausible wise, gave the husband high commendation for the prudent arguments he had used with himself, deeming it quite possible that he might in sooth have done this thing in consideraton of the end he anticipated, and, after some further discourse over the affair, they brought about a reconciliation between him and his wife; whereupon she consented to go back with him to his house, holding the belief that he would not again begin to speak to her of such matters as he had lately been in the habit of discussing. The lord cardinal, when intelligence was brought to him of what had happened, listened to the same with great bitterness of spirit, for it seemed to him that his glowing hopes were beginning to lose their warmth. Nevertheless, coerced by the fierce passion which possessed him, he still went on courting her with glances more amorous and fervent than ever, and would, now by certain signs and now by spoken words, make offer to her of everything he possessed in the world without imposing upon her restraint or condition of any sort, letting her know in conclusion that for the sake of the love he had for her he was letting himself consume like ice in the rays of the sun.

Now the lady, in sooth, was made of metal which in no way differed from that out of which the residue of the female sex is compounded; wherefore she, notwithstanding that she was in every sense a virtuous and honest woman, began to be conscious of some little tenderness towards him on account of the continual hammering he kept up, but she was careful at the same time to let him get no inkling of her change of mind. Still she never neglected, whenever she might be holding conversation with her husband, to heap commendation beyond measure upon the circumspect manner and the praiseworthy carriage of the lord cardinal. Wherefore this discourse of hers chanced to become the reason for the wretched knave of a husband to pluck up his heart afresh, and to come back once more to ply her with the arguments and persuasions he had used before. Thus, having been careful to seize upon a certain time when he knew her to be in a friendly mood, he addressed her in these words: "My Giacomina, you yourself can truthfully bear witness of the fact that, both in the past and at this present time, I have cordially and truly loved you and still love you on account of the many virtues with which you are adorned. Now if the day before yesterday I demanded of you a certain thing you wot of, I should be unwilling indeed you should still hold the belief that this request of mine was produced by any want of esteem or respect for yourself. Indeed, I was urged on to beg this favour of you against my own pleasure and inclination by two very powerful reasons. The first of these is found in the extreme necessity which has fallen upon us through the working of our evil fortune —an ill for which we are ourselves in no way to blame, and which does not let me see that there is available any other method by which we may keep ourselves alive. The other, which in sooth afflicts me with grief no less bitter, is the thought that in the approaching festival which our marchioness is minded to give for the entertainment of all the various princes who are now gathered together here in our city, and to our neighbours as well, I shall not be able, through lack of money, to provide for your appearance at the same time in such gear and fashion as I should desire, and such as is fitting to our position and to your fine presence and beauty. Thus, when I consider these things in my mind, I find in them such great force, that I suffer myself to be borne along by their arguments, not only to let ensue the affair I named to your hearing, but even to consent to be haled off to eternal torture and a cruel death. And, forsooth, nothing but the fear of consequent shame keeps us back from doing this. Still, as I told you once before, no enterprise when it is undertaken with caution and foresight can ever come home to us to our prejudice or disgrace. In order that you may be assured that I am speaking the truth, I would have you see that this lord cardinal is so keenly sensible of his own honour and of ours as well that, albeit he is pining away by reason of his passion, he could not bring himself to take any other living man into his confidence as to this affair save myself, seeing that I am the one most concerned in keeping it a secret. Now therefore, not knowing of any farther consideration which I might suggest to you concerning this affair, I will bring my words to an end by saying that you must do what your soul counsels you to do, and then I, on my part, will of a surety be contented. Still I will not fail to remind you now, that hereafter, in the hours when we shall be tormented by our wretched poverty, we shall have to let our complaint be made, not to fortune, but to you."

In this fashion was the lady urged and persuaded without ceasing by her wretch of a husband, who, by these fraudulent arguments of his, led her on towards the verge of the abyss. And beyond this she, being fully persuaded that she was loved above everything else in the world by such a gracious, rich, handsome and liberal gentleman, made up her mind that, for the aforesaid reasons and many others to boot, she would forthwith break loose from all the bonds of virtue which had hitherto restrained her, and at one and the same time gain for herself the lasting gratification of her desires, and let her husband feel the prick of that punishment which he was bringing upon himself. And when she marked that he kept silence, she addressed him in these words: "My husband, since it seemed good to my brothers not only to give me to you for your wife in the first instance, but likewise to send me back again to your house contrary to my will after I had departed thence, having just and ample reason for what I did, and, seeing that we are as we are, I dare not and cannot dispose of myself otherwise than in such manner as all other beautiful women use in dealing with their husbands. By this I mean that we must submit ourselves to our husbands, and obey them as our superiors in all matters. Therefore, as I see clearly that you have in your mind a set purpose to let this person of mine be defiled in the embraces of another man, I will submit in peace to do what you will; that same thing which you have persuaded me to assent to with so many pleas and arguments. Thus I am now fully prepared to do your bidding when and in whatsoever manner you may ordain. Nevertheless, I will not omit to give you warning that it behoves you to give this affair mature reflection, and I will bid you take care, my husband, that you do not repent thereof in that season when there will remain for you no opportunity of remedying the same."

The husband, when he heard his wife answer in this unusual strain, was mightily pleased, and, deeming that his words had indeed borne fruit, said to her: "My wife, know that people never repent of what is done after due forethought and in order. However, you may safely leave the consideration of all this to me." And with these words he went out of her presence and betook himself with all speed to the cardinal, and, having given him salutation with a joyful face, thus addressed him: "My lord, the affair is set in order for this very night; but I have assuredly met with a hard task in making her say 'yes,' and I have besides promised her three hundred ducats for this first visit, and of this sum she has instant need in order to exchange the same for fine clothes and ornaments for her person, wherewith to deck herself at the festival which is about to be holden. Wherefore I beg you let it be your special care to send her home well contented."

The amorous lord cardinal, who nevertheless was well experienced and very circumspect, understood at once that the baseness of this fellow was as great as he could wish, and made answer that not only would he with the utmost pleasure hand over to him the three hundred ducats, which sum indeed he looked upon as a mere trifle, but that he wished him to have as much money as his pockets would hold. And then, after divers other kindly and courteous words, they came to an agreement one with the other as to the time and the manner in which the husband himself should conduct the lady into the cardinal's lodging. And when he had returned to his wife he set forth to her an account of what he had settled for her to do, but he could not get her to make any reply thereto save saying, "My husband, my husband, think over and consider well what thing it is you do." And when the appointed time had come for them to set forth she still kept on carping at him as they went on their way with the same discourse: "My husband, I greatly fear me you will repent of what you are after." But he, thinking the while of naught besides the three hundred ducats which he would win for himself in so short a space of time, troubled himself very little thereanent, and even less did he understand the drift of these words of hers, seeing that the passion of avarice had in no small degree blurred and darkened his understanding, and in this wise he led his wife to the cardinal.

When the young woman had come into the chamber,

and when she found herself in the loving arms of so gracious a gentleman, who, besides kissing her times out of number, caressed her over and over again in a fashion which proved the sincerity of his affection, she was seized with the desire, even before they had come to taste together the delicious fruits of love, to confirm herself in the purpose she had already formed, that is, to submit to die rather than to go back to that worthy husband of hers. Then, when the lord cardinal had given to the husband polite dismissal, and had bidden him to return betimes in the morning and take back his wife with him, he entered the soft and luxurious bed with the young woman, and when they had come to that juncture in which love holds out to us his supreme consolation, they wandered all that night in the delightful gardens of Venus overcome by mutual desire. So that the lady, who had never hitherto tasted such a dainty repast, thought within herself that she must assuredly have come to the place where alone the highest bliss was to be found. And for the reason that she had no desire to depart from where she was, she, with discreet manner and with fitting words, made known to the lord cardinal what were her wishes, and what course would be expedient for them to take to secure their common contentment and satisfaction, saying in conclusion that, if he should not be satisfied to keep her with him, he might for the future think of her and set her down as lost entirely, and of her husband as being still bereft of her, for she had determined never to return to him.

The lord cardinal, who had never before had sense of such sweetness as flowed from these words of hers, and from the purport thereof, before he made her any reply gave her some earnest of his intentions by the many sweet and loving kisses he showered upon her, and at last addressed her in these words: "Sweet soul of mine, in sooth I know of naught else to say to you save that, because I have given to you my very soul, and because you have given your beautiful and delicate body to me, you have only to command and to dispose of me in any fashion which may seem good to you. Whatever you may ordain, I shall be content therewith." Then, after he had turned to her and kissed her again, he bade her get up and put on her attire, seeing that it was by this time broad daylight, and when this was done he let her be conducted into another room. Having heard that the husband had been there since the dawn in readiness to take his wife with him back to his house, the cardinal bade a servant bring him hither. The husband, after he had come into the room and seen his wife there, and given her good morning with a smiling face went privily up to her side and spake to her in the following words: "Ah, my Giacomina, know that I indeed sorely repent me for having brought you to this place, forasmuch as never before have I endured such bitter grief as I have endured this accursed night, wherein I have not been able to sleep at all through thinking of you." The lady, who had already got in order the reply she was minded to give, then said to him: "My husband, I too have been full of regrets, but my regret has been that I did not say 'yes' the first time you proposed that I should come hither, seeing that for the rest of my life-time I shall never be able to make up for all those delicious nights which I have lost. And if, forsooth, you have slept badly, have I not also been kept awake, albeit most pleasantly, for the reason that my lord here has treated me to more caresses during this one single night than you have bestowed upon me during the whole time I have been your wife. Again I see quite well that through my ill luck in having such a husband as you, this gentleman's liberality, concerning which you discoursed to me in such an ardent tone, has been conferred upon me more than two thousandfold, for you must know that this morning when I made known to him my final resolve to remain entirely with him, he handed over to me at once the keys of all his treasures. And for this reason take whenever you like the price for which you bargained away the honour of our relationship one with the other, and assuredly I wish that this same matter may be the last venture you undertake with regard to me or to any other affair of mine, seeing that I would vastly prefer to let myself be torn in four quarters rather than return to you."

The wretch of a husband, who now indeed was fain to

believe that the very heavens were falling down about his head, answered her in these words: "Giacomina, my fairest one, do you mean to mock me, or are you indeed speaking the truth?" She answered him, "Yes, certes, I make a mock of you, and with good cause, too. But you perhaps have made yourself believe that I am now minded to make a trial of your love, after the fashion by which, as you told my brothers, you once sought to put my constancy to the proof. Now I wish that, having made this trial of yours once for all, you should rest satisfied with the result of your essay, and that for the future you should look to have nothing further to do with me or my affairs. In sooth, you ought to remember how many times I said to you, 'My husband, have a care of what you are doing,' and to these words of mine you always made answer that I was to leave all such considerations to you. Wherefore I acted in this wise, and thus I intend to act for the future. The thought which gave rise to this thing was your own, and sprang from no other brain than yours, so find a remedy therefor if you can. I, for my part, shall in the meantime, without wasting a single thought over the matter, find myself becoming ever more beautiful and fresh in the delightful embraces of my new lord."

Having spoken these words she opened a cabinet and drew therefrom a purse into which she had shortly before counted the sum of three hundred ducats, and said to her husband, "Here, take the price for the wife you held in such light esteem, and tarry here not a moment longer." Then, as she moved away, to go into another room she said, "Now, good-bye, my husband, and another time consider well the thing you would do." Then she locked the door upon him, and never more as long as he lived was a sight of her granted to him. The wretched husband failing to find remedy of any sort for this disastrous barter of his, took the three hundred ducats, so as to make the best of a bad bargain, and overflowing with tears and sighs returned to his home, but being no less terrified by the fury of his brothers-in-law than overwhelmed by the burden of his own shame, he shortly after fled therefrom. How the lady fared, and how she spent the residue of her days in joyance and pleasure, any-one may easily understand.

MASUCCIO

IT might be looked upon as a rash and presumptuous deed on the part of any man who should set to work to visit with condemnation this young Mantuan lady on account of what she did for the chastisement of her base wretch of a husband, and for the securing for herself of a life of lasting pleasure, or to blame her because she showed herself indisposed to abandon those many delights, the existence of which she had discovered all unexpectedly and even against her will—delights which perchance had been foreordained as her portion from the very beginning of time. At the same time no one could or ought to feel any pity for the deceived husband, seeing that he himself purchased the befooling he got at his own price. In like manner, too, no one can with justice lay blame on the cardinal because he did not shut the door in the face of kindly fortune when she placed in his hands that one thing which he desired more than aught else in the world. Nay, it seems to me that we should rather hold him to be praised, in that, after having satisfied his desire with her, he did not allow himself to be conquered by avarice so as to withhold from the good easy husband the money he had covenanted to give him, as in sooth many others might have done.*

But now, seeing that we have spoken enough concerning all of these, and that there is no cause for us to wonder at the fact that men cannot always defend themselves from the snares which are set for them by others, I will in another novel let you hear of a most subtle cheat put upon one who was a saint by two of our Salernitan townsman, and in what fashion they contrived to extract many hundreds of florins out of the pockets of the wary people of Florence.

* Masuccio seems here to show that he has one law for a cardinal and another for a mendicant friar.

THE END OF THE FIFTEENTH NOVEL.

Novel the Sixteenth

ARGUMENT

San Bernardino* is tricked by two Salernitans, one of whom makes the saint believe that he has found a purse containing five hundred ducats, while the other affirms that he has lost the same, and by giving a description of its contents recovers the purse. Whereupon the saint, having in a sermon of his made mention of the poverty of the first-named man to the Florentine people, collects a large sum of money, which he hands over to the knave, who, having foregathered once more with his colleague, divides with him the booty.†

TO MY MOST ILLUSTRIOUS AND VERY REVEREND LORD, DON JOHN OF ARAGON‡

EXORDIUM

I MIND me, my illustrious and most reverend lord, that I have many a time determined within myself that I would dedicate to you, before making an end of my story-telling, a novel which should be full of divert-

* San Bernardino was born at Massa-Carrara in 1380, of noble family. He was trained for high office in the church, but in 1404 was moved by the vice and degradation he saw around him, to give up all thought of the career of wealth and ease which had been chosen for him, to sell all he had, and become a preaching Franciscan. For forty-two years he preached without ceasing in every part of Italy. In Florence he anticipated Savonarola's "bonfire of vanities," and vast crowds of listeners in Perugia were converted. He began to work for the reform of his order as soon as he joined it, seeing that the rule had grown very lax, and in 1438 became vicar-general. Afterwards he founded the Observantist branch of the Franciscans. He died in 1444, and was canonized by Nicholas V. in 1450.

† In the "Epoca" of Madrid, January 15, 1884, there is an account of a trick somewhat like the one dealt with in this novel.

‡ He was the third son of Ferdinand I. by Isabella da Chiaromonte. He was born in 1456, and became a cardinal in 1478. He died in 1485.

ing and seemly incident—to you as the highest ornament and bright particular mirror of those who follow in the footsteps of Peter, and afterwards to write down the same and include it amongst the others already written. And for the reason that I am wishing to carry the project aforenamed into effect, I now send you this novel which I have recently set down, one which you will find no less true than it is diverting. In the same, moreover, you will be led to understand how, not only men of the world, but also those who are rated as saints can be tricked, and indeed often are tricked in their lifetime here on earth by those who go about under the mask of feigned righteousness.

THE NARRATIVE

ANGELO PINTO,* one of our Salernitan citizens, must in his day have been, according to what old men who knew him affirm, a most renowned master in the art of cheating others by means of every different sort of knavery, so that, if you had searched all Italy through, you would not have found his peer.† Wherefore this said man, after he had made quest in divers parts of Italy, both within and without, and had employed his tools to good service in almost every place, betook himself at last to Florence during that very same time when our most holy San Bernardino was preaching there—a time when indeed the greater part of the dwellers in Tuscany were running after the saint aforesaid, on account of the many and manifest miracles which he worked without ceasing, and of the fame which was noised abroad in public concerning his perfect manner of life.

Now, mixed with the vast multitude who were listening to the saint's preaching, the aforesaid Angelo met one day by chance another young fellow, also a Salernitan,

* According to Signor Settembrini the family of this name still survives in Salerno.

† The Salernitans had a reputation for being clever knaves. The men of Sorrento, on the other hand, were proverbial dullards. See Novel IV.

called by name Il Vescovone, who, taking into consideration his age, was marvellously well learned in the arts which Angelo Pinto practised. When these two recognized one another, and called back to remembrance the city from which they both of them sprang, they exchanged many caresses and embraces, and set about relating a good part of the adventures which had befallen each one of them. At last, while they were conversing, Il Vescovone said: "My Angelo, you must know that I tarry here in Florence so that I may be able to put into execution a marvellously fine trick I know of; but, up to this present time, I have not been able to light upon any man in whom I could put full trust, and who might be the master of a few hundred florins."* Whereupon, after the young man had duly set forth the method of this trick of his, and after Angelo had highly approved of the same, the latter made answer and said that he was quite prepared to play his part in so noteworthy a cheat as he found this to be, and to lend his aid in the form of money and of all the cunning he possessed.

Thereupon, so as not to let any further delay stand in the way of this plan of theirs, they procured a very big satchel, having divers small pockets within side, and into this they put five hundred golden ducats—which was all that remained to Angelo out of a much greater sum, the residue of which he had expended—carefully separating the Venetian ducats from those of Florence. Besides this they divided all the other coins, according to the stamp which they bore, and placed each lot in a separate pocket; and then, having taken an exact account of them and written down a memorandum of the same on a piece of paper, Il Vescovone put this away carefully so as to have it at hand when it might be wanted. This done, they rehearsed together the scheme which they had agreed to carry out.

On the following morning, Angelo, having put on the disguise of a pilgrim, and with the satchel concealed in the breast of his mantle, went to the preaching, and when San Bernardino had come to the end of his sermon and had withdrawn to his cell, the feigned pilgrim followed

* Orig., *che sia forte di qualche centinaro di fiorini.*

him thither closely and threw himself down at his feet, begging him of his charity to grant a compassionate hearing, seeing that the matter he had in hand was one which brooked no delay. Whereupon San Bernardino made answer in benignant wise, and said that he was fully prepared to hear whatever his petitioner might have to say. Then Angelo, weeping the while, began to speak in the following words:

"My father, I would have you understand that within the last few days I have received at Rome plenary absolution of my sins, which in sooth were well-nigh unpardonable, and although I was thereby almost restored to that state of innocence which I enjoyed when I received the water of holy baptism, nevertheless, as a farther atonement for my most execrable misdeeds, an additional task of penitence was put upon me, to wit, that I should set forth on a pilgrimage to San Giacomo di Compostella. Now, after I had duly got myself in order to embark on this journey, it chanced that yesterday morning I allowed myself to be drawn to listen to your most righteous discourse, whereupon the devil, who was peradventure greatly angered because I had wrested myself out of his hands, threw down before my feet a halter with which I might well hang myself by the neck. By halter I mean this satchel here which I now hold in my hand, and in which are contained at least five hundred ducats. And while he showed me this satchel, he showed me at the same time all the many cruel ills which afflict me through my poverty, and brought before my eyes the picture of my three daughters, now come to a marriageable age, and very beautiful withal, but clad in sordid rags. Moreover, by calling to mind all the possible ills and dangers which might well be their portion through the want of all things necessary, and by many other persuasions, I was incited to turn back to my home, and to enjoy together with my poor family the many good things which have been here sent to me by fortune. However, being armed and equipped with the stout shield of the Holy Spirit, I was enabled to resist these temptations, deeming that the greatest treasures earth can afford are as naught when put in comparison with a soul which God is willing to redeem with the price of His most precious blood. Now, having brought myself to have recourse to you, having this resolve in my heart the while, I beg you, in God's name, that you will forthwith take charge of these moneys I have brought here, so that to-morrow, when you are preaching your sermon, you may declare this matter to the people assembled. If you shall do this, without doubt the owner of the satchel will be found, and then, when he shall have described to you by certain signs and tokens what may be within the same, you shall return it to him. Now, in case it should not seem just to you that I may with a good conscience take aught in the way of guerdon* thereanent from the owner, I implore you that of your kindness you will recommend my poverty to the good people of this city in such manner as may seem best to your fatherly kindness."

The illustrious saint, when he listened to the discourse of the suppliant thus tricked out in such plausible and sanctimonious wise, and when he saw how indeed there was money in the satchel as the pilgrim had said, gazed at him attentively in every feature, and, as the man seemed to him to be old in years and of an honest seeming, he not only gave undoubting credit to all the words he had just listened to, but he likewise said within himself that this thing must in sooth prove to be a miracle such as had never before been heard of, seeing that in the world as he saw it, marred and corrupted by wolfish avarice and insatiable greed of money, there should still be found a human spirit of such worth and excellence. Wherefore, after the saint had heaped upon the man before him many words of extraordinary praise in respect to the honest dealing he had practised, he said to him: "My son, I can find nothing more to say to you than to assure you that, if you had crucified Christ with your own hands, you would well deserve pardon therefor only by the merits of this righteous deed which you have wrought, without any further need of going on this pilgrimage. Nevertheless, I must hearten you on to follow the blessed path upon which your mind is set, and bid you be of good cheer, for assuredly God will not suffer this good deed of yours to pass away without its

* Orig., *pigliare aicun beveraggio.*

reward. On my own part I will, as you will be able to see for yourself, do my duty to-morrow in such a fashion that, the mercy of my Creator aiding me, I hope you will soon have provided for you a more liberal aid for your poor estate—to say nothing of keeping a good conscience—than any which would have come to you through following the course which the accursed enemy of God had prepared for you in order the better to hurl you down into perdition." When the saint had finished speaking Angelo thanked him in unmeasured terms for his goodness, and more especially for the offer which he made of his willingness to address an appeal on his behalf to the people in church on the following morning. Then, having left in the hands of the saint the satchel full of ducats, he said to him: "My father, I beg that you will let me know in what manner I must bear myself, for I must tell you, not that I am minded to make a boast thereof, but merely to speak the truth, that I am, in spite of my present poverty, sprung from a noble stock, and it would go much against my will if it were to come to the knowledge of men how I have to go about begging for alms; wherefore, if it be possible, let this be kept secret," San Bernerdino, giving ready belief to these last words, which indeed only caused him to feel still greater compassion for the speaker, straightway commanded him that he should not quit the cell where he at present found himself.

And when the morrow had come, the saint according to his wont mounted into the pulpit, and having changed the text which he had already chosen for his sermon, he gave out another in these words, "Fecit mirabilia in vita sua: quis est iste, et laudabimus eum?" and then went on to say: "Fellow-citizens, seeing that a marvellous circumstance has lately come under my notice—something which, in its working, partakes assuredly more of the miraculous than of the human—it has seemed convenient to me to trespass somewhat on the set order of the sermon I had promised to deliver to you, and to place before you the text which you have just heard me repeat. Now the circumstance to which I have made reference is that a certain poor man, who was bound on a pilgrimage to San Giacoma di Compostella in order to cleanse him of his sins, happened to find himself on the morning of the day before yesterday in the midst of a great crowd, and, standing there, he turned over with his feet a purse which was lying on the ground filled full withinside with a sum of several hundred florins—a lure which had probably been placed there by the art of the devil. Now, on account of this occurrence he has been assailed by a vast multitude of temptations, and has had to wage a fierce war against the consciousness of his own extreme poverty and the thought of his family left behind him, for whom he can with difficulty provide food enough for their nutriment, and against the other numerous miseries which afflict him. But in the end, strengthened thereto by the love of Christ, he made the sign of the cross, and blew all these temptations aside and scattered them afar. Then, weeping bitterly the while, he came to me, bringing with him in his hand the satchel full of florins, which I still hold in my keeping. In truth I know not what more Saint Peter himself could have done, or even our own seraphic Saint Francis,* the one and only despiser of earthly riches, and thereby the imitator of Christ, in that he would not claim any earthly possession as his own. Could these have done anything more than, having found this treasure I speak of, have sought to restore it to its owner? How, therefore, can we give greater praise to this man, who, being altogether perplexed with worldly troubles, steeped in poverty, burdened with the care of daughters, and, beyond all, debarred by shame from seeking alms by begging from the fact that he is of noble birth, practises nevertheless virtue in such high degree that it seems to me the Church might most deservedly this day sing on his behalf alone the text in the words of which I now appeal to your charity, 'He has wrought wondrous things in his life.'"

And after this the saint began to declaim with a loud voice the following words: "And you, most rapacious of wolves, most greedy of misers, men of lust all defiled with the dregs of this deceitful world, every day you practise

* According to the "Golden Legend," the epithet "seraphic" was applied to Saint Francis because in the vision during which he received the stigmata the marks were imprinted on his body by a crucified seraph.

usury and false contracts, and go after your ill-gotten gains. By your crafty dealing you keep as your own the goods of others, you rob the Church, you usurp the rights of the helpless, you drain the blood of the poor, you neglect to carry out the testaments with which you are charged, and in a thousand other most wicked deeds you go astray from the paths of Christ to follow those of the devil."

And thus the saintly old man, wrathful and burning ardently with the fires of love, having become somewhat awearied with much speaking, calmed himself, and having repeated the words of his text, went on to say: "I could never write down with my pen nor repeat with my tongue the words of praise which might most deservedly be applied to this man; nevertheless I would that you should here grasp the full meaning of one single instance of his goodness and purity of heart. He, when he was holding speech with me concerning this matter, made a great point of telling me that he willed not to ask for any guerdon in respect to the money which he had found, believing as he did that he could not with a good conscience accept the same. Wherefore now, my brethren, if the man who has lost this satchel be amongst you, let him come to me forthwith, and let him bring a description of the satchel and of the sum of the florins which are therein, and furthermore let him tell me exactly the number of coins of each separate impression, for you must know that they are already all divided the one sort from the other. If he shall do this, he may take the satchel and the blessing of God therewith, without having to disburse a single penny. Still I would not on this account cease from urging you to follow the teaching of Jesus our Redeemer, who has let us know it to be His will that, as every ill deed should be punished, albeit mercifully, so likewise no good deed should be allowed to pass by without its due reward. So it seems to me, my children, that this poor gentleman ought by right to have granted to him some reward in respect of the virtue he has shown in this matter; and, as I feel also that I am constrained in righteousness to commend his poverty to you, I pray that all those who are marked with the triumphant ensign of the cross of Christ will cast down upon this my cloak whatever alms God may inspire him to give, and let no one neglect to give his mite. For from the thousands of people I behold here before me, we shall surely collect a sum large enough to extricate him finally from his wretched condition, and to this good deed I exhort you, and I affirm that by it you will work greater weal than in lending aid to the needs of our hospitals, or in giving your alms to mendicants of any other sort whatever."

Having thus spoken, he threw his mantle down on the ground, and scarcely had it fallen before all the people, the greatest crowd that had ever been seen in that place, moved towards it, every man who was there reaching out the alms he desired to give in so holy a cause; and, in such fashion as I have described, the companions of San Bernardino during the whole of that day kept the mantle of the saint to receive the offerings which were made in answer to his request. By the time evening had come, it was found that they had collected a good sum of a thousand florins or thereabout.

Now while all this was being brought to pass, Il Vescovone had put on the disguise of a Genoese merchant, for the reason that he knew excellently well the idiom of that city, and now he came forward, and, crying and shouting aloud amongst the great crowd of people round about, he caused them to stand aside and make a passage for him. Then, having thrown himself weeping the while before the feet of the holy friar, he spake thus: "Sirs, these money are mine, and here or elsewhere I will give you a complete description of the stamps they may bear, for I have the same all written down here." So, taking from his breast the memorandum concerning the coins which he had kept there for this purpose, he gave it into the hands of the saint. San Bernardino, looking at him with a joyful smile, said: "My son, you have assuredly had more luck in finding your money than you had sense in keeping it safely. However, you shall come with me, and we will see whether the coins be yours or not. If they be yours, you shall have them back without the cost of a penny."

Thereupon the saint, after he had pronounced the benediction over the people, went into his cell, and having poured out the coins from the satchel, he found that they tallied exactly with the description given by Il Vescovone in his memorandum; wherefore he handed over the money with much satisfaction to the cheating knave. As soon as the latter had pocketed the same, he went as fast as he could to the place where the servants of Angelo were lodging, and, according to the plan which they had already devised between themselves, they all withdrew from Florence together and tarried for Messer Angelo at a given spot. And on the following morning there was handed over to Angelo the entire sum of money which had been collected, and this, in order to make the deception yet more complete, was, through the agency of the saint, converted into gold by certain bankers who were greatly devoted to him. Then Messer Angelo bestowed all the money about his person and took leave of the saint. returning to him many grateful words and receiving his benediction. He then went forthwith to the spot where his comrades were awaiting him; whereupon they all took their way to Pisa, holding high revel on the road, and having come there they made a friendly division of the booty between themselves, and then each one went his own way. From this we may easily believe that for the rest of their days they both went on living in jovial fashion at other men's cost.

MASUCCIO

ONE may say with truth that the jest which has been narrated in the foregoing story will seem quite as artfully constructed and diverting to its hearers as it was serviceable and full of profit to the knaves who carried it out, because, forsooth, it was such a fine trick that by it two common men were able to beguile not only a holy man of great experience, but likewise nearly all the citizens of Florence, who are of a very wily sort. Nor will you find any less laughable the story of another cheat which I am about to narrate to you, devised and carried out by two illiterate Roman fellows. This, albeit it was not of such serious moment as that which I have just told, may nevertheless be held to be in a certain sense more noteworthy, inasmuch as it was brought to pass in Bologna, a town to which nearly all the people in the world resort in order to buy their wit,* and from this place everyone assuredly might carry away a walletful, if, on departing therefrom, he did not leave too wide open the mouth of the wallet. But that this is the usage of the greater part of those who repair thither, is made manifest to us by the plainest signs.

* Orig. *dove quasi tutto il mondo manda a comparar senno.*

THE END OF THE SIXTEENTH NOVEL.

Novel the Seventeenth

ARGUMENT

A DOCTOR OF LAWS SENDS HOME TO HIS HOUSE A CUP, AND IS WATCHED BY TWO THIEVES. ONE OF THESE TAKES A FISH TO THE DOCTOR'S WIFE, BRINGING HER AT THE SAME TIME A FEIGNED MESSAGE FROM HER HUSBAND, WHICH DIRECTS HER TO PREPARE THE FISH AND TO DELIVER UP THE CUP. THIS SHE GIVES TO THE ROGUE, AND WHEN THE HUSBAND COMES BACK HE FINDS HIS CUP GONE, AND HURRIES OFF TO RECOVER IT. THEN THE OTHER ROGUE GOES TO THE HOUSE AND SAYS THAT THE CUP HAS BEEN FOUND, AND THAT HE HAS COME FOR THE FISH. THE WIFE BELIEVES HIM AND GIVES HIM THE FISH, WHICH HE STRAIGHTWAY CARRIES OFF; AND, HAVING MET HIS FRIEND, THE TWO TOGETHER ENJOY THE TRICK AND THE GAINS THEREOF.

TO THE MOST REVEREND MONSIGNORE, THE MOST ILLUSTRIOUS CARDINAL OF NAPLES.*

EXORDIUM

MOST reverend Monsignore, if it be that every claim of reason must urge and persuade those who may have given voluntary promises to their creditors to satisfy the same, I, seeing that I have made myself a debtor to your lordship's reverence by the offer of one of my novels, am forced not only by justice but by every

* Oliviero Carafa, of the house of Maddaloni. He was elevated to the archepiscopal see of Naples in 1458, and made a cardinal by Paul II. in 1467. It was under his patronage that Giovanni Pietro Carafa, afterwards Paul IV., went to Rome, and was made chamberlain to Alexander VI. He died in 1511, and was buried in the Cathedral of Naples, where there is a splendid tomb to his memory.

becoming argument to carry out this promise of mine, and thus to discharge myself of my debt. Wherefore, in the account of the doings which follows, you will be told the story of a very diverting and audacious trick which was played by two Roman rogues at the expense of a very wise and learned doctor of laws in Bologna. This man, although he had taught an enormous number of students in what manner they should sell wisdom to other, nevertheless, knew not how to impart enough of the same to his wife to enable her, either in the first case or in the last, to defend herself against the frauds of these Romans aforesaid.

THE NARRATIVE

MESSER FLORIANO DA CASTEL SAN PIERO was known in his own day amongst the people of Bologna as a most famous and excellent doctor of laws; and he, after he had come out of church one morning, was walking up and down the great piazza of the city with certain other doctors of law, his friends, and in passing it chanced that he entered the shop of a silversmith living in those parts to whom he had given orders to make for him a rich and beautiful cup of silver gilt, and before he went any further, and without holding any other discourse with the silversmith thereanent, he made out his account with the craftsman and paid it. Then, when he turned round to call his servant and bid him take the cup home, he found that the varlet was not there; so he begged the silversmith that he would as a favour send the cup to his house by the hand of his apprentice, which thing the silversmith undertook willingly to do.

Now at that time there were in Bologna two young men from the Roman states, who had come from the parts round about Trevi. These two were wandering through Italy from one place to another, carrying with them a store of false money, and loaded dice, and a thousand other crafty beguilements wherewith to defraud whomsoever they might meet, contriving the while to eat and drink and live a merry life by sponging upon others.* Of these one was named Liello de Cecco and the other Andreuccio di Vallemontone; and these two, finding themselves by chance in the great piazza at that very same time when Messer Floriana had bidden the silversmith let despatch the cup to his house, forthwith proposed one to the other to make an attempt to get this cup into their hands when they heard what orders had been given about it. It happened that they knew quite well the house where the doctor lived; and as soon as they perceived that the apprentice had come back from the discharge of his errand, Liello straightway gave command to his companion as to what course they must follow. First he betook himself to a tavern, and, after he had bought a very fine lamprey from a heap of large ones which was lying there and hidden the same carefully beneath his mantle, he hurried at full speed to the house of Messer Floriano. Then, having knocked at the door, he asked for the mistress of the house, and when he had been brought into her presence he said: "Madonna, your husband sends you this fish, and bids me tell you to have it daintily prepared at once for the table, as he is minded to dine here to-day with certain other doctors who are friends of his; and, moreover, he told me that you were to send back to him the same cup which the apprentice of the Bear† brought to you a little time agone, for the reason that he finds he has made an unprofitable bargain with the master silversmith thereanent, and wishes to have it taken back to the shop in order that it may be weighed again."

The simple woman, lending easy belief to the knave's words, immediately handed over to Liello the cup, and commanded her maidservants to lose no time in letting prepare the fish; and, having duly set in order such apparel as was needful for the reception of strangers at dinner, she awaited their coming with no little pleasure. Liello, as soon as he had got the cup safely in his possession

* Orig., *mangiare e godere a spese del crocifisso.*

† Orig., *il garzone dell' Orso.* The silversmith must have used a bear for the sign of his shop.

quickly made his way towards San Michele in Bosco,* where there dwelt a prior who was a Roman and a friend of the two sharpers, and an artist no less skilled in knavery than they themselves. This man gave Liello a friendly reception, and when he had heard the whole story, they both made merry over the good stroke which had been played, while they awaited the coming of Andreuccio, who had tarried behind in the piazza to listen to whatever might be said concerning the deed they had just wrought.

When the dinner hour had come Messer Floriano, having taken leave of his companions, went to his house, and as he drew nigh thereto, his wife, observing that he was alone, went towards him and said: "Messere, and where are the guests you have invited?" The doctor, greatly amazed at such a question as this, made answer to her, "What guests are these concerning whom you ask?" "Know you not what guests I mean?" said the wife. "I, for my part, have prepared everything for dinner in very handsome fashion." Messer Floriano, now more astonished than ever, cried out: "It seems to me that you must have lost your wits this morning." Then said the wife: "Nay, I am well assured that my wits fail me not at all. You, in sooth, sent me a fine lamprey with directions for me to get the same ready, seeing that you intended to bring hither with you several other doctors to dinner; and all the things you ordered me to do by your message I have done, and I hope these may be to your pleasure, otherwise we shall have lost our time and our trouble in no small measure." The husband replied: "Certes, my wife, I do not comprehend the meaning of what you are saying, but may God ever go on sending to us people who use us in this kindly fashion—people who bring us something out of their own store without taking away in turn aught from ours. This time, in sooth, we must have been mistaken for someone else."

Now when the wife, who with such scant caution had handed over the cup to the knave, heard that in truth her husband knew nothing at all about the matter, she said,

* San Michele in Bosco is an Olivetan monastery about a mile outside the gates of Bologna.

with her mind greatly disturbed: "Messere, in my opinion it is exactly the opposite to what you say, forasmuch as the man who brought hither the fish asked me in your name to hand over to him the silver cup which the apprentice of the Bear had brought here only a short time before, and he described to me so exactly all the marks thereof that I handed it over to him forthwith." When Messer Floriano heard that the cup had thus been cozened away from him, he understood at once that he had lost it by means of treacherous dealing; wherefore he cried out: "Ah, senseless numskull that you are! You have in sooth allowed yourself to be nicely tricked." Then he departed straightway out of the house, and when he had come to the piazza he went searching about on every side without knowing why, demanding of everyone he met if any man had been seen going in the direction of his house and carrying in his hand a fish. In sooth, the doctor gave vent to a thousand other crazy humours without getting any good therefrom. He went from place to place playing the fool and sending people to the four winds, asking all sorts of questions bearing upon the business in hand, and sometimes trying to believe, with faint hope, that it was only a harmless trick which someone had played him.

In the meantime Andreuccio was standing at the corner of the piazza with all the outward seeming of a man of good repute, and although he deemed that by this time his comrade and the cup as well must have gained a harbour of refuge, he felt nevertheless no little vexation that he himself should have lost the good round sum he had spent in the purchase of the lamprey without ever tasting a mouthful of the same. Wherefore he made up his mind to get into his possession the lamprey by means of another trick no less astute than the first. Thus, taking advantage of the time when he perceived that Messer Floriano was most hotly engaged in his search for the cup, he betook himself at the top of his speed to the doctor's house, and mounting the steps with a joyful face he said to the wife: "Madonna, I bring to you good news, forasmuch as your husband has found the cup which certain friends of his caused to be stolen from him by way of playing a jest with him; therefore he has sent me hither to fetch the fish which you have got in order, and to take it to him, seeing that he is minded to make good cheer with the same in the company of those who snatched the cup out of his sight."

The wife, who had been overwhelmed with grief and trouble for the reason that she had been the cause of the loss of the cup, rejoiced mightily when she heard that it had been found, and having taken two large dishes of pewter, with a white and scented tablecloth, she placed the well-dressed fish withinside, and, glad at heart at the turn of affairs, she delivered it into the hands of the worthy Andreuccio. And he, as soon as he was clear of the house, wrapped up everything carefully under his cloak and flew as fast as his legs could carry him towards San Michele, and, having arrived there, he met the prior and Liello, and the three held high revel over the excellent lamprey, laughing and jesting the while heartily. They afterwards handed over the pewter dishes to the prior, and then, using the greatest cunning, they sold the cup and went their way to another place without raising any hue and cry with regard to their exploit.

Messer Floriano, who had spent the whole of the day in vainly seeking to get some intelligence as to the matter, went back to his house late at night hungry and sorely out of humour; whereupon his wife, going forward to meet him, addressed him in these words: "Glory be to God! seeing that by his help you have at last found the cup, through losing which I was called a numskull." But he, with a heart filled with cruel resentment, replied: "Get out of my sight, conceited fool that you are! if you do not wish to know what bad luck really is; for it appears that, over and beyond working a grievous wrong and injury to me by reason of your brutish f lly, you now are minded to make a mock of me." The wife, utterly confounded by what she heard, answered, all trembling with fear: "Messere, in good sooth I do not mean to jeer at you;" and then she went on to tell him all about the second trick which had been put upon her. Messer Floriano when he heard this fell into a humour so overwrought and grief-stricken that he came little short of losing his wits entirely; and, after he had spent a great deal of time, and tried every scheme, with all sorts of most subtle investigations, to lay his hands on the thieves, he lived for a long season with his wife in sore hatred and ill-will, having failed altogether to discover anything about those who had duped him. And in this fashion the Romans enjoyed the fruit of their cunning deceit, and left the doctor. tricked and flouted, with his sorrow and loss.

MASUCCIO

ALTHOUGH, according to the novel which has just been related, the schemes employed by the cunning tricksters came to a successful issue, nobody will be able to deny that the said schemes were most dangerous and full of risk. And as it is a common saying in the mouths of men that the richest gains give rise to the greatest rejoicings, nevertheless it sometimes comes to pass that foxes are caught in the snare, and at the same time are mulcted both as to the loss and the profits as well. Wherefore I would the rather give my praise to those artists who know better how to work than to put their lives at stake for the sake of any trifling gain, and will gather an example from the friars of Saint Antony, who, when they set forth on one of their piratical excursions, put nothing on the table in the way of stakes except words, and never fail to draw therefrom so much profit that they always return to their homes safe and sound, and filled to the eyes with plunder. Of this saying the novel which follows next in order will give you clear and open testimony.

THE END OF THE SEVENTEENTH NOVEL.

Novel the Eighteenth

ARGUMENT

A FRIAR OF SAINT ANTONY BY MEANS OF ENCHANTED ACORNS SAVES TWO PIGS FROM DYING, WHEREUPON THE WOMEN TO WHOM THEY BELONG GIVES HIM A PIECE OF LINEN CLOTH. THE HUSBAND COMES BACK, AND, BEING GREATLY ANGERED AT WHAT SHE HAD DONE, FOLLOWS THE FRIAR TO RECOVER FROM HIM THE LINEN. THE FRIAR SEES HIM COMING FROM AFAR, AND THROWS A LIGHTED BRAND INTO THE CLOTH, AND THEN GIVES IT BACK TO THE OWNER. THE FIRE BURNS THE CLOTH, AND ALL THE PEOPLE HOLD IT FOR CERTAIN THAT A MIRACLE MUST HAVE BEEN WROUGHT; SO THEY BRING THE FRIAR BACK TO THE FARM, WHERE HE COLLECTS A GOODLY QUANTITY OF CHATTELS.

TO THE EXCELLENT LORD ANTONIO DI SANSEVERINO,* THE ELDEST SON OF THE MOST SERENE PRINCE OF SALERNO

EXORDIUM

MY excellent and virtuous lord, until the time shall come when I may, with my meagre faulty lyre, endeavour to sound in my writings the praises of the abundant virtues which dwell in that youthful and noble mind of yours, in which they must needs find their most fitting abode, I have been wishing to send you this present laughable novel as an earnest. From reading it you may at least be able to learn, by way of caution, what vast numbers of pirates of different sorts go roving about

* He was the eldest son of Roberto di Sanseverino (see note p. 86), and inherited his father's dignities when he was a child in 1474. He married Costanza, the daughter of Federico di

the world, and with what various tricks these fellows persuade each fool they may meet to fill their bellies with florins, and to look upon them as true saints. All these things will be made clear to you in a fashion that will divert you amain by the time you shall have come to the end of this novel. Farewell.

THE NARRATIVE

AS may be well known to everyone, it is a fact that a set of crafty and subtle knaves and charlatans* are at all times to be found going up and down in every part of Italy in the guise of fat, filthy friars of Saint Antony, making very sharp quest, and sweeping into their bags those votive offerings and gifts which may have been promised to their saints. Under pretext of this sort they roam about from one place to another, feigning to work miracles, and with such pretences, and with every other kind of crafty beguilement which they employ, they fill themselves amazingly well with money and with chattels of all sorts, and then go back to their houses, where they lead a life of idleness. Now of this kind of men there are more to be met every day in this kingdom of ours than in any other region, and in Calabria and Apulia they especially abound —provinces in which much almsgiving and little wisdom

Montefeltro, Duke of Urbino. He was the leader of the conspiracy of the barons, and after its defeat he fled to Paris. In 1493 he was joined by the Count of Cajazzo, his kinsman of the bastard line, who was at that time in the service of Lodovico il Moro, and they were given high command by Charles VIII. in the invading army. Antonio led the attack on Recco, where the first blood was shed in the war. He recovered his estates, and rebelled a second time against Frederick. He fled and died in Sinigaglia, 1499.

* Orig., *gli Spoletani e Cerretani*. "Cerretano" is the common term for a knavish pedlar. The people of Spoleto seem to have been famed for their shrewdness. Another use of the term in this sense is in Bandello, Part I., Nov. 34: *Il Carenzone che era astutissimo e haverebbe fatta la salsa a gli Spoletini*. The Roman ciarlatani, according to Capponi, are the lineal descendants of the earliest mimes, who come from Atella, now S. Elpidio, near Naples—their name Ciarlatani being a corruption of Atellanæ.

are to be found; wherefore these men are for ever making their way towards the districts aforesaid.*

It chanced that last year, in the month of January, there arrived in Cerignola a certain charlatan of this sort, riding on horseback and having in his train an ass laden with wallet bags and a manservant on foot. He went about collecting alms all through the country, making his horse to go down on his knees, and thus do reverence to the good knight Misser Saint Antony, according to the usage of this kind. When they had come one day into a certain village, it chanced that the fellow caught sight of two very fine pigs in front of the house of a rich farmer. The farmer himself was away from home, but his wife did not fail to give the friar an offering, and she did her alms, moreover, with a demeanour even more reverential than others were wont to use, whereupon he told himself straightway that he had here come upon soil which he might till to excellent purpose with his wonted implements. Therefore, putting on a look which seemed to tell that he was bursting with Christian charity, he turned towards his servant and whispered to him softly, but not so softly as to prevent the good woman from hearing what he said, and spake thus: "What a great pity and shame it is that such fine pigs as these must almost immediately die a sudden death!" The woman, who had stretched out her ears at the sound of these words, then said: "Missere, what is it that you are saying about these pigs of mine?" To this the friar answered: "In sooth I was saying naught else concerning them than to remark that it seemed to be a great failing of Nature's handiwork that such fine pigs as these should have to die in a few hours' time, without letting you draw aught of profit therefrom." Whereupon the woman, whose heart was wrung with grief at hearing this news, said: "Alas, man of God! I beg you that you will have a care to let me know by what working, such a curse may have fallen upon them, and whether we can by any means find a remedy therefor." The friar replied, "My good

* Calabria was proverbilaly the stupid province of Italy. In Novel IV. Fra Girolamo and his confederate go there with their arm of Saint Luke: *e fra loro conchiuso di andarsene in Calabria, provincia da grossa e incolta gente abitata.*

woman, I can tell you naught else as to the causes and the reasons of this thing. I only know that, by certain signs which I observe about them, it is bound to come to pass —signs which no living person could recognize except friars of our order, who enjoy the grace and favour of our good knight, Misser Saint Antony. I indeed should be able to find a remedy for them easily enough, had I only with me a few of our enchanted acorns."* Then said the woman: "Oh, see, for the love of God! whether you may not have one of the same about you, for I will pay you a very high price therefor."

The friar, when he heard these words, turned towards his servant, a fellow very well instructed in all tricks of this sort, and said: "Martino, look and see inside our saddle-bags, and search whether we have not therein two or three of these acorns, which I kept back for that ass of ours which so frequently falls sick in the same fashion. If you should find any, let us of our generosity give the same to this poor woman, in order that she may not lose these fine pigs through want of a remedy; then, I am well assured, she will not show herself so ungrateful as to forget that we have a hospital, or to refuse us the gift of a small quantity of linen sheets for the service of our poor sick people." In answer to this the woman said: "For the love of the cross of Christ save these poor pigs of mine from such an evil fate, and I will give you in return a quantity of new and fine linen, out of which you may make not one but two pairs of sheets for your hospital."

Then the friar forthwith contrived that Martino should hand over to him some acorns of the kind aforesaid, and having made him likewise bring a vessel of water, the friar put therein the acorns together with a good quantity of bran,† and, after he had mixed all the contents well together and had said a number of prayers over the mess, he placed it before the pigs, who straightway set themselves to devour the whole of it as if they had been famished. Then the friar, turning towards the woman, said:

* This practice of the friar is strictly in accordance with tradition, Saint Antony being the protector of animals, and of pigs especially.

† Orig., *caniglia* or *canetiglia*.

"Now, in sooth, you may rest assured that these beasts of yours will be safely delivered from the cruel death which they were bound to suffer, and if it should still please you to bear in mind the benefit which we have worked on your behalf, will you of your kindness hand over to me at once the reward, for I wish to depart forthwith and to go my way with God's blessing?"

Now this hurry on the part of the friar was caused by fear lest the husband should return and bid him take his hands off the prey he hoped to snatch. But the woman with the greatest willingness made haste to give him the linen she had promised him, and he, as soon as he had received the same and had duly stored it away, mounted his horse forthwith and rode away from the farm, taking the road which led to Tre Santi, with the view of journeying afterwards into Manfredonia, a region wherein he found every year the best of pasturage. Not long after the friar had taken his departure the farmer came back to his house from working in the fields. His wife at once went out to meet him with a joyful countenance, and told him the news how his pigs had been delivered from a sudden death by the marvellous virtue of the enchanted acorns of Saint Antony, and went on to say how she had given to the good friar some linen cloth for the hospital in remembrance of the poor and as a reward for the great benefit he had done on their behalf.

The husband, although he was mightily pleased to hear that his pigs had been delivered from the great danger which had threatened them, was nevertheless vexed and angry beyond measure when he learned that the piece of linen had changed owners, and, if he had not been held back therefrom by the great haste which drove him on to get hold of his property, he would of a surety have given his wife a good basting over the back with a stout oak sapling. So, in order that he might without delay set about that part of the business which called for more immediate attention, he asked his wife, without saying anything further about the linen, how long time had elapsed since the friar had taken his leave, and in which direction he had gone. To this the wife made answer that he had not departed thence a quarter of an hour, and that he had taken the road leading to Tre Santi. The wary farmer gathered together six others, young fellows and well armed, and in their company he set forth, following without delay in the friar's wake. They had scarcely gone a mile when they caught sight of him from afar, and then they straightway began to throw out to him a lure, calling upon him with a loud voice to await their coming, forbearing not the while to advance towards him.

The friar, turning round at the sound of their shouting, and marking how the clamorous band was drawing anigh him, immediately divined what must be the reason of their coming; whereupon, assisted at this juncture by his wonted craft and foresight, he immediately bade Martino hand over to him the linen cloth. Then, having put this in front of him on the saddle-bow, and turned his back towards his adversaries, he took the steel and dexterously struck a light and kindled therewith a piece of tinder. As soon as he heard that his pursuers were now almost upon him, he carefully put the lighted tinder withinside the folds of the linen, and then, turning himself towards those who had by this time come up to him, he said: "What would you with me, my worthy men?" The farmer, when he heard these words, came forward and said: "Vile, cowardly knave that you are, I have in sooth a good mind to run this partisan through the middle of your body. Were you not ashamed to make your way into my house, and by means of your lying cheat, to rob my wife of a piece of linen? May a curse fall upon you* for what you have done.'!

At these words the friar, without making any reply thereto, threw the linen into the farmer's arms and said: "My good man, I trust God will pardon you. I did not get this linen from your good wife by robbery; on the other hand, she gave it to me of her own free will for the use and benefit of the poor folk we have in our hospital; but here, take the linen, in God's name. I hope, more-

* Orig., *da la quale che vermicane ti nasca. Vermocane* is literally a creeping ulcer, and is sometimes used for a vine canker, but its chief use in the novelists seems to be as an imprecation. In Sacchetti, Nov. 4, *mo li nasca il vermocane*, and in 140, *che vermocane e questo.* Bandello, Part II., Novel 1, uses it in a vulgar and blasphemous sense: *Tu dici il vero al Corpo del Vermo Can.*

over, that our good knight, Misser Saint Antony, may in a very short space of time let you be witness of a miracle about which there can be no doubt, that he may rain down his fire not only into the folds of this linen, but likewise upon all the rest of your chattels." But the farmer, when once he had got the linen safely into his hands, felt very little concern about any of the curses or the hocus pocus of the friar, and straightway took the road back to his house. Scarcely, however, had he gone a stone's throw on his homeward way when he began to be conscious of a smell of burning and to see smoke rising from the linen, and those who were with him smelled and saw the same things. Thereupon the farmer, being seized with a fear more terrible than any he had ever known, immediately threw the linen down upon the ground, and then, having opened the folds thereof, found that it was all ablaze. Being now altogether overcome with fear, and terrified beyond measure lest some worse evil might befall him, he called aloud upon the friar, and besought him that, for the love of God, he would turn back and offer up a prayer to his miraculous Saint Antony, so that the cruel doom which had so quickly fallen upon him might be revoked.

Then the friar, who was in no wise anxious that the cloth should be consumed entirely, went back forthwith, and, without allowing them to spend any great time in supplicating his grace, gave orders to Martino to let quench the flames, and threw himself down upon the ground, making believe to pray devoutly with many feigned tears the while. Having done this, he gave the farmer good assurance that he need have no farther fears for his property on account of the fault he had committed, and then went back with the company to the farm.

As soon as the news of this manifest and undoubted miracle which the friar had worked became known in those parts, all the people round about, men and women, and even the young children, went running towards him crying aloud for mercy, so that on his entry into the village he was greeted with a reception no less glorious than that which Christ met when He rode into Jerusalem. And the gifts and offerings which were made to him were so abundant that ten sumpter asses would not have sufficed to carry them away; wherefore the friar, after he had converted the better part of the goods he had received into hard cash, went on his way rich and rejoicing, and took no farther care to return and fill his wallets.

MASUCCIO

THAT the arts by which all living men make it their study to gather for themselves rich spoil, without vexing their bodies with labour therefor, are very numerous and varied, the three novels which I have last told to you will give you clear demonstration. These tricks may likewise be said with truth to have been very laughable, and carried out with much astuteness and subtle ingenuity. However, the one which I propose to tell in the next place will be found no less diverting, and so much the more laughable since those who took part in it made great profit without using any device or labour thereanent, and with little or no travail of mind.

THE END OF THE EIGHTEENTH NOVEL.

Novel the Nineteenth

ARGUMENT

Two men of La Cava journey to Naples. One of them, being weary, halts at La Torre, and the other arrives late at night at Ponte Ricciardo, and lies there. Another man, an Amalfitan, passes that way during the night, one who is mightily in fear of men who have been executed, and shouts to a corpse hanging on a gibbet; whereupon the man of La Cava, deeming that it is his comrade who calls, runs towards him. The Amalfitan thinks he is being greeted by the hanged man, and takes to flight, followed by the other. He likewise flings away a bag he is carrying, and this the man of La Cava picks up, and then, having been joined by his companion, they return home.

TO THE VIRTUOUS AND MAGNIFICENT MISSERE BERNARDO DE ROGIERI.*

EXORDIUM

SEEING that in this my task of novel-telling I desire to keep in remembrance my most perfect friends, and to engrave in deep characters their names on this little work of mine, to serve as a lasting remembrance, I feel myself constrained by this obligation, before I may go any farther, to call back to memory the name of such a rare and perfect friend as yourself, and to dedicate to you this little novel, made up of very laughable matter, which I have lately finished. In reading this, over and above its diverting humour, you will be able to study the breeding and descent of the men of La Cava—who, in sooth, are

* In the later editions this novel is dedicated to "Messer Sestilio Aurelio Aliprando, reale armigero."

almost like our own compatriots—in such complete fashion that you, who are their present most discreet Podestà and Rector, may be able to give a valid judgment as to whether those who are now under your charge have in any way gone aside from treading in the footsteps of their predecessors.*

THE NARRATIVE

LA CAVA, a most ancient and very loyal town, which has in recent days, as is well known to everyone, attained in some measure to a noble status, has always been most plentifully supplied with master-masons and workers in pavement of exceptional merit. In these handicrafts they achieved such a mastery that they gathered together great stores of wealth in ready money and in household chattels and in landed estates, so that it was always held that of all the dwellers in this our kingdom there would be found none so rich as were those of La Cava.

Wherefore, if the sons had been wise enough to follow in the footsteps of their fathers, and had gone on without swerving after the manner of their ancestors of old time they would never have been reduced to that extreme and immeasurable poverty which now afflicts them. But perhaps the younger men, looking down upon the riches which had been gathered together by so laborious a handicraft, and regarding them merely as transitory gifts of fortune which can lead to nothing, have given themselves up to follow virtue and nobility, as the only things which change not and last for ever; and for this reason some have settled to become our new legists and doctors and notaries, others men at-arms, and others cavaliers. Be that as it may, you cannot now enter a house of that sort, wherein formerly you would have found nought else but implements

* Signor Settembrini remarks in a note that the people of Salerno and of Amalfi and of La Cava have always been in the habit of playing jokes one with another, and that the La Cavans as a rule get the better of the others.

of the pavior's or the mason's trade, without finding there, instead of these tools, stirrups and spurs and gilt sword-belts lying around on every side. Which one of the two courses it would better have profited them to avoid and which to follow, I leave to be decided, not merely by you yourself, but by all those others who, having no other concern with them except to read this story, may be disposed to give a righteous judgment concerning the same.

Now I, following the course of my story, go on to say that in the days when the famous master Onofrio de Jordano undertook the task of the marvellous building of the Castello Novo,* the greater part of the master-builders and workmen of La Cava betook themselves to Naples to work at the building aforesaid, and amongst the others there were two young fellows from the hamlet of Priato, who, attracted no less by their anxiety to see Naples (where they had never been hitherto) than by the desire to earn money, set out on their way on a certain Sunday morning in the wake of one of the master-builders mentioned before. And it happened that as they went thus on their way in the company of a number of other men of La Cava, that these two young fellows, who were not used to the fatigue of a long march, were left some distance behind the others, following the track of those who were in advance. And for the reason that they were ignorant of the way, they wearied themselves so greatly that it was very late when they arrived at last at Torre del Greco, and there one of them, who was very much more awearied than his comrade, proposed that he should tarry for the night. Whereupon the other took heart, and, thinking that he might perchance be able to overtake his companions, took to the road again and set out walking with the utmost speed he could put forth, but in the end his strength did not prevail to take him farther than a certain point between Torre del Greco and Naples before he was overtaken by the darkness of the night.

By this time he began to regret mightily that he had not remained with his companion, but he still kept walk-

* The Castello Novo was begun in 1283 by Charles I. of Anjou, from a design supposed to be from the hand of Giovanni da Pisa. Alfonso the Magnanimous added the five round

ing on, and, without knowing where he was, arrived at the Dritto of the Ponte Ricciardo.* When he caught sight of the walls and the doors thereof he imagined forthwith that it must be a house of entertainment; so, overcome with weariness and desiring to take shelter from a fine rain which was falling at the time, he drew near to it and began to knock at the door with a stone. After having knocked for some time without bringing anyone to open to him, he straightway made a virtue of necessity,† and stretched himself at full length on the ground, and found a resting-place for his head against the door, having made up his mind to remain there until the morning, when his comrade would pass thereby. Having thus settled himself, a light sleep soon came over him.

Now it chanced that on that selfsame morning there had likewise set forth from Amalfi a certain poor little tailor, carrying on his shoulders a sackful of doublets which he had made and was minded to sell on the following morning in the market at Naples; and he, like the young man of La Cava, had also been overtaken by fatigue and by nightfall when he had travelled as far as Torre del Greco, and had tarried there to rest over the night, having purposed in his mind to set forth betimes in the morning, so as to arrive at the place of sale at an hour which might let him have a good chance to dispose of his poor wares at a profit. As luck would have it, he woke from sleep when it was but little past midnight, and, deceived by the exceeding brightness of the light of the moon, he thought it must be near daybreak, and at once set out on his journey. He walked on and on without halting and without marking any sign of the coming of the dawn, and at last began to traverse the gravel pits which lie just beyond the monastery of the Orti, and by the time

towers in 1442, and this work is probably the one alluded to. The triumphal arch in his honour is from the design of Pietro di Martino.

* Now the Ponte della Maddalena, crossing the Sebeto between Naples and Portici. The Dritto was probably the house of the collector of dues, *e. g.*, *Dritto, per tassa o Dazio che di dovuto si paga al pubblico.*

† Orig., *convertito il bisogno in pazienza.*

he had gone so far he plainly heard the friars singing their matins,* and for this reason he became aware that a good portion of the night had yet to elapse. At this moment by chance there flashed across his brain the thought of the malefactors who had been hanged upon the Ponte Ricciardo, and, because he came from Amalfi, where men are known to be timorous by nature and faint-hearted, he began to be mightily afraid, and picking his way with loitering steps he did not dare to go far forward, and at the same time had a horrible dread of turning back on his path.

And being thus bewildered and filled with fear (for it seemed to him with every step he went that one or other of the hanged corpses must be on his traces), he came close to the spot the thought of which had smitten him with such dire terror. Then, when he had come right face to face with the gallows, and marked that not one of the criminals hanging thereon stirred at all; it seemed to him that he had by this time left behind him the most pressing part of the danger; wherefore, to rouse up some of the bravery which was within his breast, he cried: "Aha, master gallows-bird! will you go with me to Naples?" The young man from La Cava, who had slept but little during the night and very badly, when at first heard the sound of the approaching footsteps thought that they must be those of his companion, and then when he heard a voice inviting him to go on to Naples he felt quite certain that it must be as he had imagined, and promptly made answer to the invitation: "Here I am; I will soon be with you."

When the Amalfitan heard this answer given to his speech he became straightway possessed with the belief that it was the corpse of the man hanging on the gallows which had spoken, and on this account he fell into such a gruesome fit of terror that he ran no light risk of falling down dead on the spot. However, when he turned round and looked back and saw that a certain one was coming towards him, it did not appear to him that the time was a meet one for halting; wherefore, having flung away the pack which he was carrying, he began to flee at the top of his speed towards La Maddalena, crying out without ceas-

* About 3 a.m.

ing in a loud voice as he went, "Jesu! Jesu!" The man of La Cava, when he heard these cries and marked how rapidly the other was fleeing, at once deemed that he must be attacked by some others; so he straightway followed him as quickly as he could go, also shouting at the top of his voice and saying: "Here I am; I am coming to you. Wait for me, and do not be afraid." These words only served to strike still greater terror into the heart of the fugitive. After following him some distance the La Cavan saw lying upon the ground the pack of wares which the other had thrown away, whereupon he forthwith picked up the same. When he had estimated the value of the excellent goods therein, knowing at the same time that his companion had no such pack in his possession, he was well assured that the man who had fled at his approach could not possibly be his friend; wherefore, troubling himself no farther about the fellow, he made his way back to the spot where he had spent the night in no very comfortable fashion, bearing with him the booty he had captured. Then he stretched himself out once more to rest, and waited there so that at the coming of the day he might go on his way to Naples, either in the company of his friend or of some other.

In the meantime the Amalfitan, uttering the most horrible cries and sobbings, arrived at the Taverne del Ponte, and when he had come opposite to the same the collectors of the city dues, demanded to know of him what might be the reason of the clamour he was making, and to them he answered and affirmed it to be the truth that he had just seen the corpse of a man who had been hanged separate itself from the gallows, and give chase to him, pursuing him as far as the brink of the river. To this tale they all of them gave full belief, and, terrified no less than the fellow himself, they took hold of him and drew him into the house. Then, having carefully closed and locked all the doors and duly signed themselves with the sign of the cross, they did not issue forth again until it was broad daylight.

Now the other man from La Cava, who had remained behind for the night at La Torre, together with another wayfarer, also a townsman of the aforesaid place, arrived at the Dritto by the Ponte Ricciardo when the day had broken and it was quite light. The first man, who was still tarrying there, when he heard the sound of their voices knew who they were, and having gone to meet them he told them the whole story of his adventure. Whereupon his companion, who was well versed in all the ways of the country round about, perceived forthwith how the affair might have come to pass, and, so as not to let slip the booty which was inside the sack, they determined amongst themselves to go back straightway to their homes by the way of Somma.* This plan they duly carried out, and, when they had divided the plunder amongst themselves, they set out once more for Naples after a little time.

In the course of a few days the story of what had happened was spread by report through all the country, and it was told as a sure and certain fact how the corpses of the men who had been hanged were wont to give chase to any solitary wayfarer who might chance to cross the Ponte Ricciardo, each one who repeated the tale compounding many and divers fresh fables thereanent. By reason of this it came to pass that there was to be found no peasant who would go by that spot before daylight without first having signed both his beast and himself with the sign of the cross. Thus, with this and with divers other precautions the common people hereafter took their way through this perilous region.

MASUCCIO

VARIED, indeed, and strange are the terrors which the presence of the dead is wont to give to the living, a thing which we may see clearly for ourselves every day that passes. And it will happen now and again to some men who may be travelling by night, that, being assailed by an access of fear, they will see all the objects around them so indistinctly, and in such fashion

* Somma lies on the north side of Vesuvius. The travellers could make a long detour by this road, but would meet none of their townsfolk on the way to Naples.

that they judge one thing to be another, and, working afterwards upon this foundation, they compound a mass of the strangest and most marvellous fables that ever man heard—an instance of which the past novel has given us sample. This one, in sooth, has let come back into my memory the thought that I ought in the next place to write concerning another form of fear, differing from the story I have just told, inasmuch as the timorous man, being spurred on by the ardent flames of love, went of his own free will in quest of fear; from which adventure there followed many noteworthy pleasantries, as will be declared to you in the coming discourse.

THE END OF THE NINETEENTH NOVEL.

Novel the Twentieth

ARGUMENT

Giacomo Pinto is enamoured of a certain widow lady, whereupon Misser Angelo gives him a promise that he will let him have possession of her by the working of necromancy. He takes Giacomo, who fully believes this tale, to hold converse with Barabbas, and likewise gives him certain animals as offerings. But Giacomo takes to flight through fear in the end. The nature of the cheat comes to light, and Giacomo goes to the wars, wherein he serves for pay, and comes back therefrom a wise man and a rich.

TO THE GOODLY JOAN FRANCISCO CARACCIOLO*

EXORDIUM

KNOWING full well the high merits of your wit, my most worthy Joan Francisco, I can readily bring myself to believe that you will not fail to understand how many and how mighty are the difficulties which the man must needs encounter who sets himself to investigate the powers of Love, our mighty lord; and how, through his working, it continually happens that the witless become wise, and discreet men become fools; the bold are turned into cowards, and the timid into men of mettle. And over and beyond this, Love, acting belike as the doomsman of fortune, leads the rich down to the lowest pit of misery, and sometimes restores the poor to a prosperous estate. And because it does not seem to me that I need in any way give to you, who have been instant in your service to mighty Love from your very earliest youth, any fresh intelligence concerning his rule, or to tell

* This may be the same as the Duke of Melfi, to whom the forty-eighth novel is dedicated.

you how often it has chanced that men and women—wise and prudent though they be—have let themselves rush headlong to inflict a bitter and cruel death upon themselves with their own hands when scorched by the flame of their burning passion, I will only at this present moment set before you a fresh instance of his power, brought to pass in the case of a certain noble fellow-citizen of ours—one, indeed, not very richly endowed either with wit or courage—who, having been transfixed by love, became forthwith a man of the highest prudence, and acquired a degree of courage such as is scarcely to be looked for in a human soul. As a consequence of this, though he was a very poor man, he found an opportunity of enriching himself, and being freed from his many misfortunes, to lead a pleasant life in happy wise. Farewell.

THE NARRATIVE

NOT many years have passed since there lived in Salerno a youth of noble and ancient lineage, who was called by name Giacomo Pinto. He, although he sprang from the Seggio di Porta Nova, a district which is commonly reckoned to be the school of good sense in our city, would have found a dwelling more fitting and agreeable to his condition in the mountain regions of our land, whence, according to what men say, the greater part of our ancient families derive their origin. Now this young man, albeit his purse was ill garnished and his brain not overcharged with wit, was nevertheless endowed with the spirit of a gentleman, which led him to become enamoured of a certain widow lady, still young and very fair, and mother-in-law* to the governor of our city. It chanced that he had never before this been in love; wherefore he began to set about his wooing in such crafty wise that there was not a child in all Salerno who was not advised thereof, and on every side, and in every place where ladies and gentlemen were wont to foregather, they discoursed concerning the same in marvellously pleasant

* Masuccio writes *suocera; possibly suora is meant.*

strain, everyone framing jests thereanent. But he, being pierced by a dart which he had never felt before, took little or no heed of their jesting, and pursued, albeit with no success, the emprise he had begun, inflamed the while by the strongest passion.

Amongst the other young men of the quarter in which he dwelt who were wont every day to go gathering up some fresh matter of diversion from the follies he committed, was a certain one named Loisi Pagano. He, being a man of great talents, a pleasant companion, and of the finest manners, soon won the complete confidence of poor Giacomo, so that the latter would frequently discourse with him concerning the passion which was consuming him. Loisi, becoming every day more fully acquainted with the wanderings of Giacomo's brain, was seized with the notion that he might, by turning to mischievous jest the humours of his lovesick friend, bring to bear by means of these a sound chastisement upon a certain rascal, another Gonnella,* albeit he was a Salernitan. This fellow, who took to himself the name of Misser Angelo, had never yet been punished as was his due for the cheats and juggling tricks he had been wont to put in practice all his life. Though he was nothing better than a farrier, he would go running about all parts of Italy, now in the character of a physician and now in that of a merchant, and would ofttimes return home with a pocketful of money.

It chanced one day that while Loisi was holding converse with Giacomo on the wonted topic, he addressed the lover in these words: "My Giacomo, you must in sooth feel little or naught of discomfort by reason of your amorous pains, and have no wish to have done with the same, seeing that you might so easily put an end to them all. You know well that Misser Angelo is the most mighty and potent necromancer now alive on the earth; in good sooth I myself can bear you worthy testimony of this, seeing that in many adventures which I have taken up I have

* Gonnella seems to have been a professional buffoon at the court of the Marchese Niccolo d'Este. Sacchetti makes frequent mention of him, generally bringing in his name to let finish a pun, Gonnella meaning a gown. Bandello also names him. His "Book of Jests" was printed in 1506.

brought the same to a successful issue by reason of his aid. Moreover, this man is a natural kinsman of yours on the side of your mother. Why do you not betake yourself to him, and, plying him well with flattering words, beg him to exercise his art on your behalf, so that this affair of yours may come to a prosperous issue? As far as this matter is concerned, you will assuredly be fully satisfied with the result, supposing that Misser Angelo should be willing to help you. But, on the other hand, if it should happen that he should show himself minded to add to you the score of those others whom he may possibly have duped in the past, see that you lay hands upon him in such fashion that for the future he may never scheme how to put a trick upon a gentleman without calling you to his memory."

Giacomo, when he heard these words, was mightily glad of heart thereanent, and gave to his companion unbounded thanks. In sooth, he was half persuaded that everything he desired was already accomplished, and declared that he would not fail to do everything which had been commanded. Then Loisi, after he had laid bare his project with considerable trouble, went as fast as his legs could carry him to find Misser Angelo, and, overjoyed the while, gave him a full account of the trap which he proposed that they two, working together, should duly set in the course of the next few days. Misser Angelo, rejoicing greatly over this new prey thus delivered into his hands, and recking naught that Loisi was to the full as desirous that he should get his hide well basted as that a trick should be put upon Giacomo, did not quit the company of his new comrade until they had duly set the affair in order and come to an agreement as to when and how it should be carried out by them.

Not many days after this, Giacomo sent for Misser Angelo, and, almost choked with tears, laid bare to him the secret of his amorous passion, which was already known at the four corners of the market-place, and then spake to him thus: "Good kinsman, in our need those who are in truth our friends offer their help. I have just lately heard that you yourself are a great necromancer; wherefore I doubt not at all that by the help of your knowledge you will be able, supposing that you are disposed that way, to extricate me from all my troubles. So, in the name of God, I beseech you that it may be your good pleasure to set about the satisfying of my need in such fashion that I may be able to tell all men that I have not only got possession of the lady through your help, but that, along with her, I have received from yon my very life as a gift."

Hereupon Misser Angelo spake with a friendly face, and made answer that he, on his part, was fully equipped with everything he would need for the complete execution of the service which was demanded of him, and, passing on from one subject of talk to another, he said at last, "My Giacomo, I do not fully know whether you are to be trusted in this affair, seeing that what you will have to endure will require the most dauntless courage to face." Then answered Giacomo, "But how can such a thing be? I would have you know that I am ready to go to the depths of hell itself, so much has love fired my spirit for this enterprise." Misser Angelo answered him and said: "But then a worse thing than this must needs be done, forasmuch as it will be necessary for you to go and speak face to face with a very fierce demon whose name is Barabbas, a demon whom I alone have power to make subject to my will." Then answered Giacomo, "If it be your will, and if necessity demands, I will hold speech with Satan himself, who assuredly is the greater." "Well, may God grant that it shall be as you say!" replied the necromancer; "but tell me how are we to furnish ourselves with the other implements which are necessary for the despatch of our business? To begin, we must have a sword with which a man has been slain." Giacomo hastened to answer, "Oh, I have a sword, one belonging to my brother, which has been the death of ten men or more." Then said Misser Angelo, "Since we have got this, we have got the thing which seems to me the hardest to come by; everything else we may need we shall find without difficulty. Nevertheless, see that you have in readiness, at the time when I shall require them of you, a black wether of good size, and four capons well fattened. For the rest, you must wait patiently till the moon shall be on the wane, and leave all else to be done by me. I, in sooth, will deliver the spoil into your clutches, and you may make of her your mistress or your wife, whichever you list."

Giacomo, almost out of his wits for joy at the offer of such service as this, made answer that he would duly set himself to work to get everything in readiness according to the directions laid upon him. Misser Angelo then left him and went straightway in search of Loisi, to whom he set forth a complete account of the instructions he had given to Giacomo, in order that there might arise between himself and Loisi no misunderstanding as to the business, and they frequently came together, before the day came when they should set to work, rejoicing mightily the while upon the task they had in hand. When a few days had passed, during which time Giacomo never ceased importuning Misser Angelo to make a beginning, the necromancer said one day, "Good kinsman, I on my part have all things in readiness; now have you sought out everything I directed you to provide?" "In sooth I have," replied Giacomo, "and in this case fortune has assuredly been kind to me, forasmuch as my sister-in-law chanced to have just now some of the finest capons in the world, and out of these I have made them bring four of the best. And, besides this, I have happened, by a very strange chance, to come upon a wether as big as a bull and as black as night, and, as he has got four horns on his head, he is indeed a thing of terror to behold." Misser Angelo, mightily pleased at what he heard, then answered, "Kinsman, since the last few days you seem to have become quite another man; it appears, indeed, that Love has sharpened your wits in such marvellous wise that you might well go teaching sea-crabs the art of arithmetic.* What man besides yourself would have known how to get in readiness so many things and in so short a time? Now I, for my part, will set you in the way we have laid out, and this very night I will come to fetch you."

Misser Angelo then left Giacomo and went to settle with Loisi how he should await their coming at the place already determined between them when he should be assured that the appointed hour had struck. As soon as night

* Orig., *che insegnereste l' abaco ai granchi.*

had fallen, he went to Giacomo's house and said to him, "Shall we set forth, forasmuch as the time is now come?" "Certainly, Misser Angelo," replied the lover. And thus Misser Angelo, when the man-slaying sword had been handed over to him, and when he had hoisted the wether on his shoulder and hung a pair of the capons on his arm, led the way towards a spot where stood divers ruined houses, in one of which was already concealed Loisi, who had brought thither with him certain other gentlemen so that he might not enjoy such fine sport without letting others share it. When they had come to the place, Misser Angelo, turning towards Giacomo, said, "Good kinsman, you must understand that we are now come to such a point in this affair that we cannot turn round and retreat without the gravest danger to ourselves; therefore see that your courage fail not. And I must not refrain from exhorting you at all times, that however dreadful may be the things you see or hear, you will never utter the name of God or of the Virgin, or even make the sign of the cross, for if you do we shall all of us be hurled forthwith into the jaws of Lucifer. If, indeed, you should feel some qualms of fear, such as are wont to creep over men in cases like these, then you may commend yourself to the burden which the ass in Egypt bore upon his back, which burden was the Holy Mother and her Son, your Redeemer, and by these means we may, peradventure, deceive this one accursed of God."

In answer to this speech Giacomo promised that he would well observe everything which had been arranged. "Come now," said the necromancer, "and take care that you repeat after me every word which you hear me say; and, as soon as we shall have conjured up Barabbas, and you have heard him cry out, 'Give me the things with tails,' you shall at once throw to him the capons. Likewise you shall throw him the wether as soon as he cries out for the thing with horns." All these directions Giacomo promised most willingly to carry out, and Misser Angelo, having fully given his orders, drew forth the sword and made a great circle on the ground, inscribing also certain mystic characters therein. Then, by means of some fire which he had brought with him for the purpose, and certain boxes of fetid gums, he made a horrible smell, and making believe to mutter his incantations with strange movements of his head and his mouth, of his hands and his feet, he said to Giacomo: "Now put your left foot within the circle, and tell me truly which of these two things you would prefer: to see him here close before you in all his horrible deformity, or to hear him speak from that house over there?"

The poor young fellow, who, showing no little courage the while, had been led thus far by love and by his own simple nature, when he saw that the beginning of the sport promised to be of a very fearsome character, began now to feel somewhat of dread and horror, and gave answer to the magician and said that it would suffice him in the meantime to hear the demon speak. Then he put forward one of his feet within the circle, and, shaking with fear from head to foot, clean forgot all about the Jerusalem ass and called upon every saint in Heaven for succour without leaving out the name of a single one. The necromancer, perceiving by this time that the lover was persuaded they were transported into another world, said to him, "Now call three times for Barabbas." Whereupon Giacomo, fearing lest something worse should happen to him, called out the name for the first time. Loisi, who was garbed in the disguise of a devil, here made a blaze of fire, and then let follow the noise of an explosion terrible enough in sooth to have stricken fear into the breast of the bravest man you can think of. It is not for us to inquire whether or not Giacomo may have wished himself safe at home; in any case, he, being nerved to the deed by Misser Angelo, called out the name of Barabbas a second time; whereupon Loisi, in the character of the devil let blaze up a greater fire than before and frightened the poor wight more than ever.

Misser Angelo, although he failed not to perceive that the little wretch was half dead, did not give over urging him to keep his heart up and to say to him: "Have no fear, good kinsman, for we have bound him in such fashion that he will not be able to do you mischief of any sort or kind; therefore now call upon him the third time." Giacomo, however, in obeying the direction made his invocation greatly against his will, and spoke so faintly and his voice trembled so that his words could only be heard with difficulty. Then Loisi cast forth his third thunderbolt, and made such a horrible screeching that it wanted little more to let poor Giacomo fall to earth a dead man. Said Misser Angelo: "Stand firm and do not fear, for he is our captive. Besides this, you must know that through me you must work the conjuration; wherefore I bid you give out in a loud voice the words which I shall tell you under my breath." Then, having concocted a conjuration of his own, he once more bade Giacomo take courage, and urged him on to recite the same; whereupon Giacomo, as soon as he made ready to open his mouth, felt his teeth chatter mightily and his legs quake in such wise that he could not maintain himself upright on his feet. In sooth, in such piteous case did he show himself to be, that Misser Angelo began to fear whether the poor wretch might not die of alarm, and, perceiving that they had at least let the affair go far enough this time, he himself began to invoke Barabbas.

In the meantime Loisi and his companions were half dead with laughing over the fool's play, and as soon as they perceived that the disposition of things which had been settled by Misser Angelo was not like to go on to its appointed issue, they, in order not to be tricked out of their sport by Misser Angelo, cried out, yelling fiercely: "Give me now the things with tails and the thing with horns." Then said the necromancer: "Throw him at once everything you have, and take to your heels the quickest you can, and, as you do not wish to be struck dead on the spot, do not turn to look behind you." Giacomo, who indeed fancied by this time that he was in the infernal world, was pleased amain to hear these words, and having flung the capons and the black wether into the ruined house, he gave his legs such free play that not even the Barbary horses who are victors in the races could have kept pace with him.

Giacomo having got back to his house, Misser Angelo after a short space of time made his appearance there, and said to him: 'Well, good kinsman, what think you now of my skill as a necromancer? Keep a good heart, however, and the next time we will carry out our intention to the full." Then answered Giacomo: "Nay, I would rather that those who wish me ill should go there, for I would not go back thither were I to gain the empire thereby; and on this account, good kinsman, see and use your best efforts to bring my desire to pass by some other method. Then I shall be beholden to you in an eternal obligation." Misser Angelo answered: "So let it be, in God's name! I will go back to my house at once to consider the cure of your passion, so that you may in the end be thoroughly satisfied with what I shall do on your behalf." And after treating Giacomo to many other cozening speeches he went his way to his home.

Now Loisi, having taken possession of the animals which had been offered to him as a precious oblation, and bidden farewell to his companions, went home to get some rest. And when the morrow came he gave orders to his servants that they should, with the provisions aforesaid and with divers other good things, get ready a sumptuous repast to which he might bid Giacomo, and, besides him, certain of his friends who were privy to the affair. When they were seated at the banquet it seemed that not a single one of them could contain his laughter, and, going beyond this even, they all began to cry out, "Barabbas! Barabbas!" and to utter gibes of all sorts and of such a nature that Giacomo straightway perceived how he was being mocked and flouted by every one of his convives. Whereupon Loisi, taking note of what he saw, determined that the moment had now come when his original and foreordained project might be put in execution, meaning thereby that the trickster should be punished on account of his cheating in the past by the hands of his victim.

Therefore, as soon as the banquet was finished, Loisi called Giacomo and recounted to him in friendly wise, in the presence of a good number of the compony, in what fashion Misser Angelo had contrived to befool him: whereupon Giacomo, keeping well in mind the chief purport of Loisi's words, believing entirely in the truth thereof and with his mind filled with a deadly purpose, started off at once at the top of his speed in search of the pretended magician. Having found him, without uttering a word concerning aught else, he seized him by the hair of the head and, having cast him down upon the ground, he set to work to beat him in such savage fashion, and with such a shower of blows and kicks, that it was a marvel how the man attacked could endure them. And for the reason that his blood became mightily heated over his work, he caught up a stone with which, if he had not been seized and bound by the hands, with no small difficulty, by the crowd which assembled, he would assuredly have treated Misser Angelo in a way which would have put an end to all his knavish tricks for the future.

When he had shaken off the fit of rage which had thus taken hold of him, and had become conscious of all the follies he had committed, he was overcome with so great shame thereanent that he no longer felt he had the heart to sally forth from his abode, and on this account he made up his mind to depart from the city for good. Wherefore having sold a little farm of his which was all the property he possessed, he bought with the proceeds thereof a horse and arms, and then took his way to the wars in certain regions beyond our borders, where, by the favour of fortune and by his own vigour and valiant deeds, he acquired a great sum of money in a short space of time, being reputed likewise a famous man-at-arms and marvellously wise and prudent. And, seeing that Love and Misser Angelo together were the cause of all this good luck, and that one of them received just paym nt for his deeds at the hands of Giacomo, it now only remains for us to ratify for ourselves the truth of th words we spoke in the beginning, to wit, one may well say that wonderful, incomprehensible, and miraculous is the power of the quiver-bearing god. How happy are they upon whom he and fortune look with smiling faces!

MASUCCIO

I HAVE heard it said by many people at many different times that when a man's wit becomes enfeebled, and he, on this account, is found an easier prey to tricksters, he will often set to work to take revenge at one stroke, and thus punish the cheater and get satisfaction for the cheat at the same time; without taking farther thought of the matter, he will fall to the use of violence, and will make the one who may have beguiled him smart well therefor. And a certain portion of the foregoing novel will let us see that the saying I have alluded to is a true one; forasmuch as we may notice that Misser Angelo, being well advised of the slender wit of the headstrong lover Giacomo, used all his art to put a trick upon the silly fellow, but the latter, as soon as he perceived in what fashion he was being used, not being well enough endowed with cunning to pay Misser Angelo back in his own coin, or to return more than he had received, at once flew to violent means. This, in sooth, he did in such a manner that, if the succour had delayed ever so little, he would assuredly have despatched the necromancer to keep company with Barabbas.

Now, seeing that in this second part of my work which has just come to an end, I have told you enough of the accidents and the potency of love, of many singular and laughable tricks and jests, and of divers other fresh and strange occurrences, I think that it is now my duty to turn my pen to other themes, and, as I puzzle my brains in settling which target I shall now shoot at with my arrows, the fact recurs to my memory that when I began to set down in writing what I knew about those sham professors of religion, I was annoyed in cruel fashion by the complaints and reproaches of certain would-be wise, lawyer-like women; and, although at the time I gave back to them an adequate reply to all their stupid chattering, still I made myself their debtor by giving them a promise that, before I should have come to the end of this work of mine, I would not fail to let the world have full intelligence concerning their faulty and most imperfect sex, adding thereto somewhat by telling of the innate corruption, the treachery, and the wickedness of the greater number of them. And, seeing that I am now minded to acquit myself of this debt, there has come up in procession before me so many perfidies, so much unheard-of baseness, so many deeds more fiendish than human, which have been wrought by the many lawless, unbridled, and wicked women in the world, that I was almost persuaded to refrain my steps from the path I had proposed to tread. Nevertheless, feeling myself more potently urged on by the sense of justice than held back by vexatious or hostile speech, I am induced, albeit somewhat disgusted with my task, to set down here some of the failings which come to women by nature.

HERE ENDS THE SECOND PART.

PART THE THIRD

Prologue

THE SECOND PART OF THE NOVELLINO, WHICH IS MADE UP OF DIVERTING DISCOURSES, HAVING NOW COME TO AN END, THE THIRD PART HERE MAKES AUSPICIOUS BEGINNING. IN THIS THE FEMALE SEX, SO FULL OF FAILINGS, WILL BE HANDLED SOMEWHAT CRUELLY. BUT FIRST OF ALL WILL BE GIVEN THE GENERAL EXORDIUM, AND THE PROFFERED GIFT OF THE AUTHOR, AND THEN WILL FOLLOW THE NOVELS SET FORTH IN THEIR DUE ORDER.

MASUCCIO

NOW that an end has come to my seafaring adventure, which I made in the company of my pleasant and merry tales; now that my sea-boat has been drawn ashore, and its sails furled, its oars and rudder set in order; now that farewell greetings and words of gratitude, such as it is allowed to me to express, have been spoken to Æolus and Neptune—it seems that it only remains for me to carry out in some measure the work I have, after such long deliberation, resolved to do. Wherefore, having bidden farewell for good and all to these delightful shores, it will behove me to take my way through rough and gloomy paths, and to make beginning of this Third Part of my Novellino, and to go on to the end thereof, concluding perchance with speech less sharp and bitter than that which I shall employ in the beginning.

And while I was led by somewhat keen desire to direct my hurrying steps into these paths, the beaten track itself tempted me to enter into a dark and horrid wood, hedged round by knotty trunks and prickly thorns, which grew there unrestrained in their natural wise. How terrifying and cruel the ingress to this place appeared to me, standing there all alone and unarmed, each one who reads this may determine for himself. And certes, being now wellnigh overdone with fear, the ardent desire which possessed me began to grow cold, and many and many a time I came near to turn backward my footsteps. While I stood thus confused and uncertain, there appeared before me an old man, having his face garnished with a spreading beard of white hair, whom I judged, as soon as I saw him, to be of august presence, and wielding sway which I must respect. Neither his form nor the raiment he wore appeared to be aught akin to the world of human beings, but were rather those of some celestial deity, whereupon I called to mind how I had once upon a time beheld his natural form portrayed in marble sculpture, and I forthwith knew him to be Mercury, the most eloquent of the gods;* and, for the reason that my dread of him had only been made all the greater by his manifestation to me, I felt myself now too much awestricken to approach him, or even to raise my eyes to look him in the face.

Then he, observing how greatly I was afeared, himself reassured me, glancing at me in pleasant wise and calling me by my name in a gentle voice, and inspiring my heart with no little boldness thereby. Next he said to me, "My Masuccio, as you yourself can give good witness, I have known you from your tenderest years to be one much more liberally endowed by nature with inborn wit than furnished with learning by your teachers. Therefore, when I marked you standing thus laden with anxious

* This presentation of Mercury as an old man is remarkable, and it would be interesting to know where the author could have seen the marble sculpture to which he refers. The Etruscan and Pelasgic statues of Hermes were occasionally bearded; *sphenopogon Ermes* (Artemidorus, ii. 42), and Herodotus, ii. 51, obviously refers to the archaic Hermes: *Tauta men nun, kai alla pros toutoisi ta ego phraso, Ellenes ap, Aiguption nenomikasi, tou de 'Ermeo ta agalmata ortha echein ta aidoia poieuntes, ouk ap Aiguption memathekasi all apo Helasgon, protoi men Ellenon apanton 'Athenaioi paralabontes para de touton olloi* Of the later bearded effigies of the god there is one on a triangular altar in the villa Borghese in Rome, one in Wilton House—in this he bears a ram on his shoulders—and another, which, according to Winckelmann, was formerly in the gardens of the Palazzo Farnese in Rome, and is now in the Museum at Naples.

thoughts and confused in mind at the entering place to this gloomy and devious wood, I was fain to have compassion upon you, and to give you my help, knowing that in the part of your book which is to follow you are minded in your biting mood to rebuke and to punish the wicked hearts and the unbounded turpitude of the infamous female sex. Thus I will point out to you a method—what though this same may appear to you to be a path very hard to tread—whereby you may with ease find a way into this distressful labyrinth, and issue therefrom once more as a victor. Wherefore enter this wild wood straightway, and, before you shall have gone far therein, you will espy on your left hand a well-tracked road, upon which, if you shall examine it narrowly, you will recognize the footsteps left thereon by Juvenal, that satirist of old time, and by Boccaccio, our own poet so famous and so highly praised, whose florid idiom and style you have ever done your best to imitate. Take care, therefore, that you follow in the footsteps of these men, for you will assuredly find that you must perforce travel over a very wide and ample plain, and in your journeyings in every part of the same you will, on all sides, come face to face with all manner of new and wonderful things, which will, without ceasing, fill you with fresh wonder and amazement every minute that passes, so that your pen, however weary it may be, will not be suffered to rest for a moment unemployed. For, be it well known, there would not be found in the choicest eloquence power enough to set forth with due effect what there is to be said concerning this corrupt, this cruel, this miscreant sex of women, from whose treachery and wicked dealings the strivings of the immortal gods—and much less those of human creatures—can do naught to rescue us. Moreover, I will keep silence concerning the measureless deceits practised by this perverse brood against our mighty father Jove himself, against the radiant Apollo, against us and the residue of the gods; to all of whom, in sooth, every mystery is clear, and to whom the future is even as the present day.

But now, putting on one side the heavenly deities, so as not to cause you to wander aside from your destined path, I will yet further hearten you to your task by narrating to you yet other things concerning the unfaithful and variable female sex, because every step you take you will find their ways to be full of all sorts of sin and lasciviousness. For this reason see that you be well on your guard, for in the midmost point of the wood, where the trees are most shady and thickest, you will behold, long before you shall come thereto, and placed some distance from the road, a most delightsome garden fenced in with marble walls, in which are gates of alabaster adorned with sculpture which are a wonder to behold. How full it may be of green growing laurels, of fresh olive-trees, and of other varied and choice shrubs producing luscious fruits and laden with sweet-smelling flowers, it boots me not to tell you now, seeing that in a short space of time you will behold all these things with your own eyes.

This spot you must know has been called the sacristy of chastity, and has likewise been consecrated and chosen by all the celestial deities as the special possession of our lady Ipolita Maria dei Visconti, writing of whom you have already covered so many sheets of paper, and whose name you are for ever celebrating and exalting in such worthy fashion with the highest praise and honour. In this place also it is meet to sing the praises, together with hers, of the Infantas Donna Lionora and Donna Beatrice of Aragon,* her sisters-in-law, ladies who are at the same time honest, modest, and winsome, and honoured by the ensign of the snow-white ermine† in their laps. These ladies, by the virtues which are their own, have already outdone nature, and have decked their royal brows with jewels of the East, and, wrapped round in their purple-gold embroidered mantles, have withdrawn themselves altogether from intercourse with the crowd of womankind. On the highest spot within the garden you will espy a banner, on the green field of which there is pictured the semblance of a little animal of the purest white, standing as if in doubt, with its foot uplifted so as

* Daughters of Ferdinand I.

† This is an allusion to the order of Ermellino, instituted by Ferdinand I.

not to befoul the same in the mud. From its mouth there issues a scroll, upon which is written in letters of gilt the motto, "Malo mori quam fœdari."* Over and beyond this you will perceive that the boundary hedges of the garden are adorned with hangings of blue cloth of the richest texture, thickly sown with the representations of vases filled with golden rods, the vases standing in the midst of burning flames, which thus refine the purity and consummate nature of the gold, making up the notable ensign which, as you well know, this illustrious lady, a very divinity to us, has chosen as a device most fitting for her use.

Likewise you will remark how the whole of this sacred spot that is surrounded by unicorns of the fiercest nature, which have become obedient and gentle simply through perceiving the odour which hangs about the modest dames and damsels who have their dwelling within the garden aforesaid.† Therefore I bid you take good care, if you would not run in danger of smarting under our anger and indignation, that you do not, either in your thoughts or by

* The motto of the order of the Ermellino.

† One of the mediæval legends of the unicorn was that it could only be caught by the bait of a virgin, and that in her presence it would lose its fierceness and lie down at her feet. In the "Piacevoli Notti," Straparola makes the unicorn the subject of the enigma to the First Fable of the Thirteenth Book, and endows the animal with similar qualities. The Chinese tradition is very much the same, describing the beast to be of a gentle nature, and unwilling even to tread upon an insect. On the other hand, Pliny writes, viii., 21: "But the most fell and furious beast of all other is the Licorne or Monoceros: his body resembles a horse, his head a stag, his feet an elephant, his tail a bore: he loweth after a hideous manner, one black horn he hath in the mids of his forehead, bearing out two cubits in length: by report this wild beast cannot possibly be caught alive." Ælian, "De Nat. Animal.," xvi. 20, places its habitat in the mountain districts of India. "Amongst others they enumerate the unicorn, which they call cartazonon, and say that it reaches the size of a horse of mature age, possesses a mane and reddish hair, and that it excels in swiftness. One black horn projects between the eyebrows, not awkwardly, but with a certain natural twist, and terminating in a sharp point. It is said to be gentle to other beasts approaching it, but to fight with its fellows." Ludovicus Vertomanus, in "The Historie of Travayle in the East and West Indies," declares that

your words, or by what you set down with your pen, bring into notice or entangle in either great or small degree any one of these most virtuous ladies aforesaid in the course of this journey which you have undertaken. Nay, if it should happen that hereafter you should be minded to treat of their sacred perfection, it will behove you always to write them down, and to include them in the number of our divinities. Also let it not escape your mind, if at any time you should have a desire to write aught concerning them, that you may tell with truth well approved, how these ladies alone have remained true women, and have kept the purity of their sex as it was given to them by nature. Wherefore for the present time let it be sufficient to you to gaze upon and wonder at this marvellous place, both from afar and nigh thereto, and to follow diligently the path which we have pointed out to you, forasmuch as you will always have us with you for your government and your guidance."

As soon as he had brought this discourse of his to an end, he straightway disappeared from before me, and, in like manner as long seasons of wretchedness are dispersed and put to flight by the unexpected and sudden advent of good fortune, even so my terror and the fear which had hitherto possessed me were transformed into exceeding great gladness by listening to the finely-spoken and pleasing discourse of the god. Thus, having taken courage from the consolations he had just given me and from his commands, and likewise from the promises which

he saw two unicorns in a temple at Mecca, which had been given to the Sultan by a King of Ethiopia. In the "Bestiary" of Philip de Thaun is the following rhyme:

"Monosceros est Beste, un corne ad en la teste,
Purceo ad si a nun, de buc ad facun;
Par Pucele est prise; or vez en quel guise
Quant hom le volt cacer et prendre et enginner
Si vent hom ul forest u sis riparis est;
La met une Pucele hors de sein sa mamele,
Et par odurement Monosceros la sent:
Dunc vent à la Pucele, et si baiset la mamele,
En sein devant se dort, issi vent à sa mort;
Li hom suivent atant ki l'ocit en dormant
U tres tout vif le prent, si fais puis sun talent."

T. Wright, *Popular Treatises on Science*, p. 81.

he had made me with regard to the future, I took my way into the forest without further hesitation, and, passing along with hasty steps, I soon found myself within the bounds of the green and lovely little meadow in which the garden described by the god had been planned and made. But the commands which he had laid upon me did not permit me to fare any further. Nevertheless, being heartened by the sound of sweetest harmony coming from divers instruments which discoursed tuneful melodies withinside the garden, I felt content with the mere sight of the same, and having seated myself at the foot of a forest tree, I set to work, rejoicing greatly the while, to write the novel which follows.

Novel the Twenty-first

ARGUMENT

MESSER BERTRAMO D'AQUINO IS ENAMOURED OF A LADY WITHOUT GETTING A RETURN OF HIS PASSION. BUT FOR THE REASON THAT THE HUSBAND OF THE LADY AFORESAID LAVISHES GREAT PRAISE ON THIS SUITOR OF HERS UNDER THE GUISE OF A FALCON, SHE IS AT LENGTH INDUCED TO TAKE HER LOVER INTO FAVOUR. WHEN THEY FOREGATHER, MESSER BERTRAMO DEMANDS TO KNOW WHY SHE HAS LET HIM COME TO HER. HAVING HEARD THIS, THE CAVALIER BEARS HIMSELF IN GRATEFUL WISE, AND, WITHOUT SO MUCH AS TOUCHING HER, TAKES HIS DEPARTURE AND LEAVES HER IN DERISION.

TO THE MOST EXCELLENT LADY, ANTONELLA D'AQUINO, COUNTESS, AND WIFE OF THE KING'S CHAMBERLAIN*

EXORDIUM

MOST excellent Countess, being now in the humour to carry out the set purpose which I have formed, and to castigate in ten other novels of mine the evil nature, the wicked vices, and the crafty machinations of ill-minded women, it seems to me that it will be both fitting and necessary to treat of certain trifling matters in the story which follows, in such measure that you, a follower of the school and standard of virtue, you who by your own peculiar worth have overcome and conquered the natural inclination of the female sex, may deliver to us a full and true judgment, telling us in what degree the natural qualities and the habits of women differ from those of men, in quantity and in kind also, taking to yourself the while all the fame that is rightly yours. In this

* Wife of the Count d'Avalos, to whom Masuccio dedicates Novel XII. She was the only daughter of the Marquis Pescara.

fashion the extraordinary virtue and the lofty deeds practised by a most worthy cavalier, sprung from your own noble stock,* concerning which you will read near the end of the story, will afford you manifest proof of the truth of my saying.

THE NARRATIVE

IT is now not many days agone since a tale was told to me as truth undoubted by a certain cavalier of good repute, how, in those days when Manfred † was overthrown and slain by Charles, first of the name, who subsequently conquered and took possession of the whole kingdom, there was one who bore a part in the conquest aforesaid, a certain valorous and active cavalier called by the name of Messer Bertramo d'Aquino. Being a mighty shrewd fighter, he was appointed captain; over and beyond this, he was sage in counsel, far-seeing, and gallant beyond any other gentleman at that time holding service in the army of the King Charles aforesaid, and accordingly he was wont to let all his friends view with delight and his enemies taste with little pleasure, the high and daring deeds he wrought.

Therefore, after he had gained full possession of the kingdom, the king, accompanied by the whole body of

* The family of Pescara sprang from Aquino, as did also Messer Bertramo.

† Natural son of Frederic II. On the death of Conrad his brother, he governed the kingdom for Conradin his nephew. The Pope claimed the kingdom of Naples for the Holy See, and ultimately gave it in fee to Charles of Anjou. Manfred was defeated and slain by Charles at Beneventum in 1266. The battle was lost by the treachery of the Apulians in Manfred's service:

"E l'altra, il cui ossame ancor s'accoglie
A Ceperan, là dove fu bugiardo
Ciascum Pugliese."—DANTE, *Inferno*, xxviii.

After his death the church endeavoured to withhold from the body of the excommunicated Manfred the rites of burial, for although Charles had caused it to be interred, the Bishop of Cosenza afterwards rifled the grave.

his barons and courtiers, went to Naples to enjoy all the delightful and delicate fruits which the advent of peace always holds out to the conquerors. They began to devote themselves to joustings and balls and divers other feasts given in honour of their triumph, and amongst the crowd of cavaliers who took special delight in diversions of this sort—peradventure as a reward for all the dangers and fatigues undergone while serving with the army in the wars—Messer Bertramo was to be found. Now it happened that he, having one day cast eyes upon Madonna Fiola Torella at a certain ball, straightway fell in love with her so ardently that he found he could in no wise let his thoughts turn towards any other object; and, in spite of the fact that Messer Corrado, the husband of the lady, was a particular friend of his own, and one who in the prosecution of the late war had borne his part manfully, fighting side by side with Messer Bertramo, he, completely taken and bound by the charms of the lady, so that no restraint could avail anything against the strength of his passion, set himself with all his mind to bring to an issue the enterprise in which he had embarked. Thus he began to joust in her honour, and to prepare many sumptuous feasts on her behalf, spending and giving away his substance—thus letting it be made manifest to her every hour that passed how he loved her more dearly than he loved his own self.

Now it fell out, either because the lady was exceedingly true of heart, or on account of the superabundant love which she bore to her husband, that she did naught else but mock at the cavalier and the amorous courting he lavished upon her. Thus, all his labour and pains being of no effect, she showed herself every day more cruel and inflexible to his prayers; and, howbeit he perceived that with regard to this enterprise of his all hope was fled, nevertheless, as is the common use of all those who are consumed by fervent love, his desire, increasing from hour to hour, ever waxed into a fiercer flame. And while the luckless lover was in this untoward mind, without even enjoying the boon of a single glance graciously vouchsafed to him by the lady, it chanced one day, when Messer Corrado and his wife, accompanied by divers other ladies and gentlemen, were going out to enjoy a bout of hawking, they came unexpectedly upon a covey of partridges, and behind them a wild falcon, which was scattering them in such fashion that they could not in any way come together again.

When the company beheld this they were all mightily diverted thereanent, and Messer Corrado, amongst the others, declared with a merry face that it seemed to him as if he had just beheld, under the likeness of the falcon, Messer Bertramo, his valiant captain, chasing and putting to flight the foemen in some battle of the late war, bearing himself in such wise, that, as soon as he might show himself with lance and with sword, not a single one of his adversaries would find stomach to await his onslaught. And over and beyond this, he went on to say that, in the valiant deeds of arms which he wrought without ceasing, Messer Bertramo reminded him, not only of the falcon which they had just seen chasing the flying partridges, but also of a bold and savage lion amongst a herd of cowardly cattle.

Having said so much, he spake yet more in the same strain, unwitting that the cavalier whom he lauded in these terms of praise was in a certain sense fascinated by the charms of his own wife. He related so many other examples of Messer Bertramo's worth and pleasant humour and splendid liberality, that there was not a single one of the company who did not on account of this praise become more favourably disposed towards Bertramo even than was the speaker. Amongst these, too, was Madonna Fiola, who up to this time had suffered neither the thought of the cavalier himself nor of his worth to find a lodgment in her heart. But she, when she heard and considered how great were the commendations given to this gentleman by her husband, to whose words she was ever wont to give unquestioning faith, was moved straightway to change the cruelty and dislike for him which had heretofore possessed her into an excessive passion of love. Wherefore, having returned a prisoner of love to her house from which she had gone forth free as air, she began to desire most earnestly that her lover might pass that way, in order that, letting herself be seen by him in her most gracious aspect, she might let him know how completely she was changed both in her condition and temper.

As it was willed by the happy fortune of the two lovers, the lady, being still in the humour aforesaid, soon caught sight of the cavalier passing by, more elegant and comely of aspect, as it seemed to her, than was his wont; and he, without letting rise in his heart hopes of gaining any answer, made her an amorous salutation, according to his habit. The lady, as soon as she saw this, gave him back, as she had already in her mind determined, the reply his greeting demanded, feeling the greatest joy meanwhile. On this account the cavalier, delighted beyond measure, and overcome by amazement as well, went his way to his own house. There he set himself to canvass the affair fully, and to cudgel his brains as to how he should proceed in the matter, and not being able to call to mind that he had brought into practice any fresh or unwonted expedient whereby he could have induced her to show him such great kindness, and knowing not how to come to any rightful judgment in the matter, he found himself, as it were, altogether puzzled. Whereupon he sent for one of his most intimate friends, one who was well informed as to his private affairs, and to this man he narrated, point by point, the strange accident which had befallen him, and all his own astonishing reflections thereanent. This friend, who was gifted with great sense and prudence, and one, moreover, quite free from all amorous passion, began forthwith to make a jest of the lover and of his dreaming, and answered him in these words: "In sooth, I marvel not at all at your lack of judgment, seeing that love has dazzled your understanding in such wise as to keep you in ignorance as to the stuff women are made of, and of the customs they practise, and of the humours which their faulty nature produces in them. Be well assured that in no one of them, however honest and circumspect she may be, will there be found aught of constancy or stability. Of a surety the greater part of them may be set down as incontinent, faithless, wayward, vindictive, and full of suspicion, knowing little of love, and void of charity of any sort whatever. Envy, as the one passion peculiarly their own, occupies the highest place in the centre of their hearts. In them there is no reason, and they are never moved to act by sober and well-considered purpose. In any disputes which they may provoke they never keep a well-balanced mind, but with their unbridled desires they are ever wont to choose the baser part, according to the fashion in which they may be swayed by their light unstable wit. And as a proof that these words of mine are true, let us call to mind how often in these our times we may have seen some particular woman, loved and courted by many different gentlemen of worth, and lovers gifted with every virtue, who at the same time will, taking the libidinous she-wolf for her model, turn her back upon them all, and give herself to the embraces of some base villain filled full of every wickedness. Therefore, can you bring yourself to believe that this one, after having so long treated you with churlishness, on account of which you in sooth have been brought more than once nigh unto death, can have kept in this humour with any other set purpose and design except to win for herself the glory of having gulled for so long a time such a proper gentleman and lover as you yourself are, and, with a pretence of modesty, to rejoice at seeing you in travail and languishment the while, deeming by such conduct she may magnify the fame of her beauty and charm? Likewise, in the same way you may be well assured that it is not on account of any set purpose, or for the reason that you yourself have given any fresh cause therefor, that she has shown herself thus graciously disposed towards you, but simply because she is thus following the course acceptable to her own base and wicked nature, without digressing at all therefrom. Wherefore I do not doubt but that you, if you shall follow up this track rather than put faith in the planet which is now ruling, may achieve a threefold victory in this long-prosecuted undertaking of yours. Moreover, without making farther delay thereanent, write to her in seemly fashion, and try your best to have granted to you some occasion of speaking to her, thus striking the iron while it is hot, whereby of a surety you will let your design have issue in the way you so greatly desire."

Thus, with much discourse of this same character, this friend made Messer Bertramo understand full well what the quality was and the natural disposition of women at large, exhorting him at the same time to take care never to give way to overmuch joy on account of any kindness received from one of the sex, nor to be cast down with sorrow should the opposite thing befall him; forasmuch as, neither in the one case nor in the other, ought there to be found any occasion for making much ado thereanent, seeing that the affair itself was a trifling one and of no great importance. Rather he counselled Messser Bertramo to pluck the fruit which might be offered as the day and the season might allow, giving no thought to the past and nursing no hope as to the future, prosecuting this enterprise in such fashion that this woman, and every other one of her sex, might find herself flouted and befooled, and able to glean little or nothing of gratification from the malice and wickedness of their inborn selves.

The cavalier, feeling himself confirmed and encouraged by the discourse of this true friend of his, straightway took pen and paper, and in the huge delight of his new hope wrote to the lady of his love in mighty passionate words. After he had set before her the whole story of his most fervent love, called into being by her excessive beauty, he renewed the offer of himself as her servant, and, together with many other well-trimmed and loving words, he made an end by begging her that she would graciously deign to assign him a time and a place for a satisfactory interview, in order that he, simply by once having speech with her, might find recompense for all those numerous and protracted vexations which he had suffered. After this letter had been despatched in very cautious wise, and had been received and read with exceeding satisfaction on her part, she, noting well every portion thereof, let him have free access to her heart, now infected with the malady of love, in such full, free measure that, not only was she ready and willing to accord to him an audience with her such as he prayed for, but without any restraint whatsoever laid herself out entirely to grant him her favour.

Whereupon she straightway returned to him an answer in fitting wise, bidding him on the very next evening to betake himself on foot into the garden of her house and there to wait near a certain tree which she duly specified. Then, as soon as her husband should be asleep and the residue of the household settled to rest, she would go to him, even more than willingly. The cavalier, overjoyed as everyone may well imagine by this answer, and perceiving how the counsels of his friend were bearing due fruit, went as soon as the night began to fall, accompanied by certain servants of his, at the appointed hour to the spot which had been fixed, and there awaited the coming of the lady. She, on her part, when she perceived that the cavalier had come already to the place of meeting, opened in secret wise the door which led to the garden without delay, and came with mincing delicate steps to the spot where he stood. He, advancing towards her with open arms, received her very graciously, saying, the while, "Happily indeed are you come, sweet soul of mine, on whose account I have heretofore undergone so many and so great vexations."

After these lovers had given and taken back a thousand sweetest kisses, they sat down to rest beneath a sweet-smelling orange-tree, waiting for a sign to be given them by a trusty serving-woman, who should at last lead them away into a chamber on the ground floor in which a couch, prepared in dainty fashion and finely perfumed, had been got in order for them. Having gone therein, the cavalier, holding the lady by the hand, and using pleasant speech, and kissing her tenderly while he begged her to grant him the last and the long-desired end of love, was suddenly seized by the wish to inquire the reason why she had for so long time exhibited herself to him as one possessed by such inflexible severity, and again, why she had so suddenly, contrary to every hope of his, shown herself so gracious and benign, and granted him success in the undertaking he prized so highly, which thing seemed to him beyond belief.

The lady, without letting interpose any delay, thus made answer: "Dearest and sweetest lord of my life, I will reply and give satisfaction to this most pleasant question of yours in the briefest words. It is true perhaps that, during all the time in which I showed myself harsh and hostile you-ward, I was using far more severity than was needful, looking at your worth and your noble estate. Certes, this inflexibility of mine has had no other cause—over and beyond the preservation of my honour—than the most fervent love which I have ever borne and still bear towards my husband, to whom in no event, however great and pressing it might be, would I ever have proved myself in thought, much less in deed, guilty of aught which might afterwards return upon him to his dishonour. Moreover, this same love which I have towards him has, by its very nature and by a certain inherent force, led me to give myself to your loving embraces, and I will tell you how this was brought about. The other day, as I was going to the chase in the company of my husband and of certain other ladies of my acquaintance, we saw before us a falcon in pursuit of some partridges, which, as is the habit and nature of such birds, he quickly dispersed on all sides. Whereupon my husband said straightway that it seemed to him as if he saw before his eyes Messer Bertramo in the midst of the battle, putting his foes to rout. And over and beyond this he went on to discourse concerning you, telling us of so many other amazing virtues of yours, and sounding the praises of your deeds of daring in such wise that, not only did I feel myself constrained to yield you my love by the claims of reason, but likewise all those who were present prayed to God for your welfare, and we all felt desire to please you in whatever way we might. And furthermore my husband declared that, on account of your exceeding worth, he felt himself bound to love all those who loved you, and hold all those who were of a contrary mind as his chiefest enemies. Therefore I, who am regardful of his wishes in everything, perceiving at once how his highest desire was that everyone should hold you in love and affection, understood that no greater happiness could befall him than that all those about him should love you as well and cordially. Thus, before I moved from that place, I was made aware how all the chains and defences which I had wrought around my obdurate heart, in order to shut out of it all love for you, were broken and dashed to pieces; and, excited by a new

BERTRAMO'S RENUNCIATION.

FROM A DRAWING BY E. R. HUGHES. (Mas., Nov. xxi., v. ii.)

and burning flame of love, I was altogether melted with longing to be at your disposition, as in sooth I now am, and intend to be, as long as it may be granted to me to live."

Now Messer Bertramo, who from his most tender years had ever been in the habit of dealing with everybody and everything with the grandest and most magnificent generosity, as soon as he heard how that the husband of the lady herself had let him acquire her favours by reason of the excessive praises he had spoken and the love he had shown, felt stirring within himself straightway the spirit of a true-hearted and righteous cavalier; and, turning the matter over in his own mind, he said to himself: "Alas, alas! good Bertramo, wilt thou show thyself to be a caitiff knight for so base and so trifling a thing as the enjoyment of a woman's person, what though for many years past thou mayst have desired the possession of the same? And, admitting that this may be the greatest and the dearest boon that anyone could give to thee, shall not thy well tried virtue reap all the higher praise on this account? The doing of noble actions consists not in putting oneself to the proof with regard to things of little worth, but in the undertaking of deeds of high emprise when the doing thereof may not be to our liking. In all thy lifetime thou hast never met any man who has outdone thyself in the practise of courtesy and gentle usage; wherefore, by what act couldst thou make manifest the spotlessness of thy virtue better than by this one, especially as, having the lady in thy power, and deeming thou mightest take thy pleasure with her for a long time to come, thou hast gained the victory over thyself, and hast foregone the fruition of the thing thou hast desired for so long? And to speak yet farther, if the husband of this lady had been thy most bitter enemy, one who had without ceasing sought to cast down thy good name and thy renown, what vengeance more fell and more hateful couldst thou wreak upon him than to let eternal shame fall upon his head? Wherefore, what law of reason or of honesty is there which wills that our friends should be dealt with as if they were foes? And to assure thee that this man is to thee a most perfect friend, beyond any example which has ever befallen in the past, thou hast heard and understood plainly from the mouth of this lady herself how that she was led hither to grant thee the boon of her love by no other power than that of the love which her husband bears to thee. Thus, if thou shalt take this thing which is proffered thee, what a noble recompense it will be to render him for having been thy well-wisher and for loading thee with the highest praise in thy absence, as one is called to do in the case of one's closest friends! Now, may it never please God that such vileness may ever fall upon any gentleman of Aquino."

And thus, without farther calling to mind the love which possessed him or the great beauty of the lady, he said, turning towards her as he spake, "Dear lady, may God forbid that the love which your worthy husband bears towards me, and the superabundant praise which he has given me, and the many other kindly words and actions said and done by him on my behalf, should obtain so foul and base a recompense as to make me, by any act of mine whatsoever, do aught against what he holds most dear—deeds which might, either in great or in small measure, come back to him for his dishonour. Nay, always from this time forth I will place at his disposal both my body and my estate, as I should be bound to do for my own brother or my most loyal friend; and thee, lady, I shall ever hold as my sister, making offer of myself for what I am and whatsoever I may be worth, with all my possessions, as well as the service of my person, to be employed in the preservation of thy honour and good fame."

Then, having unloosed from a handkerchief certain rich jewels which he had brought with him as a love-gift for her, he cast the same into her lap, saying, "Wear these gems for the sake of my love, and in memory of the deed I am doing at this moment. Let it be your constant thought, moreover, to be more faithful to your husband than you have ever been heretofore." After he had kissed her tenderly on the brow, and had given her many thanks for the generous manner in which she had received him, he took his leave of her.

In how great measure the lady was overcome with

confusion and anger at her rejection by the cavalier, everyone will be able to understand for himself. Nevertheless, moved by the innate greed that swayed her, she gathered up the very precious gems, and went back into the house. When a certain time had elapsed, the whole story got noised abroad; whereupon it was proclaimed in Messer Bertramo's praise how he was supreme in arms, in courage, in discretion, and in foresight; likewise, how in noble deeds, in generosity, and in the loftiest virtue, he outstripped every other cavalier who had ever lived in that age, either within or without the bounds of Italy.

MASUCCIO

HOWEVER excessive the terms we may use in according our praise to Messer Bertramo for that noble behaviour of his towards his friend which has been described in the foregoing novel, his merits will still seem to demand yet more lavish commendation. Wherefore I leave this question to be solved by those who have been, and still are, possessed by fervent passion of love, so that each one, thinking of his own case, may decide what share of praise may be due—a matter which I refrain from touching through the lack of power I feel to deal therewith. Nevertheless, calling back to my mind the noteworthy counsel of that friend of his, and in what fashion he made clear the quality, the nature, and the carriage of women in that true and most praiseworthy discourse which he delivered, I myself will exhibit in this very next novel, in order that I may appear as one willing to confirm his judgment, how a wicked and abandoned woman set to work to satisfy her unbridled lust—a matter which will strike with no small astonishment the understanding of all who may read or hear tell of the same.

THE END OF THE TWENTY-FIRST NOVEL.

Novel the Twenty-second

ARGUMENT

A LADY OF TRAPANI BECOMES ENAMOURED OF A MOOR, AND LETS HIM HAVE KNOWLEDGE OF HER. SHE ROBS HER HUSBAND, AND THEN TAKES FLIGHT TO BARBARY IN COMPANY WITH THE AFORESAID MOOR AND A TURKISH GIRL. WHEREUPON THE HUSBAND, IN ORDER TO AVENGE HIMSELF, FOLLOWS THEM, HAVING PUT ON A CERTAIN DISGUISE, AND SLAYS THE MOOR AND HIS WIFE. THEN HE RETURNS WITH THE TURKISH GIRL TO TRAPANI, AND, HAVING MADE HER HIS WIFE, HE LIVES WITH HER A LONG TIME IN GREAT HAPPINESS.

TO THE MAGNIFICENT SIGNOR GALEAZZO SANSEVERINO*

EXORDIUM

FORASMUCH as my weary but still unsatiated pen is not equal to the heavy task of setting forth to you by description the deeds, more natural to monstrous beasts than to human beings, which are commonly wrought by members of that most base and wicked female sex, I mean to let all those things concerning which I myself gathered experience in the early years of my youth stand apart from what I have learned about women and their deeds in my present season of old age. Nevertheless, in order to win my way to the end of the journey I have begun, I will not hold back from writing

* Galeazzo Sanseverino was in the service of Ludovico Moro in Milan. On the death of Pietro del Verme by poison, he obtained a grant of all the possessions of the murdered man. Ludovico also gave him his natural daughter in marriage. He went a prisoner with Ludovico to France, and was killed fighting on the French side at Pavia in 1525. See Porzio, book iii., ch. 122.

in this place concerning certain wicked deeds wrought by this evil-natured brood and since become a scandal in the mouths of the vulgar, and from giving full intelligence of the same to all such as are well endowed with virtue and good manners. And, certes, while dealing with these I will not be niggard of my speech you-ward, knowing that it is meet to reckon you amongst the most virtuous, but will tell you a story anent the unnatural and libidinous desire which overcame a certain woman of Trapani. From the hearing of this I doubt not at all—supposing there should still abide within you any faith as to women at large—that you will hereafter abandon all trust in the female sex on account of the hatred you will feel for this woman's crime. Now let me wish that you, free and untrammeled as you are, may find much joy in the course of your flourishing youth. Farewell!

THE NARRATIVE

TRAPANI, a noble city of Sicily, is situated, as many know, in the furthermost regions of the island, and is, in sooth, almost a nearer neighbour to Africa than any other Christian country, for which reason the Trapanese are often wont, at such times as they may be cruising about in their ships of war, to sail up and down along the shores and the inlets of the country of the Moors, wherefrom they continually gather the most valuable booty. At certain times, however, they suffer defeat and are plundered in their turn, and on this account it often happens that, in order to negotiate as to the ransoms to be paid for the release of prisoners on one side or the other, they arrange a truce between themselves, and transport their merchandize and buy and sell, carrying on their dealings together without hindrance. For the reasons above given it is the case that there are to be found very few Trapanese who are not as well acquainted with the country of the Moors as with their own.

Not a great time ago it chanced that a gentleman of Trapani, called by name Nicolao d'Aguito, in his day renowned as a most famous corsair, after he had many times harried and despoiled the coasts of Barbary, returned to his home and took to himself as wife a young woman of great beauty; and having had born to him several children by her, he settled down to lead his life in honourable wise. Amongst the other servants and slaves whom he kept in his house was a certain Moor of Tripoli in Barbary, who was called by name Elia, a young fellow strong and robust of body, but ugly beyond all measure. The wife of Nicolao, assailed by hot and unbridled wantonness, having no regard to the breaking of her marriage vow (of which sacrament, indeed, they rarely take much account except they be compelled thereto by circumstance), considering naught either that this fellow was a slave and she a free woman, or that she was fair and he beyond measure hideous, or that she was a Christian, he a Moor, or that by reason of this last-named consideration she would give offence to God, to the law, and to her honour, remembered only that he was young and lusty, and would on this account satisfy her carnal desires better than could her husband. Wherefore she at once set to work with all her will to make trial whether the Moor would know how to bear himself as a valiant man-at-arms in as capable a manner as he used in carrying burdens of inordinate weight upon his shoulders. Having made trial of his powers once and again, and having fully satisfied herself that the judgment she had formed of him had not deceived her, she determined to follow her bent as long as her course of life and her husband's wealth should suffice therefor.

Now, although it seemed that the world must be going very well with the Moor, and that he might for many reasons be quite contented with the game he was called upon to play, nevertheless—seeing that he was by nature akin to the birds of prey, which, being left at liberty, always seek to return to their own abandoned nests, although as long as they are in the keeping of the falconer they are daily fed with excellent and delicate meats, while when they shift for themselves they rarely secure their prey—this Moor, in spite of all the flattering words and the rich gifts and the love lavished upon him without ceasing by his beautiful mistress, would constantly dream of a flight to his own home. And, as he was both cunning and wicked by nature, he began to put on sad and melancholy humours in the presence of his mistress, and was wont at such times as she showed herself wishful to take her pleasure with him to deny her the same. On account of these moods, she being mightily ill content therewith, urged him continually to let her know the cause of his melancholy, for she was disposed to leave nothing undone which might work for his cure. In answer the Moor let her know in plain terms that he would never be satisfied until he should have returned to his own home, and the lady, when she listened to these words, was smitten with a sorrow the like of which she had never felt before, and she strove with all her powers, using many and most convincing arguments the while, to persuade him to abide contented in his present condition. Nay, further, she promised, if she might thereby win the Moor's approval, to poison her husband in order that they might seize upon his estate. The Moor, however, would not assent to this proposition, but with great cunning stood firm to the resolution he had taken; wherefore she fixed upon the desperate course of eloping with him into Barbary, and when she told him her resolution he listened to her words with exceeding great pleasure.

In order that there might be no delay in carrying out their enterprise, they awaited the season when a fresh and steady Tramontano wind should be blowing, and when Messer Nicolao should be gone to Mazzara to despatch certain business of his. Then one night the Moor and certain other slaves took a ship which had been furnished with all equipment necessary for a voyage, and having carried on board the lady—who had with her a young and very beautiful Turkish girl—with as many light and delicate articles for her use as their hurried flight allowed, they issued forth from the city and took to the ship. They were so well sped by good fortune on their way that on the following day they found themselves close upon the Moorish coast. After they had landed, and all their companions had gone their divers ways into their own lands, Elia, in the company of the lady and the Turkish girl, journeyed to Tripoli, and there they were received by all his friends with the most sumptuous feasts and rejoicings.

When he had tarried a few days in his house, enjoying the booty he had taken, the Moor, either urged on thereto by the justice of God, which never suffers any wrong-doing to go long unpunished, or convinced by some thoughts which may have sprung from his own brain, determined that it was neither in his power nor in his duty to give either faith or love or hope to this wicked and abandoned woman, who, driven along by her own insatiate lechery, had deceived the husband who had loved her better than he had loved his own life; had abandoned her children, a deed which must of a surety cause no small wonderment, and had forsaken alike her country and the laws of her God. For the reasons aforesaid he began, after the lapse of a few days, to hold her in such savage hatred and disgust that not only was he unable to bestow upon her such caresses as he was wont to give her, but even found it a hard business to speak a word to her. Neither could he trust himself to look towards her; and, beyond this, whensoever she might commit the slightest fault, he would cudgel her as lustily as if he were the captain of a galley and she the slave.* Wherefore the foolish woman, finding herself reduced to a state of extreme wretchedness, began to repent when it was too late, and bewept the misery of her life, together with all the ill-doing of which she had been guilty. In sooth, she would much sooner have died outright than have lived on, and would have welcomed death with the greatest joy as the one cure for all her troubles.

When the wretched Nicolao returned to his home, and heard the most odious and most shameful tidings which awaited him there, everyone who reads will be able to judge for himself how great must have been the grief and the tears and the sorrowing which possessed the poor wight. Indeed, he fell into so desperate a mood that over and over again he came within an ace of plunging a sharp knife into his heart's core, knowing well enough

* Orig. *ed oltre cio per ogni piccola cagione le bastonate andavano da comito di galea.*

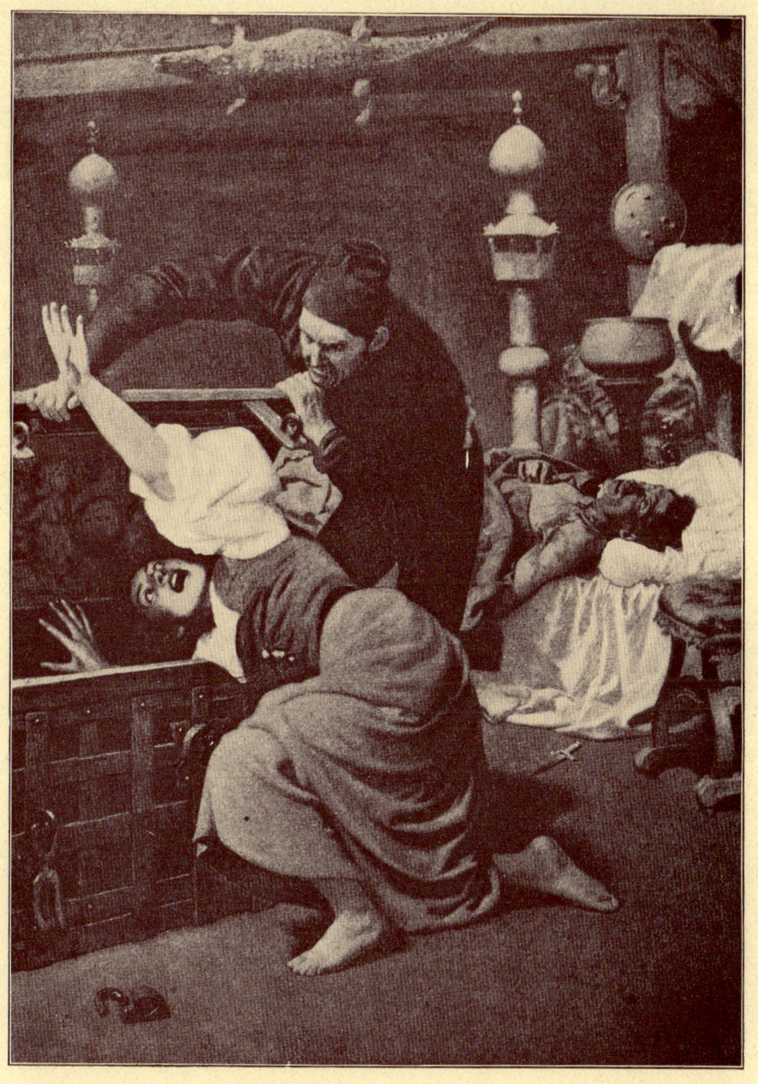

THE VENGEANCE OF NICOLAO.

FROM A DRAWING BY E. R. HUGHES. (Mas., Nov. xxii., v. ii.)

that to continue to live, weighed down by such a burden of disgrace, would be much worse than death itself. Nevertheless, after having given way to his grief for a certain time, he began to take thought that he would be greatly lacking in all that was due to the maintenance of his fair fame were he, out of cowardice, to make an end of his life. Wherefore he determined to go like a man, and to lose his life in that same place where he had already lost both his honour and his riches. Now he was at all times a man of great courage, and his nature was farther strengthened by the justice of the undertaking which he had in hand; so, without waiting to take counsel either with his friends or his relations, he bade come together secretly ten or a dozen bold and sprightly young men, and, after they had during the night armed and got in readiness a small bark fit for sea-roving, they set sail together, and directed their course towards the Barbary coast.

After a few days' voyaging, Nicolao arrived at the spot he had been seeking, and when the crew had drawn the ship up on the beach about ten miles distant from Tripoli, he covered her up with the sea-weed, which is very abundant in those parts, and bade his companions conceal themselves withinside the galley, letting no one be aware of their presence, until such time as they would have the opportunity of seizing for themselves a vast booty. Furthermore, he bade them await his return for the space of eight days and no longer; for, supposing that he should not come back within that time, they might hold it for certain that he had either met his death or had been taken prisoner by his adversaries. After he had allowed his beard to grow to some length, and had disguised himself in Moorish clothing, he, being well acquainted with the language spoken by the people of Tripoli, recommended himself to God and departed from his companions, having everything about him in order, and being very eager to carry out the vengeance he had planned against his wife and the Moor.

Now one day, when Nicolao, who indeed knew that country and all the neighbouring parts thereto belonging, but too well, was walking along beside a little river very near to the city, a spot which many women of the place were wont to frequent for the purpose of blanching their linen, it suddenly came into his mind that perchance the Turkish girl—whom he believed to be much attached to him—might have come there from the house where his wife was abiding, either to fetch water or for some other household task. And then, by the will of chance, who had likewise made ready the vengeance he was to work, and the penalty he was to exact for the losses he had suffered, it was ordained that, at the very moment when he came to the place, he espied the girl making her way back to the house bearing a vessel of water. Wherefore he, hurrying on with rapid steps, overtook her and spake thus, weeping the while: "Lucia, can it be that the great love which I have borne towards you for these many years past—a love which has led me to bring you up in my house as if you had been my own daughter—has found so little place in your heart that you, too, are ready to deceive me?" Lucia, turning round and recognizing her master both by his speech and by his countenance, was overcome by the most heartfelt compassion for him, and ran weeping to embrace him, because in sooth she loved him more than anyone else in the world, and with good reason. Then she implored his pardon, saying that her mistress had induced her to accompany herself and the Moor to that place by using the greatest deceit. Wherefore it seemed to Nicolao, when the girl went on to talk of trifling matters, that this was not the place for such discourse, he being anxious not to lose any more time before he should put into execution the cruel scheme he had devised. So, like an astute man, he determined that he would use as messenger this one who had herself been deceived in the first instance.

After he had let her tell him in a few words of the wretched life which his wife was now leading, he besought her that she would commend him lovingly to his wife, and beg her that she would be pleased to remember him who had loved her and still loved her so very dearly, and likewise to bear in mind the love of her children and her own honour. Also to say how he, having received intelligence even in Trapani of the wretchedness and misery she was suffering, had come after her to place his life in peril so as to deliver her from all her trouble, thinking not so much of forgiving her the fault she had committed against him as to take her back once more as the mistress of his life and of all his goods. And he spake to the girl many other similar words, all of them seductive and full of flattery—words which might well have moved even a heart of marble to pity. The kind-hearted slave, urged on by the prayers of her beloved master, and overcome by pity, found that for the present she could say or do nothing more than beg him come back to this place at the same hour the next day, and that, with regard to whatsoever yet remained to be done, he should leave the ordering thereof to her.

Having bidden farewell to him and gone back to the house, she told her mistress, with many bitter tears, by what means and on what errand her husband had come thither, letting her know exactly everything he had said and adding that, if in this matter she would deign to follow the advice of her poor servant, she would do well. The girl went on to say that it appeared to her, even if Messer Nicolao should play them false, it would still be better to die quickly and at once by the hand of a Christian, her husband and her lord, than to suffer daily a hundred deaths from a Moor who had formerly been her servant and slave. And thus, urging her by many kind and loving words, she heartened her mistress so much that the unhappy lady, without taking any time to consider her answer, and acting as hastily as when she had lightly, and without any good reason, let herself be carried away by her lust to commit so enormous an offence, made answer to the slave that she was prepared to carry out all the wishes of her husband, without considering at all how richly she deserved punishment at his hands. And after they had discussed together, as women are wont to do, many and various schemes, they settled that on the following night they would, in secret and cautious wise, let Nicolao gain entrance to the house, and afterwards do whatever he might command.

On the following day Lucia went at the usual time for water, and found her master already at the place she had assigned, and rejoicing amain she said to him, "Your wife is quite ready to carry out whatsoever commands you may lay upon her, and to go hence with you at any time and in whatever fashion you may please to order. Nevertheless, it has seemed good to her, and to me likewise, that you, so as not to let your presence here be known to anyone, should return with me to the house, where we will bestow you in hiding. Meantime we will keep a good watch, and when it shall appear to us that the time is ripe, we will set to work to bring our wishes and your own to the end we desire." Nicolao, lending the most perfect faith to Lucia's words, and knowing at the same time that there was no other way whereby he might bring his scheme to a successful issue, went after Lucia, following her afar off; and, having made good his entrance to the house of the Moor without being seen or heard by anyone, Lucia straightway took him and put him in hiding in a certain dark corner where the firewood was kept —a spot to which no one was wont to go save herself. Here they kept him close for six days on account of an accident which did not allow them to do otherwise, because at this particular time the Moors were celebrating a certain feast, and every evening Elia would entertain a great number of his friends at a sumptuous banquet in his own house, but in spite of this Nicolao was every day visited and fed in his darksome hole, sometimes by his wife and sometimes by Lucia.

After the feasting was over, Elia was left in the house without any other male companion, and he fell into a slumber so sound and heavy that the loudest peal of thunder would scarce have awakened him; whereupon the wife, ignorant of what Messer Nicolao was minded to do, beyond taking her and the Turkish girl away with him, let him be brought into the room where the Moor was sleeping like a log. The husband, when he saw that everything had been got in order as he desired, and that he must needs despatch quickly the affair, gave command to his wife, bidding her lay hands on all the money and jewels that she could carry away, for that he was about to depart forthwith; whereupon she lost her head somewhat and went about the house, opening now this casket and now that. In the meantime Nicolao, having chosen his time, softly approached the bed where the Moor lay asleep, and, taking in hand a knife meet for the deed, he dexterously severed the veins of the Moor's throat without making any noise, and left him lying there dead. Then he went towards his wife, who was on the floor stooping down beside an open cassone, searching for some jewels which she had seen in the Moor's possession, and having taken with both his hands the lid of the cassone, he let it descend on the neck of his wife, crushing and forcing it down upon her in such wise that he killed her then and there without even letting her cry out "Alas!"

As soon as he had brought this deed to pass he caught up certain bags filled with pistoles, and divers rich jewels and dainty little gems, and, having carefully made of the same a package, threw it into Lucia's lap, who was overwhelmed with fear at the sight of the corpses of the murdered folk, and was standing in dire terror of her own life. Then he spake thus to her: "My daughter, I have now done all the work which my heart willed me to carry out; so nothing now remains except to return to my companions, forasmuch as, with the passing of this night, will come to an end the season during which they were bound to await my return. And I will likewise take you with me, not only because it pleases me so to do, but also as a reward for the great services you have wrought on my behalf. And moreover, from the boon which I mean to confer upon you, you shall judge whether or not I ought to be charged with the vice of ingratitude." Lucia, when she listened to these words, which were in sooth vastly different from what she in her doubt and uncertainty had expected, rejoiced greatly in her heart, and forthwith declared that she was ready to do whatsoever he might command. Thereupon they went silently out of the house, and, having come to the gate of the curtilage, they opened the same by means of certain small instruments of iron which they had brought with them for the purpose. Then they took to their heels and went along at a pace which was rather quick than slow, and in due time they arrived at the place where Messer Nicolao had left his friends, who at that very same moment were launching their boat in the sea, and getting ready for their departure, for the reason that they had lost all hope of ever seeing him again.

And when they had brought to an end the manifestations of joy they made at the sight of him, they all went on board without any further delay, and, the winds and seas being propitious and calm, they made a short and prosperous voyage to Trapani. When the people heard of their arrival, and knew in what fashion Nicolao had worked his vengeance on the Moor, and how he had punished his wife for her offence, they all praised him highly thereanent, over and beyond the universal delight there was manifested on account of his return. Also Nicolao, so as not to show himself ungrateful for the many benefits he had received from Lucia, took her for his wife, and hereafter found her very dear to him, holding her in great honour as long as he lived.

MASUCCIO

IT may well be said that the wickedness of this woman of Trapani was very great and horrible in its nature—not so much perhaps for the reason that she let herself be mastered by a base slave, as for taking flight with him into Barbary. But, be this as it may, we must assuredly set down the husband as a man of singular virtue, seeing that, without the least reserve, he placed his honour before his life; and, although Fortune was prodigal of her favours in helping him on, it may not be denied that in boldness of heart he showed himself superior to any other man. And what shall we say of the generosity and gratitude which he exhibited towards Lucia, by which he not only changed her from a slave into a free woman, but also joined himself with her in matrimonial union? And certes, seeing that by her aid she restored to him his life, his honour, and his wealth, and let him issue victorious from the undertaking upon which his heart was set, no reward, however great, would have been sufficient for her, except the gift of himself to her, which in sooth he duly made. Therefore it seems to me that, in what respect soever we may give praise and give it worthily, it should be given especially in the case last named, for in the same measure as ingratitude surpasses every other vice, thankfulness for benefits received outdoes all other virtues. But now, giving over discoursing about this man, and without taking our departure from Sicily, I will tell of another most cruel and almost unheard-of story, of the fate which lately in Palermo overtook a most impious and even fiendish-hearted mother, the telling of which is scarcely in keeping with the decent honest spirit God has given me.

THE END OF THE TWENTY-SECOND NOVEL.

Novel the Twenty-third

ARGUMENT

A WIDOW WOMAN BECOMES ENAMOURED OF HER OWN SON, AND BY THE WORKING OF VERY SUBTLE DECEIT CONTRIVES THAT HE SHOULD HAVE KNOWLEDGE OF HER. AFTERWARDS, HAVING BECOME WITH CHILD, SHE CUNNINGLY DISCLOSES THIS FACT TO HER SON, WHO, BEING GREATLY INCENSED AT WHAT HAS BEEN DONE, GOES INTO EXILE. THE TRUTH OF THE DEED IS AT LAST MADE PUBLIC, AND THE MOTHER, AFTER THE BIRTH OF THE CHILD, IS BURNT TO DEATH BY THE PODESTA.

TO THE MAGNIFICENT MARINO BRANCACCIO*

EXORDIUM

IF nefarious human vices are to be condemned by the laws of nature, and by manners and customs approved as righteous, I doubt not at all but that you, you noble and valiant Parthenopean, will play the part of a virtuous man, and will give us the support of your voice in heaping condemnation upon a detestable example of lust, more devilish in sooth than human, which was exhibited by a wicked and abandoned mother in putting a shameful deceit upon her innocent son. Wherefore I trust you will read this with your accustomed prudence and foresight, for I am persuaded that, when you shall have considered well in your mind this abominable deed, you will in the future hold that no female wickedness, however great, concerning which you may have cognizance, would be impossible. Thus in the following discourse surprise and indignation will assuredly wait upon you. Farewell.

* In the later editions this novel is dedicated to Messer Anastasio Rosello Aretino.

THE NARRATIVE

WHEN, no great time ago, I came back from Palermo, a certain noble citizen, one whose word was well worthy of all belief, told to me as a fact not to be gainsaid that during the year before the last, a certain gentleman of Palermo went the way of nature and passed away from this life, leaving behind him a son who was called by the name of Pino, a youth about twenty-three years of age, rich beyond the mean, of a comely person, and as modest as a maid. Now the mother of this youth, although she was still young in years, furnished with a handsome dowry, and marvellously beautiful in face and figure, made up her mind that, on account of the great love which she had for her son, she would never again enter the married state, and this resolve of hers she made known to her son, who, on his part, ever treated her with the highest consideration and obedience.

For this reason she won the high commendation of many people, and her determination to remain a widow was especially grateful to her son, who, so as not to give her any reason to change her mind and act otherwise, bore himself towards her after a fashion more complaisant, more affectionate, and more obedient than ever yet a son had used towards a mother. Wherefore she felt pleasure and contentment beyond measure, and every day her love for her son grew greater and greater. And as they lived in this wise it came to pass that the mother, while taking heed of the worthiness and the modesty and the physical beauty of her son, was assailed and overcome by a fiery access of lust, and became inflamed with such unbridled desire for him to have knowledge of her that no contrary persuasions which she used to herself had any power to make her abandon her intent, so that she was harassed without ceasing by the thought as to how she might best carry into execution her nefarious design. And because she was sure that a project of this sort would never be brought to an issue with the knowledge and consent of her son, she determined to lure him into the deadly snare she was preparing for him by means of an artful cheat. So, having by cunning inquiry got intelligence that Pino, albeit he was of a most modest temper, had become enamoured of a certain young girl, a neighbour of theirs, the daughter of a widow of low condition and very poor, but a close friend of her own, she began to hope that she might, by working in this direction, bring her scheme to the desired end.

Therefore one day, having called the good woman to her, she said: "My Garita, as you are a mother yourself, you will be able to understand easily enough how great is the love which parents are bound to entertain towards the children who have been born to them, and more especially towards those who, on account of their singular worth, only cause our natural love to grow and expand exceedingly, as is the case with my son, who is indeed a most excellent youth, one whose accomplished and praiseworthy carriage constrains me by its merits to love him more than I love my own life. Now, for this reason, I, having learned by private inquiry that he is enamoured of your daughter, fear mightily, from the ardent nature of his passion, lest with her modesty on one side and his overpowering love on the other, he may some day or other make a fatal end to his life. And, on the other part, I recognize that you yourself are my most intimate friend, and know full well that you have ever kept intact your honour and good fame, and would never venture to demand of you aught which might in any way come home to you as a dishonour. Nay, rather, for the preservation of your fair fame, I, knowing that you are somewhat straitened in means, am filled with desire to proffer you not only all the aid which my thoughts can furnish, but likewise to make you a sharer in all my possessions, so that by these means you may be assured I am minded to treat you exactly as if I were indeed your mother. Nevertheless, I must tell you that there has just come into my mind a plan by the working of which we may at the same time give satisfaction to my dear son and let the honour of your daughter suffer no hurt, either great or little. To carry out this scheme I would wish that you should, after a manner fitted for the affair, enter into a secret plot with my son with the understanding that you are willing to sell to him, in consideration of a price to be paid by him, the virginity of your daughter. Then, when the matter shall have been duly arranged, I myself will come to your house and bring with me my waiting-maid, who, as you know, is about the same age as your own daughter, and very fair indeed in person. We will let her go into a dark room, and there, when she shall have gone to bed, she may give reception to Pino, and this in sooth will be exactly the same to him as if he had taken enjoyment of your daughter. I will bid you to have no fear lest anyone should get intelligence concerning this same affair, for the reason that my son excels all the other young men of this city in probity and in keeping private his own business. But if in the future the thing should get noised abroad through any possible accident, I give you my promise in all good faith that I will forthwith let the world know the whole truth as to how it was brought to pass. Thus, by carrying out this plan I shall no longer be in any danger of losing my son by reason of this inordinate passion of love which possesses him, and you will have won for your daughter a dowry, which indeed I am willing to commit at once to your keeping, whereby the integrity of your fair fame will not be tarnished in any degree whatever. We will let Pino enjoy the pasturage we have provided for him until such time as we shall have found a good husband for the young girl, or until he shall choose a wife. Then we will have a great sport and jest together, when we shall make known to him the cheat we have put upon him."

Garita gave faith unquestioning to these words which the lady her neighbour put before her, backed up with so many specious arguments; and, over and beyond this, she saw clearly that no small gain would ensue to her therefrom, without in any way putting a slight upon her daughter's virtue; so, feeling that she was countenanced by her exceeding poverty in doing this thing, besides being urged thereto by the thought of the pleasure she would give her dear friend, she made up her mind to satisfy her wish in full, and with a joyous countenance she made answer that she was ready to carry out all the conditions aforesaid.

Having taken her leave Garita went her way, and on the following day it chanced that she caught sight of Pino, who was passing by her house in decorous fashion, taking what diversion he could find, and spying now and then for a glimpse of the damsel; whereupon Garita in cunning wise began to hold discourse with him, and after having conversed for some time discreetly over many and divers matters, and having likewise drawn from his lips a confession of the hidden and burning passion for the young girl her daughter which consumed him, they began to bargain, and finally came to the agreement that Pino should hand over to her two hundred ducats as the dowry of her daughter, and that he should in return therefor pluck the first flower of her virginity. So as not to keep the affair any great time in suspense through long contrivance, seeing that from the accomplishment of the same there would arise advantage to one side and the other as well, they agreed before they parted that the very next night should witness the consummation of the amorous warfare. Then, having set everything discreetly in order, as to how he should betake himself to the house of Garita, Pino took leave of her.

Garita forthwith made her way to the lady's house, and with a joyful face laid before her all the plans she had prepared, in conjunction with Pino her son, so that they might compass the end which the lady desired. When the lady heard her tell of what she had done she rejoiced amazingly thereanent, and embraced and kissed Garita a hundred times, and, having once more settled between themselves the means which it would behove them to employ in procuring the fulfilment of their design, she filled the hand of Garita with money, so that she might let her depart well content; whereupon the woman went back to her own house rejoicing amain. When the appointed hour had struck, the lady, in company with her waiting-maid, went by a private path towards the house of Garita, who straightway led them into a chamber which had been made ready for them, and there left them. Thereupon the lady caused the waiting-maid to withdraw into another room, and there conceal herself; and, having got into the bed which was prepared, awaited, consumed the while by her unbridled lust, the meeting with her own son.

What words will avail to describe this accursed, abandoned woman, this lustful, swinish wretch, this inhuman and most rapacious beast? Was there in all the world any other woman so diabolically wicked in soul as this, or any other maniac distraught enough to have carried out, or even to have ventured to plan, such a monstrous and detestable incest? Ah! divine justice, tarry not to let such execrable and barbarous crime meet its punishment at the hand of earthly ministers of the law, but when this wicked woman shall make as if she would come anear thee, then quickly let fall upon her thy just wrath and vengeance, and cause the earth to open and swallow her alive.

Pino, when he deemed that the appointed hour had come, entered the house of Garita without suspicion of any sort, and met with a very gracious reception from his hostess, who then led him, like a blind man, through the darkness into the room which had been made ready for his coming. He, holding it for certain that he would find awaiting him in the bed the maiden he loved so dearly, first took off his clothes and then placed himself by her side and began to kiss her in sweet and loving wise. Next, having shown his desire to take for himself some further pleasure with her, she on her side, acting with the most consummate art, made a feeble show of giving him a rebuff and bearing herself like one whose favours could only be snatched by force. She made him believe that he had in sooth, taken the maidenhood of one who had herself greedily devoured his own. She had indeed tricked herself out by the use of certain mendicaments, and by divers arts in such a manner that a boy like Pino, and even others well skilled in the ways of women, might easily have taken her for a young virgin. With regard to the young man, what though he had never before had any experience in nightly occupation of this sort, we may presume that, thinking the while he was working in the ground of someone else and not in his own, and overcome by the great pleasure he found therein, he did not let waste in idleness a single moment.

And when at last the dawn began to whiten, Garita came, and, as it had already been planned, contrived by some fictitious reasoning to let Pino depart by stealth from the house, and then the lady and her maid likewise issued thence by a privy way. And in order to make sure that this one meeting should not be at the same time the first and the last she should have with Pino, she contrived by the employment of some new stratagem to tread the same path almost every night without letting Garita know that the young man had cognizance of anyone except the waiting-maid. Thus while both the one and the other, although for widely different reasons, were mightily well pleased with this amorous diversion, it came to pass that the guilty woman became with child, whereat she sorrowed and grieved beyond measure, and called to her aid all manner of devices in order to keep back the child she had conceived from coming to the birth. But none of these methods were of any avail, and then, when she knew that the affair had come to such a pass that she would no longer be able to keep the same a secret from her son, it would be needless to say how grievous and how many were the woes of her life, the travail of her thoughts, and the anguish of her soul. Nevertheless, helped on by her foolhardy confidence, and reckoning much upon herself and upon her own powers of persuasion that she might be able to induce her son to do, of his own free will, that which he had already done under her cunning beguilement, she determined that she would tell him everything in her own words. Having summoned him one day into a chamber alone, she began in gentle wise to address him thus: "Dear son of mine, you yourself will be able to bear true witness that, if ever a mother loved her son all in all, I assuredly am that one, seeing that I have always loved and still love you more than my own life. And this love of mine has been of such a kind, and has exercised such a power over me, that it has prevented me, what though I am rich and still young, from entering again into the married state, and from committing your wealth and my person into the keeping of strange hands, although, being a woman, I might well have been tormented by the pricks of natural desire; but, be this as it may, I have never willed to provide for the satisfying of these longings as many women are wont to do, simply in order that I might the better keep unsullied your honour and my own. Besides this, I knew that you were consumed with a fierce passion of love for the young girl who is our neighbour, and likewise that her mother would be ready to suffer death rather then let aught of disgrace fall upon the girl's good name. Wherefore I, being well advised as to the great misery and wretchedness into which lovers are wont to be led by reason of such desperate misadventures, played the part of a mother most tenderly solicitous over your life, and determined, by one and the same deed, to satisfy all the needs and longings afore-mentioned. By acting in this wise I worked an offence indeed against human laws, the work of certain officers of old time, and framed more by cunning and superstition than by right reason, in willing that both your own lusty youth and mine as well should enjoy in secret the delights of love. For know that the young woman with whom you have taken so great pleasure in the chamber of Garita our neighbour, was myself and no one else, and that things have gone with me in such wise that I now find myself with child by you."

After she had finished her speech she showed herself desirous of putting forward more ardent reasonings in order to secure the farther satisfaction of her execrable lust; but her virtuous son, enraged and confounded beyond measure by the abominable nature of the deed which he had wrought, stood as one who feels that the heavens are falling down upon his head, and the solid earth being torn from beneath his feet. Overpowered by such wrath and anguish as had never before wrung the soul of a man, he came very near to plunge a knife into her midmost heart; but, holding himself back somewhat so that he might not become voluntarily a matricide, and the slayer of that unconscious offspring still shut up in its corrupted prison-house, he resolved to leave such vengeance to the hands of those whose right and duty it was to carry out the same. Then, giving speech to all the terrible and vituperative words which it was meet for him to use in the just ruin fallen upon her, and railing and denouncing his most wicked and abandoned mother, he went forth from her presence.

He straightway gathered together his money and what jewels he possessed, and, having set the rest of his affairs in order as best he could, he awaited the coming of the galleys which were wont to put into Palermo on their voyage to Flanders. After a few days' delay the galleys arrived, and in one of them Pino took passage. But the rumour of what has been here told soon began to spread abroad in the city with all its horror, and, having come to the ears of the Podesta, he forthwith bade them seize the wicked woman, who, without letting herself suffer over much at the hands of the tormentors, confessed the truth of the whole matter exactly as it had come to pass. Then he had her placed and carefully guarded in a convent of women until such time as her child should be born, and when due period had elapsed she was delivered of a male child. Afterwards she was, according to her just deserts, burned alive upon the piazza amidst the cursing and execration of all the people.

MASUCCIO

IF there should ever be amongst those who may read or hear told the novel I have just narrated, anyone who may hold it to be a marvellous thing or impossible, that this guilty woman should have been able—as I have said in my novel—to pass herself off as a fresh young virgin by means of the cunning arts and remedies employed by her, let any such an one who troubles his brain thereanent be assured that what I have written is indeed true. Forasmuch as, when their poisonous lusts may be held in leash by necessity of any sort, women of a nature like this widow's know how to put in operation an infinite number of practices which would be strong enough to make their working felt, not only upon the libidinous bodies of those who employ them, but even upon the throat of a fierce lion. But now, bringing forward in this matter a witness well approved, I cry, "Oh! thou widow, consummate artist in thy school of knowledge, I charge thee not to let me go on to say aught that is false. Thou knowest my meaning well enough, minister of Satan as thou are! I conjure thee now that thou wilt at least make confession to thyself, if not to the public ear, that, although I may speak and write in faulty wise, I at least say and speak things which are true."

But why do I go about here and there, and thwart my fancy by writing anent the infinite meanness and treachery and wickedness of womankind? In sooth, it would be an easier task by far to number the stars of heaven. Who would ever have believed or reckoned that the widow described in the foregoing novel could have been possessed of aught but a pious and virtuous mind, seeing that she, having been left a widow while she was still young and fair and wealthy to boot, seemed to have cast aside all thoughts of earthly lust, and to have steadily set herself to live a single life on account of the love which she had for her son? Who could have known what evil disposition lay hidden under this specious exterior? But now, because she has received her due guerdon for the deeds she wrought, I will put aside all further discourse concerning her and ask, How many more of these women of honeyed* speech are there amongst us, who by means of frauds like the aforesaid, and even greater, might easily beguile another Solomon? Amongst others are those who feign to be given up entirely to things of the spirit, women whose conversation is ever with priests and monks, talking of naught else but the beatitude of the life eternal, and, with many other tricks and manners full of hypocrisy and superstition enough to make themselves a cause of offence both to God and man, they deceive everyone who may put faith in their falseness.

I say naught concerning the carriage of these as they go about the streets with demure and mincing gait, with such a modest look, and with such high disdain in their glance, as if the very ground smelt rank to them. On account of formal demeanour of this sort, they are reputed by foolish people to be most modest, and filled with the spirit of holiness; and in this mind they condemn the sprightli-

* Orig., *quante sono de le altre sputa-balsamo.*

ness of others, bringing forward as evidence in their favour that proverb which says, "I love a ready-witted woman, but not of my own house." To this dictum I can answer with ease, making a distinction the while that is very true, that women, of whatever condition they may be, ought not to be too ready with the tongue at seasons when there is no need or necessity therefor, lest they should, over and beyond any danger arising from the words they use, run the risk of incurring for themselves a lasting disgrace. But for women to speak in the hearing of all with good courage concerning such things as the necessity of the moment may require to be discussed, or when chance may let them, ought not to be rated as any falling away, or lessening of their fame and honour; and least of all for those who have a clear conscience, and who have kept their virtue intact. In this class I include those women who, however noble and beautiful and young they may be, harbour neither thought nor fear that they can in any wise injure or stain their honour by holding discourse with any man. Rarely or never does evil ensue from conversing in public; the scandals which affront our eyes arise rather from communing in private, and from words bandied in dark corners. God shield me from all such women as never speak at all, either because they know nothing, or because they are minded to play the hypocrite; such as will never open their mouths, what though you place before them ten pots full of honey; who, if a man shall doff his cap to them or greet them, will either give him no answer at all, or, if they do open their mouths, will let him see that they are disposed to make him some disdainful reply. If any gallant youth, adorned with all the virtues, should pay his court to any one of these canting females, she would let herself be killed rather than come to the determination to accede to his wishes. Not that she lets him despair of ultimately winning her good graces. She keeps him on the feed, and from time to time flings to him some vain hope or other. The reason of this demeanour is that she is fain to let the suitor act as the extoller and the herald of her virtue, so that others round about, who are privy to the affair, may be the approving witnesses of her honour, in order that no one may be led to believe that such a one as she could possibly harbour the thought of falling away from virtue; wherefore she, by these means, is raised to the dignity of Mistress of the Sentences,* and it is made to appear as if no one could or would have lived before her day.

But, on the other hand, at those times when she may chance to be in her own house, if she should foregather with some young kinsman of her own who takes her fancy, and especially if he should be one upon whose cheeks the first down of manhood is beginning to show itself, she will employ so many measures and artifices over her scheme that she will often run into breakneck dangers in order to confirm the relationship. I will let stand aside all mention of those priests who wait upon women of this sort in their houses, and who are made their gossips, following up this step by betraying God Himself, and making St. John the Baptist a go-between for the satisfaction of their libidinous passions. And if this course be denied to them, they will throw themselves at the head of whatever man they can find, and under the assaults of their inborn lust they look round about them to see whether there may not be in the house some well-grown lad who would be lusty at the work they require of him, and then, with all kind of lascivious scheming, they draw him into their embraces. In what manner they are wont to play the harlot with such as these God will let you know through these writings of mine, and if they sin not with a lad of this sort there will never be wanting some muleteer or some black Ethiopian. Let that man who does not believe I am speaking the truth take observation for himself in the well-verified matter set forth in the novel which comes hereafter, and then forsooth there may well come over him the desire to exclaim with me, Would that it had been God's pleasure and Nature's to suffer us to have been brought forth from

* *Maestra de Sententie.* The Master of the Sentences was Peter Lombard, Bishop of Paris, a famous schoolman, who died in 1160. His work, "Sententiarum Libri IV.," is a collection of arguments taken from the Fathers, and destined to meet all possible objections to orthodox doctrine. Nevertheless, the doctors of Paris detected heresy in it, and it was condemned in 1300.

the oak-trees, or indeed to have been engendered from water and mire like the frogs in the humid rains of summer, rather than to have taken our origin from so base, so corrupt, and so vilely-fashioned a sex as womankind! But now, leaving them to go to perdition in their own way, I will with gladness let follow my next novel.

THE END OF THE TWENTY-THIRD NOVEL.

Novel the Twenty-fourth

ARGUMENT

A YOUNG MAN LOVES A CERTAIN LADY WHO DOES NOT LOVE HIM IN RETURN. WHEREUPON, HAVING CONCEALED HIMSELF IN HER HOUSE, HE SEES FROM THE PLACE WHERE HE IS HIDDEN A BLACK MOOR TAKING HIS PLEASURE WITH HER. THE YOUNG MAN COMES FORWARD, AND WITH MANY INSULTING WORDS REPROVES THE WICKED NATURE OF THE WOMAN, AND FINDS HIS FORMER LOVE FOR HER TURNED TO HATRED.

TO THE EXCELLENT COUNT OF ALTAVILLA

EXORDIUM

BECAUSE it is my wish, most excellent Signor, to dedicate to you the novel which I have now in hand, I have determined, so as not to turn my pen against those who have never given me any occasion for offence, to keep silent in this story, not only concerning the present condition of the lady and of the lover, but also to conceal the name of the city in which the events of this story came to pass. In it I will let you hear of a strange and very painful adventure which befell a certain ill-starred lover, who found himself brought to such a pass that he was forced to take a par[illegible]hich could not have been, otherwise than most irksome [illegible] man of his high and gentle nature, even after car[illegible]lly the same. On this account I beg you—if a[illegible] after reading what is aforesaid written you m[illegible] find yourself hot-blooded and warmed with the fire of love—that you will give me at your pleasure a well-balanced opinion of the adventure, and tell me what course the unhappy lover should have followed, and whether or not he deserves praise with regard to the issue.

THE NARRATIVE.

IN a famous city of Italy there lived not long ago a certain youth of no mean station and influence, very comely to look upon both in face and figure, of most courteous manners, and abounding in every virtue, to whom a thing happened which in sooth happens not seldom to young men of his sort, that is to say, he became very deeply enamoured of a gracious and beautiful lady, the wife of one of the foremost gentlemen of the city aforesaid. And the lady becoming aware of this passion of his, and marking how every day he went about scheming and contriving some method by which he might win his way into her good graces, determined, as is the inborn habit of women, to entangle the poor wight by the working of her art and ingenuity, in her craftily-laid nets on the very first occasion when they might accidentally foregather. To accomplish this task did not cost her much travail; and as soon as she was assured that she had him in hold in such a fashion that it would be no easy matter for him to withdraw himself from the toils, she soon began to let him see little by little that she had scant liking for him, so that he might not for any length of time taste any pleasure or contentment by reason of his love. Thus she went on without ceasing to show him that she set very little store upon himself or upon anything that he did.

On account of this treatment the luckless lover had to endure a life of discontent and intolerable vexation, and, taking account that all his jousting and lavish spending of money, and all the other notable services which he performed on her behalf without intermission, worked no advantage to his cause, but rather seemed to furnish occasion for some fresh show of disdain from her, he essayed over and over again to withdraw himself from the enterprise which he had in hand, and to let his thoughts wander in some other direction. But whenever it became apparent to the lady that he was turning his mind towards this purpose, and that his amorous fervour showed signs of cooling, she would straightway in some fresh fashion of beguilement favour him anew, and thus induce him to set about playing the same game as heretofore. Then, when she knew that she had lured him back according to her plan, she would once more trim her sails for the contrary course, and bring him again into a state of wretchedness. And this deed she would execute with all the skill of an artist, not merely for the sake of vaunting herself as one of the company of honest and beautiful women, for the reason that she had kept so proper a lover in suspense so long, but also that the lover himself might serve as testimony of her simulated virtue, whereby everyone would be constrained to regard as false any evil doings of hers which might hereafter become publicly known.

It thus happened that the ill-fated youth, spending his life for several years in such evil and blameworthy case, without winning for himself so much as a single word to give him hope, determined that, even though he should meet his death thereby, he would stealthily break into the house of the lady, and there work out his purpose as fortune might allow. Wherefore, having got advice as to the season when the gentleman, the husband of the lady in question, would go forth from the city on certain business of his own, and be absent therefor several days, he carefully made entrance to the premises late one evening, and hid himself in an outhouse adjoining the courtyard which was used for storing fodder. He then took his stand behind some empty casks which had been bestowed there, and in this station he remained all the night through, buoyed up with the hope that when the lady should quit the house next morning and betake herself to church, he might be able to find an opportunity of gaining entrance to her chamber, and, once there, to hide himself under her bed, so that the following night he might make trial of his final venture. But, as was the will of his fate, which in sooth ever followed upon his traces, giving him a worse to-morrow for a bad to-day, the lady did not stir out of the house that morning on account of some unlooked-for accident; therefore the young man, having kept his station until the time of nones, * with all the pain and patience he was wont to feel and exercise, without any result, made up his mind still to abide there until the following morning. He took a scanty meal off some sweetmeats which he had brought with him for that purpose, and with much weariness of spirit, and with mighty little hope he kept himself without making a sound in the hiding place aforesaid.

Now when a good part of the day had rolled by, he heard a noise and saw come into the courtyard a muleteer, a black Moor who belonged to the household, bringing with him two loads of firewood, which he began to unload forthwith in the courtyard. On account of the noise which he made the lady went to her chamber-window, and at once took to rating the Moor that he had spent so long a time over his errand, and had brought back with him such a mean and miserable lot of wood. The Moor gave her little or nothing in the way of answer, but simply went on easing his mules in their harness and adjusting their packsaddles; and, this done, he entered the storehouse wherein the young man lay concealed in order to fetch some oats for his beasts. As soon as he had finished his task, lo and behold! the lady appeared and went likewise into the storehouse, and after plying the Moor with words of the kind she had lately thrown at him by way of banter, she began to sport with him in tender wise with her hand; and as she went on from one endearment to another, the wretched lover, who stood wonder-stricken, and for his own sake wishful that he could have been worse even than a Moor, if only he could have won the favour which was now being granted to the black without any labour on his part, beheld the lady go and make fast the door, and then, without further ado or demur, throw herself down upon the mules' saddles which lay there, and draw the horrible black fellow towards her. He, without waiting for any farther invitation, at once set himself to his task, and gave the vile wanton what she desired. Alas for you, you goodly youths! Alas, for you, you loyal and blameless lovers! who are wont without ceasing to place your honour and your riches and your life as well in jeopardy for the sake of women

* Three o'clock in the afternoon.

faithless and corrupt as this one. Come forward every one of you at this point of my story, and let each one, bearing in mind the while his own case, give me, according to the best judgment he can use, a righteous opinion as to what would have been the meetest course for the wretched youth to follow at this supreme juncture. Certes, according to my own humble understanding, any design of vengeance which he might have framed in his mind with respect to the deed which he had now seen done before his very eyes, would have failed to do full justice.

But to complete my story I will narrate to you truly, what the poor young man felt stirred up to do, after hastily taking counsel with himself. When he had looked upon this deed as aforesaid, and had felt that it went beyond his power to endure the same (his fervent love being changed meantime to hate), he came forth from his lurking-place with his naked sword in his hand, harbouring in his mind the fell purpose of putting an end to the lives of both of them at one thrust; but in that moment of time he felt himself withheld by a certain whisper of reason, which bade him consider well the shameful use he would be making of his sword in staining it with the death of such a base hound, and of such a vile and abandoned woman, as he now deemed her whom he had heretofore rated as the very flower of virtue. Wherefore, having rushed upon them with a terrible cry, he said: "Ah me! how woebegone and wretched is my life, how horrible, how monstrous are the deeds which my cruel fortune has brought before my eyes!" Then, turning towards the Moor, he said: "You, insolent dog that you are, I know not if there be aught for me to say to you, after giving you a word of praise anent your forecast in this matter, except to tell you that I shall remain for ever your debtor because you have delivered me out of the clutches of this savage bitch, who has, in sooth, bereft me of all my welfare and peace of mind." The lady, as soon as she beheld her lover, grew pale as one half dead, and everyone may judge for himself what manner of thoughts possessed her. She, who would sooner have been brought face to face with death—and with reason

—had in the meantime cast herself down at the feet of her lover, not to cry him mercy, but to beseech him that he would without farther tarrying give her the death-stroke which was her just meed. Thereupon he, who had by this time made ready the reply he was minded to give her, said: "Oh, wicked and most wanton she-wolf, shame and eternal infamy of all the residue of womankind! through what frenzy, through what passion, through what lustful desire have you suffered yourself to be overcome and subjected to a black hound, a brute beast, or, as it is more meet to say, a monstrous spawn of the earth, like this snarling cur to whom you have given, as a repast, your own corrupt and infected flesh? And though it might appear to you a fine thing to let me be torn and harassed all these years for the sake of this fellow, ought you not at least to have had some care for your own good repute, for the honour of mankind, and for the love which is borne to you by your husband, as well as that which you are in duty bound to bear towards him? He, certes, appears to me to be the most gallant, courteous, and accomplished gentleman now living in this land of ours. Of a surety I know not what else to say than to affirm that you women in the main, unbridled crew as you are, cannot be induced—when you are concerned with those matters which make for your lustful indulgence—by shame, or by fear, or by conscience, to draw any distinction between master and servant, noble and peasant, comely and frightful, so long as, according to your faulty judgment, the fellow upon whom your choice may fall is able and willing to play a lusty part between the sheets. As to that same death which you beg me with such persistence to give to you, it does not seem that you need ask it at my hands so pressingly, forasmuch as, with your name so blackened and disgraced and clouded with shame, you may well and truly reckon yourself as being even worse than dead in the future. Nay, rather I am fain you should still live on in the world, in order that you may be to your own self a testimony of your own unutterable crimes; and that, as often as you may get sight of me, you may suffer anew the pangs of death in calling back to memory your former life, and all the squalor thereof. Wherefore, abide still here on earth, and may bad luck cling to you; indeed, the savour which arises from your tainted person is so great and so foul that I cannot endure to remain any longer in your neighbourhood."

And then, because it was late, he went his way and returned to his own house, without being perceived of anyone, and the lady, who had not given him a single word in reply to what he had said, withdrew sadly to her own room, letting fall many piteous tears. The young man after this adventure gave up the use of the banner which he had heretofore borne in his jousting and tilting matches, and caused to be made another one which carried as a device a fierce black greyhound holding in its paws and its teeth the naked figure of a very beautiful woman, which it was rending and devouring. Every time that the lady saw this ensign it was to her as if an icy blade were being plunged into the very core of her heart, and in such wise this wicked woman, being thus vexed every day, was pierced and torn in spirit without respite.

MASUCCIO

ON account of the monstrous nature of the incident which I have just set before you, I am doubtful whether we should give the lover our highest praise in that he did the one thing which became a man of noble spirit to do, or heap our censure upon the wicked woman, seeing that she, in a way exactly similar, put into practice those same methods which all the others, who are even worse than she, use when nothing happens to interrupt the easy working of their designs. We may therefore hold it as an undoubted fact that those women are indeed rare who, when the opportunity may be given, do not go pirating the goods of whomsoever they may meet—a fact of which every day gives us clear testimony, and our belief in it may be yet further confirmed by the novel which follows. In this the young woman whom I intend to make the subject of my story, the one and singular daughter of her father, desired to be also one and singular in making choice of the very worst of all the many lovers who came to woo her.

THE END OF THE TWENTY-FOURTH NOVEL.

Novel the Twenty-fifth

ARGUMENT

A YOUNG GIRL IS BELOVED BY MANY SUITORS, AND WHILST FEEDING THEM WITH HOPE, COZENS THEM ONE AND ALL. ONE OF THESE PURSUES HER MORE CLOSELY THAN THE OTHERS. SHE, HOWEVER, HAS CRIMINAL CONVERSE WITH A SLAVE OF THE HOUSE, WHO LETS THIS THING BE KNOWN TO THE LOVER. WHEREUPON SHE DIES OF GRIEF, AND THE YOUNG MAN, HAVING PURCHASED THE SLAVE, LETS HIM GO FREE.

TO THE ILLUSTRIOUS LORD, MESSER GIULIO D'ACQUAVIVA, DUKE OF ATRI*

EXORDIUM

FOR the reason that I am advised, my illustrious and worthy sir, that you have many a time gathered no small diversion from the reading of my rude unpolished novels, and spoken fair of the same in many words of praise, I am in no way minded to withhold from you your portion of these fruits of mine which seem to please your taste. And because I have, in this part of my book, let fly my shafts at womankind as a target, I am fain to inscribe one of the missiles aforesaid to you, as one who has a good knowledge of this perverse brood, in order that, in the company of any other of their misdeeds which may have come under your notice, this one may cause you to take up, in a worthy spirit and when occasion may arise, the just quarrel which I have with the whole sex. In this wise you will every day lay me under a still greater obligation to you.

* He was one of the ablest leaders employed by Ferdinand I. He was killed fighting against the Turks in the campaign of Otranto.

THE NARRATIVE

ACCORDING to a report which I once heard from the mouth of a merchant of Ancona, there lived in that city not a great while ago a very rich merchant, well known all through Italy, who had an only daughter named Geronima, very young and beautiful, but vain beyond measure. Now this damsel, who thus gloried herself overmuch on account of her beauties of person, was firmly set in the belief that the greater the number of lovers she might each day bind to her service the greater would be the price at which her beauty would be appraised. For this reason she not only kept fast bound to her all those whom she had already ensnared, but she turned her thoughts to no other aim than to devise plans for the capture of still more victims by new arts of beguilement. So, without letting any one of them ever have a taste of the supreme fruit she held in store, she fed them with wind and leaves and flowers, but she never suffered one of them to go out of her presence altogether void of hope.

And while she went on priding herself over this game of trifling, it chanced that a certain youth of a very noble house, of a comely person and well endowed with all the virtues, applied himself with keener ardour than any others of the suitors had put forth to the task of winning this finished artist in coquetry. In sooth, he let himself be borne away so far into the depths of the sea of love that, notwithstanding the difference and disparity of their several estates, he would assuredly have taken her to wife if it had not been that he, being a poor man, deemed that others would have held him worthy of censure for that he, out of meanness of soul or greed of wealth, had thus made a market of his ancient nobility. Nevertheless, the father of the young damsel aforesaid plied him with importunity without ceasing, setting before him how great would be the profit and advantage which must accrue to him through an alliance of this sort. But the young man, albeit he did not look upon any of these proposals with favour, contrived nevertheless with great ingenuity to keep the business in suspense, so that he might determine whether he might not by a cunning trick bring this scheme to a successful issue. Thus, having planned to enter into relations with some one or other of the household of the young girl, he found that the only one of the servants he could use for this purpose was a certain black Moor belonging to her father, a youth named Alfonso, and for a Moor not ill-looking. He was wont to go about with a stout strap, and let himself out at a price, to carry burdens on his back for whomsoever might have need of his services.

Now the young man, under the pretence of employing this fellow for some errand, would often let him come to his house, treating him with much kindness and caressing, giving him plenty of good things to eat and money to spend on his pleasures, alluring him in such wise that in the end Alfonso became more devoted to him than to his rightful master. Then, as soon as the young man was fully assured that he might trust the Moor, he began to ask him to speak fair of him in the damsel's hearing; and, continuing to discourse in the same strain, he said one day, "My good Alfonso, if in sooth there be any man in the world of whom I am envious, it is of you; forasmuch as fortune gives you free leave to behold and to address your mistress whensoever you wish." And with these and with other very passionate words he went on without ceasing, tempting the slave to listen to him and to do him the service he desired. Wherefore the Moor, who was indeed in no wise lacking in wit and caution, and who was likewise in a measure cognizant of his master's intention to make a match between this young man and his daughter, determined that it would be a grievous waste if such a worthy and well-mannered gentleman as this should, under the name and guise of matrimony, be entangled in toils so fraudulent. So one day in his ill-wrought speech he bade the young man to lay aside entirely this love of his, for the reason that Geronima was a most evil-minded girl, and that he himself had many a time had intercourse with her, having done this thing rather by compulsion than of his own free will. When the poor young lover heard spoken such monstrous words as these, it seemed to him as if his soul was taking its flight from his body; however, collecting his wits somewhat, he put to the Moor many narrow and searching questions, only to find himself more clearly convinced, especially as Alfonso in the end offered to let him see the fact for himself, and as it were to touch it with his own hand—a proposition which he most readily accepted.

In order to carry out this scheme without letting waste any long time over the same, he caused to be made for himself forthwith a strap or band exactly similar to that worn by the Moor, with a certain device thereto by means of which he could put it on or take it off at will in such wise as is the habit of porters. On that same night, when he had determined to betake himself to witness the monstrous spectacle which was to be shown to him, he went to a painter who was his friend and had himself painted black from head to foot, and then, when he had put on certain rags which belonged to the Moor, together with the porter's band, and had changed himself in his carriage and in every other necessary respect, no one would have taken him for aught else than a real porter. As soon as it was nightfall he was led by Alfonso into the merchant's house, and was furthermore made to lie down on a mean, dirty bed. Then the Moor, after he had given full information as to the wonted doings of the abandoned girl, went his way to sleep in the stable.

The young man had not waited a great time before he heard a sound which told him that the door of the place where he lay was being stealthily unfastened, and when it was fully opened he saw and recognized Geronima, the damsel whom he had loved beyond all others, enter the place, bearing a little candle in her hand and glancing on every side to see whether peradventure some other one might not have come into the room. But when she saw that, according to her belief, there was no one else therein except her Alfonso, she went close beside the bed, and, remarking that he was black and suspecting nothing, she quenched the light and lay down by his side, and began straightway according to her wont to awake the sleeping beast.

The wretched lover, when he saw things had so fallen out

that, in order to accomplish what he had hitherto desired beyond aught else, he must needs have his heart wrung with grief—when he discovered that his lover's anguish had shaken his manhood in such wise that he would vainly attempt the end he had looked to attain—was several times on the point of letting it be known who he was, and assailing the unparalleled wickedness of the young girl with unbounded and scathing rebukes. But after carefully considering the affair, he reckoned that he would not himself get full satisfaction from the adventure, except it should be duly brought to its appointed issue, and except the damsel should in the end be left by him covered with shame and grief and sorrow. Whereupon he determined once for all to put compulsion on his humour, chilled as it was by grief and indignation, and then, by a punishment of the sort aforesaid, to work vengeance upon the girl, not only on his own account, but likewise on account of all the many others who had been befooled and flouted by her. So with no slight difficulty he brought to completion the course he had resolved to pursue. And when he had done this, he began to address her, his indignation raging strong and fierce as ever, in the following words: "Ah foolish, insensate, profligate wretch, headstrong and insolent beast that you are! Where are now all the charms with which you were wont to trick yourself out? Where is now your pride, you who deemed yourself fair beyond all others, and imagined in your haughtiness that, with the aid of this and of your wealth, you could touch the very heavens with your head? Where are those broods of ill-starred lovers of yours, wretches whom you fed with false hopes, while every day you mocked and derided them? Where is now that foolhardy insolence which led you to seek to get me for your husband? What manner of flesh was it you were minded to give me for my enjoyment? Was it the same which you had already given as a meet repast to a black carrion crow, to a filthy porter, to a savage hound, clad in vile rags and loaded with chains? As you must of a certainty be aware, I have ever been careful how I might with all manner of artifices deck out my person with divers fine garments, and use pleasant odours, solely with the desire of exhibiting myself in your sight in fashion which would please you; but, finding that naught I could do proved of any avail, I bethought me of putting on this dress, the habit of the basest menial, in which you saw me when you first came in. Of this you assured yourself by examining me closely with a lighted candle, and were no doubt mightily pleased with what you thought you had found. And afterwards I, as you yourself must know well, found it no light task to labour in the field which by right belongs to this Moor. Before this you will, I doubt not, have discovered by the sound of my voice that I am the man whom you have befooled and fed with wind for these many years past by means of your wheedling looks. Moreover, it grieves me to think that you, beguiled by holding me so completely under your yoke, may have been able to boast in the past that you had bettered your former condition a hundred thousandfold; though, indeed, you may now set this down as your last bit of good fortune, for be assured that I would rather let myself be cut in quarters than ever again admit that you are worthy of being mated with myself. Nor need you flatter yourself that you will be able, as heretofore, to let quench your hot lust in the arms of your beloved Moor; for it is by his hand that I now find myself unshackled from the bonds which your lures have cast around me, and as some reward for the great service he has wrought me I have determined to make a free man of him and release him from the servitude he owes to your father. And if you should ever henceforth take it upon yourself to dupe or to feed with false hopes any goodly youths in such fashion as you have befooled them in the past, or to put your flouts upon them anew, be well assured that this scheming of yours will be baulked, forasmuch as I myself will set to work to let this abominable wickedness of yours become the public talk in every part of this our city, and I will make your name the byword in the mouths of the common folk, and thereby let eternal disgrace fall upon you. In sooth, I shall never deem that I have vituperated you enough for the vile and wicked profligacy you have practised. But these rags which I now wear, and the clothes upon this bed—which have been to you heretofore so gracious and sweet-smelling and pleasant—stink in my nostrils so horribly that I am constrained to go my way forthwith; therefore get you gone quickly hence, and on your way call for me your worthy lover, who is waiting in the stable, in order that he may convey me privately out of this dark prison in which I am not inclined to tarry any longer."

The woebegone and most wretched Geronima, who indeed knew full well who was the man she had with her the very first word he spoke, would assuredly have made an end straightway to her miserable life had a knife meet for such a deed been in her hand. All the time he was speaking, she, without giving him back a single word in reply, went on with her bitter weeping, and at last, according to his command, she got up from the bed and called the Moor in a soft voice. Then, as the young man wished, she let them both out of the house, and after she had locked the door she returned to her own chamber, and there, under the colour of some excuse, she thenceforth remained grief-stricken to death, and shedding as many tears as a well full of water would have supplied. In a few days' time she died, whether by grief or by poison I know not. The noble youth, having let the whole affair get noised abroad, and having likewise enjoyed no small pleasure from the punishment and death of the young girl, purchased the Moor and set him at liberty. He himself, now that he was delivered and unfettered from his passion, lived happily for a long time, taking much pleasure in his lusty youth.

MASUCCIO

WHAT man having listened to this novel will hereafter nurse any doubts concerning the crowning profligacy of womankind? If he should turn over in his mind the stories I have told, will it not appear to him as though he had seen the same with his own eyes? I, who from very shame of myself am kept back from telling you (for I, like the rest of men, was born of a woman) how, when they are assailed by overpowering lust and unbridled rage, they employ certain means for saving their credit, in order that, as they believe, their offence may be less. If you who read this understand my meaning, there is no need for me to say anything more to you; but if you should still be in doubt, then find someone else who may declare the purport of these obscure terms of mine. I am still bound to write of divers others who, being blinded by their fiery lust, and fearing that their secret should be known, or that they should abase themselves to the conversation of men of mean estate, have not shrunk from submitting themselves to brute beasts—things of which I have heard tell as the very truth, and have myself had experience, even as a matter which I could touch with my own hands, Such nefarious working as this is in sooth for the most part practised by the very women who hold themselves to be wise beyond all others.

I may affirm for certain that motives akin to the aforesaid must have induced a certain wary and sagacious dame to act the part which I am about to describe to you in my next novel: how she, being of a sudden seized with love of a very goodly youth, still knew how to keep herself so well within bounds that the young man (although she got all from him she wanted) was never suffered to know who she might be. If other women would take an example from this one, of a surety the names of very few of them would be bandied about in the mouths of men.

THE END OF THE TWENTY-FIFTH NOVEL.

Novel the Twenty-sixth

ARGUMENT

A LADY BEING ENAMOURED OF A SEEMLY YOUTH CAUSES HIM TO BE BROUGHT BLINDFOLDED INTO HER CHAMBER BY A DISGUISED CONFIDANT OF HERS. THEN, AFTER HAVING PASSED THE NIGHT WITH HIM, SHE DIRECTS HIM TO COME THITHER AGAIN, BUT THE YOUTH HAVING TOLD HIS ADVENTURE TO A FRIEND OF HIS, THE LADY HEARS OF WHAT HE HAS DONE, AND LETS HIM COME TO HER NO MORE.

TO THE MAGNIFICENT FRANCISCHELLA DE MORISCO*

EXORDIUM

MANY a time when I have been conversing with you, my magnificent and most highly esteemed gossip, I remember having remarked in my haste that, although it is a rare thing to find a woman who may be commended as being prudent, seeing in what faulty wise Nature has made them, still there may be found some who are better advised than others—women who, while they are not strong enough to beat back their lustful desires, and on this account are ever seeking out some new and cunning schemes for the satisfying of the same, are in less degree deserving of our censure. These, indeed, go no farther than to violate the law, and work no outrage on their weak natures, but secretly satisfy their appetites. And inasmuch as in the novel which follows we shall both of us be confirmed in this our belief, so that you, taking this novel in conjunction with those which you have heard already, may by con-

* In the later editions this novel is dedicated to Madonna Fioretta Alipranda.

ferring with yourself deliver a true judgment whether, setting aside the sin of which she was guilty, the woman I shall tell of may be held to be in a certain measure worthy of praise, or whether she should be reckoned as one only meet for the company of other wicked women. Farewell!

THE NARRATIVE

DURING that time when the Pistoian was running from one end of our kingdom to the other and working such a vast number of miracles, the strange accident which is written below verily and indeed came to pass in the city of Naples. The thing happened one Saturday evening in the month of March, when the people were going in a crowd to the church of the Carmine, and amongst them was a bevy of fair ladies, who, having as they imagined received full absolution, were seized with the desire to return to their homes by traversing the outskirts of the city. When they had come to that street which crosses by the Padule, it chanced that they met a band of young men, who were no less remarkable for their grace and beauty of person than for their noble bearing, and these youths, for their diversion and for pleasant exercise, were playing the game of Palla del Maglio.* Whereupon it came to pass that a certain one of the ladies aforesaid, endowed with very great beauty and with wit still greater, let her eyes fall upon one of the young men, a youth attired in a doublet of green damask. So strongly was she moved to pleasure at the sight of him that she felt as if she must needs fall into a swoon. Nevertheless she contrived by her prudent carriage to conquer her amorous mood without let-

* The game of Pall Mall. Pepys writes, April 2nd, 1661: "To St. James's Park, where I saw the Duke of York playing at Plemele, the first time I ever saw the sport." It was probably introduced into England from France. There is an interesting article on the game in the "Archæological Journal," vol. xi., p. 253.

ting appear any sign thereof, and went back to her home in company with the others, bearing the while in her heart the most overpowering passion for the youth who had so greatly pleased her.

She began at once to run over in her mind all the many and divers methods she could employ whereby she might win for herself full and complete satisfaction of this love of hers; but, although love had now gained possession of the chief place in her heart, she was not yet so completely distraught in her wits as not to know how rarely it happens that anyone who may have resolved to give full rein to amorous passion is able for any long time to keep secret the matter, let the web have been woven ever so privily, forasmuch as there is no one in the world who has not about him some perfect friend or other to whom he is wont to tell the story of all his worthy deeds and his culpable ones as well. Then this same friend will surely possess a like confidant of his own from whom he can in no wise conceal either his own secrets or those of others, and thus, passed on from one mouth to another, the brief felicities of lovers are full often wont to come to an end in long misery.

With regard to this matter you must know that, after long pondering, the lady came to a decision either to let this passion of hers, by the working of a novel stratagem, run on to its full and perfect end, or to withdraw herself entirely therefrom; although, in this latter case, she might find her desire so powerful that the frustration of it might prove her death. To let the plan she had devised be put forthwith in execution she went to a kinsman of hers in whose fidelity she could trust, and to him she laid bare the story of her passion, and in a few words gave him command to do what she told him. This kinsman, who was well inclined to do her bidding, straightway clothed himself in a sack of the sort which the penitents of the confraternity are wont to wear, and this done he went in search of the young man he had been sent to find; and, meeting him by chance apart from the company of his friends, the messenger drew him aside, and, having a piece of cane in his mouth, spake thus to him: "Good brother, if you would meet with an adventure which cannot fail to profit you, see that you be this evening between the first and the second hour in the church of San Giovanni Maggiore." And having thus spoken he went his way.

The young man was mightily astonished when he listened to this request, and, after he had turned over the matter in his mind many times, he came to the conclusion that it must needs be somewhat of weighty import: wherefore, putting full trust in himself, inasmuch as he was young, of high courage and sprightly, and being assured, over and beyond this, that there would be no one at the place aforesaid whom he could suspect of any forethought to work him an injury, he determined, without seeking counsel from any of his friends, that he would go and put his fortune to the test; so, when the appointed hour had come, and when he had taken divers trusty weapons, he went to the place named with a stout heart and full of courage. As soon as he had come to the spot, he saw approaching him the confidant of the lady, who was now clad in a disguise differing from the sack which he had worn in the morning, so that no one would have known him for the same. He greeted the young man graciously, and, speaking in a low tone so that his voice might not betray who he was, he said: "My friend, it seems to me that kindly Fortune now approaches you, offering you the highest favours for your lasting gain as well as for your present and future contentment, if you will only show yourself wise, and give her joyful welcome. The fact is that a certain lady, young, beautiful, and beyond measure rich, is so mightily enamoured of you that she is altogether distraught and consumed by her passion, and has finally resolved to offer you the boon of taking the first fruits of enjoyment of her person before any other man, and of partaking of her wealth as well. Nevertheless, she is minded, in order that she may for a few days have experience as to whether you know how to bear yourself with silence and secrecy, that you should enter her presence with me veiled in such wise that you can gather no cognizance of herself, or of her house, or of the quarter in which she dwells. If you will consent to do this, let us at once set out on our way; but if by any chance the good fortune which now calls you, without putting upon you aught of labour or trouble, should not seem to your liking, you may go your way in God's name, for I am strictly charged not to bring you except of your own free will."

The young man, when he first heard the gist of the speech aforesaid, deemed that the enterprise would be a difficult one, and it would moreover be a strange thing to be led away thus blindfolded, almost as if he were a goat being taken to the shambles; still, when he considered that he need fear no peril to his person, seeing that the man before him had left to him the choice to go or to stay, and reckoned that beyond this there could follow naught which would not prove to be advantageous to him, he determined, without further thought thereanent, to risk the adventure, and made answer to the messenger that he was ready to go with him wherever and in whatsoever fashion it pleased him. Whereupon the other brought out a thick veil, and, after he had covered the young man's eyes and drawn off his biretta, he took him by the arm, and the two set forth on their way. He led the youth on from one street to another; they entered divers houses and issued therefrom again; and when at last it seemed to him that the time had come, he led the gallant into the lady's house. Then, after he had made him go up and down the divers staircases which were therein several times, he brought him at last into the chamber where his coming was looked for with such ardent longing, and, having removed the veil from his face, he left him there and locked the door.

The young man, as soon as he let open his eyes, knew naught else than that he was in a dark room in which there was nothing to be seen, but he soon became conscious of a delicious odour which arose from whomsoever might be near him. While he was standing somewhat overcome by amazement at his strange position he felt a woman's arms close round him in joyful wise, and a soft voice spake thus: "Welcome art thou, the sole support of my life!" And without uttering another word she gave him a sign that he should undress, which thing he did readily enough, and then, when she had duly disposed herself, they got into the bed together. Now, for the reason that at a time like this neither one of them had any need to speak a word, they occupied themselves in such manner that they lay not idle for a single moment all that night. As soon as the hour drew nigh when the lady deemed that it was meet she should let the young man go forth from her house, she took a purse full of golden florins which she had prepared for this purpose, and, once more embracing him in loving wise, and speaking softly in order that he should not be able to recognize who she was, she said to him: "My sweet soul, take now these few coins, which may be of some use to you for your present need, and leave all thought and care for the future to her who now holds you in her arms. See, moreover, that you bear yourself in prudent wise, and take care lest your tongue, while meaning only to put a slight upon my honour, may not work the ruin of your abiding joy. Indeed, when you may least look for such a thing, I will let your eyes have a feast of what will delight them not a little. But in the meantime think it not a hard thing, that you are brought hither in such wise. When I shall be in the humour to receive you again, I will send for you in similar fashion." Then, after she had once more kissed him and had received from him a countless number of sweet kisses, she bade him put on his clothes, and called for her trusty messenger, who once more bound the young man's eyes with a veil, and led him by a devious path to the spot where he had met him on the previous evening, and, having left him there, went back to his own house.

Thereupon the young man, having removed the veil from his eyes, made his way home, marvelling amain and rejoicing in heart over what had befallen him. In sooth he was wellnigh beside himself with curiosity to know who the lady might be; and, finding that he could not by his own efforts discover aught, he came to the conclusion that there was no reason why he should keep the story of his great good fortune, and his mental travail over the same, a secret from a certain comrade of his who was his particular and most trusty friend. Wherefore, having sent for him, he told him everything concerning what had recently happened, without taking any further heed as to what he did.

He now began to work in the company of this friend to try to bring to light somewhat concerning his adventure, but for the reason that neither the one nor the other could in any way hit the mark, they resolved to suffer the business to run on in whatever course should be determined by the lady herself. It chanced that this friend, who was a frequenter of the courts, found himself one day in the company of a number of other lawyers, and, as they were discussing now this argument and now that, he laid before them, point by point, as a strange and marvellous adventure, the case aforesaid just as it had occurred, making believe, however, that the thing had been brought to pass in the kingdom of France. By chance the confidant of the lady, who, as has been already told, had been, her agent, and had been cognizant of the whole affair happened to be present when these words were spoken; whereupon he went forthwith to the lady, and, grieving sorely the while, made known to her what thing he had lately heard tell by the mouth of this friend of her lover.

When she heard these words she was stricken with sorrow beyond measure, and held it for certain that, if her lover should go on to act further in this wise, the secret of her hidden passion must needs be brought to light, and her honour and good name tarnished and destroyed. For this reason she resolved, once for all, that the first pleasure and the first boon which the young man had gotten from her should at the same time be the last; and this resolution she forthwith confirmed and settled in her own mind as unchangeable. The improvident youth, unwitting as to what had come to pass, and yearning exceedingly to turn his steps once more towards the pleasant uplands of that rich pasturage, waited for many a day in vain for a summons thither, as vainly as the Jews await that Messias of theirs who will never come; and, as the days passed without letting him see any sign or token of the coming of the messenger, he learned too late that it was through the working of his own tongue that this evil had befallen him. As for the lady, although for a season she was sorely stricken with grief over what had happened, we may be sure that she found out before long some safe and convenient method for satisfying her longings with some other lover.

MASUCCIO

I CAN well believe that the young man will be shrewdly blamed by some people, for the reason that he knew not how to maintain a prudent carriage, but if in truth we are minded to consider carefully what is necessary to the conservation of true friendship, no one can with justice condemn him; for the reason that we must set down as greatly wanting in the spirit of humanity, that man who is not wont to discover every weighty secret of his to any trusty friend. And this he is especially bound to do when it may concern not only his wealth and his happiness, but even his very life, because no pleasure can be rightly enjoyed save we share the same with some well-trusted companion. Therefore, seeing that the young man put his trust in such a friend as this—what though he afterwards fared ill through the man's babbling—it cannot be denied that by his act he only followed the course in which he was constrained to go by the bonds of true friendship. So, as the result of the one merry night which he gave to the lady, he spent many months in very festive fashion, so long as the money which she had given him lasted. Now, putting on one side all farther argument as to this affair, it seems to me that a certain amount of praise is due from us to the gallant man on account of the high courage which he showed in suffering himself to be led in such fashion to the lady's house. But courage in sooth is innate in men and essential to them; but in my next story I will lay before you—and it is a wonderful tale I have to tell—an instance of the courage which was shown by a certain young woman, which would not have been deemed inadequate in a robust and stout-hearted man. Concerning this affair, judgment may be given when the story shall have been read.

THE END OF THE TWENTY-SIXTH NOVEL.

Novel the Twenty-seventh

ARGUMENT

A CERTAIN GENTLEWOMAN, HAVING BEEN ABANDONED BY HER LOVER, DISGUISES HERSELF IN MAN'S GARB, AND GOES TO KILL HIM, BUT IS TAKEN BY THE CATCHPOLES OF THE COURT. BEING BROUGHT BEFORE THE PODESTA, SHE PERSUADES HIM TO LEND HER HIS AID IN WORKING OUT HER VENGEANCE, AND HE, IN ORDER THAT HE MAY BE WITNESS OF HER COURAGE, GOES WITH HER, AND, HAVING REALIZED THE ROBUST SPIRIT THAT WAS IN HER, RESTORES THE PEACE BETWEEN HER AND HER LOVER. THEN, AFTER THE EXCHANGE OF HIGH COURTESIES, HE LEAVES THE TWO WITH THEIR FORMER LOVE RENEWED.

TO THE MOST EXCELLENT LADY, THE COUNTESS OF BUCCHIANICO

EXORDIUM

MOST magnificent and excellent lady mine, seeing that long time has passed since I visited you, either in person or by letter, I feel myself continually stirred up, by reason of this failing of mine, to atone as best I may for the fault I have committed. Wherefore I send to you the accompanying extraordinary story, as to one whom I have always held to be extraordinary amongst women. This I pray you to accept, O most worthy countess, with affection of heart like that which I myself feel in offering it, so that by reading it you may understand how women, what though nature may in some respects have been niggard towards them, can show that they are endowed with courage equal to that of a man.

THE NARRATIVE

THE day before yesterday a story was narrated to my most serene lord the prince* as an undoubted fact, telling how there lately abode in Naples a young merchant of good and honourable family, gifted with seemly manners and adequately dowered with all the goods which fortune now gives and now takes away. This young man for a long time reaped the greatest happiness in the enjoyment of the love of a gracious and beautiful young girl, who loved him and him only in return for the ardent passion he had for her; wherefore these two, each being possessed by like desire, accounted themselves blessed beyond measure in the gratification of their loves. But because those things which we are allowed to possess undisturbed and in great abundance usually pall upon our appetites after a time, it happened that the young man was taken with the desire to go a-hunting fresh game. For this reason, or for some other, without making any further sign to her who had hitherto enjoyed his love, he began to withdraw himself from her presence, and neither to go nor to send word to her, small or great; on account of which thing the lady, astonished at this strange conduct, despatched messages to him again and again to bid him either come or let her know the reason of his displeasure. But to all these inquiries of hers she could get no reply, good or bad. Furthermore, she made diligent examination of herself without being able to find that she had been guilty of any deed calculated to kindle anger or resentment against her. Wherefore she deemed for certain that the cause of this misfortune could be nothing else than some new love. And in order to have good assurance of this, she sent divers men to spy upon his traces, and these before they had searched many days found out that the lady had judged aright, forasmuch as her lover had indeed become enamoured of another damsel, upon whom he lavished all his affection. On this account the lady, when she knew for certain that this thing had come to pass, fell a-weeping bitterly, and

* Roberto di Sanseverino.

was soon brought into so cruel a state of grief that she was like to pine away; and, chafing with anger and indignation, she felt her great love change into the most malignant hatred, to such a degree that if by chance she should have held between her teeth the heart of her faithless lover she would willingly have torn and devoured the same. Moreover, being assailed and overcome by the strength of her passion, she sought out within herself all possible means whereby she might compass his death, either by steel or by poison. But finding none of these convenient, she, with a fearlessness not to be looked for in a lady so young, determined to put an end to his life with her own hands; and, being well versed in all the particular features of the young man's house, how he always lay by himself in a certain chamber near to a little garden beside a terrace, and not much elevated above the level of the high road, and how at night, the better to let fresh air come into the chamber, it was his habit in the summer time to leave open the door which communicated with the terrace, she determined at all hazard to go thither alone, putting in peril both her life and her honour, in order to avenge herself, and with her own hands to slay her false and cruel lover.

Without in any way changing her plan she took a rope-ladder which her lover had left behind in her house, and, as she possessed due skill and knowledge of the art of grappling and climbing, she disguised herself as a man, and put on all the equipment necessary for such a nocturnal excursion, and when it seemed to her that the fitting time had come she sallied forth, taking with her a poisoned knife. As she went on her quest, following the cross streets just as if she had been accustomed to such work from her earliest youth, she—either by her own evil fortune or by the good fortune of her lover—happened to encounter the guard of the governor of the city as she was passing from one street to another. Then, judging at once who they must be, and perceiving she was cut off in such wise that no chance of escape was left for her, and that it would be useless to oppose her strength to theirs in defending herself, she straightway resolved to seize upon the least compromising alternative which lay before her. So, turning towards the men who were about to lay hands upon her, she simulated as well as she could the voice of a man, and demanded of them to tell her where the governor was. Hereupon one of the guards made reply that he was close at hand, and him she answered in very courageous fashion, saying: "Let us go and find him at once, for I would fain speak with him on a matter of the highest moment." And while they were thus engaged it chanced that the governor himself came upon them; whereupon the young woman, going towards him, whispered to him that he should order his guards to withdraw themselves somewhat apart. As soon as he agreed to do this, she took him by the hand and addressed him in these terms: "Seeing that rumour has already let me know of the sincerity of your virtuous spirit, and how neither ambition nor disordinate appetite have ever prevailed to corrupt the same; how you, like a good knight, are ever ready to take in hand the righteous quarrel of an injured woman, I am moved to tell you that I am a woman, and young, and to entreat you without ceasing that you will not only suffer me now to go and carry out the project of vengeance upon which I am bound, but that you yourself, by virtue of your knighthood, will accompany me on my errand, and lend me your countenance in this matter in such fashion that I may unhindered give effect to my desire." After she had thus spoken she went on without reserve to tell him exactly everything which had passed between her lover and herself, ending by confessing to the governor the thing she was minded now to do.

After Ulzina,* the governor, had listened to this speech of hers he was greatly astonished, or even distraught with amazement, when he considered how stout was the heart of this girl, deeming that she could only have been stirred up to such passion by some grave injury. Now, although he already knew the young girl well, seeing that he had always judged her to surpass in beauty all the other damsels of Naples, and had given her all his love; neverthe-

* Some kinsman doubtless of Giovanni Olzina, the secretary of Alfonso the Magnanimous. See Porzio, "Congiura dei Baroni," Part I.

less, restrained by his great steadfastness of spirit that virtue inseparable from every true knight—and confirmed therein by the prayers and adjurations of the lady, he determined to conquer his selfishness and to drive away every froward thought, satisfying at the same time the damsel's wish and rescuing her lover from the disaster which threatened him.

When the governor remarked that she stood silent he endeavoured with many well-studied words to cause her to desist from her cruel purpose, but when he saw clearly that she was still firmly set in mind to do what she willed, and when she again requested him that, if he would not lend her his aid in this enterprise, he would at least throw no obstacle in her way, he made up his mind to go and be a witness of the final proof of the girl's skill and courage. So, having given orders to his guards that they should await his return, he took his way with her towards the lover's dwelling. When they were come to the foot of the terrace, she took a long pole and hoisted up therewith the grappling hook of iron to which the rope-ladder was attached, and having dexterously hooked the same on to the balcony she clambered up it as lightly as if she had been a cat. The governor, who found himself more and more amazed every moment, determined to see for himself what might be the issue of the affair; wherefore he too climbed up after her. When he saw her standing with the knife in her hand ready to carry out her savage design, and furthermore perceived how, on account of the heavy sleep in which her lover lay, she might easily accomplish her purpose, he had no wish to be witness of any farther proof of her intention; so, taking her by the hand, he spake thus: "My sister, I would never have believed, though it might have been told to me as something beyond doubt, that so great boldness and courage could dwell in a woman's heart, had I not seen this thing with my own eyes, and been made to understand clearly that you can only have been moved by righteous anger to inflict with your own hands a cruel death upon him whom you once held dearer than life. Nevertheless, since I am, as you must well know, the chastiser of malefactors in this city, I can find no honest or reasonable cause why I should permit myself to be made the partaker of a homicide like this. Besides, I do not doubt, after having found you engaged in such a work as this, and seen how your mind was fully made up to take the life of this sleeping man with your impious and cruel hand, that you must know perfectly well that, by every righteous judgment, you deserve yourself to be mulcted of your own life. Although I might with justice award such a doom to you, I have spared your life out of kindly consideration, and it is only becoming and seemly that they who obtain pardon should likewise grant pardon. Wherefore I beseech you be not a niggard in this respect, but, by way of recompense for the great boon you have received at my hands, grant to me the life of your lover; which life, as you have already confessed to me, you once held dearer than your own. I, forsooth, will not depart from this place until I shall have set this matter in order in such fashion that hereafter your loves shall never again be severed save only by death itself."

The young woman, although she could not for a time put aside the fury which possessed her, saw clearly in the end that she could do nothing, and when she turned to the other side of the question she found no little consolation in the good counsel given by the governor, who might, in very sooth, have taken from her her life, or at least her honour. Wherefore she seemed much appeased by what he said, and the governor, having gone into the chamber where the young man was sleeping unsuspicious of ill, took hold of him by the hair and awakened him. The young man, filled with no little fear and amazement, was brought back to his waking senses by this strange occurrence; whereupon the governor straightway commanded him to light a candle, which thing he quickly did, shaking the while with terror. And after the lady had let him know and had related to him the cause which had brought them thither, and with a torrent of befitting words had reproved his foolish doings, the governor bade him that he should, with the strap round his neck,* beg pardon of her, and from henceforth hold his life as a gift from her, promising at the same time

* Orig., *con la corregia la gola.*

that as long as life should be granted to him he would be her sole and faithful lover. And he, being convinced of his offence, straightway did all that the governor commanded him, and rendered him due thanks for all the great service and kindness that had been wrought on his behalf. Then, in obedience to the wishes of the governor, and of the lady herself, he put on his clothes, and they all together honourably escorted the gentlewoman as far as her home.

When the lady was come to her house she turned to the governor and thanked him in very graceful speech, declaring that she was quite ready to put herself under his charge, both as to her person and her goods, as to a perfect friend and good brother, recommending not only her life but also her honour to his keeping. Then, with divers other very sweet speeches, she bade him farewell. Her lover remained with her, the cruel strife between them having been transformed into soft and joyful peace; and, going back to their former love without ever recalling aught of past mischance, they reaped in bliss the full enjoyment of their love as long as they both lived.

MASUCCIO

IN truth the boldness of this love-possessed damsel may be accounted as nothing less than miraculous. (It is not for me to say whether the cause thereof may have been overpowering love or unbridled lust.) And because the virtue of the governor in the course he followed was so eminent, that any words of praise I may use thereanent must appear scanty, forasmuch as the methods he employed sprang from his natural goodness, without having been occasioned or suggested by anyone else, I will now exhibit to you an example of robust courage on the part of a certain Moorish serving-woman, which was called forth by virtue, and by her tender care for the honour of her dear master—courage which would have honoured the estate not only of a mean servant, but even that of any high-hearted man.

THE END OF THE TWENTY-SEVENTH NOVEL.

Novel the Twenty-eighth

ARGUMENT

A KNIGHT OF PROVENCE IS OVERGONE WITH LOVE FOR HIS WIFE, WHO BEING ATTACKED BY AN ACCESS OF LUST INDULGES HERSELF WITH A DWARF. A MOORISH SERVING-WOMAN KILLS THEM BOTH IN THE VERY ACT WITH A LANCE, WHEREUPON THE HUSBAND CAUSES THEIR BODIES TO BE CAST OUT AS FOOD FOR WILD BEASTS.

TO THE MOST ILLUSTRIOUS DON FRANCESCO OF ARAGON *

EXORDIUM

MY most illustrious lord, although you have not passed out of your adolescence into the full flower of your age, I, being well assured that your high ability will prove fully adequate, not merely to gather the meaning of my own unpolished writings in the mother-tongue, but also to deliver excellent and finished judgment concerning the flowery and graceful discourse of others, will not refrain from sending to you the novel which follows, so that you may have due notice and warning of the evil practices of that misbegotten brood of womankind, and in the course of time, with the prudence which you now exhibit, may acquire both the power and the knowledge to protect yourself from their snares and their treachery. Farewell!

* He was the fourth son of King Ferdinand. He was born in 1461, and was consequently not more than fifteen years of age when Masuccio dedicated to him this novel. That such a story should have been inscribed to a boy is a valuable index of the manners of the period.

THE NARRATIVE

IN the noble city of Marseilles, no very long time after the destruction by fire dealt out to it by that godlike prince, King Alfonso of Aragon of happy memory,* there lived a certain doughty knight, rich, and illustrious for his virtues, youthful, and very seemly in his person, who was called by name Messer Piero d'Orliens. He, being consumed by an ardent passion for a maiden of exceeding great beauty named Ambrosia, the daughter of a powerful baron and a countryman of his own, and having succeeded by the instrumentality of some good friends of his in transforming this passion of love into lawful matrimony, brought home to his own house Madonna Ambrosia with stately ceremonies, and sumptuous feasts. Then, having arrayed her in magnificent garments, and found that she was beautiful beyond measure, and that her manners and her carriage gave him exceeding great delight, his love for her grew a thousandfold greater than heretofore. So powerfully indeed was his inclination swayed in this particular, that he felt, whenever he might be deprived of the company of his beloved Ambrosia, that all his contentment and delight was straightway transformed into sorrow.

But although Ambrosia was furnished by her husband with a great store of rich and precious gems, and of other ornaments, more ample, indeed, than her needs demanded; although, whenever she might go abroad, she was attended by a numerous train of servants both male and female; nevertheless her husband did not show himself over-ready in furnishing that particular service which is especially to the taste of fair dames like herself, and which I will not for the sake of modesty further treat of in this place. Thus the lady passed her days blessed by fortune, without ever having need of aught that money could buy, either small or great. Amongst the troop of servants maintained in the house, it chanced

* Marseilles was attacked and partially burnt by Alfonso the Magnanimous in the course of his wars with Joanna II.

that the knight aforesaid kept for his especial amusement a certain dwarf, so horrible and deformed in his outward seeming that he was hardly to be likened to anything human. Now of this dwarf Madonna Ambrosia was wont to be mightily diverted, and from time to time she and the others of the household would make him skip about, and, for their diversion, put himself in divers and antic postures, as is the way of dwarfs and creatures of this sort, whereby they were all filled with delight and merriment.

In the course of this sport with the dwarf, it came to pass that the lady became possessed with the idea that, misshapen monster as he was, there was something about him which would make him well fitted for the purpose she had in view; and, on this account Ambrosia albeit she had for a husband so excellent and proper a gentleman, one who loved her more than he loved himself, who was endowed with all those other excellent qualities aforementioned, and who gave her such kindly and generous usage, was seized with the notion that two would serve more efficiently than one to appease and to weary out the insatiable lust which possessed her, and was overborne by an ardent and unbridled desire to make a trial whether the dwarf might not be able and willing to dance as nimbly for the satisfaction of her longings as he had danced upon the hard floor. And giving way to these wanton imaginings she fretted amain.

Now because it happens but seldom that women of this execrable breed ever take such thoughts into their heads without finding soon some occasion and commodity for putting the same into execution, this vile strumpet did not let pass more than a few hours before she was minded to glut the greedy maw of her lust with this provender almost too horrible to name. However, the savage beast within her caused her grave annoy; and she, being driven on continually by her unbridled passion, let her thoughts run only towards the encounter with the dwarf in more ardent wise with every day that passed.

Thus, while she let her humour continue in this strain of detestable lechery, it came to pass that an old Moorish woman-servant, one who had for a long time lived in the service of the father of the cavalier in question, and afterwards with the cavalier himself, holding the house in great affection, began to harbour suspicions of the lady. To her in sooth any injury which might befall either the honour or the happiness of her master would have been a greater sorrow than the loss of her own life; wherefore she made up her mind, should this suspicion of hers prove to be true, to die sooner than endure the evil thereof; but, as became a woman of age and experience, she wished to be well assured of the matter before disclosing it to her master. One day, when the knight had gone out of the city to take his pleasure in flying his hawks, the old woman, deeming that the lady with such a fair opportunity as this before her would not fail to make a fresh trial of her fine game, concealed herself beneath the bed in Madonna Ambrosia's chamber, and as she waited there she heard her mistress in artful wise give leave to all the servants of the house to go where they list, and then she beheld her come into the chamber accompanied only by the dwarf. After the door had been made fast, the old woman was conscious that they got upon the bed at once, perchance so as to waste no time over farther parley, and forthwith began to play their wicked game. Then the Moorish woman, having come out from her lurking-place, and seen clearly with what outrageous and unrestrained lechery the abandoned wanton bore herself towards the hideous toad whom she had chosen as her minion, felt herself at the same time stricken with grief and inflamed with rage in wellnigh intolerable measure. Wherefore, without taking further thought or consideration anent the thing she saw, she turned her eyes towards a corner of the room, and, espying there a wild-boar spear, finished at the point with a sharp and heavy blade, which the knight was wont to use when he went a-hunting, she seized this in her hand; and, having got upon the bed without being seen by either of them, she struck the lance through the woman's reins with the full force of her rage, and, throwing all her weight upon it, she transfixed not only Madonna Ambrosia, but the dwarf as well, even down to the sheets of the bed. Thereupon the two wretches, being unable to free themselves from the lance, in a very brief time breathed their last entangled in one another's embraces.

The Moorish woman as soon as the deed was done fell into a cooler mood, and began to doubt whether she had done well in avenging this wrong which did not concern herself. Nevertheless, having made fast the door of the chamber without moving the dead bodies from where they lay, she sent straightway a servant to fetch home the knight, and to tell him that if he wished to see his wife still alive it behoved him to come quickly, for the reason that she was like to die on account of a certain spasm of the heart which had suddenly come over her. The servant, having found the cavalier, delivered to him the message, to which he listened with no little sorrow. He at once gave over the chase and took the road back to his home with all speed; and, when he drew near, was met by the devoted and faithful Moorish woman, who, after she had conducted him into the house, took him without a word into the chamber, and there let him see the horrible work in which that wife of his, whom he held dearer than aught beside, had been engaged, and with the most overpowering grief, told him word by word, in what fashion the thing had come to this issue, and how she herself, stirred up by her exceeding great jealousy of his honour, had thus let herself outstep the bounds of her duty and commit this double homicide.

My pen, in sooth, is all inadequate to set down how great and how bitter were the inward anguish of the gentleman, and his travail and desolation of soul when he saw the deed which had been done—a deed of which the speech of his faithful servant had borne him true testimony—and realized how he had lost at one stroke his honour and his future peace of mind, together with his wife, so beautiful, and held by him in such supreme love. Each reader who has still his wits about him will be able to estimate this for himself. For it seemed to him as if his agonized heart were reft in many pieces. After he had let his grief moderate somewhat through much weeping and lamentation, he came to himself once more, and, seeing that the ill which had befallen him was one for which there was no cure, he set about taking counsel how he might as a prudent man best retrieve his honour. So, having sent straightway to fetch the father and the brothers of Madonna Ambrosia, he caused them to enter the chamber. Then, after he had let them know what had been the sin and what the punishment of these two lovers, he declared that he himself, overcome by anguish and burning indignation, had been the slayer of these wretches and the punisher of this horrible and wellnigh inhuman offence.

Thereupon the lady's kinsfolk, when they perceived and were convinced by reason in what wise the matter stood, could think of naught else to do than to commend highly the cavalier for what he had done; and he, on his part, to let the world know how severe and unflinching was the punishment of revenge which he was minded to inflict, forthwith bade them take the two dead bodies, transfixed with the lance just as they were, and place them upon the back of an ass and carry them to the top of a certain hill outside the city. There they were thrown down as food for birds and wild beasts, and in a short time naught was left of them but their naked bones.

MASUCCIO

IT would be hard to give praise enough to the old Moorish woman for that, with her affectionate love, she did her part in saving from ruin and downfall the injured honour of her beloved master, and in avenging the outrage which had been put upon him. It would be just as hard to heap adequate condemnation upon the young lady who was a Christian, seeing that by such a vile deed she blackened her own fair fame and the honour of many others who were her kinsfolk. Still, for the reason that she was punished for all the guilty pleasure she had enjoyed by one single and well-deserved stroke, I do not feel that it is my part to upbraid her more. Thus, taking my way back to the delightful shores of our Parthenope, where the pastime of jousting is much affected after divers fashions, and where people are always engaging in tourneys with marvellous vigour, I will tell you the story of another woman, who, albeit she was well approved in the jousts, was in this case more keen for sport than happy in her adventure, seeing that she was minded to run not one, but three valiant courses in a single night.

THE END OF THE TWENTY-EIGHTH NOVEL.

Novel the Twenty-ninth

ARGUMENT

Viola makes promise of her favours to three lovers in the same night. The first goes to her, but he is kept from the enjoyment of his booty by the coming of the second. Then the third arrives and is tricked by the second, and entrance is denied to him; but he discovers the cheat, and sees what is being done. Whereupon he brings craft to his aid, and takes vengeance both upon the one and the other; then, both of the others being put to heavy loss and injury, he remains in sole ownership of the prey.

TO THE MAGNIFICENT MESSER JACOMO AZZAIUOLO, A VERY NOBLE GENTLEMAN OF FLORENCE

EXORDIUM

MY work would indeed be most unfit and unsuitable for your acceptance, my magnificent and most virtuous Messer Jacomo, if I—knowing full well that you are gifted with a kindly and jovial temper—should, in writing this present novel for your pleasure, allow the same to show that it is in any way affected by dull or melancholy themes, either in its conception or in its ordering. I beg you, therefore, that you will accept it in a jocund mood, for I can tell you that you will of a surety find it made up from beginning to end of all manner of witty pleasantries, and set forth in such wise that it will not fail to rouse the loud and frequent laughter of yourself and of any others who may hear it told.

THE NARRATIVE

ONCE upon a time, which will be just a year agone when next January shall have passed, there lived in Naples a certain good fellow, a carpenter by trade, whose handicraft found no greater scope than the making of wooden shoes. He occupied a house by the side of the Sellaria,* in a little square at the back of the old Mint, and had to wife a very fair and graceful dame, who, although as a young woman she showed herself in no wise coy or averse from the courtings of everyone of the well-nigh countless swarm of her admirers, had nevertheless chosen from amongst this numerous company three whom she—and she was called Viola by name—especially favoured with her love. Of these one was a smith who lived hard by; another was a Genoese merchant, and the third was a friar; and, although I cannot now call to mind what his name was or what the colour of his frock, I well remember that he was a famous courser after such game. On a certain day it happened that, without showing one greater favour than the other, she gave her promise to all of these three, that whenever her husband might chance to be away all night from home, she would do for them what they so ardently desired.

It happened before many days had passed the husband found that he must needs go to Ponte a Selece † to bring back with him an ass-load of finished wooden shoes, in order that he might let polish the same in Naples, as was his wont; and, because on account of this business he would have perforce to remain there until the following day, his departure and his absence from home for the night soon become known to all three of the expectant wooers. Now, although each one of them had prepared himself for the meeting after his own fashion, nevertheless the first who appeared at the door of our Madonna Viola all ready for the fray was the Genoese, who was also perhaps the most ardent of the lovers. He besought her

* The saddlers' quarter.

† Probably Ponte a Sele, south of Salerno.

in most tender speech that at nightfall she would await his coming and give him a night's lodging and supper thereto, holding out to her the while the most lavish promises, as men are ever wont to do in similar cases. Indeed, he discoursed in such wise that Viola, so as not to keep him longer in suspense, assured him that she would do her best to content him, but that he must take good care to keep away until the night should be dark enough to prevent his coming from being seen by any of the people of the quarter who might be about. To this request of hers the Genoese answered gaily, "So be it, in God's name;" and, having taken his leave, he went forthwith to the Loggia, and once or twice to the Pandino, where he bought a couple of excellent capons, fat and white and big, which he sent privily to the young woman's house, together with some new bread and excellent wine of divers sorts.

The friar, after he had let celebrate his sacred office, felt himself mightily anxious that the promise which had been made to him should be duly kept; wherefore, making the ground fly from under his feet, and running through one street after another just as if he had been a greedy wolf falling upon some stray lamb which had wandered afar from the fold, he arrived in front of the house where Viola dwelt, and having called upon her aloud, he let her know that he was minded, come what might, to spend that night with her. Viola, being in no way disposed to break her faith with the Genoese, and knowing full well that she could not refuse to give to one so rash and importunate as this friar the satisfaction she had promised him, felt herself in a mighty turmoil of mind, and knew not what to do. Still, like a prudent young woman, she soon hit upon a plan by which she might settle matters in seemly and convenient fashion. Wherefore she gave the friar a pleasant answer, and told him that she would hold herself ready to do his will, but that he must on no account come to her before the fifth hour,* for the reason that she had abiding with her in the house a little cousin of hers who would not be fallen to sleep before that time, and that he should take himself off straightway, and God

* Eleven o'clock at night.

go with him, as soon as he should have appeased his appetite.

Thereupon the friar, seeing that reception would indeed be granted to him, agreed to do all that she asked him, and, caring for naught else, went his way. The smith, who had been busied until late at the custom-house, whither he had gone to attend to the withdrawal therefrom of certain iron, took his way back to his house, and as he passed along he espied Viola at the window, and said to her: "Now that your husband is away you can let me come to you, and it will be well for you if you do this, for be assured that I will mar the working of any other scheme of yours." Viola, who was mightily partial to the smith, and somewhat in awe of him to boot, now began to consider whether in the course of a long night she might not find plenty of time to let come and go all three of her customers. So, as she had provided accommodation for the first two, she determined to give reception also to the third, although he had come last; wherefore she addressed him thus: "My Mauro, you know well enough that I am looked at askance in this quarter, and that all the women—no doubt for some good and sufficient reason—seek to chase me hence, and every evening until midnight some one or other of them keeps a watch upon me; therefore, in order that no hurt may befall me from these traps of theirs, see that you delay your coming to me until the dawn, the hour when you are accustomed to rise. Then, if you will give me a signal, I will let you enter, and in this manner we may be together for a little space for our first meeting. In due time we will find for ourselves a more convenient method."

The smith, being well aware that Viola had plausible reason for what she said, and feeling sure that he would get everything he wanted, went away without another word, being well content to let the affair rest as it stood. As soon as night had fallen the Genoese stealthily made his way into Viola's house, and although he was met with a right jolly reception and got from her many kisses, nevertheless he was of such cold-blooded nature that he was unable to bring himself into the humour necessary for the occasion without the warmth of the bed and other incitements, so he disposed himself according to his liking and tried his powers; the capons meantime taking a mighty long time to roast, either through the fire being low, or from some other cause. All this time the young woman was almost fainting with eagerness, fearing amain lest her second course should be set before her ere she had disposed of the first, and the third hour* had already struck before they had so much as made a beginning of their supper. While they were thus waiting there came a knocking at the door; whereupon the Genoese, horribly frightened, cried out, "It seems to me that someone knocks at the door here." The young woman answered: "Yes, what you say is right, and in good sooth I fear very much that it may be my brother; but be not afraid, for I will take care that he does not catch sight of you. Get out of this window, and sit down in the little window arbour which is outside. Meantime I will see who is there, and what he wants, and bid him go about his business."

The Genoese, who in sooth was vastly more overcome by fear than by the ardour of love, at once followed out Viola's directions, what though the wind was very cold, and there was falling a fine rain so chilling that most people would have taken it for snow. Thereupon Viola locked him out; and, making a guess as to who was the one who knocked, she carefully hid the supper, and when she had gone down to the outer door, and had assured herself that it was the importunate priest, she said to him in a tone somewhat troubled, "You have come very early, and have not observed the directions I gave you. Bad luck to me indeed that you should be minded to be the death of me, just because you could not be kept waiting a little time." And with these and other similar words she opened the door to the friar; and, he having come in, without even tarrying to make fast the door, gave her plenary absolution at once, not indeed by any authority committed to him by his superiors, but by the power of his own lusty nature. Whereupon Viola, thinking that he had by this time got enough to let him go away contented, as soon as she saw that he was making his way into the

* Nine o'clock in the evening.

house, closed the door and followed him up the stairs, saying to him, "Go away at once, for the love of God! for my young cousin is not yet asleep, and he will hear you of a surety." But the friar, paying no heed to what she said, went up the stairs, and finding the fire still burning, warmed himself a little, and then took hold of Viola once more, and began to attune his strings for a fresh spell of dancing, making thereby a melody vastly more pleasing than that which the poor devil of a Genoese played with his teeth, which chattered grievously by reason of the excessive cold. He, forsooth, could see everything which was being brought to pass within, by peeping through a fissure of the window, and how greatly he was tormented by grief at what he beheld, and by the fear of being discovered and by the cruel cold, everyone who likes to consider the question may decide for himself.

As he stood there he made up his mind over and over again to jump down from his post, but he was held back from this deed by his inability to judge of the height on account of the darkness, and by the hope that the friar, who in sooth had swallowed far more than his share of the sweet repast, would take his departure, seeing that Viola entreated him continually to be gone. But the friar, heated by the pleasurable touch of the beautiful young woman, would in no wise let her go out of his embrace, and went on to give to her a lesson in all sorts and kinds of dances which were in fashion, and he taught, not her alone, but also the Genoese, who looked on at the sport with mighty little pleasure. At last he made up his mind that he would not depart until he should be chased away by the dawning of the day. And thus they went on until the tenth hour * struck, and then the friar heard the blacksmith knocking at Viola's door and giving the sign which had been settled; whereupon he, turning towards the young woman, spoke thus, "Who is it who knocks at your door?" To this she made answer, "Oh! that is nothing but the constant trouble I have to put up with from the smith my neighbour, a fellow I have not been able to beat off either by fair words or foul." The

* Four o'clock a. m.

friar, who was gifted with a merry humour of his own, forthwith began to cast about in his mind how he might devise some new sport or other; then he went quickly down to the door, and, speaking in a soft voice, and feigning to be Viola, he said, "Who art thou?" Then the smith replied, "It is I; do you not know me?—open quickly the door, I beg you, for I am getting wet to the skin with the rain." Then said the friar, still in a simulated voice, "Alas, woe is me, that I cannot open the door! for whenever I move it, it makes so much noise that, were I to open it now, some scandal or other would surely arise thereanent." Then the smith, knowing not where to bestow himself in order to escape the rain, called out to Viola to open the door to him straightway, inasmuch as he was dying of love for her.

The friar, who was mightily pleased at keeping the smith waiting outside so that he might get wet through, now said, "Dear soul of mine, give me just one kiss through this opening of the door, which methinks is wide enough, and then I will see whether I cannot move this accursed door without letting it make much noise." The smith took all these words for truth, and, overjoyed at his good fortune, at once disposed himself to kiss his beloved Viola; but in the meantime the friar had taken off his breeches, and now he thrust his hinder part close to the opening of the door. The smith, who thought he was about to take a kiss from the sweet lips of his Viola, was forthwith made aware, both by the touch and the odour, what thing it was he was in truth kissing, and came to the conclusion that this must be some other huntsman, who had showed himself the keener after the game, and had both robbed him of his anticipated delight and put this shameful trick upon him. So he determined at once not to suffer this insult to go unavenged, and, feigning still to be caressing his love, he said, "My Viola, while you are busying yourself in opening the door, I will go fetch a cloak from my house, for I can no longer endure this rain." To this the friar replied, "Go, in God's name, and come back as soon as possible." And when he had said this, he and Viola fell to laughing so heartily that they found it hard work to stand upright on their feet.

Meantime the smith went back to his shop and quickly got ready a rod of iron in the form of a spit, which he straightway heated red-hot in the fire, saying to his apprentice the while, "Now, take good heed of what I say, and, as soon as I shall spit, come to me as softly as you can, and bring me this rod." Having thus spoken he went back to Viola's house to let speed his plan for gaining entrance thereinto; and, passing on from one word to another, he said at last, "Kiss me once more." Whereupon the friar, who was as expert as a monkey in making such a change of front as was here called for, again put before the smith the same object to kiss. Then Mauro gave the signal to his apprentice, who at once handed to him the red-hot iron rod, which he took in his hand, and, watching his time, dealt the friar a prick with the same in his backside with such good will that it went into his flesh wellnigh a palm's breadth. The friar, when he felt the cruel pain of this, uttered perforce a howl loud enough to touch the heavens, and went on bellowing amain as if he had been a wounded bull.* All the neighbours round about, having been aroused from sleep, flocked to the windows with lights in their hands, and each one demanded to know what might be the cause of this strange uproar. The wretched Genoese, who was so benumbed with cold that a very little more would have turned him into an icicle and made an end of his life, when he heard all this clamour, and saw that lights were coming from all parts, and that the day was about to break, took heart at last and resolved to leap down from where he stood, in order that he might not be discovered standing there in shameful concealment as if he were a thief. So, recommending himself to God, he dared to do this thing. And fortune so dealt with him that, as he came to the ground, he happened to alight upon a stone, which he struck with his foot, and fell over the same in such manner that he broke one of his legs in two places. Being stricken with a pain no less cruel than that which the friar suffered, he likewise shouted his woes aloud.

The smith, hearing the noise, ran forward at once, and,

* The text of 1510 gives *fiero*, but Settembrini's emendation *ferito* seems the better sense.

when he came upon the Genoese and recognized him, and likewise perceived the cause which made him cry out in such fashion, felt somewhat of pity for him, and contrived by the aid of his apprentice to convey him within the smithy, although the task was by no means an easy one. After the smith had heard from the injured man in what manner the whole affair had come about, and the name of the friar, he rushed into the street at once and managed to silence the huge uproar which the neighbours were still making, saying that the cries had arisen from two of his apprentices who had wounded one another in a quarrel. And when everything was once more quiet, Viola, according to the wish of the friar, called softly to the smith to come; and he, having entered the house and found the wretched friar half dead, debated in his mind many and various plans for the ending of the affair. At last he and his apprentice took the friar on their shoulders and carried him to his monastery; and then, having returned, they set the Genoese upon the back of an ass and conveyed him to his lodging. As to the smith, he took his way back to the house of Viola, it being now broad daylight, and after feasting together with her off the capons, and over and beyond this attaining the full enjoyment he desired, he went back in high delight to wield his hammer. And in this wise Maestro Mauro, what though he was the last of the competitors, left the other two to suffer no slight disgrace and injury and pain.

MASUCCIO

OF a surety we may with justice praise our Viola for her care and foresight, in that she contrived in such becoming manner to give a reception to all three of her lovers on the same night. And although two of these had perforce to be accompanied back to the homes from which they had set forth, having received no slight guerdon of ill in the meantime, nevertheless Viola, fortified by the plenary absolution which the reverend friar more than once gave her during his stay, was still on the spot to teach to the worthy smith that novel fashion of dancing which the Genoese had already learnt by watching, albeit with small pleasure. Now, leaving Viola in Maestro Mauro's company to enjoy the repast which had been prepared, we will sail into deeper water, and will describe in the next novel the very artful working and the strange devices employed by a certain young gentlewoman, who, on account of some defect in her nature, was altogether wanting in bashfulness and chastity; and how she, so as not to be overlooked by careless Fortune, and thereby to lose some portion of her flowering youth, elected to become her own messenger, thus carrying into effect with greater expedition the enterprise she had so greatly at heart.

THE END OF THE TWENTY-NINTH NOVEL

Novel the Thirtieth

ARGUMENT

A YOUNG LADY BEING ENAMOURED OF THE PRINCE OF SALERNO SENDS FOR ONE OF HIS CHAPLAINS AND DECLARES TO HIM THAT SHE HAS RECEIVED FROM THE SAID PRINCE NUMEROUS LETTERS PRAYING FOR HER LOVE. THE CHAPLAIN, HAVING DIVINED HER MOTIVE, ENTERS INTO A PLOT WITH HER AND BRINGS THE AFFAIR TO THE ISSUE DESIRED.

TO THE MOST ILLUSTRIOUS LORD, GERONIMO DE SANSEVERINO, PRINCE OF BISIGNANO*

EXORDIUM

NO less out of gratitude for the many benefits which I have received at your hands, most serene prince, than because I know you are wishful, not to say eager, to test by your own experience one of my frolicsome novels, I feel myself induced, or even constrained, to send you the one I have in hand, and to include it in the collection of the others. Deign then, most gracious prince, to accept it—in sooth the most humble of gifts—with gladsome face and with benignant favour, in order that, having read the same together with the others, and having learnt that your most worshipful name is held up to lasting remembrance therein, you may give reward to the maker thereof by placing him and writing him down amongst the number of your humble servant. Farewell.

* He was Grand Chamberlain, and the leader of the Revolt of the Barons. He was executed in 1487.

THE NARRATIVE

AT that time when our most glorious lord and king, Don Fernando, was entertaining Naples, according to his constant use, with those joustings, those marvellous hunting parties, and those sumptuous festivals which were famed far and wide, it chanced that amongst the other merry-makers was a certain young damsel, of beauty almost unrivalled, and a scion of one of the noblest houses of our Parthenopean city. Now for some time past she had often let her eyes regale themselves with the beauty and the grace of form belonging to my most illustrious lord, the Prince of Salerno, and beyond this had heard sung, over and over again, the praises of his extraordinary worth. By this time she was more than ever captivated by him, wherefore she became so lovesick that she could only give thought to the gentleman by whom her fancy had been ensnared.

After she had let her thoughts—which, in sooth, were in no slight travail and confusion—engage themselves in many and divers plans by which she might honourably achieve the victory in so worthy an adventure, she found that all these schemes were over-difficult to compass; wherefore it more than once came into her head that she would follow the advice of certain other ladies of her acquaintance, who, whenever they found they could not refrain from entering the lists of love, were wont to send word to the gallant youths beloved of them and challenge them to the amorous warfare. But this damsel, who was gifted with no small prudence, and was persuaded at the same time that she would not, by following such a course, be setting a very high value either upon herself or upon her undertaking, suddenly determined that she would make trial of a novel and very crafty strategem to induce the prince aforesaid to cull the first fruits of her virgin garden. Having chosen a time when the prince had gone to other parts for diversion in the chase, she let come to her a certain priest, a man whom she could fully trust, and one who was much about the house, and to him she gave directions as to what she would have him do.

In consequence of this the priest went the very next

morning to the wonderful palace which the prince aforesaid had built for himself in the Porta Reale,* where he found a certain Fra Paulo, the chaplain and most trusted attendant of the prince. Having inquired in becoming fashion whether he was speaking to Fra Paulo, the chaplain replied that he was, saying, "I am that man." Then the other went on to say: "A noble lady I know of would fain have speech with you to-morrow morning early in such and such a church." To this the friar answered with a smiling face that he would not fail to be there according to the lady's commands, and when the appointed time had come he went thither much pleased with his task. He found the gentlewoman awaiting his coming, and she, having left for the nonce her attendant, drew aside together with the friar into a chapel, and began to speak to him in this wise: "My good Fra Paulo, inasmuch as you are reputed to be a man of great prudence, and one enjoying the intimate confidence of your lord and master, it seems to me that I shall not be trespassing beyond the bounds of reason in assuming that I may, for the safeguarding of his honour and my own, and likewise for the reassuring of my mind, lay bare to you entirely my secret affairs, as if you were my spiritual director. And, before I go on any further in this matter, I desire to hear from you—and I conjure you by the love and the fidelity which you entertain towards your lord and master that you will be truthful with me in this respect—whether you can say truly that certain letters, which I intend later on to show to you, are in the handwriting of your lord the prince. I speak to you thus for the reason that for some time past a certain young man, whom we keep in our house as the tutor of my brothers, has conveyed to me many and divers letters purporting to come from the lord prince—letters more impassioned and tempered with love than were ever before written by fervent lover to his lady. Moreover, they are all brought to an end with the request that I should agree with him as to the time and place fitted for the purpose in view. Now

* In the Largo Santa Trinita. In 1584 the palace was converted into a Jesuit church. See Porzio, "Congiura dei Baroni," p. 39.

on this account my mind has been sorely troubled, no less by this messenger than by the errand he has undertaken, so that I can get no rest, and am nearly brought to despair of my life. Over and beyond this, I have been assailed by the suspicion that this said young man may have been bribed by some one of my elder brothers by way of putting my constancy to the proof. I am the more inclined to this belief from the fact that one day, when I was holding discourse with my brothers and with divers other members of our household, concerning the valour and excellencies of some of our chief nobles, one put forward this gentleman as supreme, and another that. Whereupon I, stirred thereto by the spirit of truth, and likewise by the love which I bear the prince, and by no other motive, grew heated in the argument, and declared that your prince was not only the glory of the court but likewise the light and the mirror of this our Italian land. When he heard me utter these words one of my brothers, turning towards me, commanded me straightway to hold my peace, and from that day to this he has never looked kindly upon me. For this reason I rack my brain in debating this affair in such wise that I can scarcely eat or sleep at all. Then, on the other hand, I sometimes say to myself, 'Can it possibly be that my brother really speaks the truth, and that the prince is in sooth taken with love of me, seeing that I have at times kept my eyes fixed upon him somewhat more than was due, and has on this account been led to write to me in so passionate a strain?' And if things should come to this issue, although it would be a less matter of peril to me, I should nevertheless be cut to the heart therefor; for the reason that I desire especially that he should bear himself according to the usages of noble gentlemen, and that his love should be of a nature like to mine own passion, which in sooth, I have moderated in such wise that it does not transgress the limits which an honest woman is bound to observe, because I have not suffered myself to be so much carried away as to forget that my fair fame should be set before all gratification of sensual passion."

With these, and with other words of a like character, which had been prepared with the most consummate art, she laid before the chaplain the letters aforesaid, by way of giving him still farther assurance of the truth of her craftily devised discourse. Fra Paulo, although, as a prudent man, and as one accustomed to bring contests of this sort to a victorious issue, he had fully detected and comprehended the hidden wishes and purpose of the young lady, nevertheless, as she went on step by step with her reasonings and arguments, was astonished at finding so great ingenuity and astuteness in the brain of a damsel so delicate and youthful. Still, as he remarked more than once that, whenever she mentioned the name of his lord the prince, her face changed colour, he understood that the passion which possessed her must be indeed burning and fierce. Wherefore he determined to let this same wind speed his own bark over such a pleasant sea, and he thus made answer to her: "Lady mine, because of your kindness, you have thought well enough of me to unveil to me your secret affairs, you may rest assured that, no less for the preservation of your own good name than for the safeguarding of my lord's, I will deal with this matter with all that silence and secrecy which, according to your judgment and mine as well, the gravity and importance of the same demands. Your doubts, which have their foundation in the most valid reasons, are worthy of praise rather than rebuke, and should not be put aside without the most careful consideration; still, what though it is not to be deemed impossible that your brothers may have thus laid a plot to bring about the end they fancied they foresaw, I cannot quite persuade myself that they, being prudent folk, would be minded to place their honour, after the fashion you have described in the hands of this young scholar belonging to a foreign people, seeing that they could easily have hit upon many other and safer methods of getting certain knowledge of this thing. But letting pass the truth or the falsehood thereof, as a thing at random, and reverting to our own case, I declare once for all that these letters were never written by my lord; in sooth, if they had been his handiwork I should have marvelled amain, because it is his custom never to write with his own hand to any woman, however fiercely his passion may be kindled for her, unless he may first have made proof of her love. On this account, at the outset of all his love affairs the letters and messages thereanent are written and arranged by the agency of the chamberlain, who is in his closest confidence. Wherefore I hold it for certain that these same letters must be from the hands of this man, and besides this, it seems to me that I know somewhat of your scholar, and have seen him more than once occupied in private conversation with the chamberlain aforesaid. And it is not without good cause that I am led to entertain this belief; for many a time, when I have chanced to be discoursing concerning the beauty of women with my lord, he, with a little sigh, which he seemed fain to repress, has never ceased to place you before all other ladies. And although his words are rare and few and sententious, he has full often let me know secretly that you are the only one to whom he has entirely given his love. Therefore meseems that, although with your caution and foresight you do not need any counsel of mine, you should give me authority to act, so I may be able to place the whole matter, together with your own doubts and fears, before the notice of my lord. And this I would fain let ensue, not by means of letters or of messages, but by my own self, acting as your ambassador, for either to-morrow or the day following he ought to arrive in Salerno, and it will be in no wise irksome to me to go thither, to do a service to you and to my lord as well; and, when I shall have gathered the only true construction which can be drawn thereanent, I will come back with the best speed I can use. Supposing that I should find that the affair stands in such wise as it surely must, I can then take counsel with yourself as to what course it will be meet for you to follow, and to give such directions for the forwarding of the same as in your judgment may be the best. And in order that you may speedily be informed of the answer, and that the affair may be kept no long time in suspense, it will behove you to be on the watch for me, for when you shall see me pass by your house, and call to a certain boy who will be standing opposite thereto, you may be assured that I have done my errand, and on the following morning let us meet once more in this same spot."

The young lady, deeming that she had assuredly gulled the friar by her trick, and that her plot could not now fail to come to an issue perfectly satisfactory to her, was so greatly overjoyed that it seemed to her as if she had in sooth been crowned by Heaven. Wherefore, after the friar had brought his speech to an end, she said, "I beseech you that, as you have in a measure confirmed my doubting mind, you will furthermore assure me as to the rest; and that you will, as far as you can, disclose to me the words of your one and beloved lord, in order that my troubled spirit may repose itself somewhat." Then, having brought their discourse to an end, and each one being in a contented mood, though for a different cause, they went their several ways.

As Fortune willed it—and Fortune, be it said, ever showed herself far more favourable at the outset of the enterprises undertaken by this prince, than in letting them run on to a prosperous issue—the friar was met by the news that the prince had already taken the road with the intention of being in Naples on the following day. Wherefore Fra Paulo, having gone out to meet him, was mightily glad to let him know the whole history of the craft of the amorous damsel, and of the scheme which she had framed. The prince gave ear to the same with no less amazement than pleasure; for, albeit he had rarely cast his eyes upon this young girl, and retained no recollection of her beauty, nevertheless it seemed to him to be only just and right that he should hold dear those who loved him. So he made answer to the friar, and bade him set the business in progress in such wise that the meeting might be brought pass at the earliest possible time.

The friar, pleased beyond measure and eager to do service to the prince, betook himself towards the house of the damsel as soon as he had dismounted from his beast. Then, having made the sign which had been agreed between themselves—a sign which she observed and understood with the utmost pleasure—the damsel duly repaired on the following morning to the spot which had been chosen; and there, when she met the friar, he said to her, "My dear lord, who for your pleasure arrived last night in Naples, commends himself to you. I have set before him at full length the purport of the converse betwixt you and me, but I could not draw from his lips any other reply except that he prays and conjures you, by the perfect love which he has for so long a time borne and still bears to you, and also by that love which you should dutifully entertain towards him, that it will please you, on this same evening, to give him a kindly audience in order that he may, without needing to confide in any living man, lay bare to you those matters which he has kept hitherto, and still keeps, secured by a strong lock within his passionate breast."

The young woman, who, as she listened to these words, was so vastly overjoyed that she could with difficulty contain herself within her skin, now felt that every hour would be as a thousand years until she should find herself engaged in the supreme conclusions of love; and, after a few feeble denials and hesitations, answered that she was ready to do what the prince desired. She did not quit the friar's company until they had, in discreet wise, settled when and in what manner and in what place she and the prince should come together for the amorous battle. The friar then betook himself straightway to his beloved lord and prince, who indeed was awaiting him and his answer. Then he set forth everything to the prince, who, when himseemed that the appointed time had come, went with his attendants to the meeting-place, and there he found the lovely young damsel, who, delicately arrayed and perfumed, received him with open arms, and with exceeding great delight. Then, after countless kisses had been given and received by the prince, they got on board their bark, and after the helm had been duly set and the sails spread to the wind, the damsel, what though she was as yet greatly versed in the mariner's art, let her lover navigate the sea of love during all the time they were able to spend together. When at last they found themselves with great delight once more in port, the damsel, tenderly clasping the neck of the prince with her arms, thus addressed him: "My sweetest lord, for that I alone, aided by my own skill and forethought, have succeeded in bringing you hither this first time I have but to thank myself, but for the future I must leave to the care of you and of Love the devising of the means whereby you may be able to show me further proofs of your passion. Now there remains nothing more for me to say except that I recommend myself without ceasing to your favour." Thereupon the illustrious lord the prince heartened her with soft and tender words, and they then took leave of one another with great pleasure and delight; and if anyone should still wish to know whether, and in what fashion, this love of theirs bore further fruit, let him inquire on his own behalf.

MASUCCIO

I FOUND myself one day, not a great time ago, in a company of ladies, amongst whom there were some who were studying the book of the Master of the Sentences,* and when, as it happened, we began to discuss the miscreant wickedness, the innate malignities, the craft, and the depravity of womankind, all of which imperfections will be found in the novels lately written by me, they all of them fell upon me as if they had been so many bad bitches, reproaching me on the score of my writings, and affirming that men, who hold themselves to be, and indeed ought to be, more perfect in their way of life and in constancy than woman, continually let their sensuality get the victory over them, and plunge down into the abyss. In dealing with this subject, they came to me treating the same with such unclean and minute particulars that they far outstripped the speech of lascivious men, much more that of modest women. On this account Masuccio, who had not left his tongue in pawn with the Jews, after he had made clear the nature of his writing in a very flood of suitable and appropriate adjectives, which almost fell into verse, spake and said that men, even if they should descend to the commission of more detestable iniquities than women—a thing which was altogether beyond possibility—would still only work an offence against the laws and against their own honour, never essaying the wickedness of infecting and corrupt-

* Peter Lombard. See note to Novel XXIII.

ing the whole company of their kinsfolk—depriving them, not only of their present good name, but likewise blackening and obscuring the repute of such as these, and heaping this obloquy on the name and the memory of their descendants for ever and ever. Which profligate woman is minded to satisfy her headstrong and unbridled desire. And that this charge which I make is a true one, the laws will prove by open witness; inasmuch as these suffer any man who may discover his wife or his daughter in the sin of adultery to slay her forthwith, without being held liable to penalty; but we do not find any like privilege provided for women when they may find themselves in a similar case. And when the women aforesaid found that they had not a word to say by way of answer to my unassailable arguments, they behaved even worse than the brute beasts which in sooth they are. Nevertheless, although I have not in this Third Part spoken as much as is due, or as much as I could wish of the deeds of womankind, I must hasten on to reach the Fourth Part of my book. Wherefore I will give over the navigation of the gulfy main of their offences, and henceforth my story-telling, with the permission of Christ Jesus, my Redeemer, shall be of other themes, some of them sad, and some of a sort which may give you pleasure.

HERE ENDS THE THIRD PART

PART THE FOURTH

Prologue

THE THIRD PART OF THE NOVELLINO HAVING NOW COME TO AN END, THE FOURTH BEGINS. IN THIS WILL BE SET FORTH DIVERS THEMES; SOME MOURNFUL AND SAD, WHILE OTHERS WILL BE FOUND MERRY AND DIVERTING. FIRST WILL COME THE GENERAL EXORDIUM, AND THE STORY-TELLING WILL BEGIN WITH THE NOVEL CONCERNING THE LEPERS.

MASUCCIO

ALTHOUGH when I made a beginning of this present little work of mine I determined to deal in this, the Fourth Part thereof, only with such matters as might be of a passionate and sorrowful nature, I have nevertheless made a change in the plan I laid down originally, having been moved thereto by just and seemly reasonings, and will now let certain novels of somewhat merry complexion accompany those which are sad. Thus, by mixing the tales of terror and misfortune with those which are jocund and facetious, I may bring it to pass that the grief, which any readers or listeners may feel over the novels of the sort first named, may end in merriment; thus employing the art of wise and prudent physicians, who, in cases where they administer remedies which are sharp and violent, afterwards are wont to correct the malignity of the same with drugs which run counter thereto. Now, without giving further thought to the matter, I will, for the reason aforesaid, let follow a series of ten novels, arranged in such wise that the one, when it comes to an end, will leave the company in tears and grief, which will need to be tempered by the merry humour and gaiety of the novel which will follow it.

Thus, in the name of God, and to the honour and glory

of a celebrated and illustrious lady to whom this first novel is dedicated, I will begin with the story of the Lepers, which, being of rare merit, is now sent by me to a lady of the rarest perfection. The subject of this novel, and the issue as well, are in sooth so violent and so cruel, that when I simply think of them—to say nothing of the writing of the same—I find myself able only with difficulty to keep back my tears. Still, without letting interfere aught of delay, I will give you a counterblast to your grief by telling you next a story which shall be pleasing and comely as to its subject, and, deviating in no wise from this course, I will, under the favour of Aries,* my celestial sign, continue in like succession until the end.

* Masuccio probably means that he was born under Aries, *i. e.*, in the month of March.

Novel the Thirty-first

ARGUMENT

A COUPLE OF GRACIOUS LOVERS TAKE TO FLIGHT IN COMPANY, IN ORDER THAT THEY MAY CHANGE THEIR PRESENT CONDITION TO THAT OF MARRIED FOLK; BUT, HAVING LOST THEIR WAY THROUGH THE COMING ON OF A SUDDEN STORM, THEY LIGHT CASUALLY UPON A LEPER HOSPITAL. THERE, THE YOUNG MAN HAVING BEEN SLAIN BY THE LEPERS, THE GIRL OF HER OWN ACCORD KILLS HERSELF UPON HIS DEAD BODY.

TO THE MOST ILLUSTRIOUS INFANTA DONNA ELEONORA OF ARAGON *

EXORDIUM

IF, indeed, it be the bent of our nature to rejoice in pleasant and prosperous surroundings, made winsome with merry sporting and pleasures, and to be brought into benign and gracious mood through hearing tell of the same, it seems to me, most illustrious Madonna, that in like manner we must, whensoever we may hear or read of the unhappy mischances and horrible accidents happening to others, be constrained by our humanity to bear our part with them in their misery by according to them the tribute of our most bitter tears. Thus, seeing that a story of a very cruel mishap and lamentable misfortune which occurred to two most unhappy lovers has come to my notice (a story which tells how they were overtaken by evil fortune and led to suffer the penalty of a most cruel death), I have determined to give a special account of this sad and terrible accident to you, who, more than any other lady, are inbued with humanity and pitying love, in order that, through the

* Daughter of Ferdinand I. and wife of Ercole d'Este, Duke of Ferrara.

perusal of this story by yourself, through the hearing of the same by others, and through the compassion which will rise in your heart and the pitying tears which will fall from your eyes, some comfort may be given to the unhappy souls of these two young lovers, who, as I greatly fear, are being tormented in eternal fire. Farewell.

THE NARRATIVE

FAME, that most faithful disseminator of deeds wrought long ago, has revealed it to me how, at the time when Joan la Pucelle rose into notice in the kingdom of France, there lived in the city of Nanci, the chiefest and most noble amongst the cities of the duchy of Lorraine, two very generous and doughty knights. Each one of these was lord by a very ancient right of baronage of certain castles and villages lying round the aforesaid city, the one being called the Sieur de Condi and the other Messer Jannes de Bruscie. And even as fortune had granted to the Sieur de Condi one only daughter named Martina, a damsel well endowed with those especial virtues and praiseworthy manners which were befitting her tender years, and beautiful in person and in countenance, so also Messer Jannes was the father of one son, whose name was Lois, the only one surviving out of all those who had been born to him. Lois was about the same age as Martina, very comely in person, of noble heart, and abundantly furnished with every virtue. And although the relationship between the aforesaid families was somewhat distant, nevertheless, from the time of their remote ancestors, there had grown up by degrees so great a friendship and intimacy, that, putting aside the continual frequenting of one another's houses, it seemed as if they possessed their vassals and their goods in common, so hard would it have been to say where lay the dividing line between them.

Now it happened that when Lois had come to man's estate, he, through seeing Martina wellnigh every day and enjoying close intimacy with her, found himself to be deeply enamoured of the damsel (who, in sooth, returned his love), without having aroused the notice or suspicion of anyone. So fiercely did the flame of love burn without and within, that these lovers knew not how to find any contentment save when they were together, discoursing and diverting themselves as they were led on to do by their passion and by the fresh bloom of their years.

In lovesome play like this they spent divers years of their youth in great happiness, without ever venturing to do any illicit deed; and, although each one of them desired above everything else to taste of that last and most keenly longed-for fruit of love, nevertheless Lois, who was endowed with the more sober temper of the two, resolved to keep clear of all reproach which might fall upon the young girl and her family, and determined in his mind never to have carnal knowledge of her except he should have the right thereof granted to him by lawful matrimony. Wherefore, having many times set clearly before his Martina this honest and resolute purpose of his, he found that she was fully in agreement therewith, and she gave him constant encouragement in his suit by counselling him to let this proposition for their union be brought to the notice of their parents by the means of some trusty person. Thus Lois, who desired the fulfillment of this matter beyond everything else in the world, called in the aid of his own father, who in most seemly wise made request concerning the same to the Sieur de Condi. But this gentleman, after he had altogether refused to entertain these proposals, giving divers good reasons for his decision, went on in a straightforward and temperate manner to let Messer Jannes know it was his pleasure that, in order to keep intact the honour of both houses, the intercourse between their children should henceforth be restrained in such degree that Lois should not enter his house except when called thither by the most urgent necessity. On this account, not only was all close intimacy in divers ways denied to the lovers, but even conversation as well. It would be a lengthy task, and a needless one, to set down here how many and how great were the amorous plaints, and the bitter lamentations, and the secret and fervent sighs, of the two lovers when they understood what had been done. The trouble which weighed most heavily upon poor Lois arose chiefly from the fact that he now found himself the victim of cruel misfortune, although he had hitherto exercised such unblemished virtue, and he would often take counsel with himself and consider what was the nature of the bond which confined his soul within his wretched body. Nevertheless he did not give up the project of holding converse with his Martina by the means of letters, conveyed by a trusty messenger, and in these he besought her that, if she should be cognisant of any method by which they might compass their deliverance, she would straightway let him have intelligence thereof. Having written thus he sent the letter to her with the utmost care and discretion.

Now the young girl, borne down as she was by her intolerable grief, determined nevertheless to show how great her courage was, and as soon as she saw the messenger she took the letter from him, her face all wet with tears the while; and when she had read it, she found herself so much disturbed by the grief and trouble which oppressed her, that she could in no wise send a reply thereto in writing; wherefore she cried out to the one who had privily brought it to her: "I beseech you, who alone are cognisant of the secret and fiercely burning love there is between us two, to bear back my best greetings to him who has sent you to me, and tell him that either he shall be my husband and the one only lord of my life, or I will, by my own act, drive out my soul from this wretched body of mine by means of poison or the dagger. Tell him likewise that he, by that over-nice virtue of his, and by being more careful to guard the honour of my father's house than to enjoy the love which our youthful ardour urged us to gratify, has brought upon us, instead of the greatest joy, this most cruel separation, in which we are neither permitted to see one another or to converse together. Still, if he has the heart to come to this our castle, here beneath the window of my chamber, accompanied by certain of his followers, and provided with a rope-ladder and everything else which may help me to descend to him, I will forthwith go to him; then we together will repair to the castle of some common kinsman of ours, and there make our covenant of marriage. When our deed shall be noised abroad, if by chance my father shall be content therewith, all will be well; but if not, the thing will at least be done, and it will behove him to act prudently and to change his refusal into a wiser and more liberal mood. If Lois should find himself inclined to do this thing, charge him to come hither to me this very night in the fashion I have described to you." The trusty servant, having given due hearing to this message, and having received from the maiden a certain signal to be used between Lois and herself, so that they might run no risk of mistake, departed from her straightway, and when he had returned to his master's house, related to him, point by point, all that he had done. Lois did not need much heartening to take in hand this enterprise, and with the utmost despatch laid under his orders some twenty lusty and courageous youths, chosen from out his servants and loyal vassals. When they had duly set in order everything which was necessary for the prosecution of their design, they set forth quietly and without any uproar at nightfall on their journey, which in sooth was not a very long one, and in course of a few hours Lois found himself, together with his companions, underneath the window which the young lady had described. Then, having given the signal agreed upon—a signal which was at once heard and understood by Martina, who was awaiting it with anxiety in her heart—he forthwith threw to her a strong cord to which he had affixed the rope-ladder. This she drew up, and having hooked the grappling irons securely on to the window's ledge, she climbed down by the ladder without fear, seeming to be one who might often have had experience in such practice. Lois forthwith gathered her into his arms, and, after numberless kisses, they went hand in hand to the highway. Then they mounted the lady upon an ambling palfrey which had been duly brought thither, and took to the road, following a guide whose duty it was to lead them to the place they desired to reach. The servants, some in front and some behind, merrily accompanied them on their way.

But adverse Fortune, who must needs have set out their future in different wise, led them on to a sad and bitter end—an end more terrible, as I well believe, than had ever before been heard of—forasmuch as they had not gone a mile along the road when a storm of rain fell upon them, accompanied by such violent and baffling wind, such thick discharge of hail, and such awful thunder and lightning, that it seemed as if the universal firmament was about to fall down upon them. Around them the darkness was so dense and the tempest so violent that the greater part of the footmen—clad merely in their doublets—and the guide as well wandered out of the right path and took to flight, some in this direction and some in that, choosing whichever way seemed to offer the best chance of escape. And in like manner the two lovers themselves, the one clasping the other closely by the hand, could scarcely behold each other's faces, and were terrified and filled with dread lest this sudden manifestation of the powers of nature should prove to be a punishment sent by God on account of this forcible taking away of the damsel. Wherefore, knowing naught of the spot where they stood, nor whither they should direct their steps, hearing no sound of their companions, nor getting back any answer to the many and loud cries they uttered, they commended themselves to God, giving free rein to their horses, and committing to Heaven and to fortune the future disposition of their lives.

When they had wandered many a mile, now here, now there, as a ship labours through the sea when bereft of a steersman, they were at last lured on by pitiless death to suffer the supreme penalty; for, having espied from afar a faint light, and having for this reason let kindle a little hope, they guided the steps of their horses towards the spot where it was shining, without, alas! lessening aught the malignant purpose of fate. After faring onward for some time longer they arrived at the place where was burning the light which they had seen,

THE LOVERS IN THE STORM

FROM A DRAWING BY E. R. HUGHES. (Mas., Nov. xxxi , v. ii.)

and knocked at the door of the house. When their summons had been answered and the door opened, they found that the place to which they had come was a hospital for lepers, and straightway certain disfigured wretches out of this ghastly band demanded of them, with little show of good disposition, what had brought them there at such an hour. The young people were both of them so much benumbed and enfeebled on account of what they had undergone that they could with difficulty utter a word; wherefore Lois made answer in as brief a fashion as possible that the long endurance of the storm and their own adverse fortune had brought them to this place, passing on next to beg them that, for the love of God, they would of their bounty suffer himself and the damsel to warm themselves at the fire, and give shelter to their weary horses. The lepers, although they might well be likened to the damned, as having no hope of salvation, and being destitute alike of humanity and all charity, nevertheless, moved by a sluggish compassion, helped the two lovers to dismount, and having stabled the horses with their own asses, led the wanderers into the kitchen, and made them sit down with the other lepers before a great fire. And although the young people felt no little loathing, for that they must needs foregather with this crew of blemished and infected wretches, yet, as there was no help for it, they endeavoured to be calm and show themselves contented.

Now in a short time the comforting virtue of the fire brought back to Lois and Martina their vanished comeliness, in such wise that it seemed as if they must have stolen the forms of Narcissus and Diana, and on this account it happened that a certain ribald miscreant amongst the lepers, a fellow who had been a mercenary in the late wars, and was now more foul and diseased than any of the others, was inflamed with an unbridled desire to have carnal knowledge of the lovely damsel; and being thus overcome by savage lust, he at once conceived the notion how, by slaying her young lover, he would win for himself the enjoyment of this precious prize. Therefore, without letting go for a moment the fell design he had formed, he took into his confidence a certain comrade of his, another as wicked and inhuman as himself, and these two went together to the stable. Then one of them let loose the horses, and, making a great clamour, called out: "Sir, come hither quickly and set your horses in order, so that they may not disturb our asses;" while the other, having taken in hand a heavy axe, hid himself behind the door and waited to work the nefarious murder he had planned. Ah, wretched Fortune! who art never content to let anyone subject to thy sway enjoy lasting happiness, with what deceitful hope didst thou lure these two innocent doves into the net where they were doomed to meet with such a cruel death! And even though it might not please thee that these two wretched lovers should have prosperous voyage over calm and tranquil seas, couldst thou not have found other methods innumerable to tear them asunder in their life or in their death? In sooth thou must have kept this fate in store for them as the most barbarous one possible. Certes, I can think of naught else to say concerning thy hateful deed than to declare that wretched indeed is the man who places his faith and hope in thee!

Lois, hearing himself thus summoned—although it was irksome to him to leave the warmth of the fire—went straightway with weary steps towards the stable in order that he might pacify the horses, leaving Martina in company of a number of the lepers, both male and female. He had scarcely entered the place when the savage ruffian dealt him such a blow on the head with the axe he wielded, that before he could even cry out "Alas!" he was felled to the ground a dead man. And although the wretch must have been well assured that his victim was dead, he still kept on dealing him further unmerciful blows about the head, and at last, leaving him lying there, the two went back to the place where the luckless girl had been left. Next these ruffians, being as it were the leaders of the company, gave command to all the others that they should straightway go to bed, each unto his own place, which thing was at once done. Thus the wretched Martina was left all alone; and, after she had many times demanded what had become of her Lois without getting any answer to the question, the murderer at last came towards her, and spake thus with his coarse and failing voice: "My girl, you must have patience. We have just this minute made a dead man of your lover, wherefore you need no longer nourish any hope that he will help you; and, besides this, I am determined that as long as I shall live, I will take my pleasure of that fair body of yours." Oh, all you pitiful and weeping ladies, who have deigned so far to read or to listen to such tragic and unheard-of misfortune as I have to set forth in this sombre story of mine! have you husbands whom you love alone, or lovers for whom you burn with fierce passion? Oh, you youths, prompt to feel the amorous flame and now come to the full flower of your age! if love has ever fired the hearts of any of you with a like ardour, I implore you, if there abides in you aught of humanity, that you will let fall your saddest tears, while my pen—all unequal to the task though it be—goes on to write of the insupportable woe which fell at this moment on the unfortunate girl, of a surety more wretched than any other in all the world. Indeed, whenever the fancy seizes me to tell of her grief, there will at once rise up before me the fearsome forms of the lepers who pressed close round the unhappy girl, with their reddened eyes, and hairless brows, and inflamed noses, and festering cheeks, tinged with all the hues of corruption, and turned-up rotting lips, and hands foul, paralytic, and drawn—figures which, as we call them up to vision, may be likened to devils rather than to men, and which now sway my fancy so powerfully that my trembling hand can write thereanent no farther. All you, therefore, who listen with so much pity, imagine to yourselves what thoughts must have filled her brain, what she must have felt over and beyond the grief which oppressed her, when she found herself between these two savage hounds who were so fiercely inflamed with passion that each one seemed straining to be the first to work her ruin. She, now crying out aloud, and now beating her head against the walls several times, became as one half dead, and then came back to consciousness again, with her delicate face all scratched and covered with blood.

Knowing too well that there was now neither remedy nor help which could preserve her, she determined that, as she had in her lifetime gone fearlessly with Lois her lover, so she would now be with him, and follow him to the death. Wherefore, turning towards the two savage brutes, she said, "Oh, pitiless and inhuman as you are! by the one God there is, I now make supplication to you that, as you have bereft me of the sole treasure of my life, you will grant to me one last favour before you go on to work any other wickedness on me. This favour is that I may be permitted to behold the dead body of my unhappy lover, and to get what consolation I may by bathing his blood-stained face with my bitter tears." The ruffians, who in no way divined what scheme she had in her mind, were willing to satisfy her in this demand, and to show her some slight courtesy; so they led her to the spot where the ill-fated Lois was lying dead. She, as soon as she saw him, became as one mad and bereft of reason, and, uttering a cry which went up to heaven, and abandoning herself to grief, she threw herself upon her lover's corpse. And when she had in a manner satiated herself with weeping over him and covering him with kisses (although she had with her a small knife which would have served well enough to carry out her fell intent), she glanced at her lover's side, and her eyes fell upon his dagger, of which the ruffians had not despoiled him. So it came into her mind this would better serve her purpose, and furnish her with more prompt and expeditious means of accomplishing her design, and having secretly taken the same in her hand and concealed it between the body of her dead lover and herself, she cried out, "Before this blade, now all ready for my needs, shall enter my heart, I call upon thee, O gracious spirit of my lord, but a few short minutes ago violently torn from this maimed and tortured body here, and beg thee of thy forbearance to await my own, which will full soon gladly and willingly join itself to thee; so that, when our souls shall be burnt together in the same fiery blast, they may be conscious of close and complete union, bound by eternal love. And although in life we have not been granted the boon to enjoy, with these our mortal bodies, our love together upon earth during the time allotted to us, and to give an example of perfect love, I pray that in eternity our spirits may be united, possessing one another and abiding together continually in whatever place our lot may be cast. Oh, body of my love, noblest and dearest! take to thine own, in sacrifice and in eternal union, this body of mine, which so eagerly hastens to follow thee wherever thou mayst go—my body which has been reserved, not for thy pleasure, but as a sacrifice on thy behalf. And may the funeral incense, such as is wont to be offered at the burial of the dead, be supplied by our blood, which will be mingled and brought to corruption in this vile spot, together with the tears of our cruel parents."

Thus she spake, and although the desire was upon her to spend more time in tears and lamentations, and although there entered her mind many other and pitiful thoughts to which she was fain to give utterance, she felt that the time had now come when she must carry out her last desire; wherefore she dexterously fixed the hilt of her lover's dagger on the breast of his dead body, and brought the sharp point of the same against the spot where her own heart lay. Then she crushed herself upon it without hesitation or fear of any sort, so that the cold steel passed through her while she cried out, "Now come, remorseless hounds as you are, and seize the prey which you were so hotly set to gain." Then, having once more pressed her dead lover in a close embrace, her soul took its flight from this wretched life.

Almost as soon as the two lepers heard these last words of hers they looked and saw that more than a span's length of the steel was standing out between her shoulders. And after this the lepers, being half dead with vexation and in grievous fear of their lives, quickly dug a deep grave in the stable, and without moving the bodies of the lovers buried them therein just as they lay.

Such, then, was the woeful and cruel end of this hapless pair, which thing I, grieving sorely the while, have here written down. After the waging of many fierce and deadly wars between their fathers, and after divers of each family had fallen victims to slaughter, it seemed meet to the justice of God that vengeance should be dealt out on account of a crime so heinous as the one I have described, wherefore it let fall due punishment upon the two murderers. It chanced in the course of time that one of the lepers in the lazaret aforesaid stirred up a tumult amongst the others, and by means of this dissension all the facts of the murder were disclosed just as they had occurred. When this news came to the ears of the two nobles, the parents of Lois and Martina, they straightway agreed to send to make search in the leper hospital, and having excavated the ground where the grave was, they came upon the corpses of the gentle and ill-starred pair. Though they were now so greatly marred by corruption, the dagger which was there gave clear proof of their cruel and piteous death. After they had gathered the remains together out of the hateful spot where they had lain, and placed them in a coffin of wood, and borne the same out of the place, they set fire to the house both within and without, so that in a few hours all the inmates thereof were burnt to ashes, together with all their goods, and all the buildings and the church as well. Then they bore the dead bodies back to the city of Nanci amidst universal lamentation and weeping and display of mourning garments, not only on the part of the kinsfolk and friends, but of all strangers likewise, and with pious and solemn offices they buried them in one and the same tomb, upon which the following words were carven in remembrance of these two ill-fated ones: "Envious chance and unjust Fortune led on Lois and Martina, the two lovers who are entombed here, to a cruel death. Thus they ended their days in bitter longing. Give them your tears, give them your lamentations, ye who read this."

MASUCCIO

YOU may well set down the tale I have told you as one quite as cruel and horrible as it is mournful and piteous. I know not, forsooth, whether the subject thereof will affect the minds of others in the same manner in which it affected mine. In my case it happens that, as often as I see a leper and remember what he is, so often rises before my eyes the spectacle of these two unhappy lovers lying dead in that stable folded in a close embrace, tossed over in the mud of the floor and disfigured with their own blood. For which reason not only have I lost all the compassion and charity I felt formerly for this wretched blemished folk, but there has come to me a hatred of them so great that I am fain to believe Nature has given to me a warrant to fall upon each one I may meet by way of working vengeance for the fate of the unhappy lovers. Now, because I call to mind how I have already given my promise that I would do my best to wipe out the stains of grief I have lately caused by some new pleasantry, I will let my pen have done with all such miseries, and, leaving the two poor lovers to rest in peace, I will give you in succession thereto another history so vastly unlike the last that, as in reading the one you must needs let fall tears without ceasing, so in reading the other you will laugh from beginning to end.

THE END OF THE THIRTY-FIRST NOVEL.

Novel the Thirty-second

ARGUMENT

A WOMAN OF VENICE, AMONGST MANY OTHER ADMIRERS, IS BELOVED BY A FLORENTINE, WHO DESPATCHES TO HER HIS SERVANT WITH A MESSAGE THAT THE ABBESS OF SANTA CHIARA IS FAIN TO SEE HER. BOTH SHE AND HER HUSBAND BELIEVE THIS TO BE TRUE; WHEREUPON SHE, BY MEANS OF VERY SUBTLE CRAFT, IS LED TO THE FLORENTINE'S HOUSE, IN WHICH THAT VERY SAME NIGHT A FIRE BREAKS OUT. THE CAPTAIN OF THE WATCH GOES TO HELP QUENCH THE SAME, AND, FINDING THERE THE LADY, OF WHOM HE HIMSELF IS ENAMOURED, HE CAUSES HER TO BE CAST INTO PRISON, FROM WHICH THE WAITING WOMAN OF THE FLORENTINE LIBERATES HER BY A PRETTY STRATAGEM, AND REMAINS THERE IN THE LADY'S STEAD. THE NEXT MORNING THE OLD WOMAN IS BROUGHT BEFORE THE SIGNORIA IN PLACE OF THE YOUNG ONE, THE CAPTAIN OF THE WATCH IS PUT TO RIDICULE, AND THE LADY RETURNS TO HER HUSBAND WITHOUT ANY HURT WHATEVER.

TO THE MAGNIFICENT MESSER ZACCARIA BARBARO

EXORDIUM

BECAUSE for a long time past, my magnificent and most generous Messer Zaccaria, you have been denied all taste of the sweet and delicious fruits of your own most illustrious fatherland, I doubt not that the odour of some of its fair flowers will delight you amain. For this reason, and as a memento of our interrupted friendship, I desire, together with this present story, to make you an offering of certain of those delightsome blossoms which spring in your Venice. And albeit these blossoms were culled by a Florentine hand, still, on account of the fashion in which this deed was brought to pass, you may still find in them some diversion of that sort which the prudent and the wise are wont in their leisure time to gather from such merry conceits. Farewell.

THE NARRATIVE

IF my memory serves me aright, it happened the day before yesterday that, while we were talking pleasantly in your company, a tale was told to us, an absolute fact, by certain of your Venetian associates, how, about two years ago, there lived in Venice a man skilled in the art of beating out gold for the purpose of embroidery, who was called by name Guiliano Sulco. Upon this man Fortune, amongst many other temporal gifts, had bestowed a wife who, according to the reckoning of the people round about, was the loveliest and most graceful young woman then to be found in all Venice. She, over and above her great uprightness—for she was a woman endowed with numerous virtues—counted amongst her other accomplishments a marvellous skill in the art of embroidery. By this and by the handicraft plied by the husband, the pair gained so much money that, at the time of which I am writing, they had gathered together a handsome heap of several hundreds of florins.

The fame of the beauty of this young woman, whose name was Giustina, was already spread through the whole of Venice, and on this account many and divers youths, of noble families and of the people, Venetian citizens and strangers alike, became most ardently enamoured of her. But with regard to the dame herself, who, as it has been already stated, was no less richly endowed with honesty than with beauty, it seemed as if her virtue had let enter and abide in her young heart a hard block of ice, which effectually kept off any danger which might arise from the blazing darts of Love. Therefore she recked naught of all her crowd of lovers, or of their oglings and workings to win her favour; and, however noble and comely, rich and young these might be, she held them even of less account than the basest servants. Her husband, being advised of this conduct of his wife, not only put far away from him any jealous suspicions which might well have arisen in his heart on account of the great love he had for her, but likewise held her doubly dear, and committed to her the entire direction, charge, and government of their common honour; and she, as a wise woman, did not grow in any wise haughty or overbearing from the enjoyment of so great liberty, but, keeping a praiseworthy reputation, she seemed only bent on seeking how she might further add to her own worthiness and good name.

Now it happened that, amongst the numerous and importunate crowd which followed in vain in the footsteps of our Giustina, was a certain young Florentine, who was fully as astute and well-versed in gallantry as he was seemly and pleasant in his manner. This youth, either on his own account or in the employ of others, carried on a large traffic in merchandize in Venice, and he—having seen and duly proved by many and manifest instances how great was the young woman's integrity, how neither the greed of wealth nor the passion for any lover whomsoever could lead her to the commission of any lascivious act—took thought how he might entangle her by some artful deceit; and, as he happened to have in his household an old Slavonian woman who was well trained and experienced and intelligent in such matters, he gave to her full instructions as to what he wanted her to do. The woman forthwith gathered certain delicate herbs, and with the same she made a choice salad which she took with her to the house of Giuliano, and, having greeted him with a pleasant smile, she spake thus: "The Abbess of Santa Chiara sends you these herbs out of our own convent garden, and begs of you that you will do your best to serve her by sending to her a pound of gold thread, of which she is fain to make trial for the working of certain embroideries which, with the assistance of her nuns, she has undertaken to produce; and if she should find this sample to her liking—as indeed she thinks she will—she wili get you to draw for her several pounds of gold thread every month."

The maestro, mightily pleased at what he heard, tendered thanks to the abbess for her gift, and straightway picked out a pound of the finest gold thread he had by him, and, having notified the price thereof, told the woman that he would be able always in the future to serve her with ware of a similar quality. After she had done this errand, the messenger returned well content to her master, and having taken further counsel with him as to what they should do next, she went to the maestro a few days afterwards bearing a handbasket filled with rare fruits, and smiling as she spoke said to him: "Madonna sends you her salutation and blessing, and says that the gold thread you sent her is exactly suitable for her purpose, wherefore she desires you to send her ten other pounds of the same; so for every day's labour you will find that you reap no small advantage from this fresh customer. Likewise she sends these few fruits out of the garden of the convent as an offering to your wife, and says that she wishes by all means to know her, not only on account of the current report of her worth and honesty of carriage, but because she is, as everyone declares, the most skilful embroideress of our city, and one from whom the young damsels of the convent might well learn some dainty stitches. On this account she begs and prays of you, supposing it should not be irksome to you so to do, that on the day before the festival of our Santa Chiara, which falls in a very brief space of time, you will send her thither, where, in the company of the nieces and sisters-in-law of our abbess, she may spend two or three days with great pleasure and contentment. If you should assent to this, she will give directions to the gentlewomen aforesaid, albeit they are of the chief nobility of the city, that they take their way past this house of yours, and convey your wife away with them in honourable fashion, and afterwards bring her back to you in the same manner."

The maestro, being well aware that it was a custom amongst women of Venice to go on these occasions to stay and pass several nights in the monasteries where they might happen to have friends or kinsfolk amongst the inmates, seeing that all other times entrance to these places is forbidden to everybody, gave neither much nor little heed to the trick which was being prepared, and was all the less suspicious thereanent because he was fully assured that this invitation, and the purchase of the gold thread as well, came from the abbess herself. And because he had, as we have already said, the greatest faith in the well-approved honesty of his wife, he made answer, without giving further thought to the matter, that he was quite willing to send his wife to the convent whenever and in whatever fashion the abbess might desire, and that if at any time the gentlewomen aforesaid might deign to pass by his house, he would gladly suffer his wife to go to the convent in their company. Then, having given to the old woman the gold which she asked for, and having been paid liberally for the same, he and his wife, to whom he told what had passed, were marvellously pleased at having thus begun to have dealings with such a lady, and it seemed a thousand years to him and many more to his wife until the festival aforesaid should come, not so much in respect of the foundation of an intimacy with the abbess, which thing might prove to them a source of profit both present and to come, as for the making acquaintance of those young nuns in the convent, and of divers ladies of high rank, not under vows, and of diverting herself in the company of the same.

When the old woman returned to her master the two rejoiced amain, for that everything now seemed to be marching according to their design, and when the appointed day had come, the Florentine, as had been duly determined, conveyed cautiously into his house seven or eight women of the sort who were accustomed to ply for public gain, some of them widows, some with the seeming of matrons, and some with that of maids, handsomely dressed and decked with sumptuous gems as if they had been in truth ladies of the highest families in Venice. Then, when these had been duly settled in a barge covered after the Venetian fashion, they set forth attended by divers of their servants and handmaids, and by the old woman who had acted as messenger. They went leisurely on their way, and after they had made a long circuit through other canals they approached the piazza of Santa Croce, where Maestro Giuliano lived. Thereupon the woman at once got out of the boat and calling upon Giustina in a jocund voice, said to her, "The kinsfolk of madonna are here ready to receive you in their barge and take you back to the monastery." Then Giustina, following her husband's directions, first adorned herself richly, and afterwards entered the barge, where she was received in friendly wise by the ladies, while her husband, looking upon the company and judging from their seeming that they were of high degree, was quite content to let her go. Then they set forth, and the prow of the barge being directed towards Santo Apostolo, where the Florentine kept house, they arrived there in a very short time.

When they had come to their destination, one of the women aforesaid cried out: "Why should we not call for Madonna Teodora, seeing that she was one of the first to be invited?" And all the others having given their assent, they called to fetch her, and forthwith there came to one of the windows a black woman, who said: "My mistress begs you, in case the delay should be irksome to you, that you will come up and tarry here for a little until she shall have finished her dressing." Whereupon all the women, without waiting for any farther invitation, leaped on shore, and having taken Giustina by the hand, they went into the house in very gamesome mood. When they had gone inside, this went into one chamber, and that into another; this went out, and that came in, until at last Giustina found herself in a room alone. Very soon the Florentine entered with arms outstretched and clasped her round the neck, and, after he had in a few words let her know concerning the trick which had been put upon her, he implored her, by the long and fervent love which he had borne and still bore her, and for the sake of her own honour, that she would be ready and willing to give him, without any farther opposition, that favour which she could not now deny him even if she were so minded.

Now that this modest, well-conducted young woman, who had hitherto preserved so well her honour, saw herself brought to this difficult pass, I leave it to those ladies who may some time or other have found themselves in similar case to decide what she did; whether she acted with due discretion and made a virtue of necessity, or whether she put forth her strength in a vain resistance, let these ladies give judgment as to what most women would have said and done. All I know for certain is, that after Giustina had supped in jovial wise with the Florentine, without again seeing aught of the women who had conducted her thither, it came to pass between the second and the third hour of the night* that a fire broke out in the house, kindled either by the sumptuous preparations which had been made, or from some other cause. Whereupon a mighty uproar having arisen on account of the same, as is always the case in Venice, it chanced that one of the captains of the watch, who was himself enamoured of Giustina and one of her most persistent followers, was going through that quarter of the city, and hearing the cries of "Fire! Fire!" he, according to the duty laid upon him by his office, quickly beat down the doors and went up into the house. Then, having given orders to his following to see to the quenching of the fire, he, so as to carry out the accustomed regulations in cases of this sort, stationed himself before the door of the master of the house to prevent the crowd of people who entered from stealing any of his goods. Scarcely had he taken up his position there when he saw approach the Florentine holding Giustina by the hand, both of them apparently half-stunned and terrified and fain to flee from the burning house. On account of the number of torches carried by his followers, the captain of the watch knew for certain at once that it was Giustina he saw, and, confounded by grief and amazement, he felt that the fervent love he had hitherto borne her was forthwith changed into the fiercest hatred, and, had he not been kept back therefrom by virtue of the office he bore, he would willingly have passed his sword again and again through her body, so mad-

* Between seven and eight in the evening.

dened was he by the thought that she, whom he had always regarded as holding a particular eminence over all the women in the world for her honesty and pure life, who had never even satisfied his longings by a single kind glance, should be thus discovered by him in the guise of a common harlot in the house of a foreign trafficker, and one, most likely, who was merely the factor of others. Nevertheless, seeing that the fire was by this time put out, he kept back his anger somewhat, and determined, without giving farther thought to the matter, to have her taken on the following morning to the public brothel with the drums beating, as was permitted by law in the case of women who might be caught publicly in adultery. With a great show of rage he snatched her out of the hands of the unlucky Florentine, and then went with his following forth from the house, taking Giustina into one of the chief streets where stood the prison, and having left her there in hold, as if she had been a serving-woman of the basest sort, he charged the jailers that they should keep strict watch over her until the following morning. When he had done this he once more began to perlustrate his quarter of the city as the duties of his office required.

The Florentine, who had remained behind vexed with grief too keen to be described—and with good reason—brought after a while his harassed wits somewhat into order, and, aided by his love and by his own natural astuteness, concocted a plan by which it seemed that he might regain possession of the prey to win which he had spent so great care and labour, and which had been so quickly reft from him by misadventure. As he knew well where the prison was, and of what mettle were the officers who had charge of Giustina, he instructed the old woman what to do, and she, having filled a basket with capons and bread, and two flasks of good wine, went to the prison in the barge as quickly as she could go, taking a servant with her. When she came before the keepers she begged them tenderly that for the love of God they would suffer her to give somewhat to eat to the poor young servant of her master's who, through the fault of the captain of the watch, had been wrongly laid in hold, having been seized and taken from the house starving and weeping and grieving sorely. Wherefore, so as to win their goodwill and consent to her request, she gave them for themselves the greater part of the food, which in sooth she had conveyed thither for that same purpose, and they, what though they were greedy and very ill-conditioned, at once softened towards her, and bade her enter at her pleasure. The old woman having gone into the cell where Giustina was, at once gave her the cloak she was wearing and charged her to get forth as quickly as she could, and to embark in the boat outside where the servant was waiting. To her great joy, the young woman managed to carry out all these directions without let of any sort, or any questioning by the jailers, and having leapt into the boat, she was taken by the servant straightway back to the place whence she had been torn with so great violence only a short time before.

When the next morning had come, the captain of the watch, although his anger over the affair waxed greater every hour, and although he grew more and more infuriated in considering the cruel punishment he was determined to inflict, decided not to proceed with the case until he should first have taken counsel with certain of his friends. Wherefore, having let assemble the same, he laid before them, with no little savage joy in his heart the while, the whole of the cruel business, and furthermore told them what he was minded to do for the final chastisement of such an abandoned woman. After they had laughed heartily, and passed many a merry quip thereanent, it seemed meet to them all that the matter should be submitted to the judgment of the Signoria. So they went in a body to the palace, and having set before the Doge the affair in all its particulars, they next gave the word that the young woman should at once be brought privily thither, in order that they might be better informed as to what penalty was her due, and learn how, and for what purpose, and by whom she had been conveyed into the Florentine's house. They bade four of the prison guards to bring Giustina thither carefully wrapped up in her clothes, in such wise that

THE CAPTAIN OF THE WATCH.

FROM A DRAWING BY E. R. HUGHES. (Mas., Nov. xxxii., v. ii.)

no one could recognize her; whereupon these fellows, having gone to the prison, laid hold of the cunning old woman, and after they had tied her up closely, they took her before the Signoria, of which the greater part of the members were present. She, when she saw herself in the presence of so great state, began to cry aloud: "Justice, justice, for the love of God, against this cheating captain of the watch of yours! For last night, when a fire broke out in my master's house, he and his company forced their way in, and without any cause whatever he handed me over to his tipstaves, and kept me in prison in such evil case that I have had the worst night that ever a woman spent. Now, in sooth, he has hailed me before you, bound as though I had pilfered the treasury of Saint Mark. I do not, nor can any of you see what offence a poor old woman like me, the servant of another, can have committed against him."

The captain of the watch, prudent man as he was, felt utterly confounded in mind when he saw the old woman before him and listened to what she had to say, as everyone may well believe. Not only did he stand speechless, but his face was changed so mightily in seeming that the Doge and the whole body of the Signoria perceived he must surely have fallen into some grave error; so they at once commanded to let go free the old woman, and to send her back to her dwelling, which thing was done forthwith. Then some of them in good faith, and some of them in banter, demanded to know of the captain of the watch whether he had been waking or asleep, and by what mischance he could have laid hands on the poor old woman; whereupon he became so distraught that he failed to let them know by his reply how the thing could indeed have come to pass. Then, with all sorts of merry japes, they gave judgment in the case and decided that the burning passion and the great desire he harboured towards the wife of Maestro Giuliano had worked such havoc in his brainpan that he was led to regard an ugly old harridan as the fair and youthful dame he loved; and thus, flouted and bemused and ill-content with his day's work, he returned to his home. And the prudent and wary Florentine, who with so great contrivance and with so many strange accidents had seized and lost and regained the lady of whom he was enamoured, sent her back to her husband without letting arise any scandal, or without letting the good man know what had really happened, with the same device he had used in taking her thence.

MASUCCIO

WE may, in sooth, give our highest word of praise to the ingenious Florentine, seeing that in a strange country he was able to carry off the prize in the race against so many coursers of singular excellence, and ultimately by his aforesaid astuteness to bring the affair to a prosperous issue, after suffering a mischance so grave as that which befell him. And because, however much we may discourse concerning the vicissitudes and freaks of fortune, there will always remain somewhat more to be said, I will exhibit to you in the following novel the misfortunes, yet more strange and varied and pitiless, which befell two constant and noble lovers by reason of their excessive love—a narrative differing widely from those told hitherto, inasmuch as these two were brought to their end with tears of blood and with violent death.

THE END OF THE THIRTY-SECOND NOVEL.

Novel the Thirty-third

ARGUMENT

MARIOTTO, A YOUNG MAN OF SIENA, WHO IS ENAMOURED OF GIANNOZZA, TAKES FLIGHT TO ALEXANDRIA ON ACCOUNT OF A MURDER WHICH HE HAS COMMITTED. GIANNOZZA FEIGNS TO BE DEAD, AND, HAVING BEEN TAKEN OUT OF HER TOMB, GOES IN SEARCH OF HER LOVER. IN THE MEANTIME MARIOTTO, HAVING HEARD THE NEWS OF HER DEATH, RETURNS TO SIENA, IN ORDER THAT HE MAY DIE LIKEWISE. HE IS RECOGNIZED AND TAKEN, AND HIS HEAD IS STRICKEN OFF. THE LADY FINDING NO TRACE OF HER LOVER IN ALEXANDRIA GOES BACK TO SIENA, WHERE SHE LEARNS THAT HE HAS BEEN BEHEADED, AND THEN DIES OF GRIEF ON HIS CORPSE.

TO THE MOST ILLUSTRIOUS LORD, THE DUKE OF AMALFI *

EXORDIUM

THE more ill-starred and unhappy the varying fortunes of love may be, the more sedulously ought the man, who writes of the same, to strive to make them known to all lovers—to those who are ardent, and also to those who are discreet. And because, my most illustrious lord, I have for some years past had acquaintance with you—at a certain season when you were entangled in divers snares which Cupid set for you, and again when I beheld you enjoying the tender passion in most seemly fashion—I determined some long time ago to give you a full and true account of the most pitiful fate which befell two unhappy lovers; so that you,

* Antonio Piccolomini, a nephew of Pius II. He married a natural daughter of Ferdinand I. of Naples.

taught by your wonted prudence and your vast store of virtues, might be able to tell us rightly, after duly considering the case of these two, which of them loved in the more fervent wise.

THE NARRATIVE

IN these five days, and not a great while agone, this story was related by a certain gentleman of your city of Siena, and one of no small worship, to a company of gentle ladies, telling them how in recent times there abode in Siena a young man of good family, well-mannered and very comely in seeming, Mariotto Mignanelli by name. This youth, having become ardently enamoured of a fair and graceful damsel named Giannozza, the daughter of a notable and highly-esteemed citizen, a member, I think, of the house of the Saraceni, contrived on his part in the course of time to win from the damsel her most ardent love in return for his own. Now, after they had for some long time fed their eyesight by gazing at the sweet and pleasant flowers of love, and had nursed their amorous desire to have taste of the delicious fruits which were their due, they began to search and to devise many and diverse plans how they might compass the same; but finding none which might be essayed with security, the young girl, who was fully as prudent as she was lovely, made up her mind to take her lover for her husband by stealth; so that, if by the untoward working of circumstance their happiness should be denied to them, they would be provided with a shield herewith to hide from the world the error they had committed.

Wherefore, to secure the fulfillment of this deed, they bribed by a gift of money a certain Augustinian friar, through whose ministration they secretly became bound by the matrimonial tie, and with specious arguments of this sort they let themselves be lulled into a secure and certain frame of mind, and gave free rein to their ardent desires, the one enjoying therefrom fully as much pleasure as the other. Now, after they had spent some time thus happily over the gratification of their secret, and in a sense lawful love, it came to pass that their evil and unfriendly fortune by adverse working overturned the whole fabric of their desires both present and to come. This calamity was brought about by Mariotto, who happened one day to come to high words with another honourable citizen of the town, and not to words only, for the affair soon went on to blows in such wise that Mariotto smote his adversary on the head with a cudgel, and of this blow he died in a very short time. On this account Mariotto went into hiding, and, having been diligently sought for by the officials of the court without being found, he was not only condemned by the lords of the council and the Podesta to perpetual exile, but was likewise banished by proclamation as a rebel against the law.

Only those who have themselves been pierced by wounds like this will be able to judge aright as to the greatness and the intensity of this crowning sorrow, or to keep count of the tears shed by these two most unhappy lovers, so short a time united by secret bond, over what seemed to be a long, or even in their belief a perpetual separation. Their grief was in sooth so cruel and bitter that, when the moment came for their last farewell and they stood folded in each other's arms, they might well have been taken for those whose souls death had already seized. However, letting their grief abate for a little, they indulged in a hope that peradventure in the course of time it might be granted to Mariotto, by some turn of affairs, to come back to his native place. Wherefore they agreed it would be well for him to depart not only from Tuscany, but from Italy itself, and to make his way to Alexandria, in which city there was residing an uncle of his named Ser Niccolo Mignanelli, a man concerned in large traffic and a merchant widely known. Then, having given her full directions as to the future, and many assurances that he, though so far distant from her, would visit her in the letters he would write, the pair of lovers bade each other farewell with tears which seemed to have no end.

The wretched Mariotto took his departure after having made known to a brother of his all the details of his secret, begging him at the same time that he would, most carefully and before everything else, keep him well informed as to any accident which might befall his Giannozza, by writing constantly and setting down most particularly all that happened. Then, having set forth on his journey after giving these instructions, he took his way towards Alexandria, which city he reached in due time. He found his uncle who was living there, and by him was welcomed in joyful and friendly wise, and before long he let his kinsman know the whole story of the affair in which he had been concerned of late. The uncle, being a man of sound judgment, was greatly disquieted as he listened, not so much indeed with regard to the case of the man slain by mischance, as to the affront put thereby upon so many kinsfolk. However, knowing full well that censure of offences past and gone is worth little more than nothing, he did his best with Mariotto's help to restore peace, and gave much thought as to how they might in the course of time hit upon some remedy fitting for the case in point. He likewise committed to Mariotto's hands the care of certain of his commercial affairs, and would often come anear the youth, at such times as he might be vexed with his heavy grief and constant weeping, and console him as best he could. A month never passed in which Mariotto did not receive letters from his Giannozza and from his brother also. These letters, in sooth, coming during this cruel time of misfortune and long absence, were a marvellously great comfort and consolation to both of the lovers.

While the matter stood in this wise it happened that the father of Giannozza found himself greatly besought and importuned by divers suitors who were eager to have his daughter in marriage; but she, making use of various fictitious arguments, would have naught to say to any one of them. But in the end it came to pass that being urged and constrained by her father to take for her husband one of the suitors for whom she could find no ground of refusal, her agonized soul was torn by a

GIANNOZZA AND THE FRIARS.

FROM A DRAWING BY E R. HUGHES. (Mas., Nov. xxxiii , v. ii.)

cruel conflict so incessantly and in so grievous a fashion that death itself would have seemed to her more welcome than life under such conditions. In addition to this, she had by this time begun to look upon the return of the husband, whom she had married by stealth, and whom she loved so dearly, as a vain hope, and likewise to perceive that were she to disclose to her father the whole truth concerning the matter it could profit nothing, but would rather kindle more grievously his wrath against her; so she determined to make good all her faults by embarking in a project which was no less strange than perilous and hard of execution, one the like of which had never been heard of before, and, at the same time, apt to imperil both her honour and her life.

Thus, with her heart kept up by the great courage that was in her, she sent word to her father to tell him that she was altogether ready to do his pleasure, and then summoned to her that same friar who had been the original schemer in the business. To him she disclosed in very cautious manner what thing it was she was minded to do, and begged him that he would favour her plan by giving her his aid therein. The friar, as soon as he knew what it was she wanted, showed himself to be, as is the wonted practice of such folk, somewhat amazed and timid and slow to act; but she on her part soon roused his ardour and activity by means of the virtue and of the magic spells worked by Messer San Giovanni Bocca-d'oro,* and brought him into the mind to speed her project with all his strength. Then, on account of the pressing haste which drove her on, the friar went his way as quickly as he could, and compounded with his own hands, being in sooth an expert in such matters, a certain water made up by the blending of divers subtle powders, and limited in its action in such manner that if anyone should drink of the same he would not only remain for three days in a deep sleep, but would seem to anyone who might look upon him to be verily and indeed dead. This potion he sent forthwith to the lady.

Now Giannozza, as soon as she had despatched to her Mariotto by a courier full intelligence of what she

* The patron saint of bribery.

was minded to do, and had got clear understanding from the friar concerning all things which she must needs carry out on her own behalf, joyfully drank off the medicated water. Then there very soon came upon her so profound a stupor that she fell to the earth like one dead. Her maids, as soon as they saw what had happened, raised a loud outcry, which forthwith brought the old father, together with a large number of other people, to learn what might be the cause of the noise. When he found how his only daughter, whom he loved so dearly, was already dead, he—stricken the while with such grief as he had never tasted before—straightway made them bring in divers physicians to try by every remedy they knew how to use, to call her back to life; but, since not one of these availed aught, everyone there present was fully assured that she had met her death through the sudden stroke which had fallen upon her.*

During the whole of that day, and during the following night as well, they kept a most careful watch over her, and, for the reason that her attendants remarked in her no signs save those of death, she was buried the next day with sumptuous funeral rites in a noble tomb in the church of Santo Agostino, to the unbounded grief of her afflicted father, and with the weeping and mourning of her kinsmen and friends and of all the people of Siena. But when it was about the hour of midnight the reverend friar betook himself to the church aforesaid, and by the help of a companion of his drew Giannozza forth from the sepulchre, and, according to the plan which had been settled, bore her into his own chamber. Now, seeing that the hour was close at hand when the effect of the potion, compounded so as to act for a certain time, should have run its course, they succeeded by the help of a fire and of certain other needful provisions in bringing her back to life, though not without great difficulty. Then, when she had been restored to her right mind, and after three days had elapsed, she set forth in the company of the good brother—she herself being disguised in the habit of a friar—to Porto Pisano, where

* Orig., *da sopravenu tale goccia fosse morta.*

the galley plying between Acquamorta* and Alexandria was bound to call. Having found all things in the transit aforesaid duly in order, she set sail in the galley; but because voyages at sea are always wont to be vastly more prolonged than the travellers desire, either through contrary winds or through having to take on board fresh merchandize, it came to pass that the galley for various reasons was delayed in coming to its destination for several months beyond the time when it was due.

Now Gargano, the brother of Mariotto, by way of carrying out the directions left with him by his well-beloved brother, immediately sent a full account of the sudden death of Giannozza to the ill-starred Mariotto, sorrowing himself greatly over the news, and likewise telling his brother in what fashion she had been mourned and where her sepulchre was, and how a little time after her own death her old father, who held her in such great love, had passed away from this life by reason of the heavy sorrow he felt. And these letters written by Gargano were sped more swiftly and fortunately by the working of hostile and malignant Fate than was the messenger who had been despatched by the unhappy Giannozza; for, just as if to prepare for these devoted lovers the bitter and bloody death which in the end was their portion, it came to pass that the messenger of Giannozza, who had taken passage in a caravel laden with corn and bound for Alexandria, was taken prisoner by corsairs and slain.

On this account Mariotto, being possessed of no other intelligence than that sent by his brother, held the same indeed to be the truth. Wherefore I bid you consider, O reader, if there be any spirit of compassion within you, how mightily he found himself grief-stricken and afflicted —and with good reason—by the bitter cruelty of this news! The anguish which wrung his heart was so intense and so great that he felt no longer any wish to live, and all the persuasions and comforting words of his good uncle were of no avail to soothe him. Thus, having passed some long time in bitter weeping, he at last resolved to go back to Siena, in order that he might make

* Aigues Mortes, then an important commercial city

his way on foot, under the cover of some disguise or other, to the sepulchre in which, as he believed, his Giannozza lay buried, and there let his grief have such full course that his life must perforce come to an end thereby. If, indeed, he should by chance be recognized, he would deem himself fortunate to be put on his trial in respect to the homicide which he had committed. This scheme aforesaid he hoped to carry out in case fortune should second his efforts and keep secret for a while the news of his return. In the meantime he was possessed with the belief that she, whom he loved more dearly than he loved himself (and who, indeed, loved him in equal degree), was dead.

Having decided upon this course, he awaited the sailing of the galley of the Venetians for the parts of the west,* and without saying to his uncle a single word anent his purpose he embarked in the vessel aforesaid, hurrying eagerly towards the death which he was foreordained to meet. After a very short voyage he arrived in Naples, from which place he betook himself by land towards Tuscany with all speed, and contrived to enter Siena in the disguise of a pilgrim without being recognized by anybody. There he took lodging at a house of entertainment little frequented by guests, and then, without having let any of his acquaintance know of his presence, he made his way at an hour which suited his purpose to the church where his Giannozza was buried, and, standing in front of her sepulchre, he wept very bitterly, and, if such a thing had been possible, he would gladly have crept into the tomb itself, so that in death he might have beside him, as an abiding companion, that most lovely and delicate body, the sweetness of which he was not permitted to enjoy during his life.

And herewith all his thoughts and desires were firmly set to bring to an issue the purpose aforesaid, what though he never ceased his wonted grief and weeping. So, having got into his possession by very cautious working divers instruments of iron, and having concealed himself one evening after vespers within the church, he

* Orig., *per ponente*, towards the setting sun, opposed to *levante* the rising.

worked with such vigour during the following night that he succeeded in putting aside the covering of the sepulchre by means of his crowbar. Just as he was on the point of entering the tomb it chanced that the sacristan who had come to ring the bell for matins, heard a sound and, having gone to ascertain what might be the cause thereof, he found Mariotto engaged in the aforesaid work. The sacristan, deeming that the man he saw must be some thief who was come thither with the intent to rifle the bodies of the dead, cried out, at the top of his voice, "A thief! a thief!" whereupon all the friars ran to his cry and laid hands on Mariotto. Then, having opened the gates and let enter a great number of laymen of all sorts, they found the ill-fated lover, who was still wrapped round with his garb of basest rags, and at once knew him to be no other than Mariotto Mignanelli. There they detained him, and, soon as it was day, all Siena was full of the news of what had happened.

When the rumour had come to the ears of the Signoria orders were issued to the Podesta to go and fetch the prisoner, and to put in force straightway whatever the laws and the constitution of the city might direct to be done in such a case. And thus Mariotto, bound and a captive, was taken to the palace of the Podesta and was put to the torture of the strappado;* but, without letting himself be subjected to be tormented much, he confessed point by point wherefore he had been led to take the desperate course of returning to Siena. And, despite the fact that every single person throughout the city felt for him the deepest compassion, and that his fate was especially bewept amongst the ladies—they in their gentleness deeming that he was, in sooth, the one instance in the world of a perfect lover, and each one of them being ready and willing to redeem his life with her own blood—he was nevertheless condemned on the first day of his trial to lose his head, which sentence was duly carried out at the given time, since all the efforts of his friends and kinsfolk prevailed naught to mend his evil fortune.

* The victim was hoisted up, tied by the arms, to a lofty beam, and then suddenly let fall.

In the meantime the most unhappy Giannozza, under the guidance of the friar aforesaid, arrived in Alexandria after the lapse of several months, and after having undergone many and divers mischances on the voyage. She went forthwith to the house of Ser Niccolo, and, when she had let him know who she was and had told him her name, she added the reason which had brought her thither and every other accident which had lately befallen her, whereupon the good man was filled with amazement and distress at one and the same time. Then, after he had given her fitting reception, and caused her to put on woman's clothing once more, and taken leave of the friar, he told the hapless Giannozza in what manner and in what desperate mood her Mariotto had fled from Alexandria on account of the tidings which had come to him, without letting any one know what he was minded to do. He likewise told her how all had bewailed him as one dead already, seeing that he had turned his steps towards what could prove to be naught else than certain death.

I will let him who may have experience meet for the task consider well the situation and say in what measure the anguish which tore Giannozza's heart as she listened, exceeded—as well it might—all the griefs hitherto undergone by her lover and herself, forasmuch as I myself deem that any words which may be spoken thereanent will profit nothing. After she had in some measure come back to herself, and had taken counsel with the good merchant, who was as another father to her, they decided, after holding many and divers deliberations and shedding together many burning tears, to betake themselves with all the speed they could use to Siena, where, whether they might find Mariotto dead or alive, they would do their best by whatsoever remedial means might be vouchsafed to them in their extreme necessity at least to save spotless the honour of Giannozza. Having set his affairs in order with as little loss to himself as he could compass, and caused the lady to put on male attire once more, they found suitable means of transit; and, meeting with a prosperous wind for their voyage, they came in a short space of time to the shores of

Tuscany, and disembarked at Piombino. From this place they took their way privily to a certain farm which Ser Niccolo owned in the neighbourhood of Siena, and when they asked what might be the news they learned that three days ago their Mariotto had been beheaded.

As soon as the bitter truth of these words was fully realized by them—what though they had hitherto held for certain that the issue of the affair must be none other than this—they stood blanched and half dead with affliction when once they knew this dreadful thing had surely come to pass. How great their sorrow was, the nature of this cruel calamity will let you judge aright. The lamentations of Giannozza, crying out loudly, "Alas, woe is me!" were so passionate that they would have moved to pity even a heart of marble. Nevertheless, having been soothed and kindly tended for some time by Ser Niccolo, and having given good heed to his wise and kindly counsels, the two resolved that, in their condition of dire adversity, it behoved them to look alone to the preservation of the honour and good name of their numerous band of kinsfolk; and, in order to compass this end, to arrange that the poor young woman should secretly gain admission to some religious house of the strictest rule, where she might lament with bitter tears her own ill-fortune, the death of her beloved Mariotto, and her present misery, as long as it should be granted to her to live. This project they carried out to the full with the closest secrecy, and when she had taken up her dwelling in the convent, without having told aught of her story to anyone but the abbess herself, after a very short time had rolled away she made an end of her most wretched life in grief which consumed her inmost soul and in weeping tears of blood—in fasting by day and in waking by night, and in calling without ceasing upon her beloved Mariotto.

MASUCCIO

IT is certain that impassioned women will feel more pity than strong-souled men over the many doleful misadventures lately described; and, over and beyond this, these ladies will assuredly set down the love of Giannozza as unmatched and fervent beyond compare—greater indeed than that of Mariotto. But if perchance this question should ever come up for debate, the man who loves wisely will be able to prove by most valid reasoning that the love of the ill-starred Mariotto was, beyond comparison, the mightier and the more intense. For this reason, admitting that the young woman really did accomplish deeds which were wonderful to be done by one of her sex in her journey in search of her lover, she was nevertheless stirred up to attempt them through the belief that she would find him a living man, and would hereafter live long and joyful days with him. But as to the hapless lover, he, believing his love to be dead already, was minded to go to her as she was, with all the speed that was possible, with no other aim before him than to lay down his own life, which thing indeed came to pass. But now, letting all these doleful matters remain for the consideration of others, I will in the next place relate to you a most laughable adventure, telling how an over-jealous loon of an innkeeper, though he was a wary fellow enough, was induced to take his wife on his own mare down to the ship of the gallant who was her lover, being moved to this deed by the covetous expectation of some small gain therefrom.

THE END OF THE THIRTY-THIRD NOVEL.

Novel the Thirty-fourth

ARGUMENT

Tobia, a Ragusan, takes his pleasure with the wife of an innkeeper of Giobennazzo, and by a most subtle trick induces the husband to bring her to the ship riding on his own mare. The husband on his return home finds his wife gone; and, after having for a long time lamented over the short faith of the Ragusan, marries another woman; and, letting go all remembrance of his first wife, enjoys his life in company of the second.

TO HIS MAGNIFICENCE THE BARON OF PRIGNIANO *

EXORDIUM

FOR the reason that many and divers troubles have stood in my way, and that the leisure and the pleasant opportunity of taking up the pen which I had laid down have been denied to me, my hearty good lord, I have until now delayed to set down in writing the novel which I destined for you—the particulars of which were given to you and to me at the same time. But those sweet and delightful fruits, which I gathered during the most joyous term of our friendship, have found in me such meet resting-place that, having let quiet my labouring brain, I now apply myself to the telling of the present story with no little pleasure; so that—because you will assuredly bear in mind my affection, and will not fail to write again to me—it may be the means of letting us regard one another continually with

* In the later editions this novel is dedicated to Messer Fabiano Rosello, *regio Segretario*.

the eyes of the mind; for, as you must know well by this time, the practice of letter-writing in itself availeth greatly, inasmuch as it can make parted friends believe that they are together.

THE NARRATIVE

A YEAR or so ago there lived at Giovenazzo a certain goodman called Tonto de Leo, who, perchance for the reason that he was minded to earn for himself and his family a living with as little bodily travail as possible, had taken up the calling of an innkeeper in the chief piazza of the town. Now, as he had to wife a very comely and graceful young woman whose name was Lella, it came to pass that there was always gathered together in front of the inn a numerous and importunate crowd of young men casting amorous glances at the fair hostess. It was, in sooth, as if an unlicensed fair was being held there all day long. Wherefore the good host, albeit he was of a most jealous nature, in order to let the world see that he, as a new tavern-keeper, was able to collect a goodly crowd of customers, was fain to put up with these doings, being sometimes contented and sometimes perturbed therewith, as is the manner of jealous men.

It happened that a well-favoured young merchant of Ragusa, Tobia by name, who was at that time trafficking in the seaboard places of Apulia, and purchasing grain wherewith to load a ship of his which was lying at Monopoli, took the road and went to Giovenazzo. He had not been long in the place before certain of his friends let him know all about the beauty and the lovesome ways of the hostess aforesaid, and how, if time and opportunity should be granted to her, she would fully satisfy the longings of whomsoever might undertake to win her. Tobia, as soon as he heard this, was vastly more desirous to set eyes on the hostess than to be well lodged, and forthwith took up his quarters at the inn of our friend Tonto, who, deeming that he might draw no small profit from the arrival of such a guest, not only gave him joyful reception on his own behalf, but likewise caused his wife to welcome him in most friendly wise; for which reason, having become very intimate with them, in a very short space of time Tobia grew to long after naught else than the pleasure and delight which he took in Madonna Lella. And it fell out that she became as madly in love with the Ragusan as he was with her, but she knew well enough that the excessive caution used by her husband would never suffer them to take their pleasure one with another as they both desired, and likewise that Tobia would not be able to abide long with them. And to him it seemed a fault of nature that a young woman of such marvellous beauty should have been joined in matrimony with such a poltroon, and should be forced to remain there as the ensign of his target; * so he determined to use the best wit he possessed to carry her off with him, and thus at the same time to satisfy himself, to work an especial pleasure to Lella, and to take away from Tonto all occasion for the plague of jealousy in the future.

Therefore he and the young woman began to talk over divers plans, and after they had sought diligently through many of these—although certain of them seemed to promise all they could wish in the way of caution—they considered, nevertheless, that if at any time Tonto should search for his wife without finding her, he would assuredly make a mighty uproar and bellowing over the affair, and with the aid of his friends and of the numerous admirers of his wife would strain himself to the utmost to get her back. Wherefore Tobia hit upon a plan of carrying her off which was merrily conceived and pleasant enough, albeit somewhat strange and hazardous—one, moreover, which would ensure their safety in the many misadventures they might encounter. Thus, when the young woman had been fully instructed by him as to the plan he had formed, and when he had heard how the ship was only waiting for himself to go on board to set sail, he called the host and said to him: "My good

* Orig., *come segno al bersaglio*. The meaning seems to be that Lella was, as it were, the sign of the inn and the lure for customers.

Tonto, because you have given me so much honour and such kindly reception since I have been in your house, it seems to me that I may well confide in you, and make use of any assistance you may be disposed to lend me in a certain matter—concerning which you shall duly hear—which I am about to undertake for a friend of mine, and, in sooth, I hold you to be my friend likewise. The fact is, that I intend to depart to-morrow in God's name, for my ship is now all cleared for sailing. But there is hidden in the house of a certain citizen of this place a young boy of Venice,* whom I am determined to carry away with me eastward, so as not to let him fall again into the hands of the people who had him in charge. Now, because for many days past he has been tormented by continuous fever, he is so enfeebled in body that it would not be possible to carry him off without injury, except on a beast with a saddle. Wherefore it came into my mind that, if he should pay you somewhat more than your due, you might take him away upon your sumpter-mare this very night, disguised as a woman, and with his face veiled in such fashion that, when he shall pass through Bari, where he is well known, no one may be able to recognize him. In this wise we might convey him as far as Monopoli, and then on the following day you could make your way homewards, having gained a good round sum for yourself, and done me an especial favour. Nevertheless, I do not forget to caution you that you speak not a single word concerning this business to any living person, not even to your wife, who, albeit for a young woman she is very discreet indeed, is still a woman, and women are not over-reticent by nature. Indeed, rather than be lacking in something to chatter about, they will often speak concerning others more than they know; and furthermore, if it should happen that some privy matter be confided to them, and they be enjoined never to repeat the same, it will be as if there had seized upon them a sort of furious humour which will not pass from them until the secret be dis-

* In the text there is a passage, *il quale per non avendo in terra niente a soi maestri*, which is here omitted as incomprehensible.

closed, however great the scandal which may ensue therefrom. Wherefore see that you bear yourself warily, and leave to me all consideration of the service you will have to perform."

Tonto, giving ear to this well-devised fable, and perceiving that he would be able to serve his friend without any grave trouble to himself, and pocket a handsome profit at the same time, made answer that he was quite ready to discharge any duty which might be required of him, and that Tobia, need stand in no fear that he would let his wife know aught of the matter, for the reason that he was never wont to talk to her of anything save what might concern the kitchen. After Tobia had made divers other pleasant speeches, and paid him liberally, and given certain little presents to the wife and to the servant, as is always the custom with merchants before they take their departure, Tonto directed his wife to withdraw to her mother's house, and there abide until he should return, and gave the servant full charge of the business of the house. This done, they went to rest; but Tobia, who was in little humour for sleep, called Tonto about midnight and bade him get ready his mare, because he was minded to depart forthwith; whereupon the host got up quickly and prepared the beast for the road, and then returned to the house to lock the door on his wife. Having given the key to the servant, he directed the fellow to do everything which he had commanded, and after he had said farewell, he went to the spot where Tobia was, and said to him, "What have we to do now?" Tobia, who in the meantime had mounted his horse, answered, "You will find your way out of the city gates, taking your mare with you, and I will go and get the young lad mounted on my horse's crupper. When we meet outside the gate, we will duly set him on your mare." Then said Tonto, "So be it, in God's name!" and then he took his way towards the city gates.

Tobia, after he had taken a short turn round that quarter of the town, went back to the inn, and there he found the servant whom the host had left in charge sitting chilled and sleepy before a very poor fire, whereupon he told the varlet that he had left behind a certain wallet of his at the head of the bed. Then the servant although he could with difficulty utter a word, because he was very sleepy, made answer that he could go and fetch it if he list. On this Tobia ran upstairs, and, by the help of a certain small tool which he had brought with him, he silently opened the door of Madonna Lella's chamber, and quickly made her disguise herself by putting on some garments especially provided for the occasion. Then, having drawn a hood over her hair, and arranged her garb in such wise that no man in the world would have recognized her, he led her out of the house and made her mount on the crupper behind him, and took her away to the spot where Tonto was awaiting his coming with anxiety. They both of them set about getting her upon the mare's back, and bolstered her up well on the seat, she feigning the while to be in such sad case that she could scarcely hold herself upright on the pack-saddle, and with such cunning trickery as this they set forth on their journey.

As they were passing through Bari it chanced that Tonto was asked by certain idle fellows who were standing about what his name was, and whither he was taking the woman; whereupon he, who was of a somewhat gamesome humour, and besides this wishful to serve his friend with all loyalty, made answer: "This is my wife, and I am taking her that she may earn somewhat by catching gallants at Taranto." * And with many other merry quips such as these he passed the time all the way, jesting in this fashion with all who would know what he was about. When they came to Monopoli they found the ship with the cables drawn up and ready to bear away, for the crew were only waiting till the

* Orig., *egli e mia moglie che la porto a guadagnare a lo panaile de Taranto.* The edition of 1483 gives "*alo panayle de taranto,*" and *l' edizione della gatta* "*paniale,*" which is probably a local word formed from *pania, birdlime*, and which in a way carries out the sense of what has gone before as Tonto had already used his wife as a lure at home, and the same idea of the decoy bird may have possessed him now. "*Panaile*" is a word not to be found, and Settembrini treats the passage as incomprehensible.

Ragusan should arrive. Then the merchant duly satisfied Tonto, who, after he had returned innumerable words of gratitude for all this liberality and courtesy, was fain to help his wife on board the ship in kind and friendly wise, even as he had brought her down to the seashore. When they had taken their last farewells with divers merry words the ship set sail, and Tonto, deeming that he had made a good profit, mounted his mare in jocund mood and rode back to his home by the same road which he had lately traversed on foot.

But when he reached his home, and found that his wife was no longer there, having chosen a new lord and a new country at the same time, he became vastly cunning, albeit it was now too late, and guessing how the mischance must have come to pass, and feeling that he could do naught to remedy the same, he bewept the loss of his wife bitterly for many days. Later on, however, he married again, and made a solemn vow that, as long as he lived, he would never again give lodging to a Ragusan. And thus, while he safeguarded himself from a second disaster, Tobia and Lella lived a merry life after their elopement.

MASUCCIO

WE may judge aright the ingenuity of the Ragusan by considering the nature of the trick which he put upon the good host, which in sooth was astute and strange and astonishing. Nevertheless, for the reason that he was at the time hotly inflamed with love, we must reserve a good part of our praises for Love himself, who, as his workings daily prove to us, has power not merely over human intelligences, but likewise extends his sway over the wild and untamed beasts. The yoke of love would indeed be most easy and pleasant if it were not that he is wont to mingle with his sweet delights the most bitter wormwood, in such wise that sometimes the joys which ill-starred lovers have taken together have been brought to an end by a double and most cruel death, as I am about to show you clearly in the next novel.

THE END OF THE THIRTY-FOURTH NOVEL

Novel the Thirty-fifth

ARGUMENT

EUGENIA, BEING WITH CHILD BY A CERTAIN KNIGHT, FEARS THE WRATH OF HER BROTHERS, AND FEIGNS TO FALL SICK AND DIE OF THE PLAGUE. HER LOVER TAKES HER DISGUISED AS A YOUTH INTO LOMBARDY, WHERE, BEING ATTACKED BY THEIR FOES, THE LOVER IS SLAIN, AND THE LADY KILLS HERSELF ON HIS CORPSE.

TO THE EMINENT MESSER FRANCISCO BANDINI, A NOBLE FLORENTINE *

EXORDIUM

AN onerous burden is this, most worthy Messer Francisco, which you have laid upon my weak shoulders, in that you have with no little kindness made me a sharer of your elegant gifts of scholarship from the first day of our acquaintance. And although I do not see that I possess any means or power of discharging this debt, either in whole or in part, nevertheless, so as to forbid my name to be written in the book of the ungrateful, I have, in searching through my slender hoard, put my hand upon a new sort of coin, without stamp, and compounded of base metal, and having turned this same to account in my present great emergency, I send it to you in exchange for your own most perfect money. If any profit should come to you therefrom accept it as at least an earnest of my exceeding great obligations towards you. Farewell.

* In the later editions this novel is dedicated to Messer Francesco Tomacello.

THE NARRATIVE

NOT long ago there lived in the framed and warlike city of Perugia a noble and stout-hearted knight-at-arms, comely in person, very worthy and gallant, who was called Virginio de Baglioni. He had for a long time nursed a hapless love for a winsome and very beautiful damsel of noble family named Eugenia, and she from day to day showed herself more and more cruel towards him. At last it happened that Virginio bore himself surpassingly well in a famous jousting match, in which he carried off all the honours from divers men of approved valour, and thereby broke and shivered in pieces the hard resistance which had hitherto possessed the cold heart of his beloved Eugenia, so that she not only gave herself likewise over to love, but took him into such high favour that this passion of hers outdid a thousandfold Virginio's old love and new love taken together. And when she let him know this thing with gladsome tokens and in discreet wise, that same thing happened to them which is often wont to happen to those who find their desires leading to a common end. Because she was yet a young girl, she was kept under very sharp watch by her brothers; but in spite of this she contrived, by her foresight and craft, to let her lover enjoy the first fruit of her virginity, to the great delight of both of them, and many a time they took their pleasure together without being ever blown upon by the blasts of evil fortune.

And because the accidents and the caprices of adverse fate are so great and so horrible—as those wretched ones who from the highest bliss have been cast down into the abyss of misery can bear witness—it happened, just at that time when the plague broke out in Perugia, that the ill-starred Eugenia found herself with child by Virginio, and although at first she had made trial of divers arts to keep herself from becoming pregnant, and afterwards to rid herself of her trouble, not one of these was of any avail, and on this account the two lovers were fain to make an end of their lives. But that thing which tortured most bitterly the mind of the young girl was the necessity which lay upon her of flying from the plague in the company of her brothers to some spot where she would miss the care of old women experienced in such matters, who would know how to take charge of her and to restore her to health, and thus deliver her from the death she deserved—what though she rated death as little more than nothing, and dreaded only to die without a sight of her lover. When she perceived that her brothers had determined to quit the city forthwith, it occurred to her that, by the aid of her own wit and contrivance, she might take security against danger and death as well, and having told this same project to Virginio on the evening before the day when her brothers were minded to depart for the country, she feigned on the morning following to be stricken in the groin with the mark of the contagious disease. Whereupon, when they heard of this, her brothers straightway believed it to be true, fearing amain for themselves, and, being terrified in such wise that it seemed to each one as if he were himself wounded to death by this dreadful dart, they quickly fled from the city. They left behind them an old servant of the house, to whom they gave orders to attend to the needs of their sister, whether she lived or whether she died.

Eugenia perceived that her plan was faring prosperously, and after she had made trial of the old man left in charge of her by many and varied schemes and novel plans, she at last suceeded in bribing him by the means of money, to do and to say whatever her needs might demand; and having sent for her Virginio, who came to her straightway by stealth, they discussed with no little satisfaction the measures which they had already taken, and those which were still to be considered in order to bring the affair to a speedy issue, forasmuch as they feared not a little that the feigned attack of the plague might become a reality. So the old man let spread a report that Eugenia, whom her brothers had left sick behind them, was dead; and next, having compounded out of rags a thing shaped so that it might have been taken for a human body, he buried the same in a church hard by, with a very small following and scanty light, for the reason that the nature of the disease did not admit of any great ceremony. Then Virginio, after he had disguised his ladylove as the page of a man-at-arms, took her to Città di Castello, whither he had sent forward his horses and attendants, and there, when her time was come, she was brought to bed of a fair male child. But, by the will of hostile Fortune, who had begun already to threaten them with every evil augury, their new-found joy after a few days was changed into the deepest grief through the death of their little son. Nevertheless they prudently composed their sorrow, and, as Virginio had already determined to enter the service of the Venetians, and had equipped himself excellently well with everything that was needful therefor, he mounted on horseback in company of his new page and went towards Lombardy, taking his train with him. By this time he had determined in his mind that, as long as he lived, he would keep Eugenia with him in a page's habit. When they had made their way out of Tuscany, and had passed through Romagna, now faring well and now ill, they arrived one evening at nightfall near Brescia; and, as Heaven and their cruel fate had already determined, it happened that, as the two ill-starred lovers were going on their way in gay humour, deeming they were by this time beyond all danger, they met the captain of a troop who was riding from the camp of the Signory, to join the army of the Duke of Milan. As soon as this fellow saw how well furnished was the man-at-arms before him with horses and weapons and attendants, and with baggage of all sorts, he determined to despoil him; whereupon he gave orders to his people to fall upon the stranger, and they, without waiting for any further command, went readily to work, knocking over now one servant and now another. After they had seized the horses and the baggage, and plundered everything they could find, they marked what a very fair youth the page was, and how a rose in May was not more lovely; wherefore they did not cause him to dismount like the rest, but seized his horse by the rein and made as if they would take him into their troop. The unfortunate Virginio, who, almost dead with grief, had hitherto borne up against this calamity, and had more than once resolved to resist by force their attack so that he might be rid of his life along with his goods, although his striving single-handed against such numbers must needs have been in vain, deemed that if only the lady should be left to him the loss of all the rest would be as nothing. When, however, he saw that she was being separated from him, he, who was strong and lusty and now nerved with fresh courage through grief and love, made up his mind once for all to die like a brave knight. Although he had for accoutrements naught but his gauntlets and thigh-pieces and flankers, he took his sword in hand, and threw himself boldly into the midst of his assailants, and dealing a death-blow to the man who held the bridle of the lady's horse, and wounding divers others both in breast and back, he seemed like a fierce lion fallen upon a herd of cowardly cattle. But the leader of the company, who looked on these doings with no small disquiet, was filled with anger thereanent, and, foaming with rage at seeing one man thus put so many to the rout, he gave charge to two of his most trusty varlets to kill him at once. Whereupon they, each taking a spear, went forthwith behind him, and after striking him several times wounded him to death. The spear of one of them, driven by the impetus of the horse, pierced his back and came out more than a palm's breadth from his breast. His horse was killed by the other, whereupon he fell to the earth mortally wounded.

Eugenia, weeping and overcome with grief at the sight of him who loved her so fervently lying lifeless, resolved forthwith to die likewise, no less to carry out all that was due to their reciprocal love and to her own self, than to prevent her dainty person, in which her Virginio had taken such great delight, from ever being placed at the disposition of another man. Thus, without wavering at all in her resolution, she threw herself violently from her horse; and making as if she wished to embrace her lord, weeping the while, she seized the opportunity, before anyone could stay her, to throw her own soft white breast upon the point of the lance which stood out from the body of her hapless lover; and, letting herself fall in this wise, there was naught in the nature of things to prevent the projecting point of the weapon from piercing her delicate body. Thus embracing her lover, who was not yet dead, and clasping him close, she said: "Alas, my sweetest love! here is the wretched woman for whose sake a cruel and violent death has, against all justice, been dealt out to you: here is she who now comes of her own free will and without fear to be the sharer of your last calamity, in order that she, your own Eugenia, may never be put under the rule of another: here is she who, with her dying breath, beseeches you, by that love which possessed us equally while we lived, which our spirits will eternally give and take in that other world, that you will, at the same instant with myself, let your spirit wing its flight; so that, joined and bound together in this wise, our souls may in that dark kingdom bear true witness of our lasting and inseparable love both in life and in death." Then, with these and with many other pitiful words, they tenderly embraced one another and breathed their last at the same moment, their wretched bodies lying where they died without burial, and their bare bones giving to posterity a manifest sign of the bloody death they died.

MASUCCIO

WE may justly call Dame Fortune variable and inconstant, without saying any new thing, when we bear in mind all the histories there are, some prosperous, some ill-fated, some told, and some yet to tell; and the misfortunes just narrated of the love-stricken Perugians cannot of a surety be read or listened to without the deepest pity. But now, leaving these to the compassion of such as may themselves be victims to love, and following the plan I have laid down, I will now let you hear of a very strange and gamesome adventure, or rather a somewhat troublesome mischance, which befell two men who were mightily intimate one with the other—an adventure which is all the more notable inasmuch as these two, what though they were rough, uncultivated fellows, knew how to make the best of the business without hurt to their friendship, or to the peace of their houses.

THE END OF THE THIRTY-FIFTH NOVEL.

Novel the Thirty-sixth

ARGUMENT

Two men, neighbours and close friends, by a strange and complicated accident have carnal knowledge of one another's wives. When they both learn the nature of the thing they have done, they agree to have in common their wives and all their other goods, in order that their friendship may not be disturbed, and thus they pass their lives pleasantly in peace and quiet.

TO THE MAGNIFICENT MESSER UGOLOTTO FACINO, THE HIGHLY-HONOURED ORATOR OF THE MOST ILLUSTRIOUS DUKE OF FERRARA

EXORDIUM

IF, when grieving over my evil Fortune, most worthy Messer Ugolotto, I could find any remedy for my present needs, I should without ceasing make complaint to her for her treatment of me, because when I consider in my mind the vast number of honours, the many and sincere proofs of kindness I have received at your hands, most righteous sir, I can discover in myself no power which will enable me to do you any service, great or small, by way of recompense. Nevertheless, pressed as I am by this necessity, I must needs make use of the tasteless herbs which spring from my ill-cultivated garden, out of which I have compounded the medley salad I now send to you, river of eloquence as you are. And I furthermore beg you that you will deign to taste the same without expecting from me any more sumptuous fare; so that, should there remain on your palate any pleasant flavour from the taste thereof, you may, wherever you may happen to be at the moment, recall the memory of your Masuccio. Farewell.

THE NARRATIVE

AT no great distance from this neighbourhood of ours there is situated a certain spot, one little known and less visited, which, though it is for the most part inhabited by people of gross and lumpish nature, numbered but a short time ago amongst its dwellers two young men, the one a miller called Augustino, and the other a cobbler Petruccio by name. Now betwixt these men, from their youth up, there had been knit together as great a friendliness and comradeship as ever existed between the truest friends. Likewise these two had each one of them married a wife, young and very comely, and between the women there was in like manner so great and constant familiarity and intimacy that they were rarely or ever to be seen the one without the other. Wherefore, passing their lives thus in a state of perfect friendship, it chanced one day that the cobbler, although his own wife was very fair to look upon, found the wife of his friend something more to his taste—longing peradventure for a change of pasturage. It chanced that on a certain occasion an opportunity more favourable than usual of getting speech with her was granted to him; so in becoming manner he made known to her his passion and what he desired as well. As soon as Caterina, for so the miller's wife was named, understood the meaning of this request, she put on a little air of disdain and answered nothing thereto, although in sooth it was but little displeasing to her. But the first time she chanced to meet with Salvaggia, the wife of the cobbler, she let her know what amorous propositions Petruccio her husband had been making; whereupon Salvaggia, the cobbler's leavings, as it were, although mightily disturbed in temper at the story she heard, nevertheless kept her anger within bounds, and hit upon a plan by which she might at the same time have vengeance upon her husband and keep intact the great friendship subsisting between herself and Caterina; so, after having made answer to her dear friend in many grateful words, she begged her to give a promise to Petruccio her husband that she would, on some particular night, wait for him to come to her in her bed, and that, in change for herself, she should let be in the bed the rascal's own wife. Then they would assuredly find great sport and pleasure in what would follow. The miller's wife, being very anxious to humour her friend, agreed to do what she asked; and the result was that in the course of a few days Petruccio, finding himself alone with Caterina, preferred to her the same request as before, using stronger persuasion than he had used on the former occasion. After listening to him, and giving him many and various denials (which forsooth seemed to have but little heart in them), she showed herself ready to do his will, so that the trick which had been planned might be duly brought to an issue. Then, having had a discussion with him as to the when, the where, and the how, the young woman said, "In sooth I can find no time fitting for such an affair save when my husband may happen to be busied some night over his work at the mill. Then I could very well let you come to me while I am abed." To this speech Petruccio made answer in very joyful wise, "I come just now from the mill, where there is so large a quantity of grain that two-thirds of the night will assuredly be spent in the grinding of the same." Hearing this, Caterina said, "So be it, in God's name. Come, then, between the second and the third hour of the night,* when I shall be awaiting you, and will leave open the door, as I am accustomed to leave it for my husband. Then, without saying a word of any sort, you must straightway get into bed. Tell me, however, by what means you will keep clear of your wife, for I fear her more than I fear death." To this Petruccio made answer, "I have already hatched a plan as to how I may borrow the ass of my good gossip the arch-priest, and will tell my wife that I am minded to go away into

* Between seven and eight in the evening.

the country." Then said she, "In sooth this plan of yours pleases me greatly."

As soon as they had made an end of their colloquy, Petruccio betook himself to the mill to get due assurance that his comrade had his hands full of business, and in the meantime Caterina gave to her friend full intelligence as to the plan which had been arranged. Petruccio, when he had ascertained that the miller was at work in the mill according to his wont, went back to his house, and making believe that he was vastly busied over his affairs, told his wife that he had a mind to go forthwith to Policastro in order to buy some leather for the workshop. The wife, who knew well enough whither he was really bound, said to him, "Go at once then;" but laughing to herself she said, "this time, forsooth, you will find you have bought leather of your own, instead of skin belonging to another man." Petruccio having made a show of departure, hid himself in a certain spot in the village, and there tarried, waiting till the expected hour should come. Caterina, as soon as the night had fallen, went to the house of Salvaggia, and, according to the plan settled between them, took up her abode there for the night; while Salvaggia went to Caterina's house, and having duly got into bed, waited with no little satisfaction the coming of her husband to that amorous battle which he so keenly desired, saying to herself many times that, after the business should be finished, she herself would have something to say.

Petruccio, when it seemed to him that the time was ripe, went with gentle steps towards his neighbour's house; but, just as he went about to enter therein, he saw that the miller was coming back home—the reason for his return being that the mill, for some cause which he could not determine, had broken down in such wise that during the present night no work whatever could be done. On account of this Petruccio was stricken with fear, and, mightily ill content with this accident, stole back to his own house without having been seen or heard by anybody, saying to himself the while that, though the business had miscarried this time, it should be duly despatched the next attempt. But because there yet remained to be spent a good part of this night which had proved so unlucky to him, he began at first softly and then aloud to knock at the door, and to call out to his wife to open it and let him in. Caterina, perceiving who it was by the voice, not only refused to open to him, but furthermore, without answering a word, kept herself as quiet as a mouse, so as not to let him get wind of the plot that had been laid for him. Petruccio, being mightily perturbed at this, plied the door so vigorously that at last he gained entry thereby, and, having gone in, went straight to the bed; and then, becoming aware of the presence of the woman, who was pretending to be fast asleep, he shook her by the arm and awakened her. Believing all the while she was his wife, he compounded a fresh story to account for the fact that his journey had been abandoned, and, having taken off his clothes, he lay down beside her. And seeing that he had already prepared himself for action, he set himself now to consider whether, after he had been frustrated in his plan of tilling his neighbour's vineyard, he might not as well do a stroke of work in his own. Wherefore, deeming that of a surety he had fast hold of his Salvaggia, he took Caterina in his arms and gave her a valorous proof of his powers, which the poor woman bore with due show of pleasure and patience in order to make him believe that she was in sooth his wife.

In the meantime the miller, who had gone back wearily and with lagging steps to his house, and had laid himself down in bed in order to get some sleep, lay quite immovable without uttering a word. Salvaggia, being well assured that it was her husband who was with her, gave him a gladsome reception, keeping quite silent the while; and, after she had waited for some time without finding the lover in the way of giving any sign that he was disposed for the battle, began to handle him amorously in order that she might not be mocked and befooled in the business she had undertaken. The miller, believing that he was abed with his wife, although he felt more need of a good night's rest than any desire for skirmishing of this sort, when he felt her lustful bitings and dallyings was stirred to get to work, and duly set going the mill which was not his own. Now when it appeared to the cobbler's neglected wife that the time had come for her to let forth the angry words she had prepared, she broke the silence and took him to task in these words: "Ah! deceitful rogue, disloyal dog that you are! Who was it you deemed you were holding in your arms, the wife of your best friend, in whose field you thought this night to spend your labour, for the sake of friendship, peradventure? Here indeed you have gone to work with far more spirit than is your wont, proving yourself to be a man of mettle, while at home you are ever short of breath. But, God be thanked, this time you have missed the prize you dreamt of, and all the same I will take good care that you smart for your sins." And with discourse like this, and with words still more injurious, she importuned him and demanded his answer.

The poor miller, although he was as one dumb-stricken when he learned the conditions of affairs, understood nevertheless clearly enough, as soon as he caught the meaning of her words, that the woman abed with him was no other than the wife of his good friend. However, divining exactly how the matter had come to pass, the pleasure which he had felt heretofore was quickly turned into sorrow; but, by dint of resolutely keeping silence, he withdrew himself from her side, and, for the reason that it was not daylight, he made his way with all speed to the spot where he deemed for certain he would find his own wife. Having arrived there and called for his friend, bidding him come down on account of a pressing matter, Petruccio went forth, albeit mightily distrustful, and him the miller at once addressed in these terms: "Good brother of mine, it comes from your fault alone that we both of us have suffered injury, and have been put to shame, and have met with a mishap of a sort which renders it more seemly on our part to keep silence than to speak, while there is assuredly no need to bring about a quarrel over the same."

Then, with no small chagrin, the miller set forth the whole story in due order to his friend, giving him full description as to how everything had happened; adding, as his own judgment thereanent, that as Fortune had shown herself propitious to the cunning and malice of their wives, she had likewise shown no disposition to vent her spite upon themselves by letting happen anything which might bring to naught, or even lessen, their friendship, which had lasted so many years. He further went on to say that the mishap which had just befallen them through trickery might, through the rectification of the late lamentable error, be made to serve the common agreement and pleasure of all four of them, and that, as in times past they had possessed all their goods in common, so in the future they should likewise enjoy the possession of one another's wives. Petruccio, perceiving what was the wise determination of his good friend, and remembering that he himself had already taken his pleasure with the woman who was his special fancy, and that the whole affair was in a way to find an issue in goodwill and charity, came to the conclusion that it would be vastly more profitable to him to keep his friend, whom he might well have lost on account of this slip of his, than the mere esteem of the world (which as may be seen in this our time, sells itself as if it were a thing of little worth, or even barters itself away like goods of the basest sort). Wherefore, putting on a pleasant face, he affirmed that he was fully content with the plan which the miller had already formed in his mind for their common convenience and for the lasting peace and quiet of both their houses.

And thus, having called to Caterina and bidden her not to go away, they made it known to her that she was not the only one who had been tricked, and gave her directions to go and summon Salvaggia forthwith. And when they were once more all come together, they let it be clearly known what had been the consequence of the attempted fraud, and how great would prove to be the boon of peace and quiet agreed upon and established between them all by the happy alliance just concluded, which thing seemed to all present to be most excellent for many and divers reasons. Thus, from this time forward, neither in the matter of their wives, nor in the matter of their goods of any kind whatsoever, was any distinction recognized between the two friends, and the agreement was carried out in such manner that the only parents the children knew for their very own were their mothers.

MASUCCIO

WITHOUT doubt there will be found some to hold up to derision the bargain concluded between these two friends in the fashion which I have just described—men who set greater store on their friendship than on their common honour. Nevertheless, I suspect that in the sight of those who may come after us (if Heaven should not in the meantime work vast changes), this aforesaid honour, which to-day is held in high esteem and lauded by virtuous folk alone, will come to such a pass that, overwhelmed with universal contempt, it will not only be held as a thing of no account, but will even be chased to the uttermost parts of the earth into a perpetual exile. However, this is an affair which I will leave to posterity, merely saying that if two other noble companions, concerning whom I am minded to write, had, while commending their loves to a certain gentle maiden, taken as an example the compact made between these two clownish country fellows, there would have not ensued such grievous strife, nor would so many people have died thereby, which things you shall hear of in the story I will now gladly relate to you.

THE END OF THE THIRTY-SIXTH NOVEL.

Novel the Thirty-seventh

ARGUMENT

MARCHETTO AND LANZILAO, COMPANION KNIGHTS, BECOME ENAMOURED OF THE SAME LADY. THEY ENGAGE IN A COMBAT AND BOTH MEET THEIR DEATHS THEREFROM; WHEREUPON THE LADY, BY REASON OF THE GRIEF SHE SUFFERS, DIES OF HER OWN WILL. THERE IS UNIVERSAL MOURNING OVER THEIR FATE, AND ALL THREE ARE BURIED IN ONE GRAVE.

TO MY MOST COMELY ARIETE *

EXORDIUM

A PRISONER as I am in the bonds of our true friendship, my most comely Ariete, I desire to recall that friendship to mind as a thing untainted in these days when we are severed the one from the other, and to send to you, as to an especial friend, this novel; so that from reading the same, what though the event thereof be bitter and bloody, you in your spring of life may understand how great is the force of love, and how undisciplined and unbounded as well; and thus, when you shall have come to maturer years, you may know how to guard yourself as best you may, and with all prudence, against any such distressing accidents.

* In the later editions this novel is dedicated to Messer Francesco Tomacello.

we are forced by the Fates that one should follow the other in yielding to love; and this should be all the more acceptable to us, for in such measure as one may have knowledge of the woes of the other, so in the same degree will he be able to condole with him in his sorrow. Nevertheless, I will not refrain from telling you that, if your lady excels mine in beauty, one may with truth affirm that she stands alone in this our age." Lanzilao, pleased mightily, answered, "To-morrow, when you shall see both of them, you shall give your judgment."

When the next day was come, and the sports once more set in order, the two friends were amongst the others who went merrily to see them, and all the people gave them great honour and kindly reception. There they soon espied their beloved in company of some other ladies, whereupon each one of them began to jest afresh, and Marchetto, having taken his friend by the arm in seemly fashion, pointed to her whom Lanzilao was about to single out at the same moment. As soon as Lanzilao saw her, and realized that Love had inflamed them in like manner with the self-same brand, his passionate heart was touched with the greatest sorrow and unrest; and, almost in tears, he said to his friend: "My Marchetto, this is she about whom I spake to you in such ardent wise, and if indeed you have at any time been minded to do me a pleasure, I beseech you now to hold off from this attempt. Admitting that victory may be doubtful for each one of us, yet meseems I am almost sure of winning her, because I have discovered the fervent love which she bears to me alone." Marchetto somewhat wrathfully made answer: "I cannot persuade myself, remembering how great has been the mutual love between us, that you can even think of making this dishonourable claim upon me, for you know how I told you yesterday that this lady, together with my heart, had robbed me of my liberty, and of a surety there is naught else to be said than that it is vain for you to love her unto death, unless you desire at the same time the death of your dear friend and brother and comrade. And what though I doubt not she may love you, still you may be well assured that she, having seen me

bear myself so valiantly, has let her fancy turn towards me in such wise that she loves and ever will love me more than her own self. And the end will show these words to be true."

Lanzilao, who had listened with little pleasure, answered, with his mind mightily perturbed at these last words: "If you deem that you have won her favour on account of your prowess, I surely cannot have lost it on this ground; for I, as you knew then, having jousted as valiantly as you yourself, was willing, out of courtesy, to let the prize rest with you, seeing that this honour was for us both. But be assured that I, for the reason that I was in better mettle than you, could have better borne the fatigue, and must have won the victory. This was plain to every man present, and indeed to every woman as well." Marchetto, now waxing hot over the affair, answered: "If you say that I won the prize because of your courtesy, you say what is not true; forasmuch as I, having jousted vastly better than you or any of the others, won it by my merit. Would to God that you had not withdrawn, so that I might have added you to the tale of those—more numerous than your own—whom I have already laid low." Lanzilao, now foaming with rage, cried out, "Wrangling in words seems to me a coward's trick; and, as I have settled with myself what I mean to do, I tell you once more that you must either give over the love of this lady, or our friendship. If you are still set on seeking her love, we will take our swords in hand and will give proof with all our strength which of us two loves her the most, or shall be best beloved of her." Then said Marchetto, "I looked for no other answer from you; wherefore hold yourself in readines, for I will very speedily let you know in what wise and in what place we may have our meeting." Then, having withdrawn himself with the greatest fury, he made known to many men-at-arms what had come about, and likewise the cause thereof, and his companion having done the like, in a short time all Arimino was full of the story; and, although the lord of the city and divers of the condottieri and men-at-arms sought with diligence to make peace between them, the temper of the

lovers was so hotly angered that, each having challenged the other to combat, they got themselves in order to fight a duel to the death on horseback the following morning outside the city.

The father of the young lady—to whom news of the affair had already been brought—when he saw how comely and valorous and rich they both were, made up his mind to give his daughter in marriage, together with a good portion of his wealth, to whomsoever of the two might be the conqueror, and he moreover made known this resolve of his to the two lovers in the presence of divers ladies and gentlemen and of his daughter also. This news in itself was acceptable to them, and furthermore pricked each one on to do his best. Wherefore they both agreed thereto. Ipolita, holding them equally dear, as I have already stated, now saw that she could not look for the love and the victory of the one except death should be the portion of the other; so she awaited with intolerable torment the issue of the fight. The next morning each one of them, accompanied by divers men of mark, well mounted, and armed in fitting fashion for the arduous work to be done, took the field, not indeed merely to go a journey, and then there was given by a certain number of trumpet blasts, the signal for the beginning of the fierce duel, and for the keeping silent of all who stood around, under heavy penalty. When the final blast of battle had been blown, each champion, full of high courage, let go his horse for the encounter. Marchetto, standing up in his stirrups, smote his adversary through the vizor of his helmet in such fashion that a splinter of the broken lance, with the iron point thereof, stuck within, and going clean through his head hurled him dead to the ground. But Lanzilao, who had kept low his point, so as to first kill the horse and then without difficulty to overcome the dismounted rider by blows of his mace, wounded the steed of Marchetto in the breast in such wise that, like a bull smitten by the axe, it fell to the ground after raging now here, now there. And as poor Marchetto's ill fortune would have it, his sword came out of its scabbard while the horse was thus plunging about, and stuck with its hilt in the ground and its point towards the horse's shoulder; and now in Marchetto's fall an unheard-of thing came to pass, for the point of the sword meeting the breastplate of his cuirass, and he in the impetus of his fall lighting heavily thereupon, it pierced his wretched body up the hilt, and he too died without a word.

The spectators forthwith ran some to one and some to the other, and having drawn them from under their horses, and stripped off their armour, found both of them, as it has been said, dead already; whereupon everyone, weeping and crying aloud, began to pour forth lamentations to God and to fate on account of this cruel and ruthless calamity. Ipolita meantime was standing with some other ladies watching from the city walls, and would gladly have brought back from death either one of her lovers at the cost of her own life. When she heard how they were both dead, stricken by grief in her heart, she forthwith determined that she would linger on earth no longer, and being set with great courage to let this thing quickly ensue, she cried: "Alas, Ipolita! how unhappy and wretched is your life, and to what a horrible pass has your evil lot brought you! On your account alone has this dreadful day dawned; you were the cause of this savage combat, of the death of these two gentlemen, and of the disruption of this long-lasting friendship and brotherhood. Alas for you, ill-starred lovers! broken now is the tie between your noble selves, vanished are all your virtues and deeds of prowess, and by the coming of bitter death are quenched your comeliness and all your gracious ways, even before there could be vouchsafed to you a single embrace by her who was your sole passion, and by whom, with all reason and justice you were equally beloved. Cursed be the hour when I was born, and cursed be that beauty of mine which won such high praise from you both, seeing that it was fated to be the cause of your death. I, afflicted and grief-stricken as I am, doubt not that your lovelorn souls are now wandering solitary through this our hemisphere awaiting my own, which, going in company with yours towards another world, must bear true witness as to which one of you is dearest to me. I forsooth will quickly send it thither for the satisfying of so pious and seemly a wish."

Having thus spoken she seized the moment when the other ladies could not bar her way, and let herself fall head foremost from the top of the wall where she was standing, and as soon as she came to the ground she broke her neck and likewise shattered nearly every one of her delicate limbs. When this most cruel news was spread abroad the people all ran together, and when they found the gentle damsel a corpse and perceived the cause of her death, each heart was pierced with fresh grief and each one lamented with bitter tears over this cruel mischance. As soon as the bloody news was carried to her aged father, who because she was his only daughter gave to her alone all his love, he felt himself stricken with abiding sorrow. How many and how profound were the tears and the lamentations of the great lords and of the other nobles and of the people, of the citizens of the state and of strangers as well, it would be long to tell. Nevertheless, according to the will of the Signor Malatesta, the two bodies of the ill-starred lovers, with that of the damsel between them, were buried in a noble marble tomb upon which the occasion of their deaths was written in an inscription to their memory.

MASUCCIO

BITTER and cruel is the record of the fate of these lovers, perishing in such barbarous wise; forasmuch as in their life it was not granted to them to taste either the flower or the leaf or the fruit of love. Still I am fain to believe that their spirits as they took their flight found some comfort in the knowledge that their bodies would ever lie side by side. But although we must needs feel the greatest compassion for all three of them, I, being bound to pass on to some new pleasantry, will leave the lamenting of them to others; and, remembering only the name of Marchetto, feel myself led on to write down the most diverting history of a certain other Marco, a fisherman, who himself conveyed in his boat a noble gentleman to have enjoyment of his own wife, and to tell of all the merry doings which ensued therefrom.

THE END OF THE THIRTY-SEVENTH NOVEL.

Novel the Thirty-eighth

ARGUMENT

ANTONIO MORO IS ENAMOURED OF THE WIFE OF A MARINER, AND BY MEANS OF A TRICK INDUCES THE HUSBAND HIMSELF TO TAKE HIM TO HAVE A MERRY TIME WITH THE WIFE. NEXT, HAVING BROUGHT HER ON BOARD A BARK, ANTONIO LETS THE HUSBAND HAVE HIS PLEASURE WITH HER, WITHOUT KNOWING WHO SHE MAY BE. THE HUSBAND AFTERWARDS PAYS FOR A FEAST; BUT THE THING HAVING BECOME PUBLICLY KNOWN, HE LEAVES THE PLACE THROUGH SHAME; WHEREUPON ANTONIO AND THE WIFE LEAD A PLEASANT LIFE TOGETHER WITHOUT CONCEALMENT.

TO THE MAGNIFICENT AND VERY EXCELLENT MESSER ZORZI CONTARINO, COUNT OF ZAFFO

EXORDIUM

MY most noble Messer Zorzi, forasmuch as Heaven and our adverse fate have forbidden us to taste for our common advantage the sweet fruits of our kindly and most delightful friendship—a pleasure which, methinks, was desired in equal degree by each one of us—I have resolved in a measure to repair this loss, and the method I shall use will be the sending to you of this very laughable story of mine. When you shall read the same in the easy and delightsome life of your most pleasant city, you may perchance find something therein to call to your memory your own Masuccio, and the unbroken friendship subsisting between us. Furthermore, if some transcript of this story should survive, your name will be held in remembrance by those who come after, albeit your rare qualities deserve a much higher reward.

THE NARRATIVE

IN the wondrous and most powerful city of Venice there lived a short time ago a gentleman of ancient and noble family, young, of good bearing, and of a merry humour, who was called by name Antonio Moro. Now he, while he abode here in the Kingdom,* held me in especial friendship, and, amongst our many other pleasant discourses, he told me the following story as something which in truth befell himself—a story which I propose to write down for your sake and in remembrance of your city, and to let it join the company of the rest I have written.

I will tell you, then, that this Antonio was one day taking his diversion with a certain good friend of his in a boat, as is your custom in Venice, and when the two were crossing from one canal to the other Antonio espied a fair and lovely young woman, the wife of a Sclavonian fisherman who was named Marco de Cursola, a fellow who many a time had gone as a sailor on board a great ship which had ploughed divers seas with Antonio for captain. Now the cavalier, being mightily pleased with her, resolved not to waste time over the business, and straightway sent an old woman, practised in such matters, and on friendly terms with Marco's wife, to have speech with her. And for the reason that the message was no less pleasing to her than had been the sender thereof when she had beheld him the day before, she answered, so as not to keep the messenger long in suspense, that she on her part was ready to do as Signor Antonio willed, but that it seemed to her it would be almost impossible to carry their purpose into effect, because her husband never let her pass a night alone; neither could she receive the cavalier in her house by day, because the neighbourhood was so thick with people that not even a bird could fly past unseen. Antonio, when he learned the bent of the young woman's wishes, deemed that the

* Orig., *nel Reame*, an expression commonly used for the kingdom of Naples.

difficulty of the task before him was greatly lessened, and at once set to work by means of a cunning trick to compass what was yet to be done. Having let the young woman be fully advised of all he was minded to do, he caused Marco to be called before him one day when he thought the time was ripe, and, after speaking him soft in his usual way, he besought him to bring his boat in the evening and take him to a certain spot where would be waiting a charming lady who had promised him the boon of her love.

Marco, who was very anxious to do Signor Antonio a favour, replied forthwith that he was ready to do the service required, and having thus settled matters he went his way. When it was night Marco cautiously locked the door on his wife and went to Antonio's house, and, as it was now time to start, they went on board the boat; and Marco, using his oar in the fashion of Venice rowed the cavalier as he had been directed to the canal beside which the old woman dwelt; indeed, the other side of her lodging looked upon another canal in which was situated Marco's hired house. Anyone wishing to go from the one to the other by water would have perforce to make a long course by going the round; whereas, taking the way by land through the old woman's house, and certain others the owners of which he had bribed, Antonio woud be able to go thither easily and speedily. So when they had come to the place, he said, "My good Marco, wait for me here. I will be back in a short time." Then he entered the house of the old woman, and she, who was on the look-out for him, welcomed him gladly, and pointed out the way she had prepared for him. In a few minutes he came to the young woman's door, and this, albeit it was strongly barred, he soon opened with certain instruments handy for the purpose which he had with him. As soon as he found himself with the young woman, who had been awaiting him in high glee they enjoyed together the full and delicious ending of their amorous desires.

When they had made all plans necessary for their future diversion, Antonio returned to the boat by the same path, and there he found Marco asleep and quite unsuspicious. As soon as the fellow had roused himself and had taken on board Signor Antonio, he turned the boat's prow homewards, and inquired whether Signor Antonio had fared as well as he desired. "Indeed I have fared mightily well," Antonio replied, "and I tell you, my good Marco, that I cannot call to mind the time when I have had so pleasant a bout with a lady; for, besides being young and fair, she was so vastly kind and gracious to me that I know not how I managed to tear myself away from her." Then said Marco: "I doubt not that you had a merry time in getting into port, and while I was waiting I stepped the mast more than once, although I did not spread the sail; for when I figured to myself the pleasure which my good signor was taking with his lady, I felt awaking within me my lustful appetite in such wise that I was within an ace of setting to work with my oar and going with all speed to take a taste of my own wife. Certes I would have done this had you not told me you were coming back; for had you returned and found me gone, nothing short of a great scandal could have been the consequence."

Antonio ,when he listened to these words—what though he was now out of danger—felt no small disquiet at the peril which he had so narrowly escaped, and at once began to consider some other method more diverting even than the one just described, by which he might provide against any such untoward accident in the future. So he said, with a laugh: "My good Marco, I knew not that you had a wife; otherwise I should have bade you go to her, and to come back to the appointed place in the course of an hour." Marco answered: "Did you not know that I only a short time ago took to wife a young and very comely girl?" Then said Antonio: "Indeed I knew it not; but wives, however fair they may be, must be reckoned as part of the regular furniture of the house, something to serve our pleasant uses whenever we may stand in need of the same; wherefore we must always be on the search if we should be fain for some fresh morsel. However, as the thing has thus come to pass this time, we must let it be as it is; but to-morrow evening I hope to bring away with me my ladylove in the boat, as well as a certain companion of hers no less fair and gracious, who will of a surety prove a dainty treat for you." Marco, when he heard this, replied, mightily pleased thereanent, that he would not fail to greet the lady as a man of mettle should.

When Antonio was come to his own house, Marco left him there and went back to his lodging, and, having taken his wife in his arms, he did not forget to make up to her in full measure whatever her gallant had failed to give her through the haste and uncertainty of their foregathering. The next morning Antonio, after he had let the young woman have full intelligence of what he was minded to do in the evening, sent for Marco at the accustomed hour. Marco meantime had tricked out his boat with carpets and draperies of serge, making therewith an enclosed space at the prow in the shape of a tent. They embarked and set forth, and Antonio, having left Marco at the same spot and told him that he would be back in a trice with the ladies he had spoken of, went to the young woman's door, which he opened in his accustomed manner; and then, when he came into her presence, he spake to her of the danger they had lately incurred, telling her at the same time how he intended to guard against such peril in the future by the precautions of which he had already sent her word. Then, when she had attired herself in a silken garment which Antonio had given her the day before, and veiled her face in such wise that her husband could not possibly have known her, she went with Antonio towards the boat.

Marco, when he saw there was only one lady with his employer, asked where was she who had been promised to him; whereupon Antonio answered that, for certain good reasons, she had not been able to come, adding: "Nevertheless, I do not think of letting you come short to-night; for this one whom I have here will be enough and to spare for both of us, and so you will get your guerdon. When I shall have taken all I want there will still be left more than is needful for you; and, although I do not know your wife, I will be sworn this woman is no less fair and young and dainty than she." Then said

Marco: "I can believe that; but meseems it is not meet that I should in any wise lay hands on what is yours." Antonio answered: "I do not look at it thus. If it had not been my pleasure I should have not made offer of her to you, nor would you have presumed to take her; Wherefore get yourself in trim to do what I shall require of you; and for this boon I will ask you for nothing in return except the price of a fish dinner which I am minded to give to certain friends of mine next Saturday." But Marco was still loth to accept the invitation, albeit Antonio pressed him urgently thereto; but at last they agreed, and Marco promised to give the dinner as a payment for the use of what was his own already.

Then Marco having put out with the boat took up Signor Antonio's lute and began to strum a new tune thereon; and Antonio, having gone with the young woman into the tent, the two together performed to the sweet sound of the music many graceful measures in Trevisan fashion; and when they had taken their fill thereof, Antonio called Marco and said to him in a whisper, "Now take your turn with this pretty prize of ours; but, for the love you bear me, see that you attempt not to find out who she is, for she is of very honourable family, and it was with the greatest difficulty that I persuaded her to come here, even though I told her you were our Doge's nephew." Marco answered, "This matter is the last to trouble me, seeing that I shall not be called upon to marry her." Having thus spoken he went to her in high glee, finding her perfumed with all delicate odours, and taking heed of naught else, or of the fact that she received him with mighty little satisfaction, he did his work in real Sclavonian fashion; and when he had rejoined Messer Antonio, he said, "I could not see her face, but as for the rest of her it seemed to me as if I must of a surety be with my own wife, for the flesh and the breath of both are exactly the same; in sooth I am now inclined to give you, not only that dinner of fish, but everything I can call my own." Then Antonio, hugely diverted thereanent, conveyed the young woman back to the place from which he had taken her, and the pair laughed so heartily at having made a cuckold of Marco, fool as he was,* that they found it hard work to stand upright. When they had settled between them all that was needful for their future enjoyment, Antonio went back to Marco, who was awaiting in a merry mood, and as soon as he had been conveyed to his house he let the boatman return to his wife, who, when he came in, feigned to be mightily disturbed at his long absence, nor was he able to appease her all that night.

On the very next Saturday Marco let prepare a fine dinner of fish in Antonio's house, and, as the last-named did not wish to play such a joke without companions to witness the same, he bade come certain of his friends, and having told them of the cheat, they all made merry over the dinner which had been prepared at Marco's expense. Then in the course of the feast they began to bandy divers jests, now speaking one by one and now all together, and they threw at poor Marco so many plain-spoken quips that he must certes have comprehended the meaning of the same even had he been one of the wooden-headed sort. And albeit this thing greatly displeased Antonio, who tried by signs and words to make them hold their peace, their merry humour was so greatly tickled by the comical nature of this jest that not even the Doge himself would have been able to impose silence upon them. Then Antonio, remarking that Marco was beginning to be incensed against his wife, having gathered the full meaning of the jests cast at him, forthwith sent a message to her warning her to withdraw from her house. And when Marco returned home and found her gone, he, overwhelmed with grief, went to live at Cursola, and the young woman, remaining with Antonio her lover, made good use of the springtide of her life.

* Orig., *che aveano Marco de montone fatto becco retornare.*

OF a surety the wiles and the subtle devices so quickly put in practice by lovers are very wonderful and of such a nature that, in my opinion, neither the precautions nor the sharpest watch kept by jealous husbands will ever avail to guard against them. And, if such be the case, meseems that everyone will have perforce to submit his wares to the favour of fortune; failing this, in taking a wife a man must needs bear in mind that proverb which clownish country doctors use when they sell their prescriptions one to another, and, taking them out of their sleeves at hazard, say to their patients, "God grant it may do you good, otherwise the grain must go to the grinding." But now, leaving the world as I find it, I will show you in the next place what great unhappiness love and fate together brought upon two poor young lovers.

THE END OF THE THIRTY-EIGHTH NOVEL.

Novel the Thirty-ninth

ARGUMENT

SUSANNA LOVES JOANNI, AND FOR A SHORT TIME THEY ARE HAPPY TOGETHER. JOANNI IS CAPTURED BY MOORS, WHEREUPON THE LADY DISGUISED IN MALE ATTIRE GOES TO TUNIS, AND SELLS HERSELF IN ORDER TO RANSOM HER LOVER. HAVING RESCUED HIM, THEY FLY TOGETHER, BUT BY THE WORKING OF EVIL FORTUNE THEY ARE DRIVEN BACK INTO BARBARY AND ONCE MORE CAPTURED. JOANNI IS HANGED, AND SUSANNA HAVING BEEN RECOGNIZED TO BE A WOMAN SLAYS HERSELF.

TO THE MOST ILLUSTRIOUS THE INFANTA DONNA BEATRICE OF ARAGON *

EXORDIUM

IF there still abides amongst women of delicate nurture and prudent carriage aught of pity for the ill fortune and the terrible accidents which befall others, I will not hold back from telling to thee, most illustrious Infanta, who art so rare an example of all the virtues to other maidens, of the most piteous fate which overtook two ill-starred lovers, who, after wandering for a little space and with no great enjoyment in the kingdom of love, both perished—the one being overborne by a violent and cruel death, and the other having raised her hand against herself, desired to keep fellowship with her lover even in death. Read this story, therefore, O most lovely offspring of a royal race!

* Daughter of Ferdinand I. She married Mathias Corvinus, King of Hungary, and after his death in 1490, Ladislas, his successor, but this last marriage was annulled. She died in 1508.

in that gentle mind with which high-souled ladies are ever wont to receive the trifles which their hearty good servants offer to them; and, as you go on to read the same, I beg that you will let your pity go out to those who deserve it. Farewell.

THE NARRATIVE

ACCORDING to the account given to me by a noteworthy citizen of Gaeta, there lived in that city, shortly before the death of King Lanzilao, a goodly youth named Joanni da Piombino, who, albeit he was endowed with many virtues, remained still in the condition of a poor man through the assaults of adverse fortune. Nevertheless, being mightily expert in all matters appertaining to seafaring, as well as in the ways of traffic, he was employed by divers merchants, who were fain to place their affairs in his hands and to send him, now with one ship and now with another, into many and various regions, some anear and some afar. Now this man, although his fortunes were humble, had a mind set on the gentle life; wherefore he spent without grudge or reserve the whole of the little gain which came to him as the fruit of all his labour and trouble in acquiring politeness and making him of a seemly presence, for which reason and also on account of his praiseworthy carriage he won perforce the good will of all men.

Thus it happened that a young damsel of noble parentage, and very beautiful withal, became most ardently enamoured of this Joanni; and she, not being minded to confide in anyone for a long time, endured this passion of hers with no little pain. But at last, by certain means which love pointed out to her, she let Joanni know that he alone was master of her heart. Whereupon Joanni, being a prudent youth, took counsel with himself how he might as quickly as possible give satisfaction both to the damsel and to himself, deeming that it was, in spite of his many misadventures, most fortunate in that he had won the love of such a lady. With so great caution did both of them act that they found means of coming together, albeit such a thing might well seem impossible, and they did not fail to give to one another the complete and delightful satisfaction of their desires. Although they abode but a brief time in this felicity, they managed their meetings with such great care that no one ever got inkling of their hidden love; and though, on account of their discretion, meeting was rarely forbidden them for any long space of time, nevertheless, either because of the excessive love between them, or because of some sinister foreboding, it happened that, whenever they parted, the one would water the face and the breast of the other with scalding tears.

On a certain day it came to pass that poor Joanni found himself obliged by his employers to convey certain merchandize in a vessel to Genoa—a thing which was little to the taste of the lady and still less to his own. So having bidden her a last farewell, he set out on his voyage; and, as they were passing not far from Ponza, the ship, being at the time becalmed, was attacked and captured by some Moorish galleys. The Moors, having carried off all the goods they could lay hands on, together with the prisoners, sank the ship and returned with their booty to Barbary, where the luckless Joanni was sold as a slave to a merchant of Tunis.

This terrible and bitter news was borne in time to Gaeta, and then how profound was the inward grief and the secret tears of the wretched young girl, only those women who have suffered from affliction as cruel as hers will be able to judge. Indeed, her sorrow smote her in a fashion so sharp and so intolerable that she would have deemed it a very trifling thing to have taken her life with her own hand; but at other times, when her grief had been somewhat assuaged, it would come into her mind that, if by the help of fortune Joanni should in the course of time be ransomed; or should by some other working of chance make his way back to Gaeta, and find her no longer living, her grief in the other world would be doubled, and she herself would be the undoubted cause of her lover's death. So by this faint hope she was held back from taking her own life; and, having been let know by the letters which came to the merchant that her Joanni yet lived, albeit a captive in Tunis, she would, had she not been held back by dread of her family, have gone thither straightway of her own free will, and, without spending further thought over the business, not merely to see him but also to treat for his ransom seeing that she had not heard that anyone else was taking thought to secure his release. And while she abode thus possessed with this one desire, it came to pass that a contagious and most malignant fever broke out in the house where she dwelt, and attacked her own family in such wise that in a very brief time all the chief members thereof were dead of the malady and only she herself and a few little children left alive.

On this account, when she found that she was wellnigh alone in the world, and free also, she determined to carry out the project she had already formed; so, having disguised herself as a man and packed up in a couple of wallets certain little things of her own and two hundred golden florins, she went to Naples, where she found a Venetian ship bound for Tunis with a cargo of fruit. She engaged herself with the captain of this vessel as a servant, calling herself Raimo Ranco instead of Susanna. After she had landed in Tunis, she became in the course of a few days on very intimate terms with certain merchants of Genoa, having taken good heed meanwhile to keep secret her identity, and by various indirect ways she made inquiries about her Joanni. Thus she found out where and in what fashion he was living, and moreover she had sight of him in his miserable estate as he went about the city, laden with chains, and plying the calling of a porter. Although she was overborne with grief and pity when she beheld him, still she felt that in finding him alive and well she had found what was more acceptable to her than aught else in the world. When they had recognized one another in due and discreet manner, and had narrated all the adventures which had severally befallen them, shedding many bitter tears the while, Joanni, albeit he was overjoyed that his Susanna should thus have come to him, and proved thereby that her love for him outdid all other love, was nevertheless assailed by a proud and righteous feeling of unrest, and felt no doubt at all that if the man she served should come to know her real condition he would want to use her as something else than a ship's servant. For this reason, and for divers others to boot, he besought her in tender wise that she would do as he wished, and return to Gaeta forthwith, assuring her that by God's help, and by his own foresight, together with the assistance he expected from his friends, there would soon be provided for him means of escape.

Susanna, when she had told him of the money she had with her, bade him be of good cheer, for she hoped soon to set him at liberty herself; and, as they could not now hold longer parley together, they parted, having settled between themselves in cautious wise as to how they should proceed with the project they had undertaken. Wherefore the damsel, so as not to lose any time, agreed through the negotiation of a Genoese merchant, one of the friends she had recently made, with the master of Joanni to ransom him for the sum of sixty doubloons; and when she went on board the ship to fetch her money, which she had hitherto kept for the sake of security in the cabin of her master the captain of the ship, she discovered that she had been robbed of her money, her baggage, and every other thing she possessed by a runaway sailor. Whereupon she, being grief-smitten almost to death, came near to cast herself into the sea, but after a little she began to consider that, failing herself, there was no one else who would do aught on her lover's behalf; so, as she was now alike bereft of all worldly goods and of hope as well, she finally determined, in that she loved him most fervently, to sell her own person into slavery and to redeem her Joanni with the profit she might gather thereby. Having gone back to the Genoese merchant, she told him with great lamentation and grief of this fresh mishap which had befallen her, and at the same time let him know what was the desperate project she was firmly set to carry out, putting together divers feigned stories to serve as a pretext to explain why she was stirred to practise such unheard-of liberality and affection towards this friend whom she had found in captivity. Then, after having debated the business again and again, she caused herself to be sold by the agency of the merchant aforesaid to the king's treasurer for the sum of sixty doubloons, and the merchant, having received this money, made use of the same in benevolent fashion by purchasing freedom for Joanni.

When he was set at liberty, and was let know in what manner and for what reason the young woman had sold herself—when he learned, over and beyond this, where and in what condition she now was—his grief, bitter and unprecedented already, became doubly sharp and altogether intolerable; and, knowing quite well that no amount of treasure, however great, would avail to redeem her from the king's house, he, urged on by love and gratitude, and by the sense of loss of so dear an object, determined, even though he should suffer death a hundredfold, to endure it all rather than to leave his Susanna in slavery. And although he was sufficiently acquainted with all the landing-places and seacoasts of Tunis, nevertheless, knowing the country to be in very barbarous condition and every place vigilantly guarded, he could think of no means by which his design might possibly be brought to a successful issue. Nevertheless, like a man desperate and wishful for death, he agreed with certain other Christian captives, and they, working together by means unheard of before and seemingly impossible, contrived to store a bark with all things they required, and having fled with Susanna to a place some distance from Tunis, where they had left the vessel they had prepared, they quickly embarked therein; and, the sea and the wind being both favourable, they directed their course towards Sicily. Having fared prosperously through the night and the greater part of the next day, and having come to a spot only a few miles distant from Trapani, they found they were forced by their evil fortune to fight another severe and even mortal battle; for, after they had been cruelly stricken by the bursting of a whirlwind, they were violently driven hither and thither by the sea and the rough tramontano; so that, without being able to bring into play any skill in seamanship, they were driven back to the Mauritanian shores which they had lately left, and cast upon a sea-beach not far from Tunis. Thereupon, being recognized as fugitive Christians, they were seized and bound securely and conveyed back to the city.

When the circumstances of their flight and the fact that the slave had been carried off from the king's household became known, Joanni was forthwith hanged as a thief; and her master, having got Susanna once more into his keeping, determined to have her beaten naked with rods, as is their use with runaway slaves. But when she was stripped naked it was at once manifest that she was a woman, and the master, considering what had recently come to pass in connection with what he now saw before him, was mightily amazed, and after he had several times made inquiry of her in vain as to her condition, without desiring to give offence either to her honour or to her person, he led her before the king, who made privately a more strict examination of her, and induced her to tell him fully who she was, and who was this lover of hers who was now dead, and why she had come to Tunis to ransom him and had then taken to flight; whereupon she told him everything that had happened since the beginning of their love, shedding a flood of tears the while. And when she had told her story, to which the king gave ear with no little wonder, she resolved that she would of her own free will and with high courage go join her lover in death, while she stood in such illustrious presence. Thus, having snatched a knife from the belt of a certain Moor, she smote herself in the breast therewith, and in the presence of the king, and of the other Moors and Christians as well, she fell dead at the king's feet still calling upon the name of her Joanni.

MASUCCIO

WE cannot, certes, look upon the numerous and horrible misfortunes, with which these wretched lovers were afflicted, without feeling the deepest compassion; nevertheless it seems to me that now the time has come when it is meet for us to shake off the remembrance of such great misery, and weep no more in this the fourth part of our book. In this last merry tale I will tell of a Catalonian trick which was put upon a poor jealous fellow, one in which my judgment outdoes in jocosity all those which have been told hitherto.

THE END OF THE THIRTY-NINTH NOVEL.

Novel the Fortieth

ARGUMENT

Genefra, a Catalan, becomes enamoured of a certain woman, and because of the slender wit of her jealous husband he carries out his purpose. By a very cunning trick he induces the husband to bring his wife on board ship in exchange for some other person, and then he takes her away into Catalonia. The husband finds out too late what has been done, and is left to mourn the roguery of Catalonian tricksters.

TO THE EXCELLENT SIGNOR JOANNI DE SANSEVERINO, COUNT OF TURSI *

EXORDIUM

MOST excellent and worthy lord, seeing that you have given me many and valid reasons why I ought to dedicate to you my special love and service, I feel constrained to proffer, with the best ability I possess, some small gift. This offering is a little basket poorly filled with certain writings of mine, unelaborated and just as they were set down—things which, meseems, will not be of much service to your present needs, but may, in the course of time, do duty as a lasting memorial of your most illustrious name, together with your other rare parts.

* He was one of the adherents to the conspiracy of the barons.

THE NARRATIVE

DURING the time when there was much shrewd fighting between Naples and the adjacent towns, it was the custom of the merchants of all nations to congregate in Salerno more than in any other part of the kingdom; and a very rich Catalan, named Pietro Genefra, having gone thither amongst the others, he carried on a mighty traffic both by sea and land, as is the custom of such folk. This man, being young and of an amorous temper, became acquainted with divers of our gentlefolk, and in time it came to pass that he fell hotly in love with a very beautiful young woman named Andriana, the wife of an Amalfitan silversmith, who, either on account of the exceeding beauty of his wife, or merely because he was an Amalfitan—people who are by nature mean-spirited when it chances that jealousy of its own accord strikes root—had of late become fiercely jealous of Andriana, although she had given him no cause therefor. Genefra knew well the suspicious humours of this man; and although the young woman had shown herself kindly disposed towards him, he, understanding what vigilant guard men of this temper are wont to keep, deemed that he must needs sail through these seas under contrary winds. Wherefore, having scraped acquaintanceship with the husband, who was named Cosmo, he employed him to execute divers trifling tasks in his handicraft, paying him overmuch for the same; and, besides this, he would very often give him certain Catalonian delicacies; whereupon the silversmith made a great ado over having won such a friend.

In the course of time the intimacy between them waxed so close that Cosmo, prompted either by affection or by doubt, besought his friend to be gossip, although his wife was not with child—a favour which Genefra joyfully granted; for it seemed to him that the husband himself, together with his own good fortune, had set to work to open for him the closely-barred way through which he might now walk with good show of reason. Then, with seeming of faith and with a kiss, he gave him that sort of left-handed pledge which triflers are wont to use; whereupon Cosmo believed that the spiritual covenant between them was firmly ratified. This matter was in itself a reason why he should often at his own charges, set good cheer before his dear gossip. Therefore it happened in the course of a few days that the Catalan, having got his foot into the house, pushed his whole body therein after such a fashion that what followed fell out exactly to his liking. And although Cosmo was warned by some of our Salernitans—fellows who are little bent on minding their own business—that he should take good heed how he dealt with Catalans, he nevertheless, full of confidence in his good gossip and in his own foresight, made mock of all that the others said to him, and let the two lovers take their pleasure without any interference on his part.

In course of time it happened that Genefra was obliged to return to Catalonia on business of grave importance, and when he had made all his dispositions for the journey, he proposed, if Andriana should be consenting, to carry her off with him by a humorous trick—and somewhat dangerous also—in the ship which was about to sail from the port. He made clear to her his plan; whereupon she, a young woman of a roving mind and much enamoured of Genefra, needed but little persuasion, and, without taking farther thought of the matter, answered that she was quite ready to go away with him and to do his bidding in all things. Wherefore Genefra, having called to him his dear gossip, spake thus: "When I remember how great is the friendship between us, I cannot hold myself back from letting you know of all my needs, great and small alike. Would to God that I had spent with you and you only the time and the money which I have wasted with certain gentlemen of this place, but I hope that before long all my misadventures may be set right. What I would discuss with you, my gossip, is this. I, by the help of a gentleman, concerning whom I will speak to you later, have had great enjoyment with the wife of a certain seafaring man of this place, and, to tell the truth, I am become madly enamoured of her, no less on account of the undivided love she bears me than on account of her exceeding great beauty. And because, as you well know, I am forced by the will of God to go hence to-morrow evening, my heart will in no way suffer me to leave her here to become the spoil of others, more especially as she herself has told me without any disguise how a certain gentleman, a very dear friend of mine, has many times challenged her to an amorous bout with himself. For this reason I have determined in any case to take her away with me in the ship; and she being fully content with what I propose, I mean to try to carry out my design in such manner that I may not be interdicted from returning hither. And because the husband must needs be kept out of the house until the time when the ship will be ready to weigh anchor, I beg you that you will ask him, late to-morrow evening, to take you—paying him very liberally for his services—in his boat on board my ship, so that you and he may keep me company until the last hour of my tarrying. In the meantime I will send Galzarano, my servant, in such wise as I have already agreed with the wife, to bring her out to the ship, clad in male attire, in his boat. So we will go, the whole party of us, on board the ship, and afterwards you can return with Galzarano. I do not wish that all this service of yours should go unrewarded, for I intend on my return that your wife and my dear gossip shall be made glad by the present of a gown of the finest stuff which I will give her."

Cosmo, when he heard spoken these words so well composed and set in order, not only gave full credence to the same, but even began, before Genefra had come to the end of his lengthy discourse, thus to chide the behaviour of the gallants who had busied themselves over his affairs: "May you bring this matter, and even more untoward ones, to a good issue; for in sooth it is to me a marvel that these men have not plundered you, and done some injury to your person. I know too well what is the result of traffic with such as these, and I warn you how some of them, jealous and ill at ease on account of our friendship, have, under show of doing me a kindness, told me a thousand tales of your ill doings and have even cast suspicion on my wife on account of our spiritual brotherhood; but I, who was not minded to lose my time, let them go on talking their trash. Now, to come back to the matter in hand, I am quite ready to serve you; for this mariner you speak of is a great friend of mine, and I will take him with me to the appointed place and in the manner you require; and, besides this, because we shall be all together, he will suspect, neither you nor me; nay, he will be firmly convinced that his wife must have eloped with someone else, for as much as she is in truth vain and light-minded in temper." After this discourse, each of the two, being content with what had been settled, went his way.

The following evening, when the ship had weighed anchor and when Genefra had let Andriana know all that had been done, the Catalan summoned his gossip when the hour had come and said, "Let us now go into your house, so that I may take leave of your wife, my gossip, and then we will go and carry out our scheme." Thereupon Cosmo took his friend by the hand with great delight, and went into the house; and, after a light meal and much pleasant talk, Genefra according to his promise handed over to Andriana twenty-five ducats, and took of her a pretended last farewell. Then Cosmo, turning to his wife, said, "Now embrace our dear gossip and give him a loving kiss, seeing that by God's mercy he leaves us without having let my honour suffer in the least through his conversation, for all that certain evil-minded folk have affirmed the contrary." Whereupon the two, who found it hard work to keep back their laughter, embraced one another; and, having said farewell, Genefra took his leave, and went with Cosmo to the shore. They found the man with his boat all ready, as Cosmo had arranged in the morning, and bade him await the coming of two servants with certain baggage, and then began to walk up and down on the beach. In the meantime Galzarano had gone with all speed to Cosmo's house; whereupon Andriana, having put on male attire, and wrapped herself in a mantle with a couple of wallets on her back, went forth to deceive the man who was planning all the while to put a cheat upon his own comrade, and came to the landing-place. Then, as soon as all were on board, they dipped their oars in the water and rowed towards the ship.

Andriana, who had been slightly moved to pity at the sight of her husband speeding her on her way, all innocent of what he did, felt a little compassion for him, as is the way with young and tender women, and began to weep silently and to rail at Fortune, who had thus led her husband to such an untoward fate. On this account Cosmo, who was standing beside her, whispered, "Ah, you pretty rogue! who makes you weep? Perchance you grieve at the sight here of your husband whom you are leaving; and if this be so, you astonish me mightily, seeing that you are going to better your lot many a hundredfold. Let no doubts trouble you; for in lieu of being poor and ill-served, you will become the mistress of great riches. I well know how my good gossip loves you; wherefore be sure that he will make you the mistress of his person and of all his goods; for no men in all the world know so well as Catalans how to love and entertain fair ladies. And besides this, Fortune may be so kind to you as to let your husband die, and then of a surety my gossip will make you his wife." By heartening her in this fashion he banished at once the little regret that had possessed her light brain, and, in like manner as she had wept somewhat in thinking of these words and of him who spake them, so now, without making farther answer thereto, she began to laugh more lustily than she had ever laughed before.

By this time they had come to where the ship lay; and Genefra having embraced and kissed his dear gossip, went together with Andriana and his servant on board the ship, which had her sails set already, and forthwith they turned the prow seaward. Cosmo, as he went ashore with the boatman, was hugely diverted as he thought of the flout which had been put as he deemed upon his companion, and of what the fellow would say when he should return home and find there no wife to meet him. When they had come to land they set out for their several homes, each with mind at ease, and Cosmo, when he entered his house and found his wife was not there, was informed by divers manifest signs of the issue to which the affair had come; so, all too late, he began to bewail himself, and the wicked woman, and that false knave of a gossip, spending much time in lamenting his stupidity.

MASUCCIO

ALTHOUGH Trifone the innkeeper, being an Amalfitan, was ingeniously tricked by the gentleman of Salerno,* and treated as an outlander in that he had to pay a toll for that piece of merchandize which he had brought into our city for his own particular use, there is no doubt that the flout put upon our good Cosmo was a greater and a more lasting wrong, forasmuch as all the goods he possessed, and for which he had become a broker, and had as a merchant contracted for and warehoused, were, at one stroke, taken away from him; nay, he even had to pay the charges of the boatman who took his property off to the ship. Wherefore, things standing thus, meseems that Amalfitan folk have little cause to speak well of our city; but because Cosmo himself confessed that he had been warned of his danger by certain Salernitans, he ought to lay the blame upon himself rather than upon others. Nevertheless, I think some excuse should be found for the poor wight, seeing that in his time the ways of the Catalans were not so notorious as they now are in this kingdom of ours. Today, indeed, they are known and diligently examined in such a measure that, not only may everyone who is so minded have full cognizance of their ways, and be on his guard against them, but he may likewise put slight upon them to their shame and injury. Now I, having come to the end of my fourth part, will with God's pleasure set to work upon the next, which will be the last.

* See Novel XII.

HERE ENDS THE FOURTH PART.

PART THE FIFTH

Prologue

THE FOURTH PART OF THE NOVELLINO HAVING COME TO AN END, HERE BEGINS THE FIFTH AND LAST, WHICH WILL TREAT OF DIVERS NOTABLE DEEDS: THE HIGH MAGNIFICENCE OF GREAT PRINCES; AND OTHER ADVENTURES WHICH HAVE COME TO A HAPPY ISSUE.

MASUCCIO

HAVING now bidden farewell to that gloomy lake, filled full with other men's miseries, over which I have sailed in my ill-rigged boat, finding sighs for adverse winds and tears for heavy drops of rain, I am brought into port by my harsh and unjust Fortune, accompanied by the sad and unending train of homicides wrought by her. And, in sooth, if my pilot had not from time to time been heartened on by the breath of kindly Zephyr, no skill of seamanship would have availed to prevent the shipwreck which must needs have befallen me. However, now that I am brought hither by the favour of the Maker of us all, I have determined to leave tears, and lamentations, and the miseries springing from the workings of cruel Fortune, to those who are themselves sunk in misery; and in the fifth and last part of this Novellino—begun by me some long time ago and now wellnigh completed—I will tell any of the others. When these two entered the lists with the chosen number of competitors, so great and so valiant was their prowess that soon every one of the others left the lists, this one overthrown and that exhausted, and the two friends alone remained. Then they, not being minded to joust together, also went out, each one yielding to the other the victory. But, as it was discovered that Marchetto had broken a few more lances than Lanzilao, so was the prize and the honour awarded to the first-named, the one feeling no less pleasure and pride thereat than the other. And as they went to make merry at the palace of the Malatesta, it came to pass that during a dance the two friends fell in love with the same lady, a damsel very graceful and fair, and daughter of a noteworthy gentleman of the city; and each one, unobserved by the other, gazed at her in ardent worship. The damsel, who was called Ipolita, seeing how they were of the same age, and alike handsome and well-mannered, and how in divers other respects they were so equally matched that she, who was well advised in all this, knew not how to determine towards which of the two she should incline, found herself in such a state of uncertainty that she determined she should hold them both equally dear. Wherefore she would in secret favour now one and now the other, contenting them both with her kindness.

When the merrymaking had come to an end, to the great regret of the two knights, these two new lovers, taken and bound by the god against whose darts no foresight can give protection, went back to their lodging, and, having come there, Marchetto began to speak: "Brother, I came hither to win the prize, and now I have lost my liberty, forasmuch as I am so deeply enamoured of a damsel, whom for my woe I espied to-day at the festival, that I can find no rest whatever." Lanzilao, sighing no less ardently, replied: "Alas, O brother! I also have this day been bound in similar fetters by another maiden, the loveliest in the world." Then said Marchetto: "I marvel not at this, for the reason that we two, since we have known each other, have ever found our wishes jump together in all things; so now, meseems,

THE NARRATIVE

IN the days when that invincible and most illustrious lord, Francesco Sforza, not yet advanced to the dukedom of Milan,* ruled over the March of Ancona, he numbered amongst his picked company of men-at-arms a certain one named Marchetto da Faenza, and another called Lanzilao da Vercelli, both of them marvellously courageous and gallant young men, and as virtuous, graceful, and accomplished as anyone could wish to see. And because they had been brought up in one another's company there arose between them a friendship so great and lasting that, as is often the case between soldiers, they became brothers both in life and in death. For so perfect was their love, that not only did they have their arms, their horses, and all their possessions in common, but it even seemed to each as if he held the soul of his comrade bound up with his own. Thus, abiding for several years in this happy state, and finding their honour, their fame, and their worldly goods ever on the increase, their union was reared on so firm a foundation of love and affection that neither the desire for rank, nor the greed of gain, nor ambition of fame or glory, would ever have prevailed in any degree to mar such friendship and fraternity if adverse Fortune, the mistress of all our affairs, had not entered their hearts by means of the snares and subtle ways of love; for, by letting kindle in the breasts of both of them the self-same fire of passion, and by the working of some new and most deadly poison, she overcame and levelled with the ground every defence which had been set up against her assaults.

It happened that a truce was declared between the armies which were fighting round the city of Fano, and during this time the Signor Malatesta proclaimed a tournament in Arimino, to which many knights of various degrees betook themselves, and amongst them the two brothers, Marchetto and Lanzilao, followed by a larger train of horses and apparel and squires than came with

* He became Duke of Milan in 1450.

ten noteworthy tales of the extraordinary virtue and the high and mighty deeds wrought by certain great princes, and of other delightsome matters, some of which will be pity-moving adventures brought at last to a joyful ending; letting these follow in the company of the novels already told, we will give a last God-speed to the book, and a brief repose to this wearied hand of mine.

But before I go any farther—leaving prudent folk on one side because they need not my counsel—I say to others, to whom Nature has been niggard in her gifts, that they should keep themselves well on their guard against the new art and industry—or I should rather say against the brazen impudence—which lovesick dames have learned to use, being taught by their own wickedness. For these are not content to let their overweening passion be made known by tokens many and varied, and by novel advertisement, and to send messages to their lovers—not merely within the city, but from one kingdom to another—bidding them come in person to essay the amorous duel, and bearing themselves in a fashion like that of lustful young lovers, who are prone in their importunate humours to send word to their sweethearts. And because I am afeared that against such like dispositions of Heaven no human forethought can shelter us, I make offer and promise, before I write more, to all those who may be united to such women by marriage or by any other relationship, that if they will come to me, who am the unworthy secretary of my most serene lord, the Salernitan Prince, I will make to them a valid special grant—asking no payment therefor—by virtue of which they may, if they list, wear that crest which is only worn by right by the firstborn of the direct line of Sanseverino. Long live Love!

The general exordium of the fifth part being now ended, the details of the first Novel will begin, first the Argument, and then the Narrative.

Novel the Forty-first

ARGUMENT

Two cavaliers of France become enamoured of two Florentine sisters, but are forced to return home. One of the ladies, working judiciously by means of a false diamond, causes them both to return to Florence; whereupon they find enjoyment of their love, albeit in strange fashion.

TO THE MAGNIFICENT FRANCESCO GALIOTO *

EXORDIUM

My most noble Galioto, if the hard rocks were moved by the sweet music of Amphion, what wonder is it that your Masuccio should be constrained by the most dulcet harmony of your lyre to fashion with his unskilful hand the following novel and to dedicate it to you as the one who furnished the theme for the same? I implore you, therefore, that you will not refuse to correct it as you read; so that, if as I doubt not you may find therein any straying from the truth or any rusty phrases, you may amend these in loving wise as our ancient friendship demands. Farewell.

* He was one of the Angevin nobles who joined the revolt against Ferdinand I., and followed John of Anjou back to France. See note to Novel L.

THE NARRATIVE

I WILL tell you, therefore, that in those days when Duke Ranier of Anjou* envious of the peace and quiet, as well as of the power and the wisdom of that divine prince, King Don Alfonso, was driven from Naples and from the Kingdom, it pleased him to tarry for a certain season in Florence. There were, amongst the other Frenchmen who were involved in the ruin and shipwreck of his fortunes, two valiant and accomplished cavaliers, the one named Filippo de Lincurto and the other Ciarlo d'Amboia. Now these two, although they were very prudent and endowed with many virtues, were inclined nevertheless, being young and given over to love, to leave the burden of disaster, and the cares thereof as well, to him who was especially concerned with the same, that is, to the duke.

It happened that in their daily rides through Florence Filippo fell deeply in love with a graceful and very lovely young lady of noble parentage, and wife to a citizen of repute; and while he strove incessantly to win her, it chanced that Ciarlo, as he ranged another part of the city, became enamoured of a sister of Filippo's ladylove, who abode unmarried in her father's house. He, unwitting of this kinship, made up his mind, albeit he deemed her passing fair, to keep his passion within sober limits, forasmuch as he was well versed in the strife of love and aware that young damsels are wont to love lightly and without constancy. Filippo, finding that his fair lady was discreet and of good understanding, and being also fully prepared to become her servant, resolved to give her his love entirely; on which account the lady, realizing his humour and considering his many and praiseworthy parts, likewise determined to recompense him with all the love of her heart, and began to favour him with her kindness in such wise that he saw she was the only woman in the world who knew how to

* Alfonso, assisted by Filippo Maria Visconti, finally expelled René from Naples in June, 1442.

love. She, certes, would have let him taste at once the supreme fruit of love had she not been restrained therefrom by the continual presence of her husband; so, having given Filippo assurance, both by letter and by messages, that she was firmly set in this purpose, the two lovers longed beyond aught else for the time when the husband would take his departure to Flanders in the galley which was now expected at any hour to touch at Pisa.

While they thus abode in pleasurable expectation, Duke Ranier was obliged to return to France, whereat both the cavaliers felt mightily aggrieved, and especially that one of the two who loved and likewise was loved in return; nevertheless, being bound by necessity, they took their departure, snared as they were in amorous toils. Filippo swore to his lady that no obstacle, however great, should debar him from returning, and that, come what might, he as a loyal lover would never forsake her. Having consoled her with other speeches yet more affectionate, he and his companion set forth; and after his return it came to pass in the course of time, either through some fresh fancy or through the cares of business, that Filippo, albeit he still remembered the lady left behind, let the ardent flames of his passion grow colder every day. He not only forgot his promise to return, but beyond this neglected to answer any of the many letters writ to him by the lady. On this account she, perceiving how she was wellnigh forsaken by this lover once so ardent, was stricken with such cruel grief thereanent that she almost lost her wits; but, calling to mind the stainless virtue of the cavalier, she could not persuade herself that so noble a heart could harbour such inhumanity. However, when she remembered his latest words, both written and sent to her by the mouth of their trusted messenger, she deliberated how she might by a new and suggestive plan stimulate the virtue of her lover and thereby make a final trial on behalf of her passion. Thus she caused to be made by a skilled master a ring of gold, wrought very finely, and in this she had set a counterfeit diamond, most manifestly false, letting engrave round the ring itself the words,

"Lama sabachtani."* This, after she had wrapped it in fine cambric, she sent to her Filippo by a certain young man of Florence, who knew how things stood with her, and who was going to France after his own affairs, charging him that he should himself deliver it to Filippo with no farther words than these: "She who loves you and you only sends you this, and implores you to let her have a fitting answer thereto." In due time the envoy with his offering and his message arrived at Filippo's house and was joyfully received; but after the cavalier had marked with amazement what was the quality of the ring, and what the motto graven thereupon, he went about for several days pondering over the purport of the same, and finding himself unable to draw from it the true meaning, he determined to show it to Ciarlo and to divers other gentlemen of the court; but these, taken singularly and all together, what though they used all their wits, were unable to hit the mark. Finally its meaning was fathomed by Duke John,† who was a gentleman of great discretion, albeit more fortunate in advising others than in reaping victory in the many enterprises he undertook. What it said was this: "False diamond, why hast thou forsaken me?"

When Filippo heard this sentence he saw at once how the lady had most justly and prudently reproved him for his lover's unfaith, and began to consider how he might by a device of the same sort answer so graceful a proposition and repay so heavy a debt of love. So, being minded to conclude the matter, he went to his dear friend Ciarlo, beseeching him by the friendship there was between them, that he would go with him to Florence for the reason aforesaid. And albeit Ciarlo found this somewhat hard at first, he ended by consenting to oblige so dear a friend, deeming besides that he might peradventure thereby compass some pleasure for himself and for the damsel he loved. Thereupon they set forth, and having duly come to Florence, they began at the first chance

* St. Matthew, xxvii., 46.

† John of Anjou, Duke of Calabria, son of King René. His father ceded Lorraine to him in 1453, and it was to him that the Angevin nobles offered the crown of Naples on Alfonso's death in 1458.

to walk past the houses of their ladies in order to signify their presence; and Filippo soon sent word by his wonted messenger to his lady how he had sufficiently understood the message which the ring sent by her had borne, and how he knew no other method of disproving her false opinion of him save by bearing witness for himself, wherefore it behoved her to grant him an interview meet for the occasion.

The gracious lady, who with her sister had rejoiced amain over the return of their lovers, and had deliberated what course should be taken, as soon as she heard this kindly message, so manifestly springing from love, was filled with such joy that she felt almost jealous of herself, and so as to lose no more time over the matter she sent back a brief answer to Filippo, bidding him wait with his companion before the door of her house the next evening. Wherefore Filippo, as soon as the hour had come, betook himself merrily with his friend Ciarlo to the spot which had been named, and there they caught sight of the lady, who gave them most gladsome reception. After she had made a trusty maidservant of hers open to them the door and bring them in, she likewise gave them to understand, by the mouth of this same woman, that the only way in which the thing she so much desired could be brought about would be that, while she should be taking her pleasure with Filippo, Messer Ciarlo should go and strip naked and lie down in the bed beside her husband, in order that, if by chance the husband should wake and feel Ciarlo in bed, he might believe that his wife was still there. Unless he should consent to do this, they would all run great peril of their honour and of their lives as well; wherefore she besought them to put in practice the timely stratagem which she had provided, or else withdraw from the place forthwith.

As soon as Ciarlo heard this request, what though he would have gone down to hell to serve his comrade, he was conscious that, even if the business should come to a fortunate issue, it would be to him a great loss of good fame were he to be found there stark naked; wherefore he refused altogether to go on such service in such fashion, declaring, however, that if he might go clad and carrying his sword in his hand he would willingly do what they wanted. Now Filippo had travelled all the way from France to foregather with his ladylove, and, in considering the difficult pass to which they had come, he perceived that his friend was speaking and that the lady was acting with good show of reason; so, after many and divers arguments, for the reason that the lady remained firmly fixed in her purpose and that he himself was more than ever fired with amorous desire, he besought Ciarlo almost with tears that, by the bonds of friendship, he would consent to oblige them, what though the thing itself might be unseemly. Therefore Ciarlo, seeing how great was the passion which possessed his friend, and to what a pass the affair had come, determined that he would if need be meet death itself rather than be wanting in service to Filippo.

Thereupon the waiting-woman taking Ciarlo by the hand led him in the dark to the lady, and she, having given him kindly welcome, took him into her own chamber, and there bade him take off all his clothes and get into the bed, keeping his sword at hand. Then she softly bade him be of a good heart and have patience, for she would soon return and release him. This done she went full of joy to her Filippo, and having led him into another room they reaped the full and delightful fruit of their desire. Now when Ciarlo had waited, not two,* but four hours, he began to think that it was full time for the lady, or at least for his trusty comrade, to come and set him free; so, hearing no one coming, and perceiving that it was near daybreak, he said to himself, "If these others, all afire with love, feel no concern at having left me here to play a fool's part, it is now full time for me to take thought of myself and of my honour." Having softly got out of bed, him seeming that the lady's husband was asleep, he went with the sheet over his shoulders to try to escape, but was hugely annoyed at finding the chamber door securely locked outside; and, not knowing where the windows were, nor

* Orig., *Non che dove ore ma quattro aspettato.* The Salernitans use *dove* for *due*.

on what place they looked, he went back to the bed in a fury. He heard sounds which told him that the other occupant of the bed was awake and moving, and, though he was pricked both by fear and curiosity, he kept aloof and spake not a word. While he was thus troubled in mind he marked through the fissures of the windows that it was now broad day, and, fearing amain lest he should be espied by his bed-partner, he turned his back, and, gathering himself together and keeping his sword ready for his needs, he resolved to leave whatever might befall him to Fortune and kept still, mightily troubled in mind.

Before long he heard sounds of the fires being kindled throughout the house, and the hasty steps of the servants as they ran to fetch water; wherefore he determined at the last rather to die as beseemed a good cavalier than to be found there stark naked and making shift for a woman; so, having leapt out of bed with his drawn sword, he went to the door, and, as he was using all his force to open the same, he became aware how someone was unfastening it from without. He drew back somewhat, and then saw enter Filippo, laughing heartily and holding the lady by the hand. The two straightway began to embrace him in merry wise, albeit they saw he was bursting with rage. But when the lady perceived that he was all bemused, and unwitting where he was, she took him by the hand and said to him: "My good sir, by the sincere love I bear towards you, and also by that which you have towards certain others, I will assure myself that I may speak to you concerning a matter which intimacy such as ours will allow us to discuss. I know not whether Nature may have failed to bestow upon you French gentlemen that which she always gives to the lower animals. I mean to say that I know of no male beast, whether wild or tame, which, when under the sway of love, will not recognize the female by her odour. And you, forsooth, a wise and discreet gentleman, who have come hither all the way from France on account of love, can it be that your frozen nature is so sluggish that, when Fortune lets you spend the whole of a long night by the side of her for whom you have shown such great tokens of love, you failed to scent out who she was?" Then, having led him up to the bedside, she let him see and know clearly that it was her sister and no one else who had lain beside him during the night which was just passed.

When he perceived this thing the cavalier was not a little ashamed of himself, but finally all four laughed and joked so merrily that they could scarce stand upright on their feet; and because of the pass to which things had come, it seemed meet to all, that, for the setting right of the fault aforesaid, they should once more divide in pairs. Whereupon Ciarlo, having got into bed, plucked the fresh flower and the earliest fruit of the goodly garden which fell to his lot, and the two friends remained there, each taking delight with his own lady, until the husband came back from western parts.

MASUCCIO

IF we should give all deserving praise to the noteworthy device of the false diamond planned by the lady, we ought surely to find no less pleasure in hearing of the curious jest she put upon Ciarlo—the like of which was never played before—as well as of the travail of mind and the many anxious thoughts and fears which vexed him all that long night. But since this adventure came to a joyful issue, the only part of the same we need consider hereafter is that one which is concerned with the fate reserved for those women who are wont to importune men. And thus going on to deduce an argument from this theme, I will let follow next in order the story of a barbarous, cruel, and libidinous adventure of a certain Queen of Poland—an adventure which ended happily for all concerned therein except the queen aforesaid.

THE END OF THE FORTY-FIRST NOVEL.

Novel the Forty-second

ARGUMENT

THE QUEEN OF POLAND SENDS AWAY A SON OF HERS IN ORDER THAT HE MAY BE SLAIN, AND THEN, HAVING BECOME PREGNANT BY ONE OF HER ATTENDANT KNIGHTS, GIVES BIRTH TO A DAUGHTER. BY DIVERS CHANCES THE SON ESCAPES DEATH, AND, BEING ADVISED OF HIS MOTHER'S DOINGS, KILLS HER, AND ON BECOMING KING TAKES TO WIFE THE DAUGHTER OF THE KING OF HUNGARY.

TO THE VERY EXCELLENT AND WORTHY LORD, DON FERRANDO DE GIVARA, COUNT OF BELCASTRO

EXORDIUM

MOST magnanimous cavalier of Castile, seeing that I have for many years had knowledge of your perfect virtue, and perceived that it in no wise fails short of the worthiness of your lineage, I, having already determined to inscribe to you one of my novels, was not minded to send to you aught else than what might deal with lofty themes and the deeds of great princes, in order that you, when you should read my story, might understand how the venturesome daring which women in these days employ in sending to summon their lovers has already been used and put into practice in kingdoms other than our own, by ladies who have proved themselves the greatest mistresses of the art. Likewise I would let you see that the means they employed differed greatly from those in favour with our Italian women, in that the ultramontane ladies employ force when art fails them, as you, my excellent Count, will be mightily astonished to learn. Farewell.

THE NARRATIVE

GERONIMO, King of Poland, according to the report given to me by divers Poles, was in his day a most wise and prudent gentleman, and he, having been left without wife or child, determined to wive once more, albeit he was now drawing anigh to the season of old age, so as not to let pass the kingdom to a strange nation after his death. Wherefore he took to wife the sister of the Frankish King of Bosnia, who was young and very fair, and, having given her reception with royal pomp and found her delightsome beyond measure, he began to love her more than his own life. But the queen, dissatisfied perchance with the lot Fate had awarded her, set herself with much persistence to seek how she might enjoy the goods of others; and, having cast her eyes upon a handsome cavalier about the court, she, being unwilling to speak of the affair to any other person, called him into her chamber one day, and in very feat manner pressed him to consent to her dissolute desires, saying to him: "The love I bear you ought to be to you a very precious thing, for it is your duty to consider who I am and with what eager desire I now address you; and, although this thing is an arduous enterprise for you to essay, you must remember that I am placed in no less peril, and that Love is a mighty sovereign whose forces no mortal has ever been able to resist. And although I might now remind you of many examples of this same thing, I must bid you be content with one only, and bring to an issue this affair concerning which I have laid my commands upon you. I will speak to you therefore of the mighty Hercules, who, after he had slain Cerberus and flayed the lion for Love's sake, learned to spin wool. I will say naught of Theseus, who, having abandoned his Ariadne, gave himself over entirely to Phaedra, and cared naught for the fate of Hippolytus. These ensamples, most true and unquestionable, ought to serve the purpose which I have in view, that is, to stir you up to give satisfaction to my longings and to my love-stricken heart, which is pining through desire of you; and of a surety, if you deny my prayer, you will yourself be the cause of my death, and afterwards, when you shall vainly seek a remedy for the same, you will be grief-stricken for having hunted me from this world by your cruelty. Wherefore come to my succour while there is yet time." And having thus spoken she was silent.

The cavalier, who was a very worthy gentleman, was conscious that if he should do such a wicked deed he would affront the honour and strike at the very life of the king his master; wherefore he made answer to the queen, after he had uttered divers words of honest censure, and spake thus: "With what show of honour and with what demeanour could I set myself to work such an unspeakable sin? You are the very crown and headpiece of my lord the king, to whom my faithful service is due, bound as I am thereto by the laws of nature. What death, however cruel, what torture too fell to name, would be adequate to my offence should I trangress against His Majesty in a fashion which men might well call base beyond measure, in that my lord, should he ever come to know of my crime, would, sooner than suffer such infamy, prefer to stand in the place of the lowest varlet in his scullery; nay rather—more cruel fate—would elect to die by his own hand? Therefore, O illustrious queen, keep back your feet from this false step, and have no fear that this thing will ever come by speech of mine to the hearing of others. Nay, now that I have locked the same in my heart, I will ever hereafter keep silence thereanent, and will deem you as one far above me in all things. If perchance you desire to exile me hence, declare it to me now, and I will betake myself to some wild spot in which I may be forced to make wild herbs my meat, and there I will abide, and seek no more to behold the faces of men. And now I will end my speech, with my mind verily and indeed set rather to suffer a thousand deaths than ever to wander in such wise from the paths of righteousness."

The queen, highly angered at these words, cried out: "See now, Misser Demitrio, that you set yourself in order to satisfy my desires, and, as I am now with child by the king, I promise you by my faith that, when my labour shall be over, I will let the child, be it a boy or a girl, perish forthwith, and when I shall be with child by you—a thing which I doubt not will come to pass—I promise you that no other man but you shall ever enjoy my person or my goods as long as I shall live, and I will make the child which may be born to us the heir, even as though he had come from the king's loins. He shall be carefully brought up, and he shall succeed without fail to this our kingdom. But should you still be obstinate in your refusal, make up your mind to go hence forthwith, and see that no tidings of you come to my hearing; otherwise I swear to you that I will let befall you a shameful death, go where you will." The cavalier was mightily alarmed by these direful threats, and at the same time drawn on by the promises of present and future rewards, and inflamed by the beauty of so lofty a lady; wherefore he determined, after hastily canvassing the matter with himself, to obey the queen's commands. And thus, before they had let abate within themselves lustful humour, we may presume that they plucked the amorous fruits of love, and that hereafter they gave each other much delight whenever fortune was favourable to them. And in due time it came to pass that the queen gave birth to a very fair boy; whereupon the king and the barons of the land, and all the people as well, held high rejoicing, and the child was baptized by the name of Adrian. Then the wicked queen, although being a mother she was deeply grieved to the heart that she must perforce carry out the promise she had made to slay her child, nevertheless, so as not to give aught of offence to her paramour, who had captured her fancy so completely that she was now more than ever entangled in the snares of her amorous, or rather of her adulterous passion, she determined in part to bring to an issue the cruel and detestable thing she had promised.

By chance there had come in those days to her husband's court a certain knight of Hungary, together with his wife and children, who had been banished on account of some angry humour of the King of Hungary; and the queen, when she heard that the wife of the Hungarian had also recently given birth to a very handsome boy, took it into mind that this woman alone would be able to aid her in carrying out the scheme she had planned. Having bidden them summon the lady to her, she said after she had given to her a kindly reception: "My dear Costanza, you, like a prudent woman, will readily understand, when you shall have heard what I have to tell you, how great is the importance of the matter I have in hand, and of what nature, and how urgently it will behove you to keep the same a secret. Therefore I beseech you, by the only true God and by the benefits which you have received from me already, and by the many others still greater which you may expect in the future, that you will be ready to carry out my wishes for the sake of the reward which will come to you thereby. When this thing shall be done, let it pass away in silence, for you yourself shall judge how pressingly silence will be necessary therefor." To this speech Costanza answered with all humility that, albeit she was unworthy of the queen's high confidence, still she was ready in all ways to carry out her wishes, and would sooner die than reveal to any living person aught which the queen might tell her.

Then said the queen: "It is necessary for certain reasons which sway me, not without ample cause—reasons which I cannot at present reveal to you—that I should give in exchange for your child the son which has lately been born to the king and myself; and, if this exchange should be made, you may be sure that your son will duly succeed to this kingdom. What fate I desire for my own child I cannot tell you, seeing that I am a mother and you a prudent woman; but you may form what conclusion you list thereanent. In this matter, however, I leave my wishes to be ruled by your forethought." Costanza, a fugitive in a strange land and sunk in poverty, albeit many and varied thoughts passed through her mind as she listened to such an extraordinary proposal, made answer forthwith that she was ready to fulfil all the queen's wishes, bearing in mind the present advantage to herself and the future welfare of her son. After she had returned home and taken counsel with her husband, they both, for the reasons aforesaid, resolved to let the matter come to an issue straightway. Thus, when she had carried her child into the queen's chamber, and changed its wrapping and other clothes for those of the queen's son, the barter agreed between the two was completed. Alas, perverse Fortune, who is it can arrest your rapid and perilous wheel! Alas, Fortune, what though great princes may deny your existence, and banish you from their presence, you still let them feel the touch of your vengeance, although tardy be the working of your wrath! To you it was no secret what would be the issue of this plot. Costanza's mind was bent on one object, the queen's upon another. Costanza, desiring only to let her son become a king, beheld not the death which was swooping down so quickly upon her innocent offspring; and the queen as yet had no inkling that aught of craft was stirring in the mind of the humble foster-mother of her child; for Costanza, being a mother herself, cared for the strange child as if he had been her own son. Now let him who has understanding consider well this matter.

Costanza, taking with her the queen's fair child clad in mean garments, returned to her humble lodging, and left her own child in the high estate which he was fated to enjoy for so brief a season; and, although she had understood well enough what the wicked queen desired in her inmost heart, to wit, that Adrian should taste no drop of milk either from her own or from any other breast, nevertheless, considering well the malignant nature of this cruel mother and the innocence of the poor babe, and being likewise moved thereto by conscience, she determined, though she might perish therefor, to bring up the boy carefully as her own; and, after she had made the queen believe that he was indeed dead, she kept him secretly in her own house. The wicked queen, who was beating against contrary winds, did not suffer the child of poor Costanza to enjoy a month of life before she took his life by violence, feigning the while to be sore stricken with grief at his death, and saying to the king and the court, and to Costanza likewise, that this thing had come about in the way of nature. Whereupon all the aforesaid were grievously affected by this bitter misfortune.

Now Misser Demitrio, deeming surely that the dead child was the one lately born of the queen, what though the deed wrought by her pleased him not a little, held it for certain that the queen must surpass in cruelty all the wicked women in the world, and was filled with no little wonder thereanent; but neither this deed nor any other consideration availed aught to hold him back from the work he had begun—a work to which both he and the queen fell with great delight. Wherefore in due course the queen found herself with child by him, and at the end of her time gave birth to a fine daughter, whom the king claimed as his own, making great show of joy over her birth. Now Costanza, who with her husband had wept bitterly in secret over the death of the child, tasting an anguish never felt before, had by this time ascertained clearly the nature of the intimacy and favour of the queen with the cavalier her lover, and that the issue of the same manifestly transgressed the limits of honesty and duty; so Costanza gathered up mentally each detail of the business point by point, exactly as it had happened, and just as though she herself had been concerned in every one. Being overcome with grief and shame in consideration of such huge and nefarious wickedness, she found no peace for her soul, and as it happened that her husband, through the intercession of the King of Poland, regained the favour of his sovereign, they returned to Hungary a few days after their son's death, taking with them their other children, and in strict concealment Adrian, who was held by them as dear as if he had been their own flesh, and was brought up with the greatest care. Having returned home they were met with kindly reception and affectionate marks of esteem by all the chief nobles; and while Costanza went day by day to visit the Queen of Hungary, being received by her most joyfully, it came to pass that the nurse of the queen's son, a lovely boy about the age of Adrian, fell ill in such wise that she could no longer suckle him. Wherefore the queen, who loved her child very dearly, sent word to divers ladies bidding them lend her their aid in this strait. But—perhaps decreed thus by Heaven—the child refused to taste the milk of any one of them, save of Costanza alone, and this he relished as well as that of his nurse. Wherefore the queen was pleased beyond measure, and begged Costanza tenderly that, until the child could be otherwise provided for, she would be pleased to nurse him, a task which Costanza joyfully undertook. Then the queen forthwith let prepare a room for her and her family in the palace, in which she nursed both the children with the greatest love and carefulness. But as Fortune was not minded that she should, thus working the weal of others, live on with such a fair and noble pair of children, it was brought about that on a certain night, when she was lying betwixt the two, she, being overcome by overpowering weariness, fell asleep on the top of the child of the King of Hungary, and pressed upon him in such wise that when she awoke she found him dead by her side. Stricken with almost mortal grief—as any one may well believe—she bewept him for a long time; and then, finding that tears would not help her, and seeking to compass her own safety, she took her beloved Adrian, who resembled mightily the other, and dressed him in the clothes of the dead child. Then she and her husband buried the queen's son without being seen by anybody, and the next morning she showed the living one, as was her wont, to the queen, and neither she, nor anyone else about the court, perceived that this was not the son of the king.

Costanza, having become more careful after this misfortune, brought up her Adrian with twice as great love as heretofore, and when he was come to man's estate he grew to be the universal ensample of worth and comeliness to all the Hungarians. In the meantime, the Queen of Poland, who had been left a widow a short time after the unheard-of barter she had made of her infant, lived with the fair child of her unlawful love, and, as there had never been born to her another child, either by her lover or by anyone else, she made offer to this exchanged and re-exchanged son of the King of Hungary—albeit she deemed him to be the second born—to give him her daughter to wife and her kingdom for a dowry. And having conceived this idea, she sent her most reverend ambassadors to bear this request to the King of Hungary, and after some negotiations the match was agreed upon. When the time had come for the celebration of the marriage and the feasts, the king put everything in order in most sumptuous fashion; and when the bridegroom, together with Costanza and her husband, had set forth on their way and had entered the kingdom of Poland, it seemed to Costanza that the time had come when she should rescue her beloved foster-child from the commission of the execrable offence towards which, in his innocence, he was tending with so much delight in his heart the while. Whereupon she and her husband secretly called him aside, and, after a fitting and seemly prelude, laid bare to him the whole story, telling him whose son he really was, and how and why he had been brought up by Costanza, and by what working he had been held to be the son of the King of Hungary. Furthermore, Costanza let him know concerning all those things which, as she had got clearly to know, had passed between his own mother and the cavalier, and then told him point by point of everything which had ensued thereupon.

Adrian, who was now called by the name of Edward, having heard these words with the greatest sorrow and amazement, felt that he could never be able by mere words to reward his beloved nurse for her goodness, and made up his mind to give her a suitable guerdon in deeds in such wise that, both in the present and in the future, men might praise him for his gratitude. Although he was endowed with an understanding much more complete than might have been expected in one so young, he nevertheless took counsel with Costanza and her husband, and resolutely determined to carry out the plan which he had formed. When he had come to his destination he was received and welcomed by the Queen of Poland, and by her barons and people, with the most sumptuous rejoicings, and all the honour due to so great a prince. Next morning the mass was celebrated with due pomp, and he was married and took to wife the daughter of his own mother. But when the hour for the consummation of the marriage approached the new king artfully made believe to be affected by a bodily distemper of such a nature that, by the counsel of his physicians, the nuptial rite was deferred until such time as his health should be amended. In the meantime he took peaceful and entire possession of the kingdom and of his estates, and having received the homage of the barons and of all the people, and confirmed his power in such wise that he need fear no man, he one night caused his mother and Misser Demitrio to be privily seized. Then, after they had been put to the question by means of divers very cruel tortures, they each of them made confession how the matter had been brought to pass from beginning to end.

When he had caused this confession to be ratified by both the accused in the presence of all the people, he let follow a legal and valid trial, in which he produced the depositions of Costanza and her husband, and then sent a copy of these to all Christian princes for the clearing of his honour. On the following morning he bade them burn his wicked mother and the disloyal cavalier, as was their due, at the same stake, and he had his sister shorn of her hair and kept closely in a convent as long as she lived, albeit she was innocent of offence. Having done this, he despatched to the King of Hungary two of his chief nobles to advise him more particularly concerning what had happened, and likewise to tell the king how he, knowing full well that he enjoyed both his life and his estate only through the favour of his majesty, was willing that these should be disposed of according to the king's desire, as had been proposed when the king, deeming the boy to be his own son, had put him in the way of attaining so fine a fortune. The King of Hungary, who had already heard with mighty great astonishment and small pleasure of what had come to pass, considered well the strange news, and, being a very wise man, it occurred to him that, as he had lost the King of Poland as a son, he might gain him as a son-in-law, seeing that he had a daughter who was exceedingly fair. Wherefore, by common consent and mutual desire, he gave to Adrian the princess to wife, and she was duly welcomed by him with high festivals and regal solemnities. To Costanza and her husband he granted a good estate and took them into his closest confidence; and thus in peace and quietness, with the greatest love subsisting between them and their beautiful children, the King and Queen of Poland lived by the grace of God for many years, to the great contentment of all the people.

MASUCCIO

HOW mighty is the worth and the holiness and the perfection of truth, and how neither vice nor wickedness can ever have power either to wound it or to deface it, or in any wise to fill its place, seeing that in the end it will still never fail to rise supreme, aided either by divine or human working, or by its own intrinsic virtue, passing through the troubled waters without ever wetting her skirts or even her feet—all this, I say, may be proved by the clearest testimony in considering the adventures, lately told by me, which happened to our Adrian and his mother and his nurse. But now, leaving the new king to his joyful life with his young spouse, I—bearing in mind only that part of the story in which the son delivered the mother over to death—am moved to let follow another novel, full of pity and very worthy to be told, concerning one of our gentlemen of Salerno, who with justice doomed his daughter to death and her lover as well. But she, through the working of certain strange and unlooked-for accidents, came in the end to enjoy together with her lover her father's goods, and the affair terminated joyfully and honourably for all concerned therein.

THE END OF THE FORTY-SECOND NOVEL.

Novel the Forty-third

ARGUMENT

Misser Mazzeo Protojudice finds his daughter with Antonio Marcello, who takes to flight unrecognized. The father sends away the daughter to be killed, but those who are charged with the errand are pitiful of her, and let her go free; whereupon she, having donned male attire, goes to the court of the Duke of Calabria! She is taken by her lord to Salerno, and there finds lodging in her lover's house, and learns that he has succeeded to the goods of her father. She makes herself known to him; whereupon he takes her to wife, and they live joyfully upon the heritage.

TO THE MAGNIFICENT MISSER JOANNI GUARNA

EXORDIUM

I AM persuaded, my magnificent Misser Joanni, that, as you have let go for a season the enjoyment of your country and your associates and kinsfolk, you may find special pleasure in reading the letters of your friends and hearing report of your former compatriots. Therefore, meseems that, by writing this letter, I shall in some wise give satisfaction to yourself, and also to that friendship which has subsisted so many years between us; in order that, when you shall read the same after so long an absence, your Masuccio may be continually present to your eyes, and to your thoughts likewise. Farewell.

THE NARRATIVE

I REMEMBER that I have often heard my old grandfather* tell us a true story how, in the time of Charles II.,† there lived in Salerno a worthy gentleman of ancient and noble family who was called Messer Mazzeo Protojudice, the richest citizen of the town in money and lands. Now when he was full of years his wife died, leaving him an only daughter named Veronica, handsome, and very discreet, whom he still kept unmarried in his own house—although she had been sought by divers noble suitors—either by reason of his great love or because he desired for her a grand alliance. It happened that there was a noble youth called Antonio Marcello, who from his earliest days had closely frequented the house, for the reason that he was of near kinship with the wife of Misser Mazzeo, and to him Veronica had given her love so fully that she could find no rest. Antonio, who was a prudent and most honest-minded youth, and one loved by Veronica's father as his own son, perceived how the matter stood, and, as he was young and lusty, and unable through unstable will to beat back the assaults of love, he was fired by a similar passion. And because it happened that the lovers were granted an opportunity favourable for the gratification of their mutual desires, they contrived at their convenience to taste the sweetest fruits of their love. And albeit by using great caution they compassed their enjoyment, their foresight could not provide against the great disaster which malignant Fortune was plotting. For once, when they were passing the night in gladsome wise and unsuspicious of danger, it happened that they were espied by a servant of the house, who straightway told all to Misser Mazzeo. Thereupon the father, fired with rage and malice, flew with his servants to the spot where the lovers were and laid violent hands upon them

* Probably Tommaso Mariconda, who is named in Novel XIV.
† He reigned from 1285 to 1309.

MAZZEO AND HIS DAUGHTER.

FROM A DRAWING BY E. R. HUGHES. (Mas., Nov. xliii., v. ii.)

just at the moment when they were reaching the summit of their bliss. But Antonio, who was very active and courageous, having forcibly loosened himself from seizure and cleared a way with his sword, fled to his own house without being recognized by anyone.

Misser Mazzeo was wellnigh stricken to death by grief when he perceived to what issue the affair had come, and desired his daughter to tell him who the youth might be; but she, being a very prudent girl, and knowing well enough that her father's flawless virtue, rather than let him live out his old age under such a burden of shame, would of a surety move him to compass Antonio's death, made up her mind that her lover's life was dearer to her than her own, and spake to her father her final answer by declaring that she would sooner suffer death by all possible torture than reveal the name of her lover. The father raged against her anew, and, after he had put her to divers tortures and found her still obstinate in her denial, finally resolved most cruelly to have her put to death, what though he was hard pressed by love of his own flesh and blood. Wherefore, without desiring to behold her more, he commanded two of his most trusted servants that they should straightway take her with them in a boat, and should cast her overboard after having put out several miles to sea.

These men, albeit the task was an abhorrent one, bound her with all speed to prove their obedience, and led her away to the seashore; and, whilst they prepared the boat, one of them was seized with pity of her, and after he had dexterously felt his way with his companion, who was equally adverse to such barbarity, they went on from one word to another, and finally agreed that, even should they meet death therefor, they would spare her life and set her free. Thus, having loosened her bonds, they told her how they, being moved to pity, would go on no further with the execution of the cruel doom laid upon them by her father, begging her that, as a reward for this service and in remembrance of so great a boon, she would exile herself and let long time elapse before her father could hear of their deed. The poor girl, when she knew that she was to receive her life from the hands of her own servants, felt that her thankful words would be a very meagre reward for so great a service; wherefore she prayed to the Rewarder of all righteous actions that he would on her account repay them abundantly for their inestimable gift. Then, because of the fear and terror which assailed them for what they had done, she promised and swore by the salvation they had given her that she would hereafter rule her life so that neither her pitiless father nor any other living person should have tidings of her being.

Then, having cut off her hair and disguised her as a man as best they could in their own clothes, they gave her what little money they had, and pointed out to her the way to Naples, taking leave of her with many tears. Afterwards they made their way back, carrying with them her clothes, and assured their lord that they had killed the damsel, and then, after binding a great stone round her neck, had cast her body into the sea about ten miles from land. The ill-fated noble damsel, who had never heretofore gone forth from the city, although with every step she felt her spirits fail at the thought that she was leaving her Antonio without hope of ever beholding him again, although divers vain dreams of returning would ever and anon come into her brain; still, when she recalled to mind the boon which had been granted to her, and the promise she had made, gratitude, the very flower of all the virtues, swayed her soul so powerfully that it cast out every opposing thought, and thus she, traversing the ways in a fashion mightily strange to her, commending herself to God and pressing onward, journeyed she knew not whither in heavy sorrow for the rest of the night, and found herself at daybreak near to Nocera, where she was overtaken by a company of wayfarers who were going to Naples, and to these she joined herself in friendly wise. Amongst them was a Calabrian gentleman, who was taking certain moulting falcons to the Duke of Calabria, and he observed that this youth had a very seemly presence, wherefore he asked him whence he had come, and whether he was minded to take service. Now in her childhood Veronica had been wont often to imitate an old Apulian woman of the household, and had learnt from her many words of the Apulian dialect, so herseemed that she might well use this speech henceforth. Therefore she answered, "Missere, I am from Apulia, and have left home on purpose to find service. But, seeing that I come of noble stock, I should not be well pleased to engage myself to do mean offices." Then said the Calabrian: "Would you consent to take care of falcons?" Veronica heard this speech with no little pleasure, because at home she had been wont to tend, not one, but many falcons, using the greatest care. Wherefore she answered that from her childhood she had been accustomed to this service, and to no other, and after a few more words she got ready to hold one of the falcons. When they came to Naples the gentleman caused her to be attired in a fitting costume, so that she seemed like a graceful and well-trained squire; and, whether it was thus willed by Fate, or whether the charming presence of Veronica stirred him thereto, it came to pass that, when the falcons were brought to the duke, he wished to have, besides the birds, the Apulian squire who managed them in such excellent fashion.

The Duke's wish having been carried out, Veronica became one of the household. A Neapolitan gentleman was ordered to attend upon her, and she gave herself up to her duties and to the service of the duke with such assiduity that in a short time she won his good will and was numbered amongst his first favourites, being treated by him with no little honour. Thus, always increasing in good repute, she dwelt in the duke's household until it seemed good to Fortune to change the course of her affairs. Her old father had consumed his years with his heart full of intolerable grief, and, when the deed he had wrought came to the public ear, he passed the greater part of his time shut up in his house, withdrawing now and then into the country to spend his wretcehd and solitary days. Antonio, after he had plentifully bewept the death of his Veronica with bitter and bloody tears, ascertained by cautious questioning that Misser Mazzeo had never been able to discover who was the youth who had fled that night;

wherefore, in order to withdraw all suspicion from himself, and likewise moved thereto by pity, he went a few days after the deed had been done to visit the old man, and abode with him wellnigh continuously in his house, using towards him the utmost care and affection. More often than not he would accompany Misser Mazzeo when he withdrew from the city, bearing himself as if he had been a most devoted son. All this pleased the old man amain, for it seemed to him that Antonio alone had not forsaken him in his great struggle. On this account, and because of the singular worth of the young man, Misser Mazzeo felt constrained to love him as his own son, turning all his affection upon him in such fashion that he could not endure to pass a single hour apart from his Antonio. And, being well assured that the young man showed no abatement in attentive service and love and reverence, he resolved that, as cruel Fate had left him without an heir, he would adopt Antonio in life and in death likewise as his son. Having settled definitely to carry out this resolve, and signed his last and final testament of all his goods, in chattels and in estates, he appointed his Antonio heir to the same, and in a very brief space of time passed from this life.

Antonio, having inherited so fine an estate, went to live in Misser Mazzeo's house, in which there was no single spot which did not cause him, through remembrance of his ladylove, to sigh and shed bitter tears; and, calling to mind continually how she had chosen death rather than let it be known who he was, he felt overcome by this debt of love, and, having likewise considered her many excellencies, he determined, after taking counsel with himself, that he would never wive with another woman. And while matters stood thus it happened that the duke purposed to pass through Calabria, which thing was mightily pleasing to Veronica, for the reason that she felt she would now not only visit the land she had abandoned, but would have some intelligence of her lover and also of her father, whom, even now, she could not bring herself to hate. In order to run in no danger of recognition, she had been careful to make no inquiries after them, neither had she ever received any tidings of them. Wherefore, when they had come to Salerno, and all the household of the duke had been settled in lodgings in the city according to their rank, it pleased Fortune that it should fall to the lot of Antonio Marcello to receive into his house the Apulian squire and his attendant, and how hugely this accident must have been to Veronica's taste everyone may judge. They were honourably received and made welcome by Antonio, and in the evening he let prepare for them a most sumptuous repast in that selfsame loggia in which aforetimes he had been used to take pleasure with his ladylove. At this moment, as he looked from the one to the other of his guests, he figured to himself now and again the image of his Veronica, and, as he called to memory her life and death, he was fain to let mingle passionate sighs with every word he uttered.

Veronica perceived that she had been brought back to her own house, and, albeit she was purely glad to see her faithful lover the master of all her estate, nevertheless, because she saw naught of her father or of any of the servants she had left behind her, she was wrung with filial affection, and, though she longed for tidings of her father, she dared not ask for them. While she sat at supper, thus confused in humour, the attendant knight inquired of Antonio whether the device of arms painted in the loggia was his own, whereto Antonio replied that it was not, but that it belonged to a most illustrious cavalier named Misser Mazzeo Protojudice, who, being left in old age childless, had bequeathed to him all his substance; wherefore, as the adopted son, he had taken, over and above the estate, both the family name and the arms of the cavalier as those of his own father. When Veronica heard these words, though she was filled with joy so great and unexpected that she could only keep back her tears with difficulty, she contrived to maintain her composure till the end of supper. And when the feast was finished it seemed to her that the time was come when she should receive with open arms that bliss which kindly Fortune had reserved for her. Thus, having taken Antonio by the hand and left the others at table, she led him away into a chamber, and, albeit she was minded to say to him certain words which she had put together in her own mind—words designed to let her see whether he recognized her in any way—she was unable, by reason of her joy and her tears, to open her lips. Wherefore she let herself fall fainting into Antonio's arms, crying, "Ah, my Antonio! can it be that you know me not?" Now he, as I have already said, had more than once imagined that he beheld in her his Veronica, and, hearing these words, his doubts became certainty, and, overcome by the most tender emotion, said, "Ah, my sweet soul! are you indeed yet alive?" Having thus spoken, he clasped her in his arms.

After they had held one another for some time in close embrace in silence they came back to their wonted mood, and told each other divers of the adventures which had befallen them; and then Antonio, who was in no wise minded to keep the matter long in suspense, told her what thing he proposed to do forthwith, whereat they both rejoiced exceedingly. When they returned from the chamber to rejoin the attendant knight, what though it was now full late, Antonio bade him go quickly and summon all the kinsfolk of the lady, and his own as well, to his house on business of great weight. When the aforesaid had come without delay, and were all gathered together, he besought them to accompany him to the palace of the duke, for that he purposed, with their leave, to beg him of his grace to reinstate him in possession of a certain noble fief, some time ago held by Misser Mazzeo, but for many years occupied by another from whom no dues had been received through lack of knowledge thereanent. Whereupon all those assembled declared that they were willing to go with him; and, when they were come into the presence of the duke, Antonio took his Veronica by the hand, and then before all present they told everything which had happened to them in most exact wise, keeping back naught, and declared next how, from the beginning of their love, they had, by mutual consent and in good faith, taken each other for man and wife, and how they intended, by the favour of his highness and in the sight of this worshipful company, to make public the final celebration of this marriage. And although the duke and his barons, and the kinsfolk of both the lovers, and all the citizens and strangers there assembled, stood wonder-stricken while they listened to the story of these strange adventures, they were nevertheless overjoyed when they knew that the matter was to come to an end, honourable and prosperous to Antonio and to Veronica as well, and they gave marvellous high praise to what he had done, and to her great virtue. The duke, pleased amain with the issue, let them return home, and next morning caused mass to be said with the highest pomp and the two lovers to be united in worthy fashion in his own presence, and in the presence of a vast crowd of nobles and citizens, to the general satisfaction of all our Salernitans. Then, having received from him many generous gifts, they went their way, and in wealth and in happiness, blessed in their mutual love and in their fair offspring, they enjoyed a long term of life.

MASUCCIO

BECAUSE the ending of this novel has proved so happy, and pleasant, and honourable, and full of profit, that it must have softened down and overcome the pity which anyone may have been moved to feel for the former mischances of the lovers, I am tempted—leaving these two to make up for time lost, and bearing in mind only the virtues of the last-created Duke of Calabria, and maybe those of the first as well—to let follow in the order of my work the story of another magnificent and worthy deed of liberality wrought by our own most illustrious lord, the present Duke of Calabria; and, as he assuredly surpasses all other princes in virtue, so this tale, which I am minded to inscribe to his most illustrious consort, outstrips by a long way all which have been told hitherto, as anyone who reads the same may judge.

THE END OF THE FORTY-THIRD NOVEL.

Novel the Forty-fourth

ARGUMENT

MARINO CARACCIOLO* IS ENAMOURED OF A LADY, WHO LOVES HIM IN RETURN. THEY ARE ABOUT TO COME TO A CONCLUSION, WHEN THE LADY BEHOLDS THE DUKE OF CALABRIA, WHO PROVES MORE TO HER TASTE THAN MARINO; SO, HAVING ABANDONED HER FIRST ENTERPRISE, SHE FOLLOWS UP THE SECOND, AND CONTRIVES TO INDUCE THE DUKE TO TAKE ENJOYMENT WITH HER. HE, ON HIS WAY THITHER, BECOMES CONCERNED AT THE GRIEF OF HIS FRIEND, AND, OUT OF HIS GOODNESS, RENOUNCES THE PLEASURE, THUS LEAVING MARINO THE POSSESSOR OF THE BOOTY.

TO THE MOST ILLUSTRIOUS IPPOLITA MARIA DE' VISCONTI OF ARAGON, DUCHESS OF CALABRIA

EXORDIUM

PROVIDED that virtuous listeners ever find consolation in hearing of noble deeds wrought by those alien and unknown to them, O lady, who art to me as a star benignant and far removed, how much more deeply and deservedly must they who may be joined to such persons by friendship or the tie of blood be stirred by outward joy and inward pleasure at hearing celebrated high praise concerning them! And because my thoughts seek no other end than to write down such things as may delight you amain, I will not refrain from speaking to you, who are to-day the supreme ensample of virtue to this our time, of a singular and

* See Exordium to Novel VII.

perhaps unparalleled deed of magnanimity, practised by a certain one who is justly dearer to you than your own life—one with whom you have been made one flesh by the marriage tie, what though you own two separate bodies. So that, when this deed shall be added to all the other heaped-up virtues of your most just and worthy spouse, the perfect love you bear towards him already may, to your joy, grow greater every day, and your happiness ever increase. Farewell.

THE NARRATIVE

YOUR majesty will then understand that, after the campaign last past of the war in the Romagna, both belligerents found it necessary to retire into winter quarters because the state of the weather did not allow them to prosecute further their military operations; the one army retiring to this quarter, and the other to that, as each found most convenient. Amongst the other leaders it fell out that the illustrious prince, Alfonso, Duke of Calabria, your most worthy consort, occupied the parts around Pisa, and led thither his most valiant and unconquered Aragonese army, and cantoned his men-at-arms in the several towns and villages round about, according to the usage and discipline of war. Having done this, he found it necessary to visit in person the most famous cities and territories of Italy, to treat of high matters bearing upon the well-being and condition of the league; and after he had been welcomed in all of these, and loyally received with great rejoicing, and honoured greatly, it happened that he came to a certain town, the name of which I do not feel bound to tell, which pleased him as a resting place beyond all the others. While he abode in this city, greatly delighted therewith, and feasting without end, it came to pass that one of his most intimate courtiers, named Marino Caracciolo, a gentleman distinguished both by worth and high lienage, was one day riding through the city for his pleasure, when he caught sight of a fair dame, young and very beautiful, the wife of a citizen of repute. So strongly did she strike his fancy that he felt himself, without moving from where he stood, so completely snared in the toils of love that he knew not what road he ought to take to return home. And thus, by riding thereby every day, and by gazing upon her in seemly wise, it came to pass that she was induced to return his love.

On this account Marino was delighted beyond measure and let arise the hope of reaping some still richer harvest. Wherefore one day he gave a feast to the honour of the lord duke aforesaid, to which there repaired the greater part of the ladies of the city, and amongst them that particular one who was especially loved and worshipped by Marino himself. She, being espied by the duke, pleased him mightily as one of the fairest dames present; and he, unwitting that his good friend Marino was in any way enslaved by her, made up his mind to take her for himself, and to follow up to the end this adventure so worthy of his attempt. The fair lady, who had never before seen the duke, what though she had heard divers people praise him marvellous high, and set him down as wise and well-mannered and prudent beyond all other princes, valiant in arms, stalwart and gallant and courageous, perceived at once that the report given her had not only not exaggerated his actual excellencies, but that he was, in sooth, the very mirror and example to all living men in grace and comeliness. She, as she took heed of his many excellent parts, gazed at him long and attentively, praying God the while to give him good fortune. The duke, who, as I have already said, was particularly taken with so fair a dame, saw, while he gazed at her in order to follow up the track, that she was no less enamoured than he himself; and before they departed from the feast each one had given the other evident signs of being inflamed in similar wise. When they had returned home the duke straightway caused to be made known to him all the lady's circumstances; and, after divers letters and messages had passed between them, it seemed to both of them, when the day of the duke's departure drew anigh, that they should procure, as soon as they could, the supreme conclusion of their passion. Wherefore, by the aid of one who was privy to the affair, they arranged to come together the following night, seeing that on the previous day the lady's husband had gone to Genoa.

Now in the meantime the lady, taken up with this new and more weighty affair, had slighted Marino in such wise that not only did she refuse to glance at him as had been her wont, but she displayed towards him a humour which became every day more unbending and haughty and cruelly hostile. Marino, ill content thereat, as anyone may well believe, and all the more because he knew not what cause he could have given for this strange new mood of hers, could find no peace and was overcome by such cruel grief that he became in seeming as another man. Many times did the duke question him as to his ill condition, and to these inquiries Marino replied by some fictitious story. At last the hour approached when the duke was minded to go and take pleasure with the lady, as had been duly arranged; and, forasmuch as he was never wont to embark on such enterprises without first taking counsel of Marino, he called him into the chamber and said: "Having marked, my Marino, in what ill humour you have been all these days, and having asked in vain of you the cause thereof, I gave over troubling you further thereanent because you did not seem in the mood for such questioning. And for this reason I have not told you, who are the particular sharer of all my secrets, of a fresh and fervent passion which has seized me, and of the successful issue of the same, which will, I hope, be brought about before many hours have passed. I beg you, therefore, by the service you owe me, and by the love you bear me, that you will lay bare that real and hidden trouble which torments you, and likewise chase away somewhat your anguish and grief, and put on a joyful face, so that you may be with me this evening; for you must know that I should go my way but ill content were you not by my side."

Marino, when he listened to these most kindly words, felt that he had wrought no slight offence to his lord in having all this time kept his love a secret; wherefore, using such excuses as seemed due and sufficient, he told the duke at full length the story of his falling in love from the very beginning, the name of the lady, and every particular event, good and bad alike, which had befallen him. The duke, when he heard all this, was for many reasons ill-pleased and even somewhat angered; nevertheless, remarking the nature of Marino's passion, and deeming that with his own magnanimity and high station it behoved him to use all the greater consideration towards his follower, he quickly determined that it would be beyond all comparison more pleasant to him to content his friend's desire than to satisfy his own appetite, so he spake thus: "My Marino, as you ought to know better than anyone else, I have never from my tenderest youth held aught so dear that I was not ready to share the same with my friends if they should so will, and certes you may be sure that, if the thing which you love so greatly were of such a nature that it could be yours and mine at the same time, I would now deal with it in just the same fashion as I have ever dealt with other matters. And, albeit up to this hour I may have held her dearer than my very eye, and we have both of us looked forward to our mutual embracings this night with the warmest longing, and although I have chosen you to accompany me on my errand, I have nevertheless determined and desire that the issue may be as follows that by conquering myself I may cause my present wish to be my wish no longer, rather than to behold you languishing in sorrow and perishing in your travail of love. And if you should desire to oblige me in this matter, chase away all the grief which has heretofore possessed you, and think only of putting on a cheerful humour, and prepare to accompany me, so that I, being in this mind, may grant you possession of this lady you love so well." Marino, hearing this news, was wonder-stricken; and when he realized how great was the generosity with which the duke proposed to treat him, he felt just as much bashfulness at accepting the same. When he had as best he could returned the gratitude which was due he ended by saying that he would die rather than defile, or think of defiling, aught which the duke might have destined for his own use.

At this the duke began to laugh, and said that he was minded Marino should prosecute this enterprise on his own behalf; and, having taken him by the hand, they set forth on their way. When they had come to the lady's house, and had left their attendants in the street for better security, the duke, accompanied only by Marino, went in; and, having been led into a chamber by a serving-woman, found there the lady, who was joyfully awaiting the duke. She went to meet him in gladsome wise; and, although she knew well enough that her former lover was there present while they talked thus merrily, she took no more heed of him than as if he had been some stranger brought thither by the duke. Then, after many sweet kissings and merry play, it seemed to the duke that the time had come when he should finish the task which had brought him thither; so, taking the lady by the hand, he said: "Dear lady, I beseech you, by the love which you have been led to give me, that you will not take amiss what I am about to say. For the more unseemly my request may appear, the greater will be your love for me in granting it. For I must tell you that, when last I left the presence of the king, my most illustrious lord and sire, he gave me amongst other counsels one which bade me, whenever I should find myself in the pitfalls of love, that I should have naught to do with any woman unless I should first have made trial of her by some intimate friend of mine; because of the well-known instance of the mighty King Lanzilao, who was infected by a woman of this country while engaged in a like enterprise. And although I am well assured that you would suffer a thousand deaths on behalf of my life; nevertheless, in order to carry out to the full the counsels of that most illustrious lord aforesaid, the king my father, I am forced to beg you that you will consent, in joyous and triumphant mood, that this my perfect friend and well-trusted follower, whom I regard as another self, may do this office for me, and be, in twofold wise, your constant and only lover."

The lady, who was very well advised and prudent, quickly understood, by what had gone before, the drift of the duke's wishes, exactly as if the plain facts had been told to her word by word. She was, in sooth, cut to the heart with grief at being thus scorned and cast off by such an illustrious and seemly gentleman, whose embraces she had anticipated with no small longing, and with good reason; nevertheless, seeing that in her case it behoved her to make a virtue of necessity, she took counsel with herself, and hiding as best she could the fierce passion which possessed her, she made answer to the duke with a look of feigned pleasure on her face: "Although, most virtuous prince, love and your own exceeding comeliness, together with your so many singular and excellent parts, have led me into this my present position, which, indeed, is one demanding a proof of my virtue, I would you should be assured, before I disclose to you my intention, that I kept my wits clear, enough to perceive that your love and mine were unfairly matched. Nevertheless, having observed by many and manifest signs that my person pleased you greatly, you yourself became, for many reasons, most dear to my fancy. But now I perceive that you have other views with regard to me, likewise that your wonted and well-known virtue and noble munificence are reaching up to a yet greater height; for you, what though you are a most illustrious prince and son of so potent and excellent a king, are abnegating the place of principal in this affair, and of your own will acting as a faithful go-between, in order to satisfy the longings of another, thus preferring the pleasure of your most loyal servant to the delight which might have filled your heart and mine as well—a renunciation such as is not required by any of the laws of love. But, so as not to balk or by any deed of mine to cloud the brightness of your lofty generosity, and without aught of gainsaying, I have once for all determined to obey you, my most gracious and excellent lord duke, and to lay myself out with all my heart to please this most noble gentleman, my whilom lover. Thus, without losing your highness I shall have recovered him with all the more pleasure and delight, no less liberal of my love to him than you have been of your earnest wishes on his behalf."

Then, having taken Marino by the hand and besought the duke that he would not find it amiss to wait a while, they withdrew into another chamber, where, after they had spent some short time in close and loving embraces, and sweet kissings, and other pleasant conversation, Marino began the longed-for sport with his falcon in a mood much more eager than vigorous, and therefore managed to capture only a single partridge, and that with difficulty. And although in the recover he attempted to take a second by a back stroke, he failed in his attempt, what though he used his dogs and all other arts of venery. Thus, having taken only one, he went back to the duke. The lady, bearing herself in merry and gracious wise, came after him, carrying in her hand a lighted torch, and said to the duke in jocular fashion: "My lord, the trial which your good follower has just made is such as the most valiant esquire should make on behalf of his lord; still, as he only tasted lightly the feast, he seemed to show that he had had enough and to spare thereof." The duke as he listened laughed heartily, and they spent the greater part of the night in very seemly and pleasant discourse; and when the duke deemed that it was time to depart, and when he had given to the lady many rich and precious gems to complete his most gracious liberality, he took his leave. Whether or not Marino ever returned to take another turn of sport, or whether what he did on this occasion contented him, I have never heard him say.

MASUCCIO

WHAT eloquence, however flowery or finished it be, would suffice to tell of the many virtues which have found a permanent home in the spirit of this terrestrial god, as if it were their natural dwelling-place? Who shall be able to set down in writing the many praiseworthy accomplishments and the illustrious deeds of this true king's son and perfect gentleman? Who shall sing the glorious fame, and the enduring reputation, which this prince has by his own worth acquired for himself in all the parts of Italy? Who will find praises adequate to extol the virtue, the magnificence, and the generosity which he showed towards his well-beloved and faithful servant? What father dealing with his only son, what brother with brother, what friend with friend—and I can cite naught, beyond this—could have equalled him in virtue? I, who wished merely to touch upon this theme, feel my lyre grow harsh—know that my wit is feeble and my wanton hand insufficient to wield the pen. Forsooth, I would rather hold my peace, seeing that I cannot say enough thereanent. And, as I have now done with it, naught remains for me to say but to exclaim, Blessed are the people who will live under his rule, blessed are the servants who behold him, blessed are the ministers who wait upon him, but most blessed may you be called, immortal goddess, Ippolita Maria, his most worthy consort, to whom the Fates have granted the enjoyment of such a treasure! And no less justly may he be called thrice blessed, for that he has been joined by a holy sacrament to so noble a lady, goodly with virtue and uprightness, the fount of all beauty and grace, the stream of magnanimity, of gratitude and charity. Oh, worthy couple! Oh, glorious union! Oh, joyful and happy bond! Let us pray to the gods without ceasing that they may preserve you and yours for many years in prosperous and peaceful estate, in such wise as each one of you must especially desire. Amen.

THE END OF THE FORTY-FOURTH NOVEL.

Novel the Forty-fifth

ARGUMENT

A Castilian scholar, while journeying to Bologna, falls in love at Avignon, and in order to have his will of the lady covenants to give her a thousand ducats. Repenting of his deed, he goes his way, and by chance meets the lady's husband, to whom, unwitting who he was, he recounts his adventure. The husband discovers that it is his wife who is thus concerned, and induces the scholar to return with him to Avignon. There he restores the money, kills his wife, and bestows upon the scholar many gifts and much honourable usage.

TO THE ILLUSTRIOUS LORD, DON HENRY OF ARAGON *

EXORDIUM

THERE is a proverb, my most illustrious lord, in frequent use amongst the common people, that every promise is a debt, and if this be true—as it manifestly seems to be—reason and honesty demand that every debtor should, as soon as may be, give full satisfaction to whomsoever he may have bound himself. Therefore, as I call to mind a promise of one of my novels, by which I made myself of my own free will a debtor to you, I have undertaken to unload my weary shoulders of this onerous burden by offering to you the present tale, by which means, besides ridding myself of an obligation, I shall let you hear of a singular act of

* Natural son of Ferdinand I.

magnanimity, and of the great generosity exhibited by a French cavalier towards a noble young Castilian. And although, certes, this deed of virtue will be marvellously commended by many, I am persuaded that some of these will find it easier to praise the same than to imitate it, should they ever find themselves in like case. Farewell.

THE NARRATIVE

A NOBLE youth of Castile, a student of the law attracted by the long-continued and widely-spread renown of the University of Bologna, resolved to go thither, so that, after studying there, he might proceed to the doctorate. His name was Missere Alfonso of Toledo; he was young and of excellent parts, and, besides this, he had been left very rich by the death of his father, a cavalier of note. Wherefore, to accomplish forthwith his praiseworthy purpose, he furnished himself with an array of sumptuous books, rich garments, good horses, and suitable servants, and thus equipped, and with a thousand golden ducats in his purse, he took the road to Italy. After travelling several days he found that he had left Castile behind him, traversed Catalonia, and had arrived in France. Having come to Avignon he determined to tarry there some days, either to rest his weary cattle or for some other need. He found lodging at an inn, and the next day he and his attendants rambled about the city; and, as fate willed it, while he was passing from one street to another he caught sight of a fair lady at a window. She was indeed young and very beautiful; but in his lover's humour himseemed that he had never before beheld her equal, and so delightful was the sight of her that before he moved from the spot he found himself taken with love of her in a fashion which no argument could gainsay.

On this account, regarding no more his virtuous intention, he resolved not to quit Avignon until he should, either altogether or in part, have won the lady's favour; and as he passed by her window continually, she, who was well versed in such business, perceived that the poor young fellow was so much enamoured of her that it would now be no easy matter to keep him aloof. When she remarked that he was young and beardless, and that, judging by his garb and his following, he must be rich and of noble descent, she determined to seize upon this dainty morsel forthwith, and to strip him of his last coin. Wherefore, in order to give him the opportunity of speaking or sending word to her, she acted in the fashion which ships becalmed at sea follow when they despatch boats ashore to fetch wood; for, having let come to her an old waiting-woman of hers, well-informed and practised in such business, she set her to ply her work by the window so that Missere Alfonso might easily see her. The youth, who desired nothing better, approached the old woman and began speech with her, and before they parted each had learnt the private circumstances of the other. Then, when the crone had returned to her mistress, and after divers messages had been sent from either side, they came at last to a clear understanding that the lady would grant him the favour of her love, and would await his coming the following night, and that he should bring with him the thousand ducats of gold which was all the money he had. At the longed-for hour the ill-advised youth, with his money in his pocket, betook himself to the house of the lady, whose name was Laura; and, after she had given him joyful reception, and caressed him beyond measure, and caused him to hand over to her the thousand ducats, wherewith she was marvellously content, they went to bed together. Missere Alfonso being of that age when the end and the beginning of such work seems the same thing, we may believe that he spent all the remainder of the night in satisfying his ardent desires. Then, when it was day, he sprang out of bed, and after making divers fresh plans whereby he might again take up the work he had begun, he returned to his inn, sleepy and somewhat repenting of his deed, accompanied by his servants, who had waited wearily for him at the lady's door.

She, who with delight amain and in such brief time

had put her hand upon so rich a chance, perceived well enough that the youth was so deeply in her toils that Bologna and the study of the law had no longer any place in his thoughts, and that before his departure he would assuredly desire to take his pleasure with her again. When the day was done, Missere Alfonso, deeming that next evening, according to their agreement, he would be received by the lady joyfully and with yet more kindly welcome, went at nightfall to Madonna Laura's door. After he had given the signal several times, and had got back no sound to break the silence, he knew, too late, that he had in one and the same hour lost the lady he had enjoyed, his honour, and his money. So, having gone back to his inn grieving wellnigh to death, he spent all that night in vexation and anguish of mind. The next day, in order that he might have final proof of the trick which had been put upon him, he walked round about her house, and, finding all the doors and windows closed, and many other signs of like import, he knew that he had been betrayed and flouted by the consummate craft of this wicked woman. Having returned to his followers, such grief and desperation fell upon him that he was more than once on the point of plunging a dagger into his breast. However, restraining himself, lest a worse thing should befall him, he resolved to quit the place.

Now because there was not left in his purse a wretched solitary penny-piece wherewith to pay his host, he determined to sell a very excellent mule of his; and, having done this and discharged his score, with what little money was left to him he went on towards Italy by the County of Provence. All the way, however, he shed bitter tears, and was especially tormented by the grievous thought that, after purposing to pursue his studies as a nobleman should, he was now forced to make his way to Bologna selling and pledging his goods and lodging at mean inns, and after reaching his destination would be obliged to live there like a poor scholar. As he pursued his way in indigence and travail of mind, he came at last to Trayques, and took lodging in an inn where, by a strange and unexpected chance, the husband of

Madonna Laura was tarrying that same night. This gentleman was an accomplished and graceful knight, a man of great eloquence and power, and was now on his way back from the Papal court to the King of France, by whom he had been sent as ambassador. He had already requested the host that, should any other gentleman arrive at the inn, he would bid the same join him at table, as is the fashion used by French gentlemen on their travels; whereto the host made answer that there was in the inn a Spanish scholar who, by his servants' report, was on his way to Bologna; but that this youth, by reason of a fit of melancholy which had come over him, had eaten naught for two days. The cavalier when he heard this was stirred by his natural kindness, and resolved in any event to have the scholar to sup with him; wherefore, having gone to him in person and found him sitting sad and distraught with grief in his chamber, he took him by the hand in very familiar wise, without making any other salutation, and said: "You must without fail sup with me." The young man, remarking the cavalier, and judging from his aspect that he was a worthy gentleman, straightway sat down to table with him, and when they had supped and dismissed their attendants, the knight asked Missere Alfonso who he was, and on what errand and whither he was bound; and, beyond this, if he could tell it honestly, to say what the cause of his deep melancholy.

Missere Alfonso, who for every word he uttered let forth two sighs, replied to the first of these questions as briefly as he could, but begged the cavalier that he would not press for an answer to the other. The gentleman, when he learned who the scholar was, and for what reason he had left home—and he knew likewise by hearsay that his father was a man of great reputation—was seized afresh with the desire to learn what accident could have befallen him on the way to make him grieve thus sorely. He went on inquiring, and the youth refusing to reply, till at last Missere Alfonso, without taking farther heed, told the whole story from beginning to end: who the lady was, and how he had enjoyed her; adding that he, assailed by excessive chagrin at the flout put upon him, and at his shame and the loss of so great a sum of money, had many a time come within an ace of taking his own life. When the cavalier—thus instant to seek that which he neither expected nor desired—heard this, anyone who may have tested the truth of such a case will be able to say how great was his righteous sorrow, how he was as one half dead, and how vastly his mental torture surpassed that of the scholar. However, having discreetly suppressed his intolerable grief, giving some slight vent to his feeling the while, it occurred to him what he would do; so, turning towards the youth, he said: "My son, you by your own words let me know how ill regulated has been your conduct, and how, like a silly boy, you have let yourself be gulled by this vile wanton; and certes, if I deemed that my chiding would profit you aught, I would never weary—supposing we were to live together hereafter—of reprehending you every day for your folly. But because I see you stand vastly more in need of actual help than of reproaches, I hope your present grief, together with the consciousness of your offence, will for this once be penalty enough. Therefore, take heart, and dream not madly of making the case worse by injuring your own person, for I will let this business, end for you, as though you were my own son. And, as you see that I am a traveller and a stranger in these parts, and wanting in means to carry out my desire, I beg you will not find it amiss to return home with me for a few days, so that you may afterwards in joy and contentment finish your journey, and carry out your original intent; because for the sake of your forbears, and of your well-born and noble seeming, I cannot let you go to the university in your present mood of set despair; and, besides this, you cannot, poor as you now are, live worthily as a gentleman ought."

The young man, astonished at such kindness, returned the cavalier as much gratitude as the grief and injury oppressing him allowed him to express, and after some further discourse each went to his rest. The following morning they took horse early and returned towards France, and having covered all the distance by the knowledge of the country possessed by the cavalier, they arrived in Avignon that same evening; and when they had entered the city the gentleman took the young man by the hand and led him to his own house. The scholar not only recognized the quarter of the city and the house, but marked the lady as she came forward with lighted torches to meet her husband, rejoicing the while. Whereupon he quickly saw how the matter stood, and deemed that he must die straightway, being so greatly overcome with fear thereanent that he could scarce dismount. Nevertheless he got down at the request of his host, who took him by the arm and led him into that self-same room where, not many hours before, he had sate, finding therein such brief pleasure, and such long-abiding trouble and loss. The lady, on her part, recognized the scholar, and, because the foreboding of the fate in store for her seized upon her, everyone will be able to imagine how great was the terror and the grief which possessed her. When the supper-hour had come, they all—the terror-stricken lady amongst them—sat down; and when the meal was finished the three of them—each one filled with bitter woe, although from differing causes—sat on at table. Then the cavelier, having turned towards his wife, said: "Laura, fetch me hither those thousand golden ducats which this man gave to you, and for the price of which you sold your person, and my honour and your own, and the honour of all your kinsfolk as well." The lady, when she heard these words, deemed that the house was falling about her ears, and, like one dumb, stood without speaking a single word; whereupon the husband, looking upon her very sternly, took his dagger and said: "Vile woman, if you wish not to die this moment, do as I bid you." Then she, seeing how fierce his anger was and that no refusal was possible, went sorrowing amain to fetch the ducats, and, having brought them, cast them on the table. The cavalier poured them out, and, taking one of them, gave it to the youth, who stood looking on in terror; for he feared every moment lest the husband should slay him and the lady as well with the dagger he held in his hand.

But the cavalier said to him: "Missere Alfonso, it is right and seemly that everyone should receive due payment on account of service rendered, and if my wife here, who has given you the pleasure of her person and duped you finely to boot, has betaken herself to such work for the price of shame, she may rightly be classed as a harlot; and because, however fair a harlot may be, she deserves no higher payment than a single ducat for one night, I am minded that you, who bought this merchandize for yourself, should pay the due price therefor." Next he commanded his wife to take the ducat; and, when she had done this, he, marking how the young man was all shamed and afeared, and unable to look him in the face, and, certes, more in need of heartening than of rebuke, spake thus: "My son, take back your ill-kept and worse spent money, and beware in future that you buy not such base wares at so high a price. As you have left your home for a place wherein you hoped to acquire honour and fame and renown, never waste your time and your wealth in lasciviousness. And, as I do not wish this night to trouble you with more discourse, I bid you now get to your rest, and be assured, on the word of a true knight, that I would sooner work an injury to my own person than think of harming either you or your goods." Then, having summoned his servants, the cavalier let the scholar take his money and withdraw to a rich chamber which had been got ready for him; and before he himself went to bed he prepared carefully some poisoned viands, whereof his wife made her last supper.

When the next morning had come, the cavalier caused to be brought out a fine ambling horse and divers other rich and noble presents; and after the young man had made a light repast and taken horse with his followers, the host himself mounted also and rode in company with him for some ten miles beyond the city. When he made ready to return he said to the scholar: "My dear son, my mind is not yet easy for that I merely spared your life and returned your money; wherefore you must in addition accept these small gifts of mine, which, through hurry, I have not been able to make worthier, together with this horse, as a compensation for the mule which you sold, bidding you to have me in mind whenever you may use the same. I desire, in sooth, that for the future you should regard me as your father, and always depend upon me, whatever you do, and I, for my part, will do the same and look upon you as my son as long as I shall live." Then he tenderly embraced the young man; and when he remarked that, by the flow of his tears and by the excess of joy over so great generosity, Missere Alfonso could scarcely open his lips to thank him, he, weeping likewise, bade him hold his peace, and thus, without being able to say farewell one to the other, they parted with tears and tender kisses. The cavalier returned to the city, and Missere Alfonso in due time arrived in Bologna; and, as I have no fresh tidings concerning what may have befallen them after thus swearing mutual friendship, I will here cease writing about them.

MASUCCIO

ACCORDING to my humble opinion, the gentleman of Avignon ought to be praised no less for the punishment of his profligate wife then for the magnanimity he used towards the noble Castilian; for he was forced to undertake the punishment both by honour and the sense of duty, whereas his generous beneficence was the outcome of his noble nature. Beyond this, I do not mean to vex the gentle youth with the severe blame with which perchance certain others would visit him, seeing that the true nobility of his soul was so great that, being verily and indeed stirred by passion, he did not hesitate to sacrifice his life and his substance as well, to satisfy the great longing of his soul. But as we have spoken enough of these matters, I will now tell of three deeds of extraordinary virtue, wrought by persons of different quality, whereof it will be hard to praise one beyond another.

THE END OF THE FORTY-FIFTH NOVEL.

Novel the Forty-sixth

ARGUMENT

THE KING OF PORTUGAL CAPTURES IN BATTLE AN ARAB CHIEF, WHOSE MOTHER, WITHOUT TAKING FURTHER SECURITY, REPAIRS TO THE KING'S CAMP WITH THIRTY THOUSAND DOUBLOONS AS RANSOM. THE KING IS WILLING TO SURRENDER HIM, BUT REQUIRES CONDITIONS TO WHICH THE ARAB WILL NOT CONSENT; WHEREUPON THE KING GIVES HIM HIS LIBERTY AND HIS MONEY ALSO. AT A FUTURE TIME THE ARAB, OUT OF GRATITUDE, BRINGS A GREAT ARMY AT HIS OWN CHARGES TO AID THE KING IN WAR.

TO THE ILLUSTRIOUS AND EXCELLENT GENTLEMAN, THE COUNT OF FUNDE, ONORATO GAJITANO, PROTONOTARY OF THE KINGDOM *

EXORDIUM

BECAUSE you, my most excellent lord, would stand out illustrious even when set in the midst of great-hearted and generous men, I, who am purposed to finish my work by travelling in the paths where deeds of great courage and virtue abound, feel constrained to inscribe one of my novels to you, who have made illustrious the name of Onorato by your inborn worth. It seems, in sooth, most necessary that when writing of you I should consider virtuous deeds alone; wherefore I bid you, most illustrious lord, to enter this

* He was father-in-law to the Prince of Bisignano, the leader of the revolt of the barons, but remained loyal to Ferdinand. See Porzio, "Congiura de Baroni," p. 252.

fair and fertile garden, and, on quitting the same, to pluck and smell its odoriferous blossoms, which are faith and liberality and gratitude. Then, as a wise man, you can decide which of these should be held worthiest in the sight of mankind.

THE NARRATIVE

CONSIDERING that it is already universally known how many and how great have been the wonderful and victorious enterprises and great conquests attempted and achieved by the most Christian princes of Portugal, and how worthy of lasting commemoration the passage of the great sea into Afria, so often made by them when warring against the Aarbs, it would be more than superfluous for me to write particularly thereanent. Therefore, saying naught of the past, and dealing only with the doings of the present sovereign, the invincible lord, King Don Alfonso, I will tell how, after the time when his father, that most excellent and serene lord and king, had occupied the populous city of Agalsere Segher and divers other places taken from the powerful King of Fes, he himself conquered Tangiers, and led his following against the almost impregnable city of Arzil,* and reduced the same to such extremity that it could resist no further. He, however, received word that the King of Fes had despatched a valiant and sturdy captain, named Molefes, who was a kinsman of his, a wise and wary leader, and greatly beloved by the people, with a prodigious army of Arabs for the raising of the leaguer of Arzil. Wherefore King Don Alfonso, not wishing to await in his entrenchments the coming of Molefes, left the bastions around the city sufficiently guarded, and advanced with the greater part of his trustworthy soldiers to meet the Arab captain, disposing his troops in such wise that one morning at daybreak the two powerful hosts met. After a fierce and bloody encounter the Arabs were put to flight, routed and shattered, the greater part of them being either killed or

* In 1471.

wounded or taken. Amongst others the commander, who would not forsake his men, was seized all covered with wounds.

This capture pleased the king fully as much as his victory, for he hoped that the Arabs, having lost their captain, would quickly submit. Wherefore, after he had taken Arzil without further opposition, he determined to keep Molefes in future a prisoner, tending him well and honourably the while. When the King of Fes heard of this battle he grieved amain, and straightway sent to the king to beg him that, even though he would not restore Molefes by the usages of war, he would at least release him as a ransomed prisoner, offering in exchange a huge quantity of money and other gifts. To this request King Alfonso made a curt reply that he was firmly set against any mediation, and that no treasure would suffice to make him change his mind, begging at the same time that this question might never be opened again, forasmuch as any further application would be vain.

When the mother of the Arab leader heard the decisive terms of this reply, although she felt she was without hope, and that any action she might take would be fruitless, she determined, nevertheless, being a true mother, and single-hearted in her love, that she would make the utmost use of her wit and of her great wealth in order to redeem her only and well-beloved son. Wherefore, without asking advice of anyone, she took horse, and, attended by many servants and an honourable equipage, she met the great army of the Christian king, and, when she had without delay dismounted in front of his pavilion, the news of her arrival was forthwith taken to him. He, greatly amazed at her coming, advanced to meet her, and gave her greeting with the highest honour and respect; then, after exchanging certain words, she said to the king: "Most excellent lord, I deem that you are mightily and with good cause astonished that I have ventured to come thus suddenly and confidently into your royal presence; nevertheless, when you shall have heard the real reason of my journey, you will not only cease wondering, but will be disposed to pity me beyond measure. You, wise and exalted sovereign as you are, have received your heart direct from the hands of God, and will be able to understand well and truly how many and how great are the pains and the griefs which poor mothers must needs suffer when they hear how their sons have fallen into some untoward mischance, and especially those mothers who, as is my unhappy case, have only one son. My sorely distressed heart could find no rest nor peace. Therefore, having heard of your rare worth and divers wonderful reports of your high honour, I was so greatly heartened thereby that, led on by these reports alone, I have come thither; and standing now before you I implore and conjure you, by your God, for whose faith and honour alone you do battle, and by your virtue as a noble cavalier, that you will mercifully give me my only and beloved son. And albeit for such a boon no price would suffice, I, who am a woman, and by nature faint-hearted, have brought with me thirty thousand doubloons, which I beg you to accept merely as a remembrance of my visit, and which may serve to furnish some slight refection for your followers. Then I shall deem I have received, not only my son, but my very life as well, as a gift from you, and will promise that both he and I and all we possess—saving only our religious faith—shall ever be at your pleasure and command."

As she spake the king became more and more astounded at her wisdom and prudence and good faith; and what though he was urged by divers of his people to detain her, and thus capture at one stroke both her treasure and the rich equipage she maintained, nevertheless, harbouring none but virtuous thoughts, he determined that he would not, though he might win all the world thereby, do aught to put wrong or insult upon her. Wherefore, with courteous mien, he said: "Lady, your frankness in coming hither, and the praiseworthy reason thereof, have taken me so strongly that they have broken down the harsh design I had formed; so in brief I tell you I am willing to restore your son on these terms, to wit, that he shall, as soon as may be, return to my camp and serve under me in the campaign I have begun, and should he fail through illness to do this, he must promise that at no other time will he fight against me or my people." The lady, after thanking the king, duly made answer with no little spirit: "Most serene king, I will be wary how I promise anything the fulfillment of which lies in the power of another; nevertheless, I will remain here as long as your majesty may need me to persuade my son to agree to your demand, and to keep his word. But you must get his own promise to your condition, seeing that the discharge thereof lies with him. But I doubt not that, if he should pledge his word, he will hold his promise sacred, even if death should be the issue thereof."

The lady's noble answer pleased greatly the generous king, and his esteem of her rose yet higher. After the Arab leader had greeted his mother lovingly and had conversed with her somewhat, she and the king likewise told him the terms of his release, and when he understood the same, he, turning boldly towards the king, said: "Most worthy lord, as I know that many words are no recompense for deeds, I will refrain from that grateful speech which is due from me in acknowledgement of the great boon which you are willing to grant me. Now it only remains for me to think how in the future I may show my sense of the same by some grateful act. Still, in answer to the last of your conditions, I must say that, as I was already bound by our own laws before coming under these conditions, I might find my country in such strait that I must, in order to perform my highest duty, take up arms on her behalf; and in such case I should fail to observe my promise made to you either wholly or in part. Therefore, God forbid that I should think of promising to do what by a possible accident might be frustrated. Besides this, if the gift of liberty is to be accompanied by any condition whatsoever, I should still deem myself a prisoner, for any worthy deed of mine would be judged both now and hereafter as done by compulsion and not by free will. Deign therefore of your goodness either to give me my liberty unconditioned, or let me wearily live out my life in my present prison."

The most worthy and illustrious king perceived that in virtue the Arab cavalier showed himself the equal of his great-souled mother; wherefore, himseeming that he was somewhat under obligation to them, and desiring that no noble deed on their part should outdo his own generosity, he said, without taking time to consider his reply: "I desire not that either one of you should tarry here, nor that you should leave any of your goods in pledge or give me any promise. Therefore, lady, take back the money which you brought hither and return home together with your dear son, because it is meet that I, as a king, should act generously, especially towards you who trusted me entirely, in that you put your person, your wealth, and your honour to the hazard in your long journey. It would, in sooth, be a shameful thing to fail in faith to one so trustful; nay, even after death, the disgrace thereof would endure, and the hurt ensuing therefrom to our crown, especially after such a prosperous reign, would far outweigh any profit arising from your death or the seizure of your treasure. And to you and to him I leave the choice of peace or war, whether or not you will take arms against me; for I hope, even without your son's aid, to bring my present righteous enterprise to a victorious issue." And having brought forth many and noble gifts, such as were worthy of his high estate and of their acceptance, he bade farewell to them and sent them back to their country with an honourable escort.

When they returned home no one of the Arabs, either in secret or in public, could believe this thing; it seemed, indeed, something beyond all human chance, and they all ran in great crowds to see the lady who had thus returned with her son. She never ceased to praise the wisdom of the king, Don Alfonso, or to commend his munificence and liberality and great virtues; wherefore an amazing number of the people, incited by the words of the lady and her son, were eager to show their goodwill to him; and Molefes, having collected a great army and treasure, went at the opening of the season with fifteen thousand horse and foot, to place the same at the king's service, without his having foreknowledge thereof. When the king heard of this he was no less amazed than delig ted, and having honourably welcomed Molefes, let him abide ever near his person, and treated him as lovingly as if he had been his own brother. And Molefes, being overcome afresh every day by gratitude, served the king all his life in love and loyalty, warring ever against his foes.

MASUCCIO

WISHING to ratify this novel in my exordium, meseems the three virtues therein dealt with may each one be compared to a rare and fragrant flower. And I will not refrain from celebrating the virtue of the lady because she was a Moor. She, albeit, moved by maternal love, still showed wonderful faith in trusting so fully the word of the Chrisitan king, the foe and the assailant of herself and of her religion; and, vastly unlike women generally, who are timid, greedy, and suspicious, she, by placing her person, her life, and her honour in the king's hands, will oblige us, whenever we may speak of the faulty and defective nature of womankind, to except from our censure this Arab lady. But I, unwilling to praise her so as to slight her companions, will affirm that the generosity of our lord the king may be put on record as great beyond measure. Again, as I know not how to rate the immeasurable gratitude of the Arab captain, that most noble gentleman, I will leave this task to those better qualified by Nature with discretion, who will know how to praise one without offending another. Then, still keeping to virtuous paths, I will exhibit another royal act of justice, one as worthy to be remembered as those already told, albeit somewhat severe.

THE END OF THE FORTY-SIXTH NOVEL.

Novel the Forty-seventh

ARGUMENT

His Majesty the King of Sicily finds lodging in the house of a certain Castilian cavalier, and two of his gentlemen-in-waiting violently deflower the two daughters of their host. The King, having heard of this deed with much regret, makes the two gentlemen marry the young girls. Then, the honour of the damsels being restored, he causes the heads of the bridegrooms to be stricken off forthwith.

TO THE ILLUSTRIOUS LORD, THE DUKE OF URBINO *

EXORDIUM

If the most eloquent and skilful orators are wont, when they speak before great princes and lords, to lose their wits and tongues alike, what wonder is there, my most illustrious lord, if Masuccio, all unversed as he is, should find his wits, his bodily powers, and all the instruments he employs, fall into confusion and travail so great that he cannot do justice to others or to himself whenever he is minded to write to your lordship, who by reason of your skill in arms and military discipline may be called the new Mars, and, over and beyond this, from your eloquence and learning are worthy to be hailed as another Mercury? And although I travel by devious bypaths I have determined to let favour my little work by calling upon your illustrious and excellent name; and this I do, not merely to satisfy myself

* Federico di Montefeltro, one of the most virtuous and magnificent princes of the time. For an account of him see Symonds' "Renaissance in Italy," vol. i., p. 105.

but to observe the promise I made to you, what time you sojourned on our Parthenopean shores, to visit you as a friend, during your long absence, by the sending to you one of those forbidden letters of mine, telling of a certain noteworthy and just deed—albeit somewhat cruel and unrelenting—wrought by a prince of the house of Aragon; so that you, who are an ensample of virtue to all living men, may give your approval to such righteous dealing by reporting and making mention of the same. Farewell.

THE NARRATIVE

AFTER the rich and powerful city of Barcelona had once more returned to the fidelity due to that distinguished sovereign, King Don John of Aragon, her rightful and undoubted master, the king resolved to wreak full vengeance on the French with respect to the occupation of Perpignan. Wherefore he bade come to help this enterprise that illustrious Aragonese prince, the King of Sicily, his first-born son, who in obedience to his father's wishes forthwith forsook all the pleasures of his Spanish court and the delightful company of his newly-wedded wife, and, attended by all his barons and knights, took the road appointed. As he passed through the divers towns and villages of Castile he met with joyful welcome everywhere, being honoured almost as if he had been the king himself. When he came to Valladolid, where they prepared in honourable wise a great triumph, no less on account of his high station than because of his lately-formed relationship, he found lodging in the house of a noteworthy cavalier, one of the chief gentlemen of the city, who, after he had made lavish preparations, so as to show clearly what honours and rejoicings were due at the coming of so mighty a prince, bade come to his house on the following day the greater part of the ladies of the city to make merry for the prince with all kinds of musical instruments and divers dances, and the fairest and most modest amongst all these were the two young maidens his own daughters, who, by reason of their exceeding beauty, took the first place in the assembly.

On this account it happened that two Aragonese cavaliers, who were amongst the king's best beloved and highly favoured followers, fell hotly in love, each one of them, with one of the fair maidens aforesaid, in such wise that in a marvellously brief time they found they had sailed out into the sea of love, and that no contrary wind could have wafted them back into a haven of peace. Wherefore, having set their unbridled lust before all the honest obligations of reason, they finally resolved to reap the victory in their enterprise before they should quit this spot, even though it might cost them their lives; and, because the departure of their most worthy lord the king had been settled for the day ensuing, they agreed together to carry out to the full their wicked and iniquitous deed that very same night. After they had won over, by novel and very crafty working, a maid-servant of the gentleman's house, called by name Agnolina, who slept in the chamber occupied by the young maidens, and had bribed her with many gifts and still more promises, as is the custom of strangers, they came to an understanding with her for the carrying out of all that was necessary for their purpose.

The windows of the chamber aforesaid were very high above the street, wherefore their amorous ardour made them remember a rope ladder which they carried with them amongst their baggage—a contrivance they had used elsewhere for the scaling of convents—and it occurred to them that they might make use of this, because every other method seemed futile. At nightfall, having got in readiness everything necessary for their purpose, they went to the foot of the window, which had been carefully prepared for their entrance, and then, aided by the bribed waiting-woman, they attached the ladder to the window of the chamber wherein were the aforesaid damsels, secure as they deemed from all ill. Having clambered up one after the other and entered the chamber, which was wellnigh dark, they found the two damsels in bed, naked and uncovered, sleeping soundly and quietly. Then when each one of them through the fierce passion which possessed him, had discerned which was the lady of his love, he lay down beside her and got himself in readiness to work his evil and villainous and most wicked purpose. Their presence did not entirely arouse from sleep the poor girls, and each one for a time believed she was sporting with her sister—as indeed it was their custom sometimes to do—and before they were sensible of what had in truth befallen them, they found that their maidenhead had been rapt from them by the most cruel fraud and violence; whereupon, stricken with wellnigh mortal grief, they cried out aloud and called for succour.

When he heard the noise and the great clamour made by them, their father came straightway to the spot, and after the whole affair had been duly set forth to him by his daughters, and he had dlscovered that the cavaliers had taken to flight, and that the ladder was still fixed to the window, it seemed to him fitting to make the waiting-woman disclose by means of dire threats and even of torments who these were who had thus torn in pieces his honour and good name. Then, when she had made full confession, and when he knew certainly what had come to pass, every reader may imagine for himself what was his grief when he tried to console his daughters, who had already determined to die a terrible death by their own hands. Next morning, howbeit the anguish of his mind had almost deadened his spirit, he went inflamed with rage to the chamber of the Sicilian king, leading his daughters by the hand, and spake thus: "My lord, may it please you to listen to a few words of mine, with which I will strive to chase away any base or unseemly suspicions which might perchance infect men's minds. I come hither, bringing with me the fruits which two of your most trusted followers, using the foulest ingratitude, have culled from the garden which I had trimmed so that I might do honour to you and to them as well, and for the permanent strengthening of my due and loving disposition youward;" and having thus spoken he gave full account of all that had occurred. When he perceived how bitter was the weeping of his daughters, he too, mastered by the pity and the anguish which wrung his heart, was fain to break into a flood of tears. The king, who was very well advised and sapient, having listened to the words of the gentleman with the greatest grief and indignation, was so mightily overcome with rage and fury that he could scarce hold back his hand from dooming these two most execrable followers of his to a shameful death. But, having calmed himself somewhat, he concealed for a while the fell punishment which was the meet reward for so violent and unheard-of an offence, and, after consoling as best he could the poor father and his daughters, he determined in some measure to compensate them for their lost honour, and postpone for a little his vengeance.

On this account he put off his departure and forthwith commanded the Podestà to summon all the noteworthy folk of the city, women as well as men, to a fresh festival which he was minded to let prepare in the house of the gentleman. When the company had rapidly come together, and had been ushered into the great hall, the discreet monarch likewise entered, having on one hand the two damsels and on the other the two delinquent cavaliers, and, scarcely keeping back his tears, he made it clear to all present, point by point, the nature of the enormous offence that had been wrought. And because of what had happened, he desired, as some satisfaction for so detestable an injury lately wrought in that very place, that each of the cavaliers should take his ladylove to wife, and that each of the damsels should be granted a dowry of ten thousand golden florins. Whereupon all that the king had ordained was forthwith done, and the most illustrious and magnanimous sovereign at once ordered that the promised dowers should be paid in full to the damsels out of his own privy purse. Thus the grief and mourning which had possessed them heretofore was changed into the highest joy, and the merry-making became as merry again, and each one felt that the world was going better than ever before. Then the king betook himself to the great piazza of the city, and summoned to follow him all the nobles and townsfolk, together with the lately-wedded cavaliers under guard; and, when the heralds had proclaimed silence, the king spake thus to the listening crowd: "Gentlemen all, seeing that I have reaped some small satisfaction by furnishing to this worthy and honourable gentleman my host, and to his daughters, certain remedies such as are permitted to me to use in cases of a nature like this—as all of you can and will ever be able to vouch—I wish next to give full satisfaction to justice, whom I am bound to serve in the first instance and beyond aught else in the world, for I would sooner die than fail in any act of duty towards her. Therefore let each one of you suffer patiently, and excuse the act I am about to perform, what though, in order to free myself from this righteous obligation, it may cost me a pang such as I never felt before." Having thus spoken, the king, without another word by way of sentence, called an attendant, who brought out two black robes long enough to reach the ground, and having made the two cavaliers don the same, he ordered that their heads should be forthwith stricken off, in the midst of this noble pageant; which thing was at once done, while all those standing anear wept bitterly. And afterwards the bodies of the two were given honourable burial by the folk of the town. Then the king desired that all the goods they possessed, real and personal as well, should be given to the two widowed ladies.

When all these commands had been duly carried out, before the feastings which had been so lately begun should be overborne by this new sorrow, the king determined to give these two damsels, now mightily rich, in marriage to two of the chief noblemen of the city; and thus the festival, upon which the hot and cold blasts of so many and divers accidents had blown, came to an end. The king went his way, reputed by all as a prince most illustrious in these our times for his virtue and munificence; and the damsels lived joyfully and prosperously in the married state with their new husbands, all the sufferings they had known hitherto being changed into the greatest happiness.

MASUCCIO

THOUGH we might tell of many and divers most illustrious deeds wrought by this prince in various places, still this one here related must be held as most noteworthy. And certes if the king was minded, following his obligation, to obey the precepts binding upon kings, he could not have acted otherwise, because the princes of this world have been instituted and ordained by God, and by Nature, and by laws human and divine, for no other purpose than the ruling and governing of the people, and for the administration of justice upon earth, that they may hold the balance even, and drive out of their breasts all love and passion and all hatred and rancour as well. Those who are gifted with such laudable virtues and worthy parts may justly be celebrated, not as mortal men, but as eternal gods, and those of contrary nature will leave behind them a fame equally immortal, not as just, wise, and prudent kings, magnanimous and liberal, but as iniquitous, depraved, and vicious tyrants, as the surviving memory of the good and of the bad daily testifies to us. Thus I, following rapidly the course I have begun, will, with God's pleasure, put an end both to the next novel and to what little remains to be done of my work.

THE END OF THE FORTY-SEVENTH NOVEL.

Novel the Forty-eighth

ARGUMENT

A SON OF THE KING OF TUNIS IS TAKEN BY CORSAIRS AND SOLD AT PISA. HIS MASTER GETS TO LOVE HIM, AND IN THE COURSE OF TIME SETS HIM FREE, UNWITTING WHO HE IS, AND SENDS HIM HOME, AND THE YOUNG MAN BECOMES SHORTLY AFTER KING OF TUNIS. SOME YEARS LATER THE PISAN IS TAKEN BY SOME MOORISH GALLEYS, AND IT CHANCES THAT HE IS, WITHOUT KNOWING IT, MADE A SLAVE OF THE KING, WHO, HAVING RECOGNIZED HIM, CAUSES HIS SISTER TO BECOME A CHRISTIAN, AND OUT OF GRATITUDE GIVES HER, TOGETHER WITH A GREAT TREASURE, IN MARRIAGE TO HIS FRIEND, AND SENDS HIM BACK TO PISA A RICH MAN.

TO THE ILLUSTRIOUS LORD, JOANNI CARACCIOLO, DUKE OF MELFI *

EXORDIUM

BECAUSE I well know, my most illustrious lord, that not only is gratitude a passion innate in you, but that, in rewarding any service done for you, you excel all others in liberality and great-heartedness—as the guerdon given to me may testify to all men —I am disposed to dedicate this present novel, which deals with liberality and gratitude, to no other than your lordship, seeing that you are most worthy of the same. You, being a true judge of virtue, will be able to instruct others which of the acts I describe, ought to be published abroad with the highest praise.

* One of the leaders of the conspiracy of the barons. He was executed in the Castel Nuovo in 1486.

THE NARRATIVE

LAST year, while I was listening to divers tales of worthy deeds told by certain traders of note, I heard one told by a noble Florentine which set forth as a well-authenticated truth how, after the occupation of the island of Sicily by King Peter of Aragon, the Catalan corsairs used to harry without ceasing the Moorish coast; for which reason the King of Tunis, perceiving the daily hurt he got from these pirates, determined to build a fortified redoubt on a great rock called the Cimbalo, situated some miles out in the sea opposite Tunis, where he might maintain constantly a guard who would give signal by letting kindle a fire whensoever he might espy any galley of the Christians there lying hidden.

Therefore one day he despatched some well-armed ships, carrying many of his best-beloved chiefs, and artificers well skilled in such work, together with his first-born son, named Malem, to set in order the spot aforesaid. When they were anigh the Cimbalo, which was some miles out at sea, their ill-fortune brought upon them two Catalan galleys, which, by means of their oars, managed to get one on either side of the ships of the Moors, and, as well-trained falcons overcome their timid quarry, so the Moors, being unable either to fly or to defend themselves, and terrified to boot, were straightway seized. Malem, albeit a youth with cheeks still unmarred by the first down, was gifted with great prudence, and, having put off his royal attire, he disguised himself as a mariner. Together with the rest he was bound and sent on board the Catalan as an oarsman. The masters of the aforesaid galleys, having captured a vast number of Moors, determined to sail westward, where, taking with them the prey they had seized, they might best carry on their usual pillage. Having voyaged prosperously for many days they came to Ponza, and, being baffled and buffeted by contrary winds, they were forced after narrowly escaping shipwreck into the Foce d'Arno. Finding themselves safe there, they sold at Pisa the greater part of their Moorish captives, and amongst these was Prince Malem, a delicate and seemly youth, and him they disposed of to a young noble of Pisa, called Guidotto Gambacorta, who, seeing that Malem was of gentle presence and about his own age, and being further more swayed by his kindly nature, was not minded to let Malem be put to any base employment. He had recently become very rich through his father's death, and, having arrayed Malem in certain of his cast-off garments, he kept him always by his side.

Remarking day by day how Malem's polished manners gave token of noble and worthy nurture, he assured himself that the youth must needs belong to the highest class amongst the Moors, and, holding this belief, he made it his constant care to give him a pleasant life and good usage. He perceived, too, that Malem had a keen and noble intellect, in that he had learnt the language of Tuscany in a very brief time; wherefore he determined to let him add to his other accomplishments a knowledge of modern Latin letters.* These the youth easily acquired; so that when three years had passed no one would have taken him for aught but a well-read Tuscan. For this reason, and for the others given, he gained so completely the love and favour of his master that Messer Guidotto regarded him as another self, and gave over to him, as to his own brother and most loyal comrade, the regulation of all that concerned his body and estate. On which account Malem—who was called Martino by his master—remarking how he had fallen into such excellent keeping out of the lowest depth of misery, was highly content, praising God for the same, and taking care every day to serve his master diligently; and, what though with the liberty granted to him he might have taken to flight when he listed, nevertheless, held back by the love springing from the many benefits conferred upon him, he never let the thought of such action find place in his heart. Wherefore Guidotto, to show him

* Masuccio here bears witness of the high repute of the contemporary Latinists.

generations; so that these, having duly scanned every part thereof—each by itself and all together—may unhesitatingly believe the same when considering the spotlessness of our unblemished faith. Farewell.

THE NARRATIVE

THE Emperor Frederick Barbarossa, being strongly moved by religious fervour, determined as a Catholic and a Christian prince to visit the sepulchre of Him who willed to die upon the wood of the Cross for the redemption of us all. Wherefore he began privily to prepare everything needful for his voyage, so that he might embark without letting aught be known of the same. However, he failed to keep secret his plans from the hearing of Alexander IV.,* who was at that time exalted to the supreme pontificate and the vicarship of Christ. The Pope, because the emperor was his bitter foe, determined in his wicked heart that in the course of this most devoted and praiseworthy pilgrimage Barbarossa should be captured and slain by the enemies of Christ. And, so as not to delay his project, he commanded a certain excellent painter, to whom he promised generous reward, to go and draw the portrait of the emperor of his own natural size; and when this was shortly afterwards brought to him, wrought in such perfection that it lacked only breath to be esteemed real and living, he despatched it by his own private chamberlain to the Sultan of Babylon, whom he further instructed as to the carrying out of his wicked and detestable desire.

When the chamberlain had arrived and had been duly introduced to the sultan, he said: "Most potent lord, my sacred master the Pope sends you information—albeit you are rated as the principal adversary of the Christian religion and faith, of which he, as the successor of Saint Peter, is chief ruler and guide—that the emperor, not satisfied with the dominion of the greater part of the West, is urgently seeking to occupy the

* A misprint for Alexander III.

Novel the Forty-ninth

ARGUMENT

Frederick Barbarossa, having disguised himself, goes to visit the Holy Sepulchre. The Pope hearing this causes to be limned a portrait of Frederick, which he sends to the Sultan, wherefore Frederick is captured, and the Sultan before liberating him demands as ransom five hundred thousand ducats. Barbarossa leaves in pledge the Body of Christ, and having returned home sends the promised money. The Sultan is so greatly impressed by this integrity that he returns the ransom, and friendship having been established between the two sovereigns, the Emperor afterwards chases the Pope out of Rome.

TO THAT EXCELLENT AND DOUGHTY GENTLEMAN, MATTEO DE CAPUA, COUNT OF PALENA

EXORDIUM

EXCELLENT and valiant sir, the further time separates us from the gestes of old, the stranger must seem the narration of the same to new hearers, and as I am assured that many years have now elapsed since the following story has been duly told, I, having made it worthy of remembrance in future times by my rough penmanship, find great pleasure in dedicating it to you, who will take care that it be rated as a new story and a very true one both by present and future to yourself as the thing which is dearer to me than all aught else; so, what though I shall be injuring myself thereby, I desire to send you home rich, content, and taking with you my sister Maratra, who is, as you know, young, very fair and wise, and of good conduct. I wish her to become a Christian, and you to take her to wife. I beg you that you will do this for our common happiness." Guidotto thanked the king, and declared himself ready to carry out any wish of his; whereupon Malem caused his sister to be privily baptized, and gave her to his Guidotto to wife with a dowry of two hundred thousand doubloons in jewels and in money, and with many other noble gifts he sent them back to Pisa. There, having been welcomed by all Guidotto's friends and kinsfolk, they lived long together, and, blessed with great riches and fair children, they ended their days at the appointed time.

MASUCCIO

GREAT and wonderful were the unlooked-for and varied adventures which Fortune let befall the Moorish king as well as the Christian, and although, of a surety, the Christian, prompted by virtue and not by hope of gain, began the good deeds, we must nevertheless estimate as incomparable the unbounded gratitude of the Tunisian; but since the adventures which happened to both of them were fortunate in their ending, we may worthily extol both as virtuous men. Wherefore, considering only our Christian religion, which Guidotto refused to abandon what though he saw himself about to rise to such a lofty height, I will tell of another marvellous experience of which the Sultan of Babylon had sight and knowledge through the personal presence of Frederick Barbarossa, which instance is worthy to be held perpetually in high praise, as an example and commendation of our most true faith.

THE END OF THE FORTY-EIGHTH NOVEL.

their adventures both prosperous and adverse, the king let them array Guidotto at once in royal garments, and then led him into the hall where all his nobles were assembled. When he had told them who this man was, and how many and how great were the benefits which he himself had received from him, he charged every one of them to give to Guidotto honour and reverence equal to that which they gave to himself, and such worship as was due to their king and rightful lord.

After he had kept Guidotto by his side in this high estate and honour for about a year, he said one day: "Dear friend, since it has pleased the gods and our good fortune to satisfy my long-cherished and particular desire with such unlooked-for happiness, it seems to me right that, ever holding you in remembrance, I should try to give full satisfaction to all your wishes. Wherefore I charge you, by the perfect bond of our unspotted friendship, that you will tell me which thing would give your soul the greatest delight, to remain here with me, not merely as my companion, but as the master of myself and of all I possess, or to return to Pisa, bearing with you such a proportion of my goods as my power, rather than my duty, allows me to give you." Guidotto, although he foresaw himself seated on the royal throne, and in like manner compared his present and future estate with the past, was nevertheless drawn by the love of his country, by filial piety, by affection for his kinsfolk, by respect for his friends, and beyond all by remembering his perfect and undoubted faith in Christ, to elect at last to return to his home, with the kind permission of the king, declaring his choice and the reasons which led him thereto. Malem, albeit he grieved amain when he heard the answer, was nevertheless glad that he could give his friend this satisfaction, and said: "My Guidotto, He who alone knows all the secrets of the heart will be my judge that, after giving me so great happiness without any effort of yours or mine, He could not afflict me more than by separating us. Still, remembering that I hold my life and all my goods as a gift from you, it seems that no gratitude would avail to repay such high liberality unless I should give you

East as well; furthermore, divers of the chiefs, his allies, have persuaded him to seize upon the Holy Sepulchre. And this thing he is fain to do, not because he is a devoted follower of the banner of Christ, but because he is a wicked tyrant, greedy and ambitious of the goods of others, fighting against you and all your kindred so as to make himself the lord over all. And for the reason that he has heretofore found all his plans come to naught, and has been treated with ridicule by the Pope, he has at last become sensible of his failure, and now seeks to satisfy otherwise his insatiable greed. He has already made mighty preparations, and gathered together many Christian warriors; and besides this, trusting no one else to give him full intelligence concerning your land and your power, he has determined to come hither in person, accompanied by two knights who are in his closest confidence, disguised in pilgrim's garb; indeed, he has already set forth on his journey, and he will shortly have achieved all he is bent to do. On this account His Holiness is not only desirous to warn you, so that you may prepare to resist his fury, but he has also sent you the emperor's portrait taken from the life, by the means of which, if you shall let all your guards, in those parts through which he is like to pass, make close examination of the same, you may doubtless lay hold of him without risk."

Having thus spoken the chamberlain gave the portrait to the prudent sultan, who, albeit he had received and listened to the embassy and the ambassador with pleasure, and had shown himself exceedingly grateful to the Pope thereanent—though he afterwards dismissed the envoy rejoicing greatly at the many gifts bestowed upon him—thought privately that this deed was a most heinous crime on the part of the execrable brood of religious clerks, and let it serve to confirm all he had hitherto heard, how the supreme pastor of Christendom and the greater part of his advisers were not only besmirched with pride and avarice and envy and unlawful indulgences, but were also filled with the most wicked and nefarious vices. Nevertheless the sultan believed fully the words of the ambassador, and deeming from the aspect of the emperor's picture that he would prove to be a man of no little weight and worship, he forthwith gave directions to his officers as to the crafty stratagems they should use in ensnaring the emperor in case he should come thither. Furthermore he summoned all the pagan powers, and by vast expenditure of treasure he assembled a huge army, so that he might avert the dire shipwreck of his fortunes which was, as he deemed, being prepared for them.

When the emperor had set in order his affairs, and when himseemed that the time had come, he privily set forth on the journey which he had determined to make, taking with him two companions disguised like himself in marvellously cunning wise. After they had suffered great hardship, and discomfort of mind and of body also, both by land and by sea, they arrived at the spot where the foes of the emperor were impatiently awaiting his coming. He was at once recognized by means of his pictured presentment, and was without a word captured and led decorously into the presence of the sultan. Anyone may imagine how great was the sultan's pleasure, and although he received his prisoner somewhat sternly, nevertheless, when he considered his demeanour, he deemed that he must be a prince endowed by God and by Fortune with the highest gifts, and set him down as one wielding a power greater than he had hitherto dreamt of. Then he caused the emperor to be carefully guarded within the palace, and to be served with all the diligence due to his rank, and after a certain time he bade them bring him once more into his presence, and graciously inquired wherefore he had journeyed thither thus secretly. The emperor, who was no whit dismayed at his capture, answered with boldness: "Sire, as I have hitherto let pass my life in feasting and pomp, and in the delights and splendour and empty flattering of the world, I determined at last to do my duty towards God, and, for the saving of my soul, to journey through the midst of many and great perils and afflictions, to the lowly spot where the Son of God and Universal Redeemer lay sheltered awhile after He had been slain by the Jews. And although this praiseworthy desire of

mine has come to an untoward issue, I do not now, nor will I ever repent me, even though I should suffer thereanent not one but a thousand deaths, that I have shown myself the servant of Him who for my sake underwent death and agony, and have, in a measure, discharged my debt to Him."

The sultan at once knew by these words that he had judged aright from the outward seeming of his prisoner; wherefore he gave fuller belief to his upright and reasonable discourse than to the false and sinister intelligence, the fruit of blind envy and cruel hatred, which he had received from the Pope, and he straightway determined he would act magnanimously in this matter. So, turning towards the emperor, he said: "The great God, who knows everything and can do whatsoever He will, will bear witness on my behalf how, I having heard by report of the fame of your many virtues, felt myself mightily constrained to love you, and possessed by lively desire to work your pleasure; therefore, if you had deigned to take of me security and pledge of faith as to your coming hither, as was fitting for your dignity and state, then of a surety your great longing to visit these parts would have proved a pleasure to both of us. Nevertheless, things having fallen out in contrary wise—peradventure by the decree of Heaven—I am fain that you should find in me, whom you regard as your foe, a kindlier spirit than that which subsists in the heart of the chief ruler of your faith."

Having thus spoken, he showed to the emperor the portrait, and related how it had come to him, setting forth clearly how the Pope had sent word that he should not fail to compass the death of the original thereof. Then he said: "Although you may have come thither deeming yourself a conqueror, and are nevertheless fallen into my power and brought before me as a victim—although I might be avenged on my enemies through my enemy—I prefer to restore to you both your life and your liberty. Still the fact remains that, when I heard news of your coming, I laid out a mighty treasure in preparing to withstand you and in qualifying myself for attacking other foes; wherefore I have deemed it just that, as a return for this great boon of mine youward, you should pay me five hundred thousand ducats as some part of the money which I have spent in vain. When I shall receive this sum I will not only give you your liberty, but will likewise furnish you with a safe-conduct to your own land." As the emperor had been amazed beyond measure at hearing of the treacherous and wicked workings of the most iniquitous Pope—or rather of the precursor of Antichrist—so was he in equal degree delighted at the wellnigh incredible virtue of the sultan's nature, and that the affair was like to come to a joyful issue, seeing that the sum named appeared to him naught but a trifle. Therefore, after he had thanked the sultan for his great and unexpected liberality, and after they had discoursed together concerning the vice and adulteries of that shepherd of souls, who in sooth had become a greedy and rapacious wolf, he said: "Most worthy lord, although I looked upon the ransom you have asked of me as little greater than nothing, still I do not see, if I remain here, how I can possibly let it come hither; because, as soon as the report thereof might become known in Christendom, many men, both in Italy and in the lands without, desiring my downfall, would be stirred up by the counsel and favour of the Pope, and under the plea of feigned charity they would quickly seize upon my empire and all my treasures. Thus, not only would your design miscarry, but I likewise must perforce remain here a private person in captivity. Therefore, for the sake of your great worth, may it please you to complete the good work you have begun, by the only possible course, and I, besides my pledge of faith, will leave with you as a hostage and security another Lord incomparably greater than I myself am—by this I mean the most sacred body of my Christ Jesus. By it I swear to you that, as soon as I shall be come to my home, by the goodwill of the Lord aforesaid, I will send you without delay the whole of the debt I promise to pay, and will hold myself and all that belongs to me in everlasting bond to you."

The sultan at once understood the true and unfeigned arguments of the emperor, and he pondered much over the high value which the Christian prince seemed to set upon a little wafer made of bread and changed by the word of the priest into the body of Christ. This thought, indeed, worked in him so strongly, that it made him abandon any other plan he might have formed to gain this treasure, and persuaded him to accept the said pledge, not on account of any covetous desire for the money itself, but simply from the wish to behold so mighty a proof of the faith of these same Christians. So he answered briefly that he would agree to whatever might best please the emperor himself; whereupon everything was carried out according to the directions of Frederick. Now, as the business demanded speedy despatch, they summoned forthwith a minorite friar; and after he, in the presence of them all, had consecrated the body of Christ with much devotion and with the wonted ceremonies, they placed the same within a tabernacle most delicately wrought, and then the Christian emperor handed it with the greatest reverence to the care of the sultan, shedding many devout tears the while. Having once more ratified the vow which he had made, the emperor a few days afterwards returned as secretly as he had come.

When he had reached home, he spent much thought over the mighty boon which he had received, and having ordered certain galleys to be equipped with all despatch and caused to embark therein his honourable embassage, accompanied by a chaplain who was a very devout man, he sent by them to the sultan the five hundred thousand ducats of new coinage with a new device stamped thereon. In due time the ambassadors arrived at Alexandria and were conducted into the presence of the sultan. Their weighty and honourable mission being now accomplished, they handed over to the sultan the money, and begged him of his kindness that he would restore to them the pledge which he held. The sultan, who had received the envoys in friendly wise, and had marvelled within himself at this perfect good faith, at once caused the tabernacle of the body of Christ to be brought forth; whereupon the chaplain received the same with deep reverence, and administered the wafer to himself in the presence of the sultan and of his mamelukes and of the other courtiers. When he saw what was done the sultan was more than ever astonished, and, almost dazed with wonder, he said to himself: "In sooth, there is not in all the world another man to match this perfect friend I have lately gained." Wherefore he not only esteemed the power of the Christian faith to be most mighty, but likewise he judged the emperor to be a man of the loftiest soul, inasmuch as he had paid so high a price for a little mouthful of bread to be eaten by one of the meanest of his chaplains. Then, turning towards the ambassadors, he said: "God forbid that any sum of money or treasure should prevail to make me work any offence, or to mar by any act of mine this new friendship of ours. Wherefore go back to your lord, who is mine as well, with the money you have brought, and commend me to him, and say that, since it is his will to cultivate in his soul such great virtue, I desire that he should dispose of me and of all that is mine, as he may best please in everything, except he should require me to retain this money (which might, in sooth, remind me of him for a season), for I desire that the example of faith shown by him should stand for good as his ransom. Moreover, as I possess no pledge so valuable as that which he left with me for the fulfillment of his promise, I must employ the best I have and send him my first-born son, not as an hostage, but as an earnest and for the strengthening of our renewed friendship, and so that the emperor, who may be styled the one man of perfect virtue in all the world, may impart to my son his own excellent way of life and courtly bearing. Then, when it shall seem good to him, let him send the youth back with his morals regulated and well versed in all good manners."

Whereupon he made them bring forth a great quantity of his richest and most precious jewels, and these he sent with the returned ransom and his own son to the emperor, bidding the ambassadors likewise bear words of tenderest affection from him to their lord. After this the young man, who was received by the emperor with the highest honour and with feasting, lived at the court for about three years, and was treated as if he were Frederick's own son, and in due time was sent back to the sultan learned in letters and accomplished in divers gifts and virtues, and with no small store of presents. Having done this the emperor—in like manner as he determined to repay the benefits he had received from the sultan—resolved to punish the ill turn which the Pope had done him. Wherefore he marched against the Pope with a great army and much treasure, and—not for mere vengeance, but rather as a chastisement, and as an everlasting example to posterity of such great treason and jealousy—he drove the Pope out of Rome with all indignity, and let him die in poverty and the greatest misery in the hospital at Siena, in such wise as a vile priest ought to end his days.*

MASUCCIO

FORASMUCH as I could not in my discourse, nor in writing with my pen, censure enough the malignant nature of this Pope of times past which I have lately set forth—so completely do the reprobate lives of our present Popes afford us visible testimony of the same—I intend to keep silence entirely concerning the former Popes and their successors as well, seeing that it would be a superfluous and unnecessary trouble to point out in a few particulars a thing which is manifest to the entire universe. For which reason I will put a bridle on my tongue for good thereanent, and will refrain from speaking not only of the wicked and monstrous crimes which they commit both in public and in private, of the offices, the benefices, the prelatures, and the scarlet hats which are put up to auction at the deaths of the holders thereof, but likewise I will make no mention of the cap of the Prince of Saint Peter, which has been made the subject of barter and exchange. For this reason nothing else suggests itself to me, as an unworthy Christian, save to implore without ceasing the great majesty of God not to regard the defiled and corrupted

* Alexander III. died at Civita Castellana in 1181.

lives of such pastors as these, but rather to look upon the simple faith and prayers of the flock. We, too, being strengthened in the integrity and the perfection of the true faith of Christianity, and taking example from the virtuous conduct of the Moorish sultan and the most Christian emperor, may, as it behoves us, commend them as noble and praiseworthy to others. And, after I have added to the tales already told yet another one telling of a wonderful instance of virtue, I will, according to the desire I have long felt, say a last and pleasing farewell to my Novellino.

THE END OF THE FORTY-NINTH NOVEL.

Novel the Fiftieth and Last

ARGUMENT

A Castilian cavalier, a favourite of the Count d'Armagnac, serves the King of France, and is made field-marshal. The daughter of the count becomes enamoured of him, and makes him the offer of her person, which offer the cavalier, out of his great virtue, refuses. Whereupon the count in gratitude gives him his daughter to wife, and the king makes him a great lord.

TO THE MAGNIFICENT AND VIRTUOUSLY GIFTED SIGNOR BUFFILLO DE LO JUDICE, A NOBLE PARTHENOPEAN *

EXORDIUM

I REMEMBER, most generous and magnificent Buffillo, that you were not merely the first awakener of my sleeping intellect, but that it was through you chiefly that I am now come to be remembered by reason of my writings as an immortal amongst mortals. Wherefore, as I have in this last part of my Novellino dealt with that most worthy quality of gratitude, it seems to me only just that, if I show myself duly grateful for all the fruits culled from that fertile garden of yours, I ought not to be written down an ingrate. Accept, therefore, in your long absence, this my last novel, telling of the virtuous deeds of certain outlanders, in order that you, a most noble Parthenopean, who have made of yourself a voluntary exile, may, while reading the same at your leisure, be reminded somewhat of Masuccio, whom once you held so dear. Farewell.

* This gentleman seems to have been one of the Angevin nobles who joined the revolt at the beginning of Ferdinand's reign, and subsequently withdrew to France.

THE NARRATIVE

DURING my recent searches for stories of worthy gestes, I was told not long ago by a noble stranger as truth unquestionable that some time ago in Toledo, a notable city of Castile, there lived a cavalier of ancient and noble family, called Messer Piero Lopes d'Aiala, who had an only son gifted with much grace and comeliness and a gentle nature, and called by name Aries. As it often happens, the youth, in company with certain of his companions, was unwittingly involved in a midnight riot, when, being forced to use blows in his defence, it chanced that he slew with his own hand a noble youth, a dependent and a favourite of the king. Wherefore, fearing amain the king's wrath—albeit the nature of his involuntary deed would have warranted a defence on his part—he resolved to adventure in other lands, not being minded to tempt the extremes of Fortune. So, having taken leave of his father, he set forth with two horses and a few attendants, and as much money as his haste would allow him to collect hardly knowing whither he fared. But having heard that a deadly war was raging in France between the French and the English, he resolved to go thither in order to make a test of his valour; and, after he had joined the army of the King of France, he, as fate willed it, hired himself as a man-at-arms to the Count d'Armagnac, the captain-general of the army and a kinsman of the king. Aries, when he had received the wage due to him for this humble service, laid out the same, together with the money he had brought with him, in arraying himself as best he could, and began to bear himself bravely, not only in the throng and bloodshed of battle, but likewise in the storming of cities and castles, and in every other affair concerned with a soldier's calling; and the renown of his name increased so mightily that he was no less a pattern of valour and prowess to the French than he was a terror and alarm to his foes. Thus he gained the favour of his own captain in such wise that he was regarded by the aforesaid as another self, and the king's love towards him waxed so greatly that he was numbered amongst the most honoured and highly favoured warriors of that most powerful host. Wherefore the king made him a knight and field-marshal with much honour, and having granted him great increase of wealth, he took him still further into favour, so that, whether overthrowing his adversaries in battle or capturing their strong places, himseemed that he must always have his Aries by his side. While Aries was enjoying this high estate and honour which he had won by his valour, the winter season came on; whereupon the king, according to necessary usage, sent his army into winter quarters, and betook himself with the greater part of his comrades and knights, together with the freshly-promoted youth, to Paris. After the lapse of a few days, wishing to make some joyous festival over the victories he had gained, the king summoned a great multitude of his barons with their ladies to the merrymaking he had prepared, and amongst the first of these came the Count d'Armagnac with his only daughter and an honourable following. Now, after the joyful and sumptuous feast had gone on for several days to the delight of all the guests, it came to pass that the daughter of the count aforesaid, as she outshone all the other ladies in wit and beauty, was minded to exhibit like talent in the selection of a valorous lover. Thus, having noted the youth and comeliness as well as the worth and good repute of the Spanish knight, she became so fiercely enamoured of him that if she did not see him, or hear report of him, some hour or other of the day, she would perforce spend the night in vexation and weariness of mind.

And because she knew no one to whom she could with safety entrust the story of this fierce passion of hers, she herself gave him to understand by divers signs, some secret, and some wellnigh plain to everybody, that she was melting and consuming with desire for him. He readily gathered the purport of these signs, being well versed in the service of Love; and, albeit she seemed marvellously beautiful in his eyes, he, for the reason that he ever kept in sight the graven record of the many benefits he had received from his lord her father, determined as far as a lover could to drive away all thoughts of enjoying her, either now or in the future. And being set in this virtuous mind, he made cunning pretence not to understand the passionate looks and the other allurements of the amorous damsel, whereby he vexed her daily with bitter grief and weeping. Thus she, deeming that he was now become most careless of her and cruel to boot, held counsel with herself how she might by means both sure and easy, cause him to enter the lists of love of his own free will. So she took paper and wrote thereon a letter to him so featly expressed and full of passion that it might have moved to pity a heart of marble, much more the soul of the youth she loved, ending this epistle by saying that she had already chosen to die a violent death unless this great delight should be granted her.

Having sealed it and given it to a little page in her service, she instructed him to whom and in what fashion it should be delivered. The page, albeit he was very young, had a man's head on his shoulders, and divined at once that this letter must needs be concerned with something unseemly; so, disregarding the command given to him, he straightway went to his master and let him know of the letter and whither it was to be taken. The count opened the letter and read it, and I will let those gifted with noble hearts, and the foes of wickedness judge how great and of what nature was the heavy and heretofore unknown grief which possessed him when he learned how unbridled and criminal was the appetite of this girl, his only daughter. And being in this cruel case, he quickly canvassed the various means he might prudently employ in letting fall upon his wicked daughter due punishment, and before deciding to follow any one of the courses aforesaid he resolved that, as he had discovered to his intolerable grief how incredibly wicked this girl was, he would likewise see a final proof of the virtue and the perfection of the good cavalier, and then allow himself to be led by the issue of the affair. Thus, having carefully reclosed the letter and given it back to the page, he bade him carry out the lady's orders and take the note to Messer Aries, and when he should have received the reply thereto to bring the same to him forthwith. This service the page discharged with diligence, and was graciously received by the cavalier, who, when he had mastered the terms of the letter, made up his mind inflexibly to let virtue be his goal, although he had—while considering the many amorous propositions hitherto made to him—weighed well in his mind what meed of good or ill fortune might befall him on account of this answer.

Therefore, borrowing strength from his virtue, he took paper, and after answering honestly all the arguments of the lady's letter, he ended by saying he would rather suffer any violent death, than stain in aught the honour of the count his master either by thought or deed. But being wary of the wicked practices natural to the vile sex of women, he was unwilling to vex her too much, because when these artful creatures find themselves repulsed and despised by their lovers, they are wont in their rage to strike savage and deadly blows. So he consoled her with certain cold hopes which could never be realized, to wit, that he would give her his heart and become her husband with her father's full consent, but not otherwise. He realized clearly the difference of their positions, and could say no more than these words, which she must accept, or banish all thought of him; for, when he considered the honours and the advancement he had received from her father, neither her great beauty, nor her exalted rank, nor her wealth would ever prevail to make him let stain the fair fame of her father. And after he had sealed the letter and given it to the discreet little page, he awaited with no slight travail and disquiet of mind whatever ill fortune should befall him thereanent.

The page took the answer back to his lord, who wisely fathomed the purport of the same, and felt his former anger and heartfelt sorrow grow less, as he gathered assurance of the virtue of the knight he loved so well;

in sooth, he was so powerfully moved by this humour that he was fain not only to shower fresh honours upon the young man, but likewise to let pass from his mind all stern thoughts of punishment, and to become kindly and clement and generous towards the daughter he loved. Being firmly set upon this praiseworthy purpose, he went straightway to the king, without saying a word either to his daughter or to anyone else, and after he had told the whole story from its earliest beginning to the point it had now reached—not forgetting the new purpose in his mind—he begged the king graciously to pronounce his judgment on the question, and what he would wish to be done thereanent. The king, who was a wise and very prudent prince, did not rate the thing he heard to be any new trait in the evil and wicked nature of woman, but he was astonished and even confounded at the great constancy and strength of mind of the knight, and esteemed his virtue and seemly carriage more than hitherto. After they had discussed many and divers matters bearing on the question, the king persuaded or even commanded the count to carry out their latest formed and most praiseworthy project without farther delay. Aries, having been summoned, came forthwith, and when they were met together the king said: "Our very dear Aries, seeing that from the first of your coming hither to serve us under the count, you have shown by divers honourable deeds and by your courage, moderation, and prudence, how great is your bodily valour, there remained naught for you to do, to prove yourself the supreme exemplar of uprightness to all the world, except to let us see the hidden strength and the unrivalled virtue of your soul. Now, as you have given us a most commendable instance both of the one and the other, and as furthermore we owe to you our lives and all that we possess, it seems that we are bound, not only by duty and right-dealing, but also by the claims of your deathless virtue both in peace and in war, to bestow upon you such a reward that our gratitude shall be held worthy of praise, and you yourself be kept in eternal memory by all present and future generations."

Having spoken thus, and likewise told Aries all that had been done in the matter of the letter of the count's daughter, and her proposal, and his reply thereto, and all other things which had come to their hearing concerning the same, he went on to say: "In sooth, we ourselves, and the count as well, understood perfectly that the last expedient in your letter, touching a possible alliance which you held out to the lady, was only caused by fear lest you should leave her entirely distraught with anger; for you must have known that through disparity of blood this same was a thing not to be done. Nevertheless, if Nature had let you be born a noble, and Fortune a rich man, you, adorned as you are with your other excellent parts, might well have won as your wife a lady of a degree far higher than this one. Therefore, as you have had a great part in gaining victory for us in opportune wise, and have let great honour befall our well-beloved count thereanent, we have agreed together by an immutable decree that, after making up all the aforesaid deficiencies of yours as some reward for your renowned worth, we will give you this high-born and beautiful damsel to wife, as she so ardently desires, what though you may have held the same to be impossible." And when the king had spoken, the count with many gracious words gave full confirmation, and, almost weeping through tenderness of heart, embraced and kissed the young man and called him both his son-in-law and his only son. The discreet cavalier was as amazed as he was delighted at this good news, and could think of naught else to say than: "My lord, albeit I know quite clearly that the power of your Majesty is so great, and that the virtues of the count, my former master and now my father, are so widespread that they might together exalt me to a still higher pitch of honour and glory, the knowledge that I myself possess of my own demerits, is so sure that, even as it is impossible for me to express the thanks due to you, so it seems unmeet to me that I should in honesty and in duty accept so exalted a position. Therefore I must leave it to the wise consideration of your Majesty and his lordship, to make excuse for all I lack in one respect and another, and, holding my high position neither from fortune, nor from any merits of my own, but only through the kindness of your Majesty—undeserved and graciously bestowed as it is—I will as long as I shall live speak of myself as your own ransomed slave and the meanest servant of my lord the count." And when he had kissed the sovereign's feet they gave over talking of the matter.

The magnificent king, so as to let the affair come to an issue with all celerity, straightway commanded that a great feast should be prepared in the royal palace for the following day; which thing was done at once. And a great company of barons and knights and ladies and other noble folk having assembled there according to the king's desire, the joyous festival began without letting the damsel or anyone else know the reason thereof. When the feast was at its height the king caused the count's daughter—who was no less fair by nature than by her adornment—to be led into his presence, so that she might be seen of all; and after the heralds had proclaimed that Messer Aries had been made captain of the army and Count of Foes—that country being without a lord—the lovely damsel was joined in marriage to the new count in the midst of this memorable pageant. Wherefore the double feast was yet farther prolonged, and the joy and gladness of everyone waxed greater. After a short lapse of time, when the various causes which had brought about the recent event were made known, the king and the count and the lady and the cavalier won marvellous praise from everybody, individually and all together. After many days had passed, and the festival had come to an end, it pleased the count that the newly-married couple should retire to their dominions; whereupon they departed thither, after having been sped on their way by the king with many sumptuous gifts. When they arrived at their home they were welcomed by their people with the heartiest goodwill and with feasts and rejoicings, everyone being delighted at such joyous doings. It seemed, however, to the newly-made captain, that as a dutiful son he ought to invite his father, Messer Lopes, to share his high estate and fame. And when he caused him to be conducted thither under honourable escort at a fitting season, everyone will be able to judge how great and of what nature were the joy and gladness, filled full with love and charity, which fell upon all three of them. Now, letting them abide in such great happiness, I will for the future have done both with the writing and the telling of novels.

MASUCCIO

BECAUSE nowadays virtue is fain to lie prostrate on the ground, and to be rated of little or no value by princes, and to get for reward naught but ingratitude, it seems to me that, when we hear tell of any deed of gratitude wrought in old time, it should be written down and noted, not only as an act of virtue, but as a supernatural thing—a testimony of which we may find in the dealings of the King of France and the Count of Armagnac with the worthy Castilian knight, and the advantage which arose therefrom. But as the boons bestowed and accepted were the source and origin of the virtue afterwards displayed by Messer Aries, and at the same time opened and pointed out to him the path he should take, I deem that he who initiated the matter ought to win our highest praise; then it may be left to the discreet consideration of the reader or hearer to decide to which of the virtuous deeds aforesaid should be given the foremost place. Still, it cannot be denied that, albeit the cavalier was perforce somewhat ungracious towards the lady, the proof he gave of his constancy thereby was a marvellous one, seeing that by sheer force of virtue he overcame his desires in thus refusing such illustrious solicitation, and in considering only how he might do justice and honour to the count his master, as has been fully set forth already. But as it is now time for me to give rest to my wearied brain, forasmuch as I have finished the fifty promised novels, it only remains for me to give a last God-speed to my beloved Novellino. Having done this in brief, I, now that I have escaped shipwreck, will cast anchor in port, and henceforth will live the life of a shepherd of the woods who has no sheep to tend. Farewell.

THE END OF THE FIFTIETH NOVEL.

Masuccio

TO HIS BOOK

HAVING now by God's mercy come to the end of the task set out and undertaken by me, and having brought to a fortunate issue the special and much-desired object I had in view, it seems to me full time, and a matter of duty also, to send you, my humble little book, into the presence of that lady on whose behalf I undertook this labour, which proved to be almost more than my feeble wits could endure. And know for certain, my Novellino, that she is not only illustrious by reason of her extraordinary virtues amongst ladies now abiding upon earth, but is even worthy to be yoked together with the celestial goddesses. Wherefore let me specially exhort you to present yourself before her with all humility, and, after you shall have kissed her snowy and most beautiful hand, to offer yourself to her without any other conveyance on my part. Then, when you, lying at her feet, may have commended me to her mercy, take care that you forget not to beg her, of her especial grace, that she will not hold it irksome to accept you as the most trifling of gifts. But if, peradventure, you should perceive that, because of your mean presence, she should receive you with a disdainful face, remind her that I am well assured she must have read formerly in some excellent history in the Greek tongue* how Xerxes, the most glorious sovereign of divers kingdoms, and lord over myriads of men and vast heaps of treasure, was one day riding through his dominions, accompanied, as was due to the state of so mighty a prince, by a goodly number of nobles. As he journeyed he came to the ford of a river, and by the river's brink there was a labouring man ploughing in his master's field with his master's oxen. To him some-

* A delicate compliment to the learning of the Duchess Ippolita.

one cried, "Behold the king!" The poor fellow remembered that there prevailed in former days a very ancient custom by which everyone, the first time he might catch sight of the king, should make him some offering, this man a trifling one, that man a rich one, according to the faculty of each. Thereupon the poor man, because he was void of any means of performing this deed (which was his duty) of honouring the King, and of acknowledging his superiority, was suddenly overcome by a marvellous reverence and affection which flowed from the very core of his heart, and, having left his oxen, he ran with hasty steps and cast himself into the river, in the midst of which he at that moment beheld the king. Then, holding his hands close together, he took therein a handful of water, and went towards the king and said: "My lord, in me there is neither gold nor silver, nor any other thing which I might offer in dutiful service to you, and acknowledge you as my king and lord. I have naught besides this drop of water which you may see in my toil-wearied hands. Take it, therefore, I implore you, with cleanness of heart, like that which I feel in offering the same, and know for certain that if Fortune had given me more I would have made in becoming fashion the offering which is your due."

The benevolence displayed by the king was indeed marvellous; for, like a true gentleman of nature, he did not think it beneath him to bend down and to touch with his delicate mouth the coarse and muddy hands of the countryman, the tiller of the soil, and to drink the water therefrom, taking no regard of the quality of this trifling gift, but only mindful of the true affection of the giver. Then, having thanked the countryman for his love, he rode on and went his way, God speeding him.

Thus, as soon as you shall have brought back to the lady's memory the instance aforesaid, on the strength of the authority here produced, tell her once more—albeit I am well assured that to the loftiness of her generous and exquisite spirit even the most sumptuous gift must needs appear mean and niggard—to deign to consider, not the imperfection of your nature, but rather the depth of the affection of him who has ventured to despatch you to her. Furthermore, beg her that, with the benevolence she uses in treasuring up little things, she will place you amongst the number of those which she has collected, and, for some brief time at least, to keep in memory Masuccio, her most devoted servant. And now, because I am persuaded that, if you carry out duly and sufficiently the directions aforesaid, you will meet with kind and joyful reception at the hands of this same serene star, it seems to me meet and proper, and even necessary, for me to instruct you soberly how you must needs pass the residue of your days with all those who may become intimate with you and read your pages.

In the first place I am fain that you should never take it upon yourself to persuade, or to beg, or to constrain anyone to read you; by obeying me in this you will not let those lengthy and not very enticing novels of which you are made up, a work of clumsy composition and uncouth speech, bring irk and regret to those readers who may find them distasteful. But to all such as may read you of their own free will, you may lay bare every secret, with all the pleasure in the world. Still you must be wary, for it is most certain that there will come across your path divers murmurers to whom the faculty of fine speech has been denied by Nature, who, on the other hand, allows them to heap censure upon virtuous men by means of their own vices. These, in sooth, will be eager to crucify me for what I have written against the honesty of womankind and the wicked life of false professors of religion. See, my Novellino, when you answer such as these, that you are wary in your words, and tell them in brief and weighty speech that whatsoever I may have written concerning women was nothing more in comparison with what I might have written, than the taking of a tiny drop of water out of the vast ocean—and of the truth of this thing the greater part of women can bear witness, the one to the other. But with respect to the reprobates under religious vows—who without doubt will come to blows with you—take care you reply to them boldly, and say that you cannot see how reason can demand, or honesty allow, that those who neither lead the life nor follow the ways of men vowed to religion, can, or ought to be held or to be called religious. For if we take into account the great mass of open sins and crowning acts of wickedness and ribaldry which they have committed in the past, and, as must be plain to anyone who inquires, still commit every day that passes, we may justly write them down and call them naught else than ravening wolves, or rather soldiers of the great Satan himself. Wherefore, if I have spoken at length, but yet not enough, concerning such as these, no one can rightly cast reproaches upon me; and certes, if I had been sure that men would have taken my meaning, I would have called these wretches not men of religion, but rather ministers of Satan.

Therefore let those men of true and perfect religion remain in their hallowed solitudes, holding the faith which approves itself to them, for against such as these I never have and never will presume to utter a carping word. Nay, rather I would say once more what I have always said heretofore, to wit, that those who dedicate themselves entirely to the service of God, and to the pure and most gentle ministrations of our divine religion, flying from the world and its treacherous snares, out of which they have of their own will withdrawn themselves, should not only be honoured and loved and accepted as religious men, but should likewise be duly praised and esteemed by us as blessed ones and saints in their lives, and in their deaths as well, seeing that they may with infallible truth be called the adamantine columns and the eternal support of our Christian religion and faith.

Wherefore let these words be a sufficient answer for those who, standing afar off, make me a target for their poisoned arrows. But if they should still answer that I, not being their rightful judge, cannot be expected to know aught concerning their failings, nor how to draw distinction between the good and the bad, and that whatever has been found sufficient for the rest of mankind now living upon earth should be sufficient for me, be steadfast, O Novellino! and answer boldly that, because some of the nefarious deeds of these manglers and destroyers of religion have become the subject of common talk, it has seemed to me that, for the sake of God, and nature, and decent manners, and on account of the good men amongst those vowed to religion, it ought to be allowed to me, by distinguishing as above, to exalt the perfect and to damn the evildoers, in order that other men may not hold that all religious persons are defiled with the same pitch—a contention which has been clearly and sufficiently dealt with by me, truthfully and with due justification, in your first part.*

To meet these just and valid arguments, since they cannot and know not how to answer the same, they will at times have recourse to the words of those vile women who declare that they shall see justice done upon me at the day of judgment. If, however, they deem they can smite or harm me by such blasphemy as this, see that you answer them, without farther concern, that I, on my part, neither seek nor wish for longer time to elapse before the coming of that universal judgment in which we shall all be rewarded or punished according to our good or evil doings.

Coming after such as these, I trow, you will find others of a sort far less malignant, who will affirm that, of the fifty novels out of which you have been compounded by my hands, the greater number are naught but fables and lies. Let it therefore please you tell these that by such discourse they come not near the truth, forasmuch as I now invoke the most mighty God as my witness that all these stories are verily true, and for the most part deal with matters which have come to pass in these our days. Those which are arrayed in antique garb, and are as it were the greybeards of fiction, have been confirmed as real and true histories, what time they were told to me by personages of the highest authority.

Thus, while you both oppose and make answer to the many and various arguments, which may be advanced against the conclusions you seek to establish, you will prove an excellent and abiding protection and shield to your Masuccio. But do not marvel if I send

* Page 9 vol. i.

you forth on so momentous a journey meanly clad and stained with tears, seeing that you must surely know of the recent cruel stroke, the bitter and bloody misfortune which has been to me the cause of lasting sorrow and never-ceasing tears. Go your way, therefore, weeping, with your garb transformed and with new aspect; and until you shall have duly come to your destination, and shall have carried out the commands given to you, do not cease from letting fall your tears; because, with regard to your author, the sun is eclipsed, the moon obscured, the heavens, planets and stars bereft of their eternal light. Dead is that gracious and comely gentleman, that illustrious, rare, and magnanimous lord, the most serene Roberto, Prince of Salerno, the great and most skilful admiral of this kingdom of ours, now widowed and shrouded in gloom. Weeping the while, I can say of him, with unquestioned truth, that worthy generosity has been chased away into perpetual exile; that Death, cruel monster, with rapine and violence has put out the light of charity; that the poor will now miss their consoler, and the strong fortress of the needy is no more; and, lastly, that the gates of the common house of shelter for worthy gentlemen are closed for ever. Weep, therefore, my Novellino, since he is now dead through whom letters, both in Latin and in the vulgar tongue, were lifted to great honour; through whom military discipline in action, in the council chamber, in the royal jousts, and in the sumptuous games of Mars, was exercised with the most studious care, and through whom the fierce wild beasts of the forest were put to flight in the chase and the various birds disturbed from their haunts. Cry out aloud, therefore, my poor Novellino, forasmuch as this sublime prince in his death has let die justice as well, seeing that he was wont to administer the same with so great integrity that now justice itself, and truth as well, seem to be hidden, and every happy virtue felled prone upon the earth. Cry out with a loud voice, "O glorious prince! where is now your elegant and thoughtful eloquence, where is your marvellous wit, your wide range of vision, your excellent judgment, and the perfect counsel and advice which you the utmost proof of his affection, was fain to induce him to become a Christian, in order that he might be able to mate him with some well-born damsel, and to give him a good share of his wealth; so, having called him one day, he made clear this wish in becoming wise. To this Martino humbly answered: "My lord, when I call to mind my wretched condition what time you purchased me for mean service, and then survey the estate to which you, by your own innate goodness and virtue, and without any desert of mine, have raised me, I feel I ought not only to consent willingly to do this thing which you, acting with such love and kindness, desire for my weal, but even, should your needs demand it, to give you my very life. However, feeling that I ought not to keep secret from you any of my affairs, great or small, I would have you to know that, leaving the truth and the falsehood of our religion to the care of truth itself, I am not inclined to change my present faith for another, though refusal should cost me my life. Wherefore I beg you that, of your great virtue, you will not trouble my soul more with this matter; but if, to complete the good offices you have done me, you should deign to let me go to see my father, who is reputed as a great and noteworthy merchant amongst the Moors, I hope I may soon let you taste the fruits of his traffic and of my own to boot, to your very great satisfaction. But if you should incline to the contrary course, on account of the great love you bear me, be assured that I will never, while life is in me fail in my duty youward."

Guidotto, knowing the righteousness of Martino's disposition, and holding his words in no light esteem, felt no regret that he had bestowed upon him such great wealth and honour, and made answer thus: "My Martino, in some measure my deeds may have made it clear to you how I could not have loved any man more, or even as much, as I have loved you, even if such an one should have been bound to me by the closest ties of amity or kinship; and, if my request may have transgressed in a measure the bounds of right dealing, be assured that it sprang from naught else than the desire to unveil to you the inmost recesses of my heart. However, now that I know your desire tends otherwhere, I bid you be of good cheer, for I promise you that in a very few days I will fully bring to pass your righteous wishes."

Martino, when he heard this most gracious reply, said, weeping as he spake: "My lord, because at present I find myself utterly unable to pay my debt of gratitude, I care not to be furnished with the power of expressing the same. I resign both the one and the other* into the hands of Him who is the rewarder of all good deeds, so that He may for my sake recompense you in such wise as may give you the greatest pleasure, and to Him I commend you and myself as well."

Guidotto, weeping the while out of tenderness of heart, embraced and kissed Martino, and then, after other fitting discourse, they took counsel together as to how Martino might take passage in the Pisan galley as far as Barbary. When everything concerned with the voyage had been set in order, when Guidotto had honourably furnished his beloved Martino with all gear needful therefor, and filled his purse with money, and heaped upon him divers gracious and worthy presents, he sent him home, both of them having shed floods of tears at parting. The King of Tunis meantime had caused a diligent search for his son to be made through a greater part of the west by renegade Christians and others, without getting any news of him, and now, when he beheld the youth standing before him well clothed and in honourable seeming, he was taken with a great access of fatherly love; for, as he had abandoned all hope of ever seeing his son again, his joy and satisfaction were all the greater. Wherefore, after he had bidden him welcome home many times, and had heard of all the adventures he had met, he sent commands to all parts of his dominions that everyone should rejoice mightily over the recovery of his son Malem, which thing was duly brought to pass. A little time after these feasts and rejoicings the King of Tunis, who was already very old, passed away from this life; whereupon the people, taking heed of Malem's great worth, and how he de-

* Orig., *l'uno e l'altro*, meaning presumably both the debt and the gratitude.

served as the son of the late king to inherit the royal sceptre and throne, cried out aloud and hailed him King of all Barbary by universal assent, nursing the hope that under his rule they would enjoy prosperity. Thus, to the joy of his people, Malem became King of Tunis forthwith.

But while he entered into full enjoyment of his father's wealth there shone ever before his eyes the graven record of those unrecompensed benefits which Guidotto had so graciously conferred upon him, and he resolved that his repayment should exceed the gifts received in the same measure as his present dominion and power surpassed the estate of his friend; and all the more, because Guidotto, moved by his many virtues, had come forward thus liberally, was he himself bound to be generous out of gratitude. Wherefore his mind was firmly set to consider how he might best carry out his righteous intent, and God and his good fortune, after showing him so much favour hitherto, were minded furthermore to let satisfy his honest and laudable intent. Guidotto, albeit he was one of the chiefest citizens of Pisa, found himself olbiged to fly as an exile to Messina on account of certain civil broils; and, having embarked in a merchant ship, was captured by Moorish galleys when sailing by Faro. Having been taken to Tunis, he was through the working of his good fortune given to the king as a slave. Now anyone with understanding may realize with what satisfaction and delight and pleasure the mind of Guidotto would have been filled had he known who was his master; as it was, I can imagine that he cried many a time to himself: "Alas, my fortune! alas, my cruel lot! I, a freeborn man, am now a slave. Would that Fate might let me hear of my Martino! for certes he, being my friend, would send to Pisa for my ransom and set me at liberty, thus saving me from ending my days in slavery." And in such wise the hapless Guidotto tormented himself with bitter lamentations, deeming his lot worse than death, and living bereft of hope. On this account he felt that Fortune could not have brought him to a worse pass, and set himself down as the most wretched man alive, because he was deprived of all hope of redemption, and because, had he fallen into the hands of any other, he might have had sight of his Martino, who would have procured for him deliverance.

One day poor Guidotto was loaded with chains and sent with some other Christian captives to work in a large and very fair garden belonging to the royal palace, into which no one ever went save the king and certain of his intimate friends. Now necessity and compulsion had taught Guidotto how to till the ground, and he, filled with intolerable grief and finding no hope that things would ever be better, passed his days plying the mattock and the pruning knife, weeping plentifully as he worked. It happened one day when the king was walking in the garden that it seemed to him he espied his poor Guidotto, and, albeit for a time he deemed it impossible that the man before him could be his friend, so greatly had misery altered him, when he looked more closely his doubt became certainty, and approaching he inquired of him: "Tuscan John,* who are you and whence do you come?" The wretched Guidotto raised his head at the king's voice, and although the newly-grown beard and the royal robes had wrought a vast change, he recognized at once who it was, and was assured that his Martino had become King of Tunis. He cast himself weeping at the king's feet, and, overcome by excessive and unlooked-for joy, awaited some sign of favour. Malem was now certain that it was in sooth his Guidotto, and as he had earnestly desired this thing to come to pass, even so the sight of his friend beside him gave him the greater joy. He considered, indeed, that everything Fortune had given him was as naught compared with the coming of this friend upon whom misfortune pressed so sore. Thus, having made Guidotto rise to his feet, he kissed him tenderly on the mouth, and caused his chains to be stricken off, and led him by the hand into his apartment. After they had many times embraced and kissed one another, and recounted

* San Giovanni is the patron saint of Florence, and every citizen receives the saint's name. Masuccio has here led us to assume that all Tuscans followed the same practice.

THE FORTY-NINTH NOVEL.

This novel is a version of the same legend which is set forth in an old German popular tale, entitled, "Ein wahrhafftige historii von dem Kayser Friderich der erst seines namens, mit ainen langen rotten Bart den die Wahlen nenten Barb: derselb gewan Jerusalem unnd durch den Babst Alexander den dritten verkuntschafft ward dem Soldanischen Kunig der in gefenklich hielt etlich zeyt. Un wie der Pundtschuch auff ist khomen in Bairn." Augspurg, 1519.

In the British Museum there is a translation in MS. of the same novel as told by Masuccio by Henry Parker, Lord Morley, dedicated to Henry VIII. in the following terms:

"To the most high most myghty and most Christen King Kinge Henry the eight by the grace of God King of Englond Fraunce and Ireland Defender of the faith and in erthe supreme hede of the Churche of England and Ireland your most humble subiecte Henry Parker knyght Lord Morley desireth to your highness pptual honour helthe and victorye.

. . . .

"Scenek wryteth in one of hys epystles that he wrote to Lucilus (mostę gratiouse and most deare soveraigne lorde) that faythe is the sure fundation of mans breste. And albeit that as sum dyvers clerks wyll that he knew not the verei true faithe but as other philosophers that by natall reasone affyrmeth that there must neades be one God that must rule and gouverne all. Yet as I do suppose that he coulde not have wryten so truly of faith oneless he had had sume perticular knowlege of Chrystes teachynge by Saincte Paule as the greate Doctoure saincte Jherome affyrmeth. But lett it be so that he ment it nothynge to the faythe of God but onely that faithe the whiche a man oughte to kepe one man to another yet surely the sentence is worthy allwayes to be pryntede in our hertts for who so ever he be pore or ryche that observeth not hys faithe fyrste to hys superiour next to hys freandes and thyrdly and generally to all men. What is he to be reputede but (as Isope saith in hys fables) a very fox that promyseth frenshyppe and love to small lytle beastes to noone other intent but for to devoure theym (farre from an honeste chrysten man so false a condition) but if it be in a poore man so ascendynge up to the greatest of all in ungoodely and ungodly wyse what it is to be counted in a spyrytual man that by faithe and by his worde dothe consecrate in forme of breade the moste blessyd body of God. And not onely hymselfe to be unfaithfull but further to goo aboute to devoure and to murder the faithful servaunt of God as that false antecriste Alexander IIII bysshope of Rome dyd as this lytle hystory declareth to the moste chrysten and moste noble ffrederyke barbarouse Emperour of Rome whyche saide hystory for as muche as that youe my most redoubted and moste graciouse Sovereignte Lorde hathe bene in lyke factyon unfaithfully unjustly and falsely by dyvers and sundry tymes by Paule bysshoppe of Rome with all fraude possible to disturb your moste godly and moste faithefull wayes I thought it shulde not be unpleasant to your highnes yf so were that ye dyd votesafe to reede it to se the ungodly faction of the ungodly bysshoppe the true faithe of the goode Emperor the great nobleness and liberalite of the Sarrasyn Souldan of babylon declared and tolde by Massuccyo Salerytano in hys Novells or tales whiche he wrote in the Italyan tongue so excellently well that I thynke in noo tonge it can or may be amendyde. Nevertheles as my poore lernynge is I have transllatyde the same (as your hyghness mya perceyve) into our natural tonge. Whiche if in any pointe it dothe content you my moste Christen sovereigne Lorde It shall not onely rejoyce my verey herte but further encourage me as my moste bounden duety requyreth to pray to Criste Jesu send youe thys yere to cum and all your yeres after perpetuall helthe vyctory and honour wyth your noble wyfe Queen Katheryn and that hope of this your realme to cum prynce Edward youre sonne that after infynyte of yeres in thys worlde ye may cum to that kyngdome that ever shall endure. Amen."

THE END.

Notes

THE FIRST NOVEL.

The source of this story is probably the fabliau, "Le Sacristain de Cluni," by Jean le Chapelain (Le Grand, iv. 252). It has parallels in almost every European language. Heywood, in his "History of Women," gives one called "The Fair Lady of Norwich." This story is repeated in Bloomfield's "History of Norfolk," Sir Thomas Erpingham figuring as the avenging husband. "The Knight and the Friar," one of George Colman's "Broad Grins," is a metrical version of the story as given in Bloomfield. Both of these strongly resemble Masuccio's novel.

It occupies the thirty-first chapter in the English "Gesta Romanorum," and in the "Seven Wise Masters," History XIX., is a medley of this story and "The Three Hunchbacks." Kirkman, a contemporary of Heywood, has left a translation of "The Seven Wise Masters," called "Erastus," and substitutes in this story a lawyer for the monk. The oldest English version is probably the metrical story of Dan Hew, Munk of Leicestre.

THE SECOND NOVEL.

In a work by Pontano, "De Fortitudine," Lyons, 1514, there is a dialogue between Charon and certain unhappy spirits, and one of these, a woman, tells an experience of hers somewhat resembling Madonna Barbara's. Compare also Bandello, iii. 15, which is the same as a story in Josephus, xviii. 4.

THE THIRD NOVEL.

The fabliau, "La Culotte des Cordeliers" (Montaiglon, iii. 275), is probably the source of this novel and also of Sacchetti's CCVII. It also occurs in Sabadino and in Poggio, CCXXXII. A modern version is given in "Les Contes Remois."

THE NINTH NOVEL.

H. Stephanus in his "Apologia pro Herodoto," lib. i., c. 21, tells how in the mountainous parts of Dauphiny and

Savoy the friars were wont to persuade the peasants' wives to feign themselves possessed in order that they might enjoy the task of exorcism.

THE SEVENTEENTH NOVEL.

There is a story like this in "Comptes du Monde Avantureux." An abbreviated translation is given in Painter's "Palace of Pleasure," No. LXVI. Marston's "Dutch Courtesan" is derived from the same source.

THE TWENTY-FIRST NOVEL.

The first story in the "Pecorone" is the same as this novel. Painter's version ("Palace of Pleasure," No. XLVII.) is a translation from Ser Giovanni. "Aleria," a novel by Giovanni Francesco Loredano deals with the same subject. It is to be found in a volume called "Choice Novels and Amarous Tales, written by the most refined wits of Italy," London, 1652.

THE TWENTY-THIRD NOVEL.

This novel is a variation of the story of Œdipus, and is probably the most repulsive extant, inasmuch as the mother is the instigator of the crime and all along cognizant of her offence. In Dunlop's "History of Fiction," vol. ii., p. 219, there is a note dealing with the parallel histories which are found in every literature. An instance not there given is one shadowed forth by an inscription on a tombstone in the parish church of Martham, Norfolk. It runs as follows: "Here Lyeth the Body of Christ° Burraway, who departed this life ye 18 day of October, Anno Domini 1730, Aged 59 years. And their Lyes ☞ Alice, who by hir Life was my Sister, my Mistres, my Mother and my Wife. Dyed Feb. ye 12, 1729, Aged 76 years."

THE TWENTY-NINTH NOVEL.

The opening of this novel resembles History XIX. in the "Seven Wise Masters," and the conclusion is evidently taken from the same source which supplied Chaucer with the subject for the "Miller's Tale." No editor of Chaucer, except Mr. Skeat, has detected this parallel story.

THE THIRTY-THIRD NOVEL.

The earliest form of this story, and the one accepted by certain writers as the source of Masuccio's novel, is the romance of "Anthia and Abrocomas," by Xenophon Ephesius, a Greek writer who lived probably during the time of the Antonines. This story is extant in MS. at Monte Cassino and in several printed editions. The principal editions of the text are Vienna, 1796, Haarlem, 1818, and one in the "Corpus Scriptorum Eroticorum Græcorum," Leipzig, 1833. It has been translated into Italian by Salvini, into German by G. A. Burger (Dessau, 1782), into French by P. Bauche (1736) and J. B. Jourdan (1748), and into English by Rooke (1727). There is likewise a reference to this romance in the "Miscellanea" of Angelo Poliziano, cap. li. The story aforesaid contains the central situation of the plot, the simulated death of the heroine, but in many details it differs essentially from Masuccio's rendering, notably in the episode of Anthia's separation from her husband and capture by robbers, from whom she is rescued by one Perilaus. It is to escape from marriage with this deliverer that she takes the drowsy potion.

In the "Illustrations to Shakespeare," Mr. Douce, who apparently did not know the version of the story given in the "Novellino," remarks, when writing of the origin of "Romeo and Juliet," that although the story of Xenophon Ephesius had not been printed, Luigi da Porto might very likely have seen the same in MS.; but it is doubtful whether he would have been able to read it even had he come across it. He himself, in an epistle attached to "La Giulietta," tells how he first heard the story "from an archer of mine whose name was Peregrino, a man about fifty years old, well practised in the military art, a pleasant companion, and, like almost all his countrymen of Verona, a great talker," and Bandello, in his version of the story, also affirms that he heard it from a Captain Alessandro Peregrino, whom he met at the baths of Caldero.

The fact that Peregrino was a Veronese may be held to be the reason why the venue of the story was laid in the city of the Scaligers, and why the Montagues and

Capulets, as two of the leading families there, were chosen as the principal agents. It was a favourite practice with the Italian story-tellers to place the scene of their narrative in some place interesting to themselves or to their hearers. Masuccio has done this with reference to this same story by laying the scene in Siena, the city of the nobleman, Antonio Piccolomini, to whom the novel is dedicated.

Masuccio's rendering and Shakespeare's have one point in common, and therein differ from certain of the others, namely, that the lovers never meet again alive after their separation.

With regard to the suggestion of the plot to Masuccio, it is highly probable that he may have heard the story of Xenophon told by some one or other of the Greek scholars who flocked to Italy after 1453.

The Thirty-sixth Novel.

"Le Meunier d'Aleus," a fabliau in Montaiglon's collection, is an early form of this story. There are parallels in Sacchetti, CCVI.; in Poggio, CCLXX.; in the "Cent Nouvelles Nouvelles," No. IX.; in the "Heptameron," No. VIII., and in La Fontaine, "Les Quid, pro Quo." It is probably the same as the sixth story of the third day of the "Decameron."

The Forty-first Novel.

From the exordium to this novel it appears that Francesco Galioto, to whom it is dedicated, gave the subject therof to Masuccio. According to Costanzo, "Storia," lib. xx., Giacomo Galioto returned to France with John of Anjou after his defeat by Ferdinand, and it is quite possible that this may be some kinsman and companion in exile of the aforesaid. Bonaventure des Periers wrote a story on the same subject (No. 128, "Contes ou nouvelles Recreations"), using probably the same legend which Galioto heard and sent to Masuccio. An episode in "The Little French Lawyer" (Beaumont and Fletcher) is something like the principal one of this novel.